Jane Austen 著

王科一 譯

PRIDE AND PREJUDICE

傲慢與偏見

商務印書館

本書譯文由上海世紀出版股份有限公司譯文出版社授權使用

書　　名：*Pride and Prejudice* 傲慢與偏見

作　　者：Jane Austen

插　　圖：Hugh Thomson

譯　　者：王科一

責任編輯：仇茵晴

封面設計：涂　慧

出　　版：商務印書館（香港）有限公司

　　　　　香港筲箕灣耀興道 3 號東滙廣場 8 樓

　　　　　http://www.commercialpress.com.hk

發　　行：香港聯合書刊物流有限公司

　　　　　香港新界大埔汀麗路 36 號中華商務印刷大廈 3 字樓

印　　刷：中華商務彩色印刷有限公司

　　　　　香港新界大埔汀麗路 36 號中華商務印刷大廈

版　　次：2017 年 8 月第 1 版第 1 次印刷

　　　　　© 2017 商務印書館（香港）有限公司

　　　　　ISBN 978 962 07 0505 2

　　　　　Printed in Hong Kong

Publisher's Note 出版説明

伊莉莎白曾對達西説："我覺得你非常狂妄自大、自私自利、看不起別人……在全天下的男人中我最不願意嫁的就是你。"但是在改變了對達西的看法後，面對達西姨母的威逼，伊莉莎白卻回應道："他 (指達西) 是紳士，我是紳士的女兒，在這點上我們是平等的。"達西則説他自己"從小給父母親寵壞了……自私自利，傲慢自大……不把任何人放在眼裏……要不是多虧了你 (指伊莉莎白)，我可能到現在還是如此！……我實在得益匪淺"。憑着伊莉莎白的自信自強和達西的自我改變，兩人終於衝破世俗的偏見，給了讀者一個圓滿的結局。

初、中級英語程度讀者使用本書時，先閱讀英文原文，如遇到理解障礙，則參考中譯作為輔助。在英文原文結束之前或附註解，標註古英語、非現代詞彙拼寫形式及語法；同樣，在譯文結束之前或會附註釋，以幫助讀者理解原文故事背景。如有餘力，讀者可在閱讀原文部份段落後，查閱相應中譯，觀察同樣詞句在雙語中不同的表達。

《傲慢與偏見》問世兩百年來，歷久不衰，並且多次被翻拍成電影。小説的精彩情節功不可沒，例如懸殊的門第，錯誤的第一印象，偽君子的誘惑，勢利姨媽的威脅，無不引起讀者強烈的好奇心；然而，奧斯汀那幽默、輕快而又機智的語言風格也值得讀者細細品味。

商務印書館 (香港) 有限公司
編輯出版部

Contents 目錄

Pride and Prejudice

Chapter 1

It is a truth universally acknowledged, that a single man in possession of a good fortune, must be in want of a wife.

However little known the feelings or views of such a man may be on his first entering a neighbourhood, this truth is so well fixed in the minds of the surrounding families, that he is considered as the rightful property of some one or other of their daughters.

'My dear Mr Bennet,' said his lady to him one day, 'have you heard that Netherfield Park is let at last?'

Mr Bennet replied that he had not.

'But it is,' returned she; 'for Mrs Long has just been here, and she told me all about it.'

Mr Bennet made no answer.

'Do not you want to know who has taken it?' cried his wife impatiently.

'*You* want to tell me, and I have no objection to hearing it.'

This was invitation enough.

'Why, my dear, you must know, Mrs Long says that Netherfield is taken by a young man of large fortune from the north of England; that he came down on Monday in a chaise and four to see the place, and was so much delighted with it that he agreed with Mr Morris immediately; that he is to take possession before Michaelmas, and some of his servants are to be in the house by the end of next week.'

'What is his name?'

'Bingley.'

'Is he married or single?'

'Oh! single, my dear, to be sure! A single man of large fortune; four or five thousand a year. What a fine thing for our girls!'

'How so? how can it affect them?'

'My dear Mr Bennet,' replied his wife, 'how can you be so tiresome! You must know that I am thinking of his marrying one of them.'

'Is that his design in settling here?'

'Design! nonsense, how can you talk so! But it is very likely that he *may* fall in love with one of them, and therefore you must visit him as soon as he comes.'

'I see no occasion for that. You and the girls may go, or you may send them by themselves, which perhaps will be still better, for as you are as handsome as any of them, Mr Bingley might like you the best of the party.'

'My dear, you flatter me. I certainly *have* had my share of beauty, but I do not pretend to be any thing extraordinary now. When a woman has five grown up daughters, she ought to give over thinking of her own beauty.'

'In such cases, a woman has not often much beauty to think of.'

'But, my dear, you must indeed go and see Mr Bingley when he comes into the neighbourhood.'

'It is more than I engage for, I assure you.'

'But consider your daughters. Only think what an establishment it would be for one of them. Sir William and Lady Lucas are determined to go, merely on that account, for in general you know they visit no new comers. Indeed you must go, for it will be impossible for *us* to visit him, if you do not.'

'You are over scrupulous surely. I dare say Mr Bingley will be very glad to see you; and I will send a few lines by you to assure him of my hearty consent to his marrying which ever he chuses[1] of the girls; though I must throw in a good word for my little Lizzy.'

'I desire you will do no such thing. Lizzy is not a bit better than the others; and I am sure she is not half so handsome as Jane, nor half so good humoured as Lydia. But you are always giving *her* the preference.'

'They have none of them much to recommend them,' replied he; 'they are all silly and ignorant like other girls; but Lizzy has something more of quickness than her sisters.'

'Mr Bennet, how can you abuse your own children in such a way? You take delight in vexing me. You have no compassion on my poor nerves.'

'You mistake me, my dear. I have a high respect for your nerves. They are my old friends. I have heard you mention them with consideration these twenty years at least.'

'Ah! you do not know what I suffer.'

'But I hope you will get over it, and live to see many young men of four thousand a year come into the neighbourhood.'

'It will be no use to us, if twenty such should come since you will not visit them.'

'Depend upon it, my dear, that when there are twenty, I will visit them all.'

Mr Bennet was so odd a mixture of quick parts, sarcastic humour, reserve, and caprice, that the experience of three and twenty years had

been insufficient to make his wife understand his character. *Her* mind was less difficult to develop. She was a woman of mean understanding, little information, and uncertain temper. When she was discontented she fancied herself nervous. The business of her life was to get her daughters married; its solace was visiting and news.

Chapter 2

Mr Bennet was among the earliest of those who waited on Mr Bingley. He had always intended to visit him, though to the last always assuring his wife that he should not go; and till the evening after the visit was paid, she had no knowledge of it. It was then disclosed in the following manner. Observing his second daughter employed in trimming a hat, he suddenly addressed her with,

'I hope Mr Bingley will like it Lizzy.'

'We are not in a way to know *what* Mr Bingley likes,' said her mother resentfully, 'since we are not to visit.'

'But you forget, mama,' said Elizabeth, 'that we shall meet him at the assemblies, and that Mrs Long has promised to introduce him.'

'I do not believe Mrs Long will do any such thing. She has two nieces of her own. She is a selfish, hypocritical woman, and I have no opinion of her.'

'No more have I,' said Mr Bennet; 'and I am glad to find that you do not depend on her serving you.'

Mrs Bennet deigned not to make any reply; but unable to contain herself, began scolding one of her daughters.

'Don't keep coughing so, Kitty, for heaven's sake! Have a little

compassion on my nerves. You tear them to pieces.'

'Kitty has no discretion in her coughs,' said her father; 'she times them ill.'

'I do not cough for my own amusement,' replied Kitty fretfully.

'When is your next ball to be, Lizzy?'

'Tomorrow fortnight.'

'Aye, so it is,' cried her mother, 'and Mrs Long does not come back till the day before; so, it will be impossible for her to introduce him, for she will not know him herself.'

'Then, my dear, you may have the advantage of your friend, and introduce Mr Bingley to *her.*'

'Impossible, Mr Bennet, impossible, when I am not acquainted with him myself; how can you be so teasing?'

'I honour your circumspection. A fortnight's acquaintance is certainly very little. One cannot know what a man really is by the end of a fortnight. But if *we* do not venture, somebody else will; and after all, Mrs Long and her nieces must stand their chance; and therefore, as she will think it an act of kindness, if you decline the office, I will take it on myself.'

The girls stared at their father. Mrs Bennet said only, 'Nonsense, nonsense!'

'What can be the meaning of that emphatic exclamation?' cried he. 'Do you consider the forms of introduction, and the stress that is laid on them, as nonsense? I cannot quite agree with you *there.* What say you, Mary? for you are a young lady of deep reflection I know, and read great books, and make extracts.'

Mary wished to say something very sensible, but knew not how.

'While Mary is adjusting her ideas,' he continued, 'let us return to Mr Bingley.'

'I am sick of Mr Bingley,' cried his wife.

'I am sorry to hear *that*; but why did not you tell me so before? If I had known as much this morning, I certainly would not have called on him. It is very unlucky; but as I have actually paid the visit, we cannot escape the acquaintance now.'

The astonishment of the ladies was just what he wished; that of Mrs Bennet perhaps surpassing the rest; though when the first tumult of joy was over, she began to declare that it was what she had expected all the while.

'How good it was in you, my dear Mr Bennet! But I knew I should persuade you at last. I was sure you loved your girls too well to neglect such an acquaintance. Well, how pleased I am! and it is such a good joke, too, that you should have gone this morning, and never said a word about it till now.'

'Now, Kitty, you may cough as much as you chuse,' said Mr Bennet; and, as he spoke, he left the room, fatigued with the raptures of his wife.

'What an excellent father you have, girls,' said she, when the door was shut. 'I do not know how you will ever make him amends for his kindness; or me either, for that matter. At our time of life, it is not so pleasant I can tell you, to be making new acquaintance every day; but for your sakes, we would do any thing. Lydia, my love, though you *are* the youngest, I dare say Mr Bingley will dance with you at the next ball.'

'Oh!' said Lydia stoutly, 'I am not afraid; for though I *am* the youngest, I'm the tallest.'

The rest of the evening was spent in conjecturing how soon he would return Mr Bennet's visit, and determining when they should ask him to dinner.

Chapter 3

Not all that Mrs Bennet, however, with the assistance of her five daughters, could ask on the subject was sufficient to draw from her husband any satisfactory description of Mr Bingley. They attacked him in various ways; with barefaced questions, ingenious suppositions, and distant surmises; but he eluded the skill of them all; and they were at last obliged to accept the second-hand intelligence of their neighbour Lady Lucas. Her report was highly favourable. Sir William had been delighted with him. He was quite young, wonderfully handsome, extremely agreeable, and to crown the whole, he meant to be at the next assembly with a large party. Nothing could be more delightful! To be fond of dancing was a certain step towards falling in love; and very lively hopes of Mr Bingley's heart were entertained.

'If I can but see one of my daughters happily settled at Netherfield,' said Mrs Bennet to her husband, 'and all the others equally well married, I shall have nothing to wish for.'

In a few days Mr Bingley returned Mr Bennet's visit, and sat about ten minutes with him in his library. He had entertained hopes of being admitted to a sight of the young ladies, of whose beauty he had heard much; but he saw only the father. The ladies were somewhat more fortunate, for they had the advantage of ascertaining from an upper window, that he wore a blue coat and rode a black horse.

An invitation to dinner was soon afterwards dispatched; and already had Mrs Bennet planned the courses that were to do credit to her housekeeping, when an answer arrived which deferred it all. Mr Bingley was obliged to be in town the following day, and consequently unable to accept the honour of their invitation, &c.[2] Mrs Bennet was quite disconcerted. She could not imagine what business he could have in town so soon after his arrival in Hertfordshire; and she began to fear that he might be always flying about from one place to another, and never settled at Netherfield as he ought to be. Lady Lucas quieted her fears a little by starting the idea of his being gone to London only to get a large party for the ball; and a report soon followed that Mr Bingley was to bring twelve ladies and seven gentlemen with him to the assembly. The girls grieved over such a number of ladies; but were comforted the day before the ball by hearing, that instead of twelve, he had brought only six with him from London, his five sisters and a cousin. And when the party entered the assembly room, it consisted of only five altogether, Mr Bingley, his two sisters, the husband of the eldest, and another young man.

Mr Bingley was good looking and gentlemanlike; he had a pleasant countenance, and easy, unaffected manners. His sisters were fine women, with an air of decided fashion. His brother-in-law, Mr Hurst, merely looked the gentleman; but his friend Mr Darcy soon drew the attention of the room by his fine, tall person, handsome features, noble mien; and the report which was in general circulation within five minutes after his entrance, of his having ten thousand a year. The

gentlemen pronounced him to be a fine figure of a man, the ladies declared he was much handsomer than Mr Bingley, and he was looked at with great admiration for about half the evening, till his manners gave a disgust which turned the tide of his popularity; for he was discovered to be proud, to be above his company, and above being pleased; and not all his large estate in Derbyshire could then save him from having a most forbidding, disagreeable countenance, and being unworthy to be compared with his friend.

Mr Bingley had soon made himself acquainted with all the principal people in the room; he was lively and unreserved, danced every dance, was angry that the ball closed so early, and talked of giving one himself at Netherfield. Such amiable qualities must speak for themselves. What a contrast between him and his friend! Mr Darcy danced only once with Mrs Hurst and once with Miss Bingley, declined being introduced to any other lady, and spent the rest of the evening in walking about the room, speaking occasionally to one of his own party. His character was decided. He was the proudest, most disagreeable man in the world, and every body hoped that he would never come there again. Amongst the most violent against him was Mrs Bennet, whose dislike of his general behaviour, was sharpened into particular resentment, by his having slighted one of her daughters.

Elizabeth Bennet had been obliged, by the scarcity of gentlemen, to sit down for two dances; and during part of that time, Mr Darcy had been standing near enough for her to overhear a conversation between him and Mr Bingley, who came from the dance for a few minutes, to press his friend to join it.

'Come, Darcy,' said he, 'I must have you dance. I hate to see you standing about by yourself in this stupid manner. You had much better dance.'

'I certainly shall not. You know how I detest it, unless I am particularly acquainted with my partner. At such an assembly as this, it would be insupportable. Your sisters are engaged, and there is not another woman in the room, whom it would not be a punishment to me to stand up with.'

'I would not be so fastidious as you are,' cried Bingley, 'for a kingdom! Upon my honour, I never met with so many pleasant girls in my life, as I have this evening; and there are several of them you see uncommonly pretty.'

'*You* are dancing with the only handsome girl in the room,' said Mr Darcy, looking at the eldest Miss Bennet.

'Oh! she is the most beautiful creature I ever beheld! But there is one of her sisters sitting down just behind you, who is very pretty, and I dare say, very agreeable. Do let me ask my partner to introduce you.'

'Which do you mean?' and turning round, he looked for a moment at Elizabeth, till catching her eye, he withdrew his own and coldly said, 'She is tolerable; but not handsome enough to tempt *me*; and I am in no humour at present to give consequence to young ladies who are slighted by other men. You had better return to your partner and enjoy her smiles, for you are wasting your time with me.'

Mr Bingley followed his advice. Mr Darcy walked off; and Elizabeth remained with no very cordial feelings towards him. She told the story however with great spirit among her friends; for she had a lively, playful disposition, which delighted in any thing ridiculous.

The evening altogether passed off pleasantly to the whole family. Mrs Bennet had seen her eldest daughter much admired by the Netherfield party. Mr Bingley had danced with her twice, and she had been distinguished by his sisters. Jane was as much gratified by this, as her mother could be, though in a quieter way. Elizabeth felt Jane's pleasure. Mary had heard herself mentioned to Miss Bingley as the most accomplished girl in the neighbourhood; and Catherine and Lydia had been fortunate enough to be never without partners, which was all that they had yet learnt to care for at a ball. They returned therefore in good spirits to Longbourn, the village where they lived, and of which they were the principal inhabitants. They found Mr Bennet still up. With a book he was regardless of time; and on the present occasion he had a good deal of curiosity as to the event of an evening which had raised such splendid expectations. He had rather hoped that all his wife's views on the stranger would be disappointed; but he soon found that he had a very different story to hear.

'Oh! my dear Mr Bennet,' as she entered the room, 'we have had a most delightful evening, a most excellent ball. I wish you had been there. Jane was so admired, nothing could be like it. Every body said how well she looked; and Mr Bingley thought her quite beautiful, and danced with her twice. Only think of *that* my dear; he actually danced with her twice; and she was the only creature in the room that he asked a second time. First of all, he asked Miss Lucas. I was so vexed to see him stand up with her; but, however, he did not admire her at all: indeed, nobody can, you know; and he seemed quite struck with Jane as she was going down the dance. So, he enquired who she was, and got introduced, and asked her for the two next. Then, the two third he danced with Miss King, and the two fourth with Maria Lucas, and the two fifth with Jane again, and the two sixth with Lizzy, and the Boulanger.'

'If he had had any compassion for *me*,' cried her husband impatiently, 'he would not have danced half so much! For God's sake, say no more of his partners. Oh! that he had sprained his ankle in the first dance!'

'Oh! my dear,' continued Mrs Bennet, 'I am quite delighted with him. He is so excessively handsome! and his sisters are charming women. I never in my life saw any thing more elegant than their dresses. I dare say the lace upon Mrs Hurst's gown –'

Here she was interrupted again. Mr Bennet protested against any description of finery. She was therefore obliged to seek another branch of the subject, and related, with much bitterness of spirit and some exaggeration, the shocking rudeness of Mr Darcy.

'But I can assure you,' she added, 'that Lizzy does not lose much by not suiting *his* fancy; for he is a most disagreeable, horrid man, not at all worth pleasing. So high and so conceited that there was no enduring him! He walked here, and he walked there, fancying himself so very great! Not handsome enough to dance with! I wish you had been there, my dear, to have given him one of your set downs. I quite detest the man.'

Chapter 4

When Jane and Elizabeth were alone, the former, who had been cautious in her praise of Mr Bingley before, expressed to her sister how very much she admired him.

'He is just what a young man ought to be,' said she, 'sensible, good humoured, lively; and I never saw such happy manners! – so much ease, with such perfect good breeding!'

'He is also handsome,' replied Elizabeth, 'which a young man ought likewise to be, if he possibly can. His character is thereby complete.'

'I was very much flattered by his asking me to dance a second time. I did not expect such a compliment.'

'Did not you? *I* did for you. But that is one great difference between us. Compliments always take *you* by surprise, and *me* never. What could be more natural than his asking you again? He could not help seeing that you were about five times as pretty as every other woman in the room. No thanks to his gallantry for that. Well, he certainly is very agreeable, and I give you leave to like him. You have liked many a stupider person.'

'Dear Lizzy!'

'Oh! you are a great deal too apt you know, to like people in general. You never see a fault in any body. All the world are good and agreeable in your eyes. I never heard you speak ill of a human being in my life.'

'I would wish not to be hasty in censuring any one; but I always speak what I think.'

'I know you do; and it is *that* which makes the wonder. With *your* good sense, to be so honestly blind to the follies and nonsense of others! Affectation of candour is common enough; – one meets it every where. But to be candid without ostentation or design – to take the good of every body's character and make it still better, and say nothing of the bad – belongs to you alone. And so, you like this man's sisters too, do you? Their manners are not equal to his.'

'Certainly not; at first. But they are very pleasing women when you converse with them. Miss Bingley is to live with her brother and keep his house; and I am much mistaken if we shall not find a very charming neighbour in her.'

Elizabeth listened in silence, but was not convinced; their behaviour at the assembly had not been calculated to please in general; and with more quickness of observation and less pliancy of temper than her sister, and with a judgment too unassailed by any attention to herself, she was very little disposed to approve them. They were in fact very fine ladies; not deficient in good humour when they were pleased, nor in the power of being agreeable where they chose it; but proud and conceited. They were rather handsome, had been educated in one of the first private seminaries in town, had a fortune of twenty thousand pounds, were in the habit of spending more than they ought, and of associating with people of rank; and were therefore in every respect entitled to think well of themselves, and meanly of others. They were of a respectable family in the north of England; a circumstance more deeply impressed on their memories than that their brother's fortune and their own had been acquired by trade.

Mr Bingley inherited property to the amount of nearly an hundred thousand pounds from his father, who had intended to purchase an estate, but did not live to do it. – Mr Bingley intended it likewise, and sometimes made choice of his county; but as he was now provided with a good house and the liberty of a manor, it was doubtful to many of those who best knew the easiness of his temper, whether he might not spend the remainder of his days at Netherfield, and leave the next generation to purchase.

His sisters were very anxious for his having an estate of his own; but though he was now established only as a tenant, Miss Bingley was by no means unwilling to preside at his table, nor was Mrs Hurst, who had married a man of more fashion than fortune, less disposed to consider his house as her home when it suited her. Mr Bingley had not been of age two years, when he was tempted by an accidental recommendation to look at Netherfield House. He did look at it and into it for half an hour[3], was pleased with the situation and the principal rooms, satisfied with what the owner said in its praise, and took it immediately.

Between him and Darcy there was a very steady friendship, in spite of a great opposition of character. – Bingley was endeared to Darcy by the easiness, openness, ductility of his temper, though no disposition could offer a greater contrast to his own, and though with his own he never appeared dissatisfied. On the strength of Darcy's regard Bingley had the firmest reliance, and of his judgment the highest opinion. In understanding Darcy was the superior. Bingley was by no means deficient, but Darcy was clever. He was at the same time haughty, reserved, and fastidious, and his manners, though well bred, were not inviting. In that respect his friend had greatly the advantage. Bingley was sure of being liked wherever he appeared, Darcy was continually giving offence.

The manner in which they spoke of the Meryton assembly was sufficiently characteristic. Bingley had never met with pleasanter people or prettier girls in his life; every body had been most kind and attentive to him, there had been no formality, no stiffness, he had soon felt acquainted with all the room; and as to Miss Bennet, he could not conceive an angel more beautiful. Darcy, on the contrary, had seen a collection of people in whom there was little beauty and no fashion, for none of whom he had felt the smallest interest, and from none received either attention or pleasure. Miss Bennet he acknowledged to be pretty, but she smiled too much.

Mrs Hurst and her sister allowed it to be so – but still they admired her and liked her, and pronounced her to be a sweet girl, and one whom they should not object to know more of. Miss Bennet was therefore established as a sweet girl, and their brother felt authorised by such commendation to think of her as he chose.

Chapter 5

Within a short walk of Longbourn lived a family with whom the Bennets were particularly intimate. Sir William Lucas had been formerly in trade in Meryton, where he had made a tolerable fortune and risen to the honour of knighthood by an address to the King, during his mayoralty. The distinction had perhaps been felt too strongly. It had given him a disgust to his business and to his residence in a small market town; and quitting them both, he had removed with his family to a house about a mile from Meryton, denominated from that period Lucas Lodge, where he could think with pleasure of his own importance, and unshackled by business, occupy himself solely in being civil to all the world. For though elated by his rank, it did not render him supercilious; on the contrary, he was all attention to every body. By nature inoffensive, friendly and obliging, his presentation at St. James's had made him courteous.

Lady Lucas was a very good kind of woman, not too clever to be a valuable neighbour to Mrs Bennet. – They had several children. The eldest of them, a sensible, intelligent young woman, about twenty-seven, was Elizabeth's intimate friend.

That the Miss Lucases and the Miss Bennets should meet to talk over a ball was absolutely necessary; and the morning after the assembly brought the former to Longbourn to hear and to communicate.

'*You* began the evening well, Charlotte,' said Mrs Bennet with civil self-command to Miss Lucas. '*You* were Mr Bingley's first choice.'

'Yes; – but he seemed to like his second better.'

'Oh! – you mean Jane, I suppose – because he danced with her twice. To be sure that *did* seem as if he admired her – indeed I rather believe he *did* – I heard something about it – but I hardly know what – something about Mr Robinson.'

'Perhaps you mean what I overheard between him and Mr

Robinson; did not I mention it to you? Mr Robinson's asking him how he liked our Meryton assemblies, and whether he did not think there were a great many pretty women in the room, and *which* he thought the prettiest? and his answering immediately to the last question – Oh! the eldest Miss Bennet beyond a doubt, there cannot be two opinions on that point.'

'Upon my word! – Well, that was very decided indeed – that does seem as if – but however, it may all come to nothing you know.'

'*My* overhearings were more to the purpose than *yours*, Eliza,' said Charlotte. 'Mr Darcy is not so well worth listening to as his friend, is he? – Poor Eliza! – to be only just *tolerable*.'

'I beg you would not put it into Lizzy's head to be vexed by his ill-treatment; for he is such a disagreeable man that it would be quite a misfortune to be liked by him. Mrs Long told me last night that he sat close to her for half an hour without once opening his lips.'

'Are you quite sure, Ma'am? – is not there a little mistake?' said Jane. – 'I certainly saw Mr Darcy speaking to her.'

'Aye – because she asked him at last how he liked Netherfield, and he could not help answering her; – but she said he seemed very angry at being spoke to.'

'Miss Bingley told me,' said Jane, 'that he never speaks much unless among his intimate acquaintance. With *them* he is remarkably agreeable.'

'I do not believe a word of it, my dear. If he had been so very agreeable he would have talked to Mrs Long. But I can guess how it was; every body says that he is ate up with pride, and I dare say he had heard somehow that Mrs Long does not keep a carriage, and had come to the ball in a hack chaise.'

'I do not mind his not talking to Mrs Long,' said Miss Lucas, 'but I wish he had danced with Eliza.'

'Another time, Lizzy,' said her mother, 'I would not dance with *him*, if I were you.'

'I believe, Ma'am, I may safely promise you *never* to dance with him.'

'His pride,' said Miss Lucas, 'does not offend *me* so much as pride often does, because there is an excuse for it. One cannot wonder that so very fine a young man, with family, fortune, every thing in his favour, should think highly of himself. If I may so express it, he has a *right* to be proud.'

'That is very true,' replied Elizabeth, 'and I could easily forgive *his* pride, if he had not mortified *mine*.'

'Pride,' observed Mary, who piqued herself upon the solidity of her reflections, 'is a very common failing I believe. By all that I have ever read, I am convinced that it is very common indeed, that human nature is particularly prone to it, and that there are very few of us who do not cherish a feeling of self-complacency on the score of some quality or other, real or imaginary. From the very beginning are different things, though the words are often used synonymously. A person may be proud without being vain. Pride relates more to our opinion of ourselves, vanity to what we would have others think of us.'

'If I were as rich as Mr Darcy,' cried a young Lucas who came with his sisters, 'I should not care how proud I was. I would keep a pack of foxhounds, and drink a bottle of wine every day.'

'Then you would drink a great deal more than you ought,' said Mrs Bennet; 'and if I were to see you at it I should take away your bottle directly.'

The boy protested that she should not; she continued to declare that she would, and the argument ended only with the visit.

Chapter 6

The ladies of Longbourn soon waited on those of Netherfield. The visit was returned in due form. Miss Bennet's pleasing manners grew on the good will of Mrs Hurst and Miss Bingley; and though the mother was found to be intolerable and the younger sisters not worth speaking to, a wish of being better acquainted with *them*, was expressed towards the two eldest. By Jane this attention was received with the greatest pleasure; but Elizabeth still saw superciliousness in their treatment of every body, hardly excepting even her sister, and could not like them; though their kindness to Jane, such as it was, had a value as arising in all probability from the influence of their brother's admiration. It was generally evident whenever they met, that he *did* admire her; and to *her* it was equally evident that Jane was yielding to the preference which she had begun to entertain for him from the first, and was in a way to be very much in love; but she considered with pleasure that it was not likely to be discovered by the world in general, since Jane united with great strength of feeling, a composure of temper and a uniform cheerfulness of manner, which would guard her from the suspicions of the impertinent. She mentioned this to her friend Miss Lucas.

'It may perhaps be pleasant,' replied Charlotte, 'to be able to impose on the public in such a case; but it is sometimes a disadvantage to be so very guarded. If a woman conceals her affection with the same skill from the object of it, she may lose the opportunity of fixing him; and it will then be but poor consolation to believe the world equally in the dark. There is so much of gratitude or vanity in almost every attachment, that it is not safe to leave any to itself. We can all *begin* freely – a slight preference is natural enough; but there are very few of us who have heart enough to be really in love without encouragement. In nine cases out of ten, a woman had better show *more* affection than she feels. Bingley likes your sister undoubtedly; but he may never do more than like her, if she does not help him on.'

'But she does help him on, as much as her nature will allow. If *I* can perceive her regard for him, he must be a simpleton indeed not to discover it too.'

'Remember, Eliza, that he does not know Jane's disposition as you do.'

'But if a woman is partial to a man, and does not endeavour to conceal it, he must find it out.'

'Perhaps he must, if he sees enough of her. But though Bingley and Jane meet tolerably often, it is never for many hours together; and as they always see each other in large mixed parties, it is impossible that every moment should be employed in conversing together. Jane should therefore make the most of every half hour in which she can command his attention. When she is secure of him, there will be leisure for falling in love as much as she chuses.'

'Your plan is a good one,' replied Elizabeth, 'where nothing is in question but the desire of being well married; and if I were determined to get a rich husband, or any husband, I dare say I should adopt it. But these are not Jane's feelings; she is not acting by design. As yet, she cannot even be certain of the degree of her own regard, nor of its reasonableness. She has known him only a fortnight. She danced four dances with him at Meryton; she saw him one morning at his own house, and has since dined in company with him four times. This is not quite enough to make her understand his character.'

'Not as you represent it. Had she merely *dined* with him, she might only have discovered whether he had a good appetite; but you must remember that four evenings have been also spent together – and four evenings may do a great deal.'

'Yes; these four evenings have enabled them to ascertain that they both like Vingt-un[4] better than Commerce[5]; but with respect to any other leading characteristic, I do not imagine that much has been unfolded.'

'Well,' said Charlotte, 'I wish Jane success with all my heart; and if she were married to him tomorrow, I should think she had as good a chance of happiness, as if she were to be studying his character for a twelve-month. Happiness in marriage is entirely a matter of chance. If the dispositions of the parties are ever so well known to each other, or ever so similar beforehand, it does not advance their felicity in the least. They always continue to grow sufficiently unlike afterwards to have their share of vexation; and it is better to know as little as possible of the defects of the person with whom you are to pass your life.'

'You make me laugh, Charlotte; but it is not sound. You know it is not sound, and that you would never act in this way yourself.'

Occupied in observing Mr Bingley's attentions to her sister, Elizabeth was far from suspecting that she was herself becoming an object of some interest in the eyes of his friend. Mr Darcy had at first scarcely allowed her to be pretty; he had looked at her without admiration at the ball; and when they next met, he looked at her only to criticise. But no sooner had he made it clear to himself and his friends that she had hardly a good feature in her face, than he began to find it was rendered uncommonly intelligent by the beautiful expression of her dark eyes. To this discovery succeeded some others equally mortifying. Though he had detected with a critical eye more than one failure of perfect symmetry in her form, he was forced to acknowledge her figure to be light and pleasing; and in spite of his asserting that her manners were not those of the fashionable world, he was caught by their easy playfulness. Of this she was perfectly unaware; – to her he was only the man who made himself agreeable no where, and who had not thought her handsome enough to dance with.

He began to wish to know more of her, and as a step towards conversing with her himself, attended to her conversation with others. His doing so drew her notice. It was at Sir William Lucas's, where a large party were assembled.

'What does Mr Darcy mean,' said she to Charlotte, 'by listening to my conversation with Colonel Forster?'

'That is a question which Mr Darcy only can answer.'

'But if he does it any more I shall certainly let him know that I see what he is about. He has a very satirical eye, and if I do not begin by being impertinent myself, I shall soon grow afraid of him.'

On his approaching them soon afterwards, though without seeming to have any intention of speaking, Miss Lucas defied her friend to mention such a subject to him, which immediately provoking Elizabeth to do it, she turned to him and said,

'Did not you think, Mr Darcy, that I expressed myself uncommonly well just now, when I was teasing Colonel Forster to give us a ball at Meryton?'

'With great energy; – but it is a subject which always makes a lady energetic.'

'You are severe on us.'

'It will be *her* turn soon to be teased,' said Miss Lucas. 'I am going to open the instrument, Eliza, and you know what follows.'

'You are a very strange creature by way of a friend! – always wanting me to play and sing before any body and every body! – If my vanity had taken a musical turn, you would have been invaluable, but as it is, I would really rather not sit down before those who must be in the habit of hearing the very best performers.' On Miss Lucas's persevering, however, she added, 'Very well; if it must be so, it must.' And gravely glancing at Mr Darcy, 'There is a fine old saying, which every body here is of course familiar with – "Keep your breath to cool your porridge," – and I shall keep mine to swell my song.'

Her performance was pleasing, though by no means capital. After a song or two, and before she could reply to the entreaties of several that she would sing again, she was eagerly succeeded at the instrument by her sister Mary, who having, in consequence of being the only plain one in the family, worked hard for knowledge and accomplishments, was always impatient for display.

Mary had neither genius nor taste; and though vanity had given her application, it had given her likewise a pedantic air and conceited manner, which would have injured a higher degree of excellence than she had reached. Elizabeth, easy and unaffected, had been listened to with much more pleasure, though not playing half so well; and Mary, at the end of a long concerto, was glad to purchase praise and gratitude by Scotch and Irish airs, at the request of her younger sisters, who with some of the Lucases and two or three officers joined eagerly in dancing at one end of the room.

Mr Darcy stood near them in silent indignation at such a mode of passing the evening, to the exclusion of all conversation, and was too much engrossed by his own thoughts to perceive that Sir William Lucas was his neighbour, till Sir William thus began.

'What a charming amusement for young people this is, Mr Darcy! – There is nothing like dancing after all. – I consider it as one of the first refinements of polished societies.'

'Certainly, Sir, – and it has the advantage also of being in vogue amongst the less polished societies of the world. – Every savage can dance.'

Sir William only smiled. 'Your friend performs delightfully;' he continued after a pause, on seeing Bingley join the group; – 'and I doubt not that you are an adept in the science yourself, Mr Darcy.'

'You saw me dance at Meryton, I believe, Sir.'

'Yes, indeed, and received no inconsiderable pleasure from the sight. Do you often dance at St. James's?'

'Never, sir.'

'Do you not think it would be a proper compliment to the place?'

'It is a compliment which I never pay to any place if I can avoid it.'

'You have a house in town, I conclude.'

Mr Darcy bowed.

'I had once some thoughts of fixing in town myself – for I am fond of superior society; but I did not feel quite certain that the air of London would agree with Lady Lucas.'

He paused in hopes of an answer; but his companion was not disposed to make any; and Elizabeth at that instant moving towards them, he was struck with the notion of doing a very gallant thing, and called out to her,

'My dear Miss Eliza, why are not you dancing? – Mr Darcy, you must allow me to present this young lady to you as a very desirable partner. – You cannot refuse to dance, I am sure, when so much beauty

is before you.' And taking her hand, he would have given it to Mr Darcy, who, though extremely surprised, was not unwilling to receive it, when she instantly drew back, and said with some discomposure to Sir William,

'Indeed, Sir, I have not the least intention of dancing. – I entreat you not to suppose that I moved this way in order to beg for a partner.'

Mr Darcy with grave propriety requested to be allowed the honour of her hand; but in vain. Elizabeth was determined; nor did Sir William at all shake her purpose by his attempt at persuasion.

'You excel so much in the dance, Miss Eliza, that it is cruel to deny me the happiness of seeing you; and though this gentleman dislikes the amusement in general, he can have no objection, I am sure, to oblige us for one half hour.'

'Mr Darcy is all politeness,' said Elizabeth, smiling.

'He is indeed – but considering the inducement, my dear Miss Eliza, we cannot wonder at his complaisance; for who would object to such a partner?'

Elizabeth looked archly, and turned away. Her resistance had not injured her with the gentleman, and he was thinking of her with some complacency, when thus accosted by Miss Bingley,

'I can guess the subject of your reverie.'

'I should imagine not.'

'You are considering how insupportable it would be to pass many evenings in this manner – in such society; and indeed I am quite of your opinion. I was never more annoyed! The insipidity and yet the noise; the nothingness and yet the self-importance of all these people! – What would I give to hear your strictures on them!'

'Your conjecture is totally wrong, I assure you. My mind was more agreeably engaged. I have been meditating on the very great pleasure which a pair of fine eyes in the face of a pretty woman can bestow.'

Miss Bingley immediately fixed her eyes on his face, and desired he would tell her what lady had the credit of inspiring such reflections. Mr Darcy replied with great intrepidity,

'Miss Elizabeth Bennet.'

'Miss Elizabeth Bennet!' repeated Miss Bingley. 'I am all astonishment. How long has she been such a favourite? – and pray when am I to wish you joy?'

'That is exactly the question which I expected you to ask. A lady's imagination is very rapid; it jumps from admiration to love, from love to matrimony in a moment. I knew you would be wishing me joy.'

'Nay, if you are so serious about it, I shall consider the matter as absolutely settled. You will have a charming mother-in-law, indeed, and of course she will be always at Pemberley with you.'

He listened to her with perfect indifference, while she chose to entertain herself in this manner, and as his composure convinced her that all was safe, her wit flowed long.

Chapter 7

Mr Bennet's property consisted almost entirely in an estate of two thousand a year, which, unfortunately for his daughters, was entailed in default of heirs male, on a distant relation; and their mother's fortune, though ample for her situation in life, could but ill supply the deficiency of his. Her father had been an attorney in Meryton, and had left her four thousand pounds.

She had a sister married to a Mr Philips, who had been a clerk to their father, and succeeded him in the business, and a brother settled in London in a respectable line of trade.

The village of Longbourn was only one mile from Meryton; a most convenient distance for the young ladies, who were usually tempted thither[6] three or four times a week, to pay their duty to their aunt and to a milliner's shop just over the way. The two youngest of the family, Catherine and Lydia, were particularly frequent in these attentions; their minds were more vacant than their sisters', and when nothing better offered, a walk to Meryton was necessary to amuse their morning hours and furnish conversation for the evening; and however bare of news the country in general might be, they always contrived to learn some from their aunt. At present, indeed, they were well supplied both with news and happiness by the recent arrival of a militia regiment in the neighbourhood; it was to remain the whole winter, and Meryton was the head quarters.

Their visits to Mrs Philips were now productive of the most interesting intelligence. Every day added something to their knowledge of the officers' names and connections. Their lodgings were not long a secret, and at length they began to know the officers themselves. Mr Philips visited them all, and this opened to his nieces a source of felicity unknown before. They could talk of nothing but officers; and Mr Bingley's large fortune, the mention of which gave animation to their mother, was worthless in their eyes when opposed to the regimentals of an ensign.

After listening one morning to their effusions on this subject, Mr Bennet coolly observed,

'From all that I can collect by your manner of talking, you must be two of the silliest girls in the country. I have suspected it some time, but I am now convinced.'

Catherine was disconcerted, and made no answer; but Lydia, with perfect indifference, continued to express her admiration of Captain Carter, and her hope of seeing him in the course of the day, as he was going the next morning to London.

'I am astonished, my dear,' said Mrs Bennet, 'that you should be so ready to think your own children silly. If I wished to think slightingly of any body's children, it should not be of my own however.'

'If my children are silly I must hope to be always sensible of it.'

'Yes – but as it happens, they are all of them very clever.'

'This is the only point, I flatter myself, on which we do not agree. I had hoped that our sentiments coincided in every particular, but I must so far differ from you as to think our two youngest daughters uncommonly foolish.'

'My dear Mr Bennet, you must not expect such girls to have the sense of their father and mother. – When they get to our age I dare say they will not think about officers any more than we do. I remember the time when I liked a red-coat myself very well – and indeed so I do still at my heart; and if a smart young colonel, with five or six thousand a year, should want one of my girls, I shall not say nay to him; and I thought Colonel Forster looked very becoming the other night at Sir William's in his regimentals.'

'Mama,' cried Lydia, 'my aunt says that Colonel Forster and Captain Carter do not go so often to Miss Watson's as they did when they first came; she sees them now very often standing in Clarke's library.'

Mrs Bennet was prevented replying by the entrance of the footman with a note for Miss Bennet; it came from Netherfield, and the servant waited for an answer. Mrs Bennet's eyes sparkled with pleasure, and she was eagerly calling out, while her daughter read,

'Well, Jane, who is it from? what is it about? what does he say? Well, Jane, make haste and tell us; make haste, my love.'

'It is from Miss Bingley,' said Jane, and then read it aloud.

MY DEAR FRIEND – IF you are not so compassionate as to dine today with Louisa and me, we shall be in danger of hating each other for the rest of our lives, for a whole day's tête-à-tête between two women can never end without a quarrel. Come as soon as you can on the receipt of this. My brother and the gentlemen are to dine with the officers. Yours ever,

CAROLINE BINGLEY

'With the officers!' cried Lydia. 'I wonder my aunt did not tell us of *that.*'

'Dining out,' said Mrs Bennet, 'that is very unlucky.'

'Can I have the carriage?' said Jane.

'No, my dear, you had better go on horseback, because it seems likely to rain; and then you must stay all night.'

'That would be a good scheme,' said Elizabeth, 'if you were sure that they would not offer to send her home.'

'Oh! but the gentlemen will have Mr Bingley's chaise to go to Meryton; and the Hursts have no horses to theirs.'

'I had much rather go in the coach.'

'But, my dear, your father cannot spare the horses, I am sure. They are wanted in the farm, Mr Bennet, are not they?'

'They are wanted in the farm much oftener than I can get them.'

'But if you have got them today,' said Elizabeth, 'my mother's purpose will be answered.'

She did at last extort from her father an acknowledgment that the horses were engaged. Jane was therefore obliged to go on horseback, and her mother attended her to the door with many cheerful prognostics of a bad day. Her hopes were answered; Jane had not been gone long before it rained hard. Her sisters were uneasy for her, but her mother was delighted. The rain continued the whole evening without

intermission; Jane certainly could not come back.

'This was a lucky idea of mine, indeed!' said Mrs Bennet, more than once, as if the credit of making it rain were all her own. Till the next morning, however, she was not aware of all the felicity of her contrivance. Breakfast was scarcely over when a servant from Netherfield brought the following note for Elizabeth:

MY DEAREST LIZZY – I FIND myself very unwell this morning, which, I suppose, is to be imputed to my getting wet through yesterday. My kind friends will not hear of my returning home till I am better. They insist also on my seeing Mr Jones – therefore do not be alarmed if you should hear of his having been to me – and excepting a sore-throat and head-ache there is not much the matter with me.

Yours, &c.

'Well, my dear,' said Mr Bennet, when Elizabeth had read the note aloud, 'if your daughter should have a dangerous fit of illness, if she should die, it would be a comfort to know that it was all in pursuit of

Mr Bingley, and under your orders.'

'Oh! I am not at all afraid of her dying. People do not die of little trifling colds. She will be taken good care of. As long as she stays there, it is all very well. I would go and see her, if I could have the carriage.'

Elizabeth, feeling really anxious, was determined to go to her, though the carriage was not to be had; and as she was no horse-woman, walking was her only alternative. She declared her resolution.

'How can you be so silly,' cried her mother, 'as to think of such a thing, in all this dirt! You will not be fit to be seen when you get there.'

'I shall be very fit to see Jane – which is all I want.'

'Is this a hint to me, Lizzy,' said her father, 'to send for the horses?'

'No, indeed. I do not wish to avoid the walk. The distance is nothing, when one has a motive; only three miles. I shall be back by dinner.'

'I admire the activity of your benevolence,' observed Mary, 'but every impulse of feeling should be guided by reason; and, in my opinion, exertion should always be in proportion to what is required.'

'We will go as far as Meryton with you,' said Catherine and Lydia. – Elizabeth accepted their company, and the three young ladies set off together.

'If we make haste,' said Lydia, as they walked along, 'perhaps we may see something of Captain Carter before he goes.'

In Meryton they parted; the two youngest repaired to the lodgings of one of the officers' wives, and Elizabeth continued her walk alone, crossing field after field at a quick pace, jumping over stiles and springing over puddles with impatient activity, and finding herself at last within view of the house, with weary ankles, dirty stockings, and a face glowing with the warmth of exercise.

She was shown into the breakfast-parlour, where all but Jane were assembled, and where her appearance created a great deal of surprise. – That she should have walked three miles so early in the day, in such dirty weather, and by herself, was almost incredible to Mrs Hurst and Miss Bingley; and Elizabeth was convinced that they held her in contempt for it. She was received, however, very politely by them; and in their brother's manners there was something better than politeness; there was good humour and kindness. – Mr Darcy said very little, and Mr Hurst nothing at all. The former was divided between admiration of the brilliancy which exercise had given to her complexion, and doubt as to the occasion's justifying her coming so far alone. The latter was thinking only of his breakfast.

Her enquiries after her sister were not very favourably answered. Miss Bennet had slept ill, and though up, was very feverish and not well enough to leave her room. Elizabeth was glad to be taken to her immediately; and Jane, who had only been withheld by the fear of giving alarm or inconvenience, from expressing in her note how much she longed for such a visit, was delighted at her entrance. She was not equal, however, to much conversation, and when Miss Bingley left them together, could attempt little beside expressions of gratitude for the extraordinary kindness she was treated with. Elizabeth silently attended her.

When breakfast was over, they were joined by the sisters; and Elizabeth began to like them herself, when she saw how much affection and solicitude they showed for Jane. The apothecary came, and having examined his patient, said, as might be supposed, that she had caught a violent cold, and that they must endeavour to get the better of it; advised her to return to bed, and promised her some draughts. The advice was followed readily, for the feverish symptoms increased, and her head ached acutely. Elizabeth did not quit her room for a moment, nor were the other ladies often absent; the gentlemen being out, they had in fact nothing to do elsewhere.

When the clock struck three, Elizabeth felt that she must go; and very unwillingly said so. Miss Bingley offered her the carriage, and she only wanted a little pressing to accept it, when Jane testified such concern in parting with her, that Miss Bingley was obliged to convert the offer of the chaise into an invitation to remain at Netherfield for the present. Elizabeth most thankfully consented, and a servant was dispatched to Longbourn to acquaint the family with her stay, and bring back a supply of clothes.

Chapter 8

A t five o'clock the two ladies retired to dress, and at half past six Elizabeth was summoned to dinner. To the civil enquiries which then poured in, and amongst which she had the pleasure of distinguishing the much superior solicitude of Mr Bingley's, she could not make a very favourable answer. Jane was by no means better. The sisters, on hearing this, repeated three or four times how much they were grieved, how shocking it was to have a bad cold, and how excessively they disliked being ill themselves; and then thought no more of the matter: and their indifference towards Jane when not immediately before them, restored Elizabeth to the enjoyment of all her original dislike.

Their brother, indeed, was the only one of the party whom she could regard with any complacency. His anxiety for Jane was evident, and his attentions to herself most pleasing, and they prevented her feeling herself so much an intruder as she believed she was considered by the others. She had very little notice from any but him. Miss Bingley was engrossed by Mr Darcy, her sister scarcely less so; and as for Mr Hurst, by whom Elizabeth sat, he was an indolent man, who lived only to eat, drink, and play at cards, who when he found her prefer a plain dish to a ragout, had nothing to say to her.

When dinner was over, she returned directly to Jane, and Miss Bingley began abusing her as soon as she was out of the room. Her manners were pronounced to be very bad indeed, a mixture of pride and impertinence; she had no conversation, no stile[7], no taste, no beauty. Mrs Hurst thought the same, and added,

'She has nothing, in short, to recommend her, but being an excellent walker. I shall never forget her appearance this morning. She really looked almost wild.'

'She did indeed, Louisa. I could hardly keep my countenance. Very nonsensical to come at all! Why must *she* be scampering about the country, because her sister had a cold? Her hair so untidy, so blowsy!'

'Yes, and her petticoat; I hope you saw her petticoat, six inches deep in mud, I am absolutely certain; and the gown which had been let down to hide it, not doing its office.'

'Your picture may be very exact, Louisa,' said Bingley; 'but this was all lost upon me. I thought Miss Elizabeth Bennet looked remarkably well, when she came into the room this morning. Her dirty petticoat quite escaped my notice.'

'*You* observed it, Mr Darcy, I am sure,' said Miss Bingley; 'and I am inclined to think that you would not wish to see *your sister* make such an exhibition.'

'Certainly not.'

'To walk three miles, or four miles, or five miles, or whatever it is, above her ankles in dirt, and alone, quite alone! what could she mean by it? It seems to me to show an abominable sort of conceited independence, a most country town indifference to decorum.'

'It shows an affection for her sister that is very pleasing,' said Bingley.

'I am afraid, Mr Darcy,' observed Miss Bingley, in a half whisper, 'that this adventure has rather affected your admiration of her fine eyes.'

'Not at all,' he replied; 'they were brightened by the exercise.' – A short pause followed this speech, and Mrs Hurst began again.

'I have an excessive regard for Jane Bennet, she is really a very sweet girl, and I wish with all my heart she were well settled. But with such a father and mother, and such low connections, I am afraid there is no chance of it.'

'I think I have heard you say, that their uncle is an attorney in Meryton.'

'Yes; and they have another, who lives somewhere near Cheapside.'

'That is capital,' added her sister, and they both laughed heartily.

'If they had uncles enough to fill *all* Cheapside,' cried Bingley, 'it would not make them one jot less agreeable.'

'But it must very materially lessen their chance of marrying men of any consideration in the world,' replied Darcy.

To this speech Bingley made no answer; but his sisters gave it their hearty assent, and indulged their mirth for some time at the expense of their dear friend's vulgar relations.

With a renewal of tenderness, however, they repaired to her room on leaving the dining-parlour, and sat with her till summoned to coffee. She was still very poorly, and Elizabeth would not quit her at all, till late in the evening, when she had the comfort of seeing her asleep, and when it appeared to her rather right than pleasant that she should go down stairs herself. On entering the drawing-room she found the whole party at loo, and was immediately invited to join them; but suspecting them to be playing high she declined it, and making her sister the excuse, said she would amuse herself for the short time she could stay below with a book. Mr Hurst looked at her with astonishment.

'Do you prefer reading to cards?' said he; 'that is rather singular.'

'Miss Eliza Bennet,' said Miss Bingley, 'despises cards. She is a great reader and has no pleasure in anything else.'

'I deserve neither such praise nor such censure,' cried Elizabeth; 'I am *not* a great reader, and I have pleasure in many things.'

'In nursing your sister I am sure you have pleasure,' said Bingley; 'and I hope it will soon be increased by seeing her quite well.'

Elizabeth thanked him from her heart, and then walked towards a table where a few books were lying. He immediately offered to fetch her others; all that his library afforded.

'And I wish my collection were larger for your benefit and my own credit; but I am an idle fellow, and though I have not many, I have more than I ever look into.'

Elizabeth assured him that she could suit herself perfectly with those in the room.

'I am astonished,' said Miss Bingley, 'that my father should have left so small a collection of books. – What a delightful library you have at Pemberley, Mr Darcy!'

'It ought to be good,' he replied, 'it has been the work of many generations.'

'And then you have added so much to it yourself, you are always buying books.'

'I cannot comprehend the neglect of a family library in such days as these.'

'Neglect! I am sure you neglect nothing that can add to the beauties of that noble place. Charles, when you build *your* house, I wish it may be half as delightful as Pemberley.'

'I wish it may.'

'But I would really advise you to make your purchase in that neighbourhood, and take Pemberley for a kind of model. There is not a finer county in England than Derbyshire.'

'With all my heart; I will buy Pemberley itself if Darcy will sell it.'

'I am talking of possibilities, Charles.'

'Upon my word, Caroline, I should think it more possible to get Pemberley by purchase than by imitation.'

Elizabeth was so much caught by what passed, as to leave her very little attention for her book; and soon laying it wholly aside, she drew near the card-table, and stationed herself between Mr Bingley and his eldest sister, to observe the game.

'Is Miss Darcy much grown since the spring?' said Miss Bingley; 'will she be as tall as I am?'

'I think she will. She is now about Miss Elizabeth Bennet's height, or rather taller.'

'How I long to see her again! I never met with anybody who delighted me so much. Such a countenance, such manners! – and so extremely accomplished for her age! Her performance on the piano-forte is exquisite.'

'It is amazing to me,' said Bingley, 'how young ladies can have patience to be so very accomplished, as they all are.'

'All young ladies accomplished! My dear Charles, what do you mean?'

'Yes, all of them, I think. They all paint tables, cover screens and net purses. I scarcely know any one who cannot do all this, and I am sure I never heard a young lady spoken of for the first time, without being informed that she was very accomplished.'

'Your list of the common extent of accomplishments,' said Darcy, 'has too much truth. The word is applied to many a woman who deserves it no otherwise than by netting a purse, or covering a screen. But I am very far from agreeing with you in your estimation of ladies in general. I cannot boast of knowing more than half a dozen, in the whole range of my acquaintance, that are really accomplished.'

'Nor I, I am sure,' said Miss Bingley.

'Then,' observed Elizabeth, 'you must comprehend a great deal in your idea of an accomplished woman.'

'Yes; I do comprehend a great deal in it.'

'Oh! certainly,' cried his faithful assistant, 'no one can be really esteemed accomplished, who does not greatly surpass what is usually met with. A woman must have a thorough knowledge of music, singing, drawing, dancing, and the modern languages, to deserve the word; and besides all this, she must possess a certain something in her air and manner of walking, the tone of her voice, her address and expressions, or the word will be but half deserved.'

'All this she must possess,' added Darcy, 'and to all this she must yet add something more substantial, in the improvement of her mind

by extensive reading.'

'I am no longer surprised at your knowing *only* six accomplished women. I rather wonder now at your knowing *any*.'

'Are you so severe upon your own sex, as to doubt the possibility of all this?'

'*I* never saw such a woman. *I* never saw such capacity, and taste, and application, and elegance, as you describe, united.'

Mrs Hurst and Miss Bingley both cried out against the injustice of her implied doubt, and were both protesting that they knew many women who answered this description, when Mr Hurst called them to order, with bitter complaints of their inattention to what was going forward. As all conversation was thereby at an end, Elizabeth soon afterwards left the room.

'Eliza Bennet,' said Miss Bingley, when the door was closed on her, 'is one of those young ladies who seek to recommend themselves to the other sex, by undervaluing their own; and with many men, I dare say, it succeeds. But, in my opinion, it is a paltry device, a very mean art.'

'Undoubtedly,' replied Darcy, to whom this remark was chiefly addressed, 'there is meanness in *all* the arts which ladies sometimes condescend to employ for captivation. Whatever bears affinity to cunning is despicable.'

Miss Bingley was not so entirely satisfied with this reply as to continue the subject.

Elizabeth joined them again only to say that her sister was worse, and that she could not leave her. Bingley urged Mr Jones's being sent for immediately; while his sisters, convinced that no country advice could be of any service, recommended an express to town for one of the most eminent physicians. This, she would not hear of; but she was not so unwilling to comply with their brother's proposal; and it was settled that Mr Jones should be sent for early in the morning, if Miss Bennet were not decidedly better. Bingley was quite uncomfortable; his sisters declared that they were miserable. They solaced their wretchedness, however, by duets after supper, while he could find no better relief to his feelings than by giving his housekeeper directions that every possible attention might be paid to the sick lady and her sister.

Chapter 9

Elizabeth passed the chief of the night in her sister's room, and in the morning had the pleasure of being able to send a tolerable answer to the enquiries which she very early received from Mr Bingley by a house-maid, and some time afterwards from the two elegant ladies who waited on his sisters. In spite of this amendment, however, she requested to have a note sent to Longbourn, desiring her mother to visit Jane, and form her own judgment of her situation. The note was immediately dispatched, and its contents as quickly complied with. Mrs Bennet, accompanied by her two youngest girls, reached Netherfield soon after the family breakfast.

Had she found Jane in any apparent danger, Mrs Bennet would have been very miserable; but being satisfied on seeing her that her illness was not alarming, she had no wish of her recovering immediately, as her restoration to health would probably remove her from Netherfield. She would not listen therefore to her daughter's proposal of being carried home; neither did the apothecary, who arrived about the same time, think it at all advisable. After sitting a little while with Jane, on Miss Bingley's appearance and invitation, the mother and

three daughters all attended her into the breakfast parlour. Bingley met them with hopes that Mrs Bennet had not found Miss Bennet worse than she expected.

'Indeed I have, Sir,' was her answer. 'She is a great deal too ill to be moved. Mr Jones says we must not think of moving her. We must trespass a little longer on your kindness.'

'Removed!' cried Bingley. 'It must not be thought of. My sister, I am sure, will not hear of her removal.'

'You may depend upon it, Madam,' said Miss Bingley, with cold civility, 'that Miss Bennet shall receive every possible attention while she remains with us.'

Mrs Bennet was profuse in her acknowledgments.

'I am sure,' she added, 'if it was not for such good friends I do not know what would become of her, for she is very ill indeed, and suffers a vast deal, though with the greatest patience in the world, which is always the way with her, for she has, without exception, the sweetest temper I ever met with. I often tell my other girls they are nothing to *her*. You have a sweet room here, Mr Bingley, and a charming prospect over that gravel walk. I do not know a place in the country that is equal to Netherfield. You will not think of quitting it in a hurry I hope, though you have but a short lease.'

'Whatever I do is done in a hurry,' replied he; 'and therefore if I should resolve to quit Netherfield, I should probably be off in five minutes. At present, however, I consider myself as quite fixed here.'

'That is exactly what I should have supposed of you,' said Elizabeth.

'You begin to comprehend me, do you?' cried he, turning towards her.

'Oh! yes – I understand you perfectly.'

'I wish I might take this for a compliment; but to be so easily seen through I am afraid is pitiful.'

'That is as it happens. It does not necessarily follow that a deep, intricate character is more or less estimable than such a one as yours.'

'Lizzy,' cried her mother, 'remember where you are, and do not run on in the wild manner that you are suffered to do at home.'

'I did not know before,' continued Bingley immediately, 'that you were a studier of character. It must be an amusing study.'

'Yes; but intricate characters are the *most* amusing. They have at least that advantage.'

'The country,' said Darcy, 'can in general supply but few subjects for such a study. In a country neighbourhood you move in a very confined and unvarying society.'

'But people themselves alter so much, that there is something new to be observed in them forever.'

'Yes, indeed,' cried Mrs Bennet, offended by his manner of mentioning a country neighbourhood. 'I assure you there is quite as much of *that* going on in the country as in town.'

Every body was surprised; and Darcy, after looking at her for a moment, turned silently away. Mrs Bennet, who fancied she had gained a complete victory over him, continued her triumph.

'I cannot see that London has any great advantage over the country for my part, except the shops and public places. The country is a vast deal pleasanter, is not it, Mr Bingley?'

'When I am in the country,' he replied, 'I never wish to leave it; and when I am in town it is pretty much the same. They have each their advantages, and I can be equally happy in either.'

'Aye – that is because you have the right disposition. But that gentleman,' looking at Darcy, 'seemed to think the country was nothing at all.'

'Indeed, Mama, you are mistaken,' said Elizabeth, blushing for her mother. 'You quite mistook Mr Darcy. He only meant that there were not such a variety of people to be met with in the country as in town, which you must acknowledge to be true.'

'Certainly, my dear, nobody said there were; but as to not meeting with many people in this neighbourhood, I believe there are few neighbourhoods larger. I know we dine with four and twenty families.'

Nothing but concern for Elizabeth could enable Bingley to keep his countenance. His sister was less delicate, and directed her eye towards

Mr Darcy with a very expressive smile. Elizabeth, for the sake of saying something that might turn her mother's thoughts, now asked her if Charlotte Lucas had been at Longbourn since *her* coming away.

'Yes, she called yesterday with her father. What an agreeable man Sir William is, Mr Bingley – is not he? so much the man of fashion! So genteel and so easy! – He has always something to say to every body. – *That* is my idea of good breeding; and those persons who fancy themselves very important and never open their mouths, quite mistake the matter.'

'Did Charlotte dine with you?'

'No, she would go home. I fancy she was wanted about the mince pies. For my part, Mr Bingley, *I* always keep servants that can do their own work; *my* daughters are brought up differently. But every body is to judge for themselves, and the Lucases are very good sort of girls, I assure you. It is a pity they are not handsome! Not that *I* think Charlotte so *very* plain – but then she is our particular friend.'

'She seems a very pleasant young woman,' said Bingley.

'Oh! dear, yes; – but you must own she is very plain. Lady Lucas herself has often said so, and envied me Jane's beauty. I do not like to boast of my own child, but to be sure, Jane – one does not often see any body better looking. It is what every body says. I do not trust my own partiality. When she was only fifteen, there was a gentleman at my brother Gardiner's in town, so much in love with her, that my sister-in-law was sure he would make her an offer before we came away. But however he did not. Perhaps he thought her too young. However, he wrote some verses on her, and very pretty they were.'

'And so ended his affection,' said Elizabeth impatiently. 'There has been many a one, I fancy, overcome in the same way. I wonder who first discovered the efficacy of poetry in driving away love!'

'I have been used to consider poetry as the *food* of love,' said Darcy.

'Of a fine, stout, healthy love it may. Every thing nourishes what is strong already. But if it be only a slight, thin sort of inclination, I am convinced that one good sonnet will starve it entirely away.'

Darcy only smiled; and the general pause which ensued made

Elizabeth tremble lest her mother should be exposing herself again. She longed to speak, but could think of nothing to say; and after a short silence Mrs Bennet began repeating her thanks to Mr Bingley for his kindness to Jane, with an apology for troubling him also with Lizzy. Mr Bingley was unaffectedly civil in his answer, and forced his younger sister to be civil also, and say what the occasion required. She performed her part indeed without much graciousness, but Mrs Bennet was satisfied, and soon afterwards ordered her carriage. Upon this signal, the youngest of her daughters put herself forward. The two girls had been whispering to each other during the whole visit, and the result of it was, that the youngest should tax Mr Bingley with having promised on his first coming into the country to give a ball at Netherfield.

Lydia was a stout, well-grown girl of fifteen, with a fine complexion and good-humoured countenance; a favourite with her mother, whose affection had brought her into public at an early age. She had high animal spirits, and a sort of natural self-consequence, which the attentions of the officers, to whom her uncle's good dinners and her own easy manners recommended her, had increased into assurance. She was very equal therefore to address Mr Bingley on the subject of the ball, and abruptly reminded him of his promise; adding, that it would be the most shameful thing in the world if he did not keep it. His answer to this sudden attack was delightful to their mother's ear.

'I am perfectly ready, I assure you, to keep my engagement; and when your sister is recovered, you shall if you please name the very day of the ball. But you would not wish to be dancing while she is ill.'

Lydia declared herself satisfied. 'Oh! yes – it would be much better to wait till Jane was well, and by that time most likely Captain Carter would be at Meryton again. And when you have given *your* ball,' she added, 'I shall insist on their giving one also. I shall tell Colonel Forster it will be quite a shame if he does not.'

Mrs Bennet and her daughters then departed, and Elizabeth returned instantly to Jane, leaving her own and her relations' behaviour to the remarks of the two ladies and Mr Darcy; the latter of whom, however, could not be prevailed on to join in their censure of *her*, in spite of all Miss Bingley's witticisms on *fine eyes*.

Chapter 10

The day passed much as the day before had done. Mrs Hurst and Miss Bingley had spent some hours of the morning with the invalid, who continued, though slowly, to mend; and in the evening Elizabeth joined their party in the drawing-room. The loo table, however, did not appear. Mr Darcy was writing, and Miss Bingley, seated near him, was watching the progress of his letter, and repeatedly calling off his attention by messages to his sister. Mr Hurst and Mr Bingley were at piquet[8], and Mrs Hurst was observing their game.

Elizabeth took up some needlework, and was sufficiently amused in attending to what passed between Darcy and his companion. The perpetual commendations of the lady either on his hand-writing, or on the evenness of his lines, or on the length of his letter, with the perfect unconcern with which her praises were received, formed a curious dialogue, and was exactly in unison with her opinion of each.

'How delighted Miss Darcy will be to receive such a letter!'

He made no answer.

'You write uncommonly fast.'

'You are mistaken. I write rather slowly.'

'How many letters you must have occasion to write in the course of the year! Letters of business too! How odious I should think them!'

'It is fortunate, then, that they fall to my lot instead of to yours.'

'Pray tell your sister that I long to see her.'

'I have already told her so once, by your desire.'

'I am afraid you do not like your pen. Let me mend it for you. I mend pens remarkably well.'

'Thank you – but I always mend my own.'

'How can you contrive to write so even?'

He was silent.

'Tell your sister I am delighted to hear of her improvement on the harp, and pray let her know that I am quite in raptures with her beautiful little design for a table, and I think it infinitely superior to Miss Grantley's.'

'Will you give me leave to defer your raptures till I write again? – At present I have not room to do them justice.'

'Oh! it is of no consequence. I shall see her in January. But do you always write such charming long letters to her, Mr Darcy?'

'They are generally long; but whether always charming, it is not for me to determine.'

'It is a rule with me, that a person who can write a long letter, with ease, cannot write ill.'

'That will not do for a compliment to Darcy, Caroline,' cried her brother – 'because he does *not* write with ease. He studies too much for words of four syllables. – Do not you, Darcy?'

'My stile of writing is very different from yours.'

'Oh!' cried Miss Bingley, 'Charles writes in the most careless way imaginable. He leaves out half his words, and blots the rest.'

'My ideas flow so rapidly that I have not time to express them – by which means my letters sometimes convey no ideas at all to my correspondents.'

'Your humility, Mr Bingley,' said Elizabeth, 'must disarm reproof.'

'Nothing is more deceitful,' said Darcy, 'than the appearance of humility. It is often only carelessness of opinion, and sometimes an indirect boast.'

'And which of the two do you call *my* little recent piece of modesty?'

'The indirect boast; – for you are really proud of your defects in writing, because you consider them as proceeding from a rapidity of thought and carelessness of execution, which if not estimable, you think at least highly interesting. The power of doing any thing with quickness is always much prized by the possessor, and often without any attention to the imperfection of the performance. When you told Mrs Bennet this morning that if you ever resolved on quitting Netherfield you should be gone in five minutes, you meant it to be a sort of panegyric, of compliment to yourself – and yet what is there so very laudable in a precipitance which must leave very necessary business undone, and can be of no real advantage to yourself or any one else?'

'Nay,' cried Bingley, 'this is too much, to remember at night all the foolish things that were said in the morning. And yet, upon my honour, I believed what I said of myself to be true, and I believe it at this moment. At least, therefore, I did not assume the character of needless precipitance merely to show off before the ladies.'

'I dare say you believed it; but I am by no means convinced that you would be gone with such celerity. Your conduct would be quite as dependent on chance as that of any man I know; and if, as you were mounting your horse, a friend were to say, "Bingley, you had better stay till next week," you would probably do it, you would probably not go – and, at another word, might stay a month.'

'You have only proved by this,' cried Elizabeth, 'that Mr Bingley did not do justice to his own disposition. You have shown him off now much more than he did himself.'

'I am exceedingly gratified,' said Bingley, 'by your converting what my friend says into a compliment on the sweetness of my temper. But I am afraid you are giving it a turn which that gentleman did by no means intend; for he would certainly think the better of me, if under such a circumstance I were to give a flat denial, and ride off as fast as I could.'

'Would Mr Darcy then consider the rashness of your original intention as atoned for by your obstinacy in adhering to it?'

'Upon my word I cannot exactly explain the matter, Darcy must speak for himself.'

'You expect me to account for opinions which you chuse to call mine, but which I have never acknowledged. Allowing the case, however, to stand according to your representation, you must remember, Miss Bennet, that the friend who is supposed to desire his return to the house, and the delay of his plan, has merely desired it, asked it without offering one argument in favour of its propriety.'

'To yield readily – easily – to the *persuasion* of a friend is no merit with you.'

'To yield without conviction is no compliment to the understanding of either.'

'You appear to me, Mr Darcy, to allow nothing for the influence of friendship and affection. A regard for the requester would often make one readily yield to a request, without waiting for arguments to reason one into it. I am not particularly speaking of such a case as you have supposed about Mr Bingley. We may as well wait, perhaps, till the circumstance occurs, before we discuss the discretion of his behaviour thereupon. But in general and ordinary cases between friend and friend, where one of them is desired by the other to change a resolution of no very great moment, should you think ill of that person for complying with the desire, without waiting to be argued into it?'

'Will it not be advisable, before we proceed on this subject, to arrange with rather more precision the degree of importance which is to appertain to this request, as well as the degree of intimacy subsisting between the parties?'

'By all means,' cried Bingley; 'let us hear all the particulars, not forgetting their comparative height and size; for that will have more weight in the argument, Miss Bennet, than you may be aware of. I assure you that if Darcy were not such a great tall fellow, in comparison with myself, I should not pay him half so much deference. I declare I do not know a more awful object than Darcy, on particular occasions, and in particular places; at his own house especially, and of a Sunday evening when he has nothing to do.'

Mr Darcy smiled; but Elizabeth thought she could perceive that he was rather offended; and therefore checked her laugh. Miss Bingley warmly resented the indignity he had received, in an expostulation with her brother for talking such nonsense.

'I see your design, Bingley,' said his friend. – 'You dislike an argument, and want to silence this.'

'Perhaps I do. Arguments are too much like disputes. If you and Miss Bennet will defer yours till I am out of the room, I shall be very thankful; and then you may say whatever you like of me.'

'What you ask,' said Elizabeth, 'is no sacrifice on my side; and Mr Darcy had much better finish his letter.'

Mr Darcy took her advice, and did finish his letter.

When that business was over, he applied to Miss Bingley and Elizabeth for the indulgence of some music. Miss Bingley moved with alacrity to the piano-forte, and after a polite request that Elizabeth would lead the way, which the other as politely and more earnestly negative, she seated herself.

Mrs Hurst sang with her sister, and while they were thus employed Elizabeth could not help observing as she turned over some music books that lay on the instrument, how frequently Mr Darcy's eyes were fixed on her. She hardly knew how to suppose that she could be an object of admiration to so great a man; and yet that he should look at her because he disliked her, was still more strange. She could only imagine however at last, that she drew his notice because there was a something about her more wrong and reprehensible, according to his ideas of right, than in any other person present. The supposition did not pain her. She liked him too little to care for his approbation.

After playing some Italian songs, Miss Bingley varied the charm by a lively Scotch air; and soon afterwards Mr Darcy, drawing near Elizabeth, said to her –

'Do not you feel a great inclination, Miss Bennet, to seize such an opportunity of dancing a reel?'

She smiled, but made no answer. He repeated the question, with some surprise at her silence.

'Oh!' said she, 'I heard you before; but I could not immediately determine what to say in reply. You wanted me, I know, to say "Yes," that you might have the pleasure of despising my taste, but I always delight in overthrowing those kind of schemes, and cheating a person of their premeditated contempt. I have therefore made up my mind to tell you, that I do not want to dance a reel at all – and now despise me if you dare.'

'Indeed I do not dare.'

Elizabeth, having rather expected to affront him, was amazed at his gallantry; but there was a mixture of sweetness and archness in her manner which made it difficult for her to affront anybody; and Darcy had never been so bewitched by any woman as he was by her. He really believed, that were it not for the inferiority of her connections, he should be in some danger.

Miss Bingley saw, or suspected enough to be jealous; and her great anxiety for the recovery of her dear friend Jane, received some assistance from her desire of getting rid of Elizabeth.

She often tried to provoke Darcy into disliking her guest, by talking of their supposed marriage, and planning his happiness in such an alliance.

'I hope,' said she, as they were walking together in the shrubbery the next day, 'you will give your mother-in-law a few hints, when this desirable event takes place, as to the advantage of holding her tongue; and if you can compass it, do cure the younger girls of running after the officers. – And, if I may mention so delicate a subject, endeavour to check that little something, bordering on conceit and impertinence, which your lady possesses.'

'Have you any thing else to propose for my domestic felicity?'

'Oh! yes. – Do let the portraits of your uncle and aunt Philips be placed in the gallery at Pemberley. Put them next to your great uncle the judge. They are in the same profession, you know; only in different lines. As for your Elizabeth's picture, you must not attempt to have it taken, for what painter could do justice to those beautiful eyes?'

'It would not be easy, indeed, to catch their expression, but their colour and shape, and the eye-lashes, so remarkably fine, might be copied.'

At that moment they were met from another walk, by Mrs Hurst and Elizabeth herself.

'I did not know that you intended to walk,' said Miss Bingley, in some confusion, lest they had been overheard.

'You used us abominably ill,' answered Mrs Hurst, 'in running away without telling us that you were coming out.'

Then taking the disengaged arm of Mr Darcy, she left Elizabeth to walk by herself. The path just admitted three. Mr Darcy felt their rudeness and immediately said, –

'This walk is not wide enough for our party. We had better go into the avenue.'

But Elizabeth, who had not the least inclination to remain with them, laughingly answered,

'No, no; stay where you are. – You are charmingly group'd, and appear to uncommon advantage. The picturesque would be spoilt by admitting a fourth. Good bye.'

She then ran gaily off, rejoicing as she rambled about, in the hope of being at home again in a day or two. Jane was already so much recovered as to intend leaving her room for a couple of hours that evening.

Chapter 11

When the ladies removed after dinner, Elizabeth ran up to her sister, and seeing her well guarded from cold, attended her into the drawing-room; where she was welcomed by her two friends with many professions of pleasure; and Elizabeth had never seen them so agreeable as they were during the hour which passed before the gentlemen appeared. Their powers of conversation were considerable. They could describe an entertainment with accuracy, relate an anecdote with humour, and laugh at their acquaintance with spirit.

But when the gentlemen entered, Jane was no longer the first object. Miss Bingley's eyes were instantly turned towards Darcy, and she had something to say to him before he had advanced many steps. He addressed himself directly to Miss Bennet, with a polite congratulation; Mr Hurst also made her a slight bow, and said he was 'very glad;' but diffuseness and warmth remained for Bingley's salutation. He was full of joy and attention. The first half hour was spent in piling up the fire, lest she should suffer from the change of room; and she removed at his desire to the other side of the fire-place, that she might be farther from the door. He then sat down by her, and talked scarcely to any one else. Elizabeth, at work in the opposite corner, saw it all with great delight.

When tea was over, Mr Hurst reminded his sister-in-law of the card-table – but in vain. She had obtained private intelligence that Mr Darcy did not wish for cards; and Mr Hurst soon found even his open petition rejected. She assured him that no one intended to play, and the silence of the whole party on the subject, seemed to justify her. Mr Hurst had therefore nothing to do, but to stretch himself on one of the sofas and go to sleep. Darcy took up a book; Miss Bingley did the same; and Mrs Hurst, principally occupied in playing with her bracelets and rings, joined now and then in her brother's conversation with Miss Bennet.

Miss Bingley's attention was quite as much engaged in watching Mr Darcy's progress through *his* book, as in reading her own; and she was perpetually either making some inquiry, or looking at his page. She could not win him, however, to any conversation; he merely answered her question, and read on. At length, quite exhausted by the attempt to be amused with her own book, which she had only chosen because it was the second volume of his, she gave a great yawn and said, 'How pleasant it is to spend an evening in this way! I declare after all there is no enjoyment like reading! How much sooner one tires of any thing than of a book! – When I have a house of my own, I shall be miserable if I have not an excellent library.'

No one made any reply. She then yawned again, threw aside her book, and cast her eyes round the room in quest of some amusement; when hearing her brother mentioning a ball to Miss Bennet, she turned suddenly towards him and said,

'By the bye, Charles, are you really serious in meditating a dance at Netherfield? – I would advise you, before you determine on it, to consult the wishes of the present party; I am much mistaken if there are not some among us to whom a ball would be rather a punishment than a pleasure.'

'If you mean Darcy,' cried her brother, 'he may go to bed, if he chuses, before it begins – but as for the ball, it is quite a settled thing; and as soon as Nicholls has made white soup enough I shall send round my cards.'

'I should like balls infinitely better,' she replied, 'if they were carried on in a different manner; but there is something insufferably tedious in the usual process of such a meeting. It would surely be much more rational if conversation instead of dancing made the order of the day.'

'Much more rational, my dear Caroline, I dare say, but it would not be near so much like a ball.'

Miss Bingley made no answer; and soon afterwards got up and walked about the room. Her figure was elegant, and she walked well; – but Darcy, at whom it was all aimed, was still inflexibly studious. In the desperation of her feelings she resolved on one effort more; and, turning to Elizabeth, said,

'Miss Eliza Bennet, let me persuade you to follow my example, and take a turn about the room. – I assure you it is very refreshing after sitting so long in one attitude.'

Elizabeth was surprised, but agreed to it immediately. Miss Bingley succeeded no less in the real object of her civility; Mr Darcy looked up. He was as much awake to the novelty of attention in that quarter as Elizabeth herself could be, and unconsciously closed his book. He was directly invited to join their party, but he declined it, observing, that he could imagine but two motives for their chusing to walk up and down the room together, with either of which motives his joining them would interfere. 'What could he mean? she was dying to know what could be his meaning' – and asked Elizabeth whether she could at all understand him?

'Not at all,' was her answer; 'but depend upon it, he means to be severe on us, and our surest way of disappointing him, will be to ask nothing about it.'

Miss Bingley, however, was incapable of disappointing Mr Darcy in any thing, and persevered therefore in requiring an explanation of his two motives.

'I have not the smallest objection to explaining them,' said he, as soon as she allowed him to speak. 'You either chuse this method of passing the evening because you are in each other's confidence and have secret affairs to discuss, or because you are conscious that your figures appear to the greatest advantage in walking; – if the first, I should be completely in your way; – and if the second, I can admire you much better as I sit by the fire.'

'Oh! shocking!' cried Miss Bingley. 'I never heard any thing so abominable. How shall we punish him for such a speech?'

'Nothing so easy, if you have but the inclination,' said Elizabeth. 'We can all plague and punish one another. Tease him – laugh at him. – Intimate as you are, you must know how it is to be done.'

'But upon my honour I do *not*. I do assure you that my intimacy has not yet taught me *that*. Tease calmness of temper and presence of mind! No, no – I feel he may defy us there. And as to laughter, we will not expose ourselves, if you please, by attempting to laugh without a subject. Mr Darcy may hug himself.'

'Mr Darcy is not to be laughed at!' cried Elizabeth. 'That is an uncommon advantage, and uncommon I hope it will continue, for it would be a great loss to *me* to have many such acquaintance. I dearly love a laugh.'

'Miss Bingley,' said he, 'has given me credit for more than can be. The wisest and the best of men, nay, the wisest and best of their actions, may be rendered ridiculous by a person whose first object in life is a joke.'

'Certainly,' replied Elizabeth – 'there are such people, but I hope I am not one of *them*. I hope I never ridicule what is wise or good. Follies and nonsense, whims and inconsistencies *do* divert me, I own, and I laugh at them whenever I can. – But these, I suppose, are precisely what you are without.'

'Perhaps that is not possible for any one. But it has been the study of my life to avoid those weaknesses which often expose a strong understanding to ridicule.'

'Such as vanity and pride.'

'Yes, vanity is a weakness indeed. But pride – where there is a real superiority of mind, pride will be always under good regulation.'

Elizabeth turned away to hide a smile.

'Your examination of Mr Darcy is over, I presume,' said Miss

Bingley; – 'and pray what is the result?'

'I am perfectly convinced by it that Mr Darcy has no defect. He owns it himself without disguise.'

'No' – said Darcy, 'I have made no such pretension. I have faults enough, but they are not, I hope, of understanding. My temper I dare not vouch for. – It is I believe too little yielding – certainly too little for the convenience of the world. I cannot forget the follies and vices of others so soon as I ought, nor their offences against myself. My feelings are not puffed about with every attempt to move them. My temper would perhaps be called resentful. – My good opinion once lost is lost forever.'

'*That* is a failing indeed!' – cried Elizabeth. 'Implacable resentment *is* a shade in a character. But you have chosen your fault well. – I really cannot *laugh* at it. You are safe from me.'

'There is, I believe, in every disposition a tendency to some particular evil, a natural defect, which not even the best education can overcome.'

'And *your* defect is a propensity to hate every body.'

'And yours,' he replied with a smile, 'is wilfully to misunderstand them.'

'Do let us have a little music,' – cried Miss Bingley, tired of a conversation in which she had no share. – 'Louisa, you will not mind my waking Mr Hurst.'

Her sister made not the smallest objection, and the piano-forte was opened, and Darcy, after a few moments recollection, was not sorry for it. He began to feel the danger of paying Elizabeth too much attention.

Chapter 12

In consequence of an agreement between the sisters, Elizabeth wrote the next morning to her mother, to beg that the carriage might be sent for them in the course of the day. But Mrs Bennet, who had calculated on her daughters remaining at Netherfield till the following Tuesday, which would exactly finish Jane's week, could not bring herself to receive them with pleasure before. Her answer, therefore, was not propitious, at least not to Elizabeth's wishes, for she was impatient to get home. Mrs Bennet sent them word that they could not possibly have the carriage before Tuesday; and in her postscript it was added, that if Mr Bingley and his sister pressed them to stay longer, she could spare them very well. – Against staying longer, however, Elizabeth was positively resolved – nor did she much expect it would be asked; and fearful, on the contrary, as being considered as intruding themselves needlessly long, she urged Jane to borrow Mr Bingley's carriage immediately, and at length it was settled that their original design of leaving Netherfield that morning should be mentioned, and the request made.

The communication excited many professions of concern; and enough was said of wishing them to stay at least till the following day to work on Jane; and till the morrow[9], their going was deferred. Miss Bingley was then sorry that she had proposed the delay, for her jealousy and dislike of one sister much exceeded her affection for the other.

The master of the house heard with real sorrow that they were to go so soon, and repeatedly tried to persuade Miss Bennet that it would not be safe for her – that she was not enough recovered; but Jane was firm where she felt herself to be right.

To Mr Darcy it was welcome intelligence – Elizabeth had been at Netherfield long enough. She attracted him more than he liked – and Miss Bingley was uncivil to *her*, and more teasing than usual to himself. He wisely resolved to be particularly careful that no sign of admiration should *now* escape him, nothing that could elevate her with the hope of influencing his felicity; sensible that if such an idea had been suggested, his behaviour during the last day must have material weight in confirming or crushing it. Steady to his purpose, he scarcely spoke ten words to her through the whole of Saturday, and though they were at one time left by themselves for half an hour, he adhered most conscientiously to his book, and would not even look at her.

On Sunday, after morning service, the separation, so agreeable to almost all, took place. Miss Bingley's civility to Elizabeth increased at last very rapidly, as well as her affection for Jane; and when they parted, after assuring the latter of the pleasure it would always give her to see her either at Longbourn or Netherfield, and embracing her most tenderly, she even shook hands with the former. – Elizabeth took leave of the whole party in the liveliest spirits.

They were not welcomed home very cordially by their mother. Mrs Bennet wondered at their coming, and thought them very wrong to give so much trouble, and was sure Jane would have caught cold again. – But their father, though very laconic in his expressions of pleasure, was really glad to see them; he had felt their importance in the family circle. The evening conversation, when they were all assembled, had lost much of its animation, and almost all its sense, by the absence of Jane and Elizabeth.

They found Mary, as usual, deep in the study of thorough bass and human nature; and had some new extracts to admire, and some new observations of thread-bare morality to listen to. Catherine and Lydia had information for them of a different sort. Much had been done, and much had been said in the regiment since the preceding Wednesday; several of the officers had dined lately with their uncle, a private had been flogged, and it had actually been hinted that Colonel Forster was going to be married.

Chapter 13

'I hope, my dear,' said Mr Bennet to his wife, as they were at breakfast the next morning, 'that you have ordered a good dinner today, because I have reason to expect an addition to our family party.'

'Who do you mean, my dear? I know of nobody that is coming I am sure, unless Charlotte Lucas should happen to call in, and I hope *my* dinners are good enough for her. I do not believe she often sees such at home.'

'The person of whom I speak, is a gentleman and a stranger.' Mrs Bennet's eyes sparkled. – 'A gentleman and a stranger! It is Mr Bingley I am sure. Why Jane – you never dropt[10] a word of this; you sly thing! Well, I am sure I shall be extremely glad to see Mr Bingley. – But – good lord! how unlucky! there is not a bit of fish to be got today. Lydia, my love, ring the bell. I must speak to Hill, this moment.'

'It is *not* Mr Bingley,' said her husband; 'it is a person whom I never saw in the whole course of my life.'

This roused a general astonishment; and he had the pleasure of being eagerly questioned by his wife and five daughters at once.

After amusing himself some time with their curiosity, he thus explained. 'About a month ago I received this letter, and about a fortnight ago I answered it, for I thought it a case of some delicacy, and requiring early attention. It is from my cousin, Mr Collins, who, when I am dead, may turn you all out of this house as soon as he pleases.'

'Oh! my dear,' cried his wife, 'I cannot bear to hear that mentioned. Pray do not talk of that odious man. I do think it is the hardest thing in the world, that your estate should be entailed away from your own children; and I am sure if I had been you, I should have tried long ago to do something or other about it.'

Jane and Elizabeth attempted to explain to her the nature of an entail. They had often attempted it before, but it was a subject on which Mrs Bennet was beyond the reach of reason; and she continued to rail bitterly against the cruelty of settling an estate away from a family of five daughters, in favour of a man whom nobody cared anything about.

'It certainly is a most iniquitous affair,' said Mr Bennet, 'and nothing can clear Mr Collins from the guilt of inheriting Longbourn. But if you will listen to his letter, you may perhaps be a little softened by his manner of expressing himself.'

'No, that I am sure I shall not; and I think it was very impertinent of him to write to you at all, and very hypocritical. I hate such false friends. Why could not he keep on quarrelling with you, as his father did before him?'

'Why, indeed, he does seem to have had some filial scruples on that head, as you will hear.'

Hunsford, near Westerham, Kent,
15th October

DEAR SIR,

THE disagreement subsisting between yourself and my late honoured father, always gave me much uneasiness, and since I have had the misfortune to lose him, I have frequently wished to heal the breach; but for some time I was kept back by my own doubts, fearing lest it might seem disrespectful to his memory for me to be on good terms with any one, with whom it had always pleased him to be at variance. – 'There, Mrs Bennet.' – My mind however is now made up on the subject, for having received ordination at Easter, I have been so fortunate as to be distinguished by the patronage of the Right Honourable Lady Catherine de Bourgh, widow of Sir Lewis de Bourgh, whose bounty and beneficence has preferred me to the valuable rectory of this parish, where it shall be my earnest endeavour to demean myself with grateful respect towards her Ladyship, and be ever ready to perform those rites and ceremonies which are instituted by the Church of England. As a clergyman, moreover, I feel it my duty to promote and establish the blessing of peace in all families within the reach of my influence; and on these grounds I flatter myself that my present overtures of good-will are highly commendable, and that the circumstance of my being next in the entail of Longbourn estate, will be kindly overlooked on your side, and not lead you to reject the offered olive branch. I cannot be otherwise than concerned at being the means of injuring your amiable daughters, and beg leave to apologise for it, as well as to assure you of my readiness to make them every possible amends, – but of this hereafter. If you should have no objection to receive me into your house, I propose myself the satisfaction of waiting on you and your family, Monday, November 18th, by four o'clock, and shall probably trespass on your hospitality till the Saturday se'night following, which I can do without any inconvenience, as Lady Catherine is far from objecting to my occasional absence on a Sunday, provided that some other clergyman is engaged to do the duty of the day. I remain, dear sir, with respectful compliments to your lady and daughters, your well-wisher and friend,

WILLIAM COLLINS

'At four o'clock, therefore, we may expect this peace-making gentleman,' said Mr Bennet, as he folded up the letter. 'He seems to be a most conscientious and polite young man, upon my word; and I doubt not will prove a valuable acquaintance, especially if Lady Catherine should be so indulgent as to let him come to us again.'

'There is some sense in what he says about the girls however; and if he is disposed to make them any amends, I shall not be the person to discourage him.'

'Though it is difficult,' said Jane, 'to guess in what way he can mean to make us the atonement he thinks our due, the wish is certainly to his credit.'

Elizabeth was chiefly struck with his extraordinary deference for Lady Catherine, and his kind intention of christening, marrying, and burying his parishioners whenever it were required.

'He must be an oddity, I think,' said she. 'I cannot make him out. – There is something very pompous in his stile. – And what can he mean by apologizing for being next in the entail? – We cannot suppose he would help it, if he could. – Can he be a sensible man, sir?'

'No, my dear; I think not. I have great hopes of finding him quite the reverse. There is a mixture of servility and self-importance in his letter, which promises well. I am impatient to see him.'

'In point of composition,' said Mary, 'his letter does not seem defective. The idea of the olive branch perhaps is not wholly new, yet I think it is well expressed.'

To Catherine and Lydia, neither the letter nor its writer were in any degree interesting. It was next to impossible that their cousin should come in a scarlet coat, and it was now some weeks since they had received pleasure from the society of a man in any other colour. As for their mother, Mr Collins's letter had done away much of her ill-will, and she was preparing to see him with a degree of composure, which astonished her husband and daughters.

Mr Collins was punctual to his time, and was received with great politeness by the whole family. Mr Bennet indeed said little; but the ladies were ready enough to talk, and Mr Collins seemed neither in need of encouragement, nor inclined to be silent himself. He was a tall, heavy looking young man of five and twenty. His air was grave and stately, and his manners were very formal. He had not been long seated before he complimented Mrs Bennet on having so fine a family of daughters, said he had heard much of their beauty, but that, in this instance, fame had fallen short of the truth; and added, that he did not doubt her seeing them all in due time well disposed of in marriage. This gallantry was not much to the taste of some of his hearers, but Mrs Bennet, who quarrelled with no compliments, answered most readily,

'You are very kind, sir, I am sure; and I wish with all my heart it may prove so; for else they will be destitute enough. Things are settled so oddly.'

'You allude perhaps to the entail of this estate.'

'Ah! sir, I do indeed. It is a grievous affair to my poor girls, you must confess. Not that I mean to find fault with *you*, for such things

I know are all chance in this world. There is no knowing how estates will go when once they come to be entailed.'

'I am very sensible, madam, of the hardship to my fair cousins, – and could say much on the subject, but that I am cautious of appearing forward and precipitate. But I can assure the young ladies that I come prepared to admire them. At present I will not say more, but perhaps when we are better acquainted –'

He was interrupted by a summons to dinner; and the girls smiled on each other. They were not the only objects of Mr Collins's admiration. The hall, the dining-room, and all its furniture were examined and praised; and his commendation of every thing would have touched Mrs Bennet's heart, but for the mortifying supposition of his viewing it all as his own future property. The dinner too in its turn was highly admired; and he begged to know to which of his fair cousins, the excellence of its cookery was owing. But here he was set right by Mrs Bennet, who assured him with some asperity that they were very well able to keep a good cook, and that her daughters had nothing to do in the kitchen. He begged pardon for having displeased her. In a softened tone she declared herself not at all offended; but he continued to apologise for about a quarter of an hour.

Chapter 14

During dinner, Mr Bennet scarcely spoke at all; but when the servants were withdrawn, he thought it time to have some conversation with his guest, and therefore started a subject in which he expected him to shine, by observing that he seemed very fortunate in his patroness. Lady Catherine de Bourgh's attention to his wishes, and consideration for his comfort, appeared very remarkable. Mr Bennet could not have chosen better. Mr Collins was eloquent in her praise. The subject elevated him to more than usual solemnity of manner, and with a most important aspect he protested that he had never in his life witnessed such behaviour in a person of rank – such affability and condescension, as he had himself experienced from Lady Catherine. She had been graciously pleased to approve of both the discourses, which he had already had the honour of preaching before her. She had also asked him twice to dine at Rosings, and had sent for him only the Saturday before, to make up her pool of quadrille[11] in the evening. Lady Catherine was reckoned proud by many people he knew, but *he* had never seen any thing but affability in her. She had always spoken to him as she would to any other gentleman; she made not the smallest objection to his joining in the society of the neighbourhood, nor to his leaving his parish occasionally for a week or two, to visit his relations. She had even condescended to advise him to marry as soon as he could, provided he chose with discretion; and had once paid him a visit in his humble parsonage, where she had perfectly approved all the alterations he had been making, and had even vouchsafed to suggest some herself, – some shelves in the closets up stairs.

'That is all very proper and civil, I am sure,' said Mrs Bennet, 'and I dare say she is a very agreeable woman. It is a pity that great ladies in general are not more like her. Does she live near you, sir?'

'The garden in which stands my humble abode, is separated only by a lane from Rosings Park, her ladyship's residence.'

'I think you said she was a widow, sir? has she any family?'

'She has one only daughter, the heiress of Rosings, and of very extensive property.'

'Ah!' cried Mrs Bennet, shaking her head, 'then she is better off than many girls. And what sort of young lady is she? is she handsome?'

'She is a most charming young lady indeed. Lady Catherine herself says that in point of true beauty, Miss De Bourgh is far superior to the handsomest of her sex; because there is that in her features which marks the young woman of distinguished birth. She is unfortunately of a sickly constitution, which has prevented her making that progress in many accomplishments, which she could not otherwise have failed of; as I am informed by the lady who superintended her education, and who still resides with them. But she is perfectly amiable, and often condescends to drive by my humble abode in her little phaeton and ponies.'

'Has she been presented? I do not remember her name among the ladies at court.'

'Her indifferent state of health unhappily prevents her being in town; and by that means, as I told Lady Catherine myself one day, has deprived the British court of its brightest ornament. Her ladyship seemed pleased with the idea, and you may imagine that I am happy on every occasion to offer those little delicate compliments which are always acceptable to ladies. I have more than once observed to Lady Catherine, that her charming daughter seemed born to be a duchess, and that the most elevated rank, instead of giving her consequence, would be adorned by her. – These are the kind of little things which please her ladyship, and it is a sort of attention which I conceive myself peculiarly bound to pay.'

'You judge very properly,' said Mr Bennet, 'and it is happy for you that you possess the talent of flattering with delicacy. May I ask whether these pleasing attentions proceed from the impulse of the moment, or are the result of previous study?'

'They arise chiefly from what is passing at the time, and though I sometimes amuse myself with suggesting and arranging such little elegant compliments as may be adapted to ordinary occasions, I always wish to give them as unstudied an air as possible.'

Mr Bennet's expectations were fully answered. His cousin was as absurd as he had hoped, and he listened to him with the keenest enjoyment, maintaining at the same time the most resolute composure of countenance, and except in an occasional glance at Elizabeth, requiring no partner in his pleasure.

By tea-time however the dose had been enough, and Mr Bennet was glad to take his guest into the drawing-room again, and when tea was over, glad to invite him to read aloud to the ladies. Mr Collins readily assented, and a book was produced; but on beholding it, (for every thing announced it to be from a circulating library,) he started back, and begging pardon, protested that he never read novels. – Kitty stared at him, and Lydia exclaimed. – Other books were produced, and after some deliberation he chose Fordyce's Sermons. Lydia gaped as he opened the volume, and before he had, with very monotonous solemnity, read three pages, she interrupted him with,

'Do you know, mama, that my uncle Philips talks of turning away Richard, and if he does, Colonel Forster will hire him. My aunt told me so herself on Saturday. I shall walk to Meryton tomorrow to hear more about it, and to ask when Mr Denny comes back from town.'

Lydia was bid by her two eldest sisters to hold her tongue; but Mr Collins, much offended, laid aside his book, and said,

'I have often observed how little young ladies are interested by books of a serious stamp, though written solely for their benefit. It amazes me, I confess; – for certainly, there can be nothing so advantageous to them as instruction. But I will no longer importune my young cousin.'

Then turning to Mr Bennet, he offered himself as his antagonist at backgammon. Mr Bennet accepted the challenge, observing that he acted very wisely in leaving the girls to their own trifling amusements. Mrs Bennet and her daughters apologised most civilly for Lydia's interruption, and promised that it should not occur again, if he would resume his book; but Mr Collins, after assuring them that he bore his young cousin no ill will, and should never resent her behaviour as any affront, seated himself at another table with Mr Bennet, and prepared for backgammon.

Chapter 15

Mr Collins was not a sensible man, and the deficiency of nature had been but little assisted by education or society; the greatest part of his life having been spent under the guidance of an illiterate and miserly father; and though he belonged to one of the universities, he had merely kept the necessary terms, without forming at it any useful acquaintance. The subjection in which his father had brought him up, had given him originally great humility of manner, but it was now a good deal counteracted by the self-conceit of a weak head, living in retirement, and the consequential feelings of early and unexpected prosperity. A fortunate chance had recommended him to Lady Catherine de Bourgh when the living of Hunsford was vacant; and the respect which he felt for her high rank, and his veneration for her as his patroness, mingling with a very good opinion of himself, of his authority as a clergyman, and his rights as a rector, made him altogether a mixture of pride and obsequiousness, self-importance and humility.

Having now a good house and very sufficient income, he intended to marry; and in seeking a reconciliation with the Longbourn family he had a wife in view, as he meant to chuse one of the daughters, if he found them as handsome and amiable as they were represented by common report. This was his plan of amends – of atonement – for inheriting their father's estate; and he thought it an excellent one, full of eligibility and suitableness, and excessively generous and disinterested on his own part.

His plan did not vary on seeing them. – Miss Bennet's lovely face confirmed his views, and established all his strictest notions of what was due to seniority; and for the first evening *she* was his settled choice. The next morning, however, made an alteration; for in a quarter of an hour's tête-à-tête with Mrs Bennet before breakfast, a conversation beginning with his parsonage-house, and leading naturally to the avowal of his hopes, that a mistress for it might be found at Longbourn, produced from her, amid very complaisant smiles and general encouragement, a caution against the very Jane he had fixed on. – 'As to her *younger* daughters she could not take upon her to say – she could not positively answer – but she did not *know* of any prepossession; – her *eldest* daughter, she must just mention – she felt it incumbent on her to hint, was likely to be very soon engaged.'

Mr Collins had only to change from Jane to Elizabeth – and it was soon done – done while Mrs Bennet was stirring the fire. Elizabeth, equally next to Jane in birth and beauty, succeeded her of course.

Mrs Bennet treasured up the hint, and trusted that she might soon have two daughters married; and the man whom she could not bear to speak of the day before, was now high in her good graces.

Lydia's intention of walking to Meryton was not forgotten; every sister except Mary agreed to go with her; and Mr Collins was to attend them, at the request of Mr Bennet, who was most anxious to get rid of him, and have his library to himself; for thither Mr Collins had followed him after breakfast, and there he would continue, nominally engaged with one of the largest folios in the collection, but really talking to Mr Bennet, with little cessation, of his house and garden at Hunsford. Such doings discomposed Mr Bennet exceedingly. In his library he had been always sure of leisure and tranquillity; and though prepared, as he told Elizabeth, to meet with folly and conceit in every other room in the house, he was used to be free from them there; his civility, therefore, was most prompt in inviting Mr Collins to join his daughters in their walk; and Mr Collins, being in fact much better fitted for a walker than a reader, was extremely well pleased to close his large book, and go.

In pompous nothings on his side, and civil assents on that of his cousins, their time passed till they entered Meryton. The attention of the younger ones was then no longer to be gained by *him*. Their eyes were immediately wandering up in the street in quest of the officers, and nothing less than a very smart bonnet indeed, or a really new muslin in a shop window, could recall them.

But the attention of every lady was soon caught by a young man, whom they had never seen before, of most gentlemanlike appearance, walking with an officer on the other side of the way. The officer was the very Mr Denny, concerning whose return from London Lydia came to inquire, and he bowed as they passed. All were struck with the stranger's air, all wondered who he could be, and Kitty and Lydia, determined if possible to find out, led the way across the street, under pretence of wanting something in an opposite shop, and fortunately had just gained the pavement when the two gentlemen turning back had reached the same spot. Mr Denny addressed them directly, and entreated permission to introduce his friend, Mr Wickham, who had returned with him the day before from town, and he was happy to say had accepted a commission in their corps. This was exactly as it should be; for the young man wanted only regimentals to make him completely charming. His appearance was greatly in his favour; he had all the best part of beauty, a fine countenance, a good figure, and very pleasing address. The introduction was followed up on his side by a happy readiness of conversation – a readiness at the same time perfectly correct and unassuming; and the whole party were still standing and talking together very agreeably, when the sound of horses drew their notice, and Darcy and Bingley were seen riding down the street. On distinguishing the ladies of the group, the two gentlemen came directly towards them, and began the usual civilities. Bingley was the principal spokesman, and Miss Bennet the principal object. He was then, he said, on his way to Longbourn on purpose to inquire after her. Mr Darcy corroborated it with a bow, and was beginning to determine not to fix his eyes on Elizabeth, when they were suddenly arrested by the sight of the stranger, and Elizabeth happening to see the countenance of both as they looked at each other, was all astonishment at the effect of the meeting. Both changed colour, one looked white, the other red. Mr Wickham, after a few moments, touched his hat – a salutation which Mr Darcy just deigned to return. What could be the meaning of it? – It was impossible to imagine; it was impossible not to long to know.

In another minute Mr Bingley, but without seeming to have noticed what passed, took leave and rode on with his friend.

Mr Denny and Mr Wickham walked with the young ladies to the door of Mr Philips's house, and then made their bows, in spite of Miss Lydia's pressing entreaties that they would come in, and even in spite of Mrs Philips' throwing up the parlour window, and loudly seconding the invitation.

Mrs Philips was always glad to see her nieces, and the two eldest, from their recent absence, were particularly welcome, and she was eagerly expressing her surprise at their sudden return home, which, as their own carriage had not fetched them, she should have known nothing about, if she had not happened to see Mr Jones's shop boy in the street, who had told her that they were not to send any more draughts to Netherfield because the Miss Bennets were come away, when her civility was claimed towards Mr Collins by Jane's introduction of him. She received him with her very best politeness, which he returned with as much more, apologising for his intrusion, without any previous acquaintance with her, which he could not help flattering himself however might be justified by his relationship to the young ladies who introduced him to her notice. Mrs Philips was quite awed by such an excess of good breeding; but her contemplation of one stranger was soon put an end to by exclamations and inquiries about the other, of whom, however, she could only tell her nieces what they already knew, that Mr Denny had brought him from London, and that he was to have a lieutenant's commission in the —[12] shire. She had been watching him the last hour, she said, as he walked up and down the street, and had Mr Wickham appeared Kitty and Lydia would certainly have continued the occupation, but unluckily no one passed the windows now except a few of the officers, who in comparison with the stranger, were become 'stupid, disagreeable fellows.' Some of them were to dine with the Philipses the next day, and their aunt promised to make her husband call on Mr Wickham, and give him an invitation also, if the family from Longbourn would come in the evening. This was agreed to, and Mrs Philips protested that they would have a nice comfortable noisy game of lottery tickets, and a little bit of hot supper afterwards. The prospect of such delights was very cheering, and they parted in mutual good spirits. Mr Collins repeated his apologies in quitting the room, and was assured with unwearying civility that they were perfectly needless.

As they walked home, Elizabeth related to Jane what she had seen pass between the two gentlemen; but though Jane would have defended either or both, had they appeared to be wrong, she could no more explain such behaviour than her sister.

Mr Collins on his return highly gratified Mrs Bennet by admiring Mrs Philips's manners and politeness. He protested that except Lady Catherine and her daughter, he had never seen a more elegant woman; for she had not only received him with the utmost civility, but had even pointedly included him in her invitation for the next evening, although utterly unknown to her before. Something he supposed might be attributed to his connection with them, but yet he had never met with so much attention in the whole course of his life.

Chapter 16

As no objection was made to the young people's engagement with their aunt, and all Mr Collins's scruples of leaving Mr and Mrs Bennet for a single evening during his visit were most steadily resisted, the coach conveyed him and his five cousins at a suitable hour to Meryton; and the girls had the pleasure of hearing, as they entered the drawing-room, that Mr Wickham had accepted their uncle's invitation, and was then in the house.

When this information was given, and they had all taken their seats, Mr Collins was at leisure to look around him and admire, and he was so much struck with the size and furniture of the apartment, that he declared he might almost have supposed himself in the small summer breakfast parlour at Rosings; a comparison that did not at first convey much gratification; but when Mrs Philips understood from him what Rosings was, and who was its proprietor, when she had listened to the description of only one of Lady Catherine's drawing-rooms, and found that the chimney-piece alone had cost eight hundred pounds, she felt all the force of the compliment, and would hardly have resented a comparison with the housekeeper's room.

In describing to her all the grandeur of Lady Catherine and her mansion, with occasional digressions in praise of his own humble abode, and the improvements it was receiving, he was happily employed until the gentlemen joined them; and he found in Mrs Philips a very attentive listener, whose opinion of his consequence increased with what she heard, and who was resolving to retail it all among her neighbours as soon as she could. To the girls, who could not listen to their cousin, and who had nothing to do but to wish for an instrument, and examine their own indifferent imitations of china on the mantlepiece[13], the interval of waiting appeared very long. It was over at last however. The gentlemen did approach; and when Mr Wickham walked into the room, Elizabeth felt that she had neither been seeing him before, nor thinking of him since, with the smallest degree of unreasonable admiration. The officers of the —shire were in general a very creditable, gentlemanlike set, and the best of them were of the present party; but Mr Wickham was as far beyond them all in person, countenance, air, and walk, as *they* were superior to the broad-faced stuffy uncle Philips, breathing port wine, who followed them into the room.

Mr Wickham was the happy man towards whom almost every female eye was turned, and Elizabeth was the happy woman by whom he finally seated himself; and the agreeable manner in which he immediately fell into conversation, though it was only on its being a wet night, and on the probability of a rainy season, made her feel that the commonest, dullest, most threadbare topic might be rendered interesting by the skill of the speaker.

With such rivals for the notice of the fair, as Mr Wickham and the officers, Mr Collins seemed likely to sink into insignificance; to the young ladies he certainly was nothing; but he had still at intervals a kind listener in Mrs Philips, and was, by her watchfulness, most abundantly supplied with coffee and muffin.

When the card tables were placed, he had an opportunity of obliging her in return, by sitting down to whist[14].

'I know little of the game, at present,' said he, 'but I shall be glad to improve myself, for in my situation of life'– Mrs Philips was very thankful for his compliance, but could not wait for his reason.

Mr Wickham did not play at whist, and with ready delight was he received at the other table between Elizabeth and Lydia. At first there seemed danger of Lydia's engrossing him entirely, for she was a most determined talker; but being likewise extremely fond of lottery tickets, she soon grew too much interested in the game, too eager in making bets and exclaiming after prizes, to have attention for any one in particular. Allowing for the common demands of the game, Mr Wickham was therefore at leisure to talk to Elizabeth, and she was very willing to hear him, though what she chiefly wished to hear she could not hope to be told, the history of his acquaintance with Mr Darcy. She dared not even mention that gentleman. Her curiosity however was unexpectedly relieved. Mr Wickham began the subject himself. He inquired how far Netherfield was from Meryton; and, after receiving her answer, asked in an hesitating manner how long Mr Darcy had been staying there.

'About a month,' said Elizabeth; and then, unwilling to let the subject drop, added, 'he is a man of very large property in Derbyshire, I understand.'

'Yes,' replied Wickham; – 'his estate there is a noble one. A clear ten thousand per annum. You could not have met with a person more capable of giving you certain information on that head than myself – for I have been connected with his family in a particular manner from my infancy.'

Elizabeth could not but look surprised.

'You may well be surprised, Miss Bennet, at such an assertion, after seeing, as you probably might, the very cold manner of our meeting yesterday. – Are you much acquainted with Mr Darcy?'

'As much as I ever wish to be,' cried Elizabeth warmly, – 'I have spent four days in the same house with him, and I think him very disagreeable.'

'I have no right to give *my* opinion,' said Wickham, 'as to his being agreeable or otherwise. I am not qualified to form one. I have known him too long and too well to be a fair judge. It is impossible for *me* to be impartial. But I believe your opinion of him would in general astonish – and perhaps you would not express it quite so strongly anywhere else. – Here you are in your own family.'

'Upon my word I say no more *here* than I might say in any house in the neighbourhood, except Netherfield. He is not at all liked in Hertfordshire. Every body is disgusted with his pride. You will not find him more favourably spoken of by any one.'

'I cannot pretend to be sorry,' said Wickham, after a short interruption, 'that he or that any man should not be estimated beyond their deserts; but with *him* I believe it does not often happen. The world is blinded by his fortune and consequence, or frightened by his high and imposing manners, and sees him only as he chuses to be seen.'

'I should take him, even on *my* slight acquaintance, to be an ill-tempered man.' Wickham only shook his head.

'I wonder,' said he, at the next opportunity of speaking, 'whether he is likely to be in this country much longer.'

'I do not at all know; but I *heard* nothing of his going away when I was at Netherfield. I hope your plans in favour of the —shire will not be affected by his being in the neighbourhood.'

'Oh! no – it is not for *me* to be driven away by Mr Darcy. If *he* wishes to avoid seeing *me*, he must go. We are not on friendly terms, and it always gives me pain to meet him, but I have no reason for avoiding *him* but what I might proclaim to all the world; a sense of very great ill usage, and most painful regrets at his being what he is. His father, Miss Bennet, the late Mr Darcy, was one of the best men that ever breathed, and the truest friend I ever had; and I can never be in company with this Mr Darcy without being grieved to the soul by a thousand tender recollections. His behaviour to myself has been scandalous; but I verily believe I could forgive him any thing and every thing, rather than his disappointing the hopes and disgracing the memory of his father.'

Elizabeth found the interest of the subject increase, and listened with all her heart; but the delicacy of it prevented farther inquiry.

Mr Wickham began to speak on more general topics, Meryton, the neighbourhood, the society, appearing highly pleased with all that he had yet seen, and speaking of the latter especially, with gentle but very intelligible gallantry.

'It was the prospect of constant society, and good society,' he added, 'which was my chief inducement to enter the —shire. I knew it to be a most respectable, agreeable corps, and my friend Denny tempted me farther by his account of their present quarters, and the very great attentions and excellent acquaintance Meryton had procured them. Society, I own, is necessary to me. I have been a disappointed man, and my spirits will not bear solitude. I *must* have employment and society. A military life is not what I was intended for, but circumstances have now made it eligible. The church *ought* to have been my profession – I was brought up for the church, and I should at this time have been in possession of a most valuable living, had it pleased the gentleman we were speaking of just now.'

'Indeed!'

'Yes – the late Mr Darcy bequeathed me the next presentation of the best living in his gift. He was my godfather, and excessively attached to me. I cannot do justice to his kindness. He meant to provide for me amply, and thought he had done it; but when the living fell, it was given elsewhere.'

'Good heavens!' cried Elizabeth; 'but how could *that* be? – How could his will be disregarded? – Why did not you seek legal redress?'

'There was just such an informality in the terms of the bequest as to give me no hope from law. A man of honour could not have doubted the intention, but Mr Darcy chose to doubt it – or to treat it as a merely conditional recommendation, and to assert that I had forfeited all claim to it by extravagance, imprudence, in short any thing or nothing. Certain it is, that the living became vacant two years ago, exactly as I was of an age to hold it, and that it was given to another man; and no less certain is it, that I cannot accuse myself of having really done any thing to deserve to lose it. I have a warm, unguarded temper, and I may perhaps have sometimes spoken my opinion *of* him, and *to* him, too freely. I can recall nothing worse. But the fact is, that we are very different sort of men, and that he hates me.'

'This is quite shocking! – He deserves to be publicly disgraced.'

'Some time or other he *will* be – but it shall not be by *me*. Till I can forget his father, I can never defy or expose *him*.'

Elizabeth honoured him for such feelings, and thought him handsomer than ever as he expressed them.

'But what,' said she, after a pause, 'can have been his motive? – what can have induced him to behave so cruelly?'

'A thorough, determined dislike of me – a dislike which I cannot but attribute in some measure to jealousy. Had the late Mr Darcy liked me less, his son might have borne with me better; but his father's uncommon attachment to me, irritated him I believe very early in life. He had not a temper to bear the sort of competition in which we stood – the sort of preference which was often given me.'

'I had not thought Mr Darcy so bad as this – though I have never liked him, I had not thought so very ill of him – I had supposed him to be despising his fellow-creatures in general, but did not suspect him of descending to such malicious revenge, such injustice, such inhumanity as this!'

After a few minutes reflection, however, she continued, 'I *do* remember his boasting one day, at Netherfield, of the implacability of his resentments, of his having an unforgiving temper. His disposition must be dreadful.'

'I will not trust myself on the subject,' replied Wickham, '*I* can hardly be just to him.'

Elizabeth was again deep in thought, and after a time exclaimed, 'To treat in such a manner, the godson, the friend, the favourite of his father!' – She could have added, 'A young man too, like *you*, whose very countenance may vouch for your being amiable' – but she contented herself with 'And one, too, who had probably been his own companion from childhood, connected together, as I think you said, in the closest manner!'

'We were born in the same parish, within the same park, the greatest part of our youth was passed together; inmates of the same house, sharing the same amusements, objects of the same parental care. My father began life in the profession which your uncle, Mr Philips, appears to do so much credit to – but he gave up every thing to be of use to the late Mr Darcy, and devoted all his time to the care of the Pemberley property. He was most highly esteemed by Mr Darcy, a most intimate, confidential friend. Mr Darcy often acknowledged himself to be under the greatest obligations to my father's active superintendence, and when immediately before my father's death, Mr Darcy gave him a voluntary promise of providing for me, I am convinced that he felt it to be as much a debt of gratitude to *him*, as of affection to myself.'

'How strange!' cried Elizabeth. 'How abominable! – I wonder that the very pride of this Mr Darcy has not made him just to you! – If from no better motive, that he should not have been too proud to be dishonest, – for dishonesty I must call it.'

'It *is* wonderful,' – replied Wickham, – 'for almost all his actions may be traced to pride; – and pride has often been his best friend. It has connected him nearer with virtue than any other feeling. But we are none of us consistent; and in his behaviour to me, there were stronger impulses even than pride.'

'Can such abominable pride as his, have ever done him good?'

'Yes. It has often led him to be liberal and generous, – to give his money freely, to display hospitality, to assist his tenants, and relieve the poor. Family pride, and *filial* pride, for he is very proud of what his father was, have done this. Not to appear to disgrace his family, to degenerate from the popular qualities, or lose the influence of the Pemberley House, is a powerful motive. He has also *brotherly* pride, which with *some* brotherly affection, makes him a very kind and careful guardian of his sister; and you will hear him generally cried up as the most attentive and best of brothers.'

'What sort of a girl is Miss Darcy?'

He shook his head. – 'I wish I could call her amiable. It gives me pain to speak ill of a Darcy. But she is too much like her brother, – very, very proud. – As a child, she was affectionate and pleasing, and extremely fond of me; and I have devoted hours and hours to her amusement. But she is nothing to me now. She is a handsome girl, about fifteen or sixteen, and I understand highly accomplished. Since her father's death, her home has been London, where a lady lives with her, and superintends her education.'

After many pauses and many trials of other subjects, Elizabeth could not help reverting once more to the first, and saying,

'I am astonished at his intimacy with Mr Bingley! How can Mr Bingley, who seems good humour itself, and is, I really believe, truly amiable, be in friendship with such a man? How can they suit each other? – Do you know Mr Bingley?'

'Not at all.'

'He is a sweet tempered, amiable, charming man. He cannot know what Mr Darcy is.'

'Probably not; – but Mr Darcy can please where he chuses. He does not want abilities. He can be a conversible companion if he thinks it worth his while. Among those who are at all his equals in consequence, he is a very different man from what he is to the less prosperous.

His pride never deserts him; but with the rich, he is liberal-minded, just, sincere, rational, honourable, and perhaps agreeable, – allowing something for fortune and figure.'

The whist party soon afterwards breaking up, the players gathered round the other table, and Mr Collins took his station between his cousin Elizabeth and Mrs Philips. – The usual inquiries as to his success were made by the latter. It had not been very great; he had lost every point; but when Mrs Philips began to express her concern thereupon, he assured her with much earnest gravity that it was not of the least importance, that he considered the money as a mere trifle, and begged she would not make herself uneasy.

'I know very well, madam,' said he, 'that when persons sit down to a card table, they must take their chance of these things, – and happily I am not in such circumstances as to make five shillings any object. There are undoubtedly many who could not say the same, but thanks to Lady Catherine de Bourgh, I am removed far beyond the necessity of regarding little matters.'

Mr Wickham's attention was caught; and after observing Mr Collins for a few moments, he asked Elizabeth in a low voice whether her relation were very intimately acquainted with the family of de Bourgh.

'Lady Catherine de Bourgh,' she replied, 'has very lately given him a living. I hardly know how Mr Collins was first introduced to her notice, but he certainly has not known her long.'

'You know of course that Lady Catherine de Bourgh and Lady Anne Darcy were sisters; consequently that she is aunt to the present Mr Darcy.'

'No, indeed, I did not. – I knew nothing at all of Lady Catherine's connections. I never heard of her existence till the day before yesterday.'

'Her daughter, Miss de Bourgh, will have a very large fortune, and it is believed that she and her cousin will unite the two estates.'

This information made Elizabeth smile, as she thought of poor Miss Bingley. Vain indeed must be all her attentions, vain and useless her affection for his sister and her praise of himself, if he were already self-destined to another.

'Mr Collins,' said she, 'speaks highly both of Lady Catherine and her daughter; but from some particulars that he has related of her ladyship, I suspect his gratitude misleads him, and that in spite of her being his patroness, she is an arrogant, conceited woman.'

'I believe her to be both in a great degree,' replied Wickham; 'I have not seen her for many years, but I very well remember that I never liked her, and that her manners were dictatorial and insolent. She has the reputation of being remarkably sensible and clever; but I rather believe she derives part of her abilities from her rank and fortune, part from her authoritative manner, and the rest from the pride of her nephew, who chuses that every one connected with him should have an understanding of the first class.'

Elizabeth allowed that he had given a very rational account of it, and they continued talking together with mutual satisfaction till supper put an end to cards; and gave the rest of the ladies their share of Mr Wickham's attentions. There could be no conversation in the noise of Mrs Philips's supper party, but his manners recommended him to every body. Whatever he said, was said well; and whatever he did, done gracefully. Elizabeth went away with her head full of him. She could think of nothing but of Mr Wickham, and of what he had told her, all the way home; but there was not time for her even to mention his name as they went, for neither Lydia nor Mr Collins were once silent. Lydia talked incessantly of lottery tickets, of the fish she had lost and the fish she had won, and Mr Collins, in describing the civility of Mr and Mrs Philips, protesting that he did not in the least regard his losses at whist, enumerating all the dishes at supper, and repeatedly fearing that he crowded his cousins, had more to say than he could well manage before the carriage stopped at Longbourn House.

Chapter 17

Elizabeth related to Jane the next day, what had passed between Mr Wickham and herself. Jane listened with astonishment and concern; – she knew not how to believe that Mr Darcy could be so unworthy of Mr Bingley's regard; and yet, it was not in her nature to question the veracity of a young man of such amiable appearance as Wickham. – The possibility of his having really endured such unkindness, was enough to interest all her tender feelings; and nothing therefore remained to be done, but to think well of them both, to defend the conduct of each, and throw into the account of accident or mistake, whatever could not be otherwise explained.

'They have both,' said she, 'been deceived, I dare say, in some way or other, of which we can form no idea. Interested people have perhaps misrepresented each to the other. It is, in short, impossible for us to conjecture the causes or circumstances which may have alienated them, without actual blame on either side.'

'Very true, indeed; – and now, my dear Jane, what have you got to say in behalf of the interested people who have probably been concerned in the business? – Do clear *them* too, or we shall be obliged to think ill of somebody.'

'Laugh as much as you chuse, but you will not laugh me out of my opinion. My dearest Lizzy, do but consider in what a disgraceful light it places Mr Darcy, to be treating his father's favourite in such a manner, – one, whom his father had promised to provide for. – It is impossible. No man of common humanity, no man who had any value for his character, could be capable of it. Can his most intimate friends be so excessively deceived in him? oh! no.'

'I can much more easily believe Mr Bingley's being imposed on, than that Mr Wickham should invent such a history of himself as he gave me last night; names, facts, every thing mentioned without ceremony. – If it be not so, let Mr Darcy contradict it. Besides, there was truth in his looks.'

'It is difficult indeed – it is distressing. – One does not know what to think.'

'I beg your pardon; – one knows exactly what to think.'

But Jane could think with certainty on only one point, – that Mr Bingley, if he *had been* imposed on, would have much to suffer when the affair became public.

The two young ladies were summoned from the shrubbery where this conversation passed, by the arrival of some of the very persons of whom they had been speaking; Mr Bingley and his sisters came to give their personal invitation for the long expected ball at Netherfield, which was fixed for the following Tuesday. The two ladies were delighted to see their dear friend again, called it an age since they had met, and repeatedly asked what she had been doing with herself since their separation. To the rest of the family they paid little attention; avoiding Mrs Bennet as much as possible, saying not much to Elizabeth, and nothing at all to the others. They were soon gone again, rising from their seats with an activity which took their brother by surprise, and hurrying off as if eager to escape from Mrs Bennet's civilities.

The prospect of the Netherfield ball was extremely agreeable to every female of the family. Mrs Bennet chose to consider it as given in compliment to her eldest daughter, and was particularly flattered by receiving the invitation from Mr Bingley himself, instead of a ceremonious card. Jane pictured to herself a happy evening in the society of her two friends, and the attentions of their brother; and Elizabeth thought with pleasure of dancing a great deal with Mr Wickham, and of seeing a confirmation of every thing in Mr Darcy's looks and behaviour. The happiness anticipated by Catherine and Lydia, depended less on any single event, or any particular person, for though they each, like Elizabeth, meant to dance half the evening with Mr Wickham, he was by no means the only partner who could satisfy them, and a ball was at any rate, a ball. And even Mary could assure her family that she had no disinclination for it.

'While, I can have my mornings to myself,' said she, 'it is enough. – I think it no sacrifice to join occasionally in evening engagements. Society has claims on us all; and I profess myself one of those who consider intervals of recreation and amusement as desirable for every body.'

Elizabeth's spirits were so high on the occasion, that though she did not often speak unnecessarily to Mr Collins, she could not help asking him whether he intended to accept Mr Bingley's invitation, and if he did, whether he would think it proper to join in the evening's amusement; and she was rather surprised to find that he entertained no scruple whatever on that head, and was very far from dreading a rebuke either from the Archbishop, or Lady Catherine de Bourgh, by venturing to dance.

'I am by no means of opinion, I assure you,' said he, 'that a ball of this kind, given by a young man of character, to respectable people, can have any evil tendency; and I am so far from objecting to dancing myself that I shall hope to be honoured with the hands of all my fair cousins in the course of the evening, and I take this opportunity of soliciting yours, Miss Elizabeth, for the two first dances especially, – a preference which I trust my cousin Jane will attribute to the right cause, and not to any disrespect for her.'

Elizabeth felt herself completely taken in. She had fully proposed being engaged by Wickham for those very dances: – and to have Mr Collins instead! – her liveliness had been never worse timed. There was no help for it however. Mr Wickham's happiness and her own was per force delayed a little longer, and Mr Collins's proposal accepted with as good a grace as she could. She was not the better pleased with his gallantry, from the idea it suggested of something more. – It now first struck her, that *she* was selected from among her sisters as worthy of being the mistress of Hunsford Parsonage, and of assisting to form a quadrille table at Rosings, in the absence of more eligible visitors. The idea soon reached to conviction, as she observed his increasing civilities toward herself, and heard his frequent attempt at a compliment on her wit and vivacity; and though more astonished than gratified herself, by this effect of her charms, it was not long before her mother gave her to understand that the probability of their marriage was exceedingly agreeable to *her*. Elizabeth however did not chuse to take the hint, being well aware that a serious dispute must be the consequence of any reply. Mr Collins might never make the offer, and till he did, it was useless to quarrel about him.

If there had not been a Netherfield ball to prepare for and talk of, the younger Miss Bennets would have been in a pitiable state at this time, for from the day of the invitation, to the day of the ball, there was such a succession of rain as prevented their walking to Meryton once. No aunt, no officers, no news could be sought after; – the very shoe-roses for Netherfield were got by proxy. Even Elizabeth might have found some trial of her patience in weather, which totally suspended the improvement of her acquaintance with Mr Wickham; and nothing less than a dance on Tuesday, could have made such a Friday, Saturday, Sunday and Monday, endurable to Kitty and Lydia.

Chapter 18

Till Elizabeth entered the drawing-room at Netherfield and looked in vain for Mr Wickham among the cluster of red coats there assembled, a doubt of his being present had never occurred to her. The certainty of meeting him had not been checked by any of those recollections that might not unreasonably have alarmed her. She had dressed with more than usual care, and prepared in the highest spirits for the conquest of all that remained unsubdued of his heart, trusting that it was not more than might be won in the course of the evening. But in an instant arose the dreadful suspicion of his being purposely omitted for Mr Darcy's pleasure in the Bingleys' invitation to the officers; and though this was not exactly the case, the absolute fact of his absence was pronounced by his friend Mr Denny, to whom Lydia eagerly applied, and who told them that Wickham had been obliged to go to town on business the day before, and was not yet returned; adding, with a significant smile,

'I do not imagine his business would have called him away just now, if he had not wished to avoid a certain gentleman here.'

This part of his intelligence, though unheard by Lydia, was caught by Elizabeth, and as it assured her that Darcy was not less answerable for Wickham's absence than if her first surmise had been just, every feeling of displeasure against the former was so sharpened by immediate disappointment, that she could hardly reply with tolerable civility to the polite inquiries which he directly afterwards approached to make. – Attention, forbearance, patience with Darcy, was injury to Wickham. She was resolved against any sort of conversation with him, and turned away with a degree of ill humour, which she could not wholly surmount even in speaking to Mr Bingley, whose blind partiality provoked her.

But Elizabeth was not formed for ill-humour; and though every prospect of her own was destroyed for the evening, it could not dwell long on her spirits; and having told all her griefs to Charlotte Lucas, whom she had not seen for a week, she was soon able to make a voluntary transition to the oddities of her cousin, and to point him out to her particular notice. The two first dances, however, brought a return of distress; they were dances of mortification. Mr Collins, awkward and solemn, apologising instead of attending, and often moving wrong without being aware of it, gave her all the shame and misery which a disagreeable partner for a couple of dances can give. The moment of her release from him was exstacy[15].

She danced next with an officer, and had the refreshment of talking of Wickham, and of hearing that he was universally liked. When those dances were over she returned to Charlotte Lucas, and was in conversation with her, when she found herself suddenly addressed by Mr Darcy, who took her so much by surprise in his application for her hand, that, without knowing what she did, she accepted him. He walked away again immediately, and she was left to fret over her own want of presence of mind; Charlotte tried to console her.

'I dare say you will find him very agreeable.'

'Heaven forbid! – *That* would be the greatest misfortune of all! – To find a man agreeable whom one is determined to hate! – Do not wish me such an evil.'

When the dancing recommenced, however, and Darcy approached to claim her hand, Charlotte could not help cautioning her in a whisper not to be a simpleton and allow her fancy for Wickham to make her appear unpleasant in the eyes of a man of ten times his consequence. Elizabeth made no answer, and took her place in the set, amazed at the dignity to which she was arrived in being allowed to stand opposite to Mr Darcy, and reading in her neighbours' looks their equal amazement in beholding it. They stood for some time without speaking a word; and she began to imagine that their silence was to last through the two dances, and at first was resolved not to break it; till suddenly fancying that it would be the greater punishment to her partner to oblige him to talk, she made some slight observation on the dance. He replied, and was silent again. After a pause of some minutes she addressed him a second time with:

'It is *your* turn to say something now, Mr Darcy. – *I* talked about the dance, and *you* ought to make some kind of remark on the size of the room, or the number of couples.'

He smiled, and assured her that whatever she wished him to say should be said.

'Very well. – That reply will do for the present. – Perhaps by and bye I may observe that private balls are much pleasanter than public ones. – But *now* we may be silent.'

'Do you talk by rule then, while you are dancing?'

'Sometimes. One must speak a little, you know. It would look odd to be entirely silent for half an hour together, and yet for the advantage of *some*, conversation ought to be so arranged as that they may have the trouble of saying as little as possible.'

'Are you consulting your own feelings in the present case, or do you imagine that you are gratifying mine?'

'Both,' replied Elizabeth archly; 'for I have always seen a great similarity in the turn of our minds. – We are each of an unsocial, taciturn disposition, unwilling to speak, unless we expect to say something that will amaze the whole room, and be handed down to posterity with all the eclat of a proverb.'

'This is no very striking resemblance of your own character, I am sure,' said he. 'How near it may be to *mine*, I cannot pretend to say. – *You* think it a faithful portrait undoubtedly.'

'I must not decide on my own performance.'

He made no answer, and they were again silent till they had gone down the dance, when he asked her if she and her sisters did not very often walk to Meryton. She answered in the affirmative, and, unable to resist the temptation, added, 'When you met us there the other day, we had just been forming a new acquaintance.'

The effect was immediate. A deeper shade of hauteur overspread his features, but he said not a word, and Elizabeth, though blaming herself for her own weakness, could not go on. At length Darcy spoke, and in a constrained manner said,

'Mr Wickham is blessed with such happy manners as may ensure his *making* friends – whether he may be equally capable of *retaining* them, is less certain.'

'He has been so unlucky as to lose *your* friendship,' replied Elizabeth with emphasis, 'and in a manner which he is likely to suffer from all his life.'

Darcy made no answer, and seemed desirous of changing the subject. At that moment Sir William Lucas appeared close to them, meaning to pass through the set to the other side of the room; but on perceiving Mr Darcy he stopped with a bow of superior courtesy to compliment him on his dancing and his partner.

'I have been most highly gratified indeed, my dear Sir. Such very superior dancing is not often seen. It is evident that you belong to the first circles. Allow me to say, however, that your fair partner does not disgrace you, and that I must hope to have this pleasure often repeated, especially when a certain desirable event, my dear Miss Eliza, (glancing at her sister and Bingley,) shall take place. What congratulations will then flow in! I appeal to Mr Darcy: – but let me not interrupt you, Sir. – You will not thank me for detaining you from the bewitching converse of that young lady, whose bright eyes are also upbraiding me.'

The latter part of this address was scarcely heard by Darcy; but Sir William's allusion to his friend seemed to strike him forcibly, and his eyes were directed with a very serious expression towards Bingley and Jane, who were dancing together. Recovering himself, however, shortly, he turned to his partner, and said,

'Sir William's interruption has made me forget what we were talking of.'

'I do not think we were speaking at all. Sir William could not have interrupted any two people in the room who had less to say for themselves. – We have tried two or three subjects already without success, and what we are to talk of next I cannot imagine.'

'What do you think of books?' said he, smiling.

'Books – Oh! no. – I am sure we never read the same, or not with the same feelings.'

'I am sorry you think so; but if that be the case, there can at least be no want of subject. – We may compare our different opinions.'

'No – I cannot talk of books in a ball-room; my head is always full of something else.'

'The *present* always occupies you in such scenes – does it?' said he, with a look of doubt.

'Yes, always,' she replied, without knowing what she said, for her thoughts had wandered far from the subject, as soon afterwards appeared by her suddenly exclaiming, 'I remember hearing you once say, Mr Darcy, that you hardly ever forgave, that your resentment once created was unappeasable. You are very cautious, I suppose, as to its *being created.*'

'I am,' said he, with a firm voice.

'And never allow yourself to be blinded by prejudice?'

'I hope not.'

'It is particularly incumbent on those who never change their opinion, to be secure of judging properly at first.'

'May I ask to what these questions tend?'

'Merely to the illustration of *your* character,' said she, endeavouring to shake off her gravity. 'I am trying to make it out.'

'And what is your success?'

She shook her head. 'I do not get on at all. I hear such different accounts of you as puzzle me exceedingly.'

'I can readily believe,' answered he gravely, 'that report may vary greatly with respect to me; and I could wish, Miss Bennet, that you were not to sketch my character at the present moment, as there is reason to fear that the performance would reflect no credit on either.'

'But if I do not take your likeness now, I may never have another opportunity.'

'I would by no means suspend any pleasure of yours,' he coldly replied. She said no more, and they went down the other dance and parted in silence; on each side dissatisfied, though not to an equal degree, for in Darcy's breast there was a tolerable powerful feeling towards her, which soon procured her pardon, and directed all his anger against another.

They had not long separated when Miss Bingley came towards her, and with an expression of civil disdain thus accosted her,

'So, Miss Eliza, I hear you are quite delighted with George Wickham! – Your sister has been talking to me about him, and asking me a thousand questions; and I find that the young man forgot to tell you, among his other communications, that he was the son of old Wickham, the late Mr Darcy's steward. Let me recommend you, however, as a friend, not to give implicit confidence to all his assertions; for as to Mr Darcy's using him ill, it is perfectly false; for, on the contrary, he has been always remarkably kind to him, though George Wickham has treated Mr Darcy in a most infamous manner. I do not know the particulars, but I know very well that Mr Darcy is not in the least to blame, that he cannot bear to hear George Wickham mentioned, and that though my brother thought he could not well avoid including him in his invitation to the officers, he was excessively glad to find that he had taken himself out of the way. His coming into the country at all, is a most insolent thing indeed, and I wonder how he could presume to do it. I pity you, Miss Eliza, for this discovery of your favourite's guilt, but really considering his descent, one could not expect much better.'

'His guilt and his descent appear by your account to be the same,' said Elizabeth angrily; 'for I have heard you accuse him of nothing worse than of being the son of Mr Darcy's steward, and of *that*, I can assure you, he informed me himself.'

'I beg your pardon,' replied Miss Bingley, turning away with a sneer. 'Excuse my interference. – It was kindly meant.'

'Insolent girl!' said Elizabeth to herself. – 'You are much mistaken if you expect to influence me by such a paltry attack as this. I see nothing in it but your own wilful ignorance and the malice of Mr Darcy.' She then sought her eldest sister, who had undertaken to make inquiries on the same subject of Bingley. Jane met her with a smile of such sweet complacency, a glow of such happy expression, as sufficiently marked how well she was satisfied with the occurrences of the evening. – Elizabeth instantly read her feelings, and at that moment solicitude for Wickham, resentment against his enemies, and every thing else gave way before the hope of Jane's being in the fairest way for happiness.

'I want to know,' said she, with a countenance no less smiling than her sister's, 'what you have learnt about Mr Wickham. But perhaps you have been too pleasantly engaged to think of any third person; in which case you may be sure of my pardon.'

'No,' replied Jane, 'I have not forgotten him; but I have nothing satisfactory to tell you. Mr Bingley does not know the whole of his history, and is quite ignorant of the circumstances which have principally offended Mr Darcy; but he will vouch for the good conduct, the probity and honour of his friend, and is perfectly convinced that Mr Wickham has deserved much less attention from Mr Darcy than he has received; and I am sorry to say that by his account as well as his sister's, Mr Wickham is by no means a respectable young man. I am afraid he has been very imprudent, and has deserved to lose Mr Darcy's regard.'

'Mr Bingley does not know Mr Wickham himself?'

'No; he never saw him till the other morning at Meryton.'

'This account then is what he has received from Mr Darcy. I am perfectly satisfied. But what does he say of the living?'

'He does not exactly recollect the circumstances, though he has heard them from Mr Darcy more than once, but he believes that it was left to him *conditionally* only.'

'I have not a doubt of Mr Bingley's sincerity,' said Elizabeth warmly; 'but you must excuse my not being convinced by assurances only. Mr Bingley's defence of his friend was a very able one I dare say, but since he is unacquainted with several parts of the story, and has learnt the rest from that friend himself, I shall venture still to think of both gentlemen as I did before.'

She then changed the discourse to one more gratifying to each, and on which there could be no difference of sentiment. Elizabeth listened with delight to the happy, though modest hopes which Jane entertained of Bingley's regard, and said all in her power to heighten her confidence in it. On their being joined by Mr Bingley himself, Elizabeth withdrew to Miss Lucas; to whose inquiry after the pleasantness of her last partner she had scarcely replied, before Mr Collins came up to them and told her with great exultation that he had just been so fortunate as to make a most important discovery.

'I have found out,' said he, 'by a singular accident, that there is now in the room a near relation of my patroness. I happened to overhear the gentleman himself mentioning to the young lady who does the honours of this house the names of his cousin Miss de Bourgh, and of her mother Lady Catherine. How wonderfully these sort of things occur! Who would have thought of my meeting with – perhaps – a nephew of Lady Catherine de Bourgh in this assembly! – I am most thankful that the discovery is made in time for me to pay my respects to him, which I am now going to do, and trust he will excuse my not having done it before. My total ignorance of the connection must plead my apology.'

'You are not going to introduce yourself to Mr Darcy?'

'Indeed I am. I shall intreat[16] his pardon for not having done it earlier. I believe him to be Lady Catherine's *nephew*. It will be in my power to assure him that her ladyship was quite well yesterday se'nnight.'

Elizabeth tried hard to dissuade him from such a scheme; assuring him that Mr Darcy would consider his addressing him without introduction as an impertinent freedom, rather than a compliment to his aunt; that it was not in the least necessary there should be any notice on either side, and that if it were, it must belong to Mr Darcy, the superior in consequence, to begin the acquaintance. – Mr Collins listened to her with the determined air of following his own inclination, and when she ceased speaking, replied thus,

'My dear Miss Elizabeth, I have the highest opinion in the world of your excellent judgment in all matters within the scope of your understanding, but permit me to say that there must be a wide difference between the established forms of ceremony amongst the laity, and those which regulate the clergy; forgive me leave to observe that I consider the clerical office as equal in point of dignity with the highest rank in the kingdom – provided that a proper humility of behaviour is at the same time maintained. You must therefore allow me to follow the dictates of my conscience on this occasion, which leads me to perform what I look on as a point of duty. Pardon me for neglecting to profit by your advice, which on every other subject shall be my constant guide, though in the case before us I consider myself more fitted by education and habitual study to decide on what is right than a young lady like yourself.' And with a low bow he left her to attack Mr Darcy, whose reception of his advances she eagerly watched, and whose astonishment at being so addressed was very evident. Her cousin prefaced his speech with a solemn bow, and though she could not hear a word of it, she felt as if hearing it all, and saw in the motion of his lips the words 'apology,' 'Hunsford,' and 'Lady Catherine de Bourgh.' – It vexed her to see him expose himself to such a man. Mr Darcy was eyeing him with unrestrained wonder, and when at last Mr Collins allowed him time to speak, replied with an air of distant civility. Mr Collins, however, was not discouraged from speaking again, and Mr Darcy's contempt seemed abundantly increasing with the length of his second speech, and at the end of it he only made him a slight bow, and moved another way. Mr Collins then returned to Elizabeth.

'I have no reason, I assure you,' said he, 'to be dissatisfied with my reception. Mr Darcy seemed much pleased with the attention. He answered me with the utmost civility, and even paid me the compliment of saying, that he was so well convinced of Lady Catherine's discernment as to be certain she could never bestow a favour unworthily. It was really a very handsome thought. Upon the whole, I am much pleased with him.'

As Elizabeth had no longer any interest of her own to pursue, she turned her attention almost entirely on her sister and Mr Bingley, and the train of agreeable reflections which her observations gave birth to, made her perhaps almost as happy as Jane. She saw her in idea settled in that very house in all the felicity which a marriage of true affection could bestow; and she felt capable under such circumstances, of endeavouring even to like Bingley's two sisters. Her mother's thoughts she plainly saw were bent the same way, and she determined not to venture near her, lest she might hear too much. When they sat down to supper, therefore, she considered it a most unlucky perverseness which placed them within one of each other; and deeply was she vexed to find that her mother was talking to that one person (Lady Lucas) freely, openly, and of nothing else but of her expectation that Jane would be soon married to Mr Bingley. – It was an animating subject, and Mrs Bennet seemed incapable of fatigue while enumerating the advantages of the match. His being such a charming young man, and so rich, and living but three miles from them, were the first points of self-gratulation; and then it was such a comfort to think how fond the two sisters were of Jane, and to be certain that they must desire the connection as much as she could do. It was, moreover, such a promising thing for her younger daughters, as Jane's marrying so greatly must throw them in the way of other rich men; and lastly, it was so pleasant at her time of life to be able to consign her single daughters to the care of their sister, that she might not be obliged to go into company more than she liked. It was necessary to make this circumstance a matter of pleasure, because on such occasions it is the etiquette; but no one was less likely than Mrs Bennet to find comfort in staying at home at any period of her life. She concluded with many good wishes that Lady Lucas might soon be equally fortunate, though evidently and triumphantly believing there was no chance of it.

In vain did Elizabeth endeavour to check the rapidity of her mother's words, or persuade her to describe her felicity in a less audible whisper; for to her inexpressible vexation, she could perceive that the chief of it was overheard by Mr Darcy, who sat opposite to them. Her mother only scolded her for being nonsensical.

'What is Mr Darcy to me, pray, that I should be afraid of him? I am sure we owe him no such particular civility as to be obliged to say nothing *he* may not like to hear.'

'For heaven's sake, madam, speak lower. – What advantage can it be to you to offend Mr Darcy? – You will never recommend yourself to his friend by so doing.'

Nothing that she could say, however, had any influence. Her mother would talk of her views in the same intelligible tone. Elizabeth blushed and blushed again with shame and vexation. She could not help frequently glancing her eye at Mr Darcy, though every glance convinced her of what she dreaded; for though he was not always looking at her mother, she was convinced that his attention was invariably fixed by her. The expression of his face changed gradually from indignant contempt to a composed and steady gravity.

At length however Mrs Bennet had no more to say; and Lady Lucas, who had been long yawning at the repetition of delights which she saw no likelihood of sharing, was left to the comforts of cold ham and chicken. Elizabeth now began to revive. But not long was the interval of tranquillity; for when supper was over, singing was talked of, and she had the mortification of seeing Mary, after very little entreaty, preparing to oblige the company. By many significant looks and silent entreaties, did she endeavour to prevent such a proof of complaisance, – but in vain; Mary would not understand them; such an opportunity of exhibiting was delightful to her, and she began her song. Elizabeth's eyes were fixed on her with most painful sensations; and she watched her progress through the several stanzas with an impatience which was very ill rewarded at their close; for Mary, on receiving amongst the thanks of the table, the hint of a hope that she might be prevailed on to favour them again, after the pause of half a minute began another. Mary's powers were by no means fitted for such a display; her voice was weak, and her manner affected. – Elizabeth was in agonies. She looked at Jane, to see how she bore it; but Jane was very composedly talking to Bingley. She looked at his two sisters, and saw them making signs of derision at each other, and at Darcy, who continued however impenetrably grave. She looked at her father to entreat his interference, lest Mary should be singing all night. He took the hint, and when Mary had finished her second song, said aloud,

'That will do extremely well, child. You have delighted us long enough. Let the other young ladies have time to exhibit.'

Mary, though pretending not to hear, was somewhat disconcerted; and Elizabeth sorry for her, and sorry for her father's speech, was afraid her anxiety had done no good. – Others of the party were now applied to.

'If I,' said Mr Collins, 'were so fortunate as to be able to sing, I should have great pleasure, I am sure, in obliging the company with an air; for I consider music as a very innocent diversion, and perfectly compatible with the profession of a clergyman. – I do not mean however to assert that we can be justified in devoting too much of our time to music, for there are certainly other things to be attended to. The rector of a parish has much to do. – In the first place, he must make such an agreement for tithes as may be beneficial to himself and not offensive to his patron. He must write his own sermons; and the time that remains will not be too much for his parish duties, and the care and improvement of his dwelling, which he cannot be excused from making as comfortable as possible. And I do not think it of light importance that he should have attentive and conciliatory manners towards every body, especially towards those to whom he owes his preferment. I cannot acquit him of that duty; nor could I think well of the man who should omit an occasion of testifying his respect towards any body connected with the family.' And with a bow to Mr Darcy, he concluded his speech, which had been spoken so loud as to be heard by half the room. – Many stared. – Many smiled; but no one looked more amused than Mr Bennet himself, while his wife seriously commended Mr Collins for having spoken so sensibly, and observed in a half-whisper to Lady Lucas, that he was a remarkably clever, good kind of young man.

To Elizabeth it appeared, that had her family made an agreement to expose themselves as much as they could during the evening, it would have been impossible for them to play their parts with more spirit, or finer success; and happy did she think it for Bingley and her sister that some of the exhibition had escaped his notice, and that his feelings were not of a sort to be much distressed by the folly which he must have witnessed. That his two sisters and Mr Darcy, however, should have such an opportunity of ridiculing her relations was bad enough, and she could not determine whether the silent contempt of the gentleman, or the insolent smiles of the ladies, were more intolerable.

The rest of the evening brought her little amusement. She was teased by Mr Collins, who continued most perseveringly by her side, and though he could not prevail with her to dance with him again, put it out of her power to dance with others. In vain did she entreat him to stand up with somebody else, and offer to introduce him to any young lady in the room. He assured her that as to dancing, he was perfectly indifferent to it; that his chief object was by delicate attentions to recommend himself to her, and that he should therefore make a point of remaining close to her the whole evening. There was no arguing upon such a project. She owed her greatest relief to her friend Miss Lucas, who often joined them, and good-naturedly engaged Mr Collins's conversation to herself.

She was at least free from the offence of Mr Darcy's farther notice; though often standing within a very short distance of her, quite disengaged, he never came near enough to speak. She felt it to be the probable consequence of her allusions to Mr Wickham, and rejoiced in it.

The Longbourn party were the last of all the company to depart; and by a manoeuvre of Mrs Bennet had to wait for their carriages a quarter of an hour after every body else was gone, which gave them time to see how heartily they were wished away by some of the family. Mrs Hurst and her sister scarcely opened their mouths except to complain of fatigue, and were evidently impatient to have the house to themselves. They repulsed every attempt of Mrs Bennet at conversation, and by so doing, threw a languor over the whole party, which was very little relieved by the long speeches of Mr Collins, who was complimenting Mr Bingley and his sisters on the elegance of their entertainment, and the hospitality and politeness which had marked their behaviour to their guests. Darcy said nothing at all. Mr Bennet, in equal silence, was enjoying the scene. Mr Bingley and Jane were standing together, a little detached from the rest, and talked only to each other. Elizabeth preserved as steady a silence as either Mrs Hurst or Miss Bingley; and even Lydia was too much fatigued to utter more than the occasional exclamation of 'Lord, how tired I am!' accompanied by a violent yawn.

When at length they arose to take leave, Mrs Bennet was most pressingly civil in her hope of seeing the whole family soon at Longbourn; and addressed herself particularly to Mr Bingley, to assure him how happy he would make them, by eating a family dinner with them at any time, without the ceremony of a formal invitation. Bingley was all grateful pleasure, and he readily engaged for taking the earliest opportunity of waiting on her, after his return from London, whither[17] he was obliged to go the next day for a short time.

Mrs Bennet was perfectly satisfied; and quitted the house under the delightful persuasion that, allowing for the necessary preparations of settlements, new carriages and wedding clothes, she should undoubtedly see her daughter settled at Netherfield, in the course of three or four months. Of having another daughter married to Mr Collins, she thought with equal certainty, and with considerable, though not equal, pleasure. Elizabeth was the least dear to her of all her children; and though the man and the match were quite good enough for *her*, the worth of each was eclipsed by Mr Bingley and Netherfield.

Chapter 19

The next day opened a new scene at Longbourn. Mr Collins made his declaration in form. Having resolved to do it without loss of time, as his leave of absence extended only to the following Saturday, and having no feelings of diffidence to make it distressing to himself even at the moment, he set about it in a very orderly manner, with all the observances which he supposed a regular part of the business. On finding Mrs Bennet, Elizabeth, and one of the younger girls together, soon after breakfast, he addressed the mother in these words,

'May I hope, Madam, for your interest with your fair daughter Elizabeth, when I solicit for the honour of a private audience with her in the course of this morning?'

Before Elizabeth had time for any thing but a blush of surprise, Mrs Bennet instantly answered,

'Oh dear! – Yes – certainly. – I am sure Lizzy will be very happy – I am sure she can have no objection. – Come, Kitty, I want you up stairs.' And gathering her work together, she was hastening away, when Elizabeth called out,

'Dear Ma'am, do not go. – I beg you will not go. – Mr Collins must excuse me. – He can have nothing to say to me that any body need not hear. I am going away myself.'

'No, no, nonsense, Lizzy. – I desire you will stay where you are.' – And upon Elizabeth's seeming really, with vexed and embarrassed looks, about to escape, she added, 'Lizzy, I *insist* upon your staying and hearing Mr Collins.'

Elizabeth would not oppose such an injunction – and a moment's consideration making her also sensible that it would be wisest to get it over as soon and as quietly as possible, she sat down again, and tried to conceal by incessant employment the feelings which were divided between distress and diversion. Mrs Bennet and Kitty walked off, and as soon as they were gone Mr Collins began.

'Believe me, my dear Miss Elizabeth, that your modesty, so far from doing you any disservice, rather adds to your other perfections. You would have been less amiable in my eyes had there *not* been this little unwillingness; but allow me to assure you that I have your respected mother's permission for this address. You can hardly doubt the purport of my discourse, however your natural delicacy may lead you to dissemble; my attentions have been too marked to be mistaken. Almost as soon as I entered the house I singled you out as the companion of my future life. But before I am run away with by my feelings on this subject, perhaps it will be advisable for me to state my reasons for marrying – and moreover for coming into Hertfordshire with the design of selecting a wife, as I certainly did.'

The idea of Mr Collins, with all his solemn composure, being run away with by his feelings, made Elizabeth so near laughing that she could not use the short pause he allowed in any attempt to stop him farther, and he continued:

'My reasons for marrying are, first, that I think it a right thing for every clergyman in easy circumstances (like myself) to set the example of matrimony in his parish. Secondly, that I am convinced it will add very greatly to my happiness; and thirdly – which perhaps I ought to have mentioned earlier, that it is the particular advice and recommendation of the very noble lady whom I have the honour of calling patroness. Twice has she condescended to give me her opinion (unasked too!) on this subject; and it was but the very Saturday night before I left Hunsford – between our pools at quadrille, while Mrs Jenkinson was arranging Miss de Bourgh's foot-stool, that she said, "Mr Collins, you must marry. A clergyman like you must marry. – Chuse properly, chuse a gentlewoman for *my* sake; and for your *own*, let her be an active, useful sort of person, not brought up high, but able to make a small income go a good way. This is my advice. Find such a woman as soon as you can, bring her to Hunsford, and I will visit her." Allow me, by the way, to observe, my fair cousin, that I do not reckon the notice and kindness of Lady Catherine de Bourgh as among the least of the advantages in my power to offer. You will find her manners beyond any thing I can describe; and your wit and vivacity I think must be acceptable to her, especially when tempered with the silence and respect which her rank will inevitably excite. Thus much for my general intention in favour of matrimony; it remains to be told why my views were directed to Longbourn instead of my own neighbourhood, where I assure you there are many amiable young women. But the fact is, that being, as I am, to inherit this estate after the death of your honoured father, (who, however, may live many years longer,) I could not satisfy myself without resolving to chuse a wife from among his daughters, that the loss to them might be as little as possible, when the melancholy event takes place – which, however, as I have already said, may not be for several years. This has been my motive, my fair cousin, and I flatter myself it will not sink me in your esteem. And now nothing remains for me but to assure you in the most animated language of the violence of my affection. To fortune I am perfectly indifferent, and shall make no demand of that nature on your father, since I am well aware that it could not be complied with; and that one thousand pounds in the 4 per cents, which will not be yours till after your mother's decease, is all that you may ever be entitled to. On that head, therefore, I shall be uniformly silent; and you may assure yourself that no ungenerous reproach shall ever pass my lips when we are married.'

It was absolutely necessary to interrupt him now.

'You are too hasty, Sir,' she cried. 'You forget that I have made no answer. Let me do it without farther loss of time. Accept my thanks for the compliment you are paying me. I am very sensible of the honour of your proposals, but it is impossible for me to do otherwise than decline them.'

'I am not now to learn,' replied Mr Collins, with a formal wave of the hand, 'that it is usual with young ladies to reject the addresses of the man whom they secretly mean to accept, when he first applies for their favour; and that sometimes the refusal is repeated a second or even a third time. I am therefore by no means discouraged by what you have just said, and shall hope to lead you to the altar ere[18] long.'

'Upon my word, Sir,' cried Elizabeth, 'your hope is rather an extraordinary one after my declaration. I do assure you that I am not one of those young ladies (if such young ladies there are) who are so daring as to risk their happiness on the chance of being asked a second time. I am perfectly serious in my refusal. – You could not make *me* happy, and I am convinced that I am the last woman in the world who would make *you* so. – Nay, were your friend Lady Catherine to know me, I am persuaded she would find me in every respect ill-qualified for the situation.'

'Were it certain that Lady Catherine would think so,' said Mr Collins very gravely – 'but I cannot imagine that her ladyship would at all disapprove of you. And you may be certain that when I have the honour of seeing her again I shall speak in the highest terms of your modesty, economy, and other amiable qualifications.'

'Indeed, Mr Collins, all praise of me will be unnecessary. You must give me leave to judge for myself, and pay me the compliment of believing what I say. I wish you very happy and very rich, and by refusing your hand, do all in my power to prevent your being otherwise. In making me the offer, you must have satisfied the delicacy of your feelings with regard to my family, and may take possession of Longbourn estate whenever it falls, without any self-reproach. This matter may be considered, therefore, as finally settled.' And rising as she thus spoke, she would have quitted the room, had not Mr Collins thus addressed her,

'When I do myself the honour of speaking to you next on this subject I shall hope to receive a more favourable answer than you have now given me; though I am far from accusing you of cruelty at present, because I know it to be the established custom of your sex to reject a man on the first application, and perhaps you have even now said as much to encourage my suit as would be consistent with the true delicacy of the female character.'

'Really, Mr Collins,' cried Elizabeth with some warmth, 'you puzzle me exceedingly. If what I have hitherto said can appear to you in the form of encouragement, I know not how to express my refusal in such a way as may convince you of its being one.'

'You must give me leave to flatter myself, my dear cousin, that your refusal of my addresses is merely words of course. My reasons for believing it are briefly these: – It does not appear to me that my hand is unworthy your acceptance, or that the establishment I can offer would be any other than highly desirable. My situation in life, my connections with the family of De Bourgh, and my relationship to your own, are circumstances highly in my favour; and you should take it into farther consideration that in spite of your manifold attractions, it is by no means certain that another offer of marriage may ever be made you. Your portion is unhappily so small that it will in all likelihood undo the effects of your loveliness and amiable qualifications. As I must therefore conclude that you are not serious in your rejection of me, I shall chuse to attribute it to your wish of increasing my love by suspense, according to the usual practice of elegant females.'

'I do assure you, Sir, that I have no pretension whatever to that kind of elegance which consists in tormenting a respectable man. I would rather be paid the compliment of being believed sincere. I thank you again and again for the honour you have done me in your proposals, but to accept them is absolutely impossible. My feelings in every respect forbid it. Can I speak plainer? Do not consider me now as an elegant female intending to plague you, but as a rational creature speaking the truth from her heart.'

'You are uniformly charming!' cried he, with an air of awkward gallantry; 'and I am persuaded that when sanctioned by the express authority of both your excellent parents, my proposals will not fail of being acceptable.'

To such perseverance in wilful self-deception Elizabeth would make no reply, and immediately and in silence withdrew; determined, if he persisted in considering her repeated refusals as flattering encouragement, to apply to her father, whose negative might be uttered in such a manner as must be decisive, and whose behaviour at least could not be mistaken for the affectation and coquetry of an elegant female.

Chapter 20

Mr Collins was not left long to the silent contemplation of his successful love; for Mrs Bennet, having dawdled about in the vestibule to watch for the end of the conference, no sooner saw Elizabeth open the door and with quick step pass her towards the staircase, than she entered the breakfast-room, and congratulated both him and herself in warm terms on the happy prospect of their nearer connection. Mr Collins received and returned these felicitations with equal pleasure, and then proceeded to relate the particulars of their interview, with the result of which he trusted he had every reason to be satisfied, since the refusal which his cousin had steadfastly given him would naturally flow from her bashful modesty and the genuine delicacy of her character.

This information, however, startled Mrs Bennet; – she would have been glad to be equally satisfied that her daughter had meant to encourage him by protesting against his proposals, but she dared not to believe it, and could not help saying so.

'But depend upon it, Mr Collins,' she added, 'that Lizzy shall be brought to reason. I will speak to her about it myself directly. She is a very headstrong foolish girl, and does not know her own interest; but I will *make* her know it.'

'Pardon me for interrupting you, Madam,' cried Mr Collins; 'but if she is really headstrong and foolish, I know not whether she would altogether be a very desirable wife to a man in my situation, who naturally looks for happiness in the marriage state. If therefore she actually persists in rejecting my suit, perhaps it were better not to force her into accepting me, because if liable to such defects of temper, she could not contribute much to my felicity.'

'Sir, you quite misunderstand me,' said Mrs Bennet, alarmed. 'Lizzy is only headstrong in such matters as these. In every thing else she is as good natured a girl as ever lived. I will go directly to Mr Bennet, and we shall very soon settle it with her, I am sure.'

She would not give him time to reply, but hurrying instantly to her husband, called out as she entered the library,

'Oh! Mr Bennet, you are wanted immediately; we are all in an uproar. You must come and make Lizzy marry Mr Collins, for she vows she will not have him, and if you do not make haste he will change his mind and not have *her*.'

Mr Bennet raised his eyes from his book as she entered, and fixed them on her face with a calm unconcern which was not in the least altered by her communication.

'I have not the pleasure of understanding you,' said he, when she had finished her speech. 'Of what are you talking?'

'Of Mr Collins and Lizzy. Lizzy declares she will not have Mr Collins, and Mr Collins begins to say that he will not have Lizzy.'

'And what am I to do on the occasion? – It seems a hopeless business.'

'Speak to Lizzy about it yourself. Tell her that you insist upon her marrying him.'

'Let her be called down. She shall hear my opinion.'

Mrs Bennet rang the bell, and Miss Elizabeth was summoned to the library.

'Come here, child,' cried her father as she appeared. 'I have sent for you on an affair of importance. I understand that Mr Collins has made you an offer of marriage. Is it true?' Elizabeth replied that it was. 'Very well – and this offer of marriage you have refused?'

'I have, Sir.'

'Very well. We now come to the point. Your mother insists upon your accepting it. Is not it so, Mrs Bennet?'

'Yes, or I will never see her again.'

'An unhappy alternative is before you, Elizabeth. From this day you must be a stranger to one of your parents. – Your mother will never see you again if you do *not* marry Mr Collins, and I will never see you again if you *do*.'

Elizabeth could not but smile at such a conclusion of such

a beginning; but Mrs Bennet, who had persuaded herself that her husband regarded the affair as she wished, was excessively disappointed.

'What do you mean, Mr Bennet, by talking in this way? You promised me to *insist* upon her marrying him.'

'My dear,' replied her husband, 'I have two small favours to request. First, that you will allow me the free use of my understanding on the present occasion; and secondly, of my room. I shall be glad to have the library to myself as soon as may be.'

Not yet, however, in spite of her disappointment in her husband, did Mrs Bennet give up the point. She talked to Elizabeth again and again; coaxed and threatened her by turns. She endeavoured to secure Jane in her interest, but Jane with all possible mildness declined interfering; – and Elizabeth sometimes with real earnestness and sometimes with playful gaiety replied to her attacks. Though her manner varied however, her determination never did.

Mr Collins, meanwhile, was meditating in solitude on what had passed. He thought too well of himself to comprehend on what motive his cousin could refuse him; and though his pride was hurt, he suffered in no other way. His regard for her was quite imaginary; and the possibility of her deserving her mother's reproach prevented his feeling any regret.

While the family were in this confusion, Charlotte Lucas came to spend the day with them. She was met in the vestibule by Lydia, who, flying to her, cried in a half whisper, 'I am glad you are come, for there is such fun here! – What do you think has happened this morning? – Mr Collins has made an offer to Lizzy, and she will not have him.'

Charlotte had hardly time to answer, before they were joined by Kitty, who came to tell the same news, and no sooner had they entered the breakfast-room, where Mrs Bennet was alone, than she likewise began on the subject, calling on Miss Lucas for her compassion, and entreating her to persuade her friend Lizzy to comply with the wishes of all her family. 'Pray do, my dear Miss Lucas,' she added in a melancholy tone, 'for nobody is on my side, nobody takes part with me, I am cruelly used, nobody feels for my poor nerves.'

Charlotte's reply was spared by the entrance of Jane and Elizabeth.

'Aye, there she comes,' continued Mrs Bennet, 'looking as unconcerned as may be, and caring no more for us than if we were at York, provided she can have her own way. – But I tell you what, Miss Lizzy, if you take it into your head to go on refusing every offer of marriage in this way, you will never get a husband at all – and I am sure I do not know who is to maintain you when your father is dead. – I shall not be able to keep you – and so I warn you. – I have done with you from this very day. – I told you in the library, you know, that I should never speak to you again, and you will find me as good as my word. I have no pleasure in talking to undutiful children. – Not that I have much pleasure indeed in talking to any body. People who suffer as I do from nervous complaints can have no great inclination for talking. Nobody can tell what I suffer! – But it is always so. Those who do not complain are never pitied.'

Her daughters listened in silence to this effusion, sensible that any attempt to reason with or sooth her would only increase the irritation. She talked on, therefore, without interruption from any of them till

they were joined by Mr Collins, who entered with an air more stately than usual, and on perceiving whom, she said to the girls,

'Now, I do insist upon it, that you, all of you, hold your tongues, and let Mr Collins and me have a little conversation together.'

Elizabeth passed quietly out of the room, Jane and Kitty followed, but Lydia stood her ground, determined to hear all she could; and Charlotte, detained first by the civility of Mr Collins, whose inquiries after herself and all her family were very minute, and then by a little curiosity, satisfied herself with walking to the window and pretending not to hear. In a doleful voice Mrs Bennet thus began the projected conversation. – 'Oh! Mr Collins!' –

'My dear Madam,' replied he, 'let us be forever silent on this point. Far be it from me,' he presently continued in a voice that marked his displeasure, 'to resent the behaviour of your daughter. Resignation to inevitable evils is the duty of us all; the peculiar duty of a young man who has been so fortunate as I have been in early preferment; and I trust I am resigned. Perhaps not the less so from feeling a doubt of my positive happiness had my fair cousin honoured me with her hand; for I have often observed that resignation is never so perfect as when the blessing denied begins to lose somewhat of its value in our estimation. You will not, I hope, consider me as showing any disrespect to your family, my dear Madam, by thus withdrawing my pretensions to your daughter's favour, without having paid yourself and Mr Bennet the compliment of requesting you to interpose your authority in my behalf. My conduct may I fear be objectionable in having accepted my dismission from your daughter's lips instead of your own. But we are all liable to error. I have certainly meant well through the whole affair. My object has been to secure an amiable companion for myself, with due consideration for the advantage of all your family, and if my *manner* has been at all reprehensible, I here beg leave to apologise.'

The discussion of Mr Collins's offer was now nearly at an end, and Elizabeth had only to suffer from the uncomfortable feelings necessarily attending it, and occasionally from some peevish allusion of her mother. As for the gentleman himself, *his* feelings were chiefly expressed, not by embarrassment or dejection, or by trying to avoid her, but by stiffness of manner and resentful silence. He scarcely ever spoke to her, and the assiduous attentions which he had been so sensible of himself, were transferred for the rest of the day to Miss Lucas, whose civility in listening to him, was a seasonable relief to them all, and especially to her friend.

The morrow produced no abatement of Mrs Bennet's ill humour or ill health. Mr Collins was also in the same state of angry pride. Elizabeth had hoped that his resentment might shorten his visit, but his plan did not appear in the least affected by it. He was always to have gone on Saturday, and to Saturday he still meant to stay.

After breakfast, the girls walked to Meryton to inquire if Mr Wickham were returned, and to lament over his absence from the Netherfield ball. He joined them on their entering the town and attended them to their aunt's, where his regret and vexation, and the concern of every body was well talked over. – To Elizabeth, however, he voluntarily acknowledged that the necessity of his absence *had* been self imposed.

'I found,' said he, 'as the time drew near, that I had better not meet Mr Darcy; – that to be in the same room, the same party with him for so many hours together, might be more than I could bear, and that scenes might arise unpleasant to more than myself.'

She highly approved his forbearance, and they had leisure for a full discussion of it, and for all the commendation which they civilly bestowed on each other, as Wickham and another officer walked back with them to Longbourn, and during the walk, he particularly attended to her. His accompanying them was a double advantage; she felt all the compliment it offered to herself, and it was most acceptable as an occasion of introducing him to her father and mother.

Soon after their return, a letter was delivered to Miss Bennet; it came from Netherfield, and was opened immediately. The envelope contained a sheet of elegant, little, hot pressed paper, well covered with a lady's fair, flowing hand; and Elizabeth saw her sister's countenance change as she read it, and saw her dwelling intently on some particular passages. Jane recollected herself soon, and putting the letter away, tried to join with her usual cheerfulness in the general conversation; but Elizabeth felt an anxiety on the subject which drew off her attention even from Wickham; and no sooner had he and his companion taken leave, than a glance from Jane invited her to follow her upstairs. When they had gained their own room, Jane taking out the letter, said,

'This is from Caroline Bingley; what it contains, has surprised me a good deal. The whole party have left Netherfield by this time, and are on their way to town; and without any intention of coming back again. You shall hear what she says.'

She then read the first sentence aloud, which comprised the information of their having just resolved to follow their brother to town directly, and of their meaning to dine that day in Grosvenor street, where Mr Hurst had a house. The next was in these words. 'I do not pretend to regret any thing I shall leave in Hertfordshire,

except your society, my dearest friend; but we will hope at some future period, to enjoy many returns of the delightful intercourse we have known, and in the meanwhile may lessen the pain of separation by a very frequent and most unreserved correspondence. I depend on you for that.' To these high flown expressions, Elizabeth listened with all the insensibility of distrust; and though the suddenness of their removal surprised her, she saw nothing in it really to lament; it was not to be supposed that their absence from Netherfield would prevent Mr Bingley's being there; and as to the loss of their society, she was persuaded that Jane must soon cease to regard it, in the enjoyment of his.

'It is unlucky,' said she, after a short pause, 'that you should not be able to see your friends before they leave the country. But may we not hope that the period of future happiness to which Miss Bingley looks forward, may arrive earlier than she is aware, and that the delightful intercourse you have known as friends, will be renewed with yet greater satisfaction as sisters? – Mr Bingley will not be detained in London by them.'

'Caroline decidedly says that none of the party will return into Hertfordshire this winter. I will read it to you –

"When my brother left us yesterday, he imagined that the business which took him to London, might be concluded in three or four days, but as we are certain it cannot be so, and at the same time convinced that when Charles gets to town, he will be in no hurry to leave it again, we have determined on following him thither, that he may not be obliged to spend his vacant hours in a comfortless hotel. Many of my acquaintance are already there for the winter; I wish I could hear that you, my dearest friend, had any intention of making one in the crowd, but of that I despair. I sincerely hope your Christmas in Hertfordshire may abound in the gaieties which that season generally brings, and that your beaux will be so numerous as to prevent your feeling the loss of the three, of whom we shall deprive you." '

'It is evident by this,' added Jane, 'that he comes back no more this winter.'

'It is only evident that Miss Bingley does not mean he *should*.'

'Why will you think so? It must be his own doing. – He is his own master. But you do not know *all*. I *will* read you the passage which particularly hurts me. I will have no reserves from *you*.' 'Mr Darcy is impatient to see his sister, and to confess the truth, *we* are scarcely less eager to meet her again. I really do not think Georgiana Darcy has her equal for beauty, elegance, and accomplishments; and the affection she inspires in Louisa and myself, is heightened into something still more interesting, from the hope we dare to entertain of her being hereafter our sister. I do not know whether I ever before mentioned to you my feelings on this subject, but I will not leave the country without confiding them, and I trust you will not esteem them unreasonable. My brother admires her greatly already, he will have frequent opportunity now of seeing her on the most intimate footing, her relations all wish the connection as much as his own, and a sister's partiality is not misleading me, I think, when I call Charles most capable of engaging any woman's heart. With all these circumstances to favour an attachment and nothing to prevent it, am I wrong, my dearest Jane, in indulging the hope of an event which will secure the happiness of so many?' 'What think you of *this* sentence, my dear Lizzy?' – said Jane as she finished it. 'Is it not clear enough? – Does it not expressly declare that Caroline neither expects nor wishes me to be her sister; that she is perfectly convinced of her brother's indifference, and that if she suspects the nature of my feelings for him, she means (most kindly!) to put me on my guard? Can there be any other opinion on the subject?'

'Yes, there can; for mine is totally different. – Will you hear it?'

'Most willingly.'

'You shall have it in few words. Miss Bingley sees that her brother is in love with you, and wants him to marry Miss Darcy. She follows him to town in the hope of keeping him there, and tries to persuade you that he does not care about you.'

Jane shook her head.

'Indeed, Jane, you ought to believe me. – No one who has ever seen you together, can doubt his affection. Miss Bingley I am sure cannot. She is not such a simpleton. Could she have seen half as much love in Mr Darcy for herself, she would have ordered her wedding clothes. But the case is this. We are not rich enough, or grand enough for them; and she is the more anxious to get Miss Darcy for her brother, from the notion that when there has been *one* intermarriage, she may have less trouble in achieving a second; in which there is certainly some ingenuity, and I dare say it would succeed, if Miss de Bourgh were out of the way. But, my dearest Jane, you cannot seriously imagine that because Miss Bingley tells you her brother greatly admires Miss Darcy, he is in the smallest degree less sensible of *your* merit than when he took leave of you on Tuesday, or that it will be in her power to persuade him that instead of being in love with you, he is very much in love with her friend.'

'If we thought alike of Miss Bingley,' replied Jane, 'your representation of all this, might make me quite easy. But I know the foundation is unjust. Caroline is incapable of wilfully deceiving any one; and all that I can hope in this case is, that she is deceived herself.'

'That is right. – You could not have started a more happy idea, since you will not take comfort in mine. Believe her to be deceived by all means. You have now done your duty by her, and must fret no longer.'

'But, my dear sister, can I be happy, even supposing the best, in accepting a man whose sisters and friends are all wishing him to marry elsewhere?'

'You must decide for yourself,' said Elizabeth, 'and if upon mature deliberation, you find that the misery of disobliging his two sisters is more than equivalent to the happiness of being his wife, I advise you by all means to refuse him.'

'How can you talk so?' – said Jane faintly smiling, – 'You must know that though I should be exceedingly grieved at their disapprobation, I could not hesitate.'

'I did not think you would; – and that being the case, I cannot consider your situation with much compassion.'

'But if he returns no more this winter, my choice will never be required. A thousand things may arise in six months!'

The idea of his returning no more Elizabeth treated with the utmost contempt. It appeared to her merely the suggestion of Caroline's interested wishes, and she could not for a moment suppose that those wishes, however openly or artfully spoken, could influence a young man so totally independent of every one.

She represented to her sister as forcibly as possible what she felt on the subject, and had soon the pleasure of seeing its happy effect. Jane's temper was not desponding, and she was gradually led to hope, though the diffidence of affection sometimes overcame the hope, that Bingley would return to Netherfield and answer every wish of her heart.

They agreed that Mrs Bennet should only hear of the departure of the family, without being alarmed on the score of the gentleman's conduct; but even this partial communication gave her a great deal of concern, and she bewailed it as exceedingly unlucky that the ladies should happen to go away, just as they were all getting so intimate together. After lamenting it however at some length, she had the consolation of thinking that Mr Bingley would be soon down again and soon dining at Longbourn, and the conclusion of all was the comfortable declaration that, though he had been invited only to a family dinner, she would take care to have two full courses.

Chapter 22

The Bennets were engaged to dine with the Lucases, and again during the chief of the day, was Miss Lucas so kind as to listen to Mr Collins. Elizabeth took an opportunity of thanking her. 'It keeps him in good humour,' said she, 'and I am more obliged to you than I can express.' Charlotte assured her friend of her satisfaction in being useful, and that it amply repaid her for the little sacrifice of her time. This was very amiable, but Charlotte's kindness extended farther than Elizabeth had any conception of; – its object was nothing less, than to secure her from any return of Mr Collins's addresses, by engaging them towards herself. Such was Miss Lucas's scheme; and appearances were so favourable that when they parted at night, she would have felt almost sure of success if he had not been to leave Hertfordshire so very soon. But here, she did injustice to the fire and independence of his character, for it led him to escape out of Longbourn House the next morning with admirable slyness, and hasten to Lucas Lodge to throw himself at her feet. He was anxious to avoid the notice of his cousins, from a conviction that if they saw him depart, they could not fail to conjecture his design, and he was not willing to have the attempt known till its success could be known likewise; for though feeling almost secure, and with reason, for Charlotte had been tolerably encouraging, he was comparatively diffident since the adventure of Wednesday. His reception however was of the most flattering kind. Miss Lucas perceived him from an upper window as he walked towards the house, and instantly set out to meet him accidentally in the lane. But little had she dared to hope that so much love and eloquence awaited her there.

In as short a time as Mr Collins's long speeches would allow, every thing was settled between them to the satisfaction of both; and as they entered the house, he earnestly entreated her to name the day that was to make him the happiest of men; and though such a solicitation must

be waved for the present, the lady felt no inclination to trifle with his happiness. The stupidity with which he was favoured by nature, must guard his courtship from any charm that could make a woman wish for its continuance; and Miss Lucas, who accepted him solely from the pure and disinterested desire of an establishment, cared not how soon that establishment were gained.

Sir William and Lady Lucas were speedily applied to for their consent; and it was bestowed with a most joyful alacrity. Mr Collins's present circumstances made it a most eligible match for their daughter, to whom they could give little fortune; and his prospects of future wealth were exceedingly fair. Lady Lucas began directly to calculate with more interest than the matter had ever excited before, how many years longer Mr Bennet was likely to live; and Sir William gave it as his decided opinion, that whenever Mr Collins should be in possession of the Longbourn estate, it would be highly expedient that both he and his wife should make their appearance at St. James's. The whole family in short were properly overjoyed on the occasion.

The younger girls formed hopes of *coming out* a year or two sooner than they might otherwise have done; and the boys were relieved from their apprehension of Charlotte's dying an old maid. Charlotte herself was tolerably composed. She had gained her point, and had time to consider of it. Her reflections were in general satisfactory. Mr Collins to be sure was neither sensible nor agreeable; his society was irksome, and his attachment to her must be imaginary. But still he would be her husband. – Without thinking highly either of men or of matrimony, marriage had always been her object; it was the only honourable provision for well-educated young women of small fortune, and however uncertain of giving happiness, must be their pleasantest preservative from want. This preservative she had now obtained; and at the age of twenty-seven, without having ever been handsome, she felt all the good luck of it. The least agreeable circumstance in the business, was the surprise it must occasion to Elizabeth Bennet, whose friendship she valued beyond that of any other person. Elizabeth would wonder, and probably would blame her; and though her resolution was not to be shaken, her feelings must be hurt by such disapprobation. She resolved to give her the information herself, and therefore charged Mr Collins when he returned to Longbourn to dinner, to drop no hint of what had passed before any of the family. A promise of secrecy was of course very dutifully given, but it could not be kept without difficulty; for the curiosity excited by his long absence, burst forth in such very direct questions on his return, as required some ingenuity to evade, and he was at the same time exercising great self-denial, for he was longing to publish his prosperous love.

As he was to begin his journey too early on the morrow to see any of the family, the ceremony of leave-taking was performed when the ladies moved for the night; and Mrs Bennet with great politeness and cordiality said how happy they should be to see him at Longbourn again, whenever his other engagements might allow him to visit them.

'My dear Madam,' he replied, 'this invitation is particularly gratifying, because it is what I have been hoping to receive; and you may be very certain that I shall avail myself of it as soon as possible.'

They were all astonished; and Mr Bennet, who could by no means wish for so speedy a return, immediately said,

'But is there not danger of Lady Catherine's disapprobation here, my good sir? – You had better neglect your relations, than run the risk of offending your patroness.'

'My dear sir,' replied Mr Collins, 'I am particularly obliged to you for this friendly caution, and you may depend upon my not taking so material a step without her ladyship's concurrence.'

'You cannot be too much on your guard. Risk any thing rather than her displeasure; and if you find it likely to be raised by your coming to us again, which I should think exceedingly probable, stay quietly at home, and be satisfied that *we* shall take no offence.'

'Believe me, my dear sir, my gratitude is warmly excited by such affectionate attention; and depend upon it, you will speedily receive from me a letter of thanks for this, as well as for every other mark of your regard during my stay in Hertfordshire. As for my fair cousins, though my absence may not be long enough to render it necessary, I shall now take the liberty of wishing them health and happiness, not excepting my cousin Elizabeth.'

With proper civilities the ladies then withdrew; all of them equally surprised to find that he meditated a quick return. Mrs Bennet wished to understand by it that he thought of paying his addresses to one of her younger girls, and Mary might have been prevailed on to accept him. She rated his abilities much higher than any of the others; there was a solidity in his reflections which often struck her, and though by no means so clever as herself, she thought that if encouraged to read and improve himself by such an example as hers, he might become a very agreeable companion. But on the following morning, every hope of this kind was done away. Miss Lucas called soon after breakfast, and in a private conference with Elizabeth related the event of the day before.

The possibility of Mr Collins's fancying himself in love with her friend had once occurred to Elizabeth within the last day or two; but that Charlotte could encourage him, seemed almost as far from possibility as that she could encourage him herself, and her astonishment was consequently so great as to overcome at first the bounds of decorum, and she could not help crying out,

'Engaged to Mr Collins! my dear Charlotte, – impossible!'

The steady countenance which Miss Lucas had commanded in telling her story, gave way to a momentary confusion here on receiving so direct a reproach; though, as it was no more than she expected, she soon regained her composure, and calmly replied,

'Why should you be surprised, my dear Eliza? – Do you think it incredible that Mr Collins should be able to procure any woman's good opinion, because he was not so happy as to succeed with you?'

But Elizabeth had now recollected herself, and making a strong effort for it, was able to assure her with tolerable firmness that the prospect of their relationship was highly grateful to her, and that she wished her all imaginable happiness.

'I see what you are feeling,' replied Charlotte, – 'you must be surprised, very much surprised, – so lately as Mr Collins was wishing to marry you. But when you have had time to think it all over, I hope you will be satisfied with what I have done. I am not romantic you know. I never was. I ask only a comfortable home; and considering Mr Collins's character, connections, and situation in life, I am convinced that my chance of happiness with him is as fair, as most people can boast on entering the marriage state.'

Elizabeth quietly answered 'Undoubtedly;' – and after an awkward pause, they returned to the rest of the family. Charlotte did not stay much longer, and Elizabeth was then left to reflect on what she had heard. It was a long time before she became at all reconciled to the idea of so unsuitable a match. The strangeness of Mr Collins's making two offers of marriage within three days, was nothing in comparison of his being now accepted. She had always felt that Charlotte's opinion of matrimony was not exactly like her own, but she could not have supposed it possible that when called into action, she would have sacrificed every better feeling to worldly advantage. Charlotte the wife of Mr Collins, was a most humiliating picture! – And to the pang of a friend disgracing herself and sunk in her esteem, was added the distressing conviction that it was impossible for that friend to be tolerably happy in the lot she had chosen.

Chapter 23

Elizabeth was sitting with her mother and sisters, reflecting on what she had heard, and doubting whether she were authorised to mention it, when Sir William Lucas himself appeared, sent by his daughter to announce her engagement to the family. With many compliments to them, and much self-gratulation on the prospect of a connection between the houses, he unfolded the matter, – to an audience not merely wondering, but incredulous; for Mrs Bennet, with more perseverance than politeness, protested he must be entirely mistaken, and Lydia, always unguarded and often uncivil, boisterously exclaimed,

'Good Lord! Sir William, how can you tell such a story? – Do not you know that Mr Collins wants to marry Lizzy?'

Nothing less than the complaisance of a courtier could have borne without anger such treatment; but Sir William's good breeding carried him through it all; and though he begged leave to be positive as to the truth of his information, he listened to all their impertinence with the most forbearing courtesy.

Elizabeth, feeling it incumbent on her to relieve him from so unpleasant a situation, now put herself forward to confirm his account, by mentioning her prior knowledge of it from Charlotte herself; and endeavoured to put a stop to the exclamations of her mother and sisters, by the earnestness of her congratulations to Sir William, in which she was readily joined by Jane, and by making a variety of remarks on the happiness that might be expected from the match, the excellent character of Mr Collins, and the convenient distance of Hunsford from London.

Mrs Bennet was in fact too much overpowered to say a great deal while Sir William remained; but no sooner had he left them than her feelings found a rapid vent. In the first place, she persisted in disbelieving the whole of the matter; secondly, she was very sure that Mr Collins had been taken in; thirdly, she trusted that they would never be happy together; and fourthly, that the match might be broken off. Two inferences, however, were plainly deduced from the whole; one, that Elizabeth was the real cause of all the mischief; and the other, that she herself had been barbarously used by them all; and on these two points she principally dwelt during the rest of the day. Nothing could console and nothing appease her. – Nor did that day wear out her resentment. A week elapsed before she could see Elizabeth without scolding her, a month passed away before she could speak to Sir William or Lady Lucas without being rude, and many months were gone before she could at all forgive their daughter.

Mr Bennet's emotions were much more tranquil on the occasion, and such as he did experience he pronounced to be of a most agreeable sort; for it gratified him, he said, to discover that Charlotte Lucas, whom he had been used to think tolerably sensible, was as foolish as his wife, and more foolish than his daughter!

Jane confessed herself a little surprised at the match; but she said less of her astonishment than of her earnest desire for their happiness; nor could Elizabeth persuade her to consider it as improbable. Kitty and Lydia were far from envying Miss Lucas, for Mr Collins was only a clergyman; and it affected them in no other way than as a piece of news to spread at Meryton.

Lady Lucas could not be insensible of triumph on being able to retort on Mrs Bennet the comfort of having a daughter well married; and she called at Longbourn rather oftener than usual to say how happy she was, though Mrs Bennet's sour looks and ill-natured remarks might have been enough to drive happiness away.

Between Elizabeth and Charlotte there was a restraint which kept them mutually silent on the subject; and Elizabeth felt persuaded that no real confidence could ever subsist between them again. Her disappointment in Charlotte made her turn with fonder regard to her sister, of whose rectitude and delicacy she was sure her opinion could never be shaken, and for whose happiness she grew daily more anxious, as Bingley had now been gone a week, and nothing was heard of his return.

Jane had sent Caroline an early answer to her letter, and was counting the days till she might reasonably hope to hear again. The promised letter of thanks from Mr Collins arrived on Tuesday, addressed to their father, and written with all the solemnity of gratitude which a twelve-month's abode in the family might have prompted. After discharging his conscience on that head, he proceeded to inform them, with many rapturous expressions, of his happiness in having obtained the affection of their amiable neighbour, Miss Lucas, and then explained that it was merely with the view of enjoying her society that he had been so ready to close with their kind wish of seeing him again at Longbourn, whither he hoped to be able to return on Monday fortnight; for Lady Catherine, he added, so heartily approved his marriage, that she wished it to take place as soon as possible, which he trusted would be an unanswerable argument with his amiable Charlotte to name an early day for making him the happiest of men.

Mr Collins's return into Hertfordshire was no longer a matter of pleasure to Mrs Bennet. On the contrary she was as much disposed to complain of it as her husband. – It was very strange that he should come to Longbourn instead of to Lucas Lodge; it was also very inconvenient and exceedingly troublesome. – She hated having visitors in the house while her health was so indifferent, and lovers were of all people the most disagreeable. Such were the gentle murmurs of Mrs Bennet, and they gave way only to the greater distress of Mr Bingley's continued absence.

Neither Jane nor Elizabeth were comfortable on this subject. Day after day passed away without bringing any other tidings of him than the report which shortly prevailed in Meryton of his coming no more to Netherfield the whole winter; a report which highly incensed Mrs Bennet, and which she never failed to contradict as a most scandalous falsehood.

Even Elizabeth began to fear — not that Bingley was indifferent — but that his sisters would be successful in keeping him away. Unwilling as she was to admit an idea so destructive of Jane's happiness, and so dishonourable to the stability of her lover, she could not prevent its frequently recurring. The united efforts of his two unfeeling sister and of his overpowering friend, assisted by the attractions of Miss Darcy and the amusements of London, might be too much, she feared, for the strength of his attachment.

As for Jane, *her* anxiety under this suspense was, of course, more painful than Elizabeth's; but whatever she felt she was desirous of concealing, and between herself and Elizabeth, therefore, the subject was never alluded to. But as no such delicacy restrained her mother, an hour seldom passed in which she did not talk of Bingley, express her impatience for his arrival, or even require Jane to confess that if he did not come back, she should think herself very ill used. It needed all Jane's steady mildness to bear these attacks with tolerable tranquility.

Mr Collins returned most punctually on the Monday fortnight, but his reception at Longbourn was not quite so gracious as it had been on his first introduction. He was too happy, however, to need much attention; and luckily for the others, the business of love-making relieved them from a great deal of his company. The chief of every day was spent by him at Lucas Lodge, and he sometimes returned to Longbourn only in time to make an apology for his absence before the family went to bed.

Mrs Bennet was really in a most pitiable state. The very mention of any thing concerning the match threw her into an agony of ill humour, and wherever she went she was sure of hearing it talked of. The sight of Miss Lucas was odious to her. As her successor in that house, she regarded her with jealous abhorrence. Whenever Charlotte came to see them she concluded her to be anticipating the hour of possession; and whenever she spoke in a low voice to Mr Collins, was convinced that they were talking of the Longbourn estate, and resolving to turn herself and her daughters out of the house, as soon as Mr Bennet were dead. She complained bitterly of all this to her husband.

'Indeed, Mr Bennet,' said she, 'it is very hard to think that Charlotte Lucas should ever be mistress of this house, that I should be forced to make way for *her*, and live to see her take my place in it!'

'My dear, do not give way to such gloomy thoughts. Let us hope for better things. Let us flatter ourselves that I may be the survivor.'

This was not very consoling to Mrs Bennet, and, therefore, instead of making any answer, she went on as before,

'I cannot bear to think that they should have all this estate. If it was not for the entail I should not mind it.'

'What should not you mind?'

'I should not mind any thing at all.'

'Let us be thankful that you are preserved from a state of such insensibility.'

'I never can be thankful, Mr Bennet, for any thing about the entail. How any one could have the conscience to entail away an estate from one's own daughters I cannot understand; and all for the sake of Mr Collins too! – Why should *he* have it more than anybody else?'

'I leave it to yourself to determine,' said Mr Bennet.

Chapter 24

Miss Bingley's letter arrived, and put an end to doubt. The very first sentence conveyed the assurance of their being all settled in London for the winter, and concluded with her brother's regret at not having had time to pay his respects to his friends in Hertfordshire before he left the country.

Hope was over, entirely over; and when Jane could attend to the rest of the letter, she found little, except the professed affection of the writer, that could give her any comfort. Miss Darcy's praise occupied the chief of it. Her many attractions were again dwelt on, and Caroline boasted joyfully of their increasing intimacy, and ventured to predict the accomplishment of the wishes which had been unfolded in her former letter. She wrote also with great pleasure of her brother's being an inmate of Mr Darcy's house, and mentioned with raptures, some plans of the latter with regard to new furniture.

Elizabeth, to whom Jane very soon communicated the chief of all this, heard it in silent indignation. Her heart was divided between concern for her sister, and resentment against all the others. To Caroline's assertion of her brother's being partial to Miss Darcy she paid no credit. That he was really fond of Jane, she doubted no more than she had ever done; and much as she had always been disposed to like him, she could not think without anger, hardly without contempt, on that easiness of temper, that want of proper resolution which now made him the slave of his designing friends, and led him to sacrifice his own happiness to the caprice of their inclinations. Had his own happiness, however, been the only sacrifice, he might have been allowed to sport with it in whatever manner he thought best; but her sister's was involved in it, as she thought he must be sensible himself. It was a subject, in short, on which reflection would be long indulged, and must be unavailing. She could think of nothing else, and yet whether Bingley's regard had really died away, or were suppressed by his friends' interference; whether he had been aware of Jane's attachment, or whether it had escaped his observation; whichever were the case, though her opinion of him must be materially affected by the difference, her sister's situation remained the same, her peace equally wounded.

A day or two passed before Jane had courage to speak of her feelings to Elizabeth; but at last on Mrs Bennet's leaving them together, after a longer irritation than usual about Netherfield and its master, she could not help saying,

'Oh! that my dear mother had more command over herself; she can have no idea of the pain she gives me by her continual reflections on him. But I will not repine. It cannot last long. He will be forgot, and we shall all be as we were before.'

Elizabeth looked at her sister with incredulous solicitude, but said nothing.

'You doubt me,' cried Jane slightly colouring; 'indeed you have no reason. He may live in my memory as the most amiable man of my acquaintance, but that is all. I have nothing either to hope or fear, and nothing to reproach him with. Thank God! I have not *that* pain. A little time therefore. – I shall certainly try to get the better.'

With a stronger voice she soon added, 'I have this comfort immediately, that it has not been more than an error of fancy on my side, and that it has done no harm to any one but myself.'

'My dear Jane!' exclaimed Elizabeth, 'you are too good. Your sweetness and disinterestedness are really angelic; I do not know what to say to you. I feel as if I had never done you justice, or loved you as you deserve.'

Miss Bennet eagerly disclaimed all extraordinary merit, and threw back the praise on her sister's warm affection.

'Nay,' said Elizabeth, 'this is not fair. *You* wish to think all the world respectable, and are hurt if I speak ill of any body. *I* only want to think *you* perfect, and you set yourself against it. Do not be afraid of my running into any excess, of my encroaching on your privilege of universal good will. You need not. There are few people whom I really love, and still fewer of whom I think well. The more I see of the world, the more am I dissatisfied with it; and every day confirms my belief of the inconsistency of all human characters, and of the little dependence that can be placed on the appearance of either merit or sense. I have met with two instances lately; one I will not mention; the other is Charlotte's marriage. It is unaccountable! in every view it is unaccountable!'

'My dear Lizzy, do not give way to such feelings as these. They will ruin your happiness. You do not make allowance enough for difference of situation and temper. Consider Mr Collins's respectability, and Charlotte's prudent, steady character. Remember that she is one of a large family; that as to fortune, it is a most eligible match; and be ready to believe, for every body's sake, that she may feel something like regard and esteem for our cousin.'

'To oblige you, I would try to believe almost any thing, but no one else could be benefited by such a belief as this; for were I persuaded that Charlotte had any regard for him, I should only think worse of her understanding, than I now do of her heart. My dear Jane, Mr Collins is a conceited, pompous, narrow-minded, silly man; you know he is, as well as I do; and you must feel, as well as I do, that the woman who marries him, cannot have a proper way of thinking. You shall not defend her, though it is Charlotte Lucas. You shall not, for the sake of one individual, change the meaning of principle and integrity, nor endeavour to persuade yourself or me, that selfishness is prudence, and insensibility of danger, security for happiness.'

'I must think your language too strong in speaking of both,' replied Jane, 'and I hope you will be convinced of it, by seeing them happy together. But enough of this. You alluded to something else. You mentioned *two* instances. I cannot misunderstand you, but I intreat you, dear Lizzy, not to pain me by thinking *that person* to blame, and saying your opinion of him is sunk. We must not be so ready to fancy ourselves intentionally injured. We must not expect a lively young man to be always so guarded and circumspect. It is very often nothing but our own vanity that deceives us. Women fancy admiration means more than it does.'

'And men take care that they should.'

'If it is designedly done, they cannot be justified; but I have no idea of there being so much design in the world as some persons imagine.'

'I am far from attributing any part of Mr Bingley's conduct to design,' said Elizabeth; 'but without scheming to do wrong, or to make others unhappy, there may be error, and there may be misery. Thoughtlessness, want of attention to other people's feelings, and want of resolution, will do the business.'

'And do you impute it to either of those?'

'Yes; to the last. But if I go on, I shall displease you by saying what I think of persons you esteem. Stop me whilst[19] you can.'

'You persist, then, in supposing his sisters influence him.'

'Yes, in conjunction with his friend.'

'I cannot believe it. Why should they try to influence him? They can only wish his happiness, and if he is attached to me, no other woman can secure it.'

'Your first position is false. They may wish many things besides his happiness; they may wish his increase of wealth and consequence; they may wish him to marry a girl who has all the importance of money, great connections, and pride.'

'Beyond a doubt, they *do* wish him to chuse Miss Darcy,' replied Jane; 'but this may be from better feelings than you are supposing. They have known her much longer than they have known me; no wonder if they love her better. But, whatever may be their own wishes, it is very unlikely they should have opposed their brother's. What sister would think herself at liberty to do it, unless there were something very objectionable? If they believed him attached to me, they would not try to part us; if he were so, they could not succeed. By supposing such an affection, you make every body acting unnaturally and wrong, and me most unhappy. Do not distress me by the idea. I am not ashamed of having been mistaken – or, at least, it is slight, it is nothing in comparison of what I should feel in thinking ill of him or his sisters. Let me take it in the best light, in the light in which it may be understood.'

Elizabeth could not oppose such a wish; and from this time Mr Bingley's name was scarcely ever mentioned between them.

Mrs Bennet still continued to wonder and repine at his returning no more, and though a day seldom passed in which Elizabeth did not account for it clearly, there seemed little chance of her ever considering it with less perplexity. Her daughter endeavoured to convince her of what she did not believe herself, that his attentions to Jane had been merely the effect of a common and transient liking, which ceased when he saw her no more; but though the probability of the statement was admitted at the time, she had the same story to repeat every day. Mrs Bennet's best comfort was, that Mr Bingley must be down again in the summer.

Mr Bennet treated the matter differently. 'So, Lizzy,' said he one day, 'your sister is crossed in love I find. I congratulate her. Next to being married, a girl likes to be crossed in love a little now and then. It is something to think of, and gives her a sort of distinction among her companions. When is your turn to come? You will hardly bear to be long outdone by Jane. Now is your time. Here are officers enough at Meryton to disappoint all the young ladies in the country. Let Wickham be *your* man. He is a pleasant fellow, and would jilt you creditably.'

'Thank you, Sir, but a less agreeable man would satisfy me. We must not all expect Jane's good fortune.'

'True,' said Mr Bennet, 'but it is a comfort to think that, whatever of that kind may befall you, you have an affectionate mother who will always make the most of it.'

Mr Wickham's society was of material service in dispelling the gloom, which the late perverse occurrences had thrown on many of the Longbourn family. They saw him often, and to his other recommendations was now added that of general unreserve. The whole of what Elizabeth had already heard, his claims on Mr Darcy, and all that he had suffered from him, was now openly acknowledged and publicly canvassed; and every body was pleased to think how much they had always disliked Mr Darcy before they had known any thing of the matter.

Miss Bennet was the only creature who could suppose there might be any extenuating circumstances in the case, unknown to the society of Hertfordshire; her mild and steady candour always pleaded for allowances, and urged the possibility of mistakes – but by everybody else Mr Darcy was condemned as the worst of men.

Chapter 25

After a week spent in professions of love and schemes of felicity, Mr Collins was called from his amiable Charlotte by the arrival of Saturday. The pain of separation, however, might be alleviated on his side, by preparations for the reception of his bride, as he had reason to hope, that shortly after his next return into Hertfordshire, the day would be fixed that was to make him the happiest of men. He took leave of his relations at Longbourn with as much solemnity as before; wished his fair cousins health and happiness again, and promised their father another letter of thanks.

On the following Monday, Mrs Bennet had the pleasure of receiving her brother and his wife, who came as usual to spend the Christmas at Longbourn. Mr Gardiner was a sensible, gentlemanlike man, greatly superior to his sister, as well by nature as education. The Netherfield ladies would have had difficulty in believing that a man who lived by trade, and within view of his own warehouses, could have been so well bred and agreeable. Mrs Gardiner, who was several years younger than Mrs Bennet and Mrs Philips, was an amiable, intelligent, elegant woman, and a great favourite with all her Longbourn nieces. Between the two eldest and herself especially, there subsisted a very particular regard. They had frequently been staying with her in town.

The first part of Mrs Gardiner's business on her arrival, was to distribute her presents and describe the newest fashions. When this was done, she had a less active part to play. It became her turn to listen. Mrs Bennet had many grievances to relate, and much to complain of. They had all been very ill-used since she last saw her sister. Two of her girls had been on the point of marriage, and after all there was nothing in it.

'I do not blame Jane,' she continued, 'for Jane would have got Mr Bingley, if she could. But, Lizzy! Oh, sister! it is very hard to think that she might have been Mr Collins's wife by this time, had not it been for her own perverseness. He made her an offer in this very room, and she refused him. The consequence of it is, that Lady Lucas will have a daughter married before I have, and that Longbourn estate is just as much entailed as ever. The Lucases are very artful people indeed, sister. They are all for what they can get. I am sorry to say it of them, but so it is. It makes me very nervous and poorly, to be thwarted so in my own family, and to have neighbours who think of themselves before anybody else. However, your coming just at this time is the greatest of comforts, and I am very glad to hear what you tell us, of long sleeves.'

Mrs Gardiner, to whom the chief of this news had been given before, in the course of Jane and Elizabeth's correspondence with her, made her sister a slight answer, and in compassion to her nieces turned the conversation.

When alone with Elizabeth afterwards, she spoke more on the subject. 'It seems likely to have been a desirable match for Jane,' said she. 'I am sorry it went off. But these things happen so often! A young man, such as you describe Mr Bingley, so easily falls in love with a pretty girl for a few weeks, and when accident separates them, so easily forgets her, that these sort of inconstancies are very frequent.'

'An excellent consolation in its way,' said Elizabeth, 'but it will not do for *us*. We do not suffer by *accident*. It does not often happen that the interference of friends will persuade a young man of independent fortune to think no more of a girl, whom he was violently in love with only a few days before.'

'But that expression of "violently in love" is so hackneyed, so doubtful, so indefinite, that it gives me very little idea. It is as often applied to feelings which arise from an half-hour's acquaintance, as to a real, strong attachment. Pray, how *violent was* Mr Bingley's love?'

'I never saw a more promising inclination. He was growing quite inattentive to other people, and wholly engrossed by her. Every time they met, it was more decided and remarkable. At his own ball he offended two or three young ladies, by not asking them to dance, and I spoke to him twice myself, without receiving an answer. Could there be finer symptoms? Is not general incivility the very essence of love?'

'Oh, yes! – of that kind of love which I suppose him to have felt. Poor Jane! I am sorry for her, because, with her disposition, she may not get over it immediately. It had better have happened to *you*, Lizzy; you would have laughed yourself out of it sooner. But do you think she would be prevailed on to go back with us? Change of scene might be of service – and perhaps a little relief from home, may be as useful as anything.'

Elizabeth was exceedingly pleased with this proposal, and felt persuaded of her sister's ready acquiescence.

'I hope,' added Mrs Gardiner, 'that no consideration with regard to this young man will influence her. We live in so different a part of town, all our connections are so different, and, as you well know, we go out so little, that it is very improbable they should meet at all, unless he really comes to see her.'

'And *that* is quite impossible; for he is now in the custody of his friend, and Mr Darcy would no more suffer him to call on Jane in such a part of London! My dear aunt, how could you think of it? Mr Darcy may perhaps have *heard* of such a place as Gracechurch Street, but he would hardly think a month's ablution enough to cleanse him from its impurities, were he once to enter it; and depend upon it, Mr Bingley never stirs without him.'

'So much the better. I hope they will not meet at all. But does not Jane correspond with the sister? *She* will not be able to help calling.'

'She will drop the acquaintance entirely.'

But in spite of the certainty in which Elizabeth affected to place this point, as well as the still more interesting one of Bingley's being withheld from seeing Jane, she felt a solicitude on the subject which convinced her, on examination, that she did not consider it entirely hopeless. It was possible, and sometimes she thought it probable, that his affection might be reanimated, and the influence of his friends successfully combated by the more natural influence of Jane's attractions.

Miss Bennet accepted her aunt's invitation with pleasure; and the Bingleys were no otherwise in her thoughts at the time, than as she hoped that, by Caroline's not living in the same house with her brother, she might occasionally spend a morning with her, without any danger of seeing him.

The Gardiners staid[20] a week at Longbourn; and what with the Philipses, the Lucases, and the officers, there was not a day without its engagement. Mrs Bennet had so carefully provided for the entertainment of her brother and sister, that they did not once sit down to a family dinner. When the engagement was for home, some of the officers always made part of it, of which officers Mr Wickham was sure to be one; and on these occasions, Mrs Gardiner, rendered suspicious by Elizabeth's warm commendation of him, narrowly observed them both. Without supposing them, from what she saw, to be very seriously in love, their preference of each other was plain enough to make her a little uneasy; and she resolved to speak to Elizabeth on the subject before she left Hertfordshire, and represent to her the imprudence of encouraging such an attachment.

To Mrs Gardiner, Wickham had one means of affording pleasure, unconnected with his general powers. About ten or a dozen years ago, before her marriage, she had spent a considerable time in that very part of Derbyshire, to which he belonged. They had, therefore, many acquaintance in common; and, though Wickham had been little there since the death of Darcy's father, five years before, it was yet in his power to give her fresher intelligence of her former friends, than she had been in the way of procuring.

Mrs Gardiner had seen Pemberley, and known the late Mr Darcy by character perfectly well. Here consequently was an inexhaustible subject of discourse. In comparing her recollection of Pemberley, with the minute description which Wickham could give, and in bestowing her tribute of praise on the character of its late possessor, she was delighting both him and herself. On being made acquainted with the present Mr Darcy's treatment of him, she tried to remember something of that gentleman's reputed disposition when quite a lad, which might agree with it, and was confident at last, that she recollected having heard Mr Fitzwilliam Darcy formerly spoken of as a very proud, ill-natured boy.

Chapter 26

Mrs Gardiner's caution to Elizabeth was punctually and kindly given on the first favourable opportunity of speaking to her alone; after honestly telling her what she thought, she thus went on:

'You are too sensible a girl, Lizzy, to fall in love merely because you are warned against it; and, therefore, I am not afraid of speaking openly. Seriously, I would have you be on your guard. Do not involve yourself, or endeavour to involve him in an affection which the want of fortune would make so very imprudent. I have nothing to say against *him*; he is a most interesting young man; and if he had the fortune he ought to have, I should think you could not do better. But as it is – you must not let your fancy run away with you. You have sense, and we all expect you to use it. Your father would depend on *your* resolution and good conduct, I am sure. You must not disappoint your father.'

'My dear aunt, this is being serious indeed.'

'Yes, and I hope to engage you to be serious likewise.'

'Well, then, you need not be under any alarm. I will take care of myself, and of Mr Wickham too. He shall not be in love with me, if I can prevent it.'

'Elizabeth, you are not serious now.'

'I beg your pardon. I will try again. At present I am not in love with Mr Wickham; no, I certainly am not. But he is, beyond all comparison, the most agreeable man I ever saw – and if he becomes really attached to me – I believe it will be better that he should not. I see the imprudence of it. – Oh! *that* abominable Mr Darcy! – My father's opinion of me does me the greatest honour; and I should be miserable to forfeit it. My father, however, is partial to Mr Wickham. In short, my dear aunt, I should be very sorry to be the means of making any of you unhappy; but since we see every day that where there is affection, young people are seldom withheld by immediate want of fortune, from entering into engagements with each other, how can I promise to be wiser than so many of my fellow-creatures if I am tempted, or how am I even to know that it would be wisdom to resist? All that I can promise you, therefore, is not to be in a hurry. I will not be in a hurry to believe myself his first object. When I am in company with him, I will not be wishing. In short, I will do my best.'

'Perhaps it will be as well, if you discourage his coming here so very often. At least, you should not *remind* your Mother of inviting him.'

'As I did the other day,' said Elizabeth, with a conscious smile; 'very true, it will be wise in me to refrain from *that*. But do not imagine that he is always here so often. It is on your account that he has been so frequently invited this week. You know my mother's ideas as to the necessity of constant company for her friends. But really, and upon my honour, I will try to do what I think to be wisest; and now, I hope you are satisfied.'

Her aunt assured her that she was; and Elizabeth having thanked her for the kindness of her hints, they parted; a wonderful instance of advice being given on such a point, without being resented.

Mr Collins returned into Hertfordshire soon after it had been quitted by the Gardiners and Jane; but as he took up his abode with the Lucases, his arrival was no great inconvenience to Mrs Bennet. His marriage was now fast approaching, and she was at length so far resigned as to think it inevitable, and even repeatedly to say in an ill-natured tone that she 'wished they might be happy.' Thursday was to be the wedding day, and on Wednesday Miss Lucas paid her farewell visit; and when she rose to take leave, Elizabeth, ashamed of her mother's ungracious and reluctant good wishes, and sincerely affected herself, accompanied her out of the room. As they went down stairs together, Charlotte said,

'I shall depend on hearing from you very often, Eliza.'

'*That* you certainly shall.'

'And I have another favour to ask. Will you come and see me?'

'We shall often meet, I hope, in Hertfordshire.'

'I am not likely to leave Kent for some time. Promise me, therefore, to come to Hunsford.'

Elizabeth could not refuse, though she foresaw little pleasure in the visit.

'My father and Maria are to come to me in March,' added Charlotte, 'and I hope you will consent to be of the party. Indeed, Eliza, you will be as welcome to me as either of them.'

The wedding took place; the bride and bridegroom set off for Kent from the church door, and every body had as much to say or to hear on the subject as usual. Elizabeth soon heard from her friend; and their correspondence was as regular and frequent as it had ever been; that it should be equally unreserved was impossible. Elizabeth could never address her without feeling that all the comfort of intimacy was over, and, though determined not to slacken as a correspondent, it was for the sake of what had been, rather than what was. Charlotte's first letters were received with a good deal of eagerness; there could not but be curiosity to know how she would speak of her new home, how she would like Lady Catherine, and how happy she would dare pronounce herself to be; though, when the letters were read, Elizabeth felt that Charlotte expressed herself on every point exactly as she might have foreseen. She wrote cheerfully, seemed surrounded with comforts, and

mentioned nothing which she could not praise. The house, furniture, neighbourhood, and roads, were all to her taste, and Lady Catherine's behaviour was most friendly and obliging. It was Mr Collins's picture of Hunsford and Rosings rationally softened; and Elizabeth perceived that she must wait for her own visit there, to know the rest.

Jane had already written a few lines to her sister to announce their safe arrival in London; and when she wrote again, Elizabeth hoped it would be in her power to say something of the Bingleys.

Her impatience for this second letter was as well rewarded as impatience generally is. Jane had been a week in town, without either seeing or hearing from Caroline. She accounted for it, however, by supposing that her last letter to her friend from Longbourn, had by some accident been lost.

'My aunt,' she continued, 'is going tomorrow into that part of the town, and I shall take the opportunity of calling in Grosvenor street.'

She wrote again when the visit was paid, and she had seen Miss Bingley. 'I did not think Caroline in spirits,' were her words, 'but she was very glad to see me, and reproached me for giving her no notice of my coming to London. I was right, therefore; my last letter had never reached her. I enquired after their brother, of course. He was well, but so much engaged with Mr Darcy, that they scarcely ever saw him. I found that Miss Darcy was expected to dinner. I wish I could see her. My visit was not long, as Caroline and Mrs Hurst were going out. I dare say I shall soon see them here.'

Elizabeth shook her head over this letter. It convinced her, that accident only could discover to Mr Bingley her sister's being in town.

Four weeks passed away, and Jane saw nothing of him. She endeavoured to persuade herself that she did not regret it; but she could no longer be blind to Miss Bingley's inattention. After waiting at home every morning for a fortnight, and inventing every evening a fresh excuse for her, the visitor did at last appear; but the shortness of her stay, and yet more, the alteration of her manner, would allow Jane to deceive herself no longer. The letter which she wrote on this occasion to her sister, will prove what she felt.

My dearest Lizzy will, I am sure, be incapable of triumphing in her better judgment, at my expense, when I confess myself to have been entirely deceived in Miss Bingley's regard for me. But, my dear sister, though the event has proved you right, do not think me obstinate if I still assert, that, considering what her behaviour was, my confidence was as natural as your suspicion. I do not at all comprehend her reason for wishing to be intimate with me, but if the same circumstances were to happen again, I am sure I should be deceived again. Caroline did not return my visit till yesterday; and not a note, not a line, did I receive in the meantime. When she did come, it was very evident that she had no pleasure in it; she made a slight, formal, apology, for not calling before, said not a word of wishing to see me again, and was in every respect so altered a creature, that when she went away, I was perfectly resolved to continue the acquaintance no longer. I pity, though I cannot help blaming her. She was very wrong in singling me out as she did; I can safely say, that every advance to intimacy began on her side. But I pity her, because she must feel that she has been acting wrong, and because I am very sure that anxiety for her brother is the cause of it. I need not explain myself farther; and though *we* know this anxiety to be quite needless, yet if she feels it, it will easily account for her behaviour to me; and so deservedly dear as he is to his sister, whatever anxiety she may feel on his behalf, is natural and amiable. I cannot but wonder, however, at her having any such fears now, because, if he had at all cared about me, we must have met long, long ago. He knows of my being in town, I am certain, from something she said herself; and yet it should seem by her manner of talking, as if she wanted to persuade herself that he is really partial to Miss Darcy. I cannot understand it. If I were not afraid of judging harshly, I should be almost tempted to say, that there is a strong appearance of duplicity in all this. But I will endeavour to banish every painful thought, and think only of what will make me happy, your affection, and the invariable kindness of my dear uncle and aunt. Let me hear from you very soon. Miss Bingley said something of his never returning to Netherfield again, of giving up the house, but not with any certainty. We had better not mention it. I am extremely glad that you have such pleasant accounts from our friends at Hunsford. Pray go to see them, with Sir William and Maria. I am sure you will be very comfortable there.

Your's, &c.

This letter gave Elizabeth some pain; but her spirits returned as she considered that Jane would no longer be duped, by the sister at least. All expectation from the brother was now absolutely over. She would not even wish for any renewal of his attentions. His character sunk on every review of it; and as a punishment for him, as well as a possible advantage to Jane, she seriously hoped he might really soon marry Mr Darcy's sister, as, by Wickham's account, she would make him abundantly regret what he had thrown away.

Mrs Gardiner about this time reminded Elizabeth of her promise concerning that gentleman, and required information; and Elizabeth had such to send as might rather give contentment to her aunt than to herself. His apparent partiality had subsided, his attentions were over, he was the admirer of some one else. Elizabeth was watchful enough to see it all, but she could see it and write of it without material pain. Her heart had been but slightly touched, and her vanity was satisfied with believing that *she* would have been his only choice, had fortune permitted it. The sudden acquisition of ten thousand pounds was the most remarkable charm of the young lady, to whom he was now rendering himself agreeable; but Elizabeth, less clear-sighted perhaps in his case than in Charlotte's, did not quarrel with him for his wish of independence. Nothing, on the contrary, could be more natural; and while able to suppose that it cost him a few struggles to relinquish her, she was ready to allow it a wise and desirable measure for both, and could very sincerely wish him happy.

All this was acknowledged to Mrs Gardiner; and after relating the circumstances, she thus went on: – 'I am now convinced, my dear aunt, that I have never been much in love; for had I really experienced that pure and elevating passion, I should at present detest his very name, and wish him all manner of evil. But my feelings are not only cordial towards *him*; they are even impartial towards Miss King. I cannot find out that I hate her at all, or that I am in the least unwilling to think her a very good sort of girl. There can be no love in all this. My watchfulness has been effectual; and though I should certainly be a more interesting object to all my acquaintance, were I distractedly in love with him, I cannot say that I regret my comparative insignificance. Importance may sometimes be purchased too dearly. Kitty and Lydia take his defection much more to heart than I do. They are young in the ways of the world, and not yet open to the mortifying conviction that handsome young men must have something to live on, as well as the plain.'

With no greater events than these in the Longbourn family, and otherwise diversified by little beyond the walks to Meryton, sometimes dirty and sometimes cold, did January and February pass away. March was to take Elizabeth to Hunsford. She had not at first thought very seriously of going thither; but Charlotte, she soon found, was depending on the plan, and she gradually learned to consider it herself with greater pleasure as well as greater certainty. Absence had increased her desire of seeing Charlotte again, and weakened her disgust of Mr Collins. There was novelty in the scheme, and as, with such a mother and such uncompanionable sisters, home could not be faultless, a little change was not unwelcome for its own sake. The journey would moreover give her a peep at Jane; and, in short, as the time drew near, she would have been very sorry for any delay. Every thing, however, went on smoothly, and was finally settled according to Charlotte's first sketch. She was to accompany Sir William and his second daughter. The improvement of spending a night in London was added in time, and the plan became perfect as plan could be.

The only pain was in leaving her father, who would certainly miss her, and who, when it came to the point, so little liked her going, that he told her to write to him, and almost promised to answer her letter.

The farewell between herself and Mr Wickham was perfectly friendly; on his side even more. His present pursuit could not make him forget that Elizabeth had been the first to excite and to deserve his attention, the first to listen and to pity, the first to be admired; and in his manner of bidding her adieu, wishing her every enjoyment, reminding her of what she was to expect in Lady Catherine de Bourgh, and trusting their opinion of her – their opinion of every body – would always coincide, there was a solicitude, an interest which she felt must ever attach her to him with a most sincere regard; and she parted from him convinced, that whether married or single, he must always be her model of the amiable and pleasing.

Her fellow-travellers the next day, were not of a kind to make her think him less agreeable. Sir William Lucas, and his daughter Maria, a good humoured girl, but as empty-headed as himself, had nothing to say that could be worth hearing, and were listened to with about as much delight as the rattle of the chaise. Elizabeth loved absurdities, but she had known Sir William's too long. He could tell her nothing new of the wonders of his presentation and knighthood; and his civilities were worn out like his information.

It was a journey of only twenty-four miles, and they began it so early as to be in Gracechurch street by noon. As they drove to Mr Gardiner's door, Jane was at a drawing-room window watching their arrival; when they entered the passage she was there to welcome them, and Elizabeth, looking earnestly in her face, was pleased to see it healthful and lovely as ever. On the stairs were a troop of little boys and girls, whose eagerness for their cousin's appearance would not allow them to wait in the drawing-room, and whose shyness, as they had not seen her for a twelve-month, prevented their coming lower. All was joy and kindness. The day passed most pleasantly away; the morning in bustle and shopping, and the evening at one of the theatres.

Elizabeth then contrived to sit by her aunt. Their first subject was her sister; and she was more grieved than astonished to hear, in reply to her minute enquiries, that though Jane always struggled to support her spirits, there were periods of dejection. It was reasonable, however, to hope, that they would not continue long. Mrs Gardiner gave her the particulars also of Miss Bingley's visit in Gracechurch street, and repeated conversations occurring at different times between Jane and herself, which proved that the former had, from her heart, given up the acquaintance.

Mrs Gardiner then rallied her niece on Wickham's desertion, and complimented her on bearing it so well.

'But, my dear Elizabeth,' she added, 'what sort of girl is Miss King? I should be sorry to think our friend mercenary.'

'Pray, my dear aunt, what is the difference in matrimonial affairs, between the mercenary and the prudent motive? Where does discretion end, and avarice begin? Last Christmas you were afraid of his marrying me, because it would be imprudent; and now, because he is trying to get a girl with only ten thousand pounds, you want to find out that he is mercenary.'

'If you will only tell me what sort of girl Miss King is, I shall know what to think.'

'She is a very good kind of girl, I believe. I know no harm of her.'

'But he paid her not the smallest attention, till her grandfather's death made her mistress of this fortune.'

'No – why should he? If it was not allowable for him to gain *my* affections, because I had no money, what occasion could there be for making love to a girl whom he did not care about, and who was equally poor?'

'But there seems indelicacy in directing his attentions towards her, so soon after this event.'

'A man in distressed circumstances has not time for all those elegant decorums which other people may observe. If *she* does not object to it, why should *we*?'

'*Her* not objecting, does not justify *him*. It only shows her being deficient in something herself – sense or feeling.'

'Well,' cried Elizabeth, 'have it as you choose. *He* shall be mercenary, and *she* shall be foolish.'

'No, Lizzy, that is what I do *not* choose. I should be sorry, you know, to think ill of a young man who has lived so long in Derbyshire.'

'Oh! if that is all, I have a very poor opinion of young men who live in Derbyshire; and their intimate friends who live in Hertfordshire are not much better. I am sick of them all. Thank Heaven! I am going tomorrow where I shall find a man who has not one agreeable quality, who has neither manner nor sense to recommend him. Stupid men are the only ones worth knowing, after all.'

'Take care, Lizzy; that speech savours strongly of disappointment.'

Before they were separated by the conclusion of the play, she had the unexpected happiness of an invitation to accompany her uncle and aunt in a tour of pleasure which they proposed taking in the summer.

'We have not quite determined how far it shall carry us,' said Mrs Gardiner, 'but perhaps to the Lakes.'

No scheme could have been more agreeable to Elizabeth, and her acceptance of the invitation was most ready and grateful. 'My dear, dear aunt,' she rapturously cried, 'what delight! what felicity! You give me fresh life and vigour. Adieu to disappointment and spleen. What are men to rocks and mountains? Oh! what hours of transport we shall spend! And when we *do* return, it shall not be like other travellers, without being able to give one accurate idea of any thing. We *will* know where we have gone – we *will* recollect what we have seen. Lakes, mountains, and rivers, shall not be jumbled together in our imaginations; nor, when we attempt to describe any particular scene, will we begin quarrelling about its relative situation. Let *our* first effusions be less insupportable than those of the generality of travellers.'

Chapter 28

Every object in the next day's journey was new and interesting to Elizabeth; and her spirits were in a state for enjoyment; for she had seen her sister looking so well as to banish all fear for her health, and the prospect of her northern tour was a constant source of delight.

When they left the high road for the lane to Hunsford, every eye was in search of the Parsonage, and every turning expected to bring it in view. The paling of Rosings Park was their boundary on one side. Elizabeth smiled at the recollection of all that she had heard of its inhabitants.

At length the Parsonage was discernible. The garden sloping to the road, the house standing in it, the green pales and the laurel hedge, every thing declared they were arriving. Mr Collins and Charlotte appeared at the door, and the carriage stopped at the small gate, which led by a short gravel walk to the house, amidst[21] the nods and smiles of the whole party. In a moment they were all out of the chaise, rejoicing at the sight of each other. Mrs Collins welcomed her friend with the liveliest pleasure, and Elizabeth was more and more satisfied with coming, when she found herself so affectionately received. She saw instantly that her cousin's manners were not altered by his marriage; his formal civility was just what it had been, and he detained her some minutes at the gate to hear and satisfy his enquiries after all her family. They were then, with no other delay than his pointing out the neatness of the entrance, taken into the house; and as soon as they were in the parlour, he welcomed them a second time with ostentatious formality to his humble abode, and punctually repeated all his wife's offers of refreshment.

Elizabeth was prepared to see him in his glory; and she could not help fancying that in displaying the good proportion of the room, its aspect and its furniture, he addressed himself particularly to her, as if wishing to make her feel what she had lost in refusing him. But though

At the door

every thing seemed neat and comfortable, she was not able to gratify him by any sigh of repentance; and rather looked with wonder at her friend that she could have so cheerful an air, with such a companion. When Mr Collins said any thing of which his wife might reasonably be ashamed, which certainly was not unseldom, she involuntarily turned her eye on Charlotte. Once or twice she could discern a faint blush; but in general Charlotte wisely did not hear. After sitting long enough to admire every article of furniture in the room, from the sideboard to the fender, to give an account of their journey and of all that had happened in London, Mr Collins invited them to take a stroll in the garden, which was large and well laid out, and to the cultivation of which he attended himself. To work in his garden was one of his most respectable pleasures; and Elizabeth admired the command of countenance with which Charlotte talked of the healthfulness of the exercise, and owned she encouraged it as much as possible. Here, leading the way through every walk and cross walk, and scarcely allowing them an interval to utter the praises he asked for, every view was pointed out with a minuteness which left beauty entirely behind. He could number the fields in every direction, and could tell how many trees there were in the most distant clump. But of all the views which his garden, or which the country, or the kingdom could boast, none were to be compared with the prospect of Rosings, afforded by an opening in the trees that bordered the park nearly opposite the front of his house. It was a handsome modern building, well situated on rising ground.

From his garden, Mr Collins would have led them round his two meadows, but the ladies not having shoes to encounter the remains of a white frost, turned back; and while Sir William accompanied him, Charlotte took her sister and friend over the house, extremely well pleased, probably, to have the opportunity of showing it without her husband's help. It was rather small, but well built and convenient; and every thing was fitted up and arranged with a neatness and consistency of which Elizabeth gave Charlotte all the credit. When Mr Collins could be forgotten, there was really a great air of comfort throughout, and by Charlotte's evident enjoyment of it, Elizabeth supposed he must be often forgotten.

She had already learnt that Lady Catherine was still in the country. It was spoken of again while they were at dinner, when Mr Collins joining in, observed,

'Yes, Miss Elizabeth, you will have the honour of seeing Lady Catherine de Bourgh on the ensuing Sunday at church, and I need not say you will be delighted with her. She is all affability and condescension, and I doubt not but you will be honoured with some portion of her notice when service is over. I have scarcely any hesitation in saying that she will include you and my sister Maria in every invitation with which she honours us during your stay here. Her behaviour to my dear Charlotte is charming. We dine at Rosings twice every week, and are never allowed to walk home. Her ladyship's carriage is regularly ordered for us. I *should* say, one of her ladyship's carriages, for she has several.'

'Lady Catherine is a very respectable, sensible woman indeed,' added Charlotte, 'and a most attentive neighbour.'

'Very true, my dear, that is exactly what I say. She is the sort of woman whom one cannot regard with too much deference.'

The evening was spent chiefly in talking over Hertfordshire news, and telling again what had been already written; and when it closed, Elizabeth in the solitude of her chamber had to meditate upon Charlotte's degree of contentment, to understand her address in guiding, and composure in bearing with her husband, and to acknowledge that it was all done very well. She had also to anticipate how her visit would pass, the quiet tenor of their usual employments, the vexatious interruptions of Mr Collins, and the gaieties of their intercourse with Rosings. A lively imagination soon settled it all.

About the middle of the next day, as she was in her room getting ready for a walk, a sudden noise below seemed to speak the whole house in confusion; and after listening a moment, she heard somebody running up stairs in a violent hurry, and calling loudly after her. She opened the door, and met Maria in the landing place, who, breathless with agitation, cried out,

'Oh, my dear Eliza! pray make haste and come into the dining-room, for there is such a sight to be seen! I will not tell you what it is. Make haste, and come down this moment.'

Elizabeth asked questions in vain; Maria would tell her nothing more, and down they ran into the dining-room, which fronted the lane, in quest of this wonder; it was two ladies stopping in a low phaeton at the garden gate.

'And is this all?' cried Elizabeth. 'I expected at least that the pigs were got into the garden, and here is nothing but Lady Catherine and her daughter!'

'La! my dear,' said Maria quite shocked at the mistake, 'it is not Lady Catherine. The old lady is Mrs Jenkinson, who lives with them. The other is Miss De Bourgh. Only look at her. She is quite a little creature. Who would have thought she could be so thin and small!'

'She is abominably rude to keep Charlotte out of doors in all this wind. Why does she not come in?'

'Oh! Charlotte says, she hardly ever does. It is the greatest of favours when Miss De Bourgh comes in.'

'I like her appearance,' said Elizabeth, struck with other ideas. 'She looks sickly and cross. – Yes, she will do for him very well. She will make him a very proper wife.'

Mr Collins and Charlotte were both standing at the gate in conversation with the ladies; and Sir William, to Elizabeth's high diversion, was stationed in the doorway, in earnest contemplation of the greatness before him, and constantly bowing whenever Miss De Bourgh looked that way.

At length there was nothing more to be said; the ladies drove on, and the others returned into the house. Mr Collins no sooner saw the two girls than he began to congratulate them on their good fortune, which Charlotte explained by letting them know that the whole party was asked to dine at Rosings the next day.

Mr Collins's triumph in consequence of this invitation was complete. The power of displaying the grandeur of his patroness to his wondering visitors, and of letting them see her civility towards himself and his wife, was exactly what he had wished for, and that an opportunity of doing it should be given so soon, was such an instance of Lady Catherine's condescension as he knew not how to admire enough.

'I confess,' said he, 'that I should not have been at all surprised by her Ladyship's asking us on Sunday to drink tea and spend the evening at Rosings. I rather expected, from my knowledge of her affability, that it would happen. But who could have foreseen such an attention as this? Who could have imagined that we should receive an invitation to dine there (an invitation moreover including the whole party) so immediately after your arrival!'

'I am the less surprised at what has happened,' replied Sir William, 'from that knowledge of what the manners of the great really are, which my situation in life has allowed me to acquire. About the Court, such instances of elegant breeding are not uncommon.'

Scarcely any thing was talked of the whole day or next morning, but their visit to Rosings. Mr Collins was carefully instructing them in what they were to expect, that the sight of such rooms, so many servants, and so splendid a dinner might not wholly overpower them.

When the ladies were separating for the toilette, he said to Elizabeth,

'Do not make yourself uneasy, my dear cousin, about your apparel. Lady Catherine is far from requiring that elegance of dress in us, which becomes herself and daughter. I would advise you merely to put on whatever of your clothes is superior to the rest, there is no occasion for any thing more. Lady Catherine will not think the worse of you for being simply dressed. She likes to have the distinction of rank preserved.'

While they were dressing, he came two or three times to their different doors, to recommend their being quick, as Lady Catherine very much objected to be kept waiting for her dinner. – Such formidable accounts of her Ladyship, and her manner of living, quite frightened Maria Lucas, who had been little used to company, and she looked forward to her introduction at Rosings, with as much apprehension, as her father had done to his presentation at St. James's.

As the weather was fine, they had a pleasant walk of about half a mile across the park. – Every park has its beauty and its prospects; and Elizabeth saw much to be pleased with, though she could not be in such raptures as Mr Collins expected the scene to inspire, and was but slightly affected by his enumeration of the windows in front of the house, and his relation of what the glazing altogether had originally cost Sir Lewis De Bourgh.

When they ascended the steps to the hall, Maria's alarm was every moment increasing, and even Sir William did not look perfectly calm. – Elizabeth's courage did not fail her. She had heard nothing of Lady Catherine that spoke her awful from any extraordinary talents or miraculous virtue, and the mere stateliness of money and rank, she thought she could witness without trepidation.

From the entrance hall, of which Mr Collins pointed out, with a rapturous air, the fine proportion and finished ornaments, they followed the servants through an anti-chamber, to the room where Lady Catherine, her daughter, and Mrs Jenkinson were sitting. – Her Ladyship, with great condescension, arose to receive them; and as Mrs Collins had settled it with her husband that the office of introduction should be hers, it was performed in a proper manner, without any of those apologies and thanks which he would have thought necessary.

In spite of having been at St. James's, Sir William was so completely awed, by the grandeur surrounding him, that he had but just courage enough to make a very low bow, and take his seat without saying a word; and his daughter, frightened almost out of her senses, sat on the edge of her chair, not knowing which way to look. Elizabeth found herself quite equal to the scene, and could observe the three ladies before her composedly. – Lady Catherine was a tall, large woman, with strongly-marked features, which might once have been handsome. Her air was not conciliating, nor was her manner of receiving them, such as to make her visitors forget their inferior rank. She was not rendered formidable by silence; but whatever she said, was spoken in so authoritative a tone, as marked her self-importance, and brought Mr Wickham immediately to Elizabeth's mind; and from the observation of the day altogether, she believed Lady Catherine to be exactly what he had represented.

When, after examining the mother, in whose countenance and deportment she soon found some resemblance of Mr Darcy, she turned her eyes on the daughter, she could almost have joined in Maria's astonishment, at her being so thin, and so small. There was neither in figure nor face, any likeness between the ladies. Miss De Bourgh was pale and sickly; her features, though not plain, were insignificant; and she spoke very little, except in a low voice, to Mrs Jenkinson, in whose appearance there was nothing remarkable, and who was entirely engaged in listening to what she said, and placing a screen in the proper direction before her eyes.

After sitting a few minutes, they were all sent to one of the windows, to admire the view, Mr Collins attending them to point out its beauties, and Lady Catherine kindly informing them that it was much better worth looking at in the summer.

The dinner was exceedingly handsome, and there were all the servants, and all the articles of plate which Mr Collins had promised; and, as he had likewise foretold, he took his seat at the bottom of the table, by her ladyship's desire, and looked as if he felt that life could furnish nothing greater. – He carved, and ate, and praised with delighted alacrity; and every dish was commended, first by him, and then by Sir William, who was now enough recovered to echo whatever his son-in-law said, in a manner which Elizabeth wondered Lady Catherine could bear. But Lady Catherine seemed gratified by their excessive admiration, and gave most gracious smiles, especially when any dish on the table proved a novelty to them. The party did not supply much conversation. Elizabeth was ready to speak whenever there was an opening, but she was seated between Charlotte and Miss De Bourgh – the former of whom was engaged in listening to Lady Catherine, and the latter said not a word to her all dinner time. Mrs Jenkinson was chiefly employed in watching how little Miss De Bourgh ate, pressing her to try some other dish, and fearing she were indisposed. Maria thought speaking out of the question, and the gentlemen did nothing but eat and admire.

When the ladies returned to the drawing-room, there was little to be done but to hear Lady Catherine talk, which she did without any intermission till coffee came in, delivering her opinion on every subject in so decisive a manner as proved that she was not used to have her judgment controverted. She enquired into Charlotte's domestic concerns familiarly and minutely, and gave her a great deal of advice, as to the management of them all; told her how every thing ought to be regulated in so small a family as hers, and instructed her as to the care of her cows and her poultry. Elizabeth found that nothing was beneath this great Lady's attention, which could furnish her with an occasion of dictating to others. In the intervals of her discourse with Mrs Collins, she addressed a variety of questions to Maria and Elizabeth, but especially to the latter, of whose connections she knew the least, and who she observed to Mrs Collins, was a very genteel, pretty kind of girl. She asked her at different times, how many sisters she had, whether they were older or younger than herself, whether any of them were likely to be married, whether they were handsome, where they had been educated, what carriage her father kept, and what had been her mother's maiden name? – Elizabeth felt all the impertinence of her questions, but answered them very composedly. – Lady Catherine then observed,

'Your father's estate is entailed on Mr Collins, I think. For your sake,' turning to Charlotte, 'I am glad of it; but otherwise I see no occasion for entailing estates from the female line. – It was not thought necessary in Sir Lewis de Bourgh's family. – Do you play and sing, Miss

Bennet?'

'A little.'

'Oh! then – some time or other we shall be happy to hear you. Our instrument is a capital one, probably superior to – You shall try it some day. – Do your sisters play and sing?'

'One of them does.'

'Why did not you all learn? – You ought all to have learned. The Miss Webbs all play, and their father has not so good an income as yours. – Do you draw?'

'No, not at all.'

'What, none of you?'

'Not one.'

'That is very strange. But I suppose you had no opportunity. Your mother should have taken you to town every spring for the benefit of masters.'

'My mother would have had no objection, but my father hates London.'

'Has your governess left you?'

'We never had any governess.'

'No governess! How was that possible? Five daughters brought up at home without a governess! – I never heard of such a thing. Your mother must have been quite a slave to your education.'

Elizabeth could hardly help smiling, as she assured her that had not been the case.

'Then, who taught you? who attended to you? Without a governess you must have been neglected.'

'Compared with some families, I believe we were; but such of us as wished to learn, never wanted the means. We were always encouraged to read, and had all the masters that were necessary. Those who chose to be idle, certainly might.'

'Aye, no doubt; but that is what a governess will prevent, and if I had known your mother, I should have advised her most strenuously to engage one. I always say that nothing is to be done in education without steady and regular instruction, and nobody but a governess can give it. It is wonderful how many families I have been the means of supplying in that way. I am always glad to get a young person well placed out. Four nieces of Mrs Jenkinson are most delightfully situated through my means; and it was but the other day, that I recommended another young person, who was merely accidentally mentioned to me, and the family are quite delighted with her. Mrs Collins, did I tell you of Lady Metcalfe's calling yesterday to thank me? She finds Miss Pope a treasure. "Lady Catherine," said she, "you have given me a treasure." Are any of your younger sisters out, Miss Bennet?'

'Yes, Ma'am, all.'

'All! – What, all five out at once? Very odd! – And you only the second. – The younger ones out before the elder are married! – Your younger sisters must be very young?'

'Yes, my youngest is not sixteen. Perhaps *she* is full young to be much in company. But really, Ma'am, I think it would be very hard upon younger sisters, that they should not have their share of society and amusement because the elder may not have the means or inclination to marry early. – The last born has as good a right to the pleasures of youth, as the first. And to be kept back on *such* a motive! – I think it would not be very likely to promote sisterly affection or delicacy of mind.'

'Upon my word,' said her Ladyship, 'you give your opinion very decidedly for so young a person. – Pray, what is your age?'

'With three younger sisters grown up,' replied Elizabeth smiling, 'your Ladyship can hardly expect me to own it.'

Lady Catherine seemed quite astonished at not receiving a direct answer; and Elizabeth suspected herself to be the first creature who had ever dared to trifle with so much dignified impertinence.

'You cannot be more than twenty, I am sure, – therefore you need not conceal your age.'

'I am not one and twenty.'

When the gentlemen had joined them, and tea was over, the card tables were placed. Lady Catherine, Sir William, and Mr and Mrs Collins sat down to quadrille; and as Miss De Bourgh chose to play at cassino[22], the two girls had the honour of assisting Mrs Jenkinson to make up her party. Their table was superlatively stupid. Scarcely a syllable was uttered that did not relate to the game, except when Mrs Jenkinson expressed her fears of Miss De Bourgh's being too hot or too cold, or having too much or too little light. A great deal more passed at the other table. Lady Catherine was generally speaking – stating the mistakes of the three others, or relating some anecdote of herself. Mr Collins was employed in agreeing to every thing her Ladyship said, thanking her for every fish he won, and apologising if he thought he won too many. Sir William did not say much. He was storing his memory with anecdotes and noble names.

When Lady Catherine and her daughter had played as long as they chose, the tables were broke up, the carriage was offered to Mrs Collins, gratefully accepted, and immediately ordered. The party then gathered round the fire to hear Lady Catherine determine what weather they were to have on the morrow. From these instructions they were summoned by the arrival of the coach, and with many speeches of thankfulness on Mr Collins's side, and as many bows on Sir William's, they departed. As soon as they had driven from the door, Elizabeth was called on by her cousin, to give her opinion of all that she had seen at Rosings, which, for Charlotte's sake, she made more favourable than it really was. But her commendation, though costing her some trouble, could by no means satisfy Mr Collins, and he was very soon obliged to take her Ladyship's praise into his own hands.

Chapter 30

S ir William staid only a week at Hunsford; but his visit was long enough to convince him of his daughter's being most comfortably settled, and of her possessing such a husband and such a neighbour as were not often met with. While Sir William was with them, Mr Collins devoted his mornings to driving him out in his gig, and showing him the country; but when he went away, the whole family returned to their usual employments, and Elizabeth was thankful to find that they did not see more of her cousin by the alteration, for the chief of the time between breakfast and dinner was now passed by him either at work in the garden, or in reading and writing, and looking out of window in his own book room, which fronted the road. The room in which the ladies sat was backwards. Elizabeth at first had rather wondered that Charlotte should not prefer the dining-parlour for common use; it was a better sized room, and had a pleasanter aspect; but she soon saw that her friend had an excellent reason for what she did, for Mr Collins would undoubtedly have been much less in his own apartment, had they sat in one equally lively; and she gave Charlotte credit for the arrangement.

From the drawing-room they could distinguish nothing in the lane, and were indebted to Mr Collins for the knowledge of what carriages went along, and how often especially Miss De Bourgh drove by in her phaeton, which he never failed coming to inform them of, though it happened almost every day. She not unfrequently stopped at the Parsonage, and had a few minutes' conversation with Charlotte, but was scarcely ever prevailed on to get out.

Very few days passed in which Mr Collins did not walk to Rosings, and not many in which his wife did not think it necessary to go likewise; and till Elizabeth recollected that there might be other family livings to be disposed of, she could not understand the sacrifice of so many hours. Now and then, they were honoured with a call from her

Ladyship, and nothing escaped her observation that was passing in the room during these visits. She examined into their employments, looked at their work, and advised them to do it differently; found fault with the arrangement of the furniture, or detected the housemaid in negligence; and if she accepted any refreshment, seemed to do it only for the sake of finding out that Mrs Collins's joints of meat were too large for her family.

Elizabeth soon perceived that though this great lady was not in the commission of the peace for the county, she was a most active magistrate in her own parish, the minutest concerns of which were carried to her by Mr Collins; and whenever any of the cottagers were disposed to be quarrelsome, discontented or too poor, she sallied forth into the village to settle their differences, silence their complaints, and scold them into harmony and plenty.

The entertainment of dining at Rosings was repeated about twice a week; and, allowing for the loss of Sir William, and there being only one card table in the evening, every such entertainment was the counterpart of the first. Their other engagements were few; as the style of living of the neighbourhood in general, was beyond the Collinses' reach. This however was no evil to Elizabeth, and upon the whole she spent her time comfortably enough; there were half hours of pleasant conversation with Charlotte, and the weather was so fine for the time of year, that she had often great enjoyment out of doors. Her favourite walk, and where she frequently went while the others were calling on Lady Catherine, was along the open grove which edged that side of the park, where there was a nice sheltered path, which no one seemed to value but herself, and where she felt beyond the reach of Lady Catherine's curiosity.

In this quiet way, the first fortnight of her visit soon passed away. Easter was approaching, and the week preceding it, was to bring an addition to the family at Rosings, which in so small a circle must be important. Elizabeth had heard soon after her arrival, that Mr Darcy was expected there in the course of a few weeks, and though there were not many of her acquaintance whom she did not prefer, his coming would furnish one comparatively new to look at in their Rosings parties, and she might be amused in seeing how hopeless Miss Bingley's designs on him were, by his behaviour to his cousin, for whom he was evidently destined by Lady Catherine; who talked of his coming with the greatest satisfaction, spoke of him in terms of the highest admiration, and seemed almost angry to find that he had already been frequently seen by Miss Lucas and herself.

His arrival was soon known at the Parsonage, for Mr Collins was walking the whole morning within view of the lodges opening into Hunsford Lane, in order to have the earliest assurance of it; and after making his bow as the carriage turned into the Park, hurried home with the great intelligence. On the following morning he hastened to Rosings to pay his respects. There were two nephews of Lady Catherine to require them, for Mr Darcy had brought with him a Colonel Fitzwilliam, the younger son of his uncle, Lord — and to the great surprise of all the party, when Mr Collins returned the gentlemen accompanied him. Charlotte had seen them from her husband's room, crossing the road, and immediately running into the other, told the girls what an honour they might expect, adding,

'I may thank you, Eliza, for this piece of civility. Mr Darcy would never have come so soon to wait upon me.'

Elizabeth had scarcely time to disclaim all right to the compliment, before their approach was announced by the door-bell, and shortly afterwards the three gentlemen entered the room. Colonel Fitzwilliam, who led the way, was about thirty, not handsome, but in person and address most truly the gentleman. Mr Darcy looked just as he had been used to look in Hertfordshire, paid his compliments, with his usual reserve, to Mrs Collins; and whatever might be his feelings towards her friend, met her with every appearance of composure. Elizabeth merely curtseyed to him, without saying a word.

Colonel Fitzwilliam entered into conversation directly with the readiness and ease of a well-bred man, and talked very pleasantly; but his cousin, after having addressed a slight observation on the house and garden to Mrs Collins, sat for some time without speaking to any body. At length, however, his civility was so far awakened as to enquire of Elizabeth after the health of her family. She answered him in the usual way, and after a moment's pause, added,

'My eldest sister has been in town these three months. Have you never happened to see her there?'

She was perfectly sensible that he never had; but she wished to see whether he would betray any consciousness of what had passed between the Bingleys and Jane; and she thought he looked a little confused as he answered that he had never been so fortunate as to meet Miss Bennet. The subject was pursued no farther, and the gentlemen soon afterwards went away.

Chapter 31

Colonel Fitzwilliam's manners were very much admired at the parsonage, and the ladies all felt that he must add considerably to the pleasure of their engagements at Rosings. It was some days, however, before they received any invitation thither, for while there were visitors in the house, they could not be necessary; and it was not till Easter-day, almost a week after the gentlemen's arrival, that they were honoured by such an attention, and then they were merely asked on leaving church to come there in the evening. For the last week they had seen very little of either Lady Catherine or her daughter. Colonel Fitzwilliam had called at the parsonage more than once during the time, but Mr Darcy they had only seen at church.

The invitation was accepted of course, and at a proper hour they joined the party in Lady Catherine's drawing-room. Her ladyship received them civilly, but it was plain that their company was by no means so acceptable as when she could get nobody else; and she was,

in fact, almost engrossed by her nephews, speaking to them, especially to Darcy, much more than to any other person in the room.

Colonel Fitzwilliam seemed really glad to see them; any thing was a welcome relief to him at Rosings; and Mrs Collins's pretty friend had moreover caught his fancy very much. He now seated himself by her, and talked so agreeably of Kent and Hertfordshire, of travelling and staying at home, of new books and music, that Elizabeth had never been half so well entertained in that room before; and they conversed with so much spirit and flow, as to draw the attention of Lady Catherine herself, as well as of Mr Darcy. His eyes had been soon and repeatedly turned towards them with a look of curiosity; and that her ladyship after a while shared the feeling, was more openly acknowledged, for she did not scruple to call out,

'What is that you are saying, Fitzwilliam? What is it you are talking of? What are you telling Miss Bennet? Let me hear what it is.'

'We are speaking of music, Madam,' said he, when no longer able to avoid a reply.

'Of music! Then pray speak aloud. It is of all subjects my delight. I must have my share in the conversation, if you are speaking of music. There are few people in England, I suppose, who have more true enjoyment of music than myself, or a better natural taste. If I had ever learnt, I should have been a great proficient. And so would Anne, if her health had allowed her to apply. I am confident that she would have performed delightfully. How does Georgiana get on, Darcy?'

Mr Darcy spoke with affectionate praise of his sister's proficiency.

'I am very glad to hear such a good account of her,' said Lady Catherine; 'and pray tell her from me, that she cannot expect to excel, if she does not practise a great deal.'

'I assure you, Madam,' he replied, 'that she does not need such advice. She practises very constantly.'

'So much the better. It cannot be done too much; and when I next write to her, I shall charge her not to neglect it on any account. I often tell young ladies, that no excellence in music is to be acquired, without constant practice. I have told Miss Bennet several times, that she will never play really well, unless she practises more; and though

Mrs Collins has no instrument, she is very welcome, as I have often told her, to come to Rosings every day, and play on the piano-forte in Mrs Jenkinson's room. She would be in nobody's way, you know, in that part of the house.'

Mr Darcy looked a little ashamed of his aunt's ill breeding, and made no answer.

When coffee was over, Colonel Fitzwilliam reminded Elizabeth of having promised to play to him; and she sat down directly to the instrument. He drew a chair near her. Lady Catherine listened to half a song, and then talked, as before, to her other nephew; till the latter walked away from her, and moving with his usual deliberation towards the piano-forte, stationed himself so as to command a full view of the fair performer's countenance. Elizabeth saw what he was doing, and at the first convenient pause, turned to him with an arch smile, and said,

'You mean to frighten me, Mr Darcy, by coming in all this state to hear me? But I will not be alarmed though your sister *does* play so well. There is a stubbornness about me that never can bear to be frightened at the will of others. My courage always rises with every attempt to intimidate me.'

'I shall not say that you are mistaken,' he replied, 'because you could not really believe me to entertain any design of alarming you; and I have had the pleasure of your acquaintance long enough to know, that you find great enjoyment in occasionally professing opinions which in fact are not your own.'

Elizabeth laughed heartily at this picture of herself, and said to Colonel Fitzwilliam, 'Your cousin will give you a very pretty notion of me, and teach you not to believe a word I say. I am particularly unlucky in meeting with a person so well able to expose my real character, in a part of the world, where I had hoped to pass myself off with some degree of credit. Indeed, Mr Darcy, it is very ungenerous in you to mention all that you knew to my disadvantage in Hertfordshire – and, give me leave to say, very impolitic too – for it is provoking me to retaliate, and such things may come out, as will shock your relations to hear.'

'I am not afraid of you,' said he, smilingly.

'Pray let me hear what you have to accuse him of,' cried Colonel Fitzwilliam. 'I should like to know how he behaves among strangers.'

'You shall hear then – but prepare yourself for something very dreadful. The first time of my ever seeing him in Hertfordshire, you must know, was at a ball – and at this ball, what do you think he did? He danced only four dances! I am sorry to pain you – but so it was. He danced only four dances, though gentlemen were scarce; and, to my certain knowledge, more than one young lady was sitting down in want of a partner. Mr Darcy, you cannot deny the fact.'

'I had not at that time the honour of knowing any lady in the assembly beyond my own party.'

'True; and nobody can ever be introduced in a ball-room. Well, Colonel Fitzwilliam, what do I play next? My fingers wait your orders.'

'Perhaps,' said Darcy, 'I should have judged better, had I sought an introduction, but I am ill-qualified to recommend myself to strangers.'

'Shall we ask your cousin the reason of this?' said Elizabeth, still addressing Colonel Fitzwilliam. 'Shall we ask him why a man of sense and education, and who has lived in the world, is ill-qualified to recommend himself to strangers?'

'I can answer your question,' said Fitzwilliam, 'without applying to him. It is because he will not give himself the trouble.'

'I certainly have not the talent which some people possess,' said Darcy, 'of conversing easily with those I have never seen before. I cannot catch their tone of conversation, or appear interested in their concerns, as I often see done.'

'My fingers,' said Elizabeth, 'do not move over this instrument in the masterly manner which I see so many women's do. They have not the same force or rapidity, and do not produce the same expression. But then I have always supposed it to be my own fault – because I would not take the trouble of practising. It is not that I do not believe *my* fingers as capable as any other woman's of superior execution.'

Darcy smiled and said, 'You are perfectly right. You have employed your time much better. No one admitted to the privilege of hearing you, can think any thing wanting. We neither of us perform to strangers.'

Here they were interrupted by Lady Catherine, who called out to know what they were talking of. Elizabeth immediately began playing again. Lady Catherine approached, and, after listening for a few minutes, said to Darcy,

'Miss Bennet would not play at all amiss, if she practised more, and could have the advantage of a London master. She has a very good notion of fingering, though her taste is not equal to Anne's. Anne would have been a delightful performer, had her health allowed her to learn.'

Elizabeth looked at Darcy to see how cordially he assented to his cousin's praise; but neither at that moment nor at any other could she discern any symptom of love; and from the whole of his behaviour to Miss De Bourgh she derived this comfort for Miss Bingley, that he might have been just as likely to marry *her*, had she been his relation.

Lady Catherine continued her remarks on Elizabeth's performance, mixing with them many instructions on execution and taste. Elizabeth received them with all the forbearance of civility; and at the request of the gentlemen remained at the instrument till her Ladyship's carriage was ready to take them all home.

Chapter 32

Elizabeth was sitting by herself the next morning, and writing to Jane, while Mrs Collins and Maria were gone on business into the village, when she was startled by a ring at the door, the certain signal of a visitor. As she had heard no carriage, she thought it not unlikely to be Lady Catherine, and under that apprehension was putting away her half-finished letter that she might escape all impertinent questions, when the door opened, and to her very great surprise, Mr Darcy, and Mr Darcy only, entered the room.

He seemed astonished too on finding her alone, and apologised for his intrusion, by letting her know that he had understood all the ladies to be within.

They then sat down, and when her enquiries after Rosings were made, seemed in danger of sinking into total silence. It was absolutely necessary, therefore, to think of something, and in this emergence recollecting *when* she had seen him last in Hertfordshire, and feeling curious to know what he would say on the subject of their hasty departure, she observed,

'How very suddenly you all quitted Netherfield last November, Mr Darcy! It must have been a most agreeable surprise to Mr Bingley to see you all after him so soon; for, if I recollect right, he went but the day before. He and his sisters were well, I hope, when you left London.'

'Perfectly so – I thank you.'

She found that she was to receive no other answer – and, after a short pause, added,

'I think I have understood that Mr Bingley has not much idea of ever returning to Netherfield again?'

'I have never heard him say so; but it is probable that he may spend very little of his time there in future. He has many friends, and he is at a time of life when friends and engagements are continually increasing.'

'If he means to be but little at Netherfield, it would be better for the neighbourhood that he should give up the place entirely, for then we might possibly get a settled family there. But perhaps Mr Bingley did not take the house so much for the convenience of the neighbourhood as for his own, and we must expect him to keep or quit it on the same principle.'

'I should not be surprised,' said Darcy, 'if he were to give it up, as soon as any eligible purchase offers.'

Elizabeth made no answer. She was afraid of talking longer of his friend; and, having nothing else to say, was now determined to leave the trouble of finding a subject to him.

He took the hint, and soon began with, 'This seems a very comfortable house. Lady Catherine, I believe, did a great deal to it when Mr Collins first came to Hunsford.'

'I believe she did – and I am sure she could not have bestowed her kindness on a more grateful object.'

'Mr Collins appears very fortunate in his choice of a wife.'

'Yes, indeed; his friends may well rejoice in his having met with one of the very few sensible women who would have accepted him, or have made him happy if they had. My friend has an excellent understanding – though I am not certain that I consider her marrying Mr Collins as the wisest thing she ever did. She seems perfectly happy, however, and in a prudential light, it is certainly a very good match for her.'

'It must be very agreeable to her to be settled within so easy a distance of her own family and friends.'

'An easy distance do you call it? It is nearly fifty miles.'

'And what is fifty miles of good road? Little more than half a day's journey. Yes, I call it a *very* easy distance.'

'I should never have considered the distance as one of the *advantages* of the match,' cried Elizabeth. 'I should never have said Mrs Collins was settled *near* her family.'

'It is a proof of your own attachment to Hertfordshire. Any thing beyond the very neighbourhood of Longbourn, I suppose, would appear far.'

As he spoke there was a sort of smile, which Elizabeth fancied she understood; he must be supposing her to be thinking of Jane and Netherfield, and she blushed as she answered,

'I do not mean to say that a woman may not be settled too near her family. The far and the near must be relative, and depend on many varying circumstances. Where there is fortune to make the expense of travelling unimportant, distance becomes no evil. But that is not the case *here*. Mr and Mrs Collins have a comfortable income, but not such a one as will allow of frequent journeys – and I am persuaded my friend would not call herself *near* her family under less than *half* the present distance.'

Mr Darcy drew his chair a little towards her, and said, '*You* cannot have a right to such very strong local attachment. *You* cannot have been always at Longbourn.'

Elizabeth looked surprised. The gentleman experienced some change of feeling; he drew back his chair, took a newspaper from the table, and, glancing over it, said, in a colder voice,

'Are you pleased with Kent?'

A short dialogue on the subject of the country ensued, on either side calm and concise – and soon put an end to by the entrance of Charlotte and her sister, just returned from their walk. The tête-à-tête surprised them. Mr Darcy related the mistake which had occasioned his intruding on Miss Bennet, and after sitting a few minutes longer without saying much to any body, went away.

'What can be the meaning of this!' said Charlotte, as soon as he was gone. 'My dear Eliza he must be in love with you, or he would never have called on us in this familiar way.'

But when Elizabeth told of his silence, it did not seem very likely, even to Charlotte's wishes, to be the case; and after various conjectures, they could at last only suppose his visit to proceed from the difficulty of finding any thing to do, which was the more probable from the time of year. All field sports were over. Within doors there was Lady Catherine, books, and a billiard table, but gentlemen cannot be always within doors; and in the nearness of the Parsonage, or the pleasantness of the walk to it, or of the people who lived in it, the two cousins found a temptation from this period of walking thither almost every day. They called at various times of the morning, sometimes separately, sometimes together, and now and then accompanied by their aunt. It was plain to them all that Colonel Fitzwilliam came because he had pleasure in their society, a persuasion which of course recommended him still more; and Elizabeth was reminded by her own satisfaction in being with him, as well as by his evident admiration of her, of her former favourite George Wickham; and though, in comparing them, she saw there was less captivating softness in Colonel Fitzwilliam's manners, she believed he might have the best informed mind.

But why Mr Darcy came so often to the Parsonage, it was more difficult to understand. It could not be for society, as he frequently sat there ten minutes together without opening his lips; and when he did speak, it seemed the effect of necessity rather than of choice – a sacrifice to propriety, not a pleasure to himself. He seldom appeared really animated. Mrs Collins knew not what to make of him. Colonel Fitzwilliam's occasionally laughing at his stupidity, proved that he was generally different, which her own knowledge of him could not have told her; and as she would have liked to believe this change the effect of love, and the object of that love, her friend Eliza, she sat herself seriously to work to find it out. – She watched him whenever they were at Rosings, and whenever he came to Hunsford; but without much success. He certainly looked at her friend a great deal, but the expression of that look was disputable. It was an earnest, steadfast gaze, but she often doubted whether there were much admiration in it, and sometimes it seemed nothing but absence of mind.

She had once or twice suggested to Elizabeth the possibility of his being partial to her, but Elizabeth always laughed at the idea; and Mrs Collins did not think it right to press the subject, from the danger of raising expectations which might only end in disappointment; for in her opinion it admitted not of a doubt, that all her friend's dislike would vanish, if she could suppose him to be in her power.

In her kind schemes for Elizabeth, she sometimes planned her marrying Colonel Fitzwilliam. He was beyond comparison the pleasantest man; he certainly admired her, and his situation in life was most eligible; but, to counterbalance these advantages, Mr Darcy had considerable patronage in the church, and his cousin could have none at all.

Chapter 33

More than once did Elizabeth in her ramble within the Park, unexpectedly meet Mr Darcy. – She felt all the perverseness of the mischance that should bring him where no one else was brought; and to prevent its ever happening again, took care to inform him at first, that it was a favourite haunt of hers. – How it could occur a second time therefore was very odd! – Yet it did, and even a third. It seemed like wilful ill-nature, or a voluntary penance, for on these occasions it was not merely a few formal enquiries and an awkward pause and then away, but he actually thought it necessary to turn back and walk with her. He never said a great deal, nor did she give herself the trouble of talking or of listening much; but it struck her in the course of their third rencontre that he was asking some odd unconnected questions – about her pleasure in being at Hunsford, her love of solitary walks, and her opinion of Mr and Mrs Collins's happiness; and that in speaking of Rosings and her not perfectly understanding the house, he seemed to expect that whenever she came into Kent again she would be staying *there* too. His words seemed to imply it. Could he have Colonel Fitzwilliam in his thoughts? She supposed, if he meant any thing, he must mean an allusion to what might arise in that quarter. It distressed her a little, and she was quite glad to find herself at the gate in the pales opposite the Parsonage.

She was engaged one day as she walked, in re-perusing Jane's last letter, and dwelling on some passages which proved that Jane had not written in spirits, when, instead of being again surprised by Mr Darcy, she saw on looking up that Colonel Fitzwilliam was meeting her. Putting away the letter immediately and forcing a smile, she said,

'I did not know before that you ever walked this way.'

'I have been making the tour of the Park,' he replied, 'as I generally do every year, and intend to close it with a call at the Parsonage. Are you going much farther?'

'On looking up'

'No, I should have turned in a moment.'

And accordingly she did turn, and they walked towards the Parsonage together.

'Do you certainly leave Kent on Saturday?' said she.

'Yes – if Darcy does not put it off again. But I am at his disposal. He arranges the business just as he pleases.'

'And if not able to please himself in the arrangement, he has at least great pleasure in the power of choice. I do not know any body who seems more to enjoy the power of doing what he likes than Mr Darcy.'

'He likes to have his own way very well,' replied Colonel Fitzwilliam. 'But so we all do. It is only that he has better means of having it than many others, because he is rich, and many others are poor. I speak feelingly. A younger son, you know, must be inured to self-denial and dependence.'

'In my opinion, the younger son of an Earl can know very little of either. Now, seriously, what have you ever known of self-denial and dependence? When have you been prevented by want of money from going wherever you chose, or procuring any thing you had a fancy for?'

'These are home questions – and perhaps I cannot say that I have experienced many hardships of that nature. But in matters of greater weight, I may suffer from the want of money. Younger sons cannot marry where they like.'

'Unless where they like women of fortune, which I think they very often do.'

'Our habits of expense make us too dependent, and there are not many in my rank of life who can afford to marry without some attention to money.'

'Is this,' thought Elizabeth, 'meant for me?' and she coloured at the idea; but, recovering herself, said in a lively tone, 'And pray, what is the usual price of an Earl's younger son? Unless the elder brother is very sickly, I suppose you would not ask above fifty thousand pounds.'

He answered her in the same style, and the subject dropped. To interrupt a silence which might make him fancy her affected with what had passed, she soon afterwards said,

'I imagine your cousin brought you down with him chiefly for the sake of having somebody at his disposal. I wonder he does not marry, to secure a lasting convenience of that kind. But, perhaps his sister does as well for the present, and, as she is under his sole care, he may do what he likes with her.'

'No,' said Colonel Fitzwilliam, 'that is an advantage which he must divide with me. I am joined with him in the guardianship of Miss Darcy.'

'Are you, indeed? And pray what sort of guardians do you make? Does your charge give you much trouble? Young ladies of her age, are sometimes a little difficult to manage, and if she has the true Darcy spirit, she may like to have her own way.'

As she spoke, she observed him looking at her earnestly, and the manner in which he immediately asked her why she supposed Miss Darcy likely to give them any uneasiness, convinced her that she had somehow or other got pretty near the truth. She directly replied,

'You need not be frightened. I never heard any harm of her; and I dare say she is one of the most tractable creatures in the world. She is a very great favourite with some ladies of my acquaintance, Mrs Hurst and Miss Bingley. I think I have heard you say that you know them.'

'I know them a little. Their brother is a pleasant gentleman-like man – he is a great friend of Darcy's.'

'Oh! yes,' said Elizabeth drily – 'Mr Darcy is uncommonly kind to Mr Bingley, and takes a prodigious deal of care of him.'

'Care of him! – Yes, I really believe Darcy *does* take care of him in those points where he most wants care. From something that he told me in our journey hither[23], I have reason to think Bingley very much indebted to him. But I ought to beg his pardon, for I have no right to suppose that Bingley was the person meant. It was all conjecture.'

'What is it you mean?'

'It is a circumstance which Darcy of course would not wish to be generally known, because if it were to get round to the lady's family, it would be an unpleasant thing.'

'You may depend upon my not mentioning it.'

'And remember that I have not much reason for supposing it to be Bingley. What he told me was merely this; that he congratulated himself on having lately saved a friend from the inconveniences of a most imprudent marriage, but without mentioning names or any other particulars, and I only suspected it to be Bingley from believing him the kind of young man to get into a scrape of that sort, and from knowing them to have been together the whole of last summer.'

'Did Mr Darcy give you his reasons for this interference?'

'I understood that there were some very strong objections against the lady.'

'And what arts did he use to separate them?'

'He did not talk to me of his own arts,' said Fitzwilliam smiling. 'He only told me, what I have now told you.'

Elizabeth made no answer, and walked on, her heart swelling with indignation. After watching her a little, Fitzwilliam asked her why she was so thoughtful.

'I am thinking of what you have been telling me,' said she. 'Your cousin's conduct does not suit my feelings. Why was he to be the judge?'

'You are rather disposed to call his interference officious?'

'I do not see what right Mr Darcy had to decide on the propriety of his friend's inclination, or why, upon his own judgment alone, he was to determine and direct in what manner that friend was to be happy.' 'But,' she continued, recollecting herself, 'as we know none of the particulars, it is not fair to condemn him. It is not to be supposed that there was much affection in the case.'

'That is not an unnatural surmise,' said Fitzwilliam, 'but it is lessening the honour of my cousin's triumph very sadly.'

This was spoken jestingly, but it appeared to her so just a picture of Mr Darcy, that she would not trust herself with an answer; and, therefore, abruptly changing the conversation, talked on indifferent matters till they reached the parsonage. There, shut into her own room, as soon as their visitor left them, she could think without interruption of all that she had heard. It was not to be supposed that any other people could be meant than those with whom she was connected. There could not exist in the world *two* men, over whom Mr Darcy could have such boundless influence. That he had been concerned in the measures taken to separate Mr Bingley and Jane, she had never doubted; but she had always attributed to Miss Bingley the principal design and arrangement of them. If his own vanity, however, did not mislead him, *he* was the cause, his pride and caprice were the cause of all that Jane had suffered, and still continued to suffer. He had ruined for a while every hope of happiness for the most affectionate, generous heart in the world; and no one could say how lasting an evil he might have inflicted.

'There were some very strong objections against the lady,' were Colonel Fitzwilliam's words, and these strong objections probably were, her having one uncle who was a country attorney, and another who was in business in London. 'To Jane herself,' she exclaimed, 'there could be no possibility of objection. All loveliness and goodness as she is! Her understanding excellent, her mind improved, and her manners captivating. Neither could any thing be urged against my father, who, though with some peculiarities, has abilities which Mr Darcy himself need not disdain, and respectability which he will probably never reach.' When she thought of her mother indeed, her confidence gave way a little, but she would not allow that any objections *there* had material weight with Mr Darcy, whose pride, she was convinced, would receive a deeper wound from the want of importance in his friend's connections, than from their want of sense; and she was quite decided at last, that he had been partly governed by this worst kind of pride, and partly by the wish of retaining Mr Bingley for his sister.

The agitation and tears which the subject occasioned, brought on a headache; and it grew so much worse towards the evening that, added to her unwillingness to see Mr Darcy, it determined her not to attend her cousins to Rosings, where they were engaged to drink tea. Mrs Collins, seeing that she was really unwell, did not press her to go, and as much as possible prevented her husband from pressing her, but Mr Collins could not conceal his apprehension of Lady Catherine's being rather displeased by her staying at home.

Chapter 34

W hen they were gone, Elizabeth, as if intending to exasperate herself as much as possible against Mr Darcy, chose for her employment the examination of all the letters which Jane had written to her since her being in Kent. They contained no actual complaint, nor was there any revival of past occurrences, or any communication of present suffering. But in all, and in almost every line of each, there was a want of that cheerfulness which had been used to characterize her style, and which, proceeding from the serenity of a mind at ease with itself, and kindly disposed towards every one, had been scarcely ever clouded. Elizabeth noticed every sentence conveying the idea of uneasiness, with an attention which it had hardly received on the first perusal. Mr Darcy's shameful boast of what misery he had been able to inflict, gave her a keener sense of her sister's sufferings. It was some consolation to think that his visit to Rosings was to end on the day after the next, and a still greater, that in less than a fortnight she should herself be with Jane again, and enabled to contribute to the recovery of her spirits, by all that affection could do.

She could not think of Darcy's leaving Kent, without remembering that his cousin was to go with him; but Colonel Fitzwilliam had made it clear that he had no intentions at all, and agreeable as he was, she did not mean to be unhappy about him.

While settling this point, she was suddenly roused by the sound of the door bell, and her spirits were a little fluttered by the idea of its being Colonel Fitzwilliam himself, who had once before called late in the evening, and might now come to enquire particularly after her. But this idea was soon banished, and her spirits were very differently affected, when, to her utter amazement, she saw Mr Darcy walk into the room. In an hurried manner he immediately began an enquiry after her health, imputing his visit to a wish of hearing that she were better. She answered him with cold civility. He sat down for a few moments, and then getting up walked about the room. Elizabeth was surprised, but said not a word. After a silence of several minutes he came towards her in an agitated manner, and thus began,

'In vain have I struggled. It will not do. My feelings will not be repressed. You must allow me to tell you how ardently I admire and love you.'

Elizabeth's astonishment was beyond expression. She stared, coloured, doubted, and was silent. This he considered sufficient encouragement, and the avowal of all that he felt and had long felt for her, immediately followed. He spoke well, but there were feelings besides those of the heart to be detailed, and he was not more eloquent on the subject of tenderness than of pride. His sense of her inferiority – of its being a degradation – of the family obstacles which judgment had always opposed to inclination, were dwelt on with a warmth which seemed due to the consequence he was wounding, but was very unlikely to recommend his suit.

In spite of her deeply-rooted dislike, she could not be insensible to the compliment of such a man's affection, and though her intentions did not vary for an instant, she was at first sorry for the pain he was to receive; till, roused to resentment by his subsequent language, she lost all compassion in anger. She tried, however, to compose herself to answer him with patience, when he should have done. He concluded with representing to her the strength of that attachment which, in spite of all his endeavours, he had found impossible to conquer; and with expressing his hope that it would now be rewarded by her acceptance of his hand. As he said this, she could easily see that he had no doubt of a favourable answer. He *spoke* of apprehension and anxiety, but his countenance expressed real security. Such a circumstance could only exasperate farther, and when he ceased, the colour rose into her cheeks, and she said,

'In such cases as this, it is, I believe, the established mode to express a sense of obligation for the sentiments avowed, however unequally they may be returned. It is natural that obligation should be felt, and if I could *feel* gratitude, I would now thank you. But I cannot – I have never desired your good opinion, and you have certainly bestowed it most unwillingly. I am sorry to have occasioned pain to any one. It has been most unconsciously done, however, and I hope will be of short duration. The feelings which, you tell me, have long prevented the acknowledgment of your regard, can have little difficulty in overcoming it after this explanation.'

Mr Darcy, who was leaning against the mantlepiece with his eyes fixed on her face, seemed to catch her words with no less resentment than surprise. His complexion became pale with anger, and the disturbance of his mind was visible in every feature. He was struggling for the appearance of composure, and would not open his lips, till he believed himself to have attained it. The pause was to Elizabeth's feelings dreadful. At length, in a voice of forced calmness, he said,

'And this is all the reply which I am to have the honour of expecting! I might, perhaps, wish to be informed why, with so little *endeavour* at civility, I am thus rejected. But it is of small importance.'

'I might as well enquire,' replied she, 'why with so evident a design of offending and insulting me, you chose to tell me that you liked me against your will, against your reason, and even against your character? Was not this some excuse for incivility, if I *was* uncivil? But I have other provocations. You know I have. Had not my own feelings decided against you, had they been indifferent, or had they even been favourable, do you think that any consideration would tempt me to accept the man, who has been the means of ruining, perhaps forever, the happiness of a most beloved sister?'

As she pronounced these words, Mr Darcy changed colour; but the emotion was short, and he listened without attempting to interrupt her while she continued.

'I have every reason in the world to think ill of you. No motive can excuse the unjust and ungenerous part you acted *there*. You dare not, you cannot deny that you have been the principal, if not the only means of dividing them from each other, of exposing one to the censure of the world for caprice and instability, the other to its derision for disappointed hopes, and involving them both in misery of the acutest kind.'

She paused, and saw with no slight indignation that he was listening with an air which proved him wholly unmoved by any feeling of remorse. He even looked at her with a smile of affected incredulity.

'Can you deny that you have done it?' she repeated.

With assumed tranquility he then replied, 'I have no wish of denying that I did every thing in my power to separate my friend from your sister, or that I rejoice in my success. Towards *him* I have been kinder than towards myself.'

Elizabeth disdained the appearance of noticing this civil reflection, but its meaning did not escape, nor was it likely to conciliate her.

'But it is not merely this affair,' she continued, 'on which my dislike is founded. Long before it had taken place, my opinion of you was decided. Your character was unfolded in the recital which I received many months ago from Mr Wickham. On this subject, what can you have to say? In what imaginary act of friendship can you here defend yourself? or under what misrepresentation, can you here impose upon others?'

'You take an eager interest in that gentleman's concerns,' said Darcy in a less tranquil tone, and with a heightened colour.

'Who that knows what his misfortunes have been, can help feeling an interest in him?'

'His misfortunes!' repeated Darcy contemptuously; 'yes, his misfortunes have been great indeed.'

'And of your infliction,' cried Elizabeth with energy. 'You have reduced him to his present state of poverty, comparative poverty. You have withheld the advantages, which you must know to have been designed for him. You have deprived the best years of his life, of that independence which was no less his due than his desert. You have done all this! And yet you can treat the mention of his misfortunes with contempt and ridicule.'

'And this,' cried Darcy, as he walked with quick steps across the room, 'is your opinion of me! This is the estimation in which you hold me! I thank you for explaining it so fully. My faults, according to this calculation, are heavy indeed! But perhaps,' added he, stopping in his walk, and turning towards her, 'these offences might have been overlooked, had not your pride been hurt by my honest confession of the scruples that had long prevented my forming any serious design. These bitter accusations might have been suppressed, had I with greater policy concealed my struggles, and flattered you into the belief of my being impelled by unqualified, unalloyed inclination; by reason, by reflection, by every thing. But disguise of every sort is my abhorrence. Nor am I ashamed of the feelings I related. They were natural and just. Could you expect me to rejoice in the inferiority of your connections? To congratulate myself on the hope of relations, whose condition in life is so decidedly beneath my own?'

Elizabeth felt herself growing more angry every moment; yet she tried to the utmost to speak with composure when she said,

'You are mistaken, Mr Darcy, if you suppose that the mode of your declaration affected me in any other way, than as it spared me the concern which I might have felt in refusing you, had you behaved in a more gentleman-like manner.'

She saw him start at this, but he said nothing, and she continued,

'You could not have made me the offer of your hand in any possible way that would have tempted me to accept it.'

Again his astonishment was obvious; and he looked at her with an expression of mingled incredulity and mortification. She went on.

'From the very beginning, from the first moment I may almost say, of my acquaintance with you, your manners impressing me with the fullest belief of your arrogance, your conceit, and your selfish disdain of the feelings of others, were such as to form that ground-work of disapprobation, on which succeeding events have built so immoveable a dislike; and I had not known you a month before I felt that you were the last man in the world whom I could ever be prevailed on to marry.'

'You have said quite enough, madam. I perfectly comprehend your feelings, and have now only to be ashamed of what my own have been. Forgive me for having taken up so much of your time, and accept my best wishes for your health and happiness.'

And with these words he hastily left the room, and Elizabeth heard him the next moment open the front door and quit the house.

The tumult of her mind was now painfully great. She knew not how to support herself, and from actual weakness sat down and cried for half an hour. Her astonishment, as she reflected on what had passed, was increased by every review of it. That she should receive an offer of marriage from Mr Darcy! that he should have been in love with her for so many months! so much in love as to wish to marry her in spite of all the objections which had made him prevent his friend's marrying her sister, and which must appear at least with equal force in his own case, was almost incredible! it was gratifying to have inspired unconsciously so strong an affection. But his pride, his abominable pride, his shameless avowal of what he had done with respect to Jane, his unpardonable assurance in acknowledging, though he could not justify it, and the unfeeling manner in which he had mentioned Mr Wickham, his cruelty towards whom he had not attempted to deny, soon overcame the pity which the consideration of his attachment had for a moment excited.

She continued in very agitating reflections till the sound of Lady Catherine's carriage made her feel how unequal she was to encounter Charlotte's observation, and hurried her away to her room.

Chapter 35

Elizabeth awoke the next morning to the same thoughts and meditations which had at length closed her eyes. She could not yet recover from the surprise of what had happened; it was impossible to think of any thing else, and totally indisposed for employment, she resolved soon after breakfast to indulge herself in air and exercise. She was proceeding directly to her favourite walk, when the recollection of Mr Darcy's sometimes coming there stopped her, and instead of entering the park, she turned up the lane, which led her farther from the turnpike road. The park paling was still the boundary on one side, and she soon passed one of the gates into the ground.

After walking two or three times along that part of the lane, she was tempted, by the pleasantness of the morning, to stop at the gates and look into the park. The five weeks which she had now passed in Kent, had made a great difference in the country, and every day was adding to the verdure of the early trees. She was on the point of continuing her walk, when she caught a glimpse of a gentleman within the sort of grove which edged the park; he was moving that way; and fearful of its being Mr Darcy, she was directly retreating. But the person who advanced, was now near enough to see her, and stepping forward with eagerness, pronounced her name. She had turned away, but on hearing herself called, though in a voice which proved it to be Mr Darcy, she moved again towards the gate. He had by that time reached it also, and holding out a letter, which she instinctively took, said with a look of haughty composure, 'I have been walking in the grove some time in the hope of meeting you. Will you do me the honour of reading that letter?' – And then, with a slight bow, turned again into the plantation, and was soon out of sight.

With no expectation of pleasure, but with the strongest curiosity, Elizabeth opened the letter, and to her still increasing wonder, perceived an envelope containing two sheets of letter paper, written quite through, in a very close hand. – The envelope itself was likewise full. – Pursuing her way along the lane, she then began it. It was dated from Rosings, at eight o'clock in the morning, and was as follows: –

Be not alarmed, Madam, on receiving this letter, by the apprehension of its containing any repetition of those sentiments, or renewal of those offers, which were last night so disgusting to you. I write without any intention of paining you, or humbling myself, by dwelling on wishes, which, for the happiness of both, cannot be too soon forgotten; and the effort which the formation, and the perusal of this letter must occasion, should have been spared, had not my character required it to be written and read. You must, therefore, pardon the freedom with which I demand your attention; your feelings, I know, will bestow it unwillingly, but I demand it of your justice.

Two offences of a very different nature, and by no means of equal magnitude, you last night laid to my charge. The first mentioned was, that, regardless of the sentiments of either, I had detached Mr Bingley from your sister, – and the other, that I had, in defiance of various claims, in defiance of honour and humanity, ruined the immediate prosperity, and blasted the prospects of Mr Wickham. – Wilfully and wantonly to have thrown off the companion of my youth, the acknowledged favourite of my father, a young man who had scarcely any other dependence than on our patronage, and who had been brought up to expect its exertion, would be a depravity, to which the separation of two young persons, whose affection could be the growth of only a few weeks, could bear no comparison. – But from the severity of that blame which was last night so liberally bestowed, respecting each circumstance, I shall hope to be in future secured, when the following account of my actions and their motives has been read. – If, in the explanation of them which is due to myself, I am under the necessity of relating feelings which may be offensive to yours, I can only say that I am sorry. – The necessity must be obeyed – and farther apology would be absurd. – I had not been long in Hertfordshire, before I saw, in common with others, that Bingley preferred your eldest sister, to any other young woman in the country. – But it was not till the evening of the dance at Netherfield that I had any apprehension of his feeling a serious attachment. – I had often seen him in love before. – At that ball, while I had the honour of dancing with you, I was first made acquainted, by Sir William Lucas's accidental information, that Bingley's attentions to your sister had given rise to a general expectation of their marriage. He spoke of it as a certain event, of which the time alone could be undecided. From that moment I observed my friend's behaviour attentively; and I could then perceive that his partiality for Miss Bennet was beyond what I had ever witnessed in him. Your sister I also watched. – Her look and manners were open, cheerful and engaging as ever, but without any symptom of peculiar regard, and I remained convinced from the evening's scrutiny, that though she received his attentions with pleasure, she did not invite them by any participation of sentiment. – If *you* have not been mistaken here, *I* must have been in an error. Your superior knowledge of your sister must make the latter probable. – If it be so, if I have been misled by such error, to inflict pain on her, your resentment has not been unreasonable. But I shall not scruple to assert, that the serenity of your sister's countenance and air was such, as might have given the most acute observer, a conviction that, however amiable her temper, her heart was not likely to be easily touched. – That I was desirous of believing her indifferent is certain, – but I will venture to say that my investigations and decisions are not usually influenced by my hopes or fears. – I did not believe her to be indifferent because I wished it; – I believed it on impartial conviction, as truly as I wished it in reason. – My objections to the marriage were not merely those, which I last night acknowledged to have required the utmost force of passion to put aside, in my own case; the want of connection could not be so great an evil to my friend as to me. – But there were other causes of repugnance; –

causes which, though still existing, and existing to an equal degree in both instances, I had myself endeavoured to forget, because they were not immediately before me. – These causes must be stated, though briefly. – The situation of your mother's family, though objectionable, was nothing in comparison of that total want of propriety so frequently, so almost uniformly betrayed by herself, by your three younger sisters, and occasionally even by your father. – Pardon me. – It pains me to offend you. But amidst your concern for the defects of your nearest relations, and your displeasure at this representation of them, let it give you consolation to consider that, to have conducted yourselves so as to avoid any share of the like censure, is praise no less generally bestowed on you and your eldest sister, than it is honourable to the sense and disposition of both. – I will only say farther, that from what passed that evening, my opinion of all parties was confirmed, and every inducement heightened, which could have led me before, to preserve my friend from what I esteemed a most unhappy connection. – He left Netherfield for London, on the day following, as you, I am certain, remember, with the design of soon returning. – The part which I acted, is now to be explained. – His sisters' uneasiness had been equally excited with my own; our coincidence of feeling was soon discovered; and, alike sensible that no time was to be lost in detaching their brother, we shortly resolved on joining him directly in London. – We accordingly went – and there I readily engaged in the office of pointing out to my friend, the certain evils of such a choice. – I described, and enforced them earnestly. – But, however this remonstrance might have staggered or delayed his determination, I do not suppose that it would ultimately have prevented the marriage, had it not been seconded by the assurance which I hesitated not in giving, of your sister's indifference. He had before believed her to return his affection with sincere, if not with equal regard. – But Bingley has great natural modesty, with a stronger dependence on my judgment than on his own. – To convince him, therefore, that he had deceived himself, was no very difficult point. To persuade him against returning into Hertfordshire, when that conviction had been given, was scarcely the work of a moment. – I cannot blame myself for having done thus much. There is but one part of my conduct in the whole affair, on which I do not reflect with satisfaction; it is that I condescended to adopt the measures of art so far as to conceal from him your sister's being in town. I knew it myself, as it was known to Miss Bingley, but her brother is even yet ignorant of it. – That they might have met without ill consequence, is perhaps probable; – but his regard did not appear to me enough extinguished for him to see her without some danger. – Perhaps this concealment, this disguise, was beneath me. – It is done, however, and it was done for the best. – On this subject I have nothing more to say, no other apology to offer. If I have wounded your sister's feelings, it was unknowingly done; and though the motives which governed me may to you very naturally appear insufficient, I have not yet learnt to condemn them. – With respect to that other, more weighty accusation, of having injured Mr Wickham, I can only refute it by laying before you the whole of his connection with my family. Of what he has *particularly* accused me I am ignorant; but of the truth of what I shall relate, I can summon more than one witness of undoubted veracity. Mr Wickham is the son of a very respectable man, who had for many years the management of all the Pemberley estates; and whose good conduct in the discharge of his trust, naturally inclined my father to be of service to him, and on George Wickham, who was his god-son, his kindness was therefore liberally bestowed. My father supported him at school, and afterwards at Cambridge; – most important assistance, as his own father, always poor from the extravagance of his wife, would have been unable to give him a gentleman's education. My father was not only fond of this young man's society, whose manners were always engaging; he had also the highest opinion of him, and hoping the church would be his profession, intended to provide for him in it. As for myself, it is many, many years since I first began to think of him in a very different manner. The vicious propensities – the want of principle which he was careful to guard from the knowledge of his best friend, could not escape the observation of a young man of nearly the same age with himself, and who had opportunities of seeing him in unguarded moments, which Mr Darcy could not have. Here again I shall give you pain – to what degree you only can tell. But whatever may be the sentiments which Mr Wickham has created, a suspicion of their nature shall not prevent me from unfolding his real character. It adds even another motive. My excellent father died about five years ago; and his attachment to Mr Wickham was to the last so steady, that in his will he particularly recommended it to me, to promote his advancement in the best manner that his profession might allow, and if he took orders, desired that a valuable family living might be his as soon as it became vacant. There was also a legacy of one thousand pounds. His own father did not long survive mine, and within half a year from these events, Mr Wickham wrote to inform me that, having finally resolved against taking orders, he hoped I should not think it unreasonable for him to expect some more immediate pecuniary advantage, in lieu of the preferment, by which he could not be benefited. He had some intention, he added, of studying the law, and I must be aware that the interest of one thousand pounds would be a very insufficient support therein. I rather wished, than believed him to be sincere; but at any rate, was perfectly ready to accede to his proposal. I knew that Mr Wickham ought not to be a clergyman. The business was therefore soon settled. He resigned all claim to assistance in the church, were it possible that he could ever be in a situation to receive it, and accepted in return three thousand pounds. All connection between us seemed now dissolved. I thought too ill of him, to invite him to Pemberley, or admit his society in town. In town I believe he chiefly lived, but his studying the law was a mere pretence, and being now free from all restraint, his life was a life of idleness and dissipation. For about three years I heard little of him;

but on the decease of the incumbent of the living which had been designed for him, he applied to me again by letter for the presentation. His circumstances, he assured me, and I had no difficulty in believing it, were exceedingly bad. He had found the law a most unprofitable study, and was now absolutely resolved on being ordained, if I would present him to the living in question – of which he trusted there could be little doubt, as he was well assured that I had no other person to provide for, and I could not have forgotten my revered father's intentions. You will hardly blame me for refusing to comply with this entreaty, or for resisting every repetition of it. His resentment was in proportion to the distress of his circumstances – and he was doubtless as violent in his abuse of me to others, as in his reproaches to myself. After this period, every appearance of acquaintance was dropt. How he lived I know not. But last summer he was again most painfully obtruded on my notice. I must now mention a circumstance which I would wish to forget myself, and which no obligation less than the present should induce me to unfold to any human being. Having said thus much, I feel no doubt of your secrecy. My sister, who is more than ten years my junior, was left to the guardianship of my mother's nephew, Colonel Fitzwilliam, and myself. About a year ago, she was taken from school, and an establishment formed for her in London; and last summer she went with the lady who presided over it, to Ramsgate; and thither also went Mr Wickham, undoubtedly by design; for there proved to have been a prior acquaintance between him and Mrs Younge, in whose character we were most unhappily deceived; and by her connivance and aid, he so far recommended himself to Georgiana, whose affectionate heart retained a strong impression of his kindness to her as a child, that she was persuaded to believe herself in love, and to consent to an elopement. She was then but fifteen, which must be her excuse; and after stating her imprudence, I am happy to add, that I owed the knowledge of it to herself. I joined them unexpectedly a day or two before the intended elopement, and then Georgiana, unable to support the idea of grieving and offending a brother whom she almost looked up to as a father, acknowledged the whole to me. You may imagine what I felt and how I acted. Regard for my sister's credit and feelings prevented any public exposure, but I wrote to Mr Wickham, who left the place immediately, and Mrs Younge was of course removed from her charge. Mr Wickham's chief object was unquestionably my sister's fortune, which is thirty thousand pounds; but I cannot help supposing that the hope of revenging himself on me, was a strong inducement. His revenge would have been complete indeed. This, madam, is a faithful narrative of every event in which we have been concerned together, and if you do not absolutely reject it as false, you will, I hope, acquit me henceforth of cruelty towards Mr Wickham. I know not in what manner, under what form of falsehood he has imposed on you; but his success is not perhaps to be wondered at, ignorant as you previously were of every thing concerning either. Detection could not be in your power, and suspicion certainly not in your inclination. You may possibly wonder why all this was not told you last night. But I was not then master enough of myself to know what could or ought to be revealed. For the truth of every thing here related, I can appeal more particularly to the testimony of Colonel Fitzwilliam, who from our near relationship and constant intimacy, and still more as one of the executors of my father's will, has been unavoidably acquainted with every particular of these transactions. If your abhorrence of *me* should make *my* assertions valueless, you cannot be prevented by the same cause from confiding in my cousin; and that there may be the possibility of consulting him, I shall endeavour to find some opportunity of putting this letter in your hands in the course of the morning. I will only add, God bless you.

FITZWILLIAM DARCY

Chapter 36

I f Elizabeth, when Mr Darcy gave her the letter, did not expect it to contain a renewal of his offers, she had formed no expectation at all of its contents. But such as they were, it may be well supposed how eagerly she went through them, and what a contrariety of emotion they excited. Her feelings as she read were scarcely to be defined. With amazement did she first understand that he believed any apology to be in his power; and steadfastly was she persuaded that he could have no explanation to give, which a just sense of shame would not conceal. With a strong prejudice against every thing he might say, she began his account of what had happened at Netherfield. She read, with an eagerness which hardly left her power of comprehension, and from impatience of knowing what the next sentence might bring, was incapable of attending to the sense of the one before her eyes. His belief of her sister's insensibility, she instantly resolved to be false, and his account of the real, the worst objections to the match, made her too angry to have any wish of doing him justice. He expressed no regret for what he had done which satisfied her; his style was not penitent, but haughty. It was all pride and insolence.

But when this subject was succeeded by his account of Mr Wickham, when she read with somewhat clearer attention, a relation of events, which, if true, must overthrow every cherished opinion of his worth, and which bore so alarming an affinity to his own history of himself, her feelings were yet more acutely painful and more difficult of definition. Astonishment, apprehension, and even horror, oppressed her. She wished to discredit it entirely, repeatedly exclaiming, 'This must be false! This cannot be! This must be the grossest falsehood!' – and when she had gone through the whole letter, though scarcely knowing any thing of the last page or two, put it hastily away, protesting that she would not regard it, that she would never look in it again.

In this perturbed state of mind, with thoughts that could rest on nothing, she walked on; but it would not do; in half a minute the letter was unfolded again, and collecting herself as well as she could, she again began the mortifying perusal of all that related to Wickham, and commanded herself so far as to examine the meaning of every sentence. The account of his connection with the Pemberley family, was exactly what he had related himself; and the kindness of the late Mr Darcy, though she had not before known its extent, agreed equally well with his own words. So far each recital confirmed the other: but when she came to the will, the difference was great. What Wickham had said of the living was fresh in her memory, and as she recalled his very words, it was impossible not to feel that there was gross duplicity on one side or the other; and, for a few moments, she flattered herself that her wishes did not err. But when she read, and re-read with the closest attention, the particulars immediately following of Wickham's resigning all pretensions to the living, of his receiving in lieu, so considerable a sum as three thousand pounds, again was she forced to hesitate. She put down the letter, weighed every circumstance with what she meant to be impartiality – deliberated on the probability of each statement – but with little success. On both sides it was only assertion. Again she read on. But every line proved more clearly that the affair, which she had believed it impossible that any contrivance could so represent, as to render Mr Darcy's conduct in it less than infamous, was capable of a turn which must make him entirely blameless throughout the whole.

The extravagance and general profligacy which he scrupled not to lay to Mr Wickham's charge, exceedingly shocked her; the more so, as she could bring no proof of its injustice. She had never heard of him before his entrance into the —shire Militia, in which he had engaged at the persuasion of the young man, who, on meeting him accidentally in town, had there renewed a slight acquaintance. Of his former way of life, nothing had been known in Hertfordshire but what he told himself. As to his real character, had information been in her power, she had never felt a wish of enquiring. His countenance, voice, and manner, had established him at once in the possession of every virtue. She tried to recollect some instance of goodness, some distinguished trait of integrity or benevolence, that might rescue him from the attacks of Mr Darcy; or at least, by the predominance of virtue, atone for those casual errors, under which she would endeavour to class, what Mr Darcy had described as the idleness and vice of many years continuance. But no such recollection befriended her. She could see him instantly before her, in every charm of air and address; but she could remember no more substantial good than the general approbation of the neighbourhood, and the regard which his social powers had gained him in the mess. After pausing on this point a considerable while, she once more continued to read. But, alas! the story which followed of his designs on Miss Darcy, received some confirmation from what had passed between Colonel Fitzwilliam and herself only the morning before; and at last she was referred for the truth of every particular to Colonel Fitzwilliam himself – from whom she had previously received the information of his near concern in all his cousin's affairs, and whose character she had no reason to question. At one time she had almost resolved on applying to him, but the idea was checked by the awkwardness of the application, and at length wholly banished by the conviction that Mr Darcy would never have hazarded such a proposal, if he had not been well assured of his cousin's corroboration.

She perfectly remembered every thing that had passed in conversation between Wickham and herself, in their first evening at Mr Philips's. Many of his expressions were still fresh in her memory. She was *now* struck with the impropriety of such communications to a stranger, and wondered it had escaped her before. She saw the indelicacy of putting himself forward as he had done, and the inconsistency of his professions with his conduct. She remembered that he had boasted of having no fear of seeing Mr Darcy – that Mr Darcy might leave the country, but that *he* should stand his ground; yet he had avoided the Netherfield ball the very next week. She remembered also, that till the Netherfield family had quitted the country, he had told his story to no one but herself; but that after their removal, it had been every where discussed; that he had then no reserves, no scruples in sinking Mr Darcy's character, though he had assured her that respect for the father, would always prevent his exposing the son.

How differently did every thing now appear in which he was concerned! His attentions to Miss King were now the consequence of views solely and hatefully mercenary; and the mediocrity of her fortune proved no longer the moderation of his wishes, but his eagerness to grasp at any thing. His behaviour to herself could now have had no tolerable motive; he had either been deceived with regard to her fortune, or had been gratifying his vanity by encouraging the preference which she believed she had most incautiously shown. Every lingering struggle in his favour grew fainter and fainter; and in farther justification of Mr Darcy, she could not but allow that Mr Bingley, when questioned by Jane, had long ago asserted his blamelessness in the affair; that proud and repulsive as were his manners, she had never, in the whole course of their acquaintance, an acquaintance which had latterly brought them much together, and given her a sort of intimacy with his ways, seen any thing that betrayed him to be unprincipled or unjust – any thing that spoke him of irreligious or immoral habits. That among his own connections he was esteemed and valued – that even Wickham had allowed him merit as a brother, and that she had often heard him speak so affectionately of his sister as to prove him capable of *some* amiable feeling. That had his actions been what Wickham represented them, so gross a violation of every thing right could hardly have been concealed from the world; and that friendship between a person capable of it, and such an amiable man as Mr Bingley, was incomprehensible.

She grew absolutely ashamed of herself. – Of neither Darcy nor Wickham could she think, without feeling that she had been blind, partial, prejudiced, absurd.

'How despicably have I acted!' she cried. – 'I, who have prided myself on my discernment! – I, who have valued myself on my abilities! who have often disdained the generous candour of my sister, and gratified my vanity, in useless or blameable distrust. – How humiliating is this discovery! – Yet, how just a humiliation! – Had I been in love, I could not have been more wretchedly blind. But vanity, not love, has been my folly. – Pleased with the preference of one, and offended by the neglect of the other, on the very beginning of our acquaintance, I have courted prepossession and ignorance, and driven reason away, where either were concerned. Till this moment, I never knew myself.'

From herself to Jane – from Jane to Bingley, her thoughts were in a line which soon brought to her recollection that Mr Darcy's explanation *there*, had appeared very insufficient; and she read it again. Widely different was the effect of a second perusal. – How could she deny that credit to his assertions, in one instance, which she had been obliged to give in the other? – He declared himself to have been totally unsuspicious of her sister's attachment; – and she could not help remembering what Charlotte's opinion had always been. – Neither could she deny the justice of his description of Jane. – She felt that Jane's feelings, though fervent, were little displayed, and that there was a constant complacency in her air and manner, not often united with great sensibility.

When she came to that part of the letter in which her family were mentioned, in terms of such mortifying, yet merited reproach, her sense of shame was severe. The justice of the charge struck her too forcibly for denial, and the circumstances to which he particularly alluded, as having passed at the Netherfield ball, and as confirming all his first disapprobation, could not have made a stronger impression on his mind than on hers. The compliment to herself and her sister, was not unfelt. It soothed, but it could not console her for the contempt which had been thus self-attracted by the rest of her family; – and as she considered that Jane's disappointment had in fact been the work of her nearest relations, and reflected how materially the credit of both must be hurt by such impropriety of conduct, she felt depressed beyond any thing she had ever known before.

After wandering along the lane for two hours, giving way to every variety of thought; re-considering events, determining probabilities, and reconciling herself as well as she could, to a change so sudden and so important, fatigue, and a recollection of her long absence, made her at length return home; and she entered the house with the wish of appearing cheerful as usual, and the resolution of repressing such reflections as must make her unfit for conversation.

She was immediately told, that the two gentlemen from Rosings had each called during her absence; Mr Darcy, only for a few minutes to take leave, but that Colonel Fitzwilliam had been sitting with them at least an hour, hoping for her return, and almost resolving to walk after her till she could be found. – Elizabeth could but just *affect* concern in missing him; she really rejoiced at it. Colonel Fitzwilliam was no longer an object. She could think only of her letter.

Chapter 37

The two gentlemen left Rosings the next morning; and Mr Collins having been in waiting near the lodges, to make them his parting obeisance, was able to bring home the pleasing intelligence, of their appearing in very good health, and in as tolerable spirits as could be expected, after the melancholy scene so lately gone through at Rosings. To Rosings he then hastened to console Lady Catherine, and her daughter; and on his return, brought back, with great satisfaction, a message from her Ladyship, importing that she felt herself so dull as to make her very desirous of having them all to dine with her.

Elizabeth could not see Lady Catherine without recollecting, that had she chosen it, she might by this time have been presented to her, as her future niece; nor could she think, without a smile, of what her ladyship's indignation would have been. 'What would she have said? – how would she have behaved?' were questions with which she amused herself.

Their first subject was the diminution of the Rosings party. – 'I assure you, I feel it exceedingly,' said Lady Catherine; 'I believe nobody feels the loss of friends so much as I do. But I am particularly attached to these young men; and know them to be so much attached to me! – They were excessively sorry to go! But so they always are. The dear colonel rallied his spirits tolerably till just at last; but Darcy seemed to feel it most acutely, more I think than last year. His attachment to Rosings, certainly increases.'

Mr Collins had a compliment, and an allusion to throw in here, which were kindly smiled on by the mother and daughter.

Lady Catherine observed, after dinner, that Miss Bennet seemed out of spirits, and immediately accounting for it herself, by supposing that she did not like to go home again so soon, she added,

'But if that is the case, you must write to your mother to beg that you may stay a little longer. Mrs Collins will be very glad of your company, I am sure.'

'I am much obliged to your ladyship for your kind invitation,' replied Elizabeth, 'but it is not in my power to accept it. – I must be in town next Saturday.'

'Why, at that rate, you will have been here only six weeks. I expected you to stay two months. I told Mrs Collins so before you came. There can be no occasion for your going so soon. Mrs Bennet could certainly spare you for another fortnight.'

'But my father cannot. – He wrote last week to hurry my return.'

'Oh! your father of course may spare you, if your mother can. – Daughters are never of so much consequence to a father. And if you will stay another *month* complete, it will be in my power to take one of you as far as London, for I am going there early in June, for a week; and as Dawson does not object to the Barouche box, there will be very good room for one of you – and indeed, if the weather should happen to be cool, I should not object to taking you both, as you are neither of you large.'

'You are all kindness, Madam; but I believe we must abide by our original plan.'

Lady Catherine seemed resigned. –

'Mrs Collins, you must send a servant with them. You know I always speak my mind, and I cannot bear the idea of two young women travelling post by themselves. It is highly improper. You must contrive to send somebody. I have the greatest dislike in the world to that sort of thing. – Young women should always be properly guarded and attended, according to their situation in life. When my niece Georgiana went to Ramsgate last summer, I made a point of her having two men servants go with her. – Miss Darcy, the daughter of Mr Darcy, of Pemberley, and Lady Anne, could not have appeared with propriety in a different manner. – I am excessively attentive to all those things. You must send John with the young ladies, Mrs Collins. I am glad it occurred to me to mention it; for it would really be discreditable to *you* to let them go alone.'

'My uncle is to send a servant for us.'

'Oh! – Your uncle! – He keeps a man-servant, does he? – I am very glad you have somebody who thinks of those things. Where shall you change horses? – Oh! Bromley, of course. – If you mention my name at the Bell, you will be attended to.'

Lady Catherine had many other questions to ask respecting their journey, and as she did not answer them all herself, attention was necessary, which Elizabeth believed to be lucky for her; or, with a mind so occupied, she might have forgotten where she was. Reflection must be reserved for solitary hours; whenever she was alone, she gave way to it as the greatest relief; and not a day went by without a solitary walk, in which she might indulge in all the delight of unpleasant recollections.

Mr Darcy's letter, she was in a fair way of soon knowing by heart. She studied every sentence: and her feelings towards its writer were at times widely different. When she remembered the style of his address, she was still full of indignation; but when she considered how unjustly she had condemned and upbraided him, her anger was turned against herself; and his disappointed feelings became the object of compassion. His attachment excited gratitude, his general character respect; but she could not approve him; nor could she for a moment repent her refusal, or feel the slightest inclination ever to see him again. In her own past behaviour, there was a constant source of vexation and regret; and in the unhappy defects of her family a subject of yet heavier chagrin. They were hopeless of remedy. Her father, contented with laughing at them, would never exert himself to restrain the wild giddiness of his youngest daughters; and her mother, with manners so far from right herself, was entirely insensible of the evil. Elizabeth had frequently united with Jane in an endeavour to check the imprudence of Catherine and Lydia; but while they were supported by their mother's indulgence, what chance could there be of improvement? Catherine, weak-spirited, irritable, and completely under Lydia's guidance, had been always affronted by their advice; and Lydia, self-willed and careless, would scarcely give them a hearing. They were ignorant, idle, and vain. While there was an officer in Meryton, they would flirt with him; and while Meryton was within a walk of Longbourn, they would be going there forever.

Anxiety on Jane's behalf, was another prevailing concern, and Mr Darcy's explanation, by restoring Bingley to all her former good opinion, heightened the sense of what Jane had lost. His affection was proved to have been sincere, and his conduct cleared of all blame, unless any could attach to the implicitness of his confidence in his

friend. How grievous then was the thought that, of a situation so desirable in every respect, so replete with advantage, so promising for happiness, Jane had been deprived, by the folly and indecorum of her own family!

When to these recollections was added the development of Wickham's character, it may be easily believed that the happy spirits which had seldom been depressed before, were now so much affected as to make it almost impossible for her to appear tolerably cheerful.

Their engagements at Rosings were as frequent during the last week of her stay, as they had been at first. The very last evening was spent there; and her Ladyship again enquired minutely into the particulars of their journey, gave them directions as to the best method of packing, and was so urgent on the necessity of placing gowns in the only right way, that Maria thought herself obliged, on her return, to undo all the work of the morning, and pack her trunk afresh.

When they parted, Lady Catherine, with great condescension, wished them a good journey, and invited them to come to Hunsford again next year; and Miss De Bourgh exerted herself so far as to curtsey and hold out her hand to both.

Chapter 38

On Saturday morning Elizabeth and Mr Collins met for breakfast a few minutes before the others appeared; and he took the opportunity of paying the parting civilities which he deemed indispensably necessary.

'I know not, Miss Elizabeth,' said he, 'whether Mrs Collins has yet expressed her sense of your kindness in coming to us, but I am very certain you will not leave the house without receiving her thanks for it. The favour of your company has been much felt, I assure you. We know how little there is to tempt any one to our humble abode. Our plain manner of living, our small rooms, and few domestics, and the little we see of the world, must make Hunsford extremely dull to a young lady like yourself; but I hope you will believe us grateful for the condescension, and that we have done every thing in our power to prevent your spending your time unpleasantly.'

Elizabeth was eager with her thanks and assurances of happiness. She had spent six weeks with great enjoyment; and the pleasure of being with Charlotte, and the kind attentions she had received, must make *her* feel the obliged. Mr Collins was gratified; and with a more smiling solemnity replied,

'It gives me the greatest pleasure to hear that you have passed your time not disagreeably. We have certainly done our best; and most fortunately having it in our power to introduce you to very superior society, and from our connection with Rosings, the frequent means of varying the humble home scene, I think we may flatter ourselves that your Hunsford visit cannot have been entirely irksome. Our situation with regard to Lady Catherine's family is indeed the sort of extraordinary advantage and blessing which few can boast. You see on what a footing we are. You see how continually we are engaged there. In truth I must acknowledge that, with all the disadvantages of this humble parsonage, I should not think any one abiding in it an object of compassion, while they are sharers of our intimacy at Rosings.'

Words were insufficient for the elevation of his feelings; and he was obliged to walk about the room, while Elizabeth tried to unite civility and truth in a few short sentences.

'You may, in fact, carry a very favourable report of us into Hertfordshire, my dear cousin. I flatter myself at least that you will be able to do so. Lady Catherine's great attentions to Mrs Collins you have been a daily witness of; and altogether I trust it does not appear that your friend has drawn an unfortunate – but on this point it will be as well to be silent. Only let me assure you, my dear Miss Elizabeth, that I can from my heart most cordially wish you equal felicity in marriage. My dear Charlotte and I have but one mind and one way of thinking. There is in every thing a most remarkable resemblance of character and ideas between us. We seem to have been designed for each other.'

Elizabeth could safely say that it was a great happiness where that was the case, and with equal sincerity could add that she firmly believed and rejoiced in his domestic comforts. She was not sorry, however, to have the recital of them interrupted by the entrance of the lady from whom they sprung. Poor Charlotte! – it was melancholy to leave her to such society! – But she had chosen it with her eyes open; and though evidently regretting that her visitors were to go, she did not seem to ask for compassion. Her home and her housekeeping, her parish and her poultry, and all their dependent concerns, had not yet lost their charms.

At length the chaise arrived, the trunks were fastened on, the parcels placed within, and it was pronounced to be ready. After an affectionate parting between the friends, Elizabeth was attended to the carriage by Mr Collins, and as they walked down the garden, he was commissioning her with his best respects to all her family, not forgetting his thanks for the kindness he had received at Longbourn in the winter, and his compliments to Mr and Mrs Gardiner, though unknown. He then handed her in, Maria followed, and the door was on the point of being closed, when he suddenly reminded them, with some consternation, that they had hitherto forgotten to leave any message for the ladies of Rosings.

'But,' he added, 'you will of course wish to have your humble respects delivered to them, with your grateful thanks for their kindness to you while you have been here.'

Elizabeth made no objection; – the door was then allowed to be shut, and the carriage drove off.

'Good gracious!' cried Maria, after a few minutes silence, 'it seems but a day or two since we first came! – and yet how many things have happened!'

'A great many indeed,' said her companion with a sigh.

'We have dined nine times at Rosings, besides drinking tea there twice! – How much I shall have to tell!'

Elizabeth privately added, 'And how much I shall have to conceal.'

Their journey was performed without much conversation, or any alarm; and within four hours of their leaving Hunsford, they reached Mr Gardiner's house, where they were to remain a few days.

Jane looked well, and Elizabeth had little opportunity of studying

her spirits, amidst the various engagements which the kindness of her aunt had reserved for them. But Jane was to go home with her, and at Longbourn there would be leisure enough for observation.

It was not without an effort meanwhile that she could wait even for Longbourn, before she told her sister of Mr Darcy's proposals. To know that she had the power of revealing what would so exceedingly astonish Jane, and must, at the same time, so highly gratify whatever of her own vanity she had not yet been able to reason away, was such a temptation to openness as nothing could have conquered, but the state of indecision in which she remained, as to the extent of what she should communicate; and her fear, if she once entered on the subject, of being hurried into repeating something of Bingley, which might only grieve her sister farther.

Chapter 39

It was the second week in May, in which the three young ladies set out together from Gracechurch-street, for the town of — in Hertfordshire; and, as they drew near the appointed inn where Mr Bennet's carriage was to meet them, they quickly perceived, in token of the coachman's punctuality, both Kitty and Lydia looking out of a dining-room upstairs. These two girls had been above an hour in the place, happily employed in visiting an opposite milliner, watching the sentinel on guard, and dressing a salad and cucumber.

After welcoming their sisters, they triumphantly displayed a table set out with such cold meat as an inn larder usually affords, exclaiming, 'Is not this nice? is not this an agreeable surprise?'

'And we mean to treat you all,' added Lydia; 'but you must lend us the money, for we have just spent ours at the shop out there.' Then showing her purchases: 'Look here, I have bought this bonnet. I do not think it is very pretty; but I thought I might as well buy it as not. I shall pull it to pieces as soon as I get home, and see if I can make it up any better.'

And when her sisters abused it as ugly, she added, with perfect unconcern, 'Oh! but there were two or three much uglier in the shop; and when I have bought some prettier-coloured satin to trim it with fresh, I think it will be very tolerable. Besides, it will not much signify what one wears this summer, after the —shire have left Meryton, and they are going in a fortnight.'

'Are they indeed?' cried Elizabeth, with the greatest satisfaction.

'They are going to be encamped near Brighton; and I do so want papa to take us all there for the summer! It would be such a delicious scheme, and I dare say would hardly cost any thing at all. Mamma would like to go too of all things! Only think what a miserable summer else we shall have!'

'Yes,' thought Elizabeth, 'that would be a delightful scheme, indeed, and completely do for us at once. Good Heaven! Brighton, and a whole campful of soldiers, to us, who have been overset already by one poor regiment of militia, and the monthly balls of Meryton.'

'Now I have got some news for you,' said Lydia, as they sat down to table. 'What do you think? It is excellent news, capital news, and about a certain person that we all like.'

Jane and Elizabeth looked at each other, and the waiter was told that he need not stay. Lydia laughed, and said, 'Aye, that is just like your formality and discretion. You thought the waiter must not hear, as if he cared! I dare say he often hears worse things said than I am going to say. But he is an ugly fellow! I am glad he is gone. I never saw such a long chin in my life. Well, but now for my news: it is about dear Wickham; too good for the waiter, is not it? There is no danger of Wickham's marrying Mary King. There's for you! She is gone down to her uncle at Liverpool; gone to stay. Wickham is safe.'

'And Mary King is safe!' added Elizabeth; 'safe from a connection imprudent as to fortune.'

'She is a great fool for going away, if she liked him.'

'But I hope there is no strong attachment on either side,' said Jane.

'I am sure there is not on *his*. I will answer for it he never cared three straws about her. Who *could* about such a nasty little freckled thing?'

Elizabeth was shocked to think that, however incapable of such coarseness of *expression* herself, the coarseness of the *sentiment* was little other than her own breast had formerly harboured and fancied liberal!

As soon as all had ate, and the elder ones paid, the carriage was ordered; and after some contrivance, the whole party, with all their boxes, workbags, and parcels, and the unwelcome addition of Kitty's and Lydia's purchases, were seated in it.

'How nicely we are crammed in!' cried Lydia. 'I am glad I bought my bonnet, if it is only for the fun of having another bandbox! Well, now let us be quite comfortable and snug, and talk and laugh all the way home. And in the first place, let us hear what has happened to you all, since you went away. Have you seen any pleasant men? Have you had any flirting? I was in great hopes that one of you would have got a husband before you came back. Jane will be quite an old maid soon, I declare. She is almost three and twenty! Lord, how ashamed I should be of not being married before three and twenty! My aunt Philips wants you so to get husbands, you can't think. She says Lizzy had better have taken Mr Collins; but *I* do not think there would have been any fun in it. Lord! how I should like to be married before any of you; and then I would chaperon you about to all the balls. Dear me! we had such a good piece of fun the other day at Colonel Forster's. Kitty and me were to spend the day there, and Mrs Forster promised to have a little dance in the evening; (by the bye, Mrs Forster and me are *such* friends!) and so she asked the two Harringtons to come, but Harriet was ill, and so Pen was forced to come by herself; and then, what do you think we did? We dressed up Chamberlayne in woman's clothes, on purpose to pass for a lady, – only think what fun! Not a soul knew of it, but Col. and Mrs Forster, and Kitty and me, except my aunt, for we were forced to borrow one of her gowns; and you cannot imagine how well he looked! When Denny, and Wickham, and Pratt, and two or three more of the men came in, they did not know him in the least.

Lord! how I laughed! and so did Mrs Forster. I thought I should have died. And *that* made the men suspect something, and then they soon found out what was the matter.'

With such kind of histories of their parties and good jokes, did Lydia, assisted by Kitty's hints and additions, endeavour to amuse her companions all the way to Longbourn. Elizabeth listened as little as she could, but there was no escaping the frequent mention of Wickham's name.

Their reception at home was most kind. Mrs Bennet rejoiced to see Jane in undiminished beauty; and more than once during dinner did Mr Bennet say voluntarily to Elizabeth,

'I am glad you are come back, Lizzy.'

Their party in the dining-room was large, for almost all the Lucases came to meet Maria and hear the news: and various were the subjects which occupied them; lady Lucas was enquiring of Maria across the table, after the welfare and poultry of her eldest daughter; Mrs Bennet was doubly engaged, on one hand collecting an account of the present fashions from Jane, who sat some way below her, and on the other, retailing them all to the younger Miss Lucases; and Lydia, in a voice rather louder than any other person's, was enumerating the various pleasures of the morning to any body who would hear her.

'Oh! Mary,' said she, 'I wish you had gone with us, for we had such fun! as we went along, Kitty and me drew up all the blinds, and pretended there was nobody in the coach; and I should have gone so all the way, if Kitty had not been sick; and when we got to the George, I do think we behaved very handsomely, for we treated the other three with the nicest cold luncheon in the world, and if you would have gone, we would have treated you too. And then when we came away it was such fun! I thought we never should have got into the coach. I was ready to die of laughter. And then we were so merry all the way home! we talked and laughed so loud, that any body might have heard us ten miles off!'

To this, Mary very gravely replied, 'Far be it from me, my dear sister, to depreciate such pleasures. They would doubtless be congenial with the generality of female minds. But I confess they would have no charms for *me*. I should infinitely prefer a book.'

But of this answer Lydia heard not a word. She seldom listened to any body for more than half a minute, and never attended to Mary at all.

In the afternoon Lydia was urgent with the rest of the girls to walk to Meryton and see how every body went on; but Elizabeth steadily opposed the scheme. It should not be said, that the Miss Bennets could not be at home half a day before they were in pursuit of the officers. There was another reason too for her opposition. She dreaded seeing Wickham again, and was resolved to avoid it as long as possible. The comfort to *her*, of the regiment's approaching removal, was indeed beyond expression. In a fortnight they were to go, and once gone, she hoped there could be nothing more to plague her on his account.

She had not been many hours at home, before she found that the Brighton scheme, of which Lydia had given them a hint at the inn, was under frequent discussion between her parents. Elizabeth saw directly that her father had not the smallest intention of yielding; but his answers were at the same time so vague and equivocal, that her mother, though often disheartened, had never yet despaired of succeeding at last.

Chapter 40

Elizabeth's impatience to acquaint Jane with what had happened could no longer be overcome; and at length resolving to suppress every particular in which her sister was concerned, and preparing her to be surprised, she related to her the next morning the chief of the scene between Mr Darcy and herself.

Miss Bennet's astonishment was soon lessened by the strong sisterly partiality which made any admiration of Elizabeth appear perfectly natural; and all surprise was shortly lost in other feelings. She was sorry that Mr Darcy should have delivered his sentiments in a manner so little suited to recommend them; but still more was she grieved for the unhappiness which her sister's refusal must have given him.

'His being so sure of succeeding, was wrong,' said she; 'and certainly ought not to have appeared; but consider how much it must increase his disappointment.'

'Indeed,' replied Elizabeth, 'I am heartily sorry for him; but he has other feelings which will probably soon drive away his regard for me. You do not blame me, however, for refusing him?'

'Blame you! Oh, no.'

'But you blame me for having spoken so warmly of Wickham.'

'No – I do not know that you were wrong in saying what you did.'

'But you *will* know it, when I have told you what happened the very next day.'

She then spoke of the letter, repeating the whole of its contents as far as they concerned George Wickham. What a stroke was this for poor Jane! who would willingly have gone through the world without believing that so much wickedness existed in the whole race of mankind, as was here collected in one individual. Nor was Darcy's vindication, though grateful to her feelings, capable of consoling her for such discovery. Most earnestly did she labour to prove the probability of error, and seek to clear one, without involving the other.

'This will not do,' said Elizabeth. 'You never will be able to make both of them good for any thing. Take your choice, but you must be satisfied with only one. There is but such a quantity of merit between them; just enough to make one good sort of man; and of late it has been shifting about pretty much. For my part, I am inclined to believe it all Mr Darcy's, but you shall do as you chuse.'

It was some time, however, before a smile could be extorted from Jane.

'I do not know when I have been more shocked,' said she. 'Wickham so very bad! It is almost past belief. And poor Mr Darcy! dear Lizzy, only consider what he must have suffered. Such a disappointment and with the knowledge of your ill opinion too! and having to relate such a thing of his sister! It is really too distressing. I am sure you must feel it so.'

'Oh! no, my regret and compassion are all done away by seeing you so full of both. I know you will do him such ample justice, that I am growing every moment more unconcerned and indifferent. Your profusion makes me saving; and if you lament over him much longer, my heart will be as light as a feather.'

'Poor Wickham; there is such an expression of goodness in his countenance! such an openness and gentleness in his manner.'

'There certainly was some great mismanagement in the education of those two young men. One has got all the goodness, and the other all the appearance of it.'

'I never thought Mr Darcy so deficient in the *appearance* of it as you used to do.'

'And yet I meant to be uncommonly clever in taking so decided a dislike to him, without any reason. It is such a spur to one's genius, such an opening for wit to have a dislike of that kind. One may be continually abusive without saying any thing just; but one cannot be always laughing at a man without now and then stumbling on something witty.'

'Lizzy, when you first read that letter, I am sure you could not treat the matter as you do now.'

'Indeed I could not. I was uncomfortable enough. I was very uncomfortable, I may say unhappy. And with no one to speak to, of what I felt, no Jane to comfort me and say that I had not been so very weak and vain and nonsensical as I knew I had! Oh! how I wanted you!'

'How unfortunate that you should have used such very strong expressions in speaking of Wickham to Mr Darcy, for now they *do* appear wholly undeserved.'

'Certainly. But the misfortune of speaking with bitterness, is a most natural consequence of the prejudices I had been encouraging. There is one point, on which I want your advice. I want to be told whether I ought, or ought not to make our acquaintance in general understand Wickham's character.'

Miss Bennet paused a little and then replied, 'Surely there can be no occasion for exposing him so dreadfully. What is your own opinion?'

'That it ought not to be attempted. Mr Darcy has not authorised me to make his communication public. On the contrary every particular relative to his sister, was meant to be kept as much as possible to myself; and if I endeavour to undeceive people as to the rest of his conduct, who will believe me? The general prejudice against Mr Darcy is so violent, that it would be the death of half the good people in Meryton, to attempt to place him in an amiable light. I am not equal to it. Wickham will soon be gone; and therefore it will not signify to anybody here, what he really is. Sometime hence it will be all found out, and then we may laugh at their stupidity in not knowing it before. At present I will say nothing about it.'

'You are quite right. To have his errors made public might ruin him forever. He is now perhaps sorry for what he has done, and anxious to re-establish a character. We must not make him desperate.'

The tumult of Elizabeth's mind was allayed by this conversation. She had got rid of two of the secrets which had weighed on her for a fortnight, and was certain of a willing listener in Jane, whenever she might wish to talk again of either. But there was still something lurking behind, of which prudence forbad the disclosure. She dared not relate the other half of Mr Darcy's letter, nor explain to her sister how sincerely she had been valued by his friend. Here was knowledge in which no one could partake; and she was sensible that nothing less than a perfect understanding between the parties could justify her in throwing off this last incumbrance of mystery. 'And then,' said she, 'if that very improbable event should ever take place, I shall merely be able to tell what Bingley may tell in a much more agreeable manner himself. The liberty of communication cannot be mine till it has lost all its value!'

She was now, on being settled at home, at leisure to observe the real state of her sister's spirits. Jane was not happy. She still cherished a very tender affection for Bingley. Having never even fancied herself in love before, her regard had all the warmth of first attachment, and from her age and disposition, greater steadiness than first attachments often boast; and so fervently did she value his remembrance, and prefer him to every other man, that all her good sense, and all her attention to the feelings of her friends, were requisite to check the indulgence of those regrets, which must have been injurious to her own health and their tranquility.

'Well, Lizzy,' said Mrs Bennet one day, 'what is your opinion *now* of this sad business of Jane's? For my part, I am determined never to speak of it again to anybody. I told my sister Philips so the other day. But I cannot find out that Jane saw any thing of him in London. Well, he is a very undeserving young man – and I do not suppose there is the least chance in the world of her ever getting him now. There is no talk of his coming to Netherfield again in the summer; and I have enquired of every body too, who is likely to know.'

'I do not believe that he will ever live at Netherfield any more.'

'Oh, well it is just as he chooses. Nobody wants him to come. Though I shall always say that he used my daughter extremely ill; and if I was her, I would not have put up with it. Well, my comfort is, I am sure Jane will die of a broken heart, and then he will be sorry for what he has done.'

But as Elizabeth could not receive comfort from any such expectation, she made no answer.

'Well, Lizzy,' continued her mother soon afterwards, 'and so the Collinses live very comfortable, do they? Well, well, I only hope it will last. And what sort of table do they keep? Charlotte is an excellent manager, I dare say. If she is half as sharp as her mother, she is saving enough. There is nothing extravagant in *their* housekeeping, I dare say.'

'No, nothing at all.'

'A great deal of good management, depend upon it. Yes, yes. *They* will take care not to outrun their income. *They* will never be distressed for money. Well, much good may it do them! And so, I suppose, they often talk of having Longbourn when your father is dead. They look upon it quite as their own, I dare say, whenever that happens.'

'It was a subject which they could not mention before me.'

'No. It would have been strange if they had. But I make no doubt, they often talk of it between themselves. Well, if they can be easy with an estate that is not lawfully their own, so much the better. *I* should be ashamed of having one that was only entailed on me.'

The first week of their return was soon gone. The second began. It was the last of the regiment's stay in Meryton, and all the young ladies in the neighbourhood were drooping apace. The dejection was almost universal. The elder Miss Bennets alone were still able to eat, drink, and sleep, and pursue the usual course of their employments. Very frequently were they reproached for this insensibility by Kitty and Lydia, whose own misery was extreme, and who could not comprehend such hard-heartedness in any of the family.

'Good Heaven! What is to become of us! What are we to do!' would they often exclaim in the bitterness of woe. 'How can you be smiling so, Lizzy?' Their affectionate mother shared all their grief; she remembered what she had herself endured on a similar occasion, five and twenty years ago.

'I am sure,' said she, 'I cried for two days together when Colonel Millar's regiment went away. I thought I should have broke my heart.'

'I am sure I shall break *mine*,' said Lydia.

'If one could but go to Brighton!' observed Mrs Bennet.

'Oh, yes! – if one could but go to Brighton! But papa is so disagreeable.'

'A little sea-bathing would set me up forever.'

'And my aunt Philips is sure it would do *me* a great deal of good,' added Kitty.

Such were the kind of lamentations resounding perpetually through Longbourn-house. Elizabeth tried to be diverted by them; but all sense of pleasure was lost in shame. She felt anew the justice of Mr Darcy's objections; and never had she before been so much disposed to pardon his interference in the views of his friend.

But the gloom of Lydia's prospect was shortly cleared away; for she received an invitation from Mrs Forster, the wife of the Colonel of the regiment, to accompany her to Brighton. This invaluable friend was a very young woman, and very lately married. A resemblance in good humour and good spirits had recommended her and Lydia to each other, and out of their *three* months' acquaintance they had been intimate *two*.

The rapture of Lydia on this occasion, her adoration of Mrs Forster, the delight of Mrs Bennet, and the mortification of Kitty, are scarcely to be described. Wholly inattentive to her sister's feelings, Lydia flew about the house in restless ecstacy[24], calling for every one's congratulations, and laughing and talking with more violence than ever; whilst the luckless Kitty continued in the parlour repining at her fate in terms as unreasonable as her accent was peevish.

'I cannot see why Mrs Forster should not ask *me* as well as Lydia,' said she, 'though I am *not* her particular friend. I have just as much right to be asked as she has, and more too, for I am two years older.'

In vain did Elizabeth attempt to make her reasonable, and Jane to make her resigned. As for Elizabeth herself, this invitation was so far from exciting in her the same feelings as in her mother and Lydia, that she considered it as the death-warrant of all possibility of common sense for the latter; and detestable as such a step must make her were it known, she could not help secretly advising her father not to let her go. She represented to him all the improprieties of Lydia's general behaviour, the little advantage she could derive from the friendship of such a woman as Mrs Forster, and the probability of her being yet more imprudent with such a companion at Brighton, where the temptations must be greater than at home. He heard her attentively, and then said,

'Lydia will never be easy till she has exposed herself in some public place or other, and we can never expect her to do it with so little expense or inconvenience to her family as under the present circumstances.'

'If you were aware,' said Elizabeth, 'of the very great disadvantage to us all, which must arise from the public notice of Lydia's unguarded and imprudent manner; nay, which has already arisen from it, I am sure you would judge differently in the affair.'

'Already arisen!' repeated Mr Bennet. 'What, has she frightened away some of your lovers? Poor little Lizzy! But do not be cast down. Such squeamish youths as cannot bear to be connected with a little absurdity, are not worth a regret. Come, let me see the list of the pitiful fellows who have been kept aloof by Lydia's folly.'

'Indeed you are mistaken. I have no such injuries to resent. It is not of peculiar, but of general evils, which I am now complaining. Our importance, our respectability in the world, must be affected by the wild volatility, the assurance and disdain of all restraint which mark Lydia's character. Excuse me – for I must speak plainly. If you, my dear father, will not take the trouble of checking her exuberant spirits, and of teaching her that her present pursuits are not to be the business of her life, she will soon be beyond the reach of amendment. Her character will be fixed, and she will, at sixteen, be the most determined flirt that ever made herself and her family ridiculous. A flirt too, in the worst and meanest degree of flirtation; without any attraction beyond youth and a tolerable person; and from the ignorance and emptiness of her mind, wholly unable to ward off any portion of that universal contempt which her rage for admiration will excite. In this danger Kitty is also comprehended. She will follow wherever Lydia leads. Vain, ignorant, idle, and absolutely uncontrolled! Oh! my dear father, can you suppose it possible that they will not be censured and despised wherever they are known, and that their sisters will not be often involved in the disgrace?'

Mr Bennet saw that her whole heart was in the subject; and affectionately taking her hand, said in reply,

'Do not make yourself uneasy, my love. Whenever you and Jane are known, you must be respected and valued; and you will not appear to less advantage for having a couple of – or I may say, three very silly sisters. We shall have no peace at Longbourn if Lydia does not go to Brighton. Let her go then. Colonel Forster is a sensible man, and will keep her out of any real mischief; and she is luckily too poor to be an object of prey to any body. At Brighton she will be of less importance even as a common flirt than she has been here. The officers will find women better worth their notice. Let us hope, therefore, that her being there may teach her her own insignificance. At any rate, she cannot grow many degrees worse, without authorizing us to lock her up for the rest of her life.'

With this answer Elizabeth was forced to be content; but her own opinion continued the same, and she left him disappointed and sorry. It was not in her nature, however, to increase her vexations, by dwelling on them. She was confident of having performed her duty, and to fret over unavoidable evils, or augment them by anxiety, was no part of her disposition.

Had Lydia and her mother known the substance of her conference with her father, their indignation would hardly have found expression in their united volubility. In Lydia's imagination, a visit to Brighton comprised every possibility of earthly happiness. She saw with the creative eye of fancy, the streets of that gay bathing place covered with officers. She saw herself the object of attention, to tens and to scores of them at present unknown. She saw all the glories of the camp; its tents stretched forth in beauteous uniformity of lines, crowded with the young and the gay, and dazzling with scarlet; and to complete the view, she saw herself seated beneath a tent, tenderly flirting with at least six officers at once.

Had she known that her sister sought to tear her from such prospects and such realities as these, what would have been her sensations? They could have been understood only by her mother, who might have felt nearly the same. Lydia's going to Brighton was all that consoled her for the melancholy conviction of her husband's never intending to go there himself.

But they were entirely ignorant of what had passed; and their raptures continued with little intermission to the very day of Lydia's leaving home.

Elizabeth was now to see Mr Wickham for the last time. Having been frequently in company with him since her return, agitation was pretty well over; the agitations of former partiality entirely so. She had even learnt to detect, in the very gentleness which had first delighted her, an affectation and a sameness to disgust and weary. In his present behaviour to herself, moreover, she had a fresh source of displeasure, for the inclination he soon testified of renewing those attentions which had marked the early part of their acquaintance, could only serve, after what had since passed, to provoke her. She lost all concern for him in finding herself thus selected as the object of such idle and frivolous gallantry; and while she steadily repressed it, could not but feel the reproof contained in his believing, that however long, and for whatever

cause, his attentions had been withdrawn, her vanity would be gratified and her preference secured at any time by their renewal.

On the very last day of the regiment's remaining in Meryton, he dined with others of the officers at Longbourn; and so little was Elizabeth disposed to part from him in good humour, that on his making some enquiry as to the manner in which her time had passed at Hunsford, she mentioned Colonel Fitzwilliam's and Mr Darcy's having both spent three weeks at Rosings, and asked him if he were acquainted with the former.

He looked surprised, displeased, alarmed; but with a moment's recollection and a returning smile, replied, that he had formerly seen him often; and after observing that he was a very gentlemanlike man, asked her how she had liked him. Her answer was warmly in his favour. With an air of indifference he soon afterwards added, 'How long did you say that he was at Rosings?'

'Nearly three weeks.'

'And you saw him frequently?'

'Yes, almost every day.'

'His manners are very different from his cousin's.'

'Yes, very different. But I think Mr Darcy improves on acquaintance.'

'Indeed!' cried Wickham with a look which did not escape her. 'And pray may I ask?' but checking himself, he added in a gayer tone, 'Is it in address that he improves? Has he deigned to add ought of civility to his ordinary style? for I dare not hope,' he continued in a lower and more serious tone, 'that he is improved in essentials.'

'Oh, no!' said Elizabeth. 'In essentials, I believe, he is very much what he ever was.'

While she spoke, Wickham looked as if scarcely knowing whether to rejoice over her words, or to distrust their meaning. There was a something in her countenance which made him listen with an apprehensive and anxious attention, while she added,

'When I said that he improved on acquaintance, I did not mean that either his mind or manners were in a state of improvement, but that from knowing him better, his disposition was better understood.'

Wickham's alarm now appeared in a heightened complexion and agitated look; for a few minutes he was silent; till, shaking off his embarrassment, he turned to her again, and said in the gentlest of accents,

'You, who so well know my feelings towards Mr Darcy, will readily comprehend how sincerely I must rejoice that he is wise enough to assume even the *appearance* of what is right. His pride, in that direction, may be of service, if not to himself, to many others, for it must deter him from such foul misconduct as I have suffered by. I only fear that the sort of cautiousness, to which you, I imagine, have been alluding, is merely adopted on his visits to his aunt, of whose good opinion and judgment he stands much in awe. His fear of her, has always operated, I know, when they were together; and a good deal is to be imputed to his wish of forwarding the match with Miss De Bourgh, which I am certain he has very much at heart.'

Elizabeth could not repress a smile at this, but she answered only by a slight inclination of the head. She saw that he wanted to engage her on the old subject of his grievances, and she was in no humour to indulge him. The rest of the evening passed with the *appearance*, on his side, of usual cheerfulness, but with no farther attempt to distinguish Elizabeth; and they parted at last with mutual civility, and possibly a mutual desire of never meeting again.

When the party broke up, Lydia returned with Mrs Forster to Meryton, from whence[25] they were to set out early the next morning. The separation between her and her family was rather noisy than pathetic. Kitty was the only one who shed tears; but she did weep from vexation and envy. Mrs Bennet was diffuse in her good wishes for the felicity of her daughter, and impressive in her injunctions that she would not miss the opportunity of enjoying herself as much as possible; advice, which there was every reason to believe would be attended to; and in the clamorous happiness of Lydia herself in bidding farewell, the more gentle adieus of her sisters were uttered without being heard.

Chapter 42

Had Elizabeth's opinion been all drawn from her own family, she could not have formed a very pleasing picture of conjugal felicity or domestic comfort. Her father captivated by youth and beauty, and that appearance of good humour, which youth and beauty generally give, had married a woman whose weak understanding and illiberal mind, had very early in their marriage put an end to all real affection for her. Respect, esteem, and confidence, had vanished forever; and all his views of domestic happiness were overthrown. But Mr Bennet was not of a disposition to seek comfort for the disappointment which his own imprudence had brought on, in any of those pleasures which too often console the unfortunate for their folly or their vice. He was fond of the country and of books; and from these tastes had arisen his principal enjoyments. To his wife he was very little otherwise indebted, than as her ignorance and folly had contributed to his amusement. This is not the sort of happiness which a man would in general wish to owe to his wife; but where other powers of entertainment are wanting, the true philosopher will derive benefit from such as are given.

Elizabeth, however, had never been blind to the impropriety of her father's behaviour as a husband. She had always seen it with pain; but respecting his abilities, and grateful for his affectionate treatment of herself, she endeavoured to forget what she could not overlook, and to banish from her thoughts that continual breach of conjugal obligation and decorum which, in exposing his wife to the contempt of her own children, was so highly reprehensible. But she had never felt so strongly as now, the disadvantages which must attend the children of so unsuitable a marriage, nor ever been so fully aware of the evils arising from so ill-judged a direction of talents; talents which rightly used, might at least have preserved the respectability of his daughters, even if incapable of enlarging the mind of his wife.

When Elizabeth had rejoiced over Wickham's departure, she found little other cause for satisfaction in the loss of the regiment. Their parties abroad were less varied than before; and at home she had a mother and sister whose constant repinings at the dullness of every thing around them, threw a real gloom over their domestic circle; and, though Kitty might in time regain her natural degree of sense, since the disturbers of her brain were removed, her other sister, from whose disposition greater evil might be apprehended, was likely to be hardened in all her folly and assurance, by a situation of such double danger as a watering place and a camp. Upon the whole, therefore, she found, what has been sometimes found before, that an event to which she had looked forward with impatient desire, did not in taking place, bring all the satisfaction she had promised herself. It was consequently necessary to name some other period for the commencement of actual felicity; to have some other point on which her wishes and hopes might be fixed, and by again enjoying the pleasure of anticipation, console herself for the present, and prepare for another disappointment. Her tour to the Lakes was now the object of her happiest thoughts; it was her best consolation for all the uncomfortable hours, which the discontentedness of her mother and Kitty made inevitable; and could she have included Jane in the scheme, every part of it would have been perfect.

'But it is fortunate,' thought she, 'that I have something to wish for. Were the whole arrangement complete, my disappointment would be certain. But here, by carrying with me one ceaseless source of regret in my sister's absence, I may reasonably hope to have all my expectations of pleasure realized. A scheme of which every part promises delight, can never be successful; and general disappointment is only warded off by the defence of some little peculiar vexation.'

When Lydia went away, she promised to write very often and very minutely to her mother and Kitty; but her letters were always long expected, and always very short. Those to her mother, contained little else, than that they were just returned from the library, where such and such officers had attended them, and where she had seen such beautiful ornaments as made her quite wild; that she had a new gown, or a new parasol, which she would have described more fully, but was obliged to leave off in a violent hurry, as Mrs Forster called her, and they were going to the camp; – and from her correspondence with her sister, there was still less to be learnt – for her letters to Kitty, though rather longer, were much too full of lines under the words to be made public.

After the first fortnight or three weeks of her absence, health, good humour and cheerfulness began to re-appear at Longbourn. Everything wore a happier aspect. The families who had been in town for the winter came back again, and summer finery and summer engagements arose. Mrs Bennet was restored to her usual querulous serenity, and by the middle of June Kitty was so much recovered as to be able to enter Meryton without tears; an event of such happy promise as to make Elizabeth hope, that by the following Christmas, she might be so tolerably reasonable as not to mention an officer above once a day, unless by some cruel and malicious arrangement at the war-office, another regiment should be quartered in Meryton.

The time fixed for the beginning of their Northern tour was now fast approaching; and a fortnight only was wanting of it, when a letter arrived from Mrs Gardiner, which at once delayed its commencement and curtailed its extent. Mr Gardiner would be prevented by business from setting out till a fortnight later in July, and must be in London again within a month; and as that left too short a period for them to go so far, and see so much as they had proposed, or at least to see it with the leisure and comfort they had built on, they were obliged to give up the Lakes, and substitute a more contracted tour; and, according to the present plan, were to go no farther northward than Derbyshire. In that county, there was enough to be seen, to occupy the chief of their three weeks; and to Mrs Gardiner it had a peculiarly strong attraction. The town where she had formerly passed some years of her life, and where they were now to spend a few days, was probably as great an object of her curiosity, as all the celebrated beauties of Matlock, Chatsworth, Dovedale, or the Peak.

Elizabeth was excessively disappointed; she had set her heart on seeing the Lakes; and still thought there might have been time enough. But it was her business to be satisfied – and certainly her temper to be happy; and all was soon right again.

With the mention of Derbyshire, there were many ideas connected. It was impossible for her to see the word without thinking of Pemberley and its owner. 'But surely,' said she, 'I may enter his county with impunity, and rob it of a few petrified spars without his perceiving me.'

The period of expectation was now doubled. Four weeks were to pass away before her uncle and aunt's arrival. But they did pass away, and Mr and Mrs Gardiner, with their four children, did at length appear at Longbourn. The children, two girls of six and eight years old, and two younger boys, were to be left under the particular care of their cousin Jane, who was the general favourite, and whose steady sense and sweetness of temper exactly adapted her for attending to them in every way – teaching them, playing with them, and loving them.

The Gardiners staid only one night at Longbourn, and set off the next morning with Elizabeth in pursuit of novelty and amusement. One enjoyment was certain – that of suitableness as companions; a

suitableness which comprehended health and temper to bear inconveniences – cheerfulness to enhance every pleasure – and affection and intelligence, which might supply it among themselves if there were disappointments abroad.

It is not the object of this work to give a description of Derbyshire, nor of any of the remarkable places through which their route thither lay; Oxford, Blenheim, Warwick, Kenelworth, Birmingham, &c. are sufficiently known. A small part of Derbyshire is all the present concern. To the little town of Lambton, the scene of Mrs Gardiner's former residence, and where she had lately learned that some acquaintance still remained, they bent their steps, after having seen all the principal wonders of the country; and within five miles of Lambton, Elizabeth found from her aunt, that Pemberley was situated. It was not in their direct road, nor more than a mile or two out of it. In talking over their route the evening before, Mrs Gardiner expressed an inclination to see the place again. Mr Gardiner declared his willingness, and Elizabeth was applied to for her approbation.

'My love, should not you like to see a place of which you have heard so much?' said her aunt. 'A place too, with which so many of your acquaintance are connected. Wickham passed all his youth there, you know.'

Elizabeth was distressed. She felt that she had no business at Pemberley, and was obliged to assume a disinclination for seeing it. She must own that she was tired of great houses; after going over so many, she really had no pleasure in fine carpets or satin curtains.

Mrs Gardiner abused her stupidity. 'If it were merely a fine house richly furnished,' said she, 'I should not care about it myself; but the grounds are delightful. They have some of the finest woods in the country.'

Elizabeth said no more – but her mind could not acquiesce. The possibility of meeting Mr Darcy, while viewing the place, instantly occurred. It would be dreadful! She blushed at the very idea; and thought it would be better to speak openly to her aunt, than to run such a risk. But against this, there were objections; and she finally resolved that it could be the last resource, if her private enquiries as to the absence of the family, were unfavourably answered.

Accordingly, when she retired at night, she asked the chambermaid whether Pemberley were not a very fine place, what was the name of its proprietor, and with no little alarm, whether the family were down for the summer. A most welcome negative followed the last question – and her alarms being now removed, she was at leisure to feel a great deal of curiosity to see the house herself; and when the subject was revived the next morning, and she was again applied to, could readily answer, and with a proper air of indifference, that she had not really any dislike to the scheme.

To Pemberley, therefore, they were to go.

Chapter 43

Elizabeth, as they drove along, watched for the first appearance of Pemberley Woods with some perturbation; and when at length they turned in at the lodge, her spirits were in a high flutter.

The park was very large, and contained great variety of ground. They entered it in one of its lowest points, and drove for some time through a beautiful wood, stretching over a wide extent.

Elizabeth's mind was too full for conversation, but she saw and admired every remarkable spot and point of view. They gradually ascended for half a mile, and then found themselves at the top of a considerable eminence, where the wood ceased, and the eye was instantly caught by Pemberley House, situated on the opposite side of a valley, into which the road with some abruptness wound. It was a large, handsome, stone building, standing well on rising ground, and backed by a ridge of high woody hills; – and in front, a stream of some natural importance was swelled into greater, but without any artificial appearance. Its banks were neither formal, nor falsely adorned. Elizabeth was delighted. She had never seen a place for which nature had done more, or where natural beauty had been so little counteracted by an awkward taste. They were all of them warm in their admiration; and at that moment she felt, that to be mistress of Pemberley might be something!

They descended the hill, crossed the bridge, and drove to the door; and, while examining the nearer aspect of the house, all her apprehensions of meeting its owner returned. She dreaded lest the chambermaid had been mistaken. On applying to see the place, they were admitted into the hall; and Elizabeth, as they waited for the housekeeper, had leisure to wonder at her being where she was.

The housekeeper came; a respectable-looking, elderly woman, much less fine, and more civil, than she had any notion of finding her. They followed her into the dining-parlour. It was a large, well-proportioned room, handsomely fitted up. Elizabeth, after slightly surveying it, went to a window to enjoy its prospect. The hill, crowned with wood, from which they had descended, receiving increased abruptness from the distance, was a beautiful object. Every disposition of the ground was good; and she looked on the whole scene, the river, the trees scattered on its banks, and the winding of the valley, as far as she could trace it, with delight. As they passed into other rooms, these objects were taking different positions; but from every window there were beauties to be seen. The rooms were lofty and handsome, and their furniture suitable to the fortune of their proprietor; but Elizabeth saw, with admiration of his taste, that it was neither gaudy nor uselessly fine; with less of splendor, and more real elegance, than the furniture of Rosings.

'And of this place,' thought she, 'I might have been mistress! With these rooms I might now have been familiarly acquainted! Instead of viewing them as a stranger, I might have rejoiced in them as my own, and welcomed to them as visitors my uncle and aunt. – But no,' – recollecting herself, – 'that could never be: my uncle and aunt would have been lost to me: I should not have been allowed to invite them.'

This was a lucky recollection – it saved her from something like regret.

She longed to enquire of the housekeeper, whether her master were really absent, but had not courage for it. At length, however, the question was asked by her uncle; and she turned away with alarm, while Mrs Reynolds replied, that he was, adding, 'but we expect him tomorrow, with a large party of friends.' How rejoiced was Elizabeth that their own journey had not by any circumstance been delayed a day!

Her aunt now called her to look at a picture. She approached, and saw the likeness of Mr Wickham suspended, amongst several other miniatures, over the mantelpiece. Her aunt asked her, smilingly, how she liked it. The housekeeper came forward, and told them it was the picture of a young gentleman, the son of her late master's steward, who had been brought up by him at his own expense. – 'He is now gone into the army,' she added, 'but I am afraid he has turned out very wild.'

Mrs Gardiner looked at her niece with a smile, but Elizabeth could not return it.

'And that,' said Mrs Reynolds, pointing to another of the miniatures, 'is my master – and very like him. It was drawn at the same time as the other – about eight years ago.'

'I have heard much of your master's fine person,' said Mrs Gardiner, looking at the picture; 'it is a handsome face. But, Lizzy, you can tell us whether it is like or not.'

Mrs Reynolds's respect for Elizabeth seemed to increase on this intimation of her knowing her master.

'Does that young lady know Mr Darcy?'

Elizabeth coloured, and said – 'A little.'

'And do not you think him a very handsome gentleman, Ma'am?'

'Yes, very handsome.'

'I am sure *I* know none so handsome; but in the gallery up stairs you will see a finer, larger picture of him than this. This room was my late master's favourite room, and these miniatures are just as they used to be then. He was very fond of them.'

This accounted to Elizabeth for Mr Wickham's being among them.

Mrs Reynolds then directed their attention to one of Miss Darcy, drawn when she was only eight years old.

'And is Miss Darcy as handsome as her brother?' said Mr Gardiner.

'Oh! yes – the handsomest young lady that ever was seen; and so accomplished! – She plays and sings all day long. In the next room is a new instrument just come down for her – a present from my master; she comes here tomorrow with him.'

Mr Gardiner, whose manners were easy and pleasant, encouraged her communicativeness by his questions and remarks; Mrs Reynolds, either from pride or attachment, had evidently great pleasure in talking of her master and his sister.

'Is your master much at Pemberley in the course of the year?'

'Not so much as I could wish, Sir; but I dare say he may spend half his time here; and Miss Darcy is always down for the summer months.'

'Except,' thought Elizabeth, 'when she goes to Ramsgate.'

'If your master would marry, you might see more of him.'

'Yes, Sir; but I do not know when *that* will be. I do not know who is good enough for him.'

Mr and Mrs Gardiner smiled. Elizabeth could not help saying, 'It is very much to his credit, I am sure, that you should think so.'

'I say no more than the truth, and what every body will say that knows him,' replied the other. Elizabeth thought this was going pretty far; and she listened with increasing astonishment as the housekeeper added, 'I have never had a cross word from him in my life, and I have known him ever since he was four years old.'

This was praise, of all others most extraordinary, most opposite to her ideas. That he was not a good-tempered man, had been her firmest opinion. Her keenest attention was awakened; she longed to hear more, and was grateful to her uncle for saying,

'There are very few people of whom so much can be said. You are lucky in having such a master.'

'Yes, Sir, I know I am. If I was to go through the world, I could not meet with a better. But I have always observed, that they who are good-natured when children, are good-natured when they grow up; and he was always the sweetest-tempered, most generous-hearted, boy in the world.'

Elizabeth almost stared at her. – 'Can this be Mr Darcy!' thought she.

'His father was an excellent man,' said Mrs Gardiner.

'Yes, Ma'am, that he was indeed; and his son will be just like him – just as affable to the poor.'

Elizabeth listened, wondered, doubted, and was impatient for more. Mrs Reynolds could interest her on no other point. She related the subject of the pictures, the dimensions of the rooms, and the price of the furniture, in vain. Mr Gardiner, highly amused by the kind of family prejudice, to which he attributed her excessive commendation of her master, soon led again to the subject; and she dwelt with energy on his many merits, as they proceeded together up the great staircase.

'He is the best landlord, and the best master,' said she, 'that ever lived. Not like the wild young men nowadays, who think of nothing but themselves. There is not one of his tenants or servants but what will give him a good name. Some people call him proud; but I am sure I never saw any thing of it. To my fancy, it is only because he does not rattle away like other young men.'

'In what an amiable light does this place him!' thought Elizabeth.

'This fine account of him,' whispered her aunt, as they walked, 'is not quite consistent with his behaviour to our poor friend.'

'Perhaps we might be deceived.'

'That is not very likely; our authority was too good.'

On reaching the spacious lobby above, they were shown into a very pretty sitting-room, lately fitted up with greater elegance and lightness than the apartments below; and were informed that it was but just done, to give pleasure to Miss Darcy, who had taken a liking to the room, when last at Pemberley.

'He is certainly a good brother,' said Elizabeth, as she walked towards one of the windows.

Mrs Reynolds anticipated Miss Darcy's delight, when she should enter the room. 'And this is always the way with him,' she added. – 'Whatever can give his sister any pleasure, is sure to be done in a moment. There is nothing he would not do for her.'

The picture gallery, and two or three of the principal bed-rooms, were all that remained to be shown. In the former were many good paintings; but Elizabeth knew nothing of the art; and from such as had been already visible below, she had willingly turned to look at some drawings of Miss Darcy's, in crayons, whose subjects were usually more interesting, and also more intelligible.

In the gallery there were many family portraits, but they could have little to fix the attention of a stranger. Elizabeth walked on in quest of the only face whose features would be known to her. At last it arrested her – and she beheld a striking resemblance of Mr Darcy, with such a smile over the face, as she remembered to have sometimes seen, when he looked at her. She stood several minutes before the picture in earnest contemplation, and returned to it again before they quitted the gallery. Mrs Reynolds informed them, that it had been taken in his father's life time.

There was certainly at this moment, in Elizabeth's mind, a more gentle sensation towards the original, than she had ever felt in the height of their acquaintance. The commendation bestowed on him by Mrs Reynolds was of no trifling nature. What praise is more valuable than the praise of an intelligent servant? As a brother, a landlord, a master, she considered how many people's happiness were in his guardianship! – How much of pleasure or pain it was in his power to bestow! – How much of good or evil must be done by him! Every idea that had been brought forward by the housekeeper was favourable to his character, and as she stood before the canvas, on which he was represented, and fixed his eyes upon herself, she thought of his regard with a deeper sentiment of gratitude than it had ever raised before; she remembered its warmth, and softened its impropriety of expression.

When all of the house that was open to general inspection had been seen, they returned down stairs, and taking leave of the housekeeper, were consigned over to the gardener, who met them at the hall door.

As they walked across the lawn towards the river, Elizabeth turned back to look again; her uncle and aunt stopped also, and while the former was conjecturing as to the date of the building, the owner of it himself suddenly came forward from the road, which led behind it to the stables.

They were within twenty yards of each other, and so abrupt was his appearance, that it was impossible to avoid his sight. Their eyes instantly met, and the cheeks of each were overspread with the deepest blush. He absolutely started, and for a moment seemed immoveable from surprise; but shortly recovering himself, advanced towards the party, and spoke to Elizabeth, if not in terms of perfect composure, at least of perfect civility.

She had instinctively turned away; but, stopping on his approach, received his compliments with an embarrassment impossible to be overcome. Had his first appearance, or his resemblance to the picture they had just been examining, been insufficient to assure the other two that they now saw Mr Darcy, the gardener's expression of surprise, on beholding his master, must immediately have told it. They stood a little aloof while he was talking to their niece, who, astonished and confused, scarcely dared lift her eyes to his face, and knew not what answer she returned to his civil enquiries after her family. Amazed at the alteration in his manner since they last parted, every sentence that he uttered was increasing her embarrassment; and every idea of the impropriety of her being found there, recurring to her mind, the few minutes in which they continued together, were some of the most uncomfortable of her life. Nor did he seem much more at ease; when he spoke, his accent had none of its usual sedateness; and he repeated his enquiries as to the time of her having left Longbourn, and of her stay in Derbyshire, so often, and in so hurried a way, as plainly spoke the distraction of his thoughts.

At length, every idea seemed to fail him; and, after standing a few moments without saying a word, he suddenly recollected himself, and took leave.

The others then joined her, and expressed their admiration of his figure; but Elizabeth heard not a word, and, wholly engrossed by her own feelings, followed them in silence. She was overpowered by shame and vexation. Her coming there was the most unfortunate, the most ill-judged thing in the world! How strange must it appear to him! In what a disgraceful light might it not strike so vain a man! It might seem as if she had purposely thrown herself in his way again! Oh! why did she come? or, why did he thus come a day before he was expected? Had they been only ten minutes sooner, they should have been beyond the reach of his discrimination, for it was plain that he was that moment arrived, that moment alighted from his horse or his carriage. She blushed again and again over the perverseness of the meeting. And his behaviour, so strikingly altered, – what could it mean? That he should even speak to her was amazing! – but to speak with such civility, to enquire after her family! Never in her life had she seen his manners so little dignified, never had he spoken with such gentleness as on this unexpected meeting. What a contrast did it offer to his last address in Rosing's Park, when he put his letter into her hand! She knew not what to think, nor how to account for it.

They had now entered a beautiful walk by the side of the water, and every step was bringing forward a nobler fall of ground, or a finer reach of the woods to which they were approaching; but it was some time before Elizabeth was sensible of any of it; and, though she answered mechanically to the repeated appeals of her uncle and aunt, and seemed to direct her eyes to such objects as they pointed out, she distinguished no part of the scene. Her thoughts were all fixed on that one spot of Pemberley House, whichever it might be, where Mr Darcy then was. She longed to know what at that moment was passing in his mind; in what manner he thought of her, and whether, in defiance of every thing, she was still dear to him. Perhaps he had been civil, only because he felt himself at ease; yet there had been *that* in his voice, which was not like ease. Whether he had felt more of pain or of pleasure in seeing her, she could not tell, but he certainly had not seen her with composure.

At length, however, the remarks of her companions on her absence of mind roused her, and she felt the necessity of appearing more like herself.

They entered the woods, and bidding adieu to the river for a while, ascended some of the higher grounds; whence, in spots where the opening of the trees gave the eye power to wander, were many charming views of the valley, the opposite hills, with the long range of woods overspreading many, and occasionally part of the stream. Mr Gardiner expressed a wish of going round the whole Park, but feared it might be beyond a walk. With a triumphant smile, they were told, that it was ten miles round. It settled the matter; and they pursued the accustomed circuit; which brought them again, after some time, in a descent among hanging woods, to the edge of the water, in one of its narrowest parts. They crossed it by a simple bridge, in character with the general air of the scene; it was a spot less adorned than any they had yet visited; and the valley, here contracted into a glen, allowed room only for the stream, and a narrow walk amidst the rough coppice-wood which bordered it. Elizabeth longed to explore its windings; but when they had crossed the bridge, and perceived their distance from the house, Mrs Gardiner, who was not a great walker, could go no farther, and thought only of returning to the carriage as quickly as possible. Her niece was, therefore, obliged to submit, and they took their way towards the house on the opposite side of the river, in the nearest direction; but their progress was slow, for Mr Gardiner, though seldom able to indulge the taste, was very fond of fishing, and was so much engaged in watching the occasional appearance of some trout in the water, and talking to the man about them, that he advanced but little. Whilst wandering on in this slow manner, they were again surprised, and Elizabeth's astonishment was quite equal to what it had been at first, by the sight of Mr Darcy approaching them, and at no great distance. The walk being here less sheltered than on the other side, allowed them to see him before they met. Elizabeth, however astonished, was at least more prepared for an interview than before, and resolved to appear and to speak with calmness, if he really intended to meet them. For a few moments, indeed, she felt that he would probably strike into some other path. This idea lasted while a turning in the walk concealed him from their view; the turning past, he was immediately before them. With a glance she saw, that he had lost none of his recent civility; and, to imitate his politeness, she began, as they met, to admire the beauty of the place; but she had not got beyond the words 'delightful,' and 'charming,' when some unlucky recollections obtruded, and she fancied that praise of Pemberley from her, might be mischievously construed. Her colour changed, and she said no more.

Mrs Gardiner was standing a little behind; and on her pausing, he asked her, if she would do him the honour of introducing him to her friends. This was a stroke of civility for which she was quite unprepared; and she could hardly suppress a smile, at his being now seeking the acquaintance of some of those very people, against whom his pride had revolted, in his offer to herself. 'What will be his surprise,' thought she, 'when he knows who they are! He takes them now for people of fashion.'

The introduction, however, was immediately made; and as she named their relationship to herself, she stole a sly look at him, to see how he bore it; and was not without the expectation of his decamping as fast as he could from such disgraceful companions. That he was *surprised* by the connexion[26] was evident; he sustained it however with fortitude, and so far from going away, turned back with them, and entered into conversation with Mr Gardiner. Elizabeth could not but be pleased, could not but triumph. It was consoling, that he should know she had some relations for whom there was no need to blush. She listened most attentively to all that passed between them, and gloried in every expression, every sentence of her uncle, which marked his intelligence, his taste, or his good manners.

The conversation soon turned upon fishing, and she heard Mr Darcy invite him, with the greatest civility, to fish there as often as he chose, while he continued in the neighbourhood, offering at the same time to supply him with fishing tackle, and pointing out those parts of the stream where there was usually most sport. Mrs Gardiner, who was walking arm in arm with Elizabeth, gave her a look expressive of her wonder. Elizabeth said nothing, but it gratified her exceedingly; the compliment must be all for herself. Her astonishment, however, was extreme; and continually was she repeating, 'Why is he so altered? From what can it proceed? It cannot be for *me*, it cannot be for *my* sake that his manners are thus softened. My reproofs at Hunsford could not work such a change as this. It is impossible that he should still love me.'

After walking some time in this way, the two ladies in front, the two gentlemen behind, on resuming their places, after descending to the brink of the river for the better inspection of some curious water-plant, there chanced to be a little alteration. It originated in Mrs Gardiner, who, fatigued by the exercise of the morning, found Elizabeth's arm inadequate to her support, and consequently preferred her husband's. Mr Darcy took her place by her niece, and they walked on together. After a short silence, the lady first spoke. She wished him to know that she had been assured of his absence before she came to the place, and accordingly began by observing, that his arrival had been very unexpected – 'for your housekeeper,' she added, 'informed us that you would certainly not be here till tomorrow; and indeed, before we left Bakewell, we understood that you were not immediately expected in the country.' He acknowledged the truth of it all; and said that business with his steward had occasioned his coming forward a few hours before the rest of the party with whom he had been travelling. 'They will join me early tomorrow,' he continued, 'and among them are some who will claim an acquaintance with you, – Mr Bingley and his sisters.'

Elizabeth answered only by a slight bow. Her thoughts were instantly driven back to the time when Mr Bingley's name had been last mentioned between them; and if she might judge from his complexion, *his* mind was not very differently engaged.

'There is also one other person in the party,' he continued after a pause, 'who more particularly wishes to be known to you, – Will you allow me, or do I ask too much, to introduce my sister to your acquaintance during your stay at Lambton?'

The surprise of such an application was great indeed; it was too great for her to know in what manner she acceded to it. She immediately felt that whatever desire Miss Darcy might have of being acquainted with her, must be the work of her brother, and without looking farther, it was satisfactory; it was gratifying to know that his resentment had not made him think really ill of her.

They now walked on in silence; each of them deep in thought. Elizabeth was not comfortable; that was impossible; but she was flattered and pleased. His wish of introducing his sister to her, was a compliment of the highest kind. They soon outstripped the others, and when they had reached the carriage, Mr and Mrs Gardiner were half a quarter of a mile behind.

He then asked her to walk into the house – but she declared

herself not tired, and they stood together on the lawn. At such a time, much might have been said, and silence was very awkward. She wanted to talk, but there seemed an embargo on every subject. At last she recollected that she had been travelling, and they talked of Matlock and Dove Dale with great perseverance. Yet time and her aunt moved slowly – and her patience and her ideas were nearly worn out before the tête-à-tête was over. On Mr and Mrs Gardiner's coming up, they were all pressed to go into the house and take some refreshment; but this was declined, and they parted on each side with the utmost politeness. Mr Darcy handed the ladies into the carriage, and when it drove off, Elizabeth saw him walking slowly towards the house.

The observations of her uncle and aunt now began; and each of them pronounced him to be infinitely superior to any thing they had expected. 'He is perfectly well behaved, polite, and unassuming,' said her uncle.

'There *is* something a little stately in him to be sure,' replied her aunt, 'but it is confined to his air, and is not unbecoming. I can now say with the housekeeper, that though some people may call him proud, *I* have seen nothing of it.'

'I was never more surprised than by his behaviour to us. It was more than civil; it was really attentive; and there was no necessity for such attention. His acquaintance with Elizabeth was very trifling.'

'To be sure, Lizzy,' said her aunt, 'he is not so handsome as Wickham; or rather he has not Wickham's countenance, for his features are perfectly good. But how come you to tell us that he was so disagreeable?'

Elizabeth excused herself as well as she could; said that she had liked him better when they met in Kent than before, and that she had never seen him so pleasant as this morning.

'But perhaps he may be a little whimsical in his civilities,' replied her uncle. 'Your great men often are; and therefore I shall not take him at his word about fishing, as he might change his mind another day, and warn me off his grounds.'

Elizabeth felt that they had entirely mistaken his character, but said nothing.

'From what we have seen of him,' continued Mrs Gardiner, 'I really should not have thought that he could have behaved in so cruel a way by any body, as he has done by poor Wickham. He has not an ill-natured look. On the contrary, there is something pleasing about his mouth when he speaks. And there is something of dignity in his countenance, that would not give one an unfavourable idea of his heart. But to be sure, the good lady who showed us the house, did give him a most flaming character! I could hardly help laughing aloud sometimes. But he is a liberal master, I suppose, and *that* in the eye of a servant comprehends every virtue.'

Elizabeth here felt herself called on to say something in vindication of his behaviour to Wickham; and therefore gave them to understand, in as guarded a manner as she could, that by what she had heard from his relations in Kent, his actions were capable of a very different construction; and that his character was by no means so faulty, nor Wickham's so amiable, as they had been considered in Hertfordshire. In confirmation of this, she related the particulars of all the pecuniary transactions in which they had been connected, without actually naming her authority, but stating it to be such as might be relied on.

Mrs Gardiner was surprised and concerned; but as they were now approaching the scene of her former pleasures, every idea gave way to the charm of recollection; and she was too much engaged in pointing out to her husband all the interesting spots in its environs, to think of any thing else. Fatigued as she had been by the morning's walk, they had no sooner dined than she set off again in quest of her former acquaintance, and the evening was spent in the satisfactions of an intercourse renewed after many years discontinuance.

The occurrences of the day were too full of interest to leave Elizabeth much attention for any of these new friends; and she could do nothing but think, and think with wonder, of Mr Darcy's civility, and above all, of his wishing her to be acquainted with his sister.

Chapter 44

Elizabeth had settled it that Mr Darcy would bring his sister to visit her, the very day after her reaching Pemberley; and was consequently resolved not to be out of sight of the inn the whole of that morning. But her conclusion was false; for on the very morning after their own arrival at Lambton, these visitors came. They had been walking about the place with some of their new friends, and were just returned to the inn to dress themselves for dining with the same family, when the sound of a carriage drew them to a window, and they saw a gentleman and lady in a curricle, driving up the street. Elizabeth immediately recognising the livery, guessed what it meant, and imparted no small degree of surprise to her relations, by acquainting them with the honour which she expected. Her uncle and aunt were all amazement; and the embarrassment of her manner as she spoke, joined to the circumstance itself, and many of the circumstances of the preceding day, opened to them a new idea on the business. Nothing had ever suggested it before, but they now felt that there was no other way of accounting for such attentions from such a quarter, than by supposing a partiality for their niece. While these newly-born notions were passing in their heads, the perturbation of Elizabeth's feelings was every moment increasing. She was quite amazed at her own discomposure; but amongst other causes of disquiet, she dreaded lest the partiality of the brother should have said too much in her favour; and more than commonly anxious to please, she naturally suspected that every power of pleasing would fail her.

She retreated from the window, fearful of being seen; and as she walked up and down the room, endeavouring to compose herself, saw such looks of enquiring surprise in her uncle and aunt, as made every thing worse.

Miss Darcy and her brother appeared, and this formidable introduction took place. With astonishment did Elizabeth see, that her

new acquaintance was at least as much embarrassed as herself. Since her being at Lambton, she had heard that Miss Darcy was exceedingly proud; but the observation of a very few minutes convinced her, that she was only exceedingly shy. She found it difficult to obtain even a word from her beyond a monosyllable.

Miss Darcy was tall, and on a larger scale than Elizabeth; and, though little more than sixteen, her figure was formed, and her appearance womanly and graceful. She was less handsome than her brother, but there was sense and good humour in her face, and her manners were perfectly unassuming and gentle. Elizabeth, who had expected to find in her as acute and unembarrassed an observer as ever Mr Darcy had been, was much relieved by discerning such different feelings.

They had not been long together, before Darcy told her that Bingley was also coming to wait on her; and she had barely time to express her satisfaction, and prepare for such a visitor, when Bingley's quick step was heard on the stairs, and in a moment he entered the room. All Elizabeth's anger against him had been long done away; but, had she still felt any, it could hardly have stood its ground against the unaffected cordiality with which he expressed himself, on seeing her again. He enquired in a friendly, though general way, after her family, and looked and spoke with the same good-humoured ease that he had ever done.

To Mr and Mrs Gardiner he was scarcely a less interesting personage than to herself. They had long wished to see him. The whole party before them, indeed, excited a lively attention. The suspicions which had just arisen of Mr Darcy and their niece, directed their observation towards each with an earnest, though guarded, enquiry; and they soon drew from those enquiries the full conviction that one of them at least knew what it was to love. Of the lady's sensations they remained a little in doubt; but that the gentleman was overflowing with admiration was evident enough.

Elizabeth, on her side, had much to do. She wanted to ascertain the feelings of each of her visitors, she wanted to compose her own, and to make herself agreeable to all; and in the latter object, where she feared most to fail, she was most sure of success, for those to whom she endeavoured to give pleasure were prepossessed in her favour. Bingley was ready, Georgiana was eager, and Darcy determined, to be pleased.

In seeing Bingley, her thoughts naturally flew to her sister; and oh! how ardently did she long to know, whether any of his were directed in a like manner. Sometimes she could fancy, that he talked less than

on former occasions, and once or twice pleased herself with the notion that as he looked at her, he was trying to trace a resemblance. But, though this might be imaginary, she could not be deceived as to his behavior to Miss Darcy, who had been set up as a rival of Jane. No look appeared on either side that spoke particular regard. Nothing occurred between them that could justify the hopes of his sister. On this point she was soon satisfied; and two or three little circumstances occurred ere they parted, which, in her anxious interpretation, denoted a recollection of Jane, not untinctured by tenderness, and a wish of saying more that might lead to the mention of her, had he dared. He observed to her, at a moment when the others were talking together, and in a tone which had something of real regret, that it 'was a very long time since he had had the pleasure of seeing her;' and, before she could reply, he added, 'It is above eight months. We have not met since the 26th of November, when we were all dancing together at Netherfield.'

Elizabeth was pleased to find his memory so exact; and he afterwards took occasion to ask her, when unattended to by any of the rest, whether *all* her sisters were at Longbourn. There was not much in the question, nor in the preceding remark, but there was a look and a manner which gave them meaning.

It was not often that she could turn her eyes on Mr Darcy himself; but, whenever she did catch a glimpse, she saw an expression of general complaisance, and in all that he said, she heard an accent so far removed from hauteur or disdain of his companions, as convinced her that the improvement of manners which she had yesterday witnessed, however temporary its existence might prove, had at least outlived one day. When she saw him thus seeking the acquaintance, and courting the good opinion of people, with whom any intercourse a few months ago would have been a disgrace; when she saw him thus civil, not only to herself, but to the very relations whom he had openly disdained, and recollected their last lively scene in Hunsford Parsonage, the difference, the change was so great, and struck so forcibly on her mind, that she could hardly restrain her astonishment from being visible.

Never, even in the company of his dear friends at Netherfield, or his dignified relations at Rosings, had she seen him so desirous to please, so free from self-consequence, or unbending reserve as now, when no importance could result from the success of his endeavours, and when even the acquaintance of those to whom his attentions were addressed, would draw down the ridicule and censure of the ladies both of Netherfield and Rosings.

Their visitors staid with them above half an hour, and when they arose to depart, Mr Darcy called on his sister to join him in expressing their wish of seeing Mr and Mrs Gardiner, and Miss Bennet, to dinner at Pemberley, before they left the country. Miss Darcy, though with a diffidence which marked her little in the habit of giving invitations, readily obeyed. Mrs Gardiner looked at her niece, desirous of knowing how *she*, whom the invitation most concerned, felt disposed as to its acceptance, but Elizabeth had turned away her head. Presuming, however, that this studied avoidance spoke rather a momentary embarrassment, than any dislike of the proposal, and seeing in her husband, who was fond of society, a perfect willingness to accept it, she ventured to engage for her attendance, and the day after the next was fixed on.

Bingley expressed great pleasure in the certainty of seeing Elizabeth again, having still a great deal to say to her, and many enquiries to make after all their Hertfordshire friends. Elizabeth, construing all this into a wish of hearing her speak of her sister, was pleased; and on this account, as well as some others, found herself, when their visitors left them, capable of considering the last half hour with some satisfaction, though while it was passing, the enjoyment of it had been little. Eager to be alone, and fearful of enquiries or hints from her uncle and aunt, she stayed with them only long enough to hear their favourable opinion of Bingley, and then hurried away to dress.

But she had no reason to fear Mr and Mrs Gardiner's curiosity; it was not their wish to force her communication. It was evident that she was much better acquainted with Mr Darcy than they had before any idea of; it was evident that he was very much in love with her. They saw much to interest, but nothing to justify enquiry.

Of Mr Darcy it was now a matter of anxiety to think well; and, as far as their acquaintance reached, there was no fault to find. They could not be untouched by his politeness, and had they drawn his character from their own feelings, and his servant's report, without any reference to any other account, the circle in Hertfordshire to which he was known, would not have recognised it for Mr Darcy. There was now an interest, however, in believing the housekeeper; and they soon became sensible, that the authority of a servant who had known him since he was four years old, and whose own manners indicated respectability, was not to be hastily rejected. Neither had any thing occurred in the intelligence of their Lambton friends, that could materially lessen its weight. They had nothing to accuse him of but pride; pride he probably had, and if not, it would certainly be imputed by the inhabitants of a small market-town, where the family did not visit. It was acknowledged, however, that he was a liberal man, and did much good among the poor.

With respect to Wickham, the travellers soon found that he was not held there in much estimation; for though the chief of his concerns, with the son of his patron, were imperfectly understood, it was yet a well known fact that, on his quitting Derbyshire, he had left many debts behind him, which Mr Darcy afterwards discharged.

As for Elizabeth, her thoughts were at Pemberley this evening more than the last; and the evening, though as it passed it seemed long, was not long enough to determine her feelings towards *one* in that mansion; and she lay awake two whole hours, endeavouring to make them out. She certainly did not hate him. No; hatred had vanished long ago, and she had almost as long been ashamed of ever feeling a dislike against him, that could be so called. The respect created by the conviction of his valuable qualities, though at first unwillingly admitted, had for some time ceased to be repugnant to her feelings; and it was now heightened into somewhat of a friendlier nature, by the testimony so highly in his favour, and bringing forward his disposition in so amiable a light, which yesterday had produced. But above all, above respect and esteem, there was a motive within her of good will which could not be overlooked. It was gratitude. – Gratitude, not merely for having once loved her, but for loving her still well enough, to forgive all the petulance and acrimony of her manner in rejecting him, and all the unjust accusations accompanying her rejection. He who, she had been persuaded, would avoid her as his greatest enemy, seemed, on this accidental meeting, most eager to preserve the acquaintance, and without any indelicate display of regard, or any peculiarity of manner, where their two selves only were concerned, was soliciting the good opinion of her friends, and bent on making her known to his sister. Such a change in a man of so much pride, excited not only astonishment but gratitude – for to love, ardent love, it must be attributed; and as such its impression on her was of a sort to be encouraged, as by no means unpleasing, though it could not be exactly defined. She respected, she esteemed, she was grateful to him, she felt a real interest in his welfare; and she only wanted to know how far she wished that welfare to depend upon herself, and how far it would be for the happiness of both that she should employ the power, which her fancy told her she still possessed, of bringing on the renewal of his addresses.

It had been settled in the evening, between the aunt and niece, that such a striking civility as Miss Darcy's, in coming to them on the very day of her arrival at Pemberley, for she had reached it only to a late breakfast, ought to be imitated, though it could not be equalled, by some exertion of politeness on their side; and, consequently, that it would be highly expedient to wait on her at Pemberley the following morning. They were, therefore, to go. – Elizabeth was pleased, though, when she asked herself the reason, she had very little to say in reply.

Mr Gardiner left them soon after breakfast. The fishing scheme had been renewed the day before, and a positive engagement made of his meeting some of the gentlemen at Pemberley by noon.

Chapter 45

Convinced as Elizabeth now was that Miss Bingley's dislike of her had originated in jealousy, she could not help feeling how very unwelcome her appearance at Pemberley must be to her, and was curious to know with how much civility on that lady's side, the acquaintance would now be renewed.

On reaching the house, they were shown through the hall into the saloon, whose northern aspect rendered it delightful for summer. Its windows opening to the ground, admitted a most refreshing view of the high woody hills behind the house, and of the beautiful oaks and Spanish chesnuts[27] which were scattered over the intermediate lawn.

In this room they were received by Miss Darcy, who was sitting there with Mrs Hurst and Miss Bingley, and the lady with whom she lived in London. Georgiana's reception of them was very civil; but attended with all that embarrassment which, though proceeding from shyness and the fear of doing wrong, would easily give to those who felt themselves inferior, the belief of her being proud and reserved. Mrs Gardiner and her niece, however, did her justice, and pitied her.

By Mrs Hurst and Miss Bingley, they were noticed only by a curtsey; and on their being seated, a pause, awkward as such pauses must always be, succeeded for a few moments. It was first broken by Mrs Annesley, a genteel, agreeable-looking woman, whose endeavour to introduce some kind of discourse, proved her to be more truly well bred than either of the others; and between her and Mrs Gardiner, with occasional help from Elizabeth, the conversation was carried on. Miss Darcy looked as if she wished for courage enough to join in it; and sometimes did venture a short sentence, when there was least danger of its being heard.

Elizabeth soon saw that she was herself closely watched by Miss Bingley, and that she could not speak a word, especially to Miss Darcy, without calling her attention. This observation would not have prevented her from trying to talk to the latter, had they not been seated at an inconvenient distance; but she was not sorry to be spared the necessity of saying much. Her own thoughts were employing her. She expected every moment that some of the gentlemen would enter the room. She wished, she feared that the master of the house might be amongst them; and whether she wished or feared it most, she could scarcely determine. After sitting in this manner a quarter of an hour, without hearing Miss Bingley's voice, Elizabeth was roused by receiving from her a cold enquiry after the health of her family. She answered with equal indifference and brevity, and the other said no more.

The next variation which their visit afforded was produced by the entrance of servants with cold meat, cake, and a variety of all the finest fruits in season; but this did not take place till after many a significant look and smile from Mrs Annesley to Miss Darcy had been given, to remind her of her post. There was now employment for the whole party; for though they could not all talk, they could all eat; and the beautiful pyramids of grapes, nectarines, and peaches, soon collected them round the table.

While thus engaged, Elizabeth had a fair opportunity of deciding whether she most feared or wished for the appearance of Mr Darcy, by the feelings which prevailed on his entering the room; and then, though but a moment before she had believed her wishes to predominate, she began to regret that he came.

He had been some time with Mr Gardiner, who, with two or three other gentlemen from the house, was engaged by the river, and had left him only on learning that the ladies of the family intended a visit to Georgiana that morning. No sooner did he appear, than Elizabeth wisely resolved to be perfectly easy and unembarrassed; – a resolution the more necessary to be made, but perhaps not the more easily kept, because she saw that the suspicions of the whole party were awakened against them, and that there was scarcely an eye which did not watch his behavior when he first came into the room. In no countenance was attentive curiosity so strongly marked as in Miss Bingley's, in spite of the smiles which overspread her face whenever she spoke to one of its objects; for jealousy had not yet made her desperate, and her attentions to Mr Darcy were by no means over. Miss Darcy, on her brother's entrance, exerted herself much more to talk; and Elizabeth saw that he was anxious for his sister and herself to get acquainted, and forwarded, as much as possible, every attempt at conversation on either side. Miss Bingley saw all this likewise; and, in the imprudence of anger, took the first opportunity of saying, with sneering civility,

'Pray, Miss Eliza, are not the —shire militia removed from Meryton? They must be a great loss to *your* family.'

In Darcy's presence she dared not mention Wickham's name; but Elizabeth instantly comprehended that he was uppermost in her thoughts; and the various recollections connected with him gave her a moment's distress; but, exerting herself vigorously to repel the ill-natured attack, she presently answered the question in a tolerably disengaged tone. While she spoke, an involuntary glance showed her Darcy with an heightened complexion, earnestly looking at her, and his sister overcome with confusion, and unable to lift up her eyes. Had Miss Bingley known what pain she was then giving her beloved friend, she undoubtedly would have refrained from the hint; but she had merely intended to discompose Elizabeth, by bringing forward the idea of a man to whom she believed her partial, to make her betray a sensibility which might injure her in Darcy's opinion, and perhaps to remind the latter of all the follies and absurdities, by which some part of her family were connected with that corps. Not a syllable had ever reached her of Miss Darcy's meditated elopement. To no creature had it been revealed, where secrecy was possible, except to Elizabeth; and from all Bingley's connections her brother was particularly anxious to conceal it, from that very wish which Elizabeth had long ago attributed to him, of their becoming hereafter her own. He had certainly formed such a plan, and without meaning that it should affect his endeavour to separate him from Miss Bennet, it is probable that it might add something to his lively concern for the welfare of his friend.

Elizabeth's collected behaviour, however, soon quieted his emotion; and as Miss Bingley, vexed and disappointed, dared not approach nearer to Wickham, Georgiana also recovered in time, though not enough to be able to speak any more. Her brother, whose eye she feared to meet, scarcely recollected her interest in the affair, and the very circumstance which had been designed to turn his thoughts from Elizabeth, seemed to have fixed them on her more, and more cheerfully.

Their visit did not continue long after the question and answer above-mentioned; and while Mr Darcy was attending them to their carriage, Miss Bingley was venting her feelings in criticisms on Elizabeth's person, behaviour, and dress. But Georgiana would not join her. Her brother's recommendation was enough to ensure her favour: his judgment could not err, and he had spoken in such terms of Elizabeth, as to leave Georgiana without the power of finding her otherwise than lovely and amiable. When Darcy returned to the saloon, Miss Bingley could not help repeating to him some part of what she had been saying to his sister.

'How very ill Eliza Bennet looks this morning, Mr Darcy,' she cried; 'I never in my life saw any one so much altered as she is since the winter. She is grown so brown and coarse! Louisa and I were agreeing that we should not have known her again.'

However little Mr Darcy might have liked such an address, he contented himself with coolly replying, that he perceived no other alteration than her being rather tanned, — no miraculous consequence of travelling in the summer.

'For my own part,' she rejoined, 'I must confess that I never could see any beauty in her. Her face is too thin; her complexion has no brilliancy; and her features are not at all handsome. Her nose wants character; there is nothing marked in its lines. Her teeth are tolerable, but not out of the common way; and as for her eyes, which have sometimes been called so fine, I never could perceive any thing extraordinary in them. They have a sharp, shrewish look, which I do not like at all; and in her air altogether, there is a self-sufficiency without fashion, which is intolerable.'

Persuaded as Miss Bingley was that Darcy admired Elizabeth, this was not the best method of recommending herself; but angry people are not always wise; and in seeing him at last look somewhat nettled, she had all the success she expected. He was resolutely silent however; and, from a determination of making him speak, she continued,

'I remember, when we first knew her in Hertfordshire, how amazed we all were to find that she was a reputed beauty; and I particularly recollect your saying one night, after they had been dining at Netherfield, "*She* a beauty! – I should as soon call her mother a wit." But afterwards she seemed to improve on you, and I believe you thought her rather pretty at one time.'

'Yes,' replied Darcy, who could contain himself no longer, 'but *that* was only when I first knew her, for it is many months since I have considered her as one of the handsomest women of my acquaintance.'

He then went away, and Miss Bingley was left to all the satisfaction of having forced him to say what gave no one any pain but herself.

Mrs Gardiner and Elizabeth talked of all that had occurred, during their visit, as they returned except what had particularly interested them both. The looks and behaviour of every body they had seen were discussed, except of the person who had mostly engaged their attention. They talked of his sister, his friends, his house, his fruit, of every thing but himself; yet Elizabeth was longing to know what Mrs Gardiner thought of him, and Mrs Gardiner would have been highly gratified by her niece's beginning the subject.

Chapter 46

Elizabeth had been a good deal disappointed in not finding a letter from Jane, on their first arrival at Lambton; and this disappointment had been renewed on each of the mornings that had now been spent there; but on the third, her repining was over, and her sister justified by the receipt of two letters from her at once, on one of which was marked that it had been missent elsewhere. Elizabeth was not surprised at it, as Jane had written the direction remarkably ill.

They had just been preparing to walk as the letters came in; and her uncle and aunt, leaving her to enjoy them in quiet, set off by themselves. The one missent must be first attended to; it had been written five days ago. The beginning contained an account of all their little parties and engagements, with such news as the country afforded; but the latter half, which was dated a day later, and written in evident agitation, gave more important intelligence. It was to this effect:

'Since writing the above, dearest Lizzy, something has occurred of a most unexpected and serious nature; but I am afraid of alarming you – be assured that we are all well. What I have to say relates to poor Lydia. An express came at twelve last night, just as we were all gone to bed, from Colonel Forster, to inform us that she was gone off to Scotland with one of his officers; to own the truth, with Wickham! – Imagine our surprise. To Kitty, however, it does not seem so wholly unexpected. I am very, very sorry. So imprudent a match on both sides! – But I am willing to hope the best, and that his character has been misunderstood. Thoughtless and indiscreet I can easily believe him, but this step (and let us rejoice over it) marks nothing bad at heart. His choice is disinterested at least, for he must know my father can give her nothing. Our poor mother is sadly grieved. My father bears it better. How thankful am I, that we never let them know what has been said against him; we must forget it ourselves. They were off Saturday night about twelve, as is conjectured, but were not missed till yesterday morning at eight. The express was sent off directly. My dear Lizzy, they must have passed within ten miles of us. Colonel Forster gives us reason to expect him here soon. Lydia left a few lines for his wife, informing her of their intention. I must conclude, for I cannot be long from my poor mother. I am afraid you will not be able to make it out, but I hardly know what I have written.'

Without allowing herself time for consideration, and scarcely knowing what she felt, Elizabeth on finishing this letter, instantly seized the other, and opening it with the utmost impatience, read as follows: it had been written a day later than the conclusion of the first.

'By this time, my dearest sister, you have received my hurried letter; I wish this may be more intelligible, but though not confined for time, my head is so bewildered that I cannot answer for being coherent. Dearest Lizzy, I hardly know what I would write, but I have bad news for you, and it cannot be delayed. Imprudent as a marriage between Mr Wickham and our poor Lydia would be, we are now anxious to be assured it has taken place, for there is but too much reason to fear they are not gone to Scotland. Colonel Forster came yesterday, having left Brighton the day before, not many hours after the express. Though Lydia's short letter to Mrs F. gave them to understand that they were going to Gretna Green, something was dropped by Denny expressing his belief that W. never intended to go there, or to marry Lydia at all, which was repeated to Colonel F. who instantly taking the alarm, set off from B. intending to trace their route. He did trace them easily to Clapham, but no farther; for on entering that place they removed into a hackney-coach and dismissed the chaise that brought them from Epsom. All that is known after this is, that they were seen to continue the London road. I know not what to think. After making every possible enquiry on that side London, Colonel F. came on into Hertfordshire, anxiously renewing them at all the turnpikes, and at the inns in Barnet and Hatfield, but without any success, no such people had been seen to pass through. With the kindest concern he came on to Longbourn, and broke his apprehensions to us in a manner most creditable to his heart. I am sincerely grieved for him and Mrs F: but no one can throw any blame on them. Our distress, my dear Lizzy, is very great. My father and mother believe the worst, but I cannot think so ill of him. Many circumstances might make it more eligible for them to be married privately in town than to pursue their first plan; and even if *he* could form such a design against a young woman of Lydia's connections, which is not likely, can I suppose her so lost to every thing? – Impossible. I grieve to find, however, that Colonel F. is not disposed to depend upon their marriage; he shook his head when I expressed my hopes, and said he feared W. was not a man to be trusted. My poor mother is really ill and keeps her room. Could she exert herself it would be better, but this is not to be expected; and as to my father, I never in my life saw him so affected. Poor Kitty has anger for having concealed their attachment; but as it was a matter of confidence one cannot wonder. I am truly glad, dearest Lizzy, that you have been spared something of these distressing scenes; but now as the first shock is over, shall I own that I long for your return? I am not so selfish, however, as to press for it, if inconvenient. Adieu. I take up my pen again to do, what I have just told you I would not, but circumstances are such, that I cannot help earnestly begging you all to come here, as soon as possible. I know my dear uncle and aunt so well, that I am not afraid of requesting it, though I have still something more to ask of the former. My father is going to London with Colonel Forster instantly, to try to discover her. What he means to do, I am sure I know not; but his excessive distress will not allow him to pursue any measure in the best and safest way, and Colonel Forster is obliged to be at Brighton again tomorrow evening. In such an exigence my uncle's advice and assistance would be every thing in the world; he will immediately comprehend what I must feel, and I rely upon his goodness.'

'Oh! where, where is my uncle?' cried Elizabeth, darting from her seat as she finished the letter, in eagerness to follow him, without losing a moment of the time so precious; but as she reached the door, it was opened by a servant, and Mr Darcy appeared. Her pale face and impetuous manner made him start, and before he could recover himself enough to speak, she, in whose mind every idea was superseded by

Lydia's situation, hastily exclaimed, 'I beg your pardon, but I must leave you. I must find Mr Gardiner this moment, on business that cannot be delayed; I have not an instant to lose.'

'Good God! what is the matter?' cried he, with more feeling than politeness; then recollecting himself, 'I will not detain you a minute, but let me, or let the servant, go after Mr and Mrs Gardiner. You are not well enough; – you cannot go yourself.'

Elizabeth hesitated, but her knees trembled under her, and she felt how little would be gained by her attempting to pursue them. Calling back the servant, therefore, she commissioned him, though in so breathless an accent as made her almost unintelligible, to fetch his master and mistress home, instantly.

On his quitting the room, she sat down, unable to support herself, and looking so miserably ill, that it was impossible for Darcy to leave her, or to refrain from saying, in a tone of gentleness and commiseration, 'Let me call your maid. Is there nothing you could take, to give you present relief? – A glass of wine; – shall I get you one? – You are very ill.'

'No, I thank you;' she replied, endeavouring to recover herself. 'There is nothing the matter with me. I am quite well. I am only distressed by some dreadful news which I have just received from Longbourn.'

She burst into tears as she alluded to it, and for a few minutes could not speak another word. Darcy, in wretched suspense, could only say something indistinctly of his concern, and observe her in compassionate silence. At length, she spoke again. 'I have just had a letter from Jane, with such dreadful news. It cannot be concealed from any one. My youngest sister has left all her friends – has eloped; – has thrown herself into the power of – of Mr Wickham. They are gone off together from Brighton. *You* know him too well to doubt the rest. She has no money, no connections, nothing that can tempt him to – she is lost forever.'

Darcy was fixed in astonishment. 'When I consider,' she added, in a yet more agitated voice, 'that *I* might have prevented it! – *I* who knew what he was. Had I but explained some part of it only – some part of what I learnt, to my own family! Had his character been known, this could not have happened. But it is all, all too late now.'

'I am grieved, indeed,' cried Darcy; 'grieved – shocked. But is it certain, absolutely certain?'

'Oh yes! – They left Brighton together on Sunday night, and were traced almost to London, but not beyond; they are certainly not gone to Scotland.'

'And what has been done, what has been attempted, to recover her?'

'My father is gone to London, and Jane has written to beg my uncle's immediate assistance, and we shall be off, I hope, in half an hour. But nothing can be done; I know very well that nothing can be done. How is such a man to be worked on? How are they even to be discovered? I have not the smallest hope. It is every way horrible!'

Darcy shook his head in silent acquiesence.

'When *my* eyes were opened to his real character. – Oh! had I known what I ought, what I dared, to do! But I knew not – I was afraid of doing too much. Wretched, wretched, mistake!'

Darcy made no answer. He seemed scarcely to hear her, and was walking up and down the room in earnest meditation; his brow contracted, his air gloomy. Elizabeth soon observed, and instantly understood it. Her power was sinking; every thing *must* sink under such a proof of family weakness, such an assurance of the deepest disgrace. She could neither wonder nor condemn, but the belief of his self-conquest brought nothing consolatory to her bosom, afforded no palliation of her distress. It was, on the contrary, exactly calculated to make her understand her own wishes; and never had she so honestly felt that she could have loved him, as now, when all love must be vain.

But self, though it would intrude, could not engross her. Lydia – the humiliation, the misery, she was bringing on them all, soon swallowed up every private care; and covering her face with her handkerchief, Elizabeth was soon lost to every thing else; and, after a pause of several minutes, was only recalled to a sense of her situation by the voice of her companion, who, in a manner, which though it spoke compassion, spoke likewise restraint, said, 'I am afraid you have been long desiring my absence, nor have I any thing to plead in excuse of my stay, but real, though unavailing, concern. Would to heaven that any thing could be either said or done on my part, that might offer consolation to such distress. – But I will not torment you with vain wishes, which may seem purposely to ask for your thanks. This unfortunate affair will, I fear, prevent my sister's having the pleasure of seeing you at Pemberley today.'

'Oh, yes. Be so kind as to apologize for us to Miss Darcy. Say that urgent business calls us home immediately. Conceal the unhappy truth as long as it is possible. – I know it cannot be long.'

He readily assured her of his secrecy – again expressed his sorrow for her distress, wished it a happier conclusion than there was at present reason to hope, and leaving his compliments for her relations, with only one serious, parting, look, went away.

As he quitted the room, Elizabeth felt how improbable it was that they should ever see each other again on such terms of cordiality as had marked their several meetings in Derbyshire; and as she threw a retrospective glance over the whole of their acquaintance, so full of contradictions and varieties, sighed at the perverseness of those feelings which would now have promoted its continuance, and would formerly have rejoiced in its termination.

If gratitude and esteem are good foundations of affection, Elizabeth's change of sentiment will be neither improbable nor faulty. But if otherwise, if the regard springing from such sources is unreasonable or unnatural, in comparison of what is so often described as arising on a first interview with its object, and even before two words have been exchanged, nothing can be said in her defence, except that she had given somewhat of a trial to the latter method, in her partiality for Wickham, and that its ill-success might perhaps authorise her to seek the other less interesting mode of attachment. Be that as it may, she saw him go with regret; and in this early example of what Lydia's infamy must produce, found additional anguish as she reflected on that wretched business. Never, since reading Jane's second letter, had she entertained a hope of Wickham's meaning to marry her. No one but Jane, she thought, could flatter herself with such an expectation. Surprise was the least of her feelings on this development. While the contents of the first letter remained on her mind, she was all surprise – all astonishment that Wickham should marry a girl, whom it was impossible he could marry for money; and how Lydia could ever have attached him, had appeared incomprehensible. But now it was all too natural. For such an attachment as this, she might have sufficient charms; and though she did not suppose Lydia to be deliberately engaging in an elopement, without the intention of marriage, she had no difficulty in believing that neither her virtue nor her understanding would preserve her from falling an easy prey.

She had never perceived, while the regiment was in Hertfordshire, that Lydia had any partiality for him, but she was convinced that Lydia had wanted only encouragement to attach herself to any body. Sometimes one officer, sometimes another had been her favourite, as their attentions raised them in her opinion. Her affections had been continually fluctuating, but never without an object. The mischief of neglect and mistaken indulgence towards such a girl. – Oh! how acutely did she now feel it.

She was wild to be at home – to hear, to see, to be upon the spot, to share with Jane in the cares that must now fall wholly upon her, in a family so deranged; a father absent, a mother incapable of exertion, and requiring constant attendance; and though almost persuaded that nothing could be done for Lydia, her uncle's interference seemed of the utmost importance, and till he entered the room, the misery of her impatience was severe. Mr and Mrs Gardiner had hurried back in alarm, supposing, by the servant's account, that their niece was taken suddenly ill; – but satisfying them instantly on that head, she eagerly communicated the cause of their summons, reading the two letters aloud, and dwelling on the postscript of the last, with trembling energy. – Though Lydia had never been a favourite with them, Mr and Mrs Gardiner could not but be deeply affected. Not Lydia only, but all were concerned in it; and after the first exclamations of surprise and horror, Mr Gardiner readily promised every assistance in his power. – Elizabeth, though expecting no less, thanked him with tears of gratitude; and all three being actuated by one spirit, every thing relating to their journey was speedily settled. They were to be off as soon as possible. 'But what is to be done about Pemberley?' cried Mrs Gardiner. 'John told us Mr Darcy was here when you sent for us; – was it so?'

'Yes; and I told him we should not be able to keep our engagement. *That* is all settled.'

'That is all settled;' repeated the other, as she ran into her room to prepare. 'And are they upon such terms as for her to disclose the real truth! Oh, that I knew how it was!'

But wishes were vain; or at best could serve only to amuse her in the hurry and confusion of the following hour. Had Elizabeth been at leisure to be idle, she would have remained certain that all employment was impossible to one so wretched as herself; but she had her share of business as well as her aunt, and amongst the rest there were notes to be written to all their friends in Lambton, with false excuses for their sudden departure. An hour, however, saw the whole completed; and Mr Gardiner meanwhile having settled his account at the inn, nothing remained to be done but to go; and Elizabeth, after all the misery of the morning, found herself, in a shorter space of time than she could have supposed, seated in the carriage, and on the road to Longbourn.

Chapter 47

'I have been thinking it over again, Elizabeth,' said her uncle, as they drove from the town; 'and really, upon serious consideration, I am much more inclined than I was to judge as your eldest sister does of the matter. It appears to me so very unlikely, that any young man should form such a design against a girl who is by no means unprotected or friendless, and who was actually staying in his colonel's family, that I am strongly inclined to hope the best. Could he expect that her friends would not step forward? Could he expect to be noticed again by the regiment, after such an affront to Colonel Forster? His temptation is not adequate to the risk.'

'Do you really think so?' cried Elizabeth, brightening up for a moment.

'Upon my word,' said Mrs Gardiner, 'I begin to be of your uncle's opinion. It is really too great a violation of decency, honour, and interest, for him to be guilty of it. I cannot think so very ill of Wickham. Can you, yourself, Lizzy, so wholly give him up, as to believe him capable of it?'

'Not perhaps of neglecting his own interest. But of every other neglect I can believe him capable. If, indeed, it should be so! But I dare not hope it. Why should they not go on to Scotland, if that had been the case?'

'In the first place,' replied Mr Gardiner, 'there is no absolute proof that they are not gone to Scotland.'

'Oh! but their removing from the chaise into an hackney coach is such a presumption! And, besides, no traces of them were to be found on the Barnet road.'

'Well, then – supposing them to be in London. They may be there, though for the purpose of concealment, for no more exceptionable purpose. It is not likely that money should be very abundant on either side; and it might strike them that they could be more economically, though less expeditiously, married in London, than in Scotland.'

'But why all this secrecy? Why any fear of detection? Why must their marriage be private? Oh! no, no, this is not likely. His most particular friend, you see by Jane's account, was persuaded of his never intending to marry her. Wickham will never marry a woman without some money. He cannot afford it. And what claims has Lydia, what attractions has she beyond youth, health, and good humour, that could make him for her sake, forego every chance of benefiting himself by marrying well? As to what restraint the apprehension of disgrace in the corps might throw on a dishonourable elopement with her, I am not able to judge; for I know nothing of the effects that such a step might produce. But as to your other objection, I am afraid it will hardly hold good. Lydia has no brothers to step forward; and he might imagine, from my father's behaviour, from his indolence and the little attention he has ever seemed to give to what was going forward in his family, that *he* would do as little, and think as little about it, as any father could do, in such a matter.'

'But can you think that Lydia is so lost to every thing but love of him, as to consent to live with him on any other terms than marriage?'

'It does seem, and it is most shocking indeed,' replied Elizabeth, with tears in her eyes, 'that a sister's sense of decency and virtue in such a point should admit of doubt. But, really, I know not what to say. Perhaps I am not doing her justice. But she is very young; she has never been taught to think on serious subjects; and for the last half year, nay, for a twelvemonth, she has been given up to nothing but amusement and vanity. She has been allowed to dispose of her time in the most idle and frivolous manner, and to adopt any opinions that came in her way. Since the —shire were first quartered in Meryton, nothing but love, flirtation, and officers, have been in her head. She has been doing every thing in her power by thinking and talking on the subject, to give greater – what shall I call it? susceptibility to her feelings; which are naturally lively enough. And we all know that Wickham has every charm of person and address that can captivate a woman.'

'But you see that Jane,' said her aunt, 'does not think so ill of

Wickham, as to believe him capable of the attempt.'

'Of whom does Jane ever think ill? And who is there, whatever might be their former conduct, that she would believe capable of such an attempt, till it were proved against them? But Jane knows, as well as I do, what Wickham really is. We both know that he has been profligate in every sense of the word. That he has neither integrity nor honour. That he is as false and deceitful, as he is insinuating.'

'And do you really know all this?' cried Mrs Gardiner, whose curiosity as to the mode of her intelligence was all alive.

'I do, indeed,' replied Elizabeth, colouring. 'I told you the other day, of his infamous behaviour to Mr Darcy; and you, yourself, when last at Longbourn, heard in what manner he spoke of the man, who had behaved with such forbearance and liberality towards him. And there are other circumstances which I am not at liberty – which it is not worthwhile to relate; but his lies about the whole Pemberley family are endless. From what he said of Miss Darcy, I was thoroughly prepared to see a proud, reserved, disagreeable girl. Yet he knew to the contrary himself. He must know that she was as amiable and unpretending as we have found her.'

'But does Lydia know nothing of this? Can she be ignorant of what you and Jane seem so well to understand?'

'Oh, yes! – that, that is the worst of all. Till I was in Kent, and saw so much both of Mr Darcy and his relation, Colonel Fitzwilliam, I was ignorant of the truth myself. And when I returned home, the —shire was to leave Meryton in a week or fortnight's time. As that was the case, neither Jane, to whom I related the whole, nor I, thought it necessary to make our knowledge public; for of what use could it apparently be to any one, that the good opinion which all the neighbourhood had of him, should then be overthrown? And even when it was settled that Lydia should go with Mrs Forster, the necessity of opening her eyes to his character never occurred to me. That *she* could be in any danger from the deception never entered my head. That such a consequence as *this* should ensue, you may easily believe was far enough from my thoughts.'

'When they all removed to Brighton, therefore, you had no reason, I suppose, to believe them fond of each other.'

'Not the slightest. I can remember no symptom of affection on either side; and had any thing of the kind been perceptible, you must be aware that ours is not a family, on which it could be thrown away. When first he entered the corps, she was ready enough to admire him; but so we all were. Every girl in, or near Meryton, was out of her senses about him for the first two months; but he never distinguished *her* by any particular attention, and, consequently, after a moderate period of extravagant and wild admiration, her fancy for him gave way, and others of the regiment, who treated her with more distinction, again became her favourites.'

*

It may be easily believed, that however little of novelty could be added to their fears, hopes, and conjectures, on this interesting subject, by its repeated discussion, no other could detain them from it long, during the whole of the journey. From Elizabeth's thoughts it was never absent. Fixed there by the keenest of all anguish, self reproach, she could find no interval of ease or forgetfulness.

They travelled as expeditiously as possible; and sleeping one night on the road, reached Longbourn by dinner-time the next day. It was a comfort to Elizabeth to consider that Jane could not have been wearied by long expectations.

The little Gardiners, attracted by the sight of a chaise, were standing on the steps of the house, as they entered the paddock; and when the carriage drove up to the door, the joyful surprise that lighted up their faces, and displayed itself over their whole bodies, in a variety of capers and frisks, was the first pleasing earnest of their welcome.

Elizabeth jumped out; and, after giving each of them an hasty kiss, hurried into the vestibule, where Jane, who came running down stairs from her mother's apartment, immediately met her.

Elizabeth, as she affectionately embraced her, whilst tears filled the eyes of both, lost not a moment in asking whether any thing had been heard of the fugitives.

'Not yet,' replied Jane. 'But now that my dear uncle is come, I hope every thing will be well.'

'Is my father in town?'

'Yes, he went on Tuesday as I wrote you word.'

'And have you heard from him often?'

'We have heard only once. He wrote me a few lines on Wednesday, to say that he had arrived in safety, and to give me his directions, which I particularly begged him to do. He merely added, that he should not write again, till he had something of importance to mention.'

'And my mother – How is she? How are you all?'

'My mother is tolerably well, I trust; though her spirits are greatly shaken. She is up stairs, and will have great satisfaction in seeing you all. She does not yet leave her dressing-room. Mary and Kitty, thank Heaven! are quite well.'

'But you – How are you?' cried Elizabeth. 'You look pale. How much you must have gone through!'

Her sister, however, assured her, of her being perfectly well; and their conversation, which had been passing while Mr and Mrs Gardiner were engaged with their children, was now put an end to, by the approach of the whole party. Jane ran to her uncle and aunt, and welcomed and thanked them both, with alternate smiles and tears.

When they were all in the drawing-room, the questions which Elizabeth had already asked, were of course repeated by the others, and they soon found that Jane had no intelligence to give. The sanguine hope of good, however, which the benevolence of her heart suggested, had not yet deserted her; she still expected that it would all end well, and that every morning would bring some letter, either from Lydia or her father, to explain their proceedings, and perhaps announce the marriage.

Mrs Bennet, to whose apartment they all repaired, after a few minutes conversation together, received them exactly as might be expected; with tears and lamentations of regret, invectives against the villainous conduct of Wickham, and complaints of her own sufferings and ill usage; blaming every body but the person to whose ill judging indulgence the errors of her daughter must be principally owing.

'If I had been able,' said she, 'to carry my point of going to Brighton, with all my family, *this* would not have happened; but poor dear Lydia had nobody to take care of her. Why did the Forsters ever let her go out of their sight? I am sure there was some great neglect or other on their side, for she is not the kind of girl to do such a thing, if she had been well looked after. I always thought they were very unfit to have the charge of her; but I was overruled, as I always am. Poor dear child! And now here's Mr Bennet gone away, and I know he will fight Wickham, wherever he meets him, and then he will be killed, and what is to become of us all? The Collinses will turn us out, before he is cold in his grave; and if you are not kind to us, brother, I do not know what we shall do.'

They all exclaimed against such terrific ideas; and Mr Gardiner, after general assurances of his affection for her and all her family, told her that he meant to be in London the very next day, and would assist Mr Bennet in every endeavour for recovering Lydia.

'Do not give way to useless alarm,' added he; 'though it is right to be prepared for the worst, there is no occasion to look on it as certain. It is not quite a week since they left Brighton. In a few days more, we may gain some news of them, and till we know that they are not married, and have no design of marrying, do not let us give the matter over as lost. As soon as I get to town, I shall go to my brother, and make him come home with me to Gracechurch Street, and then we may consult together as to what is to be done.'

'Oh! my dear brother,' replied Mrs Bennet, 'that is exactly what I could most wish for. And now do, when you get to town, find them out, wherever they may be; and if they are not married already, *make* them marry. And as for wedding clothes, do not let them wait for that, but tell Lydia she shall have as much money as she chuses, to buy them, after they are married. And, above all things, keep Mr Bennet from fighting. Tell him what a dreadful state I am in, – that I am frightened out of my wits; and have such tremblings, such flutterings, all over me, such spasms in my side, and pains in my head, and such beatings at heart, that I can get no rest by night nor by day. And tell my dear Lydia, not to give any directions about her clothes, till she has seen me, for she does not know which are the best warehouses. Oh, brother, how kind you are! I know you will contrive it all.'

But Mr Gardiner, though he assured her again of his earnest endeavours in the cause, could not avoid recommending moderation to her, as well in her hopes as her fears; and, after talking with her in this manner till dinner was on table, they left her to vent all her feelings on the housekeeper, who attended, in the absence of her daughters.

Though her brother and sister were persuaded that there was no real occasion for such a seclusion from the family, they did not attempt to oppose it, for they knew that she had not prudence enough to hold her tongue before the servants, while they waited at table, and judged it better that *one* only of the household, and the one whom they could most trust, should comprehend all her fears and solicitude on the subject.

In the dining-room they were soon joined by Mary and Kitty, who had been too busily engaged in their separate apartments, to make their appearance before. One came from her books, and the other from her toilette. The faces of both, however, were tolerably calm; and no change was visible in either, except that the loss of her favourite sister, or the anger which she had herself incurred in the business, had given something more of fretfulness than usual, to the accents of Kitty. As for Mary, she was mistress enough of herself to whisper to Elizabeth with a countenance of grave reflection, soon after they were seated at table,

'This is a most unfortunate affair; and will probably be much talked of. But we must stem the tide of malice, and pour into the wounded bosoms of each other, the balm of sisterly consolation.'

Then, perceiving in Elizabeth no inclination of replying, she added, 'Unhappy as the event must be for Lydia, we may draw from it this useful lesson; that loss of virtue in a female is irretrievable – that one false step involves her in endless ruin – that her reputation is no less brittle than it is beautiful, – and that she cannot be too much guarded in her behaviour towards the undeserving of the other sex.'

Elizabeth lifted up her eyes in amazement, but was too much oppressed to make any reply. Mary, however, continued to console herself with such kind of moral extractions from the evil before them.

In the afternoon, the two elder Miss Bennets were able to be for half an hour by themselves; and Elizabeth instantly availed herself of the opportunity of making many enquiries, which Jane was equally eager to satisfy. After joining in general lamentations over the dreadful sequel of this event, which Elizabeth considered as all but certain, and Miss Bennet could not assert to be wholly impossible; the former continued the subject, by saying, 'But tell me all and every thing about it, which I have not already heard. Give me farther particulars. What did Colonel Forster say? Had they no apprehension of any thing before the elopement took place? They must have seen them together for ever.'

'Colonel Forster did own that he had often suspected some partiality, especially on Lydia's side, but nothing to give him any alarm. I am so grieved for him. His behaviour was attentive and kind to the utmost. He *was* coming to us, in order to assure us of his concern, before he had any idea of their not being gone to Scotland: when that apprehension first got abroad, it hastened his journey.'

'And was Denny convinced that Wickham would not marry? Did he know of their intending to go off? Had Colonel Forster seen Denny himself?'

'Yes; but when questioned by *him* Denny denied knowing any thing of their plan, and would not give his real opinion about it. He did not repeat his persuasion of their not marrying – and from *that*, I am inclined to hope, he might have been misunderstood before.'

'And till Colonel Forster came himself, not one of you entertained a doubt, I suppose, of their being really married?'

'How was it possible that such an idea should enter our brains! I felt a little uneasy – a little fearful of my sister's happiness with him in marriage, because I knew that his conduct had not been always quite right. My father and mother knew nothing of that, they only felt how imprudent a match it must be. Kitty then owned, with a very natural triumph on knowing more than the rest of us, that in Lydia's last letter, she had prepared her for such a step. She had known, it seems, of their being in love with each other, many weeks.'

'But not before they went to Brighton?'

'No, I believe not.'

'And did Colonel Forster appear to think ill of Wickham himself? Does he know his real character?'

'I must confess that he did not speak so well of Wickham as he formerly did. He believed him to be imprudent and extravagant. And since this sad affair has taken place, it is said, that he left Meryton greatly in debt; but I hope this may be false.'

'Oh, Jane, had we been less secret, had we told what we knew of him, this could not have happened!'

'Perhaps it would have been better;' replied her sister. 'But to expose the former faults of any person, without knowing what their present feelings were, seemed unjustifiable. We acted with the best intentions.'

'Could Colonel Forster repeat the particulars of Lydia's note to his wife?'

'He brought it with him for us to see.'

Jane then took it from her pocket-book, and gave it to Elizabeth. These were the contents:

MY DEAR HARRIET – You will laugh when you know where I am gone, and I cannot help laughing myself at your surprise tomorrow morning, as soon as I am missed. I am going to Gretna Green, and if you cannot guess with who, I shall think you a simpleton, for there is but one man in the world I love, and he is an angel. I should never be happy without him, so think it no harm to be off. You need not send them word at Longbourn of my going, if you do not like it, for it will make the surprise the greater, when I write to them, and sign my name Lydia Wickham. What a good joke it will be! I can hardly write for laughing. Pray make my excuses to Pratt, for not keeping my engagement, and dancing with him tonight. Tell him I hope he will excuse me when he knows all, and tell him I will dance with him at the next ball we meet, with great pleasure. I shall send for my clothes when I get to Longbourn; but I wish you would tell Sally to mend a great slit in my worked muslin gown, before they are packed up. Good bye. Give my love to Colonel Forster, I hope you will drink to our good journey.

Your affectionate friend,

LYDIA BENNET

'Oh! thoughtless, thoughtless Lydia!' cried Elizabeth when she had finished it. 'What a letter is this, to be written at such a moment. But at least it shows, that she was serious in the object of her journey. Whatever he might afterwards persuade her to, it was not on her side a scheme of infamy. My poor father! how he must have felt it!'

'I never saw any one so shocked. He could not speak a word for full ten minutes. My mother was taken ill immediately, and the whole house in such confusion!'

'Oh! Jane,' cried Elizabeth, 'was there a servant belonging to it, who did not know the whole story before the end of the day?'

'I do not know. – I hope there was. – But to be guarded at such a time, is very difficult. My mother was in hysterics, and though I endeavoured to give her every assistance in my power, I am afraid I did not do so much as I might have done! but the horror of what might possibly happen, almost took from me my faculties.'

'Your attendance upon her, has been too much for you. You do not look well. Oh! that I had been with you, you have had every care and anxiety upon yourself alone.'

'Mary and Kitty have been very kind, and would have shared in every fatigue, I am sure, but I did not think it right for either of them. Kitty is slight and delicate, and Mary studies so much, that her hours of repose should not be broken in on. My aunt Philips came to Longbourn on Tuesday, after my father went away; and was so good as to stay till Thursday with me. She was of great use and comfort to us all, and lady Lucas has been very kind; she walked here on Wednesday morning to condole with us, and offered her services, or any of her daughters, if they could be of use to us.'

'She had better have stayed at home,' cried Elizabeth; 'perhaps she meant well, but, under such a misfortune as this, one cannot see too little of one's neighbours. Assistance is impossible; condolence, insufferable. Let them triumph over us at a distance, and be satisfied.'

She then proceeded to enquire into the measures which her father had intended to pursue, while in town, for the recovery of his daughter.

'He meant, I believe,' replied Jane, 'to go to Epsom, the place where they last changed horses, see the postilions, and try if any thing could be made out from them. His principal object must be, to discover the number of the hackney coach which took them from Clapham. It had come with a fare from London; and as he thought the circumstance of a gentleman and lady's removing from one carriage into another, might be remarked, he meant to make enquiries at Clapham. If he could any how discover at what house the coachman had before set down his fare, he determined to make enquiries there, and hoped it might not be impossible to find out the stand and number of the coach. I do not know of any other designs that he had formed: but he was in such a hurry to be gone, and his spirits so greatly discomposed, that I had difficulty in finding out even so much as this.'

Chapter 48

The whole party were in hopes of a letter from Mr Bennet the next morning, but the post came in without bringing a single line from him. His family knew him to be on all common occasions, a most negligent and dilatory correspondent, but at such a time, they had hoped for exertion. They were forced to conclude, that he had no pleasing intelligence to send, but even of that they would have been glad to be certain. Mr Gardiner had waited only for the letters before he set off.

When he was gone, they were certain at least of receiving constant information of what was going on, and their uncle promised, at parting, to prevail on Mr Bennet to return to Longbourn, as soon as he could, to the great consolation of his sister, who considered it as the only security for her husband's not being killed in a duel.

Mrs Gardiner and the children were to remain in Hertfordshire a few days longer, as the former thought her presence might be serviceable to her nieces. She shared in their attendance on Mrs Bennet, and was a great comfort to them, in their hours of freedom. Their other aunt also visited them frequently, and always, as she said, with the design of cheering and heartening them up, though as she never came without reporting some fresh instance of Wickham's extravagance or irregularity, she seldom went away without leaving them more dispirited than she found them.

All Meryton seemed striving to blacken the man, who, but three months before, had been almost an angel of light. He was declared to be in debt to every tradesman in the place, and his intrigues, all honoured with the title of seduction, had been extended into every tradesman's family. Every body declared that he was the wickedest young man in the world; and every body began to find out, that they had always distrusted the appearance of his goodness. Elizabeth, though she did not credit above half of what was said, believed enough to make her former assurance of her sister's ruin still more certain; and even Jane, who believed still less of it, became almost hopeless, more especially as the time was now come, when if they had gone to Scotland, which she had never before entirely despaired of, they must in all probability have gained some news of them.

Mr Gardiner left Longbourn on Sunday; on Tuesday, his wife received a letter from him; it told them, that on his arrival, he had immediately found out his brother, and persuaded him to come to Gracechurch street. That Mr Bennet had been to Epsom and Clapham, before his arrival, but without gaining any satisfactory information; and that he was now determined to enquire at all the principal hotels in town, as Mr Bennet thought it possible they might have gone to one of them, on their first coming to London, before they procured lodgings. Mr Gardiner himself did not expect any success from this measure, but as his brother was eager in it, he meant to assist him in pursuing it. He added, that Mr Bennet seemed wholly disinclined at present, to leave London, and promised to write again very soon. There was also a postscript to this effect:

'I have written to Colonel Forster to desire him to find out, if possible, from some of the young man's intimates in the regiment, whether Wickham has any relations or connections, who would be likely to know in what part of the town he has now concealed himself. If there were any one, that one could apply to, with a probability of gaining such a clue as that, it might be of essential consequence. At present we have nothing to guide us. Colonel Forster will, I dare say, do every thing in his power to satisfy us on this head. But, on second thoughts, perhaps Lizzy could tell us, what relations he has now living, better than any other person.'

Elizabeth was at no loss to understand from whence this deference for her authority proceeded; but it was not in her power to give any information of so satisfactory a nature, as the compliment deserved.

She had never heard of his having had any relations, except a father and mother, both of whom had been dead many years. It was possible, however, that some of his companions in the —shire, might be able to give more information; and, though she was not very sanguine in expecting it, the application was a something to look forward to.

Every day at Longbourn was now a day of anxiety; but the most anxious part of each was when the post was expected. The arrival of letters was the first grand object of every morning's impatience. Through letters, whatever of good or bad was to be told, would be communicated, and every succeeding day was expected to bring some news of importance.

But before they heard again from Mr Gardiner, a letter arrived for their father, from a different quarter, from Mr Collins; which, as Jane had received directions to open all that came for him in his absence, she accordingly read; and Elizabeth, who knew what curiosities his letters always were, looked over her, and read it likewise. It was as follows:

MY DEAR SIR – I feel myself called upon, by our relationship, and my situation in life, to condole with you on the grievous affliction you are now suffering under, of which we were yesterday informed by a letter from Hertfordshire. Be assured, my dear Sir, that Mrs Collins and myself sincerely sympathise with you, and all your respectable family, in your present distress, which must be of the bitterest kind, because proceeding from a cause which no time can remove. No arguments shall be wanting on my part, that can alleviate so severe a misfortune; or that may comfort you, under a circumstance that must be of all others most afflicting to a parent's mind. The death of your daughter would have been a blessing in comparison of this. And it is the more to be lamented, because there is reason to suppose, as my dear Charlotte informs me, that this licentiousness of behaviour in your daughter, has proceeded from a faulty degree of indulgence, though, at the same time, for the consolation of yourself and Mrs Bennet, I am inclined to think that her own disposition must be naturally bad, or she could not be guilty of such an enormity, at so early an age. Howsoever that may be, you are grievously to be pitied, in which opinion I am not only joined by Mrs Collins, but likewise by lady Catherine and her daughter, to whom I have related the affair. They agree with me in apprehending that this false step in one daughter, will be injurious to the fortunes of all the others, for who, as lady Catherine herself condescendingly says, will connect themselves with such a family. And this consideration leads me moreover to reflect with augmented satisfaction on a certain event of last November, for had it been otherwise, I must have been involved in all your sorrow and disgrace. Let me advise you then, my dear Sir, to console yourself as much as possible, to throw off your unworthy child from your affection for ever, and leave her to reap the fruits of her own heinous offence.

I am, dear Sir, &c. &c.

Mr Gardiner did not write again, till he had received an answer from Colonel Forster; and then he had nothing of a pleasant nature to send. It was not known that Wickham had a single relation, with whom he kept up any connection, and it was certain that he had no near one living. His former acquaintance had been numerous; but since he had been in the militia, it did not appear that he was on

terms of particular friendship with any of them. There was no one therefore who could be pointed out, as likely to give any news of him. And in the wretched state of his own finances, there was a very powerful motive for secrecy, in addition to his fear of discovery by Lydia's relations, for it had just transpired that he had left gaming debts behind him, to a very considerable amount. Colonel Forster believed that more than a thousand pounds would be necessary to clear his expenses at Brighton. He owed a good deal in the town, but his debts of honour were still more formidable. Mr Gardiner did not attempt to conceal these particulars from the Longbourn family; Jane heard them with horror. 'A gamester!' she cried. 'This is wholly unexpected. I had not an idea of it.'

Mr Gardiner added in his letter, that they might expect to see their father at home on the following day, which was Saturday. Rendered spiritless by the ill-success of all their endeavours, he had yielded to his brother-in-law's intreaty that he would return to his family, and leave it to him to do, whatever occasion might suggest to be advisable for continuing their pursuit. When Mrs Bennet was told of this, she did not express so much satisfaction as her children expected, considering what her anxiety for his life had been before.

'What, is he coming home, and without poor Lydia!' she cried. 'Sure he will not leave London before he has found them. Who is to fight Wickham, and make him marry her, if he comes away?'

As Mrs Gardiner began to wish to be at home, it was settled that she and her children should go to London, at the same time that Mr Bennet came from it. The coach, therefore, took them the first stage of their journey, and brought its master back to Longbourn.

Mrs Gardiner went away in all the perplexity about Elizabeth and her Derbyshire friend, that had attended her from that part of the world. His name had never been voluntarily mentioned before them by her niece; and the kind of half-expectation which Mrs Gardiner had formed, of their being followed by a letter from him, had ended in nothing. Elizabeth had received none since her return, that could come from Pemberley.

The present unhappy state of the family, rendered any other excuse for the lowness of her spirits unnecessary; nothing, therefore, could be fairly conjectured from that, though Elizabeth, who was by this time tolerably well acquainted with her own feelings, was perfectly aware, that, had she known nothing of Darcy, she could have borne the dread of Lydia's infamy somewhat better. It would have spared her, she thought, one sleepless night out of two.

When Mr Bennet arrived, he had all the appearance of his usual philosophic composure. He said as little as he had ever been in the habit of saying; made no mention of the business that had taken him away, and it was some time before his daughters had courage to speak of it.

It was not till the afternoon, when he joined them at tea, that Elizabeth ventured to introduce the subject; and then, on her briefly expressing her sorrow for what he must have endured, he replied, 'Say nothing of that. Who should suffer but myself? It has been my own doing, and I ought to feel it.'

'You must not be too severe upon yourself,' replied Elizabeth.

'You may well warn me against such an evil. Human nature is so prone to fall into it! No, Lizzy, let me once in my life feel how much I have been to blame. I am not afraid of being overpowered by the impression. It will pass away soon enough.'

'Do you suppose them to be in London?'

'Yes; where else can they be so well concealed?'

'And Lydia used to want to go to London,' added Kitty.

'She is happy, then,' said her father, drily; 'and her residence there will probably be of some duration.'

Then, after a short silence, he continued, 'Lizzy, I bear you no ill-will for being justified in your advice to me last May, which, considering the event, shows some greatness of mind.'

They were interrupted by Miss Bennet, who came to fetch her mother's tea.

'This is a parade,' cried he, 'which does one good; it gives such an elegance to misfortune! Another day I will do the same; I will sit in my library, in my night cap and powdering gown, and give as much trouble as I can, – or, perhaps, I may defer it, till Kitty runs away.'

'I am not going to run away, Papa,' said Kitty, fretfully; 'if I should ever go to Brighton, I would behave better than Lydia.'

'You go to Brighton! – I would not trust you so near it as East Bourne, for fifty pounds! No, Kitty, I have at last learnt to be cautious, and you will feel the effects of it. No officer is ever to enter my house again, nor even to pass through the village. Balls will be absolutely prohibited, unless you stand up with one of your sisters. And you are never to stir out of doors, till you can prove, that you have spent ten minutes of every day in a rational manner.'

Kitty, who took all these threats in a serious light, began to cry.

'Well, well,' said he, 'do not make yourself unhappy. If you are a good girl for the next ten years, I will take you to a review at the end of them.'

Two days after Mr Bennet's return, as Jane and Elizabeth were walking together in the shrubbery behind the house, they saw the housekeeper coming towards them, and, concluding that she came to call them to their mother, went forward to meet her; but, instead of the expected summons, when they approached her, she said to Miss Bennet, 'I beg your pardon, madam, for interrupting you, but I was in hopes you might have got some good news from town, so I took the liberty of coming to ask.'

'What do you mean, Hill? We have heard nothing from town.'

'Dear madam,' cried Mrs Hill, in great astonishment, 'don't you know there is an express come for master from Mr Gardiner? He has been here this half hour, and master has had a letter.'

Away ran the girls, too eager to get in to have time for speech. They ran through the vestibule into the breakfast room; from thence to the library; – their father was in neither; and they were on the point of seeking him up stairs with their mother, when they were met by the butler, who said,

'If you are looking for my master, ma'am, he is walking towards the little copse.'

Upon this information, they instantly passed through the hall once more, and ran across the lawn after their father, who was deliberately pursuing his way towards a small wood on one side of the paddock.

Jane, who was not so light, nor so much in the habit of running as Elizabeth, soon lagged behind, while her sister, panting for breath, came up with him, and eagerly cried out,

'Oh, Papa, what news? what news? have you heard from my uncle?'

'Yes, I have had a letter from him by express.'

'Well, and what news does it bring? good or bad?'

'What is there of good to be expected?' said he, taking the letter from his pocket; 'but perhaps you would like to read it.'

Elizabeth impatiently caught it from his hand. Jane now came up.

'Read it aloud,' said their father, 'for I hardly know myself what it is about.'

> Gracechurch street, Monday
>
> August 2
>
> MY DEAR BROTHER – At last I am able to send you some tidings of my niece, and such as, upon the whole, I hope will give you satisfaction. Soon after you left me on Saturday, I was fortunate enough to find out in what part of London they were. The

particulars, I reserve till we meet. It is enough to know they are discovered, I have seen them both –'

'Then it is, as I always hoped,' cried Jane; 'they are married!'
Elizabeth read on:

I have seen them both. They are not married, nor can I find there was any intention of being so; but if you are willing to perform the engagements which I have ventured to make on your side, I hope it will not be long before they are. All that is required of you is, to assure to your daughter, by settlement, her equal share of the five thousand pounds, secured among your children after the decease of yourself and my sister; and, moreover, to enter into an engagement of allowing her, during your life, one hundred pounds per annum. These are conditions, which, considering every thing, I had no hesitation in complying with, as far as I thought myself privileged, for you. I shall send this by express, that no time may be lost in bringing me your answer. You will easily comprehend, from these particulars, that Mr Wickham's circumstances are not so hopeless as they are generally believed to be. The world has been deceived in that respect; and I am happy to say, there will be some little money, even when all his debts are discharged, to settle on my niece, in addition to her own fortune. If, as I conclude will be the case, you send me full powers to act in your name, throughout the whole of this business, I will immediately give directions to Haggerston for preparing a proper settlement. There will not be the smallest occasion for your coming to town again; therefore, stay quietly at Longbourn, and depend on my diligence and care. Send back your answer as soon as you can, and be careful to write explicitly. We have judged it best, that my niece should be married from this house, of which I hope you will approve. She comes to us today. I shall write again as soon as any thing more is determined on. Yours, &c.

EDW. GARDINER

'Is it possible!' cried Elizabeth, when she had finished. 'Can it be possible that he will marry her?'

'Wickham is not so undeserving, then, as we have thought him;' said her sister. 'My dear father, I congratulate you.'

'And have you answered the letter?' said Elizabeth.

'No; but it must be done soon.'

Most earnestly did she then intreat him to lose no more time before he wrote.

'Oh! my dear father,' she cried, 'come back, and write immediately. Consider how important every moment is, in such a case.'

'Let me write for you,' said Jane, 'if you dislike the trouble yourself.'

'I dislike it very much,' he replied; 'but it must be done.'

And so saying, he turned back with them, and walked towards the house.

'And may I ask?' said Elizabeth, 'but the terms, I suppose, must be complied with.'

'Complied with! I am only ashamed of his asking so little.'

'And they must marry! Yet he is such a man!'

'Yes, yes, they must marry. There is nothing else to be done. But there are two things that I want very much to know: – one is, how much money your uncle has laid down, to bring it about; and the other, how I am ever to pay him.'

'Money! my uncle!' cried Jane, 'what do you mean, Sir?'

'I mean, that no man in his senses, would marry Lydia on so slight a temptation as one hundred a-year during my life, and fifty after I am gone.'

'That is very true,' said Elizabeth; 'though it had not occurred to me before. His debts to be discharged, and something still to remain! Oh! it must be my uncle's doings! Generous, good man, I am afraid he has distressed himself. A small sum could not do all this.'

'No,' said her father, 'Wickham's a fool, if he takes her with a farthing less than ten thousand pounds. I should be sorry to think so ill of him, in the very beginning of our relationship.'

'Ten thousand pounds! Heaven forbid! How is half such a sum to be repaid?'

Mr Bennet made no answer, and each of them, deep in thought, continued silent till they reached the house. Their father then went to the library to write, and the girls walked into the breakfast-room.

'And they are really to be married!' cried Elizabeth, as soon as they were by themselves. 'How strange this is! And for this we are to be thankful. That they should marry, small as is their chance of happiness, and wretched as is his character, we are forced to rejoice! Oh, Lydia!'

'I comfort myself with thinking,' replied Jane, 'that he certainly would not marry Lydia, if he had not a real regard for her. Though our kind uncle has done something towards clearing him, I cannot believe that ten thousand pounds, or any thing like it, has been advanced. He has children of his own, and may have more. How could he spare half ten thousand pounds?'

'If we are ever able to learn what Wickham's debts have been,' said Elizabeth, 'and how much is settled on his side on our sister, we shall exactly know what Mr Gardiner has done for them, because Wickham has not six-pence of his own. The kindness of my uncle and aunt can never be requited. Their taking her home, and affording her their personal protection and countenance, is such a sacrifice to her advantage, as years of gratitude cannot enough acknowledge. By this time she is actually with them! If such goodness does not make her miserable now, she will never deserve to be happy! What a meeting for her, when she first sees my aunt!'

'We must endeavour to forget all that has passed on either side,' said Jane: 'I hope and trust they will yet be happy. His consenting to marry her is a proof, I will believe, that he is come to a right way of thinking. Their mutual affection will steady them; and I flatter myself they will settle so quietly, and live in so rational a manner, as may in time make their past imprudence forgotten.'

'Their conduct has been such,' replied Elizabeth, 'as neither you, nor I, nor any body, can ever forget. It is useless to talk of it.'

It now occurred to the girls that their mother was in all likelihood perfectly ignorant of what had happened. They went to the library, therefore, and asked their father, whether he would not wish them to make it known to her. He was writing, and, without raising his head, coolly replied,

'Just as you please.'

'May we take my uncle's letter to read to her?'

'Take whatever you like, and get away.'

Elizabeth took the letter from his writing table, and they went upstairs together. Mary and Kitty were both with Mrs Bennet: one communication would, therefore, do for all. After a slight preparation for good news, the letter was read aloud. Mrs Bennet could hardly contain herself. As soon as Jane had read Mr Gardiner's hope of Lydia's being soon married, her joy burst forth, and every following sentence added to its exuberance. She was now in an irritation as violent from delight, as she had ever been fidgetty from alarm and vexation. To know that her daughter would be married was enough. She was disturbed by no fear for her felicity, nor humbled by any remembrance of her misconduct.

'My dear, dear Lydia!' she cried: 'This is delightful indeed! – She will be married! – I shall see her again! – She will be married at sixteen! – My good, kind brother! – I knew how it would be – I knew he would manage every thing. How I long to see her! and to see dear Wickham too! But the clothes, the wedding clothes! I will write to my sister Gardiner about them directly. Lizzy, my dear, run down to your father, and ask him how much he will give her. Stay, stay, I will go myself. Ring the bell, Kitty, for Hill. I will put on my things in a moment. My dear, dear Lydia! – How merry we shall be together when we meet!'

Her eldest daughter endeavoured to give some relief to the violence of these transports, by leading her thoughts to the obligations which Mr Gardiner's behaviour laid them all under.

'For we must attribute this happy conclusion,' she added, 'in a great measure, to his kindness. We are persuaded that he has pledged himself to assist Mr Wickham with money.'

'Well,' cried her mother, 'it is all very right; who should do it but her own uncle? If he had not had a family of his own, I and my children must have had all his money you know, and it is the first time we have ever had any thing from him, except a few presents. Well! I am so happy. In a short time, I shall have a daughter married. Mrs Wickham! How well it sounds. And she was only sixteen last June. My dear Jane, I am in such a flutter, that I am sure I can't write; so I will dictate, and you write for me. We will settle with your father about the money afterwards; but the things should be ordered immediately.'

She was then proceeding to all the particulars of calico, muslin, and cambric, and would shortly have dictated some very plentiful orders, had not Jane, though with some difficulty, persuaded her to wait, till her father was at leisure to be consulted. One day's delay she observed, would be of small importance; and her mother was too happy, to be quite so obstinate as usual. Other schemes too came into her head.

'I will go to Meryton,' said she, 'as soon as I am dressed, and tell the good, good news to my sister Philips. And as I come back, I can call on Lady Lucas and Mrs Long. Kitty, run down and order the carriage. An airing would do me a great deal of good, I am sure. Girls, can I do any thing for you in Meryton? Oh! here comes Hill. My dear Hill, have you heard the good news? Miss Lydia is going to be married; and you shall all have a bowl of punch, to make merry at her wedding.'

Mrs Hill began instantly to express her joy. Elizabeth received her congratulations amongst the rest, and then, sick of this folly, took refuge in her own room, that she might think with freedom.

Poor Lydia's situation must, at best, be bad enough; but that it was no worse, she had need to be thankful. She felt it so; and though, in looking forward, neither rational happiness nor worldly prosperity, could be justly expected for her sister; in looking back to what they had feared, only two hours ago, she felt all the advantages of what they had gained.

Chapter 50

Mr Bennet had very often wished, before this period of his life, that, instead of spending his whole income, he had laid by an annual sum, for the better provision of his children, and of his wife, if she survived him. He now wished it more than ever. Had he done his duty in that respect, Lydia need not have been indebted to her uncle, for whatever of honour or credit could now be purchased for her. The satisfaction of prevailing on one of the most worthless young men in Great Britain to be her husband, might then have rested in its proper place.

He was seriously concerned, that a cause of so little advantage to any one, should be forwarded at the sole expense of his brother-in-law, and he was determined, if possible, to find out the extent of his assistance, and to discharge the obligation as soon as he could.

When first Mr Bennet had married, economy was held to be perfectly useless; for, of course, they were to have a son. This son was to join in cutting off the entail, as soon as he should be of age, and the widow and younger children would by that means be provided for. Five daughters successively entered the world, but yet the son was to come; and Mrs Bennet, for many years after Lydia's birth, had been certain that he would. This event had at last been despaired of, but it was then too late to be saving. Mrs Bennet had no turn for economy, and her husband's love of independence had alone prevented their exceeding their income.

Five thousand pounds was settled by marriage articles on Mrs Bennet and the children. But in what proportions it should be divided amongst the latter, depended on the will of the parents. This was one point, with regard to Lydia at least, which was now to be settled, and Mr Bennet could have no hesitation in acceding to the proposal before him. In terms of grateful acknowledgment for the kindness of his brother, though expressed most concisely, he then delivered on paper his perfect approbation of all that was done, and his willingness to fulfil the engagements that had been made for him. He had never before supposed that, could Wickham be prevailed on to marry his daughter, it would be done with so little inconvenience to himself, as by the present arrangement. He would scarcely be ten pounds a year the loser, by the hundred that was to be paid them; for, what with her board and pocket allowance, and the continual presents in money, which passed to her, through her mother's hands, Lydia's expenses had been very little within that sum.

That it would be done with such trifling exertion on his side, too, was another very welcome surprise; for his chief wish at present, was to have as little trouble in the business as possible. When the first transports of rage which had produced his activity in seeking her were over, he naturally returned to all his former indolence. His letter was soon dispatched; for though dilatory in undertaking business, he was quick in its execution. He begged to know farther particulars of what he was indebted to his brother; but was too angry with Lydia, to send any message to her.

The good news quickly spread through the house; and with

proportionate speed through the neighbourhood. It was borne in the latter with decent philosophy. To be sure it would have been more for the advantage of conversation, had Miss Lydia Bennet come upon the town; or, as the happiest alternative, been secluded from the world, in some distant farm house. But there was much to be talked of, in marrying her; and the good-natured wishes for her well-doing, which had proceeded before, from all the spiteful old ladies in Meryton, lost but little of their spirit in this change of circumstances, because with such an husband, her misery was considered certain.

It was a fortnight since Mrs Bennet had been down stairs, but on this happy day, she again took her seat at the head of her table, and in spirits oppressively high. No sentiment of shame gave a damp to her triumph. The marriage of a daughter, which had been the first object of her wishes, since Jane was sixteen, was now on the point of accomplishment, and her thoughts and her words ran wholly on those attendants of elegant nuptials, fine muslins, new carriages, and servants. She was busily searching through the neighbourhood for a proper situation for her daughter, and, without knowing or considering what their income might be, rejected many as deficient in size and importance.

'Haye-Park might do,' said she, 'if the Gouldings would quit it, or the great house at Stoke, if the drawing-room were larger; but Ashworth is too far off! I could not bear to have her ten miles from me; and as for Purvis Lodge, the attics are dreadful.'

Her husband allowed her to talk on without interruption, while the servants remained. But when they had withdrawn, he said to her, 'Mrs Bennet, before you take any, or all of these houses, for your son and daughter, let us come to a right understanding. Into one house in this neighbourhood, they shall never have admittance. I will not encourage the impudence of either, by receiving them at Longbourn.'

A long dispute followed this declaration; but Mr Bennet was firm: it soon led to another; and Mrs Bennet found, with amazement and horror, that her husband would not advance a guinea to buy clothes for his daughter. He protested that she should receive from him no mark of affection whatever, on the occasion. Mrs Bennet could hardly comprehend it. That his anger could be carried to such a point of inconceivable resentment, as to refuse his daughter a privilege, without which her marriage would scarcely seem valid, exceeded all that she could believe possible. She was more alive to the disgrace, which the want of new clothes must reflect on her daughter's nuptials, than to any sense of shame at her eloping and living with Wickham, a fortnight before they took place.

Elizabeth was now most heartily sorry that she had, from the distress of the moment, been led to make Mr Darcy acquainted with their fears for her sister; for since her marriage would so shortly give the proper termination to the elopement, they might hope to conceal its unfavourable beginning, from all those who were not immediately on the spot.

She had no fear of its spreading farther, through his means. There were few people on whose secrecy she would have more confidently depended; but at the same time, there was no one, whose knowledge of a sister's frailty would have mortified her so much. Not, however, from any fear of disadvantage from it, individually to herself; for at any rate, there seemed a gulf impassable between them. Had Lydia's marriage been concluded on the most honourable terms, it was not to be supposed that Mr Darcy would connect himself with a family, where to every other objection would now be added, an alliance and relationship of the nearest kind with the man whom he so justly scorned.

From such a connection she could not wonder that he should shrink. The wish of procuring her regard, which she had assured herself of his feeling in Derbyshire, could not in rational expectation survive such a blow as this. She was humbled, she was grieved; she repented, though she hardly knew of what. She became jealous of his esteem, when she could no longer hope to be benefited by it. She wanted to hear of him, when there seemed the least chance of gaining intelligence. She was convinced that she could have been happy with him; when it was no longer likely they should meet.

What a triumph for him, as she often thought, could he know

that the proposals which she had proudly spurned only four months ago, would now have been gladly and gratefully received! He was as generous, she doubted not, as the most generous of his sex. But while he was mortal, there must be a triumph.

She began now to comprehend that he was exactly the man, who, in disposition and talents, would most suit her. His understanding and temper, though unlike her own, would have answered all her wishes. It was a union that must have been to the advantage of both; by her ease and liveliness, his mind might have been softened, his manners improved, and from his judgment, information, and knowledge of the world, she must have received benefit of greater importance.

But no such happy marriage could now teach the admiring multitude what connubial felicity really was. A union of a different tendency, and precluding the possibility of the other, was soon to be formed in their family.

How Wickham and Lydia were to be supported in tolerable independence, she could not imagine. But how little of permanent happiness could belong to a couple who were only brought together because their passions were stronger than their virtue, she could easily conjecture.

*

Mr Gardiner soon wrote again to his brother. To Mr Bennet's acknowledgments he briefly replied, with assurances of his eagerness to promote the welfare of any of his family; and concluded with intreaties that the subject might never be mentioned to him again. The principal purport of his letter was to inform them, that Mr Wickham had resolved on quitting the Militia.

It was greatly my wish that he should do so [he added], as soon as his marriage was fixed on. And I think you will agree with me, in considering a removal from that corps as highly advisable, both on his account and my niece's. It is Mr Wickham's intention to go into the regulars; and, among his former friends, there are still some who are able and willing to assist him in the army. He has the promise of an ensigncy in General —'s regiment, now quartered in the North. It is an advantage to have it so far from this part of the kingdom. He promises fairly, and I hope among different people, where they may each have a character to preserve, they will both be more prudent. I have written to Colonel Forster, to inform him of our present arrangements, and to request that he will satisfy the various creditors of Mr Wickham in and near Brighton, with assurances of speedy payment, for which I have pledged myself. And will you give yourself the trouble of carrying similar assurances to his creditors in Meryton, of whom I shall subjoin a list, according to his information. He has given in all his debts; I hope at least he has not deceived us. Haggerston has our directions, and all will be completed in a week. They will then join his regiment, unless they are first invited to Longbourn; and I understand from Mrs Gardiner, that my niece is very desirous of seeing you all, before she leaves the South. She is well, and begs to be dutifully remembered to you and her mother. – Yours, &c.

E. GARDINER.

Mr Bennet and his daughters saw all the advantages of Wickham's removal from the —shire, as clearly as Mr Gardiner could do. But Mrs Bennet, was not so well pleased with it. Lydia's being settled in the North, just when she had expected most pleasure and pride in her company, for she had by no means given up her plan of their residing in Hertfordshire, was a severe disappointment; and besides, it was such a pity that Lydia should be taken from a regiment where she was acquainted with every body, and had so many favourites.

'She is so fond of Mrs Forster,' said she, 'it will be quite shocking to send her away! And there are several of the young men, too, that she likes very much. The officers may not be so pleasant in General —'s regiment.'

His daughter's request, for such it might be considered, of being admitted into her family again, before she set off for the North, received at first an absolute negative. But Jane and Elizabeth, who agreed in wishing, for the sake of their sister's feelings and consequence, that she should be noticed on her marriage by her parents, urged him so earnestly, yet so rationally and so mildly, to receive her and her husband at Longbourn, as soon as they were married, that he was prevailed on to think as they thought, and act as they wished. And their mother had the satisfaction of knowing, that she should be able to show her married daughter in the neighbourhood, before she was banished to the North. When Mr Bennet wrote again to his brother, therefore, he sent his permission for them to come; and it was settled, that as soon as the ceremony was over, they should proceed to Longbourn. Elizabeth was surprised, however, that Wickham should consent to such a scheme, and, had she consulted only her own inclination, any meeting with him would have been the last object of her wishes.

Chapter 51

Their sister's wedding day arrived; and Jane and Elizabeth felt for her probably more than she felt for herself. The carriage was sent to meet them at —, and they were to return in it, by dinner-time. Their arrival was dreaded by the elder Miss Bennets; and Jane more especially, who gave Lydia the feelings which would have attended herself, had she been the culprit, was wretched in the thought of what her sister must endure.

They came. The family were assembled in the breakfast room, to receive them. Smiles decked the face of Mrs Bennet, as the carriage drove up to the door; her husband looked impenetrably grave; her daughters, alarmed, anxious, uneasy.

Lydia's voice was heard in the vestibule; the door was thrown open, and she ran into the room. Her mother stepped forwards, embraced her, and welcomed her with rapture; gave her hand with an affectionate smile to Wickham, who followed his lady, and wished them both joy,

with an alacrity which showed no doubt of their happiness.

Their reception from Mr Bennet, to whom they then turned, was not quite so cordial. His countenance rather gained in austerity; and he scarcely opened his lips. The easy assurance of the young couple, indeed, was enough to provoke him. Elizabeth was disgusted, and even Miss Bennet was shocked. Lydia was Lydia still; untamed, unabashed, wild, noisy, and fearless. She turned from sister to sister, demanding their congratulations, and when at length they all sat down, looked eagerly round the room, took notice of some little alteration in it, and observed, with a laugh, that it was a great while since she had been there.

Wickham was not at all more distressed than herself, but his manners were always so pleasing, that had his character and his marriage been exactly what they ought, his smiles and his easy address, while he claimed their relationship, would have delighted them all. Elizabeth had not before believed him quite equal to such assurance; but she sat down, resolving within herself, to draw no limits in future to the impudence of an impudent man. She blushed, and Jane blushed; but the cheeks of the two who caused their confusion, suffered no variation of colour.

There was no want of discourse. The bride and her mother could neither of them talk fast enough; and Wickham, who happened to sit near Elizabeth, began enquiring after his acquaintance in that neighbourhood, with a good humoured ease, which she felt very unable to equal in her replies. They seemed each of them to have the happiest memories in the world. Nothing of the past was recollected with pain; and Lydia led voluntarily to subjects, which her sisters would not have alluded to for the world.

'Only think of its being three months,' she cried, 'since I went away; it seems but a fortnight I declare; and yet there have been things enough happened in the time. Good gracious! when I went away, I am sure I had no more idea of being married till I came back again! though I thought it would be very good fun if I was.'

Her father lifted up his eyes. Jane was distressed. Elizabeth looked expressively at Lydia; but she, who never heard nor saw any thing of which she chose to be insensible, gaily continued, 'Oh! mamma, do the people hereabouts know I am married today? I was afraid they might not; and we overtook William Goulding in his curricle, so I was determined he should know it, and so I let down the side glass next to him, and took off my glove, and let my hand just rest upon the window frame, so that he might see the ring, and then I bowed and smiled like any thing.'

Elizabeth could bear it no longer. She got up, and ran out of the room; and returned no more, till she heard them passing through the hall to the dining-parlour. She then joined them soon enough to see Lydia, with anxious parade, walk up to her mother's right hand, and hear her say to her eldest sister, 'Ah! Jane, I take your place now, and you must go lower, because I am a married woman.'

It was not to be supposed that time would give Lydia that embarrassment, from which she had been so wholly free at first. Her ease and good spirits increased. She longed to see Mrs Philips, the Lucases, and all their other neighbours, and to hear herself called 'Mrs Wickham,' by each of them; and in the meantime, she went after dinner to show her ring and boast of being married, to Mrs Hill and the two housemaids.

'Well, mamma,' said she, when they were all returned to the breakfast room, 'and what do you think of my husband? Is not he a charming man? I am sure my sisters must all envy me. I only hope they may have half my good luck. They must all go to Brighton. That is the place to get husbands. What a pity it is, mamma, we did not all go.'

'Very true; and if I had my will, we should. But my dear Lydia, I don't at all like your going such a way off. Must it be so?'

'Oh, lord! yes; – there is nothing in that. I shall like it of all things. You and papa, and my sisters, must come down and see us. We shall be at Newcastle all the winter, and I dare say there will be some balls, and I will take care to get good partners for them all.'

'I should like it beyond any thing!' said her mother.

'And then when you go away, you may leave one or two of my

sisters behind you; and I dare say I shall get husbands for them before the winter is over.'

'I thank you for my share of the favour,' said Elizabeth; 'but I do not particularly like your way of getting husbands.'

Their visitors were not to remain above ten days with them. Mr Wickham had received his commission before he left London, and he was to join his regiment at the end of a fortnight.

No one but Mrs Bennet, regretted that their stay would be so short; and she made the most of the time, by visiting about with her daughter, and having very frequent parties at home. These parties were acceptable to all; to avoid a family circle was even more desirable to such as did think, than such as did not.

Wickham's affection for Lydia, was just what Elizabeth had expected to find it; not equal to Lydia's for him. She had scarcely needed her present observation to be satisfied, from the reason of things, that their elopement had been brought on by the strength of her love, rather than by his; and she would have wondered why, without violently caring for her, he chose to elope with her at all, had she not felt certain that his flight was rendered necessary by distress of circumstances; and if that were the case, he was not the young man to resist an opportunity of having a companion.

Lydia was exceedingly fond of him. He was her dear Wickham on every occasion; no one was to be put in competition with him. He did every thing best in the world; and she was sure he would kill more birds on the first of September, than any body else in the country.

One morning, soon after their arrival, as she was sitting with her two elder sisters, she said to Elizabeth,

'Lizzy, I never gave you an account of my wedding, I believe. You were not by, when I told mamma, and the others, all about it. Are not you curious to hear how it was managed?'

'No really,' replied Elizabeth; 'I think there cannot be too little said on the subject.'

'La! You are so strange! But I must tell you how it went off. We were married you know, at St. Clement's, because Wickham's lodgings were in that parish. And it was settled that we should all be there by eleven o'clock. My uncle and aunt and I were to go together; and the others were to meet us at the church. Well, Monday morning came, and I was in such a fuss! I was so afraid you know that something would happen to put it off, and then I should have gone quite distracted. And there was my aunt, all the time I was dressing, preaching and talking away just as if she was reading a sermon. However, I did not hear above one word in ten, for I was thinking, you may suppose, of my dear Wickham. I longed to know whether he would be married in his blue coat.

'Well, and so we breakfasted at ten as usual; I thought it would never be over; for, by the bye, you are to understand, that my uncle and aunt were horrid unpleasant all the time I was with them. If you'll believe me, I did not once put my foot out of doors, though I was there a fortnight. Not one party, or scheme, or any thing. To be sure London was rather thin, but however the little Theatre was open. Well, and so just as the carriage came to the door, my uncle was called away upon business to that horrid man Mr Stone. And then, you know, when once they get together, there is no end of it. Well, I was so frightened I did not know what to do, for my uncle was to give me away; and if we were beyond the hour, we could not be married all day. But, luckily, he came back again in ten minutes time, and then we all set out. However, I recollected afterwards, that if he had been prevented going, the wedding need not be put off, for Mr Darcy might have done as well.'

'Mr Darcy!' repeated Elizabeth, in utter amazement.

'Oh, yes! – he was to come there with Wickham, you know. But gracious me! I quite forgot! I ought not to have said a word about it. I promised them so faithfully! What will Wickham say? It was to be such a secret!'

'If it was to be secret,' said Jane, 'say not another word on the subject. You may depend upon my seeking no further.'

'Oh! certainly,' said Elizabeth, though burning with curiosity; 'we will ask you no questions.'

'Thank you,' said Lydia, 'for if you did, I should certainly tell you all, and then Wickham would be angry.'

On such encouragement to ask, Elizabeth was forced to put it out of her power, by running away.

But to live in ignorance on such a point was impossible; or at least it was impossible not to try for information. Mr Darcy had been at her sister's wedding. It was exactly a scene, and exactly among people, where he had apparently least to do, and least temptation to go. Conjectures as to the meaning of it, rapid and wild, hurried into her brain; but she was satisfied with none. Those that best pleased her, as placing his conduct in the noblest light, seemed most improbable. She could not bear such suspense; and hastily seizing a sheet of paper, wrote a short letter to her aunt, to request an explanation of what Lydia had dropt, if it were compatible with the secrecy which had been intended.

'You may readily comprehend,' she added, 'what my curiosity must be to know how a person unconnected with any of us, and (comparatively speaking) a stranger to our family, should have been amongst you at such a time. Pray write instantly, and let me understand it – unless it is, for very cogent reasons, to remain in the secrecy which Lydia seems to think necessary; and then I must endeavour to be satisfied with ignorance.'

'Not that I shall though,' she added to herself, as she finished the letter; 'and my dear aunt, if you do not tell me in an honourable manner, I shall certainly be reduced to tricks and stratagems to find it out.'

Jane's delicate sense of honour would not allow her to speak to Elizabeth privately of what Lydia had let fall; Elizabeth was glad of it; – till it appeared whether her inquiries would receive any satisfaction, she had rather be without a confidante.

Chapter 52

Elizabeth had the satisfaction of receiving an answer to her letter, as soon as she possibly could. She was no sooner in possession of it, than hurrying into the little copse, where she was least likely to be interrupted, she sat down on one of the benches, and prepared to be happy; for the length of the letter convinced her that it did not contain a denial.

Gracechurch street, Sept. 6

MY DEAR NIECE – I have just received your letter, and shall devote this whole morning to answering it, as I foresee that a little writing will not comprise what I have to tell you. I must confess myself surprised by your application; I did not expect it from you. Don't think me angry, however, for I only mean to let you know, that I had not imagined such enquiries to be necessary on your side. If you do not choose to understand me, forgive my impertinence. Your uncle is as much surprised as I am – and nothing but the belief of your being a party concerned, would have allowed him to act as he has done. But if you are really innocent and ignorant, I must be more explicit. On the very day of my coming home from Longbourn, your uncle had a most unexpected visitor. Mr Darcy called, and was shut up with him several hours. It was all over before I arrived; so my curiosity was not so dreadfully racked as yours seems to have been. He came to tell Mr Gardiner that he had found out where your sister and Mr Wickham were, and that he had seen and talked with them both, Wickham repeatedly, Lydia once. From what I can collect, he left Derbyshire only one day after ourselves, and came to town with the resolution of hunting for them. The motive professed, was his conviction of its being owing to himself that Wickham's worthlessness had not been so well known, as to make it impossible for any young woman of character, to love or confide in him. He generously imputed the whole to his mistaken pride, and confessed that he had before thought it beneath him, to lay his private actions open to the world. His character was to speak for itself. He called it, therefore, his duty to step forward, and endeavour to remedy an evil, which had been brought on by himself. If he had another motive, I am sure it would never disgrace him. He had been some days in town, before he was able to discover them; but he had something to direct his search, which was more than we had; and the consciousness of this, was another reason for his resolving to follow us. There is a lady, it seems, a Mrs Younge, who was some time ago governess to Miss Darcy, and was dismissed from her charge on some cause of disapprobation, though he did not say what. She then took a large house in Edward street, and has since maintained herself by letting lodgings. This Mrs Younge was, he knew, intimately acquainted with Wickham; and he went to her for intelligence of him, as soon as he got to town. But it was two or three days before he could get from her what he wanted. She would not betray her trust, I suppose, without bribery and corruption, for she really did know where her friend was to be found. Wickham indeed had gone to her, on their first arrival in London, and had she been able to receive them into her house, they would have taken up their abode with her. At length, however, our kind friend procured the wished-for direction. They were in —street. He saw Wickham, and afterwards insisted on seeing Lydia. His first object with her, he acknowledged, had been to persuade her to quit her present disgraceful situation, and return to her friends as soon as they could be prevailed on to receive her, offering his assistance, as far as it would go. But he found Lydia absolutely resolved on remaining where she was. She cared for none of her friends, she wanted no help of his, she would not hear of leaving Wickham. She was sure they should be married some time or other, and it did not much signify when. Since such were her feelings, it only remained, he thought, to secure and expedite a marriage, which, in his very first conversation with Wickham, he easily learnt, had never been his design. He confessed himself obliged to leave the regiment, on account of some debts of honour, which were very pressing; and scrupled not to lay all the ill-consequences of Lydia's flight, on her own folly alone. He meant to resign his commission immediately; and as to his future situation, he could conjecture very little about it. He must go somewhere, but he did not know where, and he knew he should have nothing to live on. Mr Darcy asked him why he had not married your sister at once. Though Mr Bennet was not imagined to be very rich, he would have been able to do something for him, and his situation must have been benefited by marriage. But he found, in reply to this question, that Wickham still cherished the hope of more effectually making his fortune by marriage, in some other country. Under such circumstances, however, he was not likely to be proof against the temptation of immediate relief. They met several times, for there was much to be discussed. Wickham of course wanted more than he could get; but at length was reduced to be reasonable. Every thing being settled between them, Mr Darcy's next step was to make your uncle acquainted with it, and he first called in Gracechurch street the evening before I came home. But Mr Gardiner could not be seen, and Mr Darcy found, on further enquiry, that your father was still with him, but would quit town the next morning. He did not judge your father to be a person whom he could so properly consult as your uncle, and therefore readily postponed seeing him, till after the departure of the former. He did not leave his name, and till the next day, it was only known that a gentleman had called on business. On Saturday he came again. Your father was gone, your uncle at home, and, as I said before, they had a great deal of talk together. They met again on Sunday, and then I saw him too. It was not all settled before Monday: as soon as it was, the express was sent off to Longbourn. But our visitor was very obstinate. I fancy, Lizzy, that obstinacy is the real defect of his character after all. He has been accused of many faults at different times; but this is the true one. Nothing was to be done that he did not do himself; though I am sure (and I do not speak it to be thanked, therefore say nothing about it,) your uncle would most readily have settled the whole. They battled it together for a long time, which was more than either the gentleman or lady concerned in it deserved. But at last your uncle was forced to yield, and instead of being allowed to be of use to his niece, was forced to put up with only having the probable credit of it, which went sorely against the grain; and I really believe your letter this morning gave him great pleasure, because it required an explanation that would rob him of his borrowed feathers, and give the praise where it was due. But, Lizzy, this must go no farther than yourself, or Jane at most. You know pretty well, I suppose, what has been done for the young people. His debts are to be paid, amounting, I believe, to considerably more than a thousand pounds, another thousand in addition to her own settled upon her, and his commission purchased. The reason why all this was to be done by him alone, was such as I have given above. It was owing to him, to his reserve, and want of proper consideration, that Wickham's character had been so misunderstood, and consequently that he had been received and noticed as he was. Perhaps there was some truth in this; though I doubt whether his reserve, or anybody's reserve, can be answerable for the event. But in spite of all this fine talking, my dear Lizzy, you may rest perfectly assured, that your uncle would never have yielded, if we had not given him credit for another interest in the affair. When all this was resolved on, he returned again to his friends, who were still staying at Pemberley; but it was agreed that he should be in London once more when the wedding took place, and all money matters were then to receive the last finish. I believe I have now told you every thing. It is a relation which you tell me is to give you great surprise; I hope at least it will not afford you any displeasure. Lydia came to us; and Wickham had constant admission to the house. He was exactly what he had been, when I knew him in Hertfordshire; but

I would not tell you how little I was satisfied with her behaviour while she stayed with us, if I had not perceived, by Jane's letter last Wednesday, that her conduct on coming home was exactly of a piece with it, and therefore what I now tell you, can give you no fresh pain. I talked to her repeatedly in the most serious manner, representing to her all the wickedness of what she had done, and all the unhappiness she had brought on her family. If she heard me, it was by good luck, for I am sure she did not listen. I was sometimes quite provoked, but then I recollected my dear Elizabeth and Jane, and for their sakes had patience with her. Mr Darcy was punctual in his return, and as Lydia informed you, attended the wedding. He dined with us the next day, and was to leave town again on Wednesday or Thursday. Will you be very angry with me, my dear Lizzy, if I take this opportunity of saying (what I was never bold enough to say before) how much I like him. His behaviour to us has, in every respect, been as pleasing as when we were in Derbyshire. His understanding and opinions all please me; he wants nothing but a little more liveliness, and that, if he marry prudently, his wife may teach him. I thought him very sly; – he hardly ever mentioned your name. But slyness seems the fashion.

Pray forgive me, if I have been very presuming, or at least do not punish me so far, as to exclude me from P. I shall never be quite happy till I have been all round the park. A low phaeton, with a nice little pair of ponies, would be the very thing. But I must write no more. The children have been wanting me this half hour.

Yours, very sincerely,

M. GARDINER

The contents of this letter threw Elizabeth into a flutter of spirits, in which it was difficult to determine whether pleasure or pain bore the greatest share. The vague and unsettled suspicions which uncertainty had produced of what Mr Darcy might have been doing to forward her sister's match, which she had feared to encourage, as an exertion of goodness too great to be probable, and at the same time dreaded to be just, from the pain of obligation, were proved beyond their greatest extent to be true! He had followed them purposely to town, he had taken on himself all the trouble and mortification attendant on such a research; in which supplication had been necessary to a woman whom he must abominate and despise, and where he was reduced to meet, frequently meet, reason with, persuade, and finally bribe, the man whom he always most wished to avoid, and whose very name it was punishment to him to pronounce. He had done all this for a girl whom he could neither regard nor esteem. Her heart did whisper, that he had done it for her. But it was a hope shortly checked by other considerations, and she soon felt that even her vanity was insufficient, when required to depend on his affection for her, for a woman who had already refused him, as able to overcome a sentiment so natural as abhorrence against relationship with Wickham. Brother-in-law of Wickham! Every kind of pride must revolt from the connection. He had to be sure done much. She was ashamed to think how much. But he had given a reason for his interference, which asked no extraordinary stretch of belief. It was reasonable that he should feel he had been wrong; he had liberality, and he had the means of exercising it; and though she would not place herself as his principal inducement, she could, perhaps, believe, that remaining partiality for her, might assist his endeavours in a cause where her peace of mind must be materially concerned. It was painful, exceedingly painful, to know that they were under obligations to a person who could never receive a return. They owed the restoration of Lydia, her character, every thing to him. Oh! how heartily did she grieve over every ungracious sensation she had ever encouraged, every saucy speech she had ever directed towards him. For herself she was humbled; but she was proud of him. Proud that in a cause of compassion and honour, he had been able to get the better of himself. She read over her aunt's commendation of him again and again. It was hardly enough; but it pleased her. She was even sensible of some pleasure, though mixed with regret, on finding how steadfastly both she and her uncle had been persuaded that affection and confidence subsisted between Mr Darcy and herself.

She was roused from her seat, and her reflections, by some one's approach; and before she could strike into another path, she was overtaken by Wickham.

'I am afraid I interrupt your solitary ramble, my dear sister?' said he, as he joined her.

'You certainly do,' she replied with a smile; 'but it does not follow that the interruption must be unwelcome.'

'I should be sorry indeed, if it were. We were always good friends; and now we are better.'

'True. Are the others coming out?'

'I do not know. Mrs Bennet and Lydia are going in the carriage to Meryton. And so, my dear sister, I find, from our uncle and aunt, that you have actually seen Pemberley.'

She replied in the affirmative.

'I almost envy you the pleasure, and yet I believe it would be too much for me, or else I could take it in my way to Newcastle. And you saw the old housekeeper, I suppose? Poor Reynolds, she was always very fond of me. But of course she did not mention my name to you.'

'Yes, she did.'

'And what did she say?'

'That you were gone into the army, and she was afraid had – not turned out well. At such a distance as that, you know, things are strangely misrepresented.'

'Certainly,' he replied, biting his lips. Elizabeth hoped she had silenced him; but he soon afterwards said,

'I was surprised to see Darcy in town last month. We passed each other several times. I wonder what he can be doing there.'

'Perhaps preparing for his marriage with Miss de Bourgh,' said Elizabeth. 'It must be something particular, to take him there at this time of year.'

'Undoubtedly. Did you see him while you were at Lambton? I thought I understood from the Gardiners that you had.'

'Yes; he introduced us to his sister.'

'And do you like her?'

'Very much.'

'I have heard, indeed, that she is uncommonly improved within this year or two. When I last saw her, she was not very promising. I am very glad you liked her. I hope she will turn out well.'

'I dare say she will; she has got over the most trying age.'

'Did you go by the village of Kympton?'

'I do not recollect that we did.'

'I mention it, because it is the living which I ought to have had. A most delightful place! – Excellent Parsonage House! It would have suited me in every respect.'

'How should you have liked making sermons?'

'Exceedingly well. I should have considered it as part of my duty, and the exertion would soon have been nothing. One ought not to repine; – but, to be sure, it would have been such a thing for me! The quiet, the retirement of such a life, would have answered all my ideas of happiness! But it was not to be. Did you ever hear Darcy mention the circumstance, when you were in Kent?'

'I have heard from authority, which I thought as good, that it was left you conditionally only, and at the will of the present patron.'

'You have. Yes, there was something in that; I told you so from the first, you may remember.'

'I did hear, too, that there was a time, when sermon-making was not so palatable to you as it seems to be at present; that you actually declared your resolution of never taking orders, and that the business had been compromised accordingly.'

'You did! and it was not wholly without foundation. You may remember what I told you on that point, when first we talked of it.'

They were now almost at the door of the house, for she had walked fast to get rid of him; and unwilling, for her sister's sake, to provoke him, she only said in reply, with a good-humoured smile,

'Come, Mr Wickham, we are brother and sister, you know. Do not let us quarrel about the past. In future, I hope we shall be always of one mind.'

She held out her hand; he kissed it with affectionate gallantry, though he hardly knew how to look, and they entered the house.

Chapter 53

Mr Wickham was so perfectly satisfied with this conversation, that he never again distressed himself, or provoked his dear sister Elizabeth, by introducing the subject of it; and she was pleased to find that she had said enough to keep him quiet.

The day of his and Lydia's departure soon came, and Mrs Bennet was forced to submit to a separation, which, as her husband by no means entered into her scheme of their all going to Newcastle, was likely to continue at least a twelvemonth.

'Oh! my dear Lydia,' she cried, 'when shall we meet again?'

'Oh, lord! I don't know. Not these two or three years perhaps.'

'Write to me very often, my dear.'

'As often as I can. But you know married women have never much time for writing. My sisters may write to me. They will have nothing else to do.'

Mr Wickham's adieus were much more affectionate than his wife's. He smiled, looked handsome, and said many pretty things.

'He is as fine a fellow,' said Mr Bennet, as soon as they were out of the house, 'as ever I saw. He simpers, and smirks, and makes love to us all. I am prodigiously proud of him. I defy even Sir William Lucas himself, to produce a more valuable son-in-law.'

The loss of her daughter made Mrs Bennet very dull for several days.

'I often think,' said she, 'that there is nothing so bad as parting with one's friends. One seems so forlorn without them.'

'This is the consequence you see, Madam, of marrying a daughter,' said Elizabeth. 'It must make you better satisfied that your other four are single.'

'It is no such thing. Lydia does not leave me because she is married; but only because her husband's regiment happens to be so far off. If that had been nearer, she would not have gone so soon.'

But the spiritless condition which this event threw her into, was shortly relieved, and her mind opened again to the agitation of hope, by an article of news, which then began to be in circulation. The housekeeper at Netherfield had received orders to prepare for the arrival of her master, who was coming down in a day or two, to shoot there for several weeks. Mrs Bennet was quite in the fidgets. She looked at Jane, and smiled, and shook her head by turns.

'Well, well, and so Mr Bingley is coming down, sister,' (for Mrs Philips first brought her the news.) 'Well, so much the better. Not that I care about it, though. He is nothing to us, you know, and I am sure I never want to see him again. But, however, he is very welcome to come to Netherfield, if he likes it. And who knows what may happen? But that is nothing to us. You know, sister, we agreed long ago never to mention a word about it. And so, is it quite certain he is coming?'

'You may depend on it,' replied the other, 'for Mrs Nicholls was in Meryton last night; I saw her passing by, and went out myself on purpose to know the truth of it; and she told me that it was certain true. He comes down on Thursday at the latest, very likely on Wednesday. She was going to the butcher's, she told me, on purpose to order in some meat on Wednesday, and she has got three couple of ducks, just fit to be killed.'

Miss Bennet had not been able to hear of his coming, without changing colour. It was many months since she had mentioned his name to Elizabeth; but now, as soon as they were alone together, she said,

'I saw you look at me today, Lizzy, when my aunt told us of the present report; and I know I appeared distressed. But don't imagine it was from any silly cause. I was only confused for the moment, because I felt that I should be looked at. I do assure you, that the news does not affect me either with pleasure or pain. I am glad of one thing, that he comes alone; because we shall see the less of him. Not that I am afraid of myself, but I dread other people's remarks.'

Elizabeth did not know what to make of it. Had she not seen him in Derbyshire, she might have supposed him capable of coming there, with no other view than what was acknowledged; but she still thought him partial to Jane, and she wavered as to the greater probability of his coming there with his friend's permission, or being bold enough to come without it.

'Yet it is hard,' she sometimes thought, 'that this poor man cannot come to a house, which he has legally hired, without raising all this speculation! I will leave him to himself.'

In spite of what her sister declared, and really believed to be her feelings, in the expectation of his arrival, Elizabeth could easily perceive that her spirits were affected by it. They were more disturbed, more unequal, than she had often seen them.

The subject which had been so warmly canvassed between their parents, about a twelvemonth ago, was now brought forward again.

'As soon as ever Mr Bingley comes, my dear,' said Mrs Bennet, 'you will wait on him of course.'

'No, no. You forced me into visiting him last year, and promised if I went to see him, he should marry one of my daughters. But it ended in nothing, and I will not be sent on a fool's errand again.'

His wife represented to him how absolutely necessary such an attention would be from all the neighbouring gentlemen, on his returning to Netherfield.

''Tis[28] an etiquette I despise,' said he. 'If he wants our society, let him seek it. He knows where we live. I will not spend my hours in running after my neighbours every time they go away, and come back again.'

'Well, all I know is, that it will be abominably rude if you do not wait on him. But, however, that shan't prevent my asking him to dine here, I am determined. We must have Mrs Long and the Gouldings soon. That will make thirteen with ourselves, so there will be just room at table for him.'

Consoled by this resolution, she was the better able to bear her husband's incivility; though it was very mortifying to know that her neighbours might all see Mr Bingley in consequence of it, before they did. As the day of his arrival drew near,

'I begin to be sorry that he comes at all,' said Jane to her sister. 'It would be nothing; I could see him with perfect indifference, but I can hardly bear to hear it thus perpetually talked of. My mother means well; but she does not know, no one can know how much I suffer from what she says. Happy shall I be, when his stay at Netherfield is over!'

'I wish I could say any thing to comfort you,' replied Elizabeth; 'but it is wholly out of my power. You must feel it; and the usual satisfaction of preaching patience to a sufferer is denied me, because you have always so much.'

Mr Bingley arrived. Mrs Bennet, through the assistance of servants, contrived to have the earliest tidings of it, that the period of anxiety and fretfulness on her side, might be as long as it could. She counted the days that must intervene before their invitation could be sent; hopeless of seeing him before. But on the third morning after his arrival in Hertfordshire, she saw him from her dressing-room window, enter the paddock, and ride towards the house.

Her daughters were eagerly called to partake of her joy. Jane resolutely kept her place at the table; but Elizabeth, to satisfy her mother, went to the window – she looked, – she saw Mr Darcy with him, and sat down again by her sister.

'There is a gentleman with him, mamma,' said Kitty; 'who can it be?'

'Some acquaintance or other, my dear, I suppose; I am sure I do not know.'

'La!' replied Kitty, 'it looks just like that man that used to be with him before. Mr what's his name. That tall, proud man.'

'Good gracious! Mr Darcy! – and so it does I vow. Well, any friend of Mr Bingley's will always be welcome here to be sure; but else I must say that I hate the very sight of him.'

Jane looked at Elizabeth with surprise and concern. She knew but little of their meeting in Derbyshire, and therefore felt for the awkwardness which must attend her sister, in seeing him almost for the first time after receiving his explanatory letter. Both sisters were uncomfortable enough. Each felt for the other, and of course for themselves; and their mother talked on, of her dislike of Mr Darcy, and her resolution to be civil to him only as Mr Bingley's friend, without being heard by either of them. But Elizabeth had sources of uneasiness which could not be suspected by Jane, to whom she had never yet had courage to show Mrs Gardiner's letter, or to relate her own change of sentiment towards him. To Jane, he could be only a man whose proposals she had refused, and whose merit she had undervalued; but to her own more extensive information, he was the person, to whom the whole family were indebted for the first of benefits, and whom she regarded herself with an interest, if not quite so tender, at least as reasonable and just, as what Jane felt for Bingley. Her astonishment at his coming – at his coming to Netherfield, to Longbourn, and voluntarily seeking her again, was almost equal to what she had known on first witnessing his altered behaviour in Derbyshire.

The colour which had been driven from her face, returned for half a minute with an additional glow, and a smile of delight added lustre to her eyes, as she thought for that space of time, that his affection and wishes must still be unshaken. But she would not be secure.

'Let me first see how he behaves,' said she; 'it will then be early enough for expectation.'

She sat intently at work, striving to be composed, and without daring to lift up her eyes, till anxious curiosity carried them to the face of her sister, as the servant was approaching the door. Jane looked a little paler than usual, but more sedate than Elizabeth had expected. On the gentlemen's appearing, her colour increased; yet she received them with tolerable ease, and with a propriety of behaviour equally free from any symptom of resentment, or any unnecessary complaisance.

Elizabeth said as little to either as civility would allow, and sat down again to her work, with an eagerness which it did not often command. She had ventured only one glance at Darcy. He looked serious as usual; and she thought, more as he had been used to look in Hertfordshire, than as she had seen him at Pemberley. But, perhaps he could not in her mother's presence be what he was before her uncle and aunt. It was a painful, but not an improbable, conjecture.

Bingley, she had likewise seen for an instant, and in that short period saw him looking both pleased and embarrassed. He was received by Mrs Bennet with a degree of civility, which made her two daughters ashamed, especially when contrasted with the cold and ceremonious politeness of her curtsey and address to his friend.

Elizabeth particularly, who knew that her mother owed to the latter the preservation of her favourite daughter from irremediable infamy, was hurt and distressed to a most painful degree by a distinction so ill applied.

Darcy, after enquiring of her how Mr and Mrs Gardiner did, a question which she could not answer without confusion, said scarcely any thing. He was not seated by her; perhaps that was the reason of his silence; but it had not been so in Derbyshire. There he had talked to her friends, when he could not to herself. But now several minutes elapsed, without bringing the sound of his voice; and when occasionally, unable to resist the impulse of curiosity, she raised her eyes to his face, she as often found him looking at Jane, as at herself, and frequently on no object but the ground. More thoughtfulness, and less anxiety to please than when they last met, were plainly expressed. She was disappointed, and angry with herself for being so.

'Could I expect it to be otherwise!' said she. 'Yet why did he come?'

She was in no humour for conversation with any one but himself; and to him she had hardly courage to speak.

She enquired after his sister, but could do no more.

'It is a long time, Mr Bingley, since you went away,' said Mrs Bennet.

He readily agreed to it.

'I began to be afraid you would never come back again. People did say, you meant to quit the place entirely at Michaelmas; but, however, I hope it is not true. A great many changes have happened in the neighbourhood, since you went away. Miss Lucas is married and settled. And one of my own daughters. I suppose you have heard of it; indeed, you must have seen it in the papers. It was in the Times and the Courier, I know; though it was not put in as it ought to be. It was only said, "Lately, George Wickham, Esq to Miss Lydia Bennet," without there being a syllable said of her father, or the place where she lived, or any thing. It was my brother Gardiner's drawing up too, and I wonder how he came to make such an awkward business of it. Did you see it?'

Bingley replied that he did, and made his congratulations. Elizabeth dared not lift up her eyes. How Mr Darcy looked, therefore, she could not tell.

'It is a delightful thing, to be sure, to have a daughter well married,' continued her mother, 'but at the same time, Mr Bingley, it is very hard to have her taken such a way from me. They are gone down to Newcastle, a place quite northward, it seems, and there they are to stay, I do not know how long. His regiment is there; for I suppose you have heard of his leaving the —shire, and of his being gone into the regulars. Thank Heaven! he has some friends, though perhaps not so many as he deserves.'

Elizabeth, who knew this to be levelled at Mr Darcy, was in such misery of shame, that she could hardly keep her seat. It drew from her, however, the exertion of speaking, which nothing else had so effectually done before; and she asked Bingley, whether he meant to make any stay in the country at present. A few weeks, he believed.

'When you have killed all your own birds, Mr Bingley,' said her mother, 'I beg you will come here, and shoot as many as you please, on Mr Bennet's manor. I am sure he will be vastly happy to oblige you, and will save all the best of the coves for you.'

Elizabeth's misery increased, at such unnecessary, such officious attention! Were the same fair prospect to arise at present, as had flattered them a year ago, every thing, she was persuaded, would be hastening to the same vexatious conclusion. At that instant she felt, that years of happiness could not make Jane or herself amends, for moments of such painful confusion.

'The first wish of my heart,' said she to herself, 'is never more to be in company with either of them. Their society can afford no pleasure, that will atone for such wretchedness as this! Let me never see either one or the other again!'

Yet the misery, for which years of happiness were to offer no compensation, received soon afterwards material relief, from observing how much the beauty of her sister re-kindled the admiration of her former lover. When first he came in, he had spoken to her but little; but every five minutes seemed to be giving her more of his attention. He found her as handsome as she had been last year; as good natured, and as unaffected, though not quite so chatty. Jane was anxious that no difference should be perceived in her at all, and was really persuaded that she talked as much as ever. But her mind was so busily engaged, that she did not always know when she was silent.

When the gentlemen rose to go away, Mrs Bennet was mindful of her intended civility, and they were invited and engaged to dine at Longbourn in a few days' time.

'You are quite a visit in my debt, Mr Bingley,' she added, 'for when you went to town last winter, you promised to take a family dinner with us, as soon as you returned. I have not forgot, you see; and I assure you, I was very much disappointed that you did not come back and keep your engagement.'

Bingley looked a little silly at this reflection, and said something of his concern, at having been prevented by business. They then went away.

Mrs Bennet had been strongly inclined to ask them to stay and dine there, that day; but, though she always kept a very good table, she did not think any thing less than two courses, could be good enough for a man, on whom she had such anxious designs, or satisfy the appetite and pride of one who had ten thousand a year.

Chapter 54

As soon as they were gone, Elizabeth walked out to recover her spirits; or in other words, to dwell without interruption on those subjects that must deaden them more. Mr Darcy's behaviour astonished and vexed her.

'Why, if he came only to be silent, grave, and indifferent,' said she, 'did he come at all?'

She could settle it in no way that gave her pleasure.

'He could be still amiable, still pleasing, to my uncle and aunt, when he was in town; and why not to me? If he fears me, why come hither? If he no longer cares for me, why silent? Teasing, teasing, man! I will think no more about him.'

Her resolution was for a short time involuntarily kept by the approach of her sister, who joined her with a cheerful look, which showed her better satisfied with their visitors, than Elizabeth.

'Now,' said she, 'that this first meeting is over, I feel perfectly easy. I know my own strength, and I shall never be embarrassed again by his coming. I am glad he dines here on Tuesday. It will then be publicly seen, that on both sides, we meet only as common and indifferent acquaintance.'

'Yes, very indifferent indeed,' said Elizabeth, laughingly. 'Oh, Jane, take care.'

'My dear Lizzy, you cannot think me so weak, as to be in danger now.'

'I think you are in very great danger of making him as much in love with you as ever.'

*

They did not see the gentlemen again till Tuesday; and Mrs Bennet, in the meanwhile, was giving way to all the happy schemes, which the good humour, and common politeness of Bingley, in half an hour's visit, had revived.

On Tuesday there was a large party assembled at Longbourn; and the two, who were most anxiously expected, to the credit of their punctuality as sportsmen, were in very good time. When they repaired to the dining-room, Elizabeth eagerly watched to see whether Bingley would take the place, which, in all their former parties, had belonged to him, by her sister. Her prudent mother, occupied by the same ideas, forbore to invite him to sit by herself. On entering the room, he seemed to hesitate; but Jane happened to look round, and happened to smile: it was decided. He placed himself by her.

Elizabeth, with a triumphant sensation, looked towards his friend. He bore it with noble indifference, and she would have imagined that Bingley had received his sanction to be happy, had she not seen his eyes likewise turned towards Mr Darcy, with an expression of half-laughing alarm.

His behaviour to her sister was such, during dinner time, as showed an admiration of her, which, though more guarded than formerly, persuaded Elizabeth, that if left wholly to himself, Jane's happiness, and his own, would be speedily secured. Though she dared not depend upon the consequence, she yet received pleasure from observing his behaviour. It gave her all the animation that her spirits could boast; for she was in no cheerful humour. Mr Darcy was almost

as far from her, as the table could divide them. He was on one side of her mother. She knew how little such a situation would give pleasure to either, or make either appear to advantage. She was not near enough to hear any of their discourse, but she could see how seldom they spoke to each other, and how formal and cold was their manner, whenever they did. Her mother's ungraciousness, made the sense of what they owed him more painful to Elizabeth's mind; and she would, at times, have given any thing to be privileged to tell him, that his kindness was neither unknown nor unfelt by the whole of the family.

She was in hopes that the evening would afford some opportunity of bringing them together; that the whole of the visit would not pass away without enabling them to enter into something more of conversation, than the mere ceremonious salutation attending his entrance. Anxious and uneasy, the period which passed in the drawing-room, before the gentlemen came, was wearisome and dull to a degree, that almost made her uncivil. She looked forward to their entrance, as the point on which all her chance of pleasure for the evening must depend.

'If he does not come to me, then,' said she, 'I shall give him up forever.'

The gentlemen came; and she thought he looked as if he would have answered her hopes; but, alas! the ladies had crowded round the table, where Miss Bennet was making tea, and Elizabeth pouring out the coffee, in so close a confederacy, that there was not a single vacancy near her, which would admit of a chair. And on the gentlemen's approaching, one of the girls moved closer to her than ever, and said, in a whisper,

'The men shan't come and part us, I am determined. We want none of them; do we?'

Darcy had walked away to another part of the room. She followed him with her eyes, envied every one to whom he spoke, had scarcely patience enough to help anybody to coffee; and then was enraged against herself for being so silly!

'A man who has once been refused! How could I ever be foolish enough to expect a renewal of his love? Is there one among the sex, who would not protest against such a weakness as a second proposal to the same woman? There is no indignity so abhorrent to their feelings!'

She was a little revived, however, by his bringing back his coffee cup himself; and she seized the opportunity of saying,

'Is your sister at Pemberley still?'

'Yes, she will remain there till Christmas.'

'And quite alone? Have all her friends left her?'

'Mrs Annesley is with her. The others have been gone on to Scarborough, these three weeks.'

She could think of nothing more to say; but if he wished to converse with her, he might have better success. He stood by her, however, for some minutes, in silence; and, at last, on the young lady's whispering to Elizabeth again, he walked away.

When the tea-things were removed, and the card tables placed, the ladies all rose, and Elizabeth was then hoping to be soon joined by him, when all her views were overthrown, by seeing him fall a victim to her mother's rapacity for whist players, and in a few moments after seated with the rest of the party. She now lost every expectation of pleasure. They were confined for the evening at different tables, and she had nothing to hope, but that his eyes were so often turned towards her side of the room, as to make him play as unsuccessfully as herself.

Mrs Bennet had designed to keep the two Netherfield gentlemen to supper; but their carriage was unluckily ordered before any of the others, and she had no opportunity of detaining them.

'Well girls,' said she, as soon as they were left to themselves, 'What say you to the day? I think every thing has passed off uncommonly well, I assure you. The dinner was as well dressed as any I ever saw. The venison was roasted to a turn – and everybody said, they never saw so fat a haunch. The soup was fifty times better than what we had at the Lucas's last week; and even Mr Darcy acknowledged, that the partridges were remarkably well done; and I suppose he has two or three French cooks at least. And, my dear Jane, I never saw you look in greater beauty. Mrs Long said so too, for I asked her whether you did not. And what do you think she said besides? "Ah! Mrs Bennet, we shall have her at Netherfield at last." She did indeed. I do think Mrs Long is as good a creature as ever lived – and her nieces are very pretty behaved girls, and not at all handsome: I like them prodigiously.'

Mrs Bennet, in short, was in very great spirits; she had seen enough of Bingley's behaviour to Jane, to be convinced that she would get him at last; and her expectations of advantage to her family, when in a happy humour, were so far beyond reason, that she was quite disappointed at not seeing him there again the next day, to make his proposals.

'It has been a very agreeable day,' said Miss Bennet to Elizabeth. 'The party seemed so well selected, so suitable one with the other. I hope we may often meet again.'

Elizabeth smiled.

'Lizzy, you must not do so. You must not suspect me. It mortifies me. I assure you that I have now learnt to enjoy his conversation as an agreeable and sensible young man, without having a wish beyond it. I am perfectly satisfied from what his manners now are, that he never had any design of engaging my affection. It is only that he is blessed

with greater sweetness of address, and a stronger desire of generally pleasing than any other man.'

'You are very cruel,' said her sister, 'you will not let me smile, and are provoking me to it every moment.'

'How hard it is in some cases to be believed!'

'And how impossible in others!'

'But why should you wish to persuade me that I feel more than I acknowledge?'

'That is a question which I hardly know how to answer. We all love to instruct, though we can teach only what is not worth knowing. Forgive me; and if you persist in indifference, do not make me your confidante.'

A few days after this visit, Mr Bingley called again, and alone. His friend had left him that morning for London, but was to return home in ten days' time. He sat with them above an hour, and was in remarkably good spirits. Mrs Bennet invited him to dine with them; but, with many expressions of concern, he confessed himself engaged elsewhere.

'Next time you call,' said she, 'I hope we shall be more lucky.'

He should be particularly happy at any time, &c. &c.; and if she would give him leave, would take an early opportunity of waiting on them.

'Can you come tomorrow?'

Yes, he had no engagement at all for tomorrow; and her invitation was accepted with alacrity.

He came, and in such very good time, that the ladies were none of them dressed. In ran Mrs Bennet to her daughter's room, in her dressing gown, and with her hair half finished, crying out,

'My dear Jane, make haste and hurry down. He is come – Mr Bingley is come. – He is, indeed. Make haste, make haste. Here, Sarah, come to Miss Bennet this moment, and help her on with her gown. Never mind Miss Lizzy's hair.'

'We will be down as soon as we can,' said Jane; 'but I dare say Kitty is forwarder than either of us, for she went upstairs half an hour ago.'

'Oh! hang Kitty! what has she to do with it? Come be quick, be quick! where is your sash my dear?'

But when her mother was gone, Jane would not be prevailed on to go down without one of her sisters.

The same anxiety to get them by themselves, was visible again in the evening. After tea, Mr Bennet retired to the library, as was his custom, and Mary went upstairs to her instrument. Two obstacles of the five being thus removed, Mrs Bennet sat looking and winking at

Elizabeth and Catherine for a considerable time, without making any impression on them. Elizabeth would not observe her; and when at last Kitty did, she very innocently said, 'What is the matter mamma? What do you keep winking at me for? What am I to do?'

'Nothing child, nothing. I did not wink at you.' She then sat still five minutes longer; but unable to waste such a precious occasion, she suddenly got up, and saying to Kitty,

'Come here, my love, I want to speak to you,' took her out of the room. Jane instantly gave a look at Elizabeth, which spoke her distress at such premeditation, and her intreaty that she would not give into it. In a few minutes, Mrs Bennet half opened the door and called out,

'Lizzy, my dear, I want to speak with you.'

Elizabeth was forced to go.

'We may as well leave them by themselves you know;' said her mother as soon as she was in the hall. 'Kitty and I are going up stairs to sit in my dressing-room.'

Elizabeth made no attempt to reason with her mother, but

remained quietly in the hall, till she and Kitty were out of sight, then returned into the drawing-room.

Mrs Bennet's schemes for this day were ineffectual. Bingley was every thing that was charming, except the professed lover of her daughter. His ease and cheerfulness rendered him a most agreeable addition to their evening party; and he bore with the ill-judged officiousness of the mother, and heard all her silly remarks with a forbearance and command of countenance, particularly grateful to the daughter.

He scarcely needed an invitation to stay supper; and before he went away, an engagement was formed, chiefly through his own and Mrs Bennet's means, for his coming next morning to shoot with her husband.

After this day, Jane said no more of her indifference. Not a word passed between the sisters concerning Bingley; but Elizabeth went to bed in the happy belief that all must speedily be concluded, unless Mr Darcy returned within the stated time. Seriously, however, she felt tolerably persuaded that all this must have taken place with that gentleman's concurrence.

Bingley was punctual to his appointment; and he and Mr Bennet spent the morning together, as had been agreed on. The latter was much more agreeable than his companion expected. There was nothing of presumption or folly in Bingley, that could provoke his ridicule, or disgust him into silence; and he was more communicative, and less eccentric than the other had ever seen him. Bingley of course returned with him to dinner; and in the evening Mrs Bennet's invention was again at work to get every body away from him and her daughter. Elizabeth, who had a letter to write, went into the breakfast room for that purpose soon after tea; for as the others were all going to sit down to cards, she could not be wanted to counteract her mother's schemes.

But on returning to the drawing-room, when her letter was finished, she saw, to her infinite surprise, there was reason to fear that her mother had been too ingenious for her. On opening the door, she perceived her sister and Bingley standing together over the hearth, as if engaged in earnest conversation; and had this led to no suspicion, the faces of both as they hastily turned round, and moved away from each other, would have told it all. Their situation was awkward enough; but hers she thought was still worse. Not a syllable was uttered by either; and Elizabeth was on the point of going away again, when Bingley, who as well as the others had sat down, suddenly rose, and whispering a few words to her sister, ran out of the room.

Jane could have no reserves from Elizabeth, where confidence would give pleasure; and instantly embracing her, acknowledged, with the liveliest emotion, that she was the happiest creature in the world.

'Tis too much!' she added, 'by far too much. I do not deserve it. Oh! why is not every body as happy?'

Elizabeth's congratulations were given with a sincerity, a warmth, a delight, which words could but poorly express. Every sentence of kindness was a fresh source of happiness to Jane. But she would not allow herself to stay with her sister, or say half that remained to be said, for the present.

'I must go instantly to my mother;' she cried. 'I would not on any account trifle with her affectionate solicitude; or allow her to hear it from any one but myself. He is gone to my father already. Oh! Lizzy, to know that what I have to relate will give such pleasure to all my dear family! how shall I bear so much happiness!'

She then hastened away to her mother, who had purposely broken up the card party, and was sitting up stairs with Kitty.

Elizabeth, who was left by herself, now smiled at the rapidity and ease with which an affair was finally settled, that had given them so many previous months of suspense and vexation.

'And this,' said she, 'is the end of all his friend's anxious circumspection! of all his sister's falsehood and contrivance! the happiest, wisest, most reasonable end!'

In a few minutes she was joined by Bingley, whose conference with her father had been short and to the purpose.

'Where is your sister?' said he hastily, as he opened the door.

'With my mother up stairs. She will be down in a moment I dare say.'

He then shut the door, and coming up to her, claimed the good wishes and affection of a sister. Elizabeth honestly and heartily expressed her delight in the prospect of their relationship. They shook hands with great cordiality; and then till her sister came down, she had to listen to all he had to say, of his own happiness, and of Jane's perfections; and in spite of his being a lover, Elizabeth really believed all his expectations of felicity, to be rationally founded, because they had for basis the excellent understanding, and super-excellent disposition of Jane, and a general similarity of feeling and taste between her and himself.

It was an evening of no common delight to them all; the satisfaction of Miss Bennet's mind gave a glow of such sweet animation to her face, as made her look handsomer than ever. Kitty simpered and smiled, and hoped her turn was coming soon. Mrs Bennet could not give her consent, or speak her approbation in terms warm enough to satisfy her feelings, though she talked to Bingley of nothing else, for half an hour; and when Mr Bennet joined them at supper, his voice and manner plainly showed how really happy he was.

Not a word, however, passed his lips in allusion to it, till their visitor took his leave for the night; but as soon as he was gone, he turned to his daughter and said,

'Jane, I congratulate you. You will be a very happy woman.'

Jane went to him instantly, kissed him, and thanked him for his goodness.

'You are a good girl;' he replied, 'and I have great pleasure in thinking you will be so happily settled. I have not a doubt of your doing very well together. Your tempers are by no means unlike. You are each of you so complying, that nothing will ever be resolved on; so easy, that every servant will cheat you; and so generous, that you will always exceed your income.'

'I hope not so. Imprudence or thoughtlessness in money matters, would be unpardonable in me.'

'Exceed their income! My dear Mr Bennet,' cried his wife, 'what are you talking of? Why, he has four or five thousand a year, and very likely more.' Then addressing her daughter, 'Oh! My dear, dear Jane, I am so happy! I am sure I shan't get a wink of sleep all night. I knew how it would be. I always said it must be so, at last. I was sure you could not be so beautiful for nothing! I remember, as soon as ever I saw him, when he first came into Hertfordshire last year, I thought how likely it was that you should come together. Oh! he is the handsomest young man that ever was seen!'

Wickham, Lydia, were all forgotten. Jane was beyond competition her favourite child. At that moment, she cared for no other. Her younger sisters soon began to make interest with her for objects of happiness which she might in future be able to dispense.

Mary petitioned for the use of the library at Netherfield; and Kitty begged very hard for a few balls there every winter.

Bingley, from this time, was of course a daily visitor at Longbourn; coming frequently before breakfast, and always remaining till after supper; unless when some barbarous neighbour, who could not be enough detested, had given him an invitation to dinner, which he thought himself obliged to accept.

Elizabeth had now but little time for conversation with her sister; for while he was present, Jane had no attention to bestow on any one else; but she found herself considerably useful to both of them, in those hours of separation that must sometimes occur. In the absence of Jane, he always attached himself to Elizabeth, for the pleasure of talking of her; and when Bingley was gone, Jane constantly sought the same means of relief.

'He has made me so happy,' said she, one evening, 'by telling me, that he was totally ignorant of my being in town last spring! I had not believed it possible.'

'I suspected as much,' replied Elizabeth. 'But how did he account for it?'

'It must have been his sister's doing. They were certainly no friends to his acquaintance with me, which I cannot wonder at, since he might have chosen so much more advantageously in many respects. But when they see, as I trust they will, that their brother is happy with me, they will learn to be contented, and we shall be on good terms again; though we can never be what we once were to each other.'

'That is the most unforgiving speech,' said Elizabeth, 'that I ever heard you utter. Good girl! It would vex me, indeed, to see you again the dupe of Miss Bingley's pretended regard.'

'Would you believe it, Lizzy, that when he went to town last November, he really loved me, and nothing but a persuasion of my being indifferent, would have prevented his coming down again!'

'He made a little mistake to be sure; but it is to the credit of his modesty.'

This naturally introduced a panegyric from Jane on his diffidence, and the little value he put on his own good qualities.

Elizabeth was pleased to find, that he had not betrayed the interference of his friend, for, though Jane had the most generous and forgiving heart in the world, she knew it was a circumstance which must prejudice her against him.

'I am certainly the most fortunate creature that ever existed!' cried Jane. 'Oh! Lizzy, why am I thus singled from my family, and blessed above them all! If I could but see you as happy! If there were but such another man for you!'

'If you were to give me forty such men, I never could be so happy as you. Till I have your disposition, your goodness, I never can have your happiness. No, no, let me shift for myself; and, perhaps, if I have very good luck, I may meet with another Mr Collins in time.'

The situation of affairs in the Longbourn family could not be long a secret. Mrs Bennet was privileged to whisper it to Mrs Philips, and she ventured, without any permission, to do the same by all her neighbours in Meryton.

The Bennets were speedily pronounced to be the luckiest family in the world, though only a few weeks before, when Lydia had first run away, they had been generally proved to be marked out for misfortune.

Chapter 56

One morning, about a week after Bingley's engagement with Jane had been formed, as he and the females of the family were sitting together in the dining-room, their attention was suddenly drawn to the window, by the sound of a carriage; and they perceived a chaise and four driving up the lawn. It was too early in the morning for visitors, and besides, the equipage did not answer to that of any of their neighbours. The horses were post; and neither the carriage, nor the livery of the servant who preceded it, were familiar to them. As it was certain, however, that somebody was coming, Bingley instantly prevailed on Miss Bennet to avoid the confinement of such an intrusion, and walk away with him into the shrubbery. They both set off, and the conjectures of the remaining three continued, though with little satisfaction, till the door was thrown open, and their visitor entered. It was lady Catherine de Bourgh.

They were of course all intending to be surprised; but their astonishment was beyond their expectation; and on the part of Mrs

Bennet and Kitty, though she was perfectly unknown to them, even inferior to what Elizabeth felt.

She entered the room with an air more than usually ungracious, made no other reply to Elizabeth's salutation, than a slight inclination of the head, and sat down without saying a word. Elizabeth had mentioned her name to her mother, on her ladyship's entrance, though no request of introduction had been made.

Mrs Bennet all amazement, though flattered by having a guest of such high importance, received her with the utmost politeness. After sitting for a moment in silence, she said very stiffly to Elizabeth,

'I hope you are well, Miss Bennet. That lady I suppose is your mother.'

Elizabeth replied very concisely that she was.

'And that I suppose is one of your sisters.'

'Yes, madam,' said Mrs Bennet, delighted to speak to a lady Catherine. 'She is my youngest girl but one. My youngest of all, is lately married, and my eldest is somewhere about the grounds, walking with a young man, who I believe will soon become a part of the family.'

'You have a very small park here,' returned Lady Catherine after a short silence.

'It is nothing in comparison of Rosings, my lady, I dare say; but I assure you it is much larger than Sir William Lucas's.'

'This must be a most inconvenient sitting room for the evening, in summer; the windows are full west.'

Mrs Bennet assured her that they never sat there after dinner; and then added,

'May I take the liberty of asking your ladyship whether you left Mr and Mrs Collins well.'

'Yes, very well. I saw them the night before last.'

Elizabeth now expected that she would produce a letter for her from Charlotte, as it seemed the only probable motive for her calling. But no letter appeared, and she was completely puzzled.

Mrs Bennet, with great civility, begged her ladyship to take some refreshment; but Lady Catherine very resolutely, and not very politely, declined eating any thing; and then rising up, said to Elizabeth,

'Miss Bennet, there seemed to be a prettyish kind of a little wilderness on one side of your lawn. I should be glad to take a turn in it, if you will favour me with your company.'

'Go, my dear,' cried her mother, 'and show her ladyship about the different walks. I think she will be pleased with the hermitage.'

Elizabeth obeyed, and running into her own room for her parasol, attended her noble guest down stairs. As they passed through the hall, Lady Catherine opened the doors into the dining-parlour and drawing-room, and pronouncing them, after a short survey, to be decent looking rooms, walked on.

Her carriage remained at the door, and Elizabeth saw that her waiting-woman was in it. They proceeded in silence along the gravel walk that led to the copse; Elizabeth was determined to make no effort for conversation with a woman, who was now more than usually insolent and disagreeable.

'How could I ever think her like her nephew?' said she, as she looked in her face.

As soon as they entered the copse, Lady Catherine began in the following manner: –

'You can be at no loss, Miss Bennet, to understand the reason of my journey hither. Your own heart, your own conscience, must tell you why I come.'

Elizabeth looked with unaffected astonishment.

'Indeed, you are mistaken, Madam. I have not been at all able to account for the honour of seeing you here.'

'Miss Bennet,' replied her ladyship, in an angry tone, 'you ought to know, that I am not to be trifled with. But however insincere you may choose to be, you shall not find me so. My character has ever been celebrated for its sincerity and frankness, and in a cause of such moment as this, I shall certainly not depart from it. A report of a most alarming nature, reached me two days ago. I was told, that not only your sister was on the point of being most advantageously married, but that you, that Miss Elizabeth Bennet, would, in all likelihood, be soon afterwards united to my nephew, my own nephew, Mr Darcy. Though I know it must be a scandalous falsehood; though I would not injure him so much as to suppose the truth of it possible, I instantly resolved on setting off for this place, that I might make my sentiments known to you.'

'If you believed it impossible to be true,' said Elizabeth, colouring with astonishment and disdain, 'I wonder you took the trouble of coming so far. What could your ladyship propose by it?'

'At once to insist upon having such a report universally contradicted.'

'Your coming to Longbourn, to see me and my family,' said Elizabeth, coolly, 'will be rather a confirmation of it; if, indeed, such a report is in existence.'

'If! do you then pretend to be ignorant of it? Has it not been industriously circulated by yourselves? Do you not know that such a report is spread abroad?'

'I never heard that it was.'

'And can you likewise declare, that there is no foundation for it?'

'I do not pretend to possess equal frankness with your ladyship. You may ask questions, which I shall not choose to answer.'

'This is not to be borne. Miss Bennet, I insist on being satisfied. Has he, has my nephew, made you an offer of marriage?'

'Your ladyship has declared it to be impossible.'

'It ought to be so; it must be so, while he retains the use of his reason. But your arts and allurements may, in a moment of infatuation, have made him forget what he owes to himself and to all his family. You may have drawn him in.'

'If I have, I shall be the last person to confess it.'

'Miss Bennet, do you know who I am? I have not been accustomed to such language as this. I am almost the nearest relation he has in the world, and am entitled to know all his dearest concerns.'

'But you are not entitled to know mine, nor will such behaviour as this, ever induce me to be explicit.'

'Let me be rightly understood. This match, to which you have the presumption to aspire, can never take place. No, never. Mr Darcy is engaged to my daughter. Now what have you to say?'

'Only this; that if he is so, you can have no reason to suppose he will make an offer to me.'

Lady Catherine hesitated for a moment, and then replied,

'The engagement between them is of a peculiar kind. From their infancy, they have been intended for each other. It was the favourite wish of his mother, as well as of hers. While in their cradles, we planned the union: and now, at the moment when the wishes of both sisters would be accomplished, in their marriage, to be prevented by a young woman of inferior birth, of no importance in the world, and wholly unallied to the family! Do you pay no regard to the wishes of his friends? To his tacit engagement with Miss De Bourgh? Are you lost to every feeling of propriety and delicacy? Have you not heard me say, that from his earliest hours he was destined for his cousin?'

'Yes, and I had heard it before. But what is that to me? If there is no other objection to my marrying your nephew, I shall certainly not be kept from it, by knowing that his mother and aunt wished him to marry Miss De Bourgh. You both did as much as you could, in planning the marriage. Its completion depended on others. If Mr Darcy is neither by honour nor inclination confined to his cousin, why is not he to make another choice? And if I am that choice, why may not I accept him?'

'Because honour, decorum, prudence, nay, interest, forbid it. Yes, Miss Bennet, interest; for do not expect to be noticed by his family or friends, if you wilfully act against the inclinations of all. You will be censured, slighted, and despised, by every one connected with him. Your alliance will be a disgrace; your name will never even be mentioned by any of us.'

'These are heavy misfortunes,' replied Elizabeth. 'But the wife of Mr Darcy must have such extraordinary sources of happiness necessarily attached to her situation, that she could, upon the whole, have no cause to repine.'

'Obstinate, headstrong girl! I am ashamed of you! Is this your gratitude for my attentions to you last spring? Is nothing due to me on that score?'

'Let us sit down. You are to understand, Miss Bennet, that I came here with the determined resolution of carrying my purpose; nor will I be dissuaded from it. I have not been used to submit to any person's whims. I have not been in the habit of brooking disappointment.'

'That will make your ladyship's situation at present more pitiable; but it will have no effect on me.'

'I will not be interrupted. Hear me in silence. My daughter and my nephew are formed for each other. They are descended on the maternal side, from the same noble line; and, on the father's, from respectable, honourable, and ancient, though untitled families. Their fortune on both sides is splendid. They are destined for each other by the voice of every member of their respective houses; and what is to divide them? The upstart pretensions of a young woman without family, connections, or fortune. Is this to be endured! But it must not, shall not be. If you were sensible of your own good, you would not wish to quit the sphere, in which you have been brought up.'

'In marrying your nephew, I should not consider myself as quitting that sphere. He is a gentleman; I am a gentleman's daughter; so far we are equal.'

'True. You are a gentleman's daughter. But who was your mother? Who are your uncles and aunts? Do not imagine me ignorant of their condition.'

'Whatever my connections may be,' said Elizabeth, 'if your nephew does not object to them, they can be nothing to you.'

'Tell me once for all, are you engaged to him?'

Though Elizabeth would not, for the mere purpose of obliging Lady Catherine, have answered this question; she could not but say, after a moment's deliberation,

'I am not.'

Lady Catherine seemed pleased.

'And will you promise me, never to enter into such an engagement?'

'I will make no promise of the kind.'

'Miss Bennet, I am shocked and astonished. I expected to find a more reasonable young woman. But do not deceive yourself into a belief that I will ever recede. I shall not go away, till you have given me the assurance I require.'

'And I certainly never shall give it. I am not to be intimidated into anything so wholly unreasonable. Your ladyship wants Mr Darcy to marry your daughter; but would my giving you the wished-for promise, make their marriage at all more probable? Supposing him to be attached to me, would my refusing to accept his hand, make him wish to bestow it on his cousin? Allow me to say, Lady Catherine, that the arguments with which you have supported this extraordinary application, have been as frivolous as the application was ill-judged. You have widely mistaken my character, if you think I can be worked on by such persuasions as these. How far your nephew might approve of your interference in his affairs, I cannot tell; but you have certainly no right to concern yourself in mine. I must beg, therefore, to be importuned no farther on the subject.'

'Not so hasty, if you please. I have by no means done. To all the objections I have already urged, I have still another to add. I am no stranger to the particulars of your youngest sister's infamous elopement. I know it all; that the young man's marrying her, was a patched-up business, at the expense of your father and uncles. And is such a girl to be my nephew's sister? Is her husband, is the son of his late father's steward, to be his brother? Heaven and earth! – of what are you thinking? Are the shades of Pemberley to be thus polluted?'

'You can now have nothing farther to say,' she resentfully answered. 'You have insulted me, in every possible method. I must beg to return to the house.'

And she rose as she spoke. Lady Catherine rose also, and they turned back. Her ladyship was highly incensed.

'You have no regard, then, for the honour and credit of my nephew! Unfeeling, selfish girl! Do you not consider that a connection with you, must disgrace him in the eyes of everybody?'

'Lady Catherine, I have nothing farther to say. You know my sentiments.'

'You are then resolved to have him?'

'I have said no such thing. I am only resolved to act in that manner, which will, in my own opinion, constitute my happiness, without reference to you, or to any person so wholly unconnected with me.'

'It is well. You refuse, then, to oblige me. You refuse to obey the claims of duty, honour, and gratitude. You are determined to ruin him in the opinion of all his friends, and make him the contempt of the world.'

'Neither duty, nor honour, nor gratitude,' replied Elizabeth, 'have any possible claim on me, in the present instance. No principle of either, would be violated by my marriage with Mr Darcy. And with regard to the resentment of his family, or the indignation of the world, if the former were excited by his marrying me, it would not give me one moment's concern – and the world in general would have too much sense to join in the scorn.'

'And this is your real opinion! This is your final resolve! Very well.

I shall now know how to act. Do not imagine, Miss Bennet, that your ambition will ever be gratified. I came to try you. I hoped to find you reasonable; but depend upon it I will carry my point.'

In this manner Lady Catherine talked on, till they were at the door of the carriage, when turning hastily round, she added,

'I take no leave of you, Miss Bennet. I send no compliments to your mother. You deserve no such attention. I am most seriously displeased.'

Elizabeth made no answer; and without attempting to persuade her ladyship to return into the house, walked quietly into it herself. She heard the carriage drive away as she proceeded up stairs. Her mother impatiently met her at the door of the dressing-room, to ask why Lady Catherine would not come in again and rest herself.

'She did not choose it,' said her daughter, 'she would go.'

'She is a very fine-looking woman! and her calling here was prodigiously civil! for she only came, I suppose, to tell us the Collinses were well. She is on her road somewhere, I dare say, and so passing through Meryton, thought she might as well call on you. I suppose she had nothing particular to say to you, Lizzy?'

Elizabeth was forced to give into a little falsehood here; for to acknowledge the substance of their conversation was impossible.

Chapter 57

The discomposure of spirits, which this extraordinary visit threw Elizabeth into, could not be easily overcome; nor could she for many hours, learn to think of it less than incessantly. Lady Catherine it appeared, had actually taken the trouble of this journey from Rosings, for the sole purpose of breaking off her supposed engagement with Mr Darcy. It was a rational scheme to be sure! but from what the report of their engagement could originate, Elizabeth was at a loss to imagine; till she recollected that his being the intimate friend of Bingley, and her being the sister of Jane, was enough, at a time when the expectation of one wedding, made every body eager for another, to supply the idea. She had not herself forgotten to feel that the marriage of her sister must bring them more frequently together. And her neighbours at Lucas lodge, therefore, (for through their communication with the Collinses, the report she concluded had reached lady Catherine) had only set that down, as almost certain and immediate, which she had looked forward to as possible, at some future time.

In revolving lady Catherine's expressions, however, she could not help feeling some uneasiness as to the possible consequence of her persisting in this interference. From what she had said of her resolution to prevent their marriage, it occurred to Elizabeth that she must meditate an application to her nephew; and how he might take a similar representation of the evils attached to a connection with her, she dared not pronounce. She knew not the exact degree of his affection for his aunt, or his dependence on her judgment, but it was natural to suppose that he thought much higher of her ladyship than she could do; and it was certain, that in enumerating the miseries of a marriage with one, whose immediate connections were so unequal to his own, his aunt would address him on his weakest side. With his notions of dignity, he would probably feel that the arguments, which to Elizabeth had appeared weak and ridiculous, contained much good sense and solid reasoning.

If he had been wavering before, as to what he should do, which had often seemed likely, the advice and intreaty of so near a relation might settle every doubt, and determine him at once to be as happy, as dignity unblemished could make him. In that case he would return no more. Lady Catherine might see him in her way through town; and his engagement to Bingley of coming again to Netherfield must give way.

'If, therefore, an excuse for not keeping his promise, should come to his friend within a few days,' she added, 'I shall know how to understand it. I shall then give over every expectation, every wish of his constancy. If he is satisfied with only regretting me, when he might have obtained my affections and hand, I shall soon cease to regret him at all.'

*

The surprise of the rest of the family, on hearing who their visitor had been, was very great; but they obligingly satisfied it, with the same kind of supposition, which had appeased Mrs Bennet's curiosity; and Elizabeth was spared from much teasing on the subject.

The next morning, as she was going downstairs, she was met by her father, who came out of his library with a letter in his hand.

'Lizzy,' said he, 'I was going to look for you; come into my room.'

She followed him thither; and her curiosity to know what he had to tell her, was heightened by the supposition of its being in some manner connected with the letter he held. It suddenly struck her that it might be from Lady Catherine; and she anticipated with dismay all the consequent explanations.

She followed her father to the fire place, and they both sat down. He then said,

'I have received a letter this morning that has astonished me exceedingly. As it principally concerns yourself, you ought to know its contents. I did not know before, that I had two daughters on the brink of matrimony. Let me congratulate you, on a very important conquest.'

The colour now rushed into Elizabeth's cheeks in the instantaneous conviction of its being a letter from the nephew, instead of the aunt;

and she was undetermined whether most to be pleased that he explained himself at all, or offended that his letter was not rather addressed to herself; when her father continued,

'You look conscious. Young ladies have great penetration in such matters as these; but I think I may defy even your sagacity, to discover the name of your admirer. This letter is from Mr Collins.'

'From Mr Collins! and what can he have to say?'

'Something very much to the purpose of course. He begins with congratulations on the approaching nuptials of my eldest daughter, of which it seems he has been told, by some of the good-natured, gossiping Lucases. I shall not sport with your impatience, by reading what he says on that point. What relates to yourself, is as follows.' 'Having thus offered you the sincere congratulations of Mrs Collins and myself on this happy event, let me now add a short hint on the subject of another, of which we have been advertised by the same authority. Your daughter Elizabeth, it is presumed, will not long bear the name of Bennet, after her elder sister has resigned it, and the chosen partner of her fate, may be reasonably looked up to, as one of the most illustrious personages in this land.'

'Can you possibly guess, Lizzy, who is meant by this?' 'This young gentleman is blessed in a peculiar way, with every thing the heart of mortal can most desire, – splendid property, noble kindred, and extensive patronage. Yet in spite of all these temptations, let me warn my cousin Elizabeth, and yourself, of what evils you may incur, by a

precipitate closure with this gentleman's proposals, which, of course, you will be inclined to take immediate advantage of.'

'Have you any idea, Lizzy, who this gentleman is? But now it comes out.'

'My motive for cautioning you, is as follows. We have reason to imagine that his aunt, Lady Catherine de Bourgh, does not look on the match with a friendly eye.'

'Mr Darcy, you see, is the man! Now, Lizzy, I think I have surprised you. Could he, or the Lucases, have pitched on any man, within the circle of our acquaintance, whose name would have given the lie more effectually to what they related? Mr Darcy, who never looks at any woman but to see a blemish, and who probably never looked at you in his life! It is admirable!'

Elizabeth tried to join in her father's pleasantry, but could only force one most reluctant smile. Never had his wit been directed in a manner so little agreeable to her.

'Are you not diverted?'

'Oh! yes. Pray read on.'

'After mentioning the likelihood of this marriage to her ladyship last night, she immediately, with her usual condescension, expressed what she felt on the occasion; when it became apparent, that on the score of some family objections on the part of my cousin, she would never give her consent to what she termed so disgraceful a match. I thought it my duty to give the speediest intelligence of this to my cousin, that she and her noble admirer may be aware of what they are about, and not run hastily into a marriage which has not been properly sanctioned.' 'Mr Collins moreover adds,' 'I am truly rejoiced that my cousin Lydia's sad business has been so well hushed up, and am only concerned that their living together before the marriage took place, should be so generally known. I must not, however, neglect the duties of my station, or refrain from declaring my amazement, at hearing that you received the young couple into your house as soon as they were married. It was an encouragement of vice; and had I been the rector of Longbourn, I should very strenuously have opposed it. You ought certainly to forgive them as a Christian, but never to admit them in your sight, or allow their names to be mentioned in your hearing.'

'That is his notion of Christian forgiveness! The rest of his letter is only about his dear Charlotte's situation, and his expectation of a young olive-branch. But, Lizzy, you look as if you did not enjoy it. You are not going to be Missish, I hope, and pretend to be affronted at an idle report. For what do we live, but to make sport for our neighbours, and laugh at them in our turn?'

'Oh!' cried Elizabeth, 'I am excessively diverted. But it is so strange!'

'Yes – that is what makes it amusing. Had they fixed on any other man it would have been nothing; but his perfect indifference, and your pointed dislike, make it so delightfully absurd! Much as I abominate writing, I would not give up Mr Collins's correspondence for any consideration. Nay, when I read a letter of his, I cannot help giving him the preference even over Wickham, much as I value the impudence and hypocrisy of my son-in-law. And pray, Lizzy, what said Lady Catherine about this report? Did she call to refuse her consent?'

To this question his daughter replied only with a laugh; and as it had been asked without the least suspicion, she was not distressed by his repeating it. Elizabeth had never been more at a loss to make her feelings appear what they were not. It was necessary to laugh, when she would rather have cried. Her father had most cruelly mortified her, by what he said of Mr Darcy's indifference, and she could do nothing but wonder at such a want of penetration, or fear that perhaps, instead of his seeing too little, she might have fancied too much.

Chapter 58

Instead of receiving any such letter of excuse from his friend, as Elizabeth half expected Mr Bingley to do, he was able to bring Darcy with him to Longbourn before many days had passed after Lady Catherine's visit. The gentlemen arrived early; and, before Mrs Bennet had time to tell him of their having seen his aunt, of which her daughter sat in momentary dread, Bingley, who wanted to be alone with Jane, proposed their all walking out. It was agreed to. Mrs Bennet was not in the habit of walking, Mary could never spare time, but the remaining five set off together. Bingley and Jane, however, soon allowed the others to outstrip them. They lagged behind, while Elizabeth, Kitty, and Darcy, were to entertain each other. Very little was said by either; Kitty was too much afraid of him to talk; Elizabeth was secretly forming a desperate resolution; and perhaps he might be doing the same.

They walked towards the Lucases, because Kitty wished to call upon Maria; and as Elizabeth saw no occasion for making it a general concern, when Kitty left them, she went boldly on with him alone. Now was the moment for her resolution to be executed, and, while her courage was high, she immediately said,

'Mr Darcy, I am a very selfish creature; and, for the sake of giving relief to my own feelings, care not how much I may be wounding yours. I can no longer help thanking you for your unexampled kindness to my poor sister. Ever since I have known it, I have been most anxious to acknowledge to you how gratefully I feel it. Were it known to the rest of my family, I should not have merely my own gratitude to express.'

'I am sorry, exceedingly sorry,' replied Darcy, in a tone of surprise and emotion, 'that you have ever been informed of what may, in a mistaken light, have given you uneasiness. I did not think Mrs Gardiner was so little to be trusted.'

'You must not blame my aunt. Lydia's thoughtlessness first betrayed to me that you had been concerned in the matter; and, of course, I could not rest till I knew the particulars. Let me thank you again and again, in the name of all my family, for that generous compassion which induced you to take so much trouble, and bear so many mortifications, for the sake of discovering them.'

'If you will thank me,' he replied, 'let it be for yourself alone. That the wish of giving happiness to you, might add force to the other inducements which led me on, I shall not attempt to deny. But your family owe me nothing. Much as I respect them, I believe, I thought only of you.'

Elizabeth was too much embarrassed to say a word. After a short pause, her companion added, 'You are too generous to trifle with me. If your feelings are still what they were last April, tell me so at once. My affections and wishes are unchanged, but one word from you will silence me on this subject forever.'

Elizabeth feeling all the more than common awkwardness and anxiety of his situation, now forced herself to speak; and immediately, though not very fluently, gave him to understand, that her sentiments had undergone so material a change, since the period to which he alluded, as to make her receive with gratitude and pleasure, his present assurances. The happiness which this reply produced, was such as he had probably never felt before; and he expressed himself on the occasion as sensibly and as warmly as a man violently in love can be supposed to do. Had Elizabeth been able to encounter his eye, she might have seen how well the expression of heartfelt delight, diffused over his face, became him; but, though she could not look, she could listen, and he told her of feelings, which, in proving of what importance she was to him, made his affection every moment more valuable.

They walked on, without knowing in what direction. There was too much to be thought; and felt, and said, for attention to any other objects. She soon learnt that they were indebted for their present good understanding to the efforts of his aunt, who did call on him in her return through London, and there relate her journey to Longbourn, its motive, and the substance of her conversation with Elizabeth; dwelling emphatically on every expression of the latter, which, in her ladyship's apprehension, peculiarly denoted her perverseness and assurance, in the belief that such a relation must assist her endeavours to obtain that promise from her nephew, which she had refused to give. But, unluckily for her ladyship, its effect had been exactly contrariwise.

'It taught me to hope,' said he, 'as I had scarcely ever allowed myself to hope before. I knew enough of your disposition to be certain, that, had you been absolutely, irrevocably decided against me, you would have acknowledged it to Lady Catherine, frankly and openly.'

Elizabeth coloured and laughed as she replied, 'Yes, you know enough of my frankness to believe me capable of that. After abusing you so abominably to your face, I could have no scruple in abusing you to all your relations.'

'What did you say of me, that I did not deserve? For, though your accusations were ill-founded, formed on mistaken premises, my behaviour to you at the time, had merited the severest reproof. It was unpardonable. I cannot think of it without abhorrence.'

'We will not quarrel for the greater share of blame annexed to that evening,' said Elizabeth. 'The conduct of neither, if strictly examined,

will be irreproachable; but since then, we have both, I hope, improved in civility.'

'I cannot be so easily reconciled to myself. The recollection of what I then said, of my conduct, my manners, my expressions during the whole of it, is now, and has been many months, inexpressibly painful to me. Your reproof, so well applied, I shall never forget: "had you behaved in a more gentleman-like manner." Those were your words. You know not, you can scarcely conceive, how they have tortured me; – though it was some time, I confess, before I was reasonable enough to allow their justice.'

'I was certainly very far from expecting them to make so strong an impression. I had not the smallest idea of their being ever felt in such a way.'

'I can easily believe it. You thought me then devoid of every proper feeling, I am sure you did. The turn of your countenance I shall never forget, as you said that I could not have addressed you in any possible way, that would induce you to accept me.'

'Oh! do not repeat what I then said. These recollections will not do at all. I assure you, that I have long been most heartily ashamed of it.'

Darcy mentioned his letter. 'Did it,' said he, 'did it soon make you think better of me? Did you, on reading it, give any credit to its contents?'

She explained what its effect on her had been, and how gradually all her former prejudices had been removed.

'I knew,' said he, 'that what I wrote must give you pain, but it was necessary. I hope you have destroyed the letter. There was one part especially, the opening of it, which I should dread your having the power of reading again. I can remember some expressions which might justly make you hate me.'

'The letter shall certainly be burnt, if you believe it essential to the preservation of my regard; but, though we have both reason to think my opinions not entirely unalterable, they are not, I hope, quite so easily changed as that implies.'

'When I wrote that letter,' replied Darcy, 'I believed myself perfectly calm and cool, but I am since convinced that it was written in a dreadful bitterness of spirit.'

'The letter, perhaps, began in bitterness, but it did not end so. The adieu is charity itself. But think no more of the letter. The feelings of the person who wrote, and the person who received it, are now so widely different from what they were then, that every unpleasant circumstance attending it, ought to be forgotten. You must learn some of my philosophy. Think only of the past as its remembrance gives you pleasure.'

'I cannot give you credit for any philosophy of the kind. Your retrospections must be so totally void of reproach, that the contentment arising from them, is not of philosophy, but what is much better, of ignorance. But with me, it is not so. Painful recollections will intrude, which cannot, which ought not to be repelled. I have been a selfish being all my life, in practice, though not in principle. As a child I was taught what was right, but I was not taught to correct my temper. I was given good principles, but left to follow them in pride and conceit. Unfortunately an only son, (for many years an only child) I was spoilt by my parents, who though good themselves, (my father particularly, all that was benevolent and amiable,) allowed, encouraged, almost taught me to be selfish and overbearing, to care for none beyond my own family circle, to think meanly of all the rest of the world, to wish at least to think meanly of their sense and worth compared with my own. Such I was, from eight to eight and twenty; and such I might still have been but for you, dearest, loveliest Elizabeth! What do I not owe you! You taught me a lesson, hard indeed at first, but most advantageous. By you, I was properly humbled. I came to you without a doubt of my reception. You showed me how insufficient were all my pretensions to please a woman worthy of being pleased.'

'Had you then persuaded yourself that I should?'

'Indeed I had. What will you think of my vanity? I believed you to be wishing, expecting my addresses.'

'My manners must have been in fault, but not intentionally I assure you. I never meant to deceive you, but my spirits might often lead me wrong. How you must have hated me after that evening?'

'Hate you! I was angry perhaps at first, but my anger soon began to take a proper direction.'

'I am almost afraid of asking what you thought of me; when we met at Pemberley. You blamed me for coming?'

'No indeed; I felt nothing but surprise.'

'Your surprise could not be greater than mine in being noticed by you. My conscience told me that I deserved no extraordinary politeness, and I confess that I did not expect to receive more than my due.'

'My object then,' replied Darcy, 'was to show you, by every civility in my power, that I was not so mean as to resent the past; and I hoped to obtain your forgiveness, to lessen your ill opinion, by letting you see that your reproofs had been attended to. How soon any other wishes introduced themselves I can hardly tell, but I believe in about half an hour after I had seen you.'

He then told her of Georgiana's delight in her acquaintance, and of her disappointment at its sudden interruption; which naturally leading to the cause of that interruption, she soon learnt that his resolution of following her from Derbyshire in quest of her sister, had been formed before he quitted the inn, and that his gravity and thoughtfulness there, had arisen from no other struggles than what such a purpose must comprehend.

She expressed her gratitude again, but it was too painful a subject to each, to be dwelt on farther.

After walking several miles in a leisurely manner, and too busy to know any thing about it, they found at last, on examining their watches, that it was time to be at home.

'What could become of Mr Bingley and Jane!' was a wonder which introduced the discussion of their affairs. Darcy was delighted with their engagement; his friend had given him the earliest information of it.

'I must ask whether you were surprised?' said Elizabeth.

'Not at all. When I went away, I felt that it would soon happen.'

'That is to say, you had given your permission. I guessed as much.'

And though he exclaimed at the term, she found that it had been pretty much the case.

'On the evening before my going to London,' said he 'I made a confession to him, which I believe I ought to have made long ago. I told him of all that had occurred to make my former interference in his affairs, absurd and impertinent. His surprise was great. He had never had the slightest suspicion. I told him, moreover, that I believed myself mistaken in supposing, as I had done, that your sister was indifferent to him; and as I could easily perceive that his attachment to her was unabated, I felt no doubt of their happiness together.'

Elizabeth could not help smiling at his easy manner of directing his friend.

'Did you speak from your own observation,' said she, 'when you told him that my sister loved him, or merely from my information last spring?'

'From the former. I had narrowly observed her during the two visits which I had lately made her here; and I was convinced of her affection.'

'And your assurance of it, I suppose, carried immediate conviction to him.'

'It did. Bingley is most unaffectedly modest. His diffidence had prevented his depending on his own judgment in so anxious a case, but his reliance on mine, made every thing easy. I was obliged to confess one thing, which for a time, and not unjustly, offended him. I could not allow myself to conceal that your sister had been in town three months last winter, that I had known it, and purposely kept it from him. He was angry. But his anger, I am persuaded, lasted no longer than he remained in any doubt of your sister's sentiments. He has heartily forgiven me now.'

Elizabeth longed to observe that Mr Bingley had been a most delightful friend; so easily guided that his worth was invaluable; but she checked herself. She remembered that he had yet to learn to be laughed at, and it was rather too early to begin. In anticipating the happiness of Bingley, which of course was to be inferior only to his own, he continued the conversation till they reached the house. In the hall they parted.

Chapter 59

'My dear Lizzy, where can you have been walking to?' was a question which Elizabeth received from Jane as soon as she entered the room, and from all the others when they sat down to table. She had only to say in reply, that they had wandered about, till she was beyond her own knowledge. She coloured as she spoke; but neither that, nor any thing else, awakened a suspicion of the truth.

The evening passed quietly, unmarked by any thing extraordinary. The acknowledged lovers talked and laughed, the unacknowledged were silent. Darcy was not of a disposition in which happiness overflows in mirth; and Elizabeth, agitated and confused, rather knew that she was happy, than felt herself to be so; for, besides the immediate embarrassment, there were other evils before her. She anticipated what would be felt in the family when her situation became known; she was aware that no one liked him but Jane; and even feared that with the others it was a dislike which not all his fortune and consequence might do away.

At night she opened her heart to Jane. Though suspicion was very far from Miss Bennet's general habits, she was absolutely incredulous here.

'You are joking, Lizzy. This cannot be! – engaged to Mr Darcy! No, no, you shall not deceive me. I know it to be impossible.'

'This is a wretched beginning indeed! My sole dependence was on you; and I am sure nobody else will believe me, if you do not. Yet, indeed, I am in earnest. I speak nothing but the truth. He still loves me, and we are engaged.'

Jane looked at her doubtingly. 'Oh, Lizzy! it cannot be. I know how much you dislike him.'

'You know nothing of the matter. That is all to be forgot. Perhaps I did not always love him so well as I do now. But in such cases as these, a good memory is unpardonable. This is the last time I shall ever remember it myself.'

Miss Bennet still looked all amazement. Elizabeth again, and more seriously assured her of its truth.

'Good Heaven! can it be really so! Yet now I must believe you,' cried Jane. 'My dear, dear Lizzy, I would – I do congratulate you – but are you certain? forgive the question – are you quite certain that you can be happy with him?'

'There can be no doubt of that. It is settled between us already, that we are to be the happiest couple in the world. But are you pleased, Jane? Shall you like to have such a brother?'

'Very, very much. Nothing could give either Bingley or myself more delight. But we considered it, we talked of it as impossible. And do you really love him quite well enough? Oh, Lizzy! do any thing rather than marry without affection. Are you quite sure that you feel what you ought to do?'

'Oh, yes! You will only think I feel more than I ought to do, when I tell you all.'

'What do you mean?'

'Why, I must confess, that I love him better than I do Bingley. I am afraid you will be, angry.'

'My dearest sister, now be serious. I want to talk very seriously. Let me know every thing that I am to know, without delay. Will you tell me how long you have loved him?'

'It has been coming on so gradually, that I hardly know when it began. But I believe I must date it from my first seeing his beautiful grounds at Pemberley.'

Another intreaty that she would be serious, however, produced the desired effect; and she soon satisfied Jane by her solemn assurances of attachment. When convinced on that article, Miss Bennet had nothing farther to wish.

'Now I am quite happy,' said she, 'for you will be as happy as myself. I always had a value for him. Were it for nothing but his love of you, I must always have esteemed him; but now, as Bingley's friend and your husband, there can be only Bingley and yourself more dear to me.

But Lizzy, you have been very sly, very reserved with me. How little did you tell me of what passed at Pemberley and Lambton! I owe all that I know of it, to another, not to you.'

Elizabeth told her the motives of her secrecy. She had been unwilling to mention Bingley; and the unsettled state of her own feelings had made her equally avoid the name of his friend. But now she would no longer conceal from her, his share in Lydia's marriage. All was acknowledged, and half the night spent in conversation.

*

'Good gracious!' cried Mrs Bennet, as she stood at a window the next morning, 'if that disagreeable Mr Darcy is not coming here again with our dear Bingley! What can he mean by being so tiresome as to be always coming here? I had no notion but he would go a shooting, or something or other, and not disturb us with his company. What shall we do with him? Lizzy, you must walk out with him again, that he may not be in Bingley's way.'

Elizabeth could hardly help laughing at so convenient a proposal; yet was really vexed that her mother should be always giving him such an epithet.

As soon as they entered, Bingley looked at her so expressively, and shook hands with such warmth, as left no doubt of his good information; and he soon afterwards said aloud, 'Mr Bennet, have you no more lanes hereabouts in which Lizzy may lose her way again today?'

'I advise Mr Darcy, and Lizzy, and Kitty,' said Mrs Bennet, 'to walk to Oakham Mount this morning. It is a nice long walk, and Mr Darcy has never seen the view.'

'It may do very well for the others,' replied Mr Bingley; 'but I am sure it will be too much for Kitty. Wont it, Kitty?'

Kitty owned that she had rather stay at home. Darcy professed a great curiosity to see the view from the Mount, and Elizabeth silently consented. As she went upstairs to get ready, Mrs Bennet followed her, saying,

'I am quite sorry, Lizzy, that you should be forced to have that disagreeable man all to yourself. But I hope you will not mind it: it is all for Jane's sake, you know; and there is no occasion for talking to him, except just now and then. So, do not put yourself to inconvenience.'

During their walk, it was resolved that Mr Bennet's consent should be asked in the course of the evening. Elizabeth reserved to herself the application for her mother's. She could not determine how her mother would take it; sometimes doubting whether all his wealth and grandeur would be enough to overcome her abhorrence of the man. But whether she were violently set against the match, or violently delighted with it, it was certain that her manner would be equally ill adapted to do credit to her sense; and she could no more bear that Mr Darcy should hear the first raptures of her joy, than the first vehemence of her disapprobation.

*

In the evening, soon after Mr Bennet withdrew to the library, she saw Mr Darcy rise also and follow him, and her agitation on seeing it was extreme. She did not fear her father's opposition, but he was going to be made unhappy, and that it should be through her means, that she, his favourite child, should be distressing him by her choice, should be filling him with fears and regrets in disposing of her, was a wretched reflection, and she sat in misery till Mr Darcy appeared again, when, looking at him, she was a little relieved by his smile. In a few minutes he approached the table where she was sitting with Kitty; and, while pretending to admire her work, said in a whisper, 'Go to your father, he wants you in the library.' She was gone directly.

Her father was walking about the room, looking grave and anxious. 'Lizzy,' said he, 'what are you doing? Are you out of your senses, to be accepting this man? Have not you always hated him?'

How earnestly did she then wish that her former opinions had been more reasonable, her expressions more moderate! It would have spared her from explanations and professions which it was exceedingly awkward to give; but they were now necessary, and she assured him with some confusion, of her attachment to Mr Darcy.

'Or in other words, you are determined to have him. He is rich, to be sure, and you may have more fine clothes and fine carriages than Jane. But will they make you happy?'

'Have you any other objection,' said Elizabeth, 'than your belief of my indifference?'

'None at all. We all know him to be a proud, unpleasant sort of man; but this would be nothing if you really liked him.'

'I do, I do like him,' she replied, with tears in her eyes, 'I love him. Indeed he has no improper pride. He is perfectly amiable. You do not know what he really is; then pray do not pain me by speaking of him in such terms.'

'Lizzy,' said her father, 'I have given him my consent. He is the kind of man, indeed, to whom I should never dare refuse any thing, which he condescended to ask. I now give it to you, if you are resolved on having him. But let me advise you to think better of it. I know your disposition, Lizzy. I know that you could be neither happy nor respectable, unless you truly esteemed your husband; unless you looked up to him as a superior. Your lively talents would place you in the greatest danger in an unequal marriage. You could scarcely escape discredit and misery. My child, let me not have the grief of seeing you unable to respect your partner in life. You know not what you are about.'

Elizabeth, still more affected, was earnest and solemn in her reply; and at length, by repeated assurances that Mr Darcy was really the object of her choice, by explaining the gradual change which her estimation of him had undergone, relating her absolute certainty that his affection was not the work of a day, but had stood the test of many months suspense, and enumerating with energy all his good qualities, she did conquer her father's incredulity, and reconcile him to the match.

'Well, my dear,' said he, when she ceased speaking, 'I have no more to say. If this be the case, he deserves you. I could not have parted with you, my Lizzy, to any one less worthy.'

To complete the favourable impression, she then told him what Mr Darcy had voluntarily done for Lydia. He heard her with astonishment.

'This is an evening of wonders, indeed! And so, Darcy did every thing; made up the match, gave the money, paid the fellow's debts, and got him his commission! So much the better. It will save me a world of trouble and economy. Had it been your uncle's doing, I must and would have paid him; but these violent young lovers carry every thing their own way. I shall offer to pay him tomorrow; he will rant and storm about his love for you, and there will be an end of the matter.'

He then recollected her embarrassment a few days before, on his reading Mr Collins's letter; and after laughing at her some time, allowed her at last to go – saying, as she quitted the room, 'If any young men come for Mary or Kitty, send them in, for I am quite at leisure.'

Elizabeth's mind was now relieved from a very heavy weight; and, after half an hour's quiet reflection in her own room, she was able to join the others with tolerable composure. Every thing was too recent for gaiety, but the evening passed tranquilly away; there was no longer any thing material to be dreaded, and the comfort of ease and familiarity would come in time.

When her mother went up to her dressing-room at night, she followed her, and made the important communication. Its effect was most extraordinary; for on first hearing it, Mrs Bennet sat quite still,

and unable to utter a syllable. Nor was it under many, many minutes, that she could comprehend what she heard; though not in general backward to credit what was for the advantage of her family, or that came in the shape of a lover to any of them. She began at length to recover, to fidget about in her chair, get up, sit down again, wonder, and bless herself.

'Good gracious! Lord bless me! only think! dear me! Mr Darcy! Who would have thought it! And is it really true? Oh! my sweetest Lizzy! how rich and how great you will be! What pin-money, what jewels, what carriages you will have! Jane's is nothing to it – nothing at all. I am so pleased – so happy. Such a charming man! – so handsome! so tall! – Oh, my dear Lizzy! pray apologise for my having disliked him so much before. I hope he will overlook it. Dear, dear Lizzy. A house in town! Every thing that is charming! Three daughters married! Ten thousand a year! Oh, Lord! What will become of me. I shall go distracted.'

This was enough to prove that her approbation need not be doubted: and Elizabeth, rejoicing that such an effusion was heard only by herself, soon went away. But before she had been three minutes in her own room, her mother followed her.

'My dearest child,' she cried, 'I can think of nothing else! Ten thousand a year, and very likely more! 'Tis as good as a Lord! And a special licence. You must and shall be married by a special licence. But my dearest love, tell me what dish Mr Darcy is particularly fond of, that I may have it tomorrow.'

This was a sad omen of what her mother's behaviour to the gentleman himself might be; and Elizabeth found, that though in the certain possession of his warmest affection, and secure of her relations' consent, there was still something to be wished for. But the morrow passed off much better than she expected; for Mrs Bennet luckily stood in such awe of her intended son-in-law, that she ventured not to speak to him, unless it was in her power to offer him any attention, or mark her deference for his opinion.

Elizabeth had the satisfaction of seeing her father taking pains to get acquainted with him; and Mr Bennet soon assured her that he was rising every hour in his esteem.

'I admire all my three sons-in-law highly,' said he. 'Wickham, perhaps, is my favourite; but I think I shall like your husband quite as well as Jane's.'

Chapter 60

Elizabeth's spirits soon rising to playfulness again, she wanted Mr Darcy to account for his having ever fallen in love with her. 'How could you begin?' said she. 'I can comprehend your going on charmingly, when you had once made a beginning; but what could set you off in the first place?'

'I cannot fix on the hour, or the spot, or the look, or the words, which laid the foundation. It is too long ago. I was in the middle before I knew that I had begun.'

'My beauty you had early withstood, and as for my manners – my behavior to you was at least always bordering on the uncivil, and I never spoke to you without rather wishing to give you pain than not. Now be sincere; did you admire me for my impertinence?'

'For the liveliness of your mind, I did.'

'You may as well call it impertinence at once. It was very little less. The fact is, that you were sick of civility, of deference, of officious attention. You were disgusted with the women who were always speaking and looking, and thinking for your approbation alone. I roused, and interested you, because I was so unlike them. Had you not been really amiable you would have hated me for it; but in spite of the pains you took to disguise yourself, your feelings were always noble and just; and in your heart, you thoroughly despised the persons who so assiduously courted you. There – I have saved you the trouble of accounting for it; and really, all things considered, I begin to think it perfectly reasonable. To be sure, you knew no actual good of me – but nobody thinks of that when they fall in love.'

'Was there no good in your affectionate behaviour to Jane, while she was ill at Netherfield?'

'Dearest Jane! who could have done less for her? But make a virtue of it by all means. My good qualities are under your protection, and you are to exaggerate them as much as possible; and, in return, it belongs to me to find occasions for teasing and quarrelling with you as often as may be; and I shall begin directly by asking you what made you so unwilling to come to the point at last. What made you so shy of me, when you first called, and afterwards dined here? Why, especially, when you called, did you look as if you did not care about me?'

'Because you were grave and silent, and gave me no encouragement.'

'But I was embarrassed.'

'And so was I.'

'You might have talked to me more when you came to dinner.'

'A man who had felt less, might.'

'How unlucky that you should have a reasonable answer to give, and that I should be so reasonable as to admit it! But I wonder how long you would have gone on, if you had been left to yourself. I wonder when you would have spoken, if I had not asked you! My resolution of thanking you for your kindness to Lydia had certainly great effect. Too much, I am afraid; for what becomes of the moral, if our comfort springs from a breach of promise, for I ought not to have mentioned the subject? This will never do.'

'You need not distress yourself. The moral will be perfectly fair. Lady Catherine's unjustifiable endeavours to separate us, were the means of removing all my doubts. I am not indebted for my present happiness to your eager desire of expressing your gratitude. I was not in a humour to wait for any opening of yours. My aunt's intelligence had given me hope, and I was determined at once to know every thing.'

'Lady Catherine has been of infinite use, which ought to make her happy, for she loves to be of use. But tell me, what did you come down to Netherfield for? Was it merely to ride to Longbourn and be embarrassed? or had you intended any more serious consequence?'

'My real purpose was to see you, and to judge, if I could, whether I might ever hope to make you love me. My avowed one, or what I avowed to myself, was to see whether your sister were still partial to Bingley, and if she were, to make the confession to him which I have since made.'

'Shall you ever have courage to announce to Lady Catherine, what is to befall her?'

'I am more likely to want time than courage, Elizabeth. But it ought to be done, and if you will give me a sheet of paper, it shall be done directly.'

'And if I had not a letter to write myself, I might sit by you, and admire the evenness of your writing, as another young lady once did. But I have an aunt, too, who must not be longer neglected.'

From an unwillingness to confess how much her intimacy with Mr Darcy had been over-rated, Elizabeth had never yet answered Mrs Gardiner's long letter, but now, having that to communicate which she knew would be most welcome, she was almost ashamed to find, that her uncle and aunt had already lost three days of happiness, and immediately wrote as follows:

I would have thanked you before, my dear aunt, as I ought to have done, for your long, kind, satisfactory, detail of particulars; but to say the truth, I was too cross to write. You supposed more than really existed. But now suppose as much as you chuse; give a loose to your fancy, indulge your imagination in every possible flight which the subject will afford, and unless you believe me actually married, you cannot greatly err. You must write again very soon, and praise him a great deal more than you did in your last. I thank you, again and again, for not going to the Lakes. How could I be so silly as to wish it! Your idea of the ponies is delightful. We will go round the Park every day. I am the happiest creature in the world. Perhaps other people have said so before, but not one with such justice. I am happier even than Jane; she only smiles, I laugh. Mr Darcy sends you all the love in the world, that he can spare from me. You are all to come to Pemberley at Christmas. Yours, &c.

Mr Darcy's letter to Lady Catherine, was in a different style; and still different from either, was what Mr Bennet sent to Mr Collins, in reply to his last.

DEAR SIR – I must trouble you once more for congratulations. Elizabeth will soon be the wife of Mr Darcy. Console Lady Catherine as well as you can. But, if I were you, I would stand by the nephew. He has more to give.

Yours sincerely, &c.

Miss Bingley's congratulations to her brother, on his approaching marriage, were all that was affectionate and insincere. She wrote even to Jane on the occasion, to express her delight, and repeat all her former professions of regard. Jane was not deceived, but she was affected; and though feeling no reliance on her, could not help writing her a much kinder answer than she knew was deserved.

The joy which Miss Darcy expressed on receiving similar information, was as sincere as her brother's in sending it. Four sides of paper were insufficient to contain all her delight, and all her earnest desire of being loved by her sister.

Before any answer could arrive from Mr Collins, or any congratulations to Elizabeth, from his wife, the Longbourn family heard that the Collinses were come themselves to Lucas lodge. The reason of this sudden removal was soon evident. Lady Catherine had been rendered so exceedingly angry by the contents of her nephew's letter, that Charlotte, really rejoicing in the match, was anxious to get away till the storm was blown over. At such a moment, the arrival of her friend was a sincere pleasure to Elizabeth, though in the course of their meetings she must sometimes think the pleasure dearly bought, when she saw Mr Darcy exposed to all the parading and obsequious civility of her husband. He bore it however with admirable calmness. He could even listen to Sir William Lucas, when he complimented him on carrying away the brightest jewel of the country, and expressed his hopes of their all meeting frequently at St. James's, with very decent composure. If he did shrug his shoulders, it was not till Sir William was out of sight.

Mrs Philips's vulgarity was another, and perhaps a greater tax on his forbearance; and though Mrs Philips, as well as her sister, stood in too much awe of him to speak with the familiarity which Bingley's good humour encouraged, yet, whenever she did speak, she must be vulgar. Nor was her respect for him, though it made her more quiet, at all likely to make her more elegant. Elizabeth did all she could, to shield him from the frequent notice of either, and was ever anxious to keep him to herself, and to those of her family with whom he might converse without mortification; and though the uncomfortable feelings arising from all this took from the season of courtship much of its pleasure, it added to the hope of the future; and she looked forward with delight to the time when they should be removed from society so little pleasing to either, to all the comfort and elegance of their family party at Pemberley.

Chapter 61

Happy for all her maternal feelings was the day on which Mrs Bennet got rid of her two most deserving daughters. With what delighted pride she afterwards visited Mrs Bingley and talked of Mrs Darcy may be guessed. I wish I could say, for the sake of her family, that the accomplishment of her earnest desire in the establishment of so many of her children, produced so happy an effect as to make her a sensible, amiable, well-informed woman for the rest of her life; though perhaps it was lucky for her husband, who might not have relished domestic felicity in so unusual a form, that she still was occasionally nervous and invariably silly.

Mr Bennet missed his second daughter exceedingly; his affection for her drew him oftener from home than any thing else could do. He delighted in going to Pemberley, especially when he was least expected.

Mr Bingley and Jane remained at Netherfield only a twelvemonth. So near a vicinity to her mother and Meryton relations was not desirable even to his easy temper, or her affectionate heart. The darling wish of his sisters was then gratified; he bought an estate in a neighbouring county to Derbyshire, and Jane and Elizabeth, in addition to every other source of happiness, were within thirty miles of each other.

Kitty, to her very material advantage, spent the chief of her time with her two elder sisters. In society so superior to what she had generally known, her improvement was great. She was not of so ungovernable a temper as Lydia, and, removed from the influence of Lydia's example, she became, by proper attention and management, less irritable, less ignorant, and less insipid. From the farther disadvantage of Lydia's society she was of course carefully kept, and though Mrs Wickham frequently invited her to come and stay with her, with the promise of balls and young men, her father would never consent to her going.

Mary was the only daughter who remained at home; and she was necessarily drawn from the pursuit of accomplishments by Mrs Bennet's being quite unable to sit alone. Mary was obliged to mix more with the world, but she could still moralize over every morning visit; and as she was no longer mortified by comparisons between her sisters' beauty and her own, it was suspected by her father that she submitted to the change without much reluctance.

As for Wickham and Lydia, their characters suffered no revolution from the marriage of her sisters. He bore with philosophy the conviction that Elizabeth must now become acquainted with whatever of his ingratitude and falsehood had before been unknown to her; and in spite of every thing, was not wholly without hope that Darcy might yet be prevailed on to make his fortune. The congratulatory letter which Elizabeth received from Lydia on her marriage, explained to her that, by his wife at least, if not by himself, such a hope was cherished. The letter was to this effect:

MY DEAR LIZZY – I wish you joy. If you love Mr Darcy half as well as I do my dear Wickham, you must be very happy. It is a great comfort to have you so rich, and when you have nothing else to do, I hope you will think of us. I am sure Wickham would like a place at court very much, and I do not think we shall have quite money enough to live upon without some help. Any place would do, of about three or four hundred a year; but, however, do not speak to Mr Darcy about it, if you had rather not.

Yours, &c.

As it happened that Elizabeth had much rather not, she endeavoured in her answer to put an end to every intreaty and expectation of the kind. Such relief, however, as it was in her power to afford, by the practice of what might be called economy in her own private expenses, she frequently sent them. It had always been evident to her that such an income as theirs, under the direction of two persons so extravagant in their wants, and heedless of the future, must be very insufficient to their support; and whenever they changed their quarters, either Jane or herself were sure of being applied to, for some little assistance towards discharging their bills. Their manner of living, even when the restoration of peace dismissed them to a home, was unsettled in the extreme. They were always moving from place to place in quest of a cheap situation, and always spending more than they ought. His affection for her soon sunk into indifference; hers lasted a little longer; and in spite of her youth and her manners, she retained all the claims to reputation which her marriage had given her.

Though Darcy could never receive him at Pemberley, yet, for Elizabeth's sake, he assisted him farther in his profession. Lydia was occasionally a visitor there, when her husband was gone to enjoy himself in London or Bath; and with the Bingleys they both of them frequently staid so long, that even Bingley's good humour was overcome, and he proceeded so far as to talk of giving them a hint to be gone.

Miss Bingley was very deeply mortified by Darcy's marriage; but as she thought it advisable to retain the right of visiting at Pemberley, she dropt all her resentment; was fonder than ever of Georgiana, almost as attentive to Darcy as heretofore, and paid off every arrear of civility to Elizabeth.

Pemberley was now Georgiana's home; and the attachment of the sisters was exactly what Darcy had hoped to see. They were able to love each other, even as well as they intended. Georgiana had the highest opinion in the world of Elizabeth; though at first she often listened with an astonishment bordering on alarm, at her lively, sportive, manner of talking to her brother. He, who had always inspired in herself a respect which almost overcame her affection, she now saw the object of open pleasantry. Her mind received knowledge which had never before fallen in her way. By Elizabeth's instructions she began to comprehend that a woman may take liberties with her husband, which a brother will not always allow in a sister more than ten years younger than himself.

Lady Catherine was extremely indignant on the marriage of her nephew; and as she gave way to all the genuine frankness of her character, in her reply to the letter which announced its arrangement, she sent him language so very abusive, especially of Elizabeth, that for some time all intercourse was at an end. But at length, by Elizabeth's persuasion, he was prevailed on to overlook the offence, and seek a reconciliation; and, after a little farther resistance on the part of his aunt, her resentment gave way, either to her affection for him, or her curiosity to see how his wife conducted herself; and she condescended to wait on them at Pemberley, in spite of that pollution which its woods had received, not merely from the presence of such a mistress, but the visits of her uncle and aunt from the city.

With the Gardiners, they were always on the most intimate terms. Darcy, as well as Elizabeth, really loved them; and they were both ever sensible of the warmest gratitude towards the persons who, by bringing her into Derbyshire, had been the means of uniting them.

THE END

Notes

1. Chuse : An archaic variant of "choose".
2. &c: An abbreviation of "etc".
3. half an hour : The use of "an" before words beginning with an "h" that is pronounced was standard in Jane Austen's day. See *Useful Jane Austen* by Martin Manser.
4. Vingt-un: French card game, predecessor of modern blackjack games.
5. Commerce : A 19th-century gambling French card game.
6. thither : An archaic variant of "to there".
7. stile : An obsolete variant of style.
8. piquet : An early 16th-century trick-taking card game for two players.
9. morrow : An obsolete variant of "tomorrow".
10. dropt : An obsolete variant of "dropped".
11. Quadrille : A dance that was fashionable in late 18th- and 19th-century Europe and its colonies.
12. — : As a means to leave certain names blank, in order to allow readers to personalize the story.
13. mantlepiece : A variant of "mantelpiece".
14. Whist : A classic English trick-taking card game which was widely played in the 18th and 19th centuries.
15. exstacy : An obsolete variant of "ecstasy".
16. intreat : An archaic variant of "entreat".
17. whither : An archaic variant of "where".
18. ere: An obsolete variant of "before".
19. whilst : An obsolete variant of "while".
20. staid : An archaic variant of "stayed".
21. amidst : Formal / British variation of "amid".
22. cassino : An Italian fishing card game.
23. hither : An archaic variant of "to here".
24. ecstacy : An obsolete variant of "ecstasy".
25. whence: An obsolete variant of "where".
26. Connexion : An obsolete variant of "connection".
27. Chesnuts : An obsolete variant of "chestnut".
28. 'Tis : 'Tis means it is.

傲慢與偏見

Preface to the Chinese Translation
中文譯本序

關於簡・奧斯汀，應該從哪裏說起呢？著名英國女作家維吉尼亞・伍爾夫有句名言說："在所有偉大作家當中，簡・奧斯汀是最難在偉大的那一瞬間捕捉的。"簡・奧斯汀（1775—1817）生長於英國南部有文化教養的牧師家庭，一生四十多個年頭的歲月基本上是在英國的鄉間度過的，她的六部完整作品——《理智與情感》（1795）、《傲慢與偏見》（1796）、《諾桑覺寺》（1798）、《曼斯費爾德莊園》（1812）、《愛瑪》（1814）、《勸導》（1816）——大都是描寫她自己熟悉的鄉間所謂體面家庭的生活與交往，看來平凡而瑣碎。在她的六部小說中，沒有拜倫式慷慨激昂的抒發，也極少見驚心動魄的現實主義描寫。對於簡・奧斯汀，要想捕捉她的"偉大"之所在，應從何處下手呢？她筆下那一場場的舞會、一次次的串門喝茶、一頓頓的家宴和一桌桌的紙牌，還有那些數不清的散步、閒談等如何能體現她的小說藝術的偉大呢？

　　評價奧斯汀，無可避免地要涉及題材問題。毫無疑問，奧斯汀是寫小題材的。據她自己說："鄉間村莊裏的三四個家庭"是她"得心應手的好材料"。她還把自己的藝術比作在"兩寸象牙"上"細細地描畫"。這是奧斯汀在藝術上自覺的選擇。當有人建議她在創作上改變風格寫這寫那,她都婉言謝絕,堅持說:"不,我必須保持自己的風格,按自己的方式寫下去……"

小天地可以反映出大問題。別小看"鄉間村莊裏的三四個家庭"的家務事,英國社會的階級狀況和經濟關係盡在其中。至少在奧斯汀的作品裏是如此。以《傲慢與偏見》為例,僅第二十九章洛欣莊園的一次宴請和飯後的一桌牌就說明了多少問題。凱瑟琳·德·包爾夫人[1]僅憑自己的家產、地位便在柯林斯牧師夫婦面前那樣驕橫,柯林斯牧師竟對她那樣謙卑。他被邀請為夫人湊上一桌牌,便感到不勝榮幸,"他贏一次要謝她一次,如果贏得太多,還得向她道歉"[2]。其實這不是一般的阿諛奉承問題。要知道,柯林斯教區牧師的職務是凱瑟琳夫人提拔的,他視夫人為"恩人",當然不好意思再贏她的錢。這僅是個小小的細節,卻有趣地反映了當時教會對產業的依附。至於威廉·盧卡斯爵士,既然本身已經封了爵位,何至於在牌桌上"不大說話,只顧把一件件軼事和一個個高貴的名字裝進腦子裏去"[3]?原來,他是在鎮上做生意起家的,曾在當市長的任內向國王獻過辭,從而獲得爵士頭銜。他是個商人變貴人的典型例子,骨子裏還是個商人,難怪羨慕貴族,從莫里哀的茹爾丹先生以來就是如此,或許可追溯到更早的羅馬喜劇。再如,賓利先生和他的兩個姊妹出場不久,第四章便交代說,"她們出生於英格蘭北部的一個體面家族。她們對自己的出身牢牢銘記,可是卻幾乎忘了她們兄弟的財產以及她們自己的財產都是做生意賺來的"[4]。對於細心的讀者,看到這"北部"一詞,就一目了然。賓利一家是在工業首先發達起來的北部發家致富的,這樣賺來的錢帶着銅臭氣,與貴族攀交的賓利小姐當然不願意正視它。這是當時普遍的階級心理。後來的蓋斯凱爾夫人在小說《北部與南部》中對照了農業的南部與工業的北部,更充份地描寫了發了財的北部企業家在文化教養上的欠缺與自卑。奧斯汀這裏輕輕一筆帶過,起了畫龍點睛的作用。

不過，要論證奧斯汀作品的歷史社會意義，要從根本上解決對奧斯汀的評價，還得從她大量描寫的"鄉間村莊裏的三四個家庭"入手來說明問題。

　　《傲慢與偏見》開卷第一句話便宣稱："凡是有財產的單身漢，必定需要娶位太太，這已經成了一條舉世公認的真理。"在這裏，關鍵的字是兩個：有"財產"和有"需要"。原文中的 in want of 是指客觀需要，不是主觀"想要"，這種提法使命題更具有"真理"的客觀性。

　　《傲慢與偏見》便以班奈特一家為典型來檢驗這條舉世公認的真理。住在朗伯恩村的班奈特一家是當地的第一大戶，班奈特先生的地產年賺兩千鎊，剛夠一家人的開支。根據遺囑上的附加條款，這份產業必須傳給男性繼承人，班奈特夫婦沒有兒子，產業要由一位遠親繼承。他們的五個女兒沒有生活保障，只能等着結婚。因此，當有十萬鎊遺產的賓利先生租下鄰近的尼德斐莊園時，這就難怪班奈特太太，像四鄰八舍所有那些家裏有女兒的太太一樣，要把這位尚未見過面的賓利當作自己女兒"理所應得的一筆財產"——"一個有錢的單身漢；每年有四五千鎊的收入。真是女兒們的福氣！"[5]

　　《傲慢與偏見》就是這樣開始的。這裏所說的婚姻，顯然不涉及感情，純粹是個經濟問題及生存問題。對於那些待嫁的女孩子，賓利只是個抽象存在，她們遠遠看見他"身穿藍上衣，騎着一匹黑馬"就足夠了。關鍵是有"財產"。人們常常籠統地認為奧斯汀專門描寫愛情與婚姻，其實她首先主要是寫婚姻問題，不是作為愛情結果的婚姻，而是作為經濟需要的婚姻。因此，我們可以說，與作者的宣稱相反，所謂"有財產的單身漢需要娶位太太"根本不是甚麼"舉世公認"的"真理"，而只是班奈特太太的一廂情願。我們也可以說，在《傲慢與偏見》中，真正的"舉世公認的真理"，不是"有財產的單身漢需要娶位太太"，而是"沒有財產的婦女需要嫁有財產的丈夫"！

　　從《傲慢與偏見》的整個描寫來看，作者探索的是資本主義社會，即佔有慾泛濫成災的社會條件下的婚姻關係；推而廣之，也是考察經濟關係在婚姻、在人們生活中的決定作用。

《傲慢與偏見》裏描寫了各種不同的婚姻關係,珍妮與賓利、達西與伊莉莎白、韋翰與麗迪亞、柯林斯牧師與夏綠蒂·盧卡斯⋯⋯夏綠蒂與麗迪亞代表兩種極端,前者只追求"可靠的儲藏室,日後可以不致受凍受飢"[6];後者卻純粹出於性的衝動,完全不顧後果。《傲慢與偏見》也描寫了人們對婚姻的不同追求與看法。如凱瑟琳夫人一心要把女兒安娜小姐嫁給外甥達西,以便"把兩家的地產合起來",她並且認為達西"有義務"、"有責任"這樣做。有兩萬鎊嫁妝的卡洛琳·賓利小姐一貫揮霍無度,喜歡與有身份地位的人結交,緊緊盯住年賺一萬鎊的達西先生。賓利小姐還極力阻止她哥哥與班奈特家的大女兒珍妮之間的愛情,她希望哥哥娶達西的妹妹喬治安娜小姐,一來可以"增加財產、提高地位",二來親上加親,可以此促成她自己與達西的婚事⋯⋯達西的表兄費茨威廉上校是位伯爵的小兒子,不能繼承家產和爵位,他坦白地向伊莉莎白說,自己揮霍慣了,在婚姻大事上不能不考慮錢財。他說,在婚姻問題上只有達西有條件不受錢財的約束而自由選擇。

對這形形色色的婚姻關係和婚姻觀,作道義上的譴責是無濟於事的。值得我們注意的是,在《傲慢與偏見》中作者始終把婚姻問題放在各種社會和經濟關係中去考察,使整個故事扎根於現實生活的土壤。

歷來英國小說描寫婚姻的不知有多少,但像奧斯汀在《傲慢與偏見》中那樣透徹地從經濟關係方面抓住資產階級婚姻制度的本質,在英國小說裏確實是不可多得的。奧斯汀用最透徹的眼光向人們表明,資產階級婚姻的實質無非是金錢的交易、利益的結合。柯林斯牧師與夏綠蒂·盧卡斯的婚姻是個典型。柯林斯牧師繼承了父親的產業又受到凱瑟琳·德·包爾夫人的提拔,獲得了教區牧師的職位,他有了房子,有了很不錯的收入,就缺個會理家又會陪伴他的馴服太太,加之他"恩人"的慫恿,因此他急於娶妻。從夏綠蒂方面而言,她從這件婚事中得到了房子、小園子、傢具陳設等一個舒服的小家。伊莉莎白去看望她時發現，"操持家務，飼養家禽，教區事物以及與此有關的一切，對她還沒有失去其吸引力……"[7]，"只要把柯林斯忘掉，其餘一切都很舒適融洽"[8]。在這種婚姻關係中，有趣的是，沒有財產的婦女的確嫁了有財產的單身漢，但在婚姻帶給她的樂趣中，恰恰沒有丈夫的地位。這不是對小說一開始提出的"舉世公認的真理"的一種絕妙的諷刺嗎？

但問題不僅止於此。柯林斯牧師與夏綠蒂以最快的速度完成這種標準化的婚姻關係，令人特別不舒服，為他們感到難堪。在奧斯汀筆下，它之所以令人不舒服，關鍵在於事情辦得那樣倉促，採取純粹的、赤裸裸的交易形式。我們由此便可以理解，在《傲慢與偏見》第一章中，班奈特太太要抓住新遷來的賓利先生，為甚麼非要催着自己的丈夫出發先去拜訪他不可。按照資產階級婚姻"儀式"的要求，必須得由一家之主的班奈特先生率先去拜訪新來者，等對方做過禮節性的回訪後，主婦方可出面設家宴招待客人，而在家宴上，女兒們便露面了。這是促使有財產的單身漢陷入情網的第一步。緊接着便是舞會，喜歡跳舞被視為一個"好兆頭"，是"導致談情說愛的一個必經步驟"[9]，這也許是奧斯汀小說裏舞會場面多的一個原因吧。總之，通過夏綠蒂的婚姻，通過她做到的和沒有做到的，奧斯汀不僅揭露了資產階級婚姻的實質，而且還審視了它的形式方面，即它的"儀式"。在珍妮與賓利的關係中，珍妮雖然默默地愛上了賓利，卻從不表露，直等到最後賓利向她求婚。他們的結合完全合乎"儀式"，是資產階級"自由選擇"、"有愛情"的婚姻的"典範"。

奧斯汀在《傲慢與偏見》中通過不同類型的婚姻關係把資產階級婚姻從經濟實質到禮儀形式揭露得多麼透徹啊！

然而，問題還不止於此。既然，如奧斯汀所表示的，婚姻不過是某種"儀式"底下的利益的權衡，那又怎麼解釋達西與伊莉莎白的不平等婚姻呢？故事從一開始就在他們兩人之間設置障礙，如達西傲慢地拒絕請她跳舞，使伊莉莎白對他產生偏見，達西方面則早就認定她們有那些不體面的親戚，"如果想嫁給有地位的男人，機會可就大大減少了"，更沒有想到自己會向她求婚！那麼他們最後又是怎麼結合起來的？在回答這個問題以前，也許有必要先談談 manners 的問題。

英語中 manners 的概念包括許多內容——舉止、言談、禮貌、風度、待人接物的態度，總之，一個人的文明教養的綜合表現，暫且稱之為"教養"吧。在當時的社會，"教養"在生活中起着重要作用。十八世紀末政治家、思想家勃克曾寫過這樣的話："教養（manners）比法律還重要……它們依着自己的性能，或推動道德，或促成道德，或完全毀滅道德。"[10] 當時十分流行的所謂"世態小説"就注重從舉止言談，即教養方面描寫人物，奧斯汀的小説實際上是屬於"世態小説"傳統的。比如，她對人物不做道德倫理的判斷，而是多從舉止言談方面刻畫。manners 一詞，在《傲慢與偏見》一書中出現竟有一百一十三次之多不是偶然的。在這個意義上，《傲慢與偏見》中的人物可以以有無教養來劃分。我們從一些不起眼的細節可以體會出奧斯汀在這方面所做的微妙區別。以人們在窗前的表現而言，伊莉莎白從窗戶看見達西帶着他妹妹喬治安娜來看望她，便趕快"從窗前閃開，生怕被人看見"[11]，在窗前張望對於像伊莉莎白這種所謂體面家庭的女孩子來説，是不合體統的。相比之下，伊莉莎白的姨媽，嫁了鎮上的律師的菲力普太太，則打開客廳窗戶，大聲向過路的熟人叫喊，請他們進屋坐坐。這個細節鮮明地突出了她的缺乏教養，使我們理解了，達西以及賓利小姐等人何以認為班奈特一家有這樣的親戚是不配與有身份的人攀親的。在奧斯汀筆下，舉止、言談、風度、教養在現實生活中是會產生作用的。比如，珍妮一度失去了賓利，正是她的至親骨肉的行為失禮造成的。[12] 別的不説，單憑班奈特太太在大庭廣眾之下滔滔不絕地議論這件婚事的好處，就足以把賓利嚇退了。

現在回到本節開始提出的問題。在《傲慢與偏見》中達西與伊莉莎白之間終於克服了財產與門第的懸殊，結為夫婦，manners 在這裏起了很大作用。如前所述，他們兩人之間的隔閡首先是由達西在舞會上對伊莉莎白無禮引起的。可是，後來又是 manners 把達西與伊莉莎白結合起來。他們在龐百利莊園偶然相遇，達西發現，伊莉莎白的舅舅、倫敦商人賈汀納先生及其夫人是極有教養的體面人。班奈特太太固然缺乏教養，但他自己的親姨凱瑟琳夫人也同樣不懂規矩。至於說麗迪亞私奔造成醜聞，其實達西自己的妹妹喬治安娜也曾打算私奔，總之在親屬的教養問題上，他們兩人的"賬"互相抵消了。純粹屬於兩個人之間的隔閡，在龐百利的新的條件下也完全煙消雲散。達西第一次求婚被伊莉莎白拒絕，他認識到了自己的居高臨下，自我中心；在龐百利再次見面時，他彬彬有禮，與昔日舞會上的達西判若兩人，使伊莉莎白大為感動……這時伊莉莎白才開始認識到，只有他（她）們兩人在思想、感情、志趣上最投契。當姐姐珍妮問她，怎麼會愛上達西先生的，伊莉莎白回答說："應該從我看到龐百利莊園那美麗的園林算起。"[13] 這話好像是指達西的財產，因此珍妮要妹妹別開玩笑，其實這話是雙關語，除了指具體的莊園外，還指在龐百利的園林裏見到的一個新的達西。也就是說，達西改了待人接物的態度，才贏得伊莉莎白的心。可以想像，如果達西還是那麼傲慢無禮，那麼即使其他誤會排解了，他們之間也不會產生愛情的。

這樣說，奧斯汀是不是以達西與伊莉莎白的婚姻而否定了自己對資產階級婚姻本質的揭示呢？當然不是。誠然，在達西與伊莉莎白疏遠與和解的關係中，manners 起了很大的作用。manners 克服了他們之間的鴻溝，包括財產地位的懸殊，但是 manners 本身不是超階級的。如前所述，manners 包括舉止言談、禮貌風度，歸根結底是社會身份的標誌。達西與伊莉莎白在財產地位上有一定的懸殊，但他們基本上屬於同一階級，即伊莉莎白說的，"他（指達西）是紳士，我是紳士的女兒，在這點上我們是平等的。"[14] 我們重溫恩格斯那段名言，應該注意到他說的資產階級的婚姻自由，是"從本階級選擇"。我們通過表面的"儀式"看到了選擇過程。更重要的是，manners 的要求則保證這選擇限於本階級。因此，奧斯汀對"儀式"和"教養"的強調不僅不削弱她在《傲慢與偏見》中對資產階級婚姻本質的揭示，相反從"儀式"到實質，奧斯汀圍繞資產階級婚姻揭示了一系列社會、經濟、道德的真理。若說奧斯汀的《傲慢與偏見》實際上是為恩格斯的論斷做了形象的註釋，這話也不為過吧。奧斯汀素來善於刻畫人物，有的批評家還認為在這點上她可以與莎士比亞媲美。英國著名作家 E・M・福斯特的小說理論名著《小說面面觀》在分析"立體"人物（與"扁平"人物相對而言）時便以奧斯汀的人物為例。實際上，奧斯汀的某些人物基本上只是漫畫，是扁平的。班奈特太太和柯林斯牧師，他們身上只有一個基本特徵，這個特徵從一開始就交代清楚了。如小說的第一章寥寥數百字的對話就把班奈特太太的過去、現在和將來呈現在讀者面前，人物後來的言行不過是他們固有特徵在新的條件下的不同表現，如同音樂中的變調。同樣，柯林斯牧師的第一封信也是一幅自畫像，他後來的言行（和書信）只不過是進一步的自我暴露而已。奧斯汀的另外一些人物，如女主人公伊莉莎白・班奈特的性格就有發展，而且還是令人意想不到的變化，正合了福斯特對立體人物的要求。但是無論如何，扁平也好，立體也好，《傲慢與偏見》中描寫得最出色的人物形象——伊莉莎白、班奈特太太、柯林斯牧師——都刻畫得栩栩如生，好像可以從書本中走出來，我們彷彿聽到伊莉莎白爽朗而調皮的笑聲、班奈特太太那喋喋不休的抱怨和柯林斯牧師滔滔不絕的廢話。

特別值得我們注意的還有奧斯汀在描寫人物形象時使用的嘲諷語調和喜劇手法，當她說班奈特太太"智力貧乏、不學無術、喜怒無常"[15] 時，她的語言還僅是簡潔而準確的。但當她接着寫到"只要碰到不稱心的事，她就自以為神經衰弱"[16] 時，就含有嘲諷了。奧斯汀還善於自己躲在後面，讓人物通過最普通的語言自己暴露自己。
《傲慢與偏見》一開始，班奈特太太急於搶先認識賓利，不指望靠郎
格太太的介紹，她說"我不相信郎格太太肯這麼做。她自己有兩個
親姪女。她是個自私自利、假仁假義的女人，我看不起她"[17]。而第
五十四章到了故事的結尾，珍妮與賓利的婚事已成定局，班奈特太
太心裏高興，又提起這位始終沒有露面的郎格太太，說："我覺得郎
格太太這個人真是太好了；她的姪女兒們都是些規規矩矩的好女孩，
只可惜長得一點也不好看。我真喜歡她們。"[18] 這兩段話一前一後，
遙相呼應，不是把班奈特太太嫁女兒的競爭心理以及她的反覆無常、
自我中心表現得淋漓盡致嗎？再如柯林斯牧師把班奈特一家攪了半
天也沒有娶他們的女兒，班奈特太太早就對他煩透了，而柯林斯牧
師臨走時還"答應"給他們"再來一封謝函"！"答應"二字用得好，
充份點出這個令人討厭的人物的遲鈍，竟絲毫沒有覺察出班奈特一
家人永遠也不想見到他或收到他的片言隻語！又如對凱瑟琳夫人的
描寫。凱瑟琳夫人的馬車路過門口，柯林斯牧師全家手忙腳亂出去
迎接，伊莉莎白卻說："就是這麼回事嗎？我還以為是豬闖進了花園
呢，原來只不過是凱瑟琳夫人母女兩人。"[19] 這話雖然說得挖苦，戳
破了凱瑟琳夫人自己吹起來的嚇人架勢，但過於直率不夠含蓄。再
看下文中對凱瑟琳夫人的描寫："只要哪一個佃戶不馴服、不知足或
窮得活不下去，她就親自出馬到村莊裏去調解糾紛、壓制怨言，把他
們罵得恢復太平與富足！"[20] 她請柯林斯等人吃飯，飯前"請客人到
窗口去欣賞風景"，飯後又要大家聆聽她來"斷定第二天的天氣會如
何"[21]。這裏僅僅通過幾個小詞的安排，一個專橫跋扈的老太婆的諷
刺畫像便躍然紙上了。

　　在《傲慢與偏見》這樣一部以喜劇性為基調的作品中，沒有嚴格
意義上的正面人物或反面人物，基本上只有理性的人和愚蠢的人，
騙子韋翰也許除外。但讀者可能會注意到，韋翰完全是從外部描寫
的，讀者無法真正了解他。他在故事中主要起道具的作用。而對書

中的蠢人，作者不僅讓他們自己暴露自己，並且還用喜劇手法讓他們以自己的愚蠢懲罰自己。如凱瑟琳夫人勞師動眾跑到班奈特家向伊莉莎白問罪，原是要扼殺達西與伊莉莎白的愛情。可是，事實上，正是她這一舉動為這一對相愛的人溝通資訊，促成了他們的結合。伊莉莎白調皮地說：「凱瑟琳夫人倒幫了極大的忙，她自己也應該高興，因為她喜歡幫別人的忙」[22]，作者就這樣把這位又霸道又可笑的老太婆給解決了。

在《傲慢與偏見》中，伊莉莎白是全書的中心人物，其他人物的愚蠢都是通過她反映出來的。如在尼德斐莊園舉行的舞會上，班奈特太太和她的小女兒們的不得體的言行都是通過伊莉莎白的眼睛看見的；當時珍妮與賓利眉目傳情，根本沒有注意，只有伊莉莎白為她們臉紅。她「覺得她家裏人好像是約定今天晚上到這裏來盡量出醜，而且可以說是從來沒有那樣起勁，從來沒有那樣成功」[23]。同樣，關於賓利小姐的種種心計，珍妮總是從最好的方面去理解，也還是伊莉莎白敏銳地覺察出她們姐妹兩人的不懷好意。班奈特先生在第一章裏，當伊莉莎白還沒有露面時就說過「別的女兒都糊塗，只有伊莉莎白聰明」等話，也給我們從心理上作了準備，使我們產生一種印象、一種期待，似乎伊莉莎白是全書的中心人物，作者通過她而對全書的人和事作出判斷，好像勃朗特之於簡·愛一樣。的確，在《傲慢與偏見》中，作者花了很多筆墨刻畫她的性格，她資質聰明，思想活潑，性格開朗，有幽默感，喜歡笑別人，也同樣能笑自己。對於賓利小姐的暗箭，她反唇相譏，對凱瑟琳夫人的無禮，她膽敢頂撞。她憑自己的聰明大方博得了眾目所矚的男子達西先生的愛慕，擊敗了「情敵」賓利小姐，有如簡·愛擊敗了布蘭奇小姐而與羅契斯特先生相愛一樣。但所有這一切只能說明，伊莉莎白是全書中興趣的中心，但還不是判斷是非曲直的尺度，即不是「意識」的中心。事實上，伊莉莎白不是嚴格意義上的正面主人公形象，作者並沒有始終一貫地從讚賞的角度描寫她。讀者會注意到《傲慢與偏見》進行到四份之一，即到第十六章的時候，作者對伊莉莎白的描寫在基調上發生了變化：她從"聰明人"變成了"愚人"。事情是從伊莉莎白在麥里頓碰到民兵自衛團的軍官韋翰開始的，伊莉莎白立刻被韋翰一副"討人喜歡"的儀表迷住了。韋翰跟她一見如故，滔滔不絕地洗刷自己，中傷達西先生，那話裏破綻百出，聰明過人的伊莉莎白竟然毫無察覺，完全被韋翰牽着鼻子走。這時奧斯汀筆鋒一轉，改用嘲諷的筆調描寫伊莉莎白，如説她看着韋翰，心裏覺得，他"越説話越顯得英俊了"[24]。其實他正在那裏編排一席謊言呢！她為他抱屈，心裏責怪達西，"怎麼竟如此對待像你這樣的一個青年，光憑你相貌堂堂，一看就知道你是個和藹可親的人"[25]。她與韋翰分手時"滿腦子是他的形象"，"一心盼着跟他跳舞"，"穿着打扮格外用心"[26]。總之，現在伊莉莎白自己成了被嘲諷的愚人了。她對韋翰的着迷已為別人所察覺，如她的舅媽就提醒她要"謹慎"[27]，她的朋友夏綠蒂也勸她"別做傻瓜，為一個韋翰而得罪比他身價高十倍的達西"[28]，而伊莉莎白恰恰當了這樣的"傻瓜"，傲慢地拒絕了達西的求婚。這完全不能跟《簡·愛》的簡·愛拒絕嫁給羅契斯特相提並論。《傲慢與偏見》第三十五章伊莉莎白拒絕達西的求婚沒有任何保衛婦女人格不受侵犯的含義。當我們想到伊莉莎白是在對韋翰着迷，聽信他的讒言的情況下才拒絕達西的求婚時，她的那副姿態不是有點可笑嗎？第三十七章是伊莉莎白成長過程的重要轉折。看了達西的信，她不僅知道了韋翰與達西關係的真相，更重要的是，她對自己達到了一種新的認識。她現在突然認識到，當初，第一次見面，韋翰就滔滔不絕，自稱自讚，是多麼有失體統，何況又言行不一，而她自己竟毫無察覺，上了大當。她悔恨自己"盲目、偏心、有偏見、荒唐"，"完全被虛榮心牽着走……"。最後她説："在此之前，我根本不認識我自己"[29]，這或者就是西方評論所謂的 epiphany，亦可稱為"頓悟"吧。伊莉莎白克服了偏見，達西也收斂了傲慢，兩人在新的境界裏結合起來。至此，小説也達到頂點與高潮。在此之後，就是收拾故事的各條線索而已；就人物塑造而言，已全部完成，不再有甚麼發展。失去了嘲諷的、喜劇性的基調，《傲慢與偏見》的最後部份就少了奧斯汀特有的韻味。如伊莉莎白與達西最後定情的那段話：“她立刻吞吞吐吐地告訴他說，……她的心情已經起了很大的變化，現在她願意以愉快和感激的心情來接受他這一番盛情美意。這個回答簡直使他感到從來沒有過的快樂，他正像一個熱戀中的人一樣，立刻抓住這個機會，無限乖巧、無限熱烈地向她傾訴衷曲……” 30 比起先前那些機智的鬥嘴和帶挖苦的敘述，這段交代多麼乏味！顯而易見，對奧斯汀來說，嘲諷是她的小說藝術的精髓。

縱觀《傲慢與偏見》，可以說，奧斯汀對於決定婚姻關係，乃至人的一切關係的物質原因可謂揭露得深刻，但這種揭露，在這部喜劇性的世態小說中，不是兇狠的，不是傷感的，不是道德義憤的，也不是玩世不恭的，而是嘲諷的。奧斯汀的嘲諷滲透於全書的字裏行間，在人物塑造上起了關鍵作用，也是敘述中的靈魂。但這種嘲諷不是文字遊戲，也不在抽象品格上兜圈，而是緊緊圍繞着對人們的現實關係的揭露。

總之，觀察的深度與才氣橫溢的嘲諷在《傲慢與偏見》中凝煉為一部閃耀着喜劇光彩的現實主義傑作，擺在世界名著的行列中間毫不遜色。

吳勞

註解：

1 轉引自伊揚・瓦特編：《奧斯汀：批評文選》1963 年美國版第 15 頁。原為書評，發表於《民族》報 1923 年 12 月 15 日，收入論文集時本段被刪去。《書信》1814 年 9 月 9 日。《書信》1816 年 12 月 16 日。《書信》1816 年 4 月 1 日。

2 見本書第 29 章。

3 同上。

4 見本書第 4 章。

5 見本書第 1 章。

6 見本書第 22 章。

7 見本書第 38 章。

8 見本書第 28 章。

9 見本書第 3 章。

10 埃德蒙德・勃克書信《論謀求與法國弒君政權媾發》，見《埃德蒙德・勃克作品集》，牛津大學出版社，1928 年版，第 6 卷，第 150 頁。

11 見本書第 44 章。

12 見本書第 36 章。

13 見本書第 59 章。

14 見本書第 56 章。

15 見本書第 1 章。

16 同上。

17 見本書第 2 章

18 見本書第 54 章。

19 見本書第 28 章。

20 見本書第 30 章。

21 見本書第 29 章。

22 見本書第 60 章。

23 見本書第 18 章。

24 見本書第 16 章。

25 見本書第 16 章。

26 見本書第 16、17 和 18 章。

27 見本書第 25 章。

28 見本書第 18 章。

29 見本書第 36 章。

30 見本書第 58 章。

第一章

凡是有財產的單身漢，必定需要娶位太太，這已經成了一條舉世公認的真理。

這樣的單身漢，每逢新搬到一個地方，四鄰八舍雖然完全不了解他的性情和想法，可是，既然這樣的一條真理早已在人們心目中根深蒂固，人們就總是把他看作是自己某個女兒理所應得的一筆財產。

有一天，班奈特太太對她的丈夫說："我的好老爺，尼德斐莊園終於租出去了，你聽說過沒有？"

班奈特先生回答道，他沒有聽說過。

"的確租出去了，"她說，"郎格太太剛剛上這裏來過，她把這件事的底細，一五一十地都告訴了我。"

班奈特先生沒有理睬她。

"你難道不想知道是誰租去的嗎？"太太不耐煩地大聲說道。

"既然你要說給我聽，我聽聽也無妨。"

這句話足夠鼓勵她講下去了。

"哦，親愛的，你得知道，郎格太太說，租尼德斐莊園的是個闊少爺，他是英格蘭北部的人；聽說他星期一那天，乘着一輛駟馬大轎車來看房子，看得非常合意，當場就和莫理斯先生談妥了；他要在'米迦勒節'¹以前搬進來，打算下個週末先讓幾個傭人來住。"

"這人叫甚麼名字？"

"賓利。"

"有太太的呢，還是個單身漢？"

"噢！是個單身漢，親愛的，確確實實是個單身漢！一個有錢的單身漢；每年有四五千鎊的收入。真是女兒們的福氣！"

"這怎麼說？關女兒們甚麼事？"

"我的好老爺，"太太回答道，"你怎麼這樣讓人討厭！告訴你吧，我正在盤算，他要是娶我們其中一個女兒為妻，該多好啊！"

"他住到這裏來，就是為了這個打算嗎？"

"打算！胡扯，這是甚麼話！不過，他倒或許看中我們的某一個女兒呢。他一搬來，你就得去拜訪拜訪他。"

"我不用去。你帶着女兒們去就得了，要不你乾脆讓她們自己去，那或許倒更好些，因為你跟女兒們比起來，她們哪一個都不能勝過你的美貌，你去了，賓利先生倒可能挑中你呢。"

"我的好老爺，你太抬舉我了。從前也的確有人讚賞過我的美貌，但現在我可不敢說有甚麼出眾的地方了。一個女人有了五個成年的女兒，就不該想着自己的美貌了。"

"這樣看來，一個女人並沒有多少時候會想到自己的美貌了。"

"不過，我的好老爺，賓利一搬到我們的附近來，你就應該去見見他。"

"老實跟你説吧，這不是我份內的事。"

"看女兒們份上吧。只請你想一想，她們不論哪一個，要是攀上了這樣一頭親事，該多好。威廉爵士夫婦已經決定去拜訪他，他們也無非是這個用意。你知道，他們通常是不會拜訪新搬來的鄰居的。你的確應該去一次，要是你不去，我們怎麼能去。"

"你實在過份細心了。賓利先生一定很高興看到你的；我可以寫封信給你帶去，就説隨便他挑中了我哪一個女兒，我都心甘情願地答應他把她娶過去；不過，我在信上要特別替小莉茲²吹噓幾句。"

"我希望你別這麼做。莉茲沒有一點地方勝過別的幾個女兒；我敢説，論漂亮，她抵不上珍妮一半；論性子，她抵不上麗迪亞一半。可你老是偏愛她。"

"她們沒有哪一個值得誇獎的，"他回答道；"她們跟別人家的女兒一樣，又傻，又無知；倒是莉茲要比她的幾個姐妹伶俐些。"

"我的好老爺，你怎麼捨得這樣糟蹋自己的親生女兒？你就是在故意氣我，好讓你自己得意吧。你半點也不體諒我的神經衰弱。”

“你真錯怪了我，我的好太太。我非常尊重你的神經。它們是我的老朋友。至少在最近二十年以來，我一直聽到你鄭重其事地提到它們。”

“啊！你不知道我怎樣受苦呢！”

“不過我希望你這毛病會好起來，那麼，像這種每年有四千鎊收入的闊少爺，你就可以眼看着他們一個個搬來做你的鄰居了。”

“你既然不願意去拜訪他們，即使有二十個搬了來，對我們又有甚麼好處！”

“放心吧，我的好太太，等到有了二十個，我一定一個一個都去拜訪。”

班奈特先生真是個古怪人，他一方面喜歡插科打諢，愛挖苦人，同時又不苟言笑，變幻莫測，使他那位太太積了二十三年的經驗，還摸不透他的性格。太太的腦子倒是很容易分析的。她是個智力貧乏、不學無術、喜怒無常的女人，只要碰到不稱心的事，就自以為神經衰弱。她生平的大事就是嫁女兒；她生平的安慰就是訪友拜客和打聽小道消息。

第二章

班奈特先生儘管在自己太太面前由始至終都說不想去拜訪賓利先生，事實上一直都打算去拜訪他，而且還是第一批拜訪者之一。等到他去拜訪過之後，當天晚上太太才知道實情。這消息透露出來的經過是這樣的——他看到第二個女兒在裝飾帽子，就突然對她說：

"我希望賓利先生會喜歡你這頂帽子，莉茲。"

她母親憤憤地說："我們既然不準備去看賓利先生，當然就無從知道他喜歡甚麼。"

"可是你忘了，媽媽，"伊莉莎白說，"我們將來可以在舞會上碰到他的，郎格太太不是答應過把他介紹給我們嗎？"

"我不相信郎格太太肯這麼做。她自己有兩個親姪女。她是個自私自利、假仁假義的女人，我看不起她。"

"我也看不起她，"班奈特先生說，"你倒不指望她來替你效勞，這讓我聽了高興。"

班奈特太太沒有理睬他，可是忍不下心頭之氣，便罵起女兒來。

"別那麼咳個不停，凱蒂，看老天爺份上吧！稍稍體諒一下我的神經吧。你簡直快把我弄得崩潰了。"

"凱蒂真不知趣，"她的父親說，"咳嗽也不懂選擇時機。"

"我又不是故意咳着玩，"凱蒂氣惱地回答道。

"你們的舞會定在哪一天，莉茲？"

"從明天算起，還要再過兩個星期。"

"唔，原來如此，"她的母親大聲說道，"郎格太太可要到舞會的前一天才能趕回來；那麼，她可來不及把他介紹給你們了，她自己也還不認識他呢。"

"那麼，好太太，你大可以佔你朋友的上風，反過來替她介紹這位貴人了。"

　　"做不到，我的好老爺，做不到，我自己還不認識他呢；你怎麼可以這樣嘲笑人？"

　　"我真佩服你想得這般周到。只認識兩個星期當然算不上甚麼。跟一個人相處了兩個星期，不可能就此了解他究竟是怎樣的一個人。不過，要是我們不去嘗試嘗試，別人可少不了要嘗試的。話說到底，郎格太太和她的姪女一定不肯錯過這個良機。因此，要是你不願意辦這件事，我自己來辦好了，反正她會覺得這是我們對她的一片好意。"

　　女兒們都對父親瞪着眼。班奈特太太只隨口説了聲："真胡扯！"

　　"你怎麼這樣大驚小怪！"他大聲説道，"你以為替別人效點勞介紹介紹是毫無意思的事嗎？你這樣的説法我可不大同意。你説呢，瑪莉？我知道你是個有獨到見解的少女，讀的書都是些巨著，而且還要做摘錄筆記。"

　　瑪莉想説幾句有見識的話，可又不知道怎麼説才好。

　　於是班奈特先生接下去説："讓瑪莉仔細想一想再發表意見吧，我們還是重新來談談賓利先生。"

　　"我就討厭談賓利先生，"他的太太叫了起來。

　　"遺憾得很，你竟會跟我説這種話；你怎麼不早説呢？要是今天上午聽到你這樣説，那我當然就不會去拜訪他了。這真叫做不湊巧。現在既然拜訪也拜訪過了，我們今後就少不了要結交這個朋友。"

　　果然不出他所料，太太女兒們一聽此話，一個個都大為詫異，尤其是班奈特太太，比誰都詫異得厲害；不過，這樣歡天喜地地喧鬧了一陣以後，她便當眾宣佈，説這件事她早就料到。

　　"你真是個好心腸的人，我的好老爺！我早就知道你終究會給我説服的。你既然疼愛自己的女兒，當然就不會把這樣一個朋友不放在心上。我真太高興了！你這個玩笑開得太有意思，誰想到你竟會今天上午去拜訪他，而且到現在隻字不提。”

“凱蒂，現在你可以放心大膽地咳嗽了，”班奈特先生一面說，一面走出房間。太太那樣得意忘形，把他鬧得有些煩了。

門一關上，班奈特太太便對她的幾個女兒說：“孩子們，你們的爸爸真是太好了，我不知道你們怎樣才能報答他的好心；再說，你們還應該好好地報答我一番呢。老實跟你們說吧，我們老夫婦活到這麼一大把年紀了，哪裏有興致天天去結交朋友；可是為了你們，我們任何事都樂意去做。麗迪亞，乖寶貝，雖然你年紀最小，開起舞會來，賓利先生或許就偏偏要跟你跳呢。”

“噢！”麗迪亞滿不在乎地說。“我才不當它一回事。年紀雖然是我最小，個子卻是我最高。”

於是她們一方面猜測那位貴人甚麼時候會來回訪班奈特先生，一方面盤算着甚麼時候請他來吃飯，就這樣把一個晚上的時間在閒談中度過了。

第三章

儘管班奈特太太有了五個女兒幫腔,向她丈夫問起賓利先生這樣那樣,可是丈夫的回答總不能令她滿意。母女們想盡辦法對付他——赤裸裸的問句,巧妙的設想,離題很遠的猜測,甚麼辦法都用到了;可是他並沒有上她們的圈套。最後,她們迫不得已,只得聽取鄰居盧卡斯太太的間接消息。她的報導全是好話。據說威廉爵士很喜歡他。他非常年輕,長得特別英俊,為人又極其謙和,最重要的一點是,他打算請一大羣客人來參加下次的舞會。這真是再好也沒有的事!喜歡跳舞是談情說愛的一個必經步驟;大家都熱烈地希望能俘獲賓利先生的心。

"我只要能看到有一個女兒在尼德斐莊園幸福地安了家,"班奈特太太對她的丈夫說,"看到其他幾個也匹配得這樣門戶對,此生就沒有別的奢望了。"

幾天之後,賓利先生上門回訪班奈特先生,在他的書房裏跟他盤桓了十分鐘左右。他久仰班奈特先生幾位小姐的年輕美貌,很希望能夠見見她們;但是他只見到了她們的父親。倒是小姐們比他幸運,她們利用樓上的窗戶,看清了他穿的是藍外套,騎的是一匹黑馬。

班府不久就發請帖請他吃飯;班奈特太太已經計劃了好幾道菜,每道菜都足以增加她的體面,說明她是個會當家的賢主婦。可是事不湊巧,賓利先生第二天非進城不可,他們這一番盛意他無法領情,因此回信給他們,說是要遲一點再說。班奈特太太大為不安。她想,此人剛來到赫福德郡[3],怎麼就要進城有事,於是她開始擔心了;照理他應該在尼德斐莊園安安定定住下來,看現在的情形,莫非他經常都得這樣東漂西泊,行蹤不定?虧得盧卡斯太太對她說,可能他是到倫敦去邀請那一大羣客人來參加舞會,這才使她稍微減少了一些顧慮。外面馬上就紛紛傳說賓利先生將要帶來七男十二女參加舞會。小姐們聽到有這麼多女賓，不禁擔心起來。幸好開舞會的前一天，她們聽到賓利先生並沒有帶來十二個女賓，僅僅帶來六個，其中五個是他自己的姐妹，一個是表姐妹，這個消息才使小姐們放了心。後來等到這羣貴客走進舞場的時候，卻一共只有五個人——賓利先生，他的兩個姐妹，姐夫，還有另外一個青年。

賓利先生儀表堂堂，大有紳士風度，而且和顏悅色，沒有拘泥做作的習慣。他的姐妹也都是些優雅的女性，態度落落大方。他的姐夫赫斯托只不過像個普通紳士，不大引人注目，但是他的朋友達西卻立刻引起了全場的注意，因為他身材偉岸，眉清目秀，舉止高貴。他進場不到五分鐘，大家都紛紛傳說他每年有一萬鎊的收入。男賓們都稱讚他的一表人才，女賓們都說他比賓利先生英俊得多。人們差不多有半個晚上都帶着愛慕的目光看着他，但後來人們發現他為人驕傲，看不起人，巴結不上他，因此對他起了厭惡的感覺，他那眾望所歸的極盛一時的場面才黯然失色。他既然擺出那麼一副討人嫌惹人厭的神情，那麼，不管他在德比郡有多大的財產，也挽救不了他，況且和他的朋友比起來，他更沒有甚麼大不了。

賓利先生很快就熟悉了全場所有的主要人物。他生氣勃勃，為人又不拘泥，每一場舞都少不了要跳。使他氣惱的是，舞會怎麼散場散得這樣早。他又談起他自己要在尼德斐莊園開一次舞會。他這些可愛的地方自然會引得大家對他產生好感。他跟他的朋友是多麼顯著的一個對照啊！達西先生只跟赫斯托太太跳了一次舞，跟賓利小姐跳了一次舞，此外就在室內踱來踱去，偶爾找他自己人談談；別人要介紹他跟別的小姐跳舞，他怎麼也不肯。大家都斷定他是世界上最驕傲，最討人厭的人，希望他不要再來。其中對他反感最厲害的是班奈特太太，她對他的整個舉止都感到討厭，而且這種厭惡竟變本加厲，形成了一種特殊的氣憤，因為他得罪了她的一個女兒。

由於男賓少，伊莉莎白‧班奈特有兩場舞都不得不空坐着。達西先生當時曾一度站在她的身旁，賓利先生特地休息了幾分鐘沒有跳舞，走到他這位朋友面前，硬要他去跳，兩個人的談話給她偷聽到了。

"來吧，達西，"賓利說，"我一定要你跳。我不願意看到你獨自一人傻站在這裏。還是去跳吧。"

"我絕對不跳。你知道我一向多麼討厭跳舞，除非跟特別熟的人跳。在這樣的舞會上跳舞，簡直令人受不了。你的姐妹們都在跟別人跳，要是讓舞場裏別的女人跟我跳，沒有一個不令我活受罪的。"

"我可不願意像你那樣挑肥揀瘦，"賓利大聲說道，"隨便怎樣我也不願意！不瞞你說，我生平沒有見過今天晚上這麼多可愛的小姐；你看，其中有幾位真是美貌絕倫。"

"你的舞伴是全場唯一稱得上漂亮的！"達西先生說，一面望着班府的長女。

"噢！我從來沒見過這麼美麗的一個尤物！可是她的一個妹妹就坐在你後面，她也很漂亮，而且我敢說，她也很討人喜愛。讓我來請我的舞伴給你們兩人介紹一下吧。"

"你說的是哪一位？"他轉過身來，朝着伊莉莎白望了一會，等她也看見了他，他才收回自己的目光，冷冷地說："她還可以，但還沒有漂亮到能夠打動我的心，眼前我可沒有興趣去抬舉那些受別人冷眼看待的小姐。你還是回到你的舞伴身邊去欣賞她的笑臉吧，犯不着把時間浪費在我身上。"

賓利先生依了達西先生的話走開以後，達西自己也走開了。伊莉莎白依舊坐在那裏，對達西先生委實沒甚麼好感。不過她卻蠻有興致地把這段偷聽到的話去講給她的朋友聽，因為她的個性活潑調皮，遇到任何可笑的事情都會感到有趣。

班府全家人這一個晚上大致都過得很高興。大小姐蒙賓利先生邀她跳了兩次舞，而且這位貴人的姐妹們都對她另眼相看。班太太看到尼德斐莊園的一家人都這麼喜愛她的大女兒，覺得非常得意。

珍妮跟她母親一樣得意，只不過沒有像她母親那樣張揚。伊莉莎白也為珍妮感到快活。瑪莉曾聽到人們在賓利小姐面前提到她自己，說她是鄰近一帶最有才幹的女子；凱瑟琳 4 和麗迪亞運氣最好，沒有哪一輪舞缺少舞伴，這是她們每逢去舞會時惟一關心的一件事。母女們高高興興地回到她們所住的朗伯恩村，而她們算是這個村莊裏的主要家族，看見班奈特先生還沒有睡覺。這位班先生平常只要捧上一本書，就忘了時間，可是這次沒有睡覺，卻是因為他極想知道大家朝思暮想的這一個盛會，情形究竟如何。他滿以為他太太對那位貴客一定很失望，但是他立刻就發覺事實並非如此。

"噢！我的好老爺，"她一走進房間就這麼說，"我們這一個晚上過得太快活了，舞會太好了。你沒有去真可惜。珍妮那麼受歡迎，簡直是無法形容。甚麼人都說她長得好；賓利先生認為她很美，跟她跳了兩場舞！你光是想想這一點吧，親愛的；他確實跟她跳了兩場！全場那麼多女賓，就只有她一個人蒙受了他第二次邀請。他第一場舞是邀請盧卡斯小姐跳的。我看到他站到她身邊去，不禁有些氣惱！不過，他對她根本沒意思，其實，甚麼人也不會對她有意思；當珍妮走下舞池的時候，他可就顯得非常着迷了。他立即打聽她的姓名，請人介紹，然後邀她跳下一輪舞。他第三輪舞是跟金小姐跳的，第四輪跟瑪麗雅·盧卡斯跳，第五輪又跟珍妮跳，第六輪跟莉茲跳，還有布朗格家的——"

"要是他稍稍體諒我一點，"她的丈夫不耐煩地叫起來了，"他就不會跳這麼多，一半也不會！天哪，不要提他那些舞伴了吧。噢！但願他第一場舞就跳得扭傷腳踝！"

"噢！親愛的，"班奈特太太接下去說，"我非常喜歡他。他真是太英俊了！他的姐妹們也都很討人喜歡。我生平沒有見過任何東西比她們的衣飾更講究。我敢說，赫斯托太太衣服上的花邊——"

她說到這裏又給打斷了。班奈特先生不願意聽人談到衣飾。她因此不得不另找話題，於是就談到達西先生那不可一世的傲慢無禮的態度，她的措辭辛辣刻薄，而又帶有幾分誇張。

「不過我可以告訴你，」她補充道，「莉茲不合他的心意，這對於莉茲並沒有甚麼可惜，因為他是個最討厭、最可惡的人，不值得去奉承他。那麼高傲，那麼自大，讓人不可容忍！他走到這裏又走到那裏，把他自己看得那麼了不起！還要嫌別人不夠漂亮，配不上跟他跳舞呢！要是你在場的話，你就可以好好地教訓他一頓。我厭惡透了那個人。」

第四章

珍妮本來並不輕易讚揚賓利先生，可是當她和伊莉莎白兩個人在一起的時候，她就向她的妹妹傾訴衷曲，説她自己多麼愛慕他。

"他真是一個典型的好青年，"她説，"有見識，有趣味，人又活潑；我從來沒見過他那種討人喜歡的舉止！——那麼大方，又有十全十美的教養！"

"他也長得很英俊，"伊莉莎白回答道，"一個年輕的男子也應該弄得英俊些，除非辦不到，那又另當別論。他真稱得上一個完美無瑕的人。"

"他第二次又來請我跳舞，我真領他的情。我真想不到他會這樣抬舉我。"

"你真沒想到嗎？我倒替你想到了。不過，這正是我和你大不相同的地方。你遇到別人抬舉你，總是受寵若驚，我就不是這樣。他第二次再來請你跳舞，這不是再自然不過的事嗎？你比起舞場裏任何一位小姐都要漂亮不知多少倍，他長了眼睛自然會看得出。他向你獻殷勤你又何必感激。説起來，他的確很可愛，我也不反對你喜歡他。不過你以前可也喜歡過許多蠢貨啊。"

"我親愛的莉茲！"

"唔！你知道，你總是太容易對別人產生好感。你從來看不出別人的短處。在你眼裏看來，天下都是好人，你都看得順眼。我生平從來沒聽見過你説別人的壞話。"

"我總希望不要輕易責難一個人，可是我一向都是想到甚麼就説甚麼。"

"我知道你是這樣的，我對你感到奇怪的也就是這種地方。憑你這樣一個聰明人，為甚麼竟會忠厚到看不出別人的愚蠢和無聊！你走遍天下，到處都可以遇到偽裝坦白的人。可是，——坦白得不加任何炫耀，不帶一點企圖，承認別人的優點，而且把別人的長處多誇獎幾分，卻絕口不提別人的短處——這可只有你做得到。那麼，你也喜歡那位先生的姐妹們嗎？她們的風度可比不上他呀。」

「初看上去——的確比不上。不過，跟她們攀談起來，就覺得她們也都是些討人喜歡的女子。聽說賓利小姐將要跟她兄弟住在一起，替他管家；她若不是個好鄰居，那才怪呢。」

伊莉莎白聽着姐姐說話，嘴上一聲不響，心裏可並不信服。她比她姐姐的觀察力來得敏銳，脾氣也沒有姐姐那麼好惹，因此提到賓家姐妹，她只要想想她們在舞場裏的那種舉止，就知道她們並不打算要討一般人的好。而且她很有主見，決不因為別人對她好就改變主張，她不會對她們產生多大好感的。事實上，她們都是些非常好的小姐；她們並不是不會談笑風生，問題是要碰到她們高興的時候；她們也不是不會待人和顏悅色，問題在於她們是否樂意這樣做。可惜的是，她們一味驕傲自大。她們都長得很漂亮，曾經在一個上流的私立名校裏受過教育，有兩萬鎊的財產，花起錢來總是太隨便了，愛結交有身價地位的人，因此才造成了她們在各方面都自視甚高，不把別人放在眼裏。她們出生於英格蘭北部的一個體面家族。她們牢牢記住自己的出身，可是卻幾乎忘了她們兄弟的財產以及她們自己的財產都是做生意賺來的。

賓利先生從他父親那裏繼承了一筆將近十萬鎊的遺產。他父親生前本來打算購置些田產，可惜沒有了卻心願就與世長辭了。賓利先生同樣有這個打算，並且一度打算就在自己的故鄉購置，不過目前他既然有了一幢很好的房子，而且有莊園供他任意使用，於是那些了解他的性格的人都說，像他這樣一個隨遇而安的人，下半輩子恐怕就在尼德斐莊園度過，購置田產的事又要留給下一代去做了。

他的姐妹們倒反而替他着急，希望他早些購置產業；不過，儘管他現在僅僅是以一個租戶的身份在這裏住下來，賓利小姐還是非常願意替他掌管家務，再說那位嫁了個虛有其表的夫家的赫斯托太太，每逢到弟弟這裏來做客，依舊像是到了自己家裏一樣。當時賓利先生成年還不滿兩年，只因為偶然聽到別人推薦尼德斐莊園的房子，他便來到這裏看看。他裏裏外外看了半個小時，地段和幾間主要的房間都很符合他的心意，加上房東又把那幢房子大大讚美了一番，那番話對他也是正中下懷，於是他就當場租了下來。

他和達西雖然性格大不相同，彼此之間的友誼卻始終如一。達西之所以喜歡賓利，是因為賓利為人溫柔敦厚、坦白直爽，儘管個性方面和他自己極端相反，而他自己也從來不曾覺得自己的個性有甚麼不完美的地方。達西很看重賓利，因此賓利對他極其信賴，對他的見解也推崇備至。從智力方面講，達西比他強——這並不是説賓利呆笨，而是說達西顯得聰明些。達西為人兼有傲慢、含蓄和愛挑剔的性子，他雖說受過良好的教養，可是他的風度總不受人歡迎。從這一方面講，他的朋友可比他高明了。賓利無論走到哪裏，一定都會討人喜歡，達西卻始終得罪人。

從他們兩人談起麥里頓舞會的態度來看，就足見兩人性格的不同。賓利説，他生平從來沒有遇到過甚麼人比這裏的人更和藹，也沒有遇到過甚麼小姐比這裏的小姐更漂亮；在他看來，這裏每個人都極其和善，極其殷勤，不拘禮，不侷促，他一下子就覺得和全場的人都相處得很相熟了；講起班奈特小姐[5]，他想像不出人間會有一個比她更美麗的天使。至於達西，他總覺得他所看到的這些人既不美，又談不上風度，沒有一個人使他感興趣，也沒有一個人對他獻殷勤，博取他的歡心。他承認班奈特小姐是漂亮的，可惜她笑得太多。

赫斯托太太姐妹兩人同意他這種看法——可是她們仍然羨慕她，喜歡她，説她是個甜美佳人，她們並不反對跟她這樣的一位小姐深交。班奈特小姐就這樣成為一個甜美佳人了，她們的兄弟聽到了這番讚美，便覺得今後可以愛怎麼樣想她就怎麼樣想她了。

第五章

距離朗伯恩不遠的地方，住着一家人，這就是威廉·盧卡斯爵士府上。班奈特府上跟他們特別友好。爵士從前是在麥里頓做生意起家發跡的，曾在當市長的任內上書國王，獲得了一個爵士的頭銜。這個顯要的身份使他覺得太榮幸，從此他就討厭做生意，討厭住在一個小市鎮上，於是結束了生意，告別了小鎮，帶着家屬遷到那離開麥里頓大約一英里路的一幢房子裏去住。從那時候起就把那地方叫做盧家莊。他可以在這裏自得其樂，以顯要自居，而且，既然擺脫了生意的糾纏，他大可以一心一意地從事社交活動。他儘管以自己的地位欣然自得，卻並不因此而目空一切，反而對甚麼人都應酬得非常周到。他生來不肯得罪人，待人接物總是和藹可親，殷勤體貼，而且自從覲見國王以來，更加彬彬有禮。

盧卡斯太太是個很善良的女人，真是班奈特太太一位可貴的鄰居。盧府有好幾個孩子。大女兒是個明理懂事的年輕小姐，年紀大約二十六七歲，她是伊莉莎白的好朋友。

盧府幾位小姐跟班府幾位小姐這回非要見見面，談談這次舞會上的事不可。於是在開完了舞會的第二天上午，盧府的小姐們到朗伯恩來跟班府的小姐交換意見。

班奈特太太一看見盧卡斯小姐，便客客氣氣、從容不迫地說："那天晚上全靠你開場開得好，你做了賓利先生的第一個意中人。"

"是呀；可是他喜歡的倒是第二個意中人。"

"哦，我想你是說珍妮吧，因為他跟她跳了兩次。看起來，他是真的愛上了她呢——我的確相信他是真的——我聽到了一些話——可是不太清楚內容———些有關魯賓遜先生的話。"

"說不定你指的是我偷聽到他和魯賓遜先生的談話吧；我不是跟

你說過了嗎？魯賓遜先生問他喜不喜歡我們麥里頓的舞會，問他是否覺得到場的女賓們中間有許多人很美，問他認為哪一個最美？他立刻回答了最後一個問題：'毫無疑問是班奈特家的大小姐最美。關於這一點，人們決不會有別的看法。'"

"一定的！說起來，那的確成了定論了——看上去的確像是——不過，也許會全部落空呢，你知道。"

"我偷聽到的話比你聽到的要更有意思呢，伊麗莎，"夏綠蒂[6]說。"達西先生的話沒有他朋友的話中聽，不是嗎？可憐的伊麗莎！他只不過認為她還可以！"

"我請求你別讓莉茲想起了他這種無禮的舉動又生起氣來；他是那麼討厭的一個人，被他看上了才叫倒霉呢。郎格太太告訴我說，昨天晚上他坐在她身邊有半個小時，可是始終不開口。"

"你的話靠得住嗎，媽媽？——一點沒有說錯嗎？"珍妮說。"我清清楚楚看到達西先生跟她說話的。"

"嘿——那是後來她問起他喜歡不喜歡尼德斐莊園，他才不得已敷衍了她一下；可是據她說，他似乎非常生氣，好像怪她不該跟他說話似的。"

"賓利小姐告訴我，"珍妮說，"他從來不愛多說話，除非跟知己的朋友們談談。他對待知己的朋友非常和藹可親。"

"我根本不相信這種話，要是他果真和藹可親，就該跟郎格太太說話了。可是這裏面的奧妙是可想而知的，大家都說他非常驕傲，他之所以沒跟郎格太太說話，或許是因為聽到郎格太太連馬車也沒有一部，臨時僱了車子來參加舞會吧。"

"他沒跟郎格太太說話，我倒不計較，"盧卡斯小姐說，"我只怪他當時沒跟伊麗莎跳舞。"

"莉茲，假如我是你，"她的母親說，"我下次偏不跟他跳舞。"

"媽媽，我相信我可以萬無一失地向你保證，我怎麼也不跟他跳舞呢。"

"他雖然驕傲，"盧卡斯小姐說，"可是不像一般人的驕傲那樣使我生氣，因為他的驕傲還勉強說得過去。這麼優秀的一個青年，門第好，又有錢，樣樣都比別人強，也難怪他要自以為了不起。照我的說法，他有權利驕傲。"

　　"這倒是真話，"伊莉莎白回答道，"要是他沒有觸犯我的驕傲，我也很容易原諒他的驕傲。"

　　"我以為驕傲是一般人的通病，"瑪莉說。她覺得自己的見解很高明，因此提高了談話的興致。"從我所讀過的許多書看來，我相信那的確是非常普遍的一種通病，人性特別容易趨向於這方面，簡直誰都不免因為自己具有了某種品質，或是自以為具有了某種品質而自命不凡。虛榮與驕傲是截然不同的兩件事，儘管字面上常常當作同義詞用。一個人可以驕傲而不虛榮。驕傲多半不外乎我們對我們自己的估價，虛榮卻牽涉到我們希望別人對我們的看法。"

　　盧家一個小公子（他是跟他姐姐們一起來的）忽然說道："要是我也像達西先生那麼有錢，我真不知道會驕傲到甚麼地步呢。我要養一羣獵狗，還要每天喝一瓶酒。"

　　班奈特太太說："那你就喝得太過份了，要是給我看見了，我就馬上奪掉你的酒瓶。"

　　那孩子抗議道，她不應該那樣做；她接着又宣佈了一遍，說她一定要那樣，一場辯論直到客人告別時才結束。

第六章

朗伯恩的小姐們不久就去拜訪尼德斐莊園的小姐們了。那家人也照例回訪了她們。班奈特小姐那種討人喜愛的舉止，使赫斯托太太和賓利小姐對她越來越有好感。儘管班家老太太令人不可容忍，幾個小妹妹也不值得攀談，可是兩位賓利小姐還是願意跟年紀大的兩位小姐作進一步的深交，珍妮極其喜悅地領受了這份盛意；可是伊莉莎白看出她們對待任何人仍然很高傲，甚至對待珍妮也幾乎沒有兩樣，因此頗不喜歡她們；不過，她們之所以對珍妮好，看來多半還是由於她們兄弟愛慕她的緣故。只要你看見他們兩人在一起，你就看得出他的確是愛慕她的。伊莉莎白又很清楚地看出珍妮一開始就對賓利先生有好感，現在已不由自主地傾心於他，也可以說是愛上了他。可是她高興地想到，珍妮雖說感情豐富，好在性格很鎮定，外表上仍然保持着正常的和顏悅色，那就不會引起那些魯莽人的懷疑，因此她的心意也就不會讓外人察覺了。伊莉莎白曾經跟自己的朋友盧卡斯小姐談到過這一點。

夏綠蒂當時說道："這種事要想瞞過大家，也許是挺有意思的，不過，這樣提心吊膽，有時候反而不妙。要是一個女人在她自己心愛的人面前，也用這種技巧遮遮掩掩，不讓他知道她對他有意思，那她就可能沒有機會博取他的歡心；那麼，就是把天下人都蒙在鼓裏，也無補於事。男女戀愛大都免不了要借重於雙方的感恩圖報之心和虛榮自負之感，順其自然是很難成其好事的。戀愛的開端都是隨隨便便——某人對某人產生點好感，本是極其自然的一回事；只可惜沒有對方的鼓勵而自己就肯沒頭沒腦去鍾情的人，簡直太少了。女人十有八九都是心裏有一分愛表面上就露出兩分。毫無疑問，賓利喜歡你姐姐；可是你姐姐如果不幫他一把，他也許喜歡她就算了。"

"不過她已經盡心竭力在幫他的忙了。要是我都能看出她對他的好感，而他卻看不出，那他未免太蠢了。"

"伊麗莎，你得記住，他可不像你那麼懂得珍妮的性格。"

"假如一個女人愛上了一個男人，只要女方不故意瞞住男方，男方一定會看得出的。"

"要是男方和女方見面的機會很多，或許他總會看得出。雖然賓利和珍妮見面的次數相當多，卻從來沒有連續幾個小時聚在一起，何況他們見起面來，總是跟一些雜七雜八的人在一起，不可能讓他們兩人暢談。因此如果珍妮想令他對她一心一意，她就千萬不能錯過任何一個機會。等到能夠把他抓到手，再從從容容盡量去談戀愛還來得及。"

伊莉莎白回答道："倘若只求嫁一個有錢的男人，你這個辦法妙極了，我如果決心找個闊丈夫，或者乾脆只要隨便找個丈夫，我或許會照你的辦法去做。可惜珍妮不是這樣想的；她為人處世，就是不願意使心計。而且，她自己也還拿不準她究竟對他鍾情到甚麼地步，鍾情是否得體。她認識他才不過兩個星期。她在麥里頓跟他跳了四次舞；有天上午她在他家裏跟他見過一次面，此後又跟他吃過四次晚飯，可是總有別人在一起。就這麼點來往，讓她怎麼能了解他的性格呢。"

"事情並不像你所說的那樣。要是她只跟他吃吃晚飯，那她或許只看得出他的飯量好不好；可是你得記住，他們既在一起吃過四頓飯也就是在一起相處了四個晚上呀——四個晚上的作用可大着呢。"

"是的；這四個晚上讓他們兩人弄清楚了一件事，那就是他們兩人都喜歡玩二十一點，不喜歡玩'康梅司'[7]；講到別的重要的特點，我看他們彼此之間還了解得很少。"

"唔，"夏綠蒂說，"我一心一意祝珍妮成功。我以為即使她明天就跟他結婚，她所能獲得的幸福，比起她花上一年時間、研究了他的性格、再去跟他結婚所能獲得的幸福，並不見得會少到哪裏去。

婚姻生活是否能幸福，完全是個機會問題。一對情人婚前脾氣摸得非常透，或者脾氣非常相同，這並不能保證他們兩人就會幸福。他們總是弄到後來距離越來越遠，彼此煩惱。你既然得和這個人過一輩子，你最好盡量少了解他的缺點。"

"你這番話妙極了，夏綠蒂。不過這種說法未必可靠。你也明知道未必可靠，你自己就不肯那麼做。"

伊莉莎白一心只知道談論賓利先生對她姐姐的殷勤，卻一點沒想到她自己已經成了賓利那位朋友的意中人。說到達西先生，他一開始並不認為她怎麼漂亮；他在舞會上望着她的時候，並沒有帶着絲毫的愛慕之意；第二次見面的時候，他也不過用吹毛求疵的眼光去看待她。不過，他剛剛在朋友們面前，在自己心裏，說她的面貌一無可取，立刻就發覺她那雙烏黑的眼睛美麗非凡，使她的整個臉龐顯得極其聰慧。緊接着這個發現之後，他又在她身上發現了幾個同樣令人慪氣的地方。他帶着挑剔的眼光，發覺她的身段這裏也不勻稱，那裏也不勻稱，可是他到底不得不承認她體態輕盈，惹人喜愛；雖然他嘴上一口咬定她缺少上流社會的翩翩風采，可是她那落落大方愛打趣的作風，又把他迷住了。伊莉莎白完全不明白這些情形，她只覺得達西是個到處不討人喜歡的男人，何況他曾經認為她不夠漂亮，不配跟他跳舞。

達西開始希望跟她深交。他為了想要慢慢地跟她攀談攀談，因此她跟別人談話的時候，他總是留神去聽。於是，有一次威廉·盧卡斯爵士請客，他這樣的做法當場引起了她的注意。

當時伊莉莎白對夏綠蒂說："你看，達西先生是甚麼意思呢，我跟弗斯托上校談話，為甚麼他要到那裏來聽？"

"這個問題只有達西先生自己能夠回答。"

"要是他再這樣，我一定要令他明白我並不是糊塗蟲。他挖苦人的本領特別高明，要是我不先給他點顏色看看，我馬上就會見他怕了。"

過了不久，達西又走到她的身邊來了，他表面上雖然並不想跟她們攀談，盧卡斯小姐卻還是慫恿伊莉莎白向他把這個問題正面提出來。伊莉莎白給她這樣一激，便立刻轉過臉來跟他說：

　　"達西先生，我剛剛纏住弗斯托上校要他給我們在麥里頓開一次舞會，你看我的話是不是說得非常得體？"

　　"的確說得起勁極了，不過這件事本來就是小姐們非常起勁的。"

　　"你這樣說我們，未免太尖刻了些吧。"

　　"馬上要有人來揶揄她了，"盧卡斯小姐說。"我去打開琴，伊麗莎，接下來該怎麼辦，你自己明白。"

　　"你這種朋友真是世上少有！——不管當着甚麼人的面，總是要我彈琴唱歌！——要是我存心要在音樂上出風頭，我真要對你感激不盡。可是賓客們都是聽慣了一流的演奏家的，我實在不好意思在他們面前坐下來獻醜。"話雖如此，怎奈盧卡斯小姐再三要求，她便說道："好吧，既是非獻醜不可，只得獻獻醜吧。"她又板着臉看了達西一眼，說道："有句老古話說得好，在場的人當然也都知道這句話：'留口氣吹涼稀飯'；我也就留口氣唱歌吧。"

　　她的表演雖然說不上奇妙絕倫，也還娓娓動聽。唱了一兩支歌以後，大家要求她再唱幾支。她還沒來得及回答，她的妹妹瑪莉早就急切地接替她坐到鋼琴前去了。原來在她們幾個姐妹之間，就只有瑪莉長得不好看，因此她發奮鑽研學問，講究才藝，老是急着要賣弄賣弄自己的本領。

　　瑪莉既沒有天份，格調也不高。雖說虛榮心促使她刻苦用功，但是同樣也造成了她一臉的女才子氣派和自高自大的態度。有了這種氣派和態度，即使她的修養再好些也無補於事，何況她不過如此而已。再說伊莉莎白，雖說彈琴彈得遠不如她，可是她落落大方，沒有矯揉造作的習慣，因此大家聽起來就高興得多了。瑪莉的幾位妹妹，本在房間那頭和盧家小姐們在一起，正在跟兩三個軍官興高采烈地跳着舞，瑪莉奏完了一支很長的協奏曲之後，她們便要求她再奏幾支蘇格蘭和愛爾蘭的小調，她也高高興興地照辦了，為的是要博得別人的誇獎和感激。

達西先生就站在她們附近，悶悶不樂，對於這種消遣的方式非常地不屑。他專注地想着心事，威廉‧盧卡斯爵士站在他身邊他也不知道，最後他才聽到爵士這樣跟他說：

「達西先生，跳舞對於年輕人是多麼可愛的一種娛樂！說來說去，甚麼都比不上跳舞，我認為這是上流社會裏最出色的才藝。」

「當然，盧卡斯爵士。而且跳舞還有一個好處，就是它在不那麼上流的社會裏也流行，即使是粗人也會跳。」

威廉爵士笑了笑沒出聲。後來他看見賓利也來參加跳舞，便對達西這麼說：「你的朋友跳得很不錯，我相信你對此道也是駕輕就熟吧，達西先生。」

「你大概在麥里頓看見過我跳舞的吧，先生。」

「見過，不錯，而且看得非常高興。你常到宮裏去跳舞嗎？」

「從來沒去過，先生。」

「你連在宮裏都不肯賞臉嗎？」

「無論在甚麼地方，我也不願意賞這種臉，能避免總是避免。」

「你在城裏一定有住宅吧？」

達西先生聳了聳身子。

「我一度曾經想在城裏住家，因為我喜歡上流社會；不過我不敢說倫敦的空氣是否適合盧卡斯太太。」

他停了一會，指望對方回答；可是對方根本就懶得回答。不久伊莉莎白朝他們走來，他靈機一動，想乘此獻一下殷勤，便對她叫道：

「親愛的伊麗莎小姐，你為甚麼不跳舞呀？——達西先生，讓我把這位年輕的小姐介紹給你，這是位最理想的舞伴。有了這樣一個美人做你的舞伴，我想你總不會不跳了吧。」他拉住了伊莉莎白的手，預備送往達西面前，達西雖然極為驚奇，卻也不是不願意接住那隻玉手，卻不料伊莉莎白立刻把手縮了回去，好像還有些神色倉皇地對威廉爵士説：

「先生，我的確一點也不想跳舞。你可千萬別以為我是跑到這邊來找舞伴的。」

達西先生非常有禮貌地要求她賞光，跟他跳一場，可是他白白地要求了。伊莉莎白下定了決心就不動搖，任憑威廉爵士怎麼勸説也沒有用。

「伊麗莎小姐，你跳舞跳得那麼高明，可是卻不肯讓我享享眼福，看你跳一場，這未免太説不過去了吧。再説，這位先生雖説平常並不喜歡這種娛樂，可是要他賞我們半個小時的臉，我相信他也不會不肯的。」

伊莉莎白笑着説：「達西先生未免太客氣了。」

「他真的太客氣了——可是，親愛的伊麗莎小姐，看他這樣求你，你總不會怪他多禮吧。誰不想要像你這樣的一個舞伴？」

伊莉莎白笑盈盈地瞟了一眼就轉身走開了。她的拒絕並沒有使達西覺得難過。達西正在相當高興地想念着她，恰巧賓利小姐走過來招呼他：

「我猜中你現在在幻想些甚麼。」

「諒你也猜不中。」

「你心裏正在想：許多個晚上都是跟這些人在一起無聊度過的，這實在讓人受不了，我跟你頗有同感。我從來不曾這樣煩悶過！既枯燥乏味，又吵鬧不堪，無聊到了極點。這批人又一個個都自以為了不起！我就想聽聽你指責他們幾句。」

「老實對你説吧，你完全猜錯了。我心裏想的東西要妙得多呢。我正在玩味着心中的雀躍：一個漂亮女人的美麗的雙眸竟會給人這麼大的快樂。」

賓利小姐立刻把眼睛盯在他的臉上，要他告訴她，究竟是哪位小姐有這種妙處，使他這樣想入非非。達西先生鼓起極大的勇氣回答道：

"伊莉莎白‧班奈特小姐。"

"伊莉莎白‧班奈特小姐！"賓利小姐重複了一遍。"我真感到驚奇。你看中她多久了？——請你告訴我，我幾時可以向你道喜啊？"

"我料到你會問出這種話來的。女人的想像力真敏捷；從敬慕一跳就跳到愛情，轉眼間又從愛情跳到結婚。我知道你要預備來向我道喜了。"

"唔，要是你這麼一本正經，我就認為這件事百份之百地決定了。你一定會得到一位有趣的岳母大人，而且當然她會永遠在龐百利跟你住在一起。"

她說得那麼得意，他卻完全似聽非聽。她看他那般鎮定自若，便放了心，於是那張利嘴更加滔滔不絕了。

第七章

班奈特先生的全部家當幾乎都在一宗產業上，每年可以借此獲得兩千鎊的收入。說起這宗產業，真是他女兒們的不幸。他因為沒有兒子，產業得由一個遠親來繼承，至於她們母親的家私，在這樣的家庭，本來也算得上一筆大數目，事實上卻還不夠補償他的損失。班奈特太太的父親曾經在麥里頓當過律師，給了她四千鎊遺產。

她有個妹妹，嫁給了她爸爸的書記菲力普，妹夫後來就承繼了她爸爸的行業；她還有個兄弟，住在倫敦，生意做得很不錯。

朗伯恩這個村莊和麥里頓相隔只有一英里路，這麼一段距離對於那幾位年輕的小姐們是再便利不過的了，她們每星期總得上那裏去三四次，看看她們的姨母，還可以順便看看那邊一家賣女人帽子的商店。兩個最小的妹妹凱瑟琳和麗迪亞特別傾心於這方面，她們的心事比姐姐們要少得多，每當沒有更好的消遣辦法時，就必定到麥里頓去走一趟，消遣一下美好的晨光，並且晚上也就有了更多話題。儘管這村莊裏通常沒有甚麼新聞可以打聽，她們還老是千方百計地從她們姨媽那裏裏打聽到一些。附近地方最近新到了一個民兵團，她們的消息來源當然從此就豐富了，真讓她們高興非凡。這一團人要在這裏駐紮整個冬天，麥里頓就是司令部的所在地。

從此她們每次拜訪菲力普太太都獲得最有趣的消息。她們每天都會打聽到幾個軍官的名字和他們的社會關係。軍官們的住宅不久就讓大家知道了，再後來小姐們就直接跟他們熟絡了。菲力普先生一一拜訪了那些軍官，這真是替他的外甥女們開闢了一道意想不到的幸福的源泉。她們現在開口閉口都離不了那些軍官。在這以前，只要提到賓利先生偌大的財產，她們的母親就會眉飛色舞，如今跟軍官們的制服對比起來，她們就覺得偌大的財產簡直一文不值了。

一天早晨，班奈特先生聽到她們滔滔不絕地談到這個問題，他不禁冷言冷語地說：

"看你們談話的神情，我覺得你們真是些再蠢不過的女孩子。以前我還是半信半疑，現在我可完全相信了。"

凱瑟琳一聽此話，頗感不安，可是並沒有回答。麗迪亞卻完全沒有把爸爸的話當一回事，還是接着說下去，說她自己多麼愛慕卡特上尉，還希望當天能夠跟他見面，因為他明天上午就要到倫敦去。

班奈特太太對她丈夫說："我真奇怪，親愛的，你總是喜歡說你自己的孩子蠢。要是我呀，甚麼人的孩子我都可以看不起，可決不會看不起自己的孩子。"

"要是我自己的孩子果真蠢，我決不願意沒有自知之明。"

"你說得不錯，可是事實上，她們卻個個都很聰明。"

"我們兩個人總算只有在這一點上看法不同。我本來希望你我在任何方面的意見都能融洽一致，可是說起我們的兩個小女兒，的確非常蠢；關於這一點，到目前為止，我不得不跟你持有不同的見解。"

"我的好老爺，你不能指望這些女孩子都跟她們爸媽一樣有見識呀。等她們到了我們這麼大年紀，她們也許就會跟我們一樣，不會再想到甚麼軍官們了。我記得從前有個時期，我也很喜愛'紅制服'[8]——當然，到現在我心裏還喜愛'紅制服'呢；要是有位英俊的年輕上校，每年有五六千鎊收入，隨便向我的哪一個女兒求婚，我決不會拒絕他的；有天晚上在威廉爵士家裏，看見弗斯托上校全副軍裝，真是一表人才！"

"媽媽，"麗迪亞叫道，"姨媽說，弗斯托上校跟卡特上尉這一陣子上沃森小姐家裏去的次數，不像初來的時候那麼勤了；她近來常常看到他們站在'克拉克借書處'等人。"

班奈特太太正要答話，不料一個男僕走了進來，拿來一封信給班奈特小姐。這是尼德斐莊園送來的一封信，男僕等着取回信。班奈特太太高興得眼睛也閃亮起來。珍妮讀信的時候，她心急地叫道：

"嘿，珍妮，誰來的信？信上說些甚麼？是怎麼說的？喂，珍妮，趕快看完說給我們聽吧；快點呀，寶貝！"

"是賓利小姐寫來的，"珍妮說，一面把信讀出來：

我親愛的朋友：

要是你不肯發發慈悲，今天光臨舍下跟路易莎和我一同吃晚飯，我和她兩個人就要結下終生的仇怨了。兩個女人成天在一起談心，最後沒有不吵架的。接信後希望盡快前來。我的哥哥和他的幾位朋友們都要上軍官們那裏去吃飯。

你永遠的朋友卡洛琳·賓利

"上軍官們那裏去吃飯！"麗迪亞叫道，"這件事怎麼姨媽沒告訴我們呢？"

"上別人家去吃飯，"班奈特太太說；"這真是晦氣。"

"我可以乘着馬車去嗎？"珍妮問。

"不行，親愛的，你最好騎着馬去。天好像要下雨的樣子，下了雨你就可以在那裏過夜。"

"這倒是個好辦法，"伊莉莎白說。"只要你拿得準他們不會送她回來。"

"噢，賓利先生的馬車要送他的朋友們到麥里頓去，赫斯托夫婦又是有車無馬。"

"我倒還是願意乘着馬車去。"

"可是，乖孩子，我包管你爸爸勻不出幾匹馬來拖車。——農莊上正要用馬，我的好老爺，是不是？"

"農莊上常常要用馬，可惜到我手裏的時候並不多。"

伊莉莎白說："可是，如果今天到了你的手裏，就如了媽媽的願了。"

她終於逼得父親不得不承認——那幾匹拉車子的馬已經有了別的用處。於是珍妮只得騎着另外一匹馬去，母親送她到門口，高高興興地説了許多預祝天氣會變壞的話。她果真如願了；珍妮走了不久，就下起大雨來。妹妹們都替她擔憂，只有她反而高興。大雨整個黃昏沒有停。珍妮當然無法回來了。

班奈特太太一遍又一遍地説："真虧我想出了這個好辦法！"好像天下雨都是她一手造成的。不過，她的神機妙算究竟造成了多大的幸福，她一直到第二天早上才知道。早飯還沒吃完，尼德斐莊園就派了人送來一封信給伊莉莎白：

我親愛的莉茲：

今晨我覺得很不舒服，我想這可能是昨天淋了雨的緣故。承蒙這裏好朋友們的關切，要我等到身體舒適一些才回家來。朋友們再三要請鍾斯醫生來替我看病，因此，要是你們聽到他上我這裏來過，可別驚訝。我只不過有點喉嚨痛和頭痛，並沒有甚麼大不了的毛病。

姐字

伊莉莎白讀信的時候，班奈特先生對他太太説："唔，好太太，要是你的女兒得了重病——萬一她一病不起——倒也值得安慰呀，因為她是奉了你的命令去追求賓利先生的。"

"噢！她難道這麼一下子就會送命！哪有小傷風就會送命的道理。他們自會好好服侍她。只要她留在那裏，包管沒事。如果有車子的話，我也想去看看她。"

真正着急的倒是伊莉莎白，她才不管有車沒車，決定非去一趟不可。她既然不會騎馬，惟一的辦法便只有步行。她把自己的打算説了出來。

她媽媽叫道："你怎麼這樣蠢！路上這麼泥濘，虧你想得出來！等你走到那裏，你那副樣子怎麼見人。"

"我只要能見到珍妮就可以。"

"莉茲，"她的父親説，"你的意思是讓我替你弄幾匹馬來駕馬車嗎？"

"當然不是這個意思。我不怕步行，只要存心去，這點路算得上甚麼。才不過三英里路。我可以趕回來吃晚飯。"

這時瑪莉說道："你完全是出於一片手足之情，我很佩服，可是你千萬不能感情用事，你得理智一點，而且我覺得盡力也不要盡得過份。"

凱瑟琳和麗迪亞同聲說道："我們陪你到麥里頓。"伊莉莎白表示贊成，於是三位年輕的小姐就一起出發了。

"要是我們走得快些，"麗迪亞邊走邊這麼說，"或許我們還來得及趕在卡特上尉臨走之前看看他。"

三姐妹到了麥里頓便分了手；兩位妹妹上一個軍官太太的家裏去，留下伊莉莎白獨自繼續往前走，急急忙忙地大踏步走過了一片片田野，跨過了一道道圍柵，跳過了一個個水窪，終於看見了尼德斐莊園。她這時候已經雙腳乏力，襪子髒了，臉上也熱得通紅。

她被領進了餐廳，只見他們全家人都在那裏，只有珍妮不在場。她一走進門就引起全場人的驚奇。赫斯托太太和賓利小姐心想，這麼一大早，路上又這麼泥濘，她竟從三英里路外趕到這裏來，而且是獨自走來的，這事情簡直令人無法相信。伊莉莎白料定她們看不起她這種舉動。不過事實上她們倒很客氣地接待了她，特別是她們的兄弟，不僅是客客氣氣接待她，而且非常殷勤多禮。達西先生說話不多，赫斯托先生完全一言不發。達西先生的心裏被兩種情感弄得七上八下：一方面愛慕她那步行之後的鮮豔的臉色，另一方面又懷疑她是否值得為了這麼點事情獨自從那麼遠走來。至於赫斯托先生，他一心一意只想要吃早飯。

她問起姐姐的病情如何，可沒有得到滿意的回答。據說班奈特小姐晚上睡不好，現在雖然已經起牀，發熱的熱度卻很高，不能出房門。使伊莉莎白高興的是，他們馬上就把她領到她姐姐那裏去了。珍妮看到她來，非常高興，原來她為了不願意讓家裏人着急和麻煩，所以信裏並沒有説明她極其盼望有個親人來看看她。可是她沒有力氣多説話，因此，當賓利小姐走開以後，剩下她們姐妹兩人在一起的時候，她只説到她們對她真是太好了，使她非常感激——除了這些話以外，就沒有再説甚麼。伊莉莎白靜悄悄地侍候着她。

　　早飯吃過以後，賓利家的姐妹也來陪伴她們，伊莉莎白看到她們對珍妮那麼親切和關懷，便不禁對她們有了好感。醫生來檢查了病人的症狀，説她是重傷風（其實這也是可想而知的），他囑咐她們要盡量當心，又勸珍妮上牀去睡覺，並且給她開了幾種藥。醫生的囑咐立刻照辦了，因為病人發熱的熱度又高了一些，而且頭痛得很厲害。伊莉莎白片刻也沒離開她的房間，另外兩位小姐也不大走開；男客們都不在家裏，其實她們到別處去也沒甚麼事好幹。

　　三點正的時候，伊莉莎白覺得應該走了，於是勉強向主人家告別。賓利小姐要她乘着馬車回去。她正打算稍微推辭一下就接受主人的盛意，不料珍妮説是捨不得讓她走，於是賓利小姐便不得不改變了請她坐馬車回去的主意，請她在尼德斐莊園小住一陣。伊莉莎白感激不盡地答應了。接下來就是差人上朗伯恩去，把她在這裏暫住的事情告訴她家裏一聲，同時讓她家裏給她帶些衣服來。

第八章

五點鐘的時候，主人家兩姐妹出去更衣；六點半的時候，伊莉莎白被請去吃晚飯。大家都禮貌周全，紛紛來探問珍妮的病情，其中尤其以賓利先生問得特別關切，這讓伊莉莎白非常愉快。只可惜珍妮的病情一點沒有好轉，因此她無法提供滿意的回答。那姐妹兩人聽到這話，便三番四次地說她們是多麼擔心，說重傷風是多麼可怕，又說她們自己多麼討厭生病，——說過了這些話以後就不當它一回事了。伊莉莎白看到她們當珍妮不在她們面前的時候就對珍妮這般冷淡，於是她本來那種討厭她們的心情現在又重新滋長了起來。

的確，她們這家人裏面只有她們的兄弟能使她稱心滿意。你一眼便可以看出他是真的在為珍妮擔憂，再說他對於伊莉莎白也殷勤和悦到極點。伊莉莎白本以為別人會把她看作一個不速之客，可是有了這份殷勤，她就不這麼想了。除他以外，別人都不大理睬她。賓利小姐的心在達西先生身上，赫斯托太太差不多也沒有甚麼兩樣；再說到赫斯托先生，他就坐在伊莉莎白身旁，他天生一副懶骨頭，活在世上就是為了吃、喝、玩牌，他看到伊莉莎白寧可吃一碟普通的菜而不喜歡吃燴肉，便和她沒甚麼話說了。

伊莉莎白一吃過晚飯就回到珍妮那裏去。她一走出飯廳，賓利小姐就開始說她的壞話，把她的禮儀風度說得壞透了，說她既傲慢又無禮貌：不懂得跟人攀談，儀表不佳，風趣索然，人又長得難看。赫斯托太太也是同樣的看法，而且還補充了幾句：

"總而言之，她除了跑路的本領以外，沒有一樣別的長處。她今天早上那副樣子我才永遠忘不了呢，簡直像個瘋子。"

"她的確像個瘋子，路易莎。我簡直忍不住要笑出來。她這一趟真來得無聊極了！姐姐得了點小傷風，為何就得要她那麼大驚小怪地跑遍了整個村莊？──頭髮給弄得那麼蓬亂，那麼邋遢！」

「是呀，還有她的襯裙──可惜你沒看到她的襯裙。我絕對不是瞎說，那上面糊上了有足足六英寸泥，她把外面的裙子放低了些，想用來遮蓋，可是遮蓋不住。」

賓利先生說：「你形容得並沒有過火的地方，路易莎，可是我並不以為然。我倒覺得伊莉莎白·班奈特小姐今天早上走進屋來的時候，那種神情風度很不錯呢。我並沒有看到她的骯髒的襯裙。」

「你一定看到的，達西先生，」賓利小姐說，「我想，你總不願意看到你自己的姐妹弄成那副狼狽樣子吧。」

「當然不願意。」

「無緣無故走上那麼三英里路、四英里路、五英里路，誰知道多少英里呢，泥土蓋沒了踝骨，而且是孤孤單單的一個人！她這究竟是甚麼意思？我看她十足表現了沒有家教的野態，完全是鄉下人不懂禮貌的輕狂。」

賓利先生說：「那正說明了她的手足情深，真是好極了。」

賓利小姐陰陽怪氣地說：「達西先生，我倒擔心，她這次的冒失行為，會影響你對她那對美麗雙眸的愛慕吧？」

達西回答道：「一點影響也沒有，她跑過了這趟路以後，那雙眼睛更加明亮了。」說完這句話，大家沉默了一會，然後赫斯托太太又開口說話：

「我非常關心珍妮·班奈特──她倒的確是位可愛的小姐──我誠心誠意地希望她好好地攀頭親事。只可惜遇到那樣的父母，加上還有那麼些低微的親戚，我怕她沒有甚麼指望了。」

「我不是聽你說過，她有個姨丈在麥里頓當律師嗎？」

「是呀；她們還有個舅舅住在齊普賽⁹附近。」

「那真妙極了，」她的妹妹補充了一句，於是姐妹兩人都縱情大笑。

賓利先生一聽此話，便大叫起來：「即使她們有多得數不清的舅舅，可以把整個齊普賽都塞滿，也不能把她們討人喜愛的地方減損分毫。」

「可是，她們如果想嫁給有地位的男人，機會可就大大減少了，」達西回答道。

賓利先生沒有理睬這句話；他的姐妹們卻聽得非常得意，於是更加肆無忌憚地拿班奈特小姐微賤的親戚開玩笑，開了老半天。

不過她們一離開了飯廳，就重新做出百般溫柔體貼的樣子，來到珍妮房間裏，一直陪着她坐到喝咖啡的時候。珍妮的病還不見好轉，伊莉莎白寸步不離地守着她，一直到黃昏，看見她睡着了，才放下了心，覺得自己應該到樓下去一趟（雖說她並不樂意下樓去）。走進客廳，她發覺大家正在玩牌，大家當時立刻邀她也來玩。可是她恐怕他們輸贏很大，便謝絕了，只推說放心不下姐姐，很快就得上樓去，她可以拿本書來消遣消遣。赫斯托先生驚奇地朝她望了一下。

「你寧可看書，不要玩牌嗎？」他說。「這真是少有。」

賓利小姐說：「伊莉莎白・班奈特小姐看不起玩牌，她是個了不起的讀書人，對別的事都不感興趣。」

伊莉莎白大聲說道：「這樣的誇獎我不敢當，這樣的責備我也不敢領受，我並不是甚麼了不起的讀書人，很多東西我都感興趣。」

賓利先生說：「我斷定你很樂意照料你自己的姐姐，但願她快些復元，那你就會更加快活了。」

伊莉莎白從心底裏感謝他，然後走到一張放了幾本書的桌子前。他立刻要另外拿些書來給她——把他書房裏所有的書都拿來。

「要是我的藏書多一些就好了，無論是為你的益處着想，還是為我自己的面子着想；可是我是個懶鬼，藏書不多，讀過的就更少了。」

伊莉莎白跟他說，房間裏那幾本書夠她看了。

賓利小姐說：「我很奇怪，爸爸怎麼只遺留下來了這麼幾本書。——達西先生，你在龐百利的那個藏書室真是好極了！」

達西説：「那有甚麼稀奇，那是好幾代的成績啊。」

「你自己又添置了不少書，看見你老是在買書。」

「我現在這樣過日子，自然不好意思疏忽家裏的藏書室。」

「疏忽！我相信凡是能為你那個高貴的地方增加美觀的東西，你一件也沒有疏忽過。——查理斯[10]，以後你自己興建住宅的時候，我只希望有龐百利一半那麼美麗就好了。」

「但願如此。」

「可是我還要竭力奉勸你就在那裏附近購買房產，而且要拿龐百利做個榜樣。全英國沒有哪一個郡比德比郡[11]更好的了。」

「我非常高興那麼辦。我真想乾脆就把龐百利買下來，只要達西肯賣。」

「我是在談談可能辦到的事情，查理斯。」

「卡洛琳，我敢説，買下龐百利比仿照龐百利的式樣造房子，可能性要大些。」

伊莉莎白聽這些話聽得出了神，弄得沒心情看書了，索性把書放在一旁，走到牌桌前，坐在賓利先生和他的妹妹之間，看他們鬥牌。

這時賓利小姐又問達西：「從春天到現在，達西小姐長高了很多吧？她將來會長到我這麼高吧？」

「我想會吧。她現在大概有伊莉莎白・班奈特小姐那麼高了，恐怕還要高一點。」

「我真想再見見她！我從來沒碰到過這麼使我喜愛的人。模樣那麼好，又那樣懂得禮貌，小小年紀就這樣多才多藝，她的鋼琴真彈得高明極了。」

賓利先生説：「這真讓我感到驚奇，年輕的小姐們怎麼一個個都有那麼大的能耐，把自己訓練得多才多藝。」

「一個個年輕的小姐們都是多才多藝！親愛的查理斯，你這話是甚麼意思呀？」

「是的，我認為一個個都是那樣。她們都會裝飾桌子，點綴屏風，編織錢袋。我簡直就沒見過哪一位不是樣樣都會，而且每逢聽人談起一個年輕小姐，沒有哪一次不聽說她是多才多藝的。」

達西說：「你列舉的這一套平庸的所謂才藝，倒是千真萬確。許多女人只不過會編織錢袋，點綴屏風，就享有了多才多藝的美名；可是我卻不能同意你對一般婦女的估價。我不敢說謊言：我認識很多女人，而真正多才多藝的實在不過半打。」

「我也的確不敢說謊言，」賓利小姐說。

伊莉莎白說：「那麼，在你的想像中，一個多才多藝的女人，應該包括很多條件的了。」

「不錯，我認為應該包括很多條件。」

「噢，當然，」達西的忠實幫手喊道，「要稱得上多才多藝，就一定要比一般的女人強。必須要懂音律，善歌舞，工繪畫，懂多國語言，才能擔得起這個美名。除此以外，她的儀表和步態，她的聲調，她的談吐和表情，都得有相當風趣，否則她就不夠資格。」

達西接着說：「她除了具備這些條件以外，還應該多讀書，長見識，有點真才實學。」

「怪不得你只認識六個才女了。我現在簡直疑心你連一個也不認識呢。」

「你怎麼對你們女人這般苛求，竟以為她們不可能具備這些條件？」

「我從來沒見過這樣的女人。我從來沒見過哪一個人像你所說的這樣有才幹，有情趣，又那麼好學，那麼儀態優雅。」

赫斯托太太和賓利小姐都叫起來了，說她不應該表示懷疑，因為這種懷疑是不公平的，而且她們還一致提出反證，說她們自己就知道有很多女人都具備這些條件。一直等到赫斯托先生讓她們好好打牌，怪她們不該對牌場上的事那麼漫不經心，她們才住嘴，一場爭論就這樣結束了，伊莉莎白沒有多久也走開了。

門關上之後，賓利小姐說：「有些女人們為了自抬身價，往往在男人們面前説其他女人的不是，伊莉莎白・班奈特就是這樣一個女人。這種手段在某些男人身上也許會產生效果，但是我認為這是一種下賤的詭計，一種卑鄙的手腕。"

達西聽出她這幾句話是有意説給他自己聽的，便連忙答道："毫無疑問，小姐們為了勾引男子，有時竟不擇手段，使用巧計，這真是卑鄙。只要你的做法帶有幾分狡詐，都應該受到鄙棄。"

賓利小姐不太滿意他這個回答，因此也就沒有再談下去。

伊莉莎白又到他們這裏來了一次，只是為了告訴他們一聲：她姐姐的病更加嚴重了，她不能離開。賓利再三主張立刻請鍾斯大夫來，他的姐妹們卻都以為鄉下郎中無濟於事，主張趕快到城裏去請一位最有名的大夫來。伊莉莎白不贊成，不過她也不便太辜負她們兄弟的一番盛意，於是大家協商出了一個辦法：如果班奈特小姐明天一大早依舊毫無起色，就馬上去請鍾斯大夫來。賓利先生心裏非常不安，他的姐姐和妹妹也説是十分擔憂。吃過宵夜之後，她們兩人總算合奏了幾支歌來消除了一些煩悶，而賓利先生因為想不出好辦法來解除焦慮，便只有關照他那女管家盡心盡意地照料病人和病人的妹妹。

第九章

伊莉莎白那一晚上的大部份時間都是在她姐姐房間裏度過的，第二天一大早，賓利先生就派了個女傭人來問候她們。過了一會，賓利的姐姐妹妹也派了兩個文雅的侍女來探病，伊莉莎白總算可以聊以自慰地告訴她們說，病人已略見好轉。不過，她雖然寬了一下心，卻還是要求他們府上替她差人送封信到朗伯恩去，要她的媽媽來看看珍妮，來親自判斷她的病情如何。信立刻就送去了，信上所說的事也很快就照辦了。班奈特太太帶着兩個最小的女兒來到尼德斐莊園的時候，他們家裏剛剛吃過早飯。

如果班奈特太太發覺珍妮有甚麼危險，那她真要傷心死了；但是一看到珍妮的病並不怎麼嚴重，她就滿意了；她也並不希望珍妮馬上復元，因為，要是一復元，她就得離開尼德斐莊園回家去。所以，她的女兒一提起要她帶她回家去，她聽也不要聽，況且那位差不多跟她同時來到的醫生，也認為搬回去不是個好辦法。母親陪着珍妮坐了一會，賓利小姐便來請她吃早飯，於是她就帶着三個女兒一起上飯廳去。賓利先生前來迎接她們，說是希望班奈特太太看到了小姐的病一定會覺得並不像想像中那般嚴重。

班奈特太太回答道："我卻沒有想像到會這般嚴重呢，先生，她病得太厲害了，根本不能搬動。鍾斯大夫也説，千萬不可以搬動她。我們只得勞煩你們多照顧幾天了。"

"搬動！"賓利叫道，"絕對不可以。我相信我的妹妹也絕對不肯讓她搬走的。"

賓利小姐冷淡而有禮貌地説："你放心好了，老太太，班奈特小姐留在我們這裏，我們一定盡心盡意地照顧她。"

班奈特太太連聲道謝。

接着她又説道："要不是靠好朋友們照顧，我相信她真不知道變成甚麼樣子了；因為她實在病得很重，也吃了很多苦頭，不過好在她有極大的耐性——她一貫都是那樣的，我生平簡直沒見過第二個人有她這般溫柔到極點的性格。我常常跟別的幾個女兒們説，她們比起她來簡直太差了。賓利先生，你這所房子很可愛呢，從那條鵝卵石鋪道上望出去，景致也很美麗。在這個村莊裏，我從來沒見過一個地方比得上尼德斐莊園。雖然你的租期很短，我勸你千萬別急着搬走。"

賓利先生説："我隨便做甚麼事，都是説做就做，要是打定主意要離開尼德斐莊園，我可能在五分鐘之內就搬走。不過目前我算是在這裏住定了。"

"我猜想得一點也不錯，"伊莉莎白説。

賓利馬上轉過身去對她大聲説道："你開始了解我了，是嗎？"

"噢，是呀——我完全了解你。"

"但願你這句話是恭維我，不過，這麼容易被人看透，那恐怕也是件可憐的事吧。"

"那得看情況説話。一個深沉複雜的人，未必比你這樣的人更難令人捉摸。"

她的母親連忙大聲説道："莉茲，別忘了你在作客，家裏讓你撒野慣了，你可不能到這裏來胡鬧。"

"我以前倒不知道你是個研究人的性格的專家。"賓利馬上接下去説，"那一定是一門很有趣的學問吧。"

"不錯；可是最有趣味的還是研究複雜的性格。至少這樣的性格有研究的價值。"

達西説："一般來説，鄉下可以做這種研究的對象就很少。因為在鄉下，你四周圍的人都非常不開通、非常單調。"

"可是人們本身的變動很多，他們身上永遠有新的東西值得你去注意。"

班奈特太太聽到剛剛達西以那樣一種口氣提到鄉下，不禁頗為生氣，便連忙大聲說道：「這才說得對呀，告訴你吧，鄉下可供研究的對象並不比城裏少。」

大家都吃了一驚。達西朝她望了一會便靜悄悄地走開了。班奈特太太自以為完全佔了他的上風，便一鼓作氣說下去：

「我覺得倫敦除了店鋪和公共場所以外，比起鄉下來並沒有甚麼大不了的好處。鄉下可舒服得多了──不是嗎，賓利先生？」

「我到了鄉下就不想走，」他回答道；「我住到城裏也就不想走。鄉下和城裏各有各的好處，我隨便住在哪裏都一樣快樂。」

「啊，那是因為你的性格好。可是那位先生，」她說到這裏，便朝達西望了一眼，「就會覺得鄉下一文不值。」

「媽媽，你根本弄錯了，」伊莉莎白說道，為她母親臉都紅了。「你完全弄錯了達西先生的意思。他只不過說，鄉下碰不到像城裏那些各色各樣的人，這你可得承認是事實呀。」

「當然，寶貝，誰說不是了。不過要是說這個村莊裏還碰不到多少人，我相信比這個大的村莊也就沒有幾個了。就我所知，平常跟我們來往吃飯的可也有二十四家呀。」

要不是顧全伊莉莎白的面子，賓利簡直忍不住要笑出來了。他的妹妹可沒有他那麼用心周到，便不由得帶着富有表情的笑容望着達西先生。伊莉莎白為了找個藉口轉移一下她母親的注意力，便問她母親說，自從她離家以後，夏綠蒂・盧卡斯有沒有到朗伯恩來過。

「來過；她是昨天跟她父親一起來的。威廉爵士是個多麼和藹的人呀，賓利先生──不是嗎？那麼時髦的一個人！那麼溫文爾雅，又那麼隨和！他見到甚麼人總要談上幾句。這就是我所說的有良好的教養；那些自以為了不起、金口難開的人，他們的想法真是大錯特錯。」

「夏綠蒂在我們家裏吃飯的嗎？」

「沒有，她硬要回去。據我猜想，大概是她家裏等着她回去做肉餅。賓利先生，我僱起傭人來，總得要她們能夠做好份內的事，我的女兒就不是像別人家那樣教養大的。可是一切要看各人自己，告訴你，盧卡斯家裏的幾個小姐倒全是些很好的女孩子。只可惜長得不漂亮！當然並不是我個人認為夏綠蒂長得很平凡，她畢竟是我們的好朋友。"

"她看來是位很可愛的小姐，"賓利說。

"是呀，可是你要承認，她的確長得很平庸。盧卡斯太太本人也那麼說，她還羨慕我的珍妮長得美呢。我並不喜歡誇耀自己的孩子，可是說老實話，提起珍妮——比她長得更好看的人也就不多見了。誰都那麼說。這並不是我說話有偏心。還在她十五歲的那一年，在我城裏那位兄弟買汀納家裏，有位先生就愛上了她，我的弟婦看準了那位先生一定會在臨走以前向她求婚。不過後來他卻沒有提。也許是他以為她年紀太小了吧。不過他卻為珍妮寫了好些詩，而且寫得很好。"

"那位先生的一場戀愛就這麼結束了，"伊莉莎白不耐煩地說。"我想，多少有情人都是這樣把自己克服過來的。詩居然有這種功能——能夠趕走愛情，這倒不知道是誰第一個發現的！"

"我卻一貫認為，詩是愛情的食糧 [12]，"達西說。

"那必須是一種優美、堅貞、健康的愛情才行。本身強健了，吃甚麼東西都可以獲得滋補。要是只不過有一點蛛絲馬跡，那麼我相信，一首十四行詩肯定會斷送掉它。"

達西只笑了一下，接着大家都沉默了一陣子，這時候伊莉莎白很是着急，怕她母親又要出醜。她想說點甚麼，可是又想不出甚麼可說的。沉默了一下以後，班奈特太太又重新向賓利先生道謝，多謝他對珍妮照顧周到，同時又向他道歉說，莉茲也來打擾了他。賓利先生回答得極其懇切而有禮貌，弄得他的妹妹也不得不講禮貌，說了些很得體的話。她說話的態度並不十分自然，可是班奈特太太已經夠滿意的了。過了一會，班奈特太太就預備馬車。這個號令一發，她那位最小的女兒立刻走上前來。原來自從她們母女來到此地，兩個女兒就一直在交頭接耳地商量，最後說定了由最小的女兒來要求賓利先生兌現他剛到鄉下時的諾言，在尼德斐莊園開一次舞會。

麗迪亞是個胖胖的、發育得很好的女孩，今年才十五歲，細皮白肉，笑顏常開。她是她母親的掌上明珠，由於嬌縱過度，她很小就進入了社交界。她生性好動，天生有些不知分寸，加上她的姨丈一次次以美酒佳餚宴請那些軍官們，軍官們又見她頗有幾分浪蕩的風情，便對她產生了相當的好感，於是她更加肆無忌憚了。所以她就有資格向賓利先生提出開舞會的事，而且冒冒失失地提醒他先前的諾言，而且還說，要是他不實踐諾言，那就是天下最丟人的事。賓利先生對她這一番突如其來的挑釁回答得令她的母親很是高興。

"我可以向你保證，我非常願意實踐我的諾言；只要等你姐姐復元後，由你隨便訂個日期就行。你總不願意在姐姐生病的時候跳舞吧？！"

麗迪亞表示滿意。"你這話說得不錯。等到珍妮復元以後再跳，那真好極了，而且到那時候，卡特上尉也許又可能回到麥里頓來。等你開過舞會以後，我一定非要他們也開一次不可。我一定會跟弗斯托上校說，要是他不開，可真丟人哪。"

於是班奈特太太帶着她的兩個女兒走了。伊莉莎白立刻回到珍妮身邊去，也不去管賓利府上的兩位小姐怎樣在背後議論她跟她家裏人有失體統。不過，儘管賓利小姐怎麼樣說俏皮話，怎麼樣拿她的美麗的眼睛開玩笑，達西卻始終不肯受她們的慫恿，跟她們一起來說她的不是。

第十章

這一天過得和前一天沒有多大的不同。赫斯托太太和賓利小姐上午陪了病人幾個小時，病人儘管好轉得很慢，卻在不斷地好轉。晚上，伊莉莎白跟她們一起留在客廳裏。不過這一回卻沒看見有人打"盧牌 [13]"。達西先生在寫信，賓利小姐坐在他身旁看他寫，一再糾纏不清地要他代她附筆問候他的妹妹。赫斯托先生和賓利先生在打"皮克牌"，赫斯托太太在一旁看他們打。

伊莉莎白在做針線，一面留神地聽着達西跟賓利小姐的談話。只聽到賓利小姐恭維話說個不停，不是說他的字寫得好，就是說他的字跡一行行很整齊，要不就是讚美他的信寫得仔細，可是對方卻完全是冷冰冰愛理不理。這兩個人你問我答，形成了一段奇妙的對白。照這樣看來，伊莉莎白的確沒有把他們兩人看錯。

"達西小姐收到了這樣的一封信，將會怎樣高興啊！"

他沒有回答。

"你寫信寫得這樣快，真是少見。"

"你這話可說得不對。我寫得相當慢。"

"你一年裏得寫多少封信啊。還得寫事務上的信，我看這是夠厭煩的吧！"

"這麼說，這些信總算幸虧碰到了我，沒有碰到你。"

"請告訴令妹，我很想和她見見面。"

"我已經遵命告訴過她了。"

"我怕你那支筆不大好用了吧。讓我來代你修理修理。修筆真是我的拿手好戲。"

"謝謝你的好意，我一向都是自己修理。"

"你怎麼能寫得那麼整齊？"

他沒有作聲。

"請告訴令妹，就說我聽到她的豎琴彈得進步了，真覺得高興，還請你告訴她說，她寄來給我裝飾桌子的那張美麗的小圖案，我真喜歡極了，我覺得比起格蘭特萊小姐的那張，真不知好了多少。"

"可否請你通融一下，讓我把你的喜悅，延遲到下一次寫信時再告訴她？這一次我可寫不下這麼多了。"

"噢，不要緊。正月裏我就可以跟她見面。不過，你老是寫那麼動人的長信給她嗎，達西先生？"

"我的信一般都寫得很長；不過是否每封都寫得動人，那就不能由我自己來說了。"

"不過我總覺得，凡是寫起長信來一揮而就的人，無論如何也不會寫得不好。"

她的哥哥大聲說道："這種恭維話可不能用在達西身上，卡洛琳，因為他並不能夠大筆一揮而就，他還得在那些文縐縐的字眼上面多多推敲。——達西，不是這樣嗎？"

"我寫信的風格和你很不同。"

"噢，"賓利小姐叫起來了，"查理斯寫起信來，那種潦草隨便的態度，簡直不可想像。他要漏掉一半字，塗掉一半字。"

"我念頭轉得太快，簡直來不及寫，因此有時候收信人讀到我的信，只覺得不知所云。"

"賓利先生，"伊莉莎白說，"你這樣謙虛，真讓人不好意思責備你。"

達西說："假裝謙虛最令人上當了，往往是信口開河，有時候簡直是轉彎抹角的自誇。"

"那麼，我剛剛那幾句謙虛的話，究竟是信口開河呢，還是轉彎抹角的自誇？"

"要算是轉彎抹角的自誇，因為你對於你自己寫信方面的缺點覺得很得意，你認為你思想敏捷，懶得去注意書法，而且你認為你這些方面即使算不上了不起，至少也非常有趣。凡是事情做得快的人總是自以為了不起，完全不考慮到做出來的成績是不是完美。你今天早上跟班奈特太太說，如果你決定要從尼德斐莊園搬走，你五分鐘之內就可以搬走，這種話無非是誇耀自己，恭維自己。再說，急躁的結果只會使得應該要做好的事情沒有做好，無論對人對己，都沒有真正的好處，這有甚麼值得讚美的呢？"

"算了吧，"賓利先生大聲說道，"晚上還記起早上的事，真是太不值得。而且老實說，我相信我對於自己的看法並沒有錯，我到現在還相信沒有錯。因此，我至少不是故意要顯得那麼神速，想要在小姐們面前炫耀自己。"

"也許你真的相信你自己的話；可是我怎麼也不相信你做事情會那麼當機立斷。我知道你也跟一般人一樣，都是見機行事。比如你正跨上馬要走了，忽然有個朋友跟你說：'賓利，你最好還是等到下個星期再走吧，'那你可能就會聽他的話，可能就不走了；要是他再跟你說句甚麼，你也許就會再住上一個月。"

伊莉莎白叫道："你這一番話只不過說明了賓利先生並沒有任着他自己的性子說做就做。你這樣一說，比他自己說更光彩了。"

賓利說："我真是太高興了，我的朋友所說的話，經你這麼一轉，反而變成恭維我的話了。不過，我只怕你這種解釋並不合那位先生的本意，因為：我如果真遇到這種事，我會爽爽快快地謝絕那位朋友，騎上馬就走，那他一定更看得起我。"

"那麼，難道達西先生認為，不管你本來的打算是多麼輕率魯莽，只要你一打定主意就堅持到底，也就情有可原了嗎？"

"老實說，我也解釋不清楚；那得由達西自己來說明。"

"你想要把這些意見說成我的意見，我可從來沒承認過。不過，班奈特小姐，即使把你所說的這種種情形假定為真有其事，你可別忘了這一點：那個朋友固然讓他留下來，讓他不要那麼說做就做，可是，那也不過是那位朋友有那麼一種希望，對他提出那麼一個要求，可並沒有堅持要他非那樣做不可。"

"說到隨隨便便地輕易聽從一個朋友的勸告，在你身上可還找不出這個優點。"

"如果不問是非，隨隨便便就聽從，恐怕對於兩個人都不能算是一種恭維吧。"

"達西先生，我覺得你未免否定了友誼和感情對於一個人的影響。要知道，一個人如果尊重別人提出的要求，通常都是用不着說服就會心甘情願地聽從的。我並不是因為你說到賓利先生而就借題發揮。也許我們可以等到真有這種事情發生的時候，再來討論他處理得是否適當。不過一般來說，朋友與朋友相處，遇到一件無關緊要的事情的時候，一個已經打定主意，另一個要他改變一下主意，如果被要求的人不等到對方加以說服，就聽從了對方的意見，你能說他有甚麼不是嗎？"

"我們稍後討論這個問題，不妨先仔細研究一下，那個朋友提出的要求究竟重要到甚麼程度，他們兩個人的交情又深到甚麼程度，這樣好不好？"

賓利大聲說道："好極了，請你仔細講吧，連他們身材的高矮和大小也別忘了講，因為，班奈特小姐，你一定想像不到討論起問題來的時候這一點是多麼重要。老實對你說，要是達西先生不比我高那麼多，大那麼多，你才休想讓我那麼尊敬他。在某些時候，某些場合，達西是個再討厭不過的傢伙——特別是禮拜天晚上在他家裏，當他沒有事情做的時候。"

達西先生微笑了一下，伊莉莎白本來要笑，可是覺得他好像有些生氣了，便忍住了沒有笑。賓利小姐看見別人拿他開玩笑，很是生氣，便怪她的哥哥為何要談這樣沒意思的話。

達西說："我明白你的用意，賓利，你不喜歡辯論，要把這場辯論壓下去。"

"我也許真是這樣。辯論往往很像爭論。假若你和班奈特小姐能夠稍緩一下，等我走出房間以後再辯論，那我是非常感激的。我走出去以後，你們便可以愛怎麼說我就怎麼說我了。"

伊莉莎白說："你要這樣做，對我並沒有甚麼損失；達西先生還是去把信寫好吧。"

達西先生聽從了她的意見，去把那封信寫好。

這件事過去以後，達西要求賓利小姐和伊莉莎白小姐賞賜他一點音樂聽聽，賓利小姐便敏捷地走到鋼琴前面，先客氣了一番，請伊莉莎白帶頭，伊莉莎白卻更加客氣、更加誠懇地推辭了，然後賓利小姐才在琴旁坐下來。

赫斯托太太替她妹妹伴唱。當她們姐妹兩人演奏的時候，伊莉莎白翻閱着鋼琴上的幾本琴譜，只見達西先生的眼睛總是望着她。如果說，這位了不起的人這樣望着她是出於愛慕之意，她倒是不大敢存這種奢望；不過，要是說達西是因為討厭她所以才望着她，那就更說不通了。最後，她只得這樣想：她之所以引起了達西的注意，大概是因為達西認為她比起在座的任何人來，都令人看不順眼。她作出了這個假想之後，並沒有感到痛苦，因為她根本不喜歡他，因此不稀罕他的垂青。

賓利小姐彈了幾支意大利歌曲以後，便改彈了一些活潑的蘇格蘭曲子來變換一下情調。不久，達西先生走到伊莉莎白面前來，跟她說：

"班奈特小姐，你是不是很想趁這個機會來跳一次蘇格蘭舞？"

伊莉莎白沒有回答他，只是笑了笑。他見她悶聲不響，覺得有點奇怪，便又問了她一次。

"噢，"她說，"我早就聽見了；可是我一下子拿不準應該怎樣回答你。當然，我知道你希望我回答一聲'是的'，那你就會蔑視我的低級趣味，好讓你自己得意一番，只可惜我一向喜歡戳穿別人的詭計，作弄一下那些存心想要蔑視我的人。因此，我決定跟你說，我根本不愛跳蘇格蘭舞；這下你不敢蔑視我了吧。"

"果真不敢。"

伊莉莎白本來打算使他難堪一下，這時見他那麼體貼，倒愣住了。其實，伊莉莎白的為人一貫溫柔乖巧，不輕易得罪任何人，而達西又對她非常着迷，以前任何女人也不曾使他這樣着迷過。他不由得一本正經地想道，要不是她的親戚出身微賤，那我就難免危險了。

賓利小姐見到這般情形，很是嫉妒，或者也可以説是她疑心病重，因此由疑生妒。於是她越想把伊莉莎白攆走，就越盼望她的好朋友珍妮身體趕快復元。

為了挑撥達西厭惡這位客人，她常常閒言閒語，説他跟伊莉莎白終將結成美滿良緣，而且估計着這一段良緣會給達西帶來多大的幸福。

第二天賓利小姐跟達西兩人在矮樹林裏散步，賓利小姐説："我希望將來有一天好事如願的時候，你得委婉地奉勸你那位岳母出言吐語要謹慎些，還有你那幾位小姨子，要是你能力辦得到，最好也得把她們那種醉心追求軍官的毛病醫治好。還有一件事，我真不好意思説出口：尊夫人有一點小脾氣，好像是自高自大，又好像是不懂禮貌，你也得盡力幫助她克制一下。"

"關於促進我的家庭幸福方面，你還有甚麼別的意見嗎？"

"噢，有的是。一定要把你姨丈人姨丈母的像掛到龐百利畫廊裏面去，就掛在你那位當法官的伯祖父大人遺像旁邊。你知道他們都是同行，只不過部門不同而已。至於尊夫人伊莉莎白，可千萬別讓別人替她畫像，天下哪一個畫家能夠把她那一雙美麗的眼睛畫得惟妙惟肖？"

"那雙眼睛的神韻的確不容易描畫；可是眼睛的形狀和顏色，以及她的睫毛，都非常美妙，也許描畫得出來。"

他們正談得起勁的時候，忽然看見赫斯托太太和伊莉莎白從另外一條路走過來。

賓利小姐連忙招呼她們説："我不知道你們也想出來散散步，"

她説這話的時候，心裏很有些惴惴不安，因為她恐怕剛才的話讓她們聽見了。

"你們太對不起我們了，"赫斯托太太回答道："只顧自己出來，也不告訴我們一聲。"

接着她就挽住達西空着的那條臂膀，丟下伊莉莎白，讓她獨自一個人走。這條路恰巧只容得下三個人並排走。達西先生覺得她們太冒昧了，便説道：

"這條路太窄，不能讓我們大家一起並排走。我們還是走到大道上去吧。"

伊莉莎白本不想跟他們在一起，一聽這話，便笑嘻嘻地説：

"不用了，不用了；你們就在這裏走走吧。你們三個人在一起走非常好看，而且很出色。加上第四個人，畫面就給破壞了。再見。"

於是她就得意洋洋地跑開了。她一面溜達，一面想到一兩天內就可以回家，覺得很高興。珍妮的病已經大為好轉，當天晚上就想走出房間去玩兩個小時。"

第十一章

女客們吃過晚飯以後，伊莉莎白就上樓到她姐姐那裏去，看她穿戴得妥妥貼貼，不會着涼，便陪着她上客廳去。她的女朋友們見到她，都表示歡迎，一個個都說非常高興。在男客們沒有來的那一個小時裏，她們是那麼和藹可親，伊莉莎白從來不曾看到過。她們的健談本領真是嚇人，描述起宴會來纖毫入微，說起故事來風趣橫溢，譏笑起一個朋友來也是有聲有色。

可是男客們一走進來，她們的心目中就不再有珍妮了。達西一進門，賓利小姐的眼睛立即轉到他身上去，要跟他說話。達西首先向班奈特小姐問好，客客氣氣地祝賀她病體康復；赫斯托先生也對她微微一鞠躬，說是見到她“非常高興”；但是說到語氣周到，情意懇切，可就比不上賓利先生那幾聲問候。賓利先生才算得上情深意切，滿懷歡欣。剛開始半小時完全消磨在添柴上面，生怕換了房間，病人會受不了。珍妮依照賓利的話，移坐到火爐的另一邊去，那樣她就離開門口遠一些，免得着涼。接着他自己在她身旁坐下，一心跟她說話，簡直不理睬別人。伊莉莎白正在對面角落裏做針線活，把這全部情景都看在眼裏，感到無限高興。

喝過茶以後，赫斯托先生提醒她的小姨子把牌桌擺好，可是沒有用。她早就看出達西先生不想打牌，因此赫斯托先生後來公開提出要打牌也被她拒絕了。她跟他說，誰都不想玩牌，只見全場對這件事都不作聲，看來她的確沒有說錯。因此，赫斯托先生無事可做，只得躺在沙發上去打瞌睡。達西拿起一本書來。賓利小姐也拿起一本書來。赫斯托太太聚精會神地在玩弄自己的手鐲和指環，偶爾也在她弟弟跟班奈特小姐的對話中插幾句嘴。

賓利小姐一面看達西讀書，一面自己讀書，兩件事同時並做，都是半心半意。她老是向他問幾句話，或者是看他讀到哪一頁。不過，她總是沒有辦法逗他說話；她問一句他就答一句，答過以後便繼續讀他的書。賓利小姐之所以要挑選那一本書讀，只不過因為那是達西所讀的那本書的第二卷，她蠻想讀個津津有味，不料這時倒讀得筋疲力盡了。她打了個呵欠，說道："這樣地度過一個晚上，真是多麼愉快啊！我說呀，甚麼娛樂也抵不上讀書的樂趣。無論幹甚麼事，都是一上手就要厭倦，讀書卻不會這樣！將來有一天我自己有了家，要是沒有個很好的書房，那會多麼遺憾啊。"

誰也沒有理睬她。於是她又打了個呵欠，拋開書本，把整個房間裏望了一轉，要想找點甚麼東西消遣消遣，這時忽然聽到她哥哥跟班奈特小姐說要開一次舞會，她就猛地掉過頭來對他說：

"這樣說，查理斯，你真打算在尼德斐莊園開一次舞會嗎？我勸你最好還是先徵求一下在場朋友們的意見再作決定吧。這裏面就會有人覺得跳舞是受罪，而不是娛樂，要是沒有這種人，你怪我好了。"

"如果你指的是達西，"她的哥哥大聲說，"那麼，他可以在跳舞開始以前就上牀睡覺，隨他的便好了。舞會已經決定了，是非開不可的，只等尼可爾斯太太把一切都準備好了，我就下請帖。"

賓利小姐說："要是開舞會能換些新花樣，那我就更高興了，通常舞會上的那老一套，實在討厭極了。你如果能把那一天的日程改一改，用談話來代替跳舞，那一定有意思得多。"

"也許有意思得多，卡洛琳，可是那還像甚麼舞會呢？"

賓利小姐沒有回答。不久，她就站起身來，在房間裏踱來踱去，故意在達西面前賣弄她優美的體態和矯健的步伐，只可惜達西只顧在那裏一心一意地看書，因此她只落得枉費心機。她絕望之餘，決定再作一次努力，於是轉過身來對伊莉莎白說：

"伊莉莎白·班奈特小姐，我勸你還是學學我的樣子，在房間裏走動走動吧。告訴你，坐了那麼久，走動一下可以提提精神。"

伊莉莎白覺得很詫異，可是立刻依了她的意思。於是賓利小姐獻殷勤的真正目的達到了——達西先生果然抬起了頭來。原來達西也和伊莉莎白一樣,看出了她在耍花招引人注目,便不知不覺地放下了書本。兩位小姐立刻請他來一起踱步,可是他謝絕了。說是她們兩人之所以要在房間裏踱來踱去,據他的理解,無非有兩個動機,如果他參加她們一起散步,他的參與對於她們的任何一個動機,都會造成妨礙。他這話是甚麼意思?賓利小姐極想知道他講這話的用意何在,便問伊莉莎白懂不懂。

伊莉莎白回答道:"完全不懂,他一定是存心奚落我們,不過你最好不要理睬他,讓他失望一下。"

可惜賓利小姐遇到任何事情都不忍心讓達西先生失望,於是再三要求他非把他的所謂兩個動機解釋一下不可。

達西等她一住口,便馬上說:"我非常願意解釋一下。事情不外乎是這樣的:你們是心腹之交,所以選擇了這個辦法來消磨黃昏,還要談談私事,否則就是你們自以為散起步來,體態顯得特別好看,所以要散散步。倘若是出於第一個動機,我夾在你們中間就會妨礙你們;假若是出於第二個動機,那麼,我坐在火爐旁邊可以更好地欣賞你們。"

"噢,嚇壞人!"賓利小姐叫起來了。"我從來沒聽到過這麼討厭的話。——虧他說得出,該怎麼罰他呀?"

"要是你存心罰他,那是再容易不過的事,"伊莉莎白說。"彼此都可以罰來罰去,折磨來折磨去。作弄他一番吧——譏笑他一番吧。你們既然這麼相熟,你該懂得怎麼對付他呀。"

"天地良心,我不懂得。不瞞你說,我們雖然相熟,可是要懂得怎樣來對付他,還差得遠呢。想要對付這種性格冷靜和頭腦機靈的人,可不容易!不行,不行,我想我們是搞不過他的。至於譏笑他,說句你不生氣的話,我們不能憑空笑別人,弄得反而惹人笑話。讓達西先生去自鳴得意吧。"

"原來達西先生是不能給人笑話的!"伊莉莎白大聲說道。"這種優越的條件倒真少有，我希望一直不要多，這樣的朋友多了，我的損失可大了。我特別喜歡笑話。"

"賓利小姐過獎我了。"他說。"要是一個人把開玩笑當作人生最重要的事，那麼，最聰明最優秀的人——不，最聰明最優秀的行為——也就會變得可笑了。"

"那當然，"伊莉莎白回答道，"這樣的人是有的，但願我不是其中之一。我希望我永遠不會嘲笑美好和聰明的行為。但對於那些蠢話、蠢事，反覆無常和前後矛盾的行為，我能嘲笑就嘲笑。我覺得這些弱點在你身上是沒有的吧。"

"或許誰都不會有這些弱點，否則可真糟了，絕頂的聰慧也要招人嘲笑了。我一生都在研究該怎麼樣避免這些弱點。"

"假如虛榮和傲慢就是屬於這一類的弱點。"

"不錯，虛榮的確是個弱點。可是傲慢——只要你果真聰明過人——你就會傲慢得比較有分寸。"

伊莉莎白掉過頭去，免得別人看見她發笑。

"你考問達西先生考問好了吧，我想，"賓利小姐說。"請問結論如何？"

"我完全承認達西先生沒有缺點。他自己也承認了這一點，並沒有掩飾。"

"不，"達西說，"我並沒有說過這種裝場面的話。我的毛病可多了，不過這些毛病與頭腦並沒有關係。至於我的性格，我不敢自誇。我認為我的性格太不能委曲求全，這當然是說我在處世方面太不能委曲求全地附和跟隨別人。別人的愚蠢和過錯我本應該趕快忘掉，卻偏偏忘不掉；別人得罪了我，我也忘不掉。說到我的一些情緒，也並不是我一打算把它們去除掉，它們就會煙消雲散，我的脾氣可以說是夠令人厭惡的。我對於某個人一旦沒有了好感，就永遠沒有好感。"

"這倒的的確確是個大缺點！"伊莉莎白大聲說道。"跟別人怨恨不解，的確是性格上的一個陰影。可是你對於自己的缺點，已經挑剔得很嚴格。我的確不能再譏笑你了。你放心好了。”

“我相信，一個人不管是怎樣的脾氣，都免不了有某種短處，這是一種天生的缺陷，即使受教育受得再好，也還是克服不了。”

“你有一種傾向，——對甚麼人都感到厭惡，這就是你的缺陷。”

“而你的缺陷呢，”達西笑着回答。“就是故意去誤解別人。”

賓利小姐眼見這場談話沒有她的份，不禁有些厭倦，便大聲説道：“讓我們來聽聽音樂吧，路易莎，你不怕我吵醒赫斯托先生嗎？”

她的姐姐毫不反對，於是鋼琴便打開了。達西想了一下，覺得這樣也不錯。他開始感覺到對伊莉莎白似乎已經過份親近了一些。

第十二章

班奈特姐妹兩人商量妥當了以後，伊莉莎白第二天早上就寫信給她母親，請她當天就派馬車來接她們。可是，班奈特太太早就打算讓她兩個女兒在尼德斐莊園住到下星期二，以便讓珍妮正好住滿一個星期，因此不大樂意提前接她們回家，回信也寫得使她們不大滿意，——至少使伊莉莎白不十分滿意，因為她急於要回家。班奈特太太信上說，非到星期二，家裏弄不出馬車來。她寫完之後，又補寫了幾句，說是倘若賓利先生兄妹挽留她們多住幾天，她非常願意讓她們住下去。怎奈伊莉莎白就是不肯住下去，她打定主意非回家不可——也不怎麼指望主人家挽留她們，她反而怕別人以為她們賴在那裏不肯走。於是她催促珍妮馬上去向賓利借馬車。她們最後決定向主人家說明，她們當天上午就要離開尼德斐莊園，而且把借馬車的事也提出來。

主人家聽到這話，表示百般關切，便再三挽留她們，希望她們至少等到第二天再走，珍妮讓他們說服了，於是姐妹兩人只得再耽擱一天。這下可讓賓利小姐後悔挽留她們，她對伊莉莎白又嫉妒又討厭，因此也就顧不得對珍妮的感情了。

賓利聽到她們馬上要走，非常發愁，便一遍又一遍地勸導珍妮，說她還沒有完全復元，馬上就走不大妥當，可是珍妮既然覺得自己的主張是對的，便再三堅持。

不過達西卻覺得這是個好消息，他認為伊莉莎白在尼德斐莊園住得夠久了。他沒想到這次會給她弄得這般地心醉，加上賓利小姐一方面對她沒有禮貌，另一方面更拿他自己開玩笑。他睿智地決定讓自己特別當心些，目前決不要流露出對她有甚麼愛慕的意思——一點形跡也不要流露出來，免得她存非份之想，就此要操縱我達西的終身幸福。他感覺到，假如她存了那種心，那麼一定是他昨天對待她的態度起了舉足輕重的作用——讓她不是對他更有好感，便是把他完全厭棄。他這樣拿定了主意，於是星期六一整天幾乎沒有跟她說上十句話。雖然他那天曾經有一次跟她單獨在一起有半小時之久，他卻正大光明地用心看書，看也沒看她一眼。

星期日做過晨禱以後，班家兩姐妹立即告辭，主人家幾乎人人樂意。賓利小姐對伊莉莎白一下子變得有禮貌起來了，對珍妮也一下子變得更親熱了。分手的時候，她先跟珍妮說，非常盼望以後有機會在朗伯恩或者在尼德斐莊園跟她重逢，接着又十分親切地擁抱了她一番，甚至還跟伊莉莎白握了握手。伊莉莎白高高興興地告別了大家。

到家以後，母親並不怎麼熱誠地歡迎她們。班奈特太太奇怪她們兩人怎麼竟會提前回來，非常埋怨她們給家裏招來那麼多麻煩，說是珍妮十拿九穩地又要傷風了。倒是她們的父親，看到兩個女兒回家來了，嘴上雖然沒有說甚麼歡天喜地的話，心裏確實非常高興。他早就體會到，這兩個女兒在家裏的地位多麼重要。晚上一家人聚在一起聊天的時候，要是珍妮和伊莉莎白不在場，就沒有勁，甚至毫無意義。

她們發覺瑪莉還像以往一樣，在埋頭研究和聲學以及人性問題，她拿出了一些新的摘錄筆記給她們欣賞，又發表對舊道德的新見解給她們聽。凱瑟琳和麗迪亞也告訴了她們一些新聞，可是性質完全不同。據她們說，民兵團自從上星期三以來又發生許多事，添了很多傳說：有幾個軍官最近和她們的姨丈吃過飯；一個士兵挨了鞭打，又聽說弗斯托上校的確快要結婚了。

第十三章

第二天吃早飯的時候，班奈特先生對他的太太說：“我的好太太，我希望你今天的晚餐準備得豐盛一些，因為我預料今天一定有客人來。”

“你指的是哪位客人，我的好老爺？我一點也不知道有誰要來，除非夏綠蒂·盧卡斯碰巧會來看我們，我覺得拿我們平常的飯餐招待她也夠好了。我不相信她在家裏經常吃得這麼好。”

“我所說到的這位客人是位男賓，又是個生客。”班奈特太太的眼睛閃亮了起來。“一位男賓又是一位生客！那一定是賓利先生，沒有錯。——哦，珍妮，你從來沒漏出過半點風聲，你這個狡猾的東西！——嘿，賓利先生要來，真讓我太高興了。可是——老天爺呀！運氣真不好，今天連一點魚也買不到。——麗迪亞寶貝，代我按一按鈴。我要馬上吩咐希爾一下。”

她的丈夫連忙說：“並不是賓利先生要來；說起這位客人，我一生都沒有見過他。”

這句話令全家都吃了一驚。他的太太和五個女兒立刻迫切地追問他，使他頗為得意。

拿他太太和女兒們的好奇心打趣了一陣以後，他便原原本本地說：“大約在一個月以前，我就收到了一封信，兩星期之前我寫了回信，因為我覺得這是件相當傷腦筋的事，得趁早留意。信是我的表姪柯林斯先生寄來的。我死了以後，這位表姪可以高興甚麼時候把你們攆出這所宅子，就甚麼時候攆你們出去。”

“噢，天啊，”他的太太叫了起來。“聽你提起這件事我就受不了。請你別談那個討厭的傢伙吧。你自己的產業不能讓自己的孩子繼承，卻要讓別人來繼承，這是世界上最難堪的事。如果我是你，一定早就想出辦法來補救這個問題了。"

珍妮和伊莉莎白設法把繼承權的問題跟她解釋了一下。其實她們一直設法跟她解釋，可是這個問題跟她是講不明白的。她老是破口大罵，說是自己的產業不能由五個親生女兒繼承，卻白白送給一個和她們毫不相干的人，這實在是太不合情理。

"這的確是一件最不公道的事，"班奈特先生說，"柯林斯先生要繼承朗伯恩的產業，他這個罪過是洗也洗不清的。不過，要是你聽聽他這封信裏所說的話，那你就會心腸軟一些，因為他這番表明心跡還算不錯。"

"不，我相信我絕對不會心軟下來；我覺得他寫信給你真是既沒有禮貌，又非常虛偽。我恨這種虛偽的朋友。他為甚麼不像他爸爸那樣跟你吵得不可開交呢？"

"哦，真的，他對這個問題，好像也有些為了顧全孝道，猶豫不決，且讓我把信讀給你們聽吧：

親愛的堂叔：

以前你與先父之間曾有些芥蒂，這一直使我感到不安。自先父不幸去世以來，我常常想到要彌補這個裂痕；但我一時猶豫，沒有這樣做，怕的是先父生前既然對閣下惟恐仇視不及，而我今天卻來與閣下修好，這未免有辱先人。留心聽呀，我的好太太。不過目前我對此事已經拿定主張，因為我已在復活節那天領受了聖職。多蒙故路易斯·德·包爾公爵的孀妻凱瑟琳·包爾夫人寵禮有加，恩惠並施，提拔我擔任該教區的教士，此後可以盡心盡力，恭侍夫人左右，奉行英國教會所規定的一切儀節，這真是三生有幸。況且以一個教士的身份來說，我覺得我有責任盡我力之所及，使家家戶戶得以敦穆親誼，促進友好。因此我自信這番好意一定會受到你的重視，而關於我繼承朗伯恩產權一事，你也不必介意，並請接受我獻上的這一枝橄欖枝[14]。我這樣侵犯了諸位令嬡的利益，真是深感不安，萬分抱歉。但請你放心，我極願給她們一切可能的補償，此事容待以後詳談。如果你不反對我登門拜候，我建議於十一月十八日，星期一，四點鐘前來拜謁，或在府上叨擾至下星期六為止。這對於我毫無不便之處，因為凱瑟琳夫人決不會反對我星期日偶爾離開教堂一下，只要有另一個教士主持這一天的事情就可以了。敬向尊夫人及諸位令嬡致候。

你的祝福者和朋友威廉・柯林斯

十月十五日寫於威斯特漢附近的肯特郡漢斯福村

"那麼，四點鐘的時候，這位息事寧人的先生就要來了，"班奈特先生一邊把信折好，一邊說。"他倒是個很有良心，很有禮貌的青年，一定是的；我相信他一定會成為一個值得器重的朋友，只要凱瑟琳夫人能夠開開恩，讓他以後再上我們這裏來，那更好了。"

"他講到女兒們的那幾句話，倒還說得不錯；要是他果真打算設法補償，我倒不反對。"

珍妮說："他說要給我們補償，我們雖然猜不出他究竟是甚麼意思，可是他這一片好意，也的確難得。"

伊莉莎白聽到他對凱瑟琳夫人尊敬得那麼出奇，而且他竟那麼好心好意，隨時替他自己教區裏的居民們行洗禮，主持婚禮和喪禮，不禁大吃一驚。

"我看他一定是個古怪人，"她說。"我真弄不懂他。他的文筆似乎有些浮誇。他所謂因為繼承了我們的產權而感到萬分抱歉，這話是甚麼意思呢？即使這件事可以取消，我們也不要以為他就肯取消，他是個頭腦清楚的人嗎，爸爸？"

"不，寶貝，我想他不是。我完全認為他是恰恰相反。從他信裏那種既謙卑又自大的口氣上就可以看得出來。我倒真想見見他。"

瑪莉說："就文章而論，他的信倒好像寫得沒有甚麼毛病。橄欖枝這種說法雖然並不新穎，可是我覺得用得倒很恰當。"

在凱瑟琳和麗迪亞看來，無論是那封信也好，寫信的人也好，都沒有一點意思。反正她們覺得她們的表兄絕不會穿着"紅制服"來，而這幾個星期以來，穿其他任何顏色的衣服的人，她們都不樂意結交。至於她們的母親，原來的一股怨氣已經被柯林斯先生一封信打消了不少，她倒準備相當平心靜氣地會見他，這使得她的丈夫和女兒們都覺得奇怪。

柯林斯先生準時來了，全家都非常客氣地接待他。班奈特先生幾乎沒有說甚麼話；可是太太和幾位小姐都十分願意暢談一下，而柯林斯先生本人好像既不需要別人鼓勵他多說話，也不打算不說話。他是個二十五歲的青年，高高的個子，看上去很肥胖。他的氣派端莊而堂皇，又很拘泥禮節。他剛一坐下來就恭維班奈特太太福氣好，養了這麼多好女兒。他說，早就聽到人們對她們的美貌讚揚備至，今天一見面，才知道她們的美貌遠遠地超過了她們的名聲；他又說，他相信小姐們到時候都會結下美滿良緣。他這些奉承話，大家真不大愛聽，只有班奈特太太，沒有哪句恭維話聽不下去，於是極其乾脆地回答道：

"我相信你是個好心腸的人，先生；我一心希望能如你的金口，否則她們就不堪設想了。事情實在辦得太古怪了。"

"你大概是說產業的繼承權問題吧。"

"唉，先生，我的確是說到這方面。你得承認，這對於我可憐的女兒們真是件不幸的事。我並不想怪你，因為我也知道，世界上這一類的事完全靠命運。一個人的產業一旦要限定繼承人，那你就無從知道它會落到誰的手裏去。"

"太太，我深深知道，這件事苦了表妹們，我在這個問題上有很多意見，一時卻不敢莽撞冒失。可是我可以向年輕的小姐們保證，我上這裏來，就是為了要向她們表示我的敬慕。目前我也不打算多說，或許等到將來我們相處得更熟一些的時候——"

主人家請他吃晚餐了，於是他的話不得不被打斷。小姐們彼此相視而笑。柯林斯先生所愛慕的才不光光是她們呢。他把客廳、飯廳以及房間裏所有的傢具，都仔細看了一遍，讚美了一番。班奈特太太本當聽到他讚美一句，心裏就得意一陣。怎奈她也想到，他原來是把這些東西都看作他自己未來的財產，因此她又非常難受。連一頓飯也蒙他稱賞不置，他請求主人告訴他，究竟是哪位表妹煮得這一手好菜。班奈特太太聽到他這句話，不禁把他指責了一番。她相當不客氣地跟他說，她們家裏現在還僱得起一個像樣的廚師，根本用不到女兒們過問廚房裏的事。他請求她原諒，不要見怪。於是她用柔和的聲調說，她根本沒有怪他，可是他卻接連道歉了十五分鐘之久。

第十四章

吃飯的時候，班奈特先生幾乎一句話也沒有説；可是等到傭人們走開以後，他就想道，現在可以跟這位客人談談了。他料想到，如果一開始就談到凱瑟琳夫人身上去，這位貴客一定會笑逐顏開的，於是他便拿這個話題做開場白，説是柯林斯先生有了那樣一個女恩人，真是幸運極了，又説凱瑟琳・德・包爾夫人對他這樣言聽計從，而且極其周到地照顧到他生活方面的安逸，真是十分難得。班奈特先生這個話題選得不能再好了。柯林斯先生果然滔滔不絕地讚美起那位夫人來。這個問題一談開了頭，他本來的那種嚴肅態度便顯得更嚴肅了。他帶着非常自負的神氣説，他一輩子也沒有看到過任何有身價地位的人，能夠像凱瑟琳夫人那樣的有德行，那樣的親切謙和。他很榮幸，曾經當着她的面講過兩次道，多蒙夫人垂愛，對他那兩次講道讚美不絕。夫人曾經請他到洛欣莊園去吃過兩次飯，上星期六晚上還請他到她家裏去打過"誇錐"牌[15]。據他所知，許多人都認為凱瑟琳夫人為人驕傲，可是他只覺得她親切。她平常跟他攀談起來，總是把他當作一個有身份的人看待。她絲毫不反對他和鄰居們來往，也不反對他偶爾離開教區一兩個星期，去拜訪親友們。多蒙她體恤下情，曾經親自勸他及早結婚，只要他能夠謹慎選擇對象。她還到他的寒舍去拜訪過一次，對於他住宅裏所有經過他修整過的地方都十分滿意，並且蒙她親自賜予指示，讓他把樓上的壁櫥添置幾個架子。

班奈特太太説："我相信這一切都做得很得體，很有禮貌，我看她一定是個和顏悅色的女人。可惜一般貴夫人們都比不上她。她住的地方離你很近嗎，先生？"

"寒舍那個花園跟她老夫人住的洛欣莊園，只隔着一條胡同。"

"你説她是個寡婦嗎，先生？她還有家屬嗎？"

"她只有一個女兒，——也就是洛欣莊園的繼承人，將來可以繼承到一筆非常大的遺產呢。"

"哎呀，"班奈特太太聽得叫了起來，一面又搖了搖頭。"那麼，她比許多小姐們都福氣好。她是怎樣的一位小姐？長得漂亮嗎？"

"她真是個極可愛的小姐。凱瑟琳夫人自己也説過，講到真正的漂亮，德·包爾小姐要勝過天下最漂亮的女性；因為她眉清目秀，與眾不同，一看上去就知道她出身高貴。她本來可以多才多藝，只可惜她體質欠佳，沒有進修，否則她一定琴棋書畫樣樣通曉，這話是她的女教師説給我聽的，那教師現在還跟她們母女住在一起。她的確是可愛極了，常常不拘名份，乘着她那輛小馬車光臨寒舍。"

"她覲見過國王嗎？在進過宮的仕女們裏面，我好像沒有聽見過她的名字。"

"不幸她身體柔弱，不能進京城去，正如我有一天跟凱瑟琳夫人所説的，這實在使英國的宮廷裏損失了一顆最耀眼的明珠；老夫人對我這種説法很是滿意。你們可以想像得到，在任何場合下，我都樂於説幾句巧妙的恭維話，讓太太小姐們聽得高興。我跟凱瑟琳夫人説過好多次，她的美麗的小姐是一位天生的公爵夫人，將來不管嫁給哪一位公爵姑爺，不論那位姑爺地位有多高，非但不是增加小姐的體面，反而要讓小姐來為他爭光。這些話都讓老夫人聽得高興極了，我總覺得我應該在這方面特別留意。"

班奈特先生説："你説得很恰當，你既然有這種才能，能夠非常巧妙地捧別人的場，這對於你自己也會有好處。我是否可以請教你一下：你這種討人喜歡的奉承話，是臨時想起來的呢，還是老早想好了的？"

"大半是看臨時的情形想起來的；不過有時候我也自己跟自己打趣，預先想好一些很好的小恭維話，平常有機會就拿來應用，而且臨説的時候，總是要裝出是自然流露出來的。"

班奈特先生果然料想得完全正確，他這位表姪確實像他所想像的那樣荒謬，他聽得非常有趣，不過表面上卻竭力保持鎮靜，除了偶爾朝着伊莉莎白望一眼以外，他並不需要別人來分享他這份愉快。

　　不過到喝茶的時候，這一場罪總算受完了。班奈特先生高高興興地把客人帶到會客室裏，等到茶喝完了，他又高高興興地邀請他朗誦點甚麼給他的太太和小姐們聽。柯林斯先生立刻就答應了，於是她們就拿了一本書給他，可是一看到那本書（因為那本書一眼就可以看出是從流通圖書館借來的），他就吃驚得往後一退，連忙表明他從來不讀小說[16]，請求她們原諒。凱蒂對他瞪着眼，麗迪亞叫了起來。於是她們另外拿了幾本書來，他仔細考慮了一下以後，選了一本弗迪斯[17]的《講道集》。他一攤開那本書，麗迪亞不禁目瞪口呆，等到他那麼單調無味、一本正經地剛要讀完三頁的時候，麗迪亞趕快岔斷了他：

　　“媽媽，你知不知道菲力普姨丈要解僱理查？要是他真的要解僱他，弗斯托上校一定願意僱用他。這是星期六那一天姨媽親自告訴我的。我打算明天上麥里頓去多了解一些情況，順便問問他們，丹尼先生甚麼時候從城裏回來。”

　　兩個姐姐都吩咐麗迪亞住嘴；柯林斯先生非常生氣，放下了書本，說道：

　　“我老是看到年輕的小姐們對正經書不感興趣，不過這些書完全是為了她們的好處寫的。老實說，這不能不令我驚奇，因為對她們最有利益的事情，當然莫過於聖哲的教訓。可是我也不願意勉強我那年輕的表妹。”

　　於是他轉過身來要求班奈特先生跟他玩“雙陸棋”[18]，班奈特先生一面答應了他，一面說，這倒是個聰明的辦法，還是讓這些女孩子們去搞她們自己的小玩藝吧。班奈特太太和她幾個女兒極有禮貌地向他道歉，請他原諒麗迪亞岔斷了他朗誦聖書，並且說，他要是重新讀那本書，她保證決不會有同樣的事件發生。柯林斯先生請她們不要介意，説是他一點也不怪表妹，決不會認為她冒犯了他而懷恨在心。他解釋過以後，就跟班奈特先生坐到另一張桌子上去，準備玩雙陸棋。

第十五章

柯林斯先生並不是個通情達理的人，他雖然也受過教育，也踏進了社會，但是先天的缺陷卻簡直沒有彌補甚麼。他大部份日子是在他那守財奴的文盲父親的教導下度過的。他也算進過大學[19]，實際上不過照例住了幾個學期，並沒有結交到一個有用的朋友。他父親管他管得十分嚴厲，因此他的為人本來很是謙卑，不過他本是個蠢材，現在生活又過得很悠閒，當然不免自高自大，何況年紀輕輕就發了意外之財，自視甚高，哪裏還談得上謙卑。當時漢斯福教區有個牧師空缺，他鴻運亨通，得到了凱瑟琳‧德‧包爾夫人的提拔。他看到他的女恩人地位頗高，便悉心崇拜，備加尊敬；另一方面又自命不凡，自以為當上了教士，該有怎樣怎樣的權力，作為一個教區的主管牧師，又該享受怎樣怎樣的權利，於是他一身兼有了驕傲自大和謙卑順從的兩重性格。

他現在已經有了一幢好房子，一筆可觀的收入，想要結婚了。他之所以要和朗伯恩這家人講和修好，原是想要在他們府上找個太太。要是這家人的幾位小姐果真像大家所傳聞的那麼美麗可愛，他一定要挑選一個。這就是他所謂補償的計劃，贖罪的計劃，為的是將來繼承她們父親的遺產時可以問心無愧。他認為這真是個獨出心裁的辦法，既極其妥善得體，又來得慷慨豪爽。

他看到這幾位小姐之後，並沒有變更本來的計劃。一看到珍妮那張可愛的臉龐，他便拿定了主張，而且更加確定了他那些傳統想法，認為一切應當長幼有序。第一個晚上他就選中了她。不過第二天早上他又變更了主張，因為他和班奈特太太親密地談了十五分鐘的話，剛開始時談談他自己那幢牧師住所，後來自然而然地把自己的心願招供了出來，說是要在朗伯恩找一位太太，而且要在她的令媛們中間找一位。班奈特太太親切地微笑着，而且一再鼓勵他，不過談到他選定了珍妮，她就不免要提請他注意一下了。"講到我幾個小女兒，我沒有甚麼意見——當然也不能一口答應——不過我還沒有聽說她們有甚麼對象；至於我的大女兒，我不得不提一提——我覺得有責任提醒你一下——大女兒可能很快就要訂婚了。"

柯林斯先生只得撇開珍妮不談，改選伊莉莎白，一下子就選定了——就在班奈特太太撥火的那一刹那之間選定的。伊莉莎白無論是年齡，美貌，比珍妮都只差一步，當然第二個就要輪到她。

班奈特太太得到這個暗示，如獲至寶，她相信很快就可以嫁出兩個女兒了；昨天她提都不願意提到的這個人，現在卻讓她極為重視了。

麗迪亞原說要到麥里頓去走走，她這個念頭到現在還沒有打消。除了瑪莉之外，姐姐們都願意跟她同去；班奈特先生為了要把柯林斯先生攆走，好讓自己在書房裏清靜一陣，便請他也伴着她們一起去。原來柯林斯先生吃過早飯以後，就跟着他到書房裏來了，一直留到那時候還不想走。名義上在看他所收藏的那本大型的對開本，事實上卻在滔滔不絕地跟班奈特先生大談他自己在漢斯福的房產和花園，弄得班奈特先生心煩意亂。他平常留在書房裏就是為了要圖個悠閒清靜。他曾經跟伊莉莎白說過，他願意在任何一間房間裏接見愚蠢和自高自大的傢伙，書房裏可就不能讓那些人插足了。因此他立刻恭恭敬敬地請柯林斯先生伴着他女兒們一起去走走，而柯林斯先生本來也適合做一個步行家，不適合做一個讀書人，於是非常高興地合上書本走了。

他一路廢話連篇，表妹們只得客客氣氣地隨聲附和，就這樣消磨着時間，來到了麥里頓。幾位年紀小的表妹一到那裏，就再也不去理會他了。她們的眼睛立刻向着街頭看來看去，看看有沒有軍官們走過，此外就只有商店櫥窗裏極漂亮的女帽，或者是最新式的花洋布，才能吸引住她們。

很快，這許多小姐都注意到一位年輕人。那人她們從來沒見過，一副道地的紳士氣派，正跟一個軍官在街道那邊散步。這位軍官就是丹尼先生，麗迪亞正要打聽他從倫敦回來了沒有。當她們從那裏走過的時候，他鞠了一個躬。大家看到那個陌生人風度翩翩，都愣了一下，只是不知道這人是誰。凱蒂和麗迪亞決定想辦法去打聽，便藉口要到對面鋪裏去買點東西，帶頭走到街那邊去了。也正是事有湊巧，她們剛剛走到人行道上，那兩個男人也正轉過身來，走到那地方。丹尼馬上招呼她們，並請求她們讓他把他的朋友韋翰先生介紹給她們。他說韋翰是前一天跟他一起從城裏回來的，而且說來很高興，韋翰已經被任命為他們團裏的軍官。這真是再好不過了，因為韋翰這位青年，只要穿上一身軍裝，便會十全十美。他的容貌舉止確實討人喜歡。他沒有一處長得不好看，眉目清秀，身材魁梧，談吐又十分動人。一經介紹之後，他就高高興興、懇懇切切地談起話來——既懇切，又顯得非常正派，而且又有分寸。他們正站在那裏談得很投機的時候，忽然聽到一陣馬蹄聲，只見達西和賓利騎着馬從街上過來。這新來的兩位紳士看見人堆裏有這幾位小姐，便連忙來到她們面前，照常寒暄了一番。帶頭說話的是賓利，他大部份的話都是對班奈特小姐說的。他說他正要趕到朗伯恩去拜訪她。達西先生證明他沒有撒謊，同時鞠了個躬。達西正打算從伊莉莎白身上移開目光，這時突然看到了那個陌生人。只見他們兩人面面相覷，大驚失色，伊莉莎白看到這個邂逅相遇的場合，覺得很是驚奇。兩個人都變了臉色，一個慘白，一個通紅。過了一會，韋翰先生按了按帽子，達西先生勉強回了一下禮。這是甚麼意思呢？既讓人無從想像，又令人不能不想去打聽一下。

　　又過了一會，賓利先生若無其事地跟他們告別了，騎着馬跟他朋友走了。

　　丹尼先生和韋翰先生陪着幾位年輕的小姐，走到菲力普家門口，麗迪亞小姐硬要他們進去，甚至菲力普太太也打開了窗戶，大聲地幫着她邀請，他們卻鞠了個躬告辭而去。

菲力普太太一向喜歡看到她的外甥女們，那大的兩個最近不常見面，因此特別受歡迎。她懇切地説，她們姐妹兩人突然回家來，真令她非常驚奇。要不是碰巧在街上遇到鍾斯醫生的藥鋪裏那個跑街的小伙子告訴她，説是班奈特家的兩位小姐都已回家，不用再送藥到尼德斐莊園去，那她到現在還不知道她們回來了呢，這是因為她們家裏沒有派馬車去接她們的緣故。正當她們這樣閒談的時候，珍妮向她介紹柯林斯先生。她不得不跟他寒暄幾句，她極其客氣地表示歡迎他。他也加倍客氣地應酬她，而且向她道歉，説是素昧生平，不該這麼冒失，闖到她府上來；又説他畢竟還是非常高興，因為介紹他的那幾位年輕小姐和他還有些親戚關係，因此他的冒昧前來也還勉強説得過去。這種過份的禮貌使菲力普太太受寵若驚。不過，正當她仔細打量着這一位生客的時候，她們姐妹兩人卻又把另一位生客的事情，大驚小怪地提出來向她問長問短，她只得又來回答她們的話，可是她能夠説給外甥女們聽的，也無非是她們早已知道了的一些情形。她説那位生客是丹尼先生剛從倫敦帶來的，他將要在某某郡擔任起一個中尉的職責，又説，他剛剛在街上走來走去的時候，她曾經對他望了整整一個小時之久。這時如果韋翰先生從這裏經過，凱蒂和麗迪亞一定還要繼續張望他一番；可惜現在除了幾位軍官之外，根本沒有人從窗外走過，而這些軍官們同韋翰一比較，都變成一些"愚蠢討厭的傢伙"了。有幾個軍官明天要上菲力普家裏吃飯。姨母説，倘若她們一家人明晚能從朗伯恩趕來，那麼她就要讓她的丈夫去拜訪韋翰先生一次，也約他來。大家都同意了。菲力普太太説，明天要給她們來一次熱鬧而有趣的抓彩票的玩藝，玩過之後再吃一頓熱騰騰的宵夜。想到了明天這一場歡樂，真令人興奮，因此大家分別的時候都很快樂。柯林斯先生走出門來，又再三道謝，主人也禮貌周全地請他不必過份客氣。

回家的時候，伊莉莎白一路上把剛剛親眼看見的那兩位先生之間的一幕情景說給珍妮聽。假如他們兩人之間真有甚麼宿怨，珍妮一定要為他們兩人中間的一人辯護，或是為兩人辯護，只可惜她跟她妹妹一樣，對於這兩個人的事情完全摸不着頭腦。

柯林斯先生回來之後，大大稱讚菲力普太太的殷勤好客，班奈特太太聽得很滿意。柯林斯說，除了凱瑟琳夫人母女之外，他生平從來沒見過更風雅的女人，因為他雖然和她素昧生平，她卻對他禮貌周全，甚至還指明要請他明天晚上一同去作客。他想，這件事多少應該歸功於他和她們的親戚關係，可是這樣殷勤好客的事，他還是生平第一次碰到呢。

第十六章

年輕的小姐們跟她們姨媽的約會，並沒有遭受到反對。柯林斯只覺得來此作客，反而把班奈特夫婦整晚丟在家裏，未免有些過意不去，可是他們讓他千萬不要放在心上。於是他和他的五個表妹便乘着馬車，準時到了麥里頓。小姐們一走進客廳，就聽說韋翰先生接受了她們姨丈的邀請，而且已經到了，覺得很是高興。

大家聽到這個消息之後，便都坐了下來。柯林斯先生悠閒自在地朝周圍望望，瞻仰瞻仰一切；房間的尺寸和裏面的傢具使他十分驚羨，他說他好像進了凱瑟琳夫人在洛欣莊園的那間消暑的小飯廳。這個比喻一開始並不怎麼令主人家滿意，可是後來菲力普太太弄明白了洛欣莊園是一個甚麼地方，它的主人是誰，又聽他說起凱瑟琳夫人的一個會客間的情形，光是一隻壁爐架就要值八百英鎊，她這才體會到他那個比喻實在太恭維她了，即使把她家裏比作洛欣莊園的女管家的房間，她也不反對了。

柯林斯在講述凱瑟琳夫人和她那莊園的富麗堂皇時，偶然還要插上幾句話，來誇耀他自己的寒舍，說他的住宅正在裝潢改善中等等，他就這樣自得其樂地一直扯到男客們進來為止。他發覺菲力普太太很留心聽他的話，她越聽就越把他看得了不起，而且決定一有空就把他的話傳播出去。至於小姐們，實在覺得等得太久，因為她們不樂意聽她們表兄的閒扯，又沒事可做，想彈彈琴又不行，只有照着壁爐架上那些瓷器的樣子，漫不經心地畫些小玩藝消遣消遣。等待的時間終於過去了，男客們來了。韋翰先生一走進來，伊莉莎白就覺得，無論是上次看見他的時候也好，從上次見面以來想起他也好，她都並沒對他產生過哪怕一丁點的盲目愛慕。某某郡的軍官們都是一批名譽很好的紳士氣派的人物，參加這次宴會的尤其是他們之中的精華。韋翰先生無論在人品上，相貌上，風度上，地位上，都遠遠地超過他們，正如他們遠遠地超過那位姨丈一樣——看那位肥頭胖耳、大腹便便的姨丈，他正帶着滿口葡萄酒味，跟着他們走進屋來。

韋翰先生是當天最得意的男子，差不多每個女人的眼睛都朝着他看；伊莉莎白是當天最得意的女子，韋翰終於在她的身旁坐了下來。他馬上就跟她攀談，雖然談的只是些當天晚上下雨和雨季可能就要到來之類的話，可是他那麼和顏悅色，使她不禁感覺到即使最平凡、最無聊、最陳舊的話，只要說話的人有技巧，還是一樣可以說得動聽。

說起要博得女性的青眼，柯林斯先生遇到像韋翰先生和軍官們這樣的勁敵，真變得無足輕重了。他在小姐們眼睛裏實在算不上甚麼，幸虧好心的菲力普太太有時候還聽聽他談話，她又十分細心，盡量把咖啡和鬆餅不斷地端給他吃。

一張張牌桌擺好以後，柯林斯便坐下來一同玩“惠斯特”[20]，總算有了一個機會報答她的好意。

他說：“我對這玩藝簡直一竅不通，不過我很願意把它學會，以我這樣的身份來說——”菲力普太太很感激他的好意，可是卻不願意聽他談論甚麼身份地位。

韋翰先生沒有玩“惠斯特”，因為他被小姐們高高興興地請到另一張桌子上去玩牌，坐在伊莉莎白和麗迪亞之間。剛開始的形勢很令人擔憂，因為麗迪亞是個十足的健談家，大有獨佔他的可能；好在她對於摸獎也同樣愛好，立刻對那玩意大感興趣，不停下注，得獎之後又大叫大喊，因此就無從特別注意到某一個人身上去了。韋翰先生一面跟大家應付這玩藝，一面從容不迫地跟伊莉莎白談話。伊莉莎白很願意聽他說話，很想了解一下他和達西先生過去的關係，可是她要聽的他未必肯講。於是她提也不敢提到那位先生。後來出人意料之外，韋翰先生竟自動地談到那個問題上去了，因此她的好奇心到底還是得到了滿足。韋翰先生問起尼德斐莊園離開麥里頓有多遠。她回答了他以後，他又吞吞吐吐地問起達西先生已經在那裏住了多久。

伊莉莎白説："大概有一個月了。"她不願意放過這個話題，又接着説："據我所知，他是德比郡的一個大財主。"

"是的，"韋翰回答道。"他的財產很可觀——每年有一萬鎊的淨收入。説起這方面，誰也沒有我知道得確切，因為我從小就和他家裏有特別關係。"

伊莉莎白不禁顯出詫異的神色。

"班奈特小姐，你昨天也許看到我們見面時那種冷冰冰的樣子吧，難怪你聽了我的話會覺得詫異。你和達西先生相熟嗎？"

"我也只希望跟他這麼熟就夠了，"伊莉莎白冒火地叫道。"我和他在一起相處了四天，覺得他很討厭。"

韋翰説："他究竟討人喜歡還是討人厭，我可沒有權利説出我的意見。我不便發表意見。我認識他太久，跟他也太熟，因此很難做一個判斷公正的人。我不可能做到大公無私。不過我敢説，你對他的看法會讓人嚇一跳的，或許你在別的地方就不會説得這樣過火吧。這裏都是你自己人呢。"

"老實説，除了在尼德斐莊園以外，我到附近任何人家裏去都會這樣説。赫福德郡根本就沒有人喜歡他。他那副傲慢的氣派，哪一個見了都討厭。你絕不會聽到任何人説他一句好話。"

停了一會，韋翰説："説句問心無愧的話，不管是他也好，是別人也好，都不應該受到人們過份的抬舉。不過對於他這個人，情況往往不是這樣。他有財有勢蒙蔽了天下人的耳目，他那目空一切、盛氣凌人的氣派又嚇壞了天下人，弄得大家只有順着他的心意去看待他。"

"我雖然跟他並不太熟，可是我認為他是個脾氣很壞的人。"韋翰聽了這話，只是搖頭。

等到有了説話的機會，他又接下去説："我不知道他是否打算在這個村莊裏多住些時候。”

“我完全不知道；不過，我在尼德斐莊園的時候，可沒有聽說他要走。你既然喜歡某某郡，打算在那裏工作，我但願你不要因為他在附近而影響了你原來的計劃。”

“噢，不；我才不會讓達西先生趕走呢。要是他不願意看到我，那就得他走。我們兩個人的交情搞壞了，我見到他就不好受，可是我沒有理由要避開他，我只是要讓大家知道他是怎樣虧待了我，他的為人處世怎樣使我痛心。班奈特小姐，他那去世的父親，那位老達西老先生，卻是天下最好心的人，也是我生平最真心的朋友；每當我和現在這位達西在一起的時候，就免不了勾起千絲萬縷溫存的回憶，從心底裏感到痛苦。他對待我的行為真是惡劣萬分；可是我千真萬確地相信，我一切都能原諒他，只是不能容忍他辜負他先人的厚望，辱沒他先人的名聲。”

伊莉莎白對這件事越來越感興趣，因此聽得很專心。但是這件事很蹊蹺，她不便進一步追問。

韋翰先生又隨便談了些一般的事情。他談到麥里頓，談到四鄰八舍和社交之類的事，凡是他所看到的事情，他談起來都非常欣喜，特別是談到社交問題的時候，他的談吐舉止更顯得文雅殷勤。

他又說：“我之所以喜歡某某郡，主要是因為這裏的社交界都是些上等人，又講交情，我又知道這支部隊名聲很好，受到大家愛護，加上我的朋友丹尼為了勸我上這裏來，又講起他們目前的營房是多麼好，麥里頓的人們對待他們又多麼殷勤，他們在麥里頓又結交了許多好朋友。我承認我是少不了社交生活的。我是個失意的人，精神上受不了孤寂。我一定要有職業和社交生活。我本來不打算過行伍生活，可是由於環境所迫，現在也只好加入軍隊了。我本應該做牧師的，家裏的意思本來也是要培養我做牧師；要是我博得了我們剛剛談到的這位先生的喜歡，說不定我現在也有一份很可觀的牧師俸祿呢。”

"是嗎？"

"怎麼會不是！老達西先生遺囑上說明，牧師職位一有了空缺就給我。他是我的教父，非常疼愛我。他對我的好意，我真無法形容。他要使我衣食豐裕，而且他自以為已經做到了這一點，可是等到牧師職位有了空缺的時候，卻落到別人名下去了。"

"天哪！"伊莉莎白叫道；"怎麼會有那種事情，怎麼能夠不依照他的遺囑辦事？你為何不依法申訴？"

"遺囑上講到遺產的地方，措辭很含混，因此我未必可以依法申訴。照理說，一個要面子的人是不會懷疑先人的意圖的；可是達西先生偏偏要懷疑，或者說，他認為遺囑上也只是說明有條件地提拔我，他硬要說我浪費和荒唐，因此要取消我的一切權利。總而言之，不說則已，說起來樣樣壞話都說到了。那個牧師位置居然在兩年前空出來了，那正是我夠年齡掌握那份俸祿的那年，可是卻給了另一個人。我實在無從責備我自己犯了甚麼過錯而活該失掉那份俸祿，除非說我性子急躁，心直口快，有時候難免在別人面前說出我對他的想法，甚至還當面頂撞他。也不過如此而已。只不過我們兩個性格差別太大，他因此懷恨我。"

"這真是駭人聽聞！應該讓他在公開場合丟丟臉。"

"遲早總會有人來讓他丟臉，可是我決不會去難為他的。除非我對他的先人忘恩負義，我決不會揭發他，跟他作對。"

伊莉莎白十分欽佩他這種見地，而且覺得他把這種見地講出來以後，他更加顯得英俊了。

停了一會，她又說道："可是他究竟是何居心？他為甚麼要這樣冷酷無情呢？"

"無非是決心要跟我結成不解的怨恨，我認為他這種結怨是出於某種程度上的嫉妒。要是老達西先生對我差一些，他的兒子自然就會和我相處得好一些。我相信就是因為他的父親太疼愛我了，這才使他從小就感到氣惱。他肚量狹窄，不能容忍我跟他競爭，不能容忍我比他強。"

"我想不到達西先生竟會這麼壞。雖說我從來沒有對他有過好感,可也不十分厭惡他。我只以為他看不起人,卻不曾想到他卑鄙到這樣的地步——竟懷着這樣惡毒的報復心,這樣的不講理,沒有人道!"

她思索了一下,便接下去說:"我的確記得,有一次他還在尼德斐莊園裏自鳴得意地說起,他跟別人結下了怨恨就無法消解,他生性就愛記仇。他的性格一定讓人很厭惡。"

韋翰回答道:"在這件事情上,我的意見不一定靠得住,因為我對他難免有成見。"

伊莉莎白又沉思了一會,然後大聲說道:"你是他父親的教子,朋友,是他父親所器重的人,他竟然這樣對待你!"她幾乎把這樣的話也說出口來:"他怎麼竟如此對待像你這樣的一個青年,光憑你相貌堂堂,一看就知道你是個和藹可親的人。"不過,她到底還是改成了這樣幾句話:"何況你從小就和他在一起,而且像你所說的,關係非常密切。"

"我們是在同一個教區,同一個花園裏長大的。我們的少年時代大部份是一起度過的——同住一幢房子,同在一起玩耍,受到同一個父親的疼愛。我父親所幹的行業就是您姨丈菲力普先生得心應手的那門行業,可是先父生前為了替老達西先生效勞,把自己的事都擱在一邊,用出全副精力來管理龐百利的財產。老達西先生對他極為器重,把他看做最知己的心腹朋友。老達西先生一向承認先父管家有方,使他受益匪淺,因此在先父臨終的時候,他便自動提出要負擔我一切的生活費用。我相信他之所以這樣做,一方面是對先父感恩,另一方面是因為疼愛我。"

伊莉莎白叫道:"多奇怪!多可惡!我真不明白,這位達西先生既然這樣有自尊心,怎麼又這樣虧待你!要是沒有別的更好的理由,那麼,他既是這麼驕傲,就應該不屑於這樣陰險——我一定要說這是陰險。"

"的確稀奇，"韋翰回答道；"歸根結底來說，差不多他的一切行動都是出於傲慢，傲慢成了他最好的朋友。照理說他既然傲慢，就應該最講求道德。可是人總免不了有自相矛盾的地方，他對待我就是意氣用事多於傲慢。"

"像他這種可惡的傲慢，對他自己有甚麼好處？"

"有好處；常常使他做起人來慷慨豪爽——花錢不吝嗇，待人殷勤、資助佃戶，救濟貧苦人。他之所以會這樣，都是因為門第祖先使他感到驕傲，他對於他父親的為人也很引以為傲。他主要就是為了不要有辱家聲，有違眾望，不要失掉龐百利族的聲勢。他還具有做哥哥身份的驕傲，這種驕傲，再加上一些手足的情份，使他成了他妹妹的親切而細心的監護人；你自會聽到大家都一致稱讚他是位體貼入微的最好的哥哥。"

"達西小姐是個怎麼樣的女子？"

韋翰搖搖頭。"我但願能夠說她一聲可愛。凡是達西家裏的人，我都不忍心說他們一句壞話。可是她的確太像她的哥哥了——非常非常傲慢。她小時候很親切，很討人喜愛，而且特別喜歡我。我常常陪她接連玩上幾個小時。可是現在我可不把她放在心上了。她是個漂亮小姐，大約十五六歲，而且據我所知，她也極有才幹。她父親去世以後，她就住在倫敦，有位太太陪她住在一起，教她讀書。"

他們又東拉西扯地談了好些別的話，談談歇歇，後來伊莉莎白不禁又扯到原來的話題上來。她說：

"我真奇怪，他竟會和賓利先生成為知己。賓利先生的性情那麼好，而且他的為人也極其和藹可親，怎麼會跟這樣一個人交起朋友來？他們怎麼能夠相處呢？你認識賓利先生嗎？"

"我不認識。"

"他的確是個和藹可親，脾氣好的人。他根本不會明白達西先生是怎樣一個人。"

"也許不明白；不過達西先生要討人喜歡的時候，他自有辦法。他的手腕很高明。只要他認為值得攀談，他也會談笑風生。他在那些地位跟他相等的人面前，在那些處境不及他的人面前，完全判若兩人。他處處傲慢，可是跟有錢人在一起的時候，他就顯得胸襟磊落、公正誠實、講道理、要面子，也許還會和和氣氣，這都是看在別人身價地位的份上。"

"惠斯特"牌散場了，玩牌的人都圍到另一張桌子上來，柯林斯先生站在他的表妹伊莉莎白和菲力普太太之間。菲力普太太照例問他贏了沒有。他沒有贏，他完全輸了。菲力普太太表示為他惋惜，於是他鄭重其事地告訴她說，區區小事何足掛齒，因為他根本不看重錢，請她不要覺得心裏不安。

他說："我很明白，太太，人只要坐上了牌桌，一切就得看自己的運氣了，幸好我並不把五個先令當作一回事。當然有些人就不會像我這樣說，也是幸虧了凱瑟琳‧德‧包爾夫人，有了她，我就不必為這點小數目心痛了。"

這話引起了韋翰先生的注意。韋翰看了柯林斯先生幾眼，便低聲問伊莉莎白，她這位親戚是不是和德‧包爾家很熟。

伊莉莎白回答道："凱瑟琳‧德‧包爾夫人最近給了他一個牧師職位。我完全不明白柯林斯先生是怎麼受到她賞識的，不過他一定沒有認識她多久。"

"想你一定知道凱瑟琳‧德‧包爾夫人和安妮‧達西夫人是姐妹吧。凱瑟琳夫人正是現在這位達西先生的姨母呢。"

"不知道，我的確不知道。關於凱瑟琳夫人的親戚，我半點都不知道。我還是前天才知道有她這個人的。"

"她的女兒德‧包爾小姐將來會繼承到一筆很大的財產，大家都相信她和她的表兄將來會把兩份家產合併起來。"

這話不禁讓伊莉莎白笑了起來，因為這使她想起了可憐的賓利小姐。要是達西果真已經另有心上人，那麼，賓利小姐的百般殷勤都是枉然。她對達西妹妹的關懷以及對達西本人的讚美，也完全白費了。

"柯林斯先生對凱瑟琳夫人母女兩人真是讚不絕口，可是聽他説起那位夫人來，有些地方真讓我不得不懷疑他説得有些過頭，對她感激得迷住了心竅。儘管她是他的恩人，她仍然是個既狂妄又自大的女人。"

"我相信她這兩種毛病都很嚴重，"韋翰回答道。"我有許多年沒見過她了，可是我記得我自己一向討厭她，因為她為人處世既專橫又無禮。大家都説她非常通情達理；不過我總認為大家之所以誇她能幹，一方面是因為她有財有勢，一方面因為她盛氣凌人，加上她又有那麼了不起的一個外甥，只有那些具有上流社會教養的人，才巴結得上他。"

伊莉莎白承認他這番話説得很有理。他們兩人繼續談下去，彼此十分投機，一直談到打牌散場吃宵夜的時候，別的小姐們才有機會分享一點韋翰先生的殷勤。菲力普太太宴請的這些客人們正在大聲喧嘩，簡直令人無法談話，好在光憑他的舉止風度，也就足以博得每個人的歡心了。他一言一語十分風趣，一舉一動非常文雅。伊莉莎白臨走時，腦子裏只想到他一個人。她在回家的路上一心只想到韋翰先生，想到他跟她説過的那些話，可是一路上麗迪亞和柯林斯先生完全沒有停過嘴，因此她連提到他名字的機會也沒有。麗迪亞不停地談到抓彩票，談到她哪一次輸了又哪一次贏了；柯林斯先生盡説些菲力普先生和菲力普太太的殷勤款待，又説打"惠斯特"輸了幾個錢他毫不在乎，又將晚餐的菜名一盤盤背出來，反覆説是怕自己讓表妹們覺得太擠。他要説的話太多，當馬車停在朗伯恩的屋門口時，他的話還沒有説完。

第十七章

第二天，伊莉莎白把韋翰先生跟她自己說的那些話全告訴了珍妮。珍妮聽得又是驚奇又是關心。她簡直不能相信，達西先生會這樣地不值得賓利先生器重；可是，像韋翰這樣一個青年美男子，她實在無從懷疑他說話不誠實。一想到韋翰可能真的受到這些虐待，她就不禁起了憐惜之心；因此她只得認為他們兩位先生都是好人，替他們雙方辯白，把一切無法解釋的事都解釋作意外和誤會。

珍妮說：「我認為他們雙方都受了別人的蒙蔽，至於是怎樣受到蒙蔽的，我們當然無從猜測，也許是哪一個有關的人從中挑撥是非。簡單地說，除非我們有確確實實的根據可以責怪任何一方，我們就無從憑空猜想出他們是為了甚麼事才不和睦的。」

「你這話說得不錯。那麼，親愛的珍妮，你將替這種有關的人說些甚麼話呢？你也得替這種人辯白一下呀，否則我們又不得不怪到某一個人身上去了。」

「你愛怎麼取笑就怎麼取笑吧，反正你總不能把我的意見笑掉。親愛的莉茲，你且想一想，達西先生的父親生前那樣地疼愛這個人，而且答應要贍養他，如今達西先生本人卻這般虐待他，那他簡直太不像話了。這是不可能的。一個人只要還有丁點的人道之心，只要多少還尊重自己的人格，就不會做出這種事來。難道他自己最知己的朋友，竟會被他蒙蔽到這種地步嗎？噢！不會的。」

「我還是認為賓利先生受了他的蒙蔽，並不認為韋翰先生昨天晚上跟我說的話是捏造的。他把一個個的人名，一件件的事實，都說得有根有據，毫無虛偽做作。倘若事實並非如此，那麼讓達西先生自己來辯白吧。你只要看看韋翰那副神情，就知道他沒有說假話。」

「這的確讓人很難說——也令人難受。讓人不知道怎麼去想才好。"

"説句你不見怪的話，我完全知道該怎麼樣去想。"

珍妮只有一件事情是猜得準的，那就是説，要是賓利先生果真受了蒙蔽，那麼，一旦真相大白，他一定會萬分痛心。

兩位年輕的小姐正在矮樹林裏談得起勁，忽然家裏派人來讓她們回去，因為有客人上門來——事情真湊巧，來的正是她們所談到的那幾位。原來尼德斐莊園下星期二要舉行一次期待已久的舞會，賓利先生跟他的姐妹們特地親自前來邀請她們參加。那兩位小姐非常高興與自己的好朋友重逢。她們認為自從分別以來，恍若隔世，而珍妮又一再被問起自分別以來做了些甚麼。她們對班奈特府上其餘的人簡直置若罔聞。她們盡量避免班奈特太太的糾纏，又很少跟伊莉莎白交談，至於對別的人，那就根本一句話也不説了。她們很快就告辭了，而且出乎她們的兄弟賓利先生的意料之外，那兩位小姐一骨碌從座位上站了起來，拔腿就走，好像急於要避開班奈特太太那些糾纏不清的繁文縟節似的。

尼德斐莊園要舉行舞會，這一件事使這一家的太太小姐都高興到極點。班奈特太太認為這次舞會是為了恭維她的大女兒才開的，而且這次舞會由賓利先生親自登門邀請，而不是發請帖來請，這令她更加高興。珍妮心裏只是想像着，到了那天晚上，便可以和兩個好朋友促膝談心，又可以受到她們兄弟的殷勤款待；伊莉莎白高興地想到可以跟韋翰先生跳好多好多次舞，又可以從達西先生的神情舉止中把事情的底細看個水落石出。至於凱瑟琳和麗迪亞，她們才不把開心作樂寄託於某一件事或某一個人身上，雖然她們兩人也跟伊莉莎白一樣，想要和韋翰先生跳上個大半夜，可是舞會上能夠使她們跳個痛快的舞伴決不止他一個人，何況舞會究竟是舞會。甚至連瑪莉也告訴家裏人説，她對於這次舞會也不是完全不感興趣。

瑪莉説："只要每天上午的時間能夠由我自己支配就夠了。我認為偶然參加參加晚會並不是甚麼犧牲。我們大家都應該有社交生活。我認為誰都少不了要有些消遣和娛樂。"

伊莉莎白這時真太高興了；她雖然本來不大跟柯林斯先生多話，現在也不禁問他是不是願意上賓利先生那裏去作客，如果願意，參加晚會又是否合適。出乎伊莉莎白的意料之外，柯林斯先生對於作客問題毫無猶豫，而且還敢跳舞，絲毫不怕大主教或凱瑟琳·德·包爾夫人的指責。

他說："老實告訴你，這樣的舞會，主人是一個品格高尚的青年，賓客又是些體面人，我決不認為會有甚麼不好的傾向。我非但不反對自己跳舞，而且希望當天晚上表妹們都肯賞臉。伊莉莎白小姐，我就利用這次機會請你陪我跳頭兩場舞，我相信珍妮表妹一定不會怪我對她有任何失禮吧，因為我這樣做有正當的理由。"

伊莉莎白覺得自己完全上了當。她本來一心要跟韋翰跳頭幾場舞，如今卻來了個柯林斯先生從中作梗！她從來沒有像現在這樣掃興過，不過事到如今，已無法補救。韋翰先生跟她自己的幸福不得不耽擱一下了，她於是極其和顏悅色地答應了柯林斯先生的請求。她一想到柯林斯此番殷勤乃是別有用心，她就不太樂意。她首先就想到他已經在她的幾個姐妹中間看中了自己，認為她配做漢斯福牧師家裏的主婦，而且當洛欣莊園沒有更適合的賓客時，打起牌來要是三缺一，她也可以湊湊數。她這個想法立刻得到了證實，因為她觀察到他對她越來越殷勤，老是恭維她聰明活潑。雖然從這場風波中足以看出她誘人的魅力，她可並不因此得意，反而感到驚奇。她的母親不久又跟她說，他們兩人是可能結婚的，這可讓她這個做母親的很滿意。伊莉莎白對母親這句話只當作沒有聽見，因為她非常明白，只要跟母親搭起腔來，就免不了要大吵一場。柯林斯先生也許不會提出求婚，既然他還沒有明白提出，那又何必為了他爭吵。

自從尼德斐莊園邀請班奈特家的幾位小姐參加舞會的那天起，到開舞會的那天為止，雨一直下個不停，弄得班家幾個年紀小的女兒們沒有到麥里頓去過一次，也無從去看望姨母，訪問軍官和打聽新聞。要不是把參加舞會的事拿來談談，準備準備，那她們真要可憐死了。她們連跳舞鞋子上要用的玫瑰花也是請別人去代買的。甚至伊莉莎白也對這種天氣厭惡極了，就是這種天氣弄得她和韋翰先生的友誼毫無進展。總算下星期二有個舞會，這才能夠令凱蒂和麗迪亞熬過星期五、星期六、星期日和星期一。

第十八章

伊莉莎白走進尼德斐莊園的會客室，在一羣穿着"紅制服"的人裏面尋找韋翰先生，找來找去都找不到，她從來沒有一絲懷疑他會不來。雖然想起了過去的種種事情而頗為擔心，可是她的信心並沒有因此受到影響，她比平常更小心地打扮了一番，高高興興地準備要把他那顆沒有被征服的心完全征服。她相信在今天的晚會上，一定會讓她把他那顆心完全贏到手。但是過了一會，她起了一種可怕的懷疑：莫非賓利先生請軍官們的時候，為了討達西先生的好，故意沒有請韋翰嗎？雖然事實並非如此，不過他缺席的原委馬上就由他的朋友丹尼先生宣佈了。這是因為麗迪亞迫不及待地問丹尼，丹尼就告訴她們說，韋翰前一天上城裏辦事去了，還沒有回來，又帶着意味深長的微笑補充了幾句：

"我想，他要不是為了要迴避這裏的某一位先生，決不會就這麼湊巧，偏偏這時候因事缺席。"

他這個消息麗迪亞雖然沒有理解，卻讓伊莉莎白參透了。伊莉莎白因此斷定：關於韋翰缺席的原因，雖然她開始沒有猜對，卻依舊是達西先生一手造成的。她覺得非常掃興，對達西也就更加起了反感，因此後來當達西走上前來向她問好的時候，她簡直不能好聲好氣地回答他。要知道，對達西殷勤、寬容、忍耐，就等於傷害韋翰。她決定不跟他說一句話，快快不樂地掉過頭來就走，甚至跟賓利先生說起話來也不大快樂，因為他對達西的盲目偏愛引起了她的氣憤。

伊莉莎白天生不大會發脾氣，雖然她今天晚上大為掃興，可是她情緒上並沒有不愉快多少時候。她先把滿腔的愁苦都告訴了那位一星期沒有見面的夏綠蒂·盧卡斯小姐，過了一會又自告奮勇地把她表兄奇奇怪怪的情形訴說給她，一面又特別把他指出來給她看。

頭兩場舞重新使她覺得煩惱，那是兩場活受罪的舞。柯林斯先生又呆笨又刻板，只知道道歉，卻不知道小心一些，往往腳步弄錯了而不自知。他真是個十足令人討厭的舞伴，使她丟盡了臉，受盡了罪。因此，從他手裏解脫出來，真讓她欣喜若狂。

她接着跟一位軍官跳舞，跟他談起韋翰的事。聽他説，韋翰是個到處討人喜愛的人，於是她精神上舒服了許多。跳過這幾場舞以後，她就回到夏綠蒂‧盧卡斯身邊，跟她談話。這時候突然聽到達西先生叫她，出其不意地請她跳舞，她吃了一驚，竟然不由自主地答應了他。達西又立刻走開了，於是她口口聲聲怪自己為甚麼這樣沒有主意。夏綠蒂盡力安慰她。

"你將來一定會發覺他很討人喜歡的。"

"天理不容！那才是倒了天大的霉呢！下定了決心去恨一個人，竟會一下子又接受起他來！別這樣咒我吧。"

當跳舞重新開始、達西又走到她面前來請她跳舞的時候，夏綠蒂禁不住跟她咬了咬耳朵，提醒她別做傻瓜，別為了對韋翰有好感，就寧可得罪一個比韋翰的身價高上十倍的人。伊莉莎白沒有回答便下了舞池，她想不到居然會有這樣的體面，跟達西先生面對面跳舞，她看見身旁的人們也同樣露出了驚奇的目光。他們兩人跳了一會，一句話也沒有交談。她想像着這兩場舞可能一直要沉默到底，剛開始時決定不要打破這種沉默，後來突然異想天開，認為如果逼得她的舞伴不得不説幾句話，那就會讓他受更大的罪，於是她就説了幾句關於跳舞方面的話。他回答了她的話，接着又是沉默。停了幾分鐘，她第二次跟他攀談——

"現在該輪到你談談了，達西先生。我既然談了跳舞，你就得談談舞池的大小以及有多少對舞伴之類的問題。"

他笑了笑，告訴她説，她要他説甚麼他就説甚麼。

"好極了；這種回答目前也説得過去了。過一會我或許會談到私人舞會比公共場所的舞會來得好；不過，我們現在可以不必作聲了。"

"那麼説，你跳起舞來照例總得要談上幾句嗎？"

"有時候要的。你知道，一個人總得要説些話。接連半個小時在一起一聲不響，那是夠彆扭的。不過有些人就偏偏覺得説話越少越好，為這些人着想，談話也不妨可以少一點。"

"在目前這樣的情況下，你是在照顧你自己的情緒呢，還是想要使我情緒上快慰？"

"一舉兩得，"伊莉莎白油滑地回答道。"因為我老是感覺到我們兩人的念頭很相同。你我的性格跟別人都不太合得來，又不願意多説話，難得開口，除非想説幾句一鳴驚人的話，讓大家當作格言來流傳千古。"

他説："我覺得你的性格並不見得就是這樣，我的性格是否很近似這方面，我也不敢説。你一定覺得你自己形容得很恰當吧。"

"我當然不能為自己下斷語。"

他沒有回答，他們兩人又沉默了，直等到又跳了一陣舞，他這才問她是不是常常和姐妹們上麥里頓去溜達。她回答説常常去。她説到這裏，實在按捺不住了，便接下去説："你那天在那裏碰到我們的時候，我們正在結交一個新朋友呢。"

這句話立刻產生了效果。一陣傲慢的陰影罩上了他的臉，可是他一句話也沒有説。伊莉莎白也説不下去了，不過她心裏卻在埋怨自己軟弱。後來還是達西很勉強地先開口説：

"韋翰先生生來滿面春風，交起朋友來得心應手。至於他是不是能和朋友們長久相處，那就不太靠得住了。"

伊莉莎白加重語氣回答道："他真不幸，竟失去了您的友誼，而且弄成那麼尷尬的局面，可能會使他一輩子都感受痛苦。"

達西沒有回答，好像想要換個話題。就在這時，威廉·盧卡斯爵士走近他們身邊，打算穿過舞池走到房間的那一邊去，可是一看到達西先生，他就停住了，禮貌周全地向他鞠了一躬，滿口稱讚他跳舞跳得好，舞伴又找得好。

“我真太高興了，親愛的先生，舞跳得這麼好，真是少見。你毫無疑問是屬於第一流的人才。讓我再嘮叨一句，你這位漂亮的舞伴也真配得上你，我真希望常常有這種眼福，特別是將來有一天某一件好事如願的時候，親愛的伊麗莎小姐。”（他朝着她的姐姐和賓利望了一眼）“那時候將會有怎樣熱鬧的祝賀場面啊。我要求達西先生：——可是我還是別打擾你吧，先生。你正在和這位小姐談得心醉神迷，如果我耽擱了你，你是不會感激我的，她那一雙明亮的眼睛也在責備我呢。”

後半段話達西幾乎沒有聽見。可是威廉爵士提起他那位朋友，卻不免讓他心頭大受震動，於是他一本正經地去望着那正在跳舞的賓利和珍妮。他馬上又鎮定了下來，掉轉頭來對他自己的舞伴說：

“威廉爵士打斷了我們的話，我簡直記不起我們剛剛談些甚麼了。”

“我覺得我們根本就沒有談甚麼。這舞廳裏隨便哪兩個人都不比我們說話說得少，因此威廉爵士打斷不了甚麼話。我們已經換過兩三次話題，總是談不投機，以後還要談些甚麼，我實在想不出了。”

“談談書本如何？”他笑着說。

“書本！噢，不；我相信我們讀過的書不會一樣，我們的體會也各有不同。”

“你會這樣想，我真抱歉；假定真是那樣，也不見得就無從談起。我們也可以把不同的見解比較一下。”

“不——我無法在舞場裏談書本；我腦子裏老是想着些別的事。”

“目前的場面老是吸引你的注意力，是不是？”他帶着猶疑的眼光問。

“是的，老是這樣，”她答道。其實她並不知道自己在說些甚麼，她的思想跑到老遠的地方去了，你且聽她突然一下子說出這樣的話吧：“達西先生，我記得有一次聽見你說，你素來不能原諒別人——

你和別人一旦結下仇怨，就消除不掉。我想，你結怨的時候總該是很慎重的吧？"

"正是，"他堅決地說。

"你從來不會受到偏見的蒙蔽嗎？"

"我想不會。"

"對於某些堅持己見的人來說，在拿定一個主張的時候，首先應該特別慎重地考慮一下。"

"是否可以允許我請教你一聲，你問我這些話用意何在？"

她竭力裝出若無其事的神情說："只不過為了要解釋解釋你的性格罷了，我想要把你的性格弄個明白。"

"那麼你究竟弄明白了沒有？"

她搖搖頭。"我一點也弄不明白。我聽到大家對於你的看法極不一致，讓我不知道相信誰的話才好。"

他嚴肅地答道："別人對於我的看法極不一致，我相信其中一定大有出入。班奈特小姐，我希望你目前還是不要刻畫我的性格，我怕這樣做，結果對於你我都沒有好處。"

"可是，倘若我現在不了解你一下，以後就沒有機會了。"

於是他冷冷地答道："我決不會打斷你的興頭。"她便沒有再說下去。他們兩人又跳了一次舞，於是就默默無言地分手了。兩個人都快快不樂，不過程度上不同罷了。達西心裏對她頗有好感，因此一下子就原諒了她，把一肚子氣憤都轉到另一個人身上去了。

他們兩人剛分開不久，賓利小姐就走到伊莉莎白面前來，帶着一種又輕蔑又客氣的態度對她說：

"噢，伊麗莎小姐，我聽說你對喬治·韋翰很有好感！你姐姐剛才還跟我談到他，問了我一大堆的話。我發覺那年輕人雖然把甚麼事都說給你聽了，可就偏偏忘了說他自己是老達西先生的賬房老韋翰的兒子。他說達西先生對他不好，那完全是胡說，讓我站在朋友的立場奉勸你，不要盲目相信他的話。達西先生一直對他太好了，只是喬治・韋翰用卑鄙的手段對付達西先生。詳細情形我不清楚，不過這件事我完全知道，一點也不應該怪達西先生。達西一聽見別人提到喬治・韋翰就受不了。我哥哥這次宴請軍官們，本來也很難把他踢開，總算他自己知趣迴避了，我哥哥才免卻擔憂。他跑到這個村裏來真是太荒謬了，我不懂他怎麼竟敢這樣做。伊麗莎小姐，我對你不起，揭穿了你心上人的過錯。可是事實上你只要看看他那種出身，當然就不會指望他會幹出甚麼好事來。”

伊莉莎白生氣地說：“照你的說法，他的過錯和他的出身好像是一回事了，我倒沒有聽到你說他別的不是，只聽到你罵他是達西先生的賬房的兒子，老實告訴你，這一點他早已親自跟我講過了。”

“對不起，請原諒我好管閒事；不過我是出於一片好意。”賓利小姐說完這話，冷笑了一下，便走開了。

“無禮的女人！”伊莉莎白自言自語地說。“你可是大錯特錯了，你以為這樣卑鄙地攻擊別人一下，就能影響我對他的看法嗎？你這種攻擊，倒讓我看穿了你自己的頑固無知和達西先生的陰險。”她接着便去找她自己的姐姐，因為姐姐也向賓利問起過這件事。只見珍妮滿臉堆笑，容光煥發，這足以說明當天晚會上的種種情景使她多麼滿意。伊莉莎白頓時就看出了她的心情；於是頃刻之間就把她自己對於韋翰的關懷、對於他仇人們的怨憤，以及其他種種感覺，都打消了，一心只希望珍妮能夠順利地走上幸福的道路。

她也和姐姐同樣滿面堆笑地說道：“我想問問你，你有沒有聽到甚麼有關韋翰先生的事？也許你太高興了，想不到第三個人身上去吧；果真是那樣的話，我一定可以諒解你的。”

“沒有，”珍妮回答道，“我並沒有忘記他，可惜我沒有甚麼滿意的消息可以告訴你。賓利先生並不清楚他的全部底細，至於他主要在哪些方面得罪了達西先生，賓利先生更是一無所知；不過他可以擔保他自己的朋友品行良好，誠實正派，他並且以為達西先生過去對待韋翰先生已經好得過份了。說來遺憾，從他的話和她妹妹的話來看，韋翰先生決不是一個正派的青年。我怕他果真是太莽撞，而招致達西先生不去理睬他。"

"難道賓利先生自己不認識韋翰先生嗎？"

"不認識，那天上午在麥里頓他還是初次和他見面。"

"那麼，他這一番話是從達西先生那裏聽來的了。我滿意極了。關於那個牧師職位的問題，他是怎麼說的？"

"他只不過聽達西先生說起過幾次，詳細情況他可記不清了，可是他相信，那個職位雖然規定了是給韋翰先生的，可也是有條件的。"

伊莉莎白懇切地說："賓利先生當然是個誠實君子了，可是請你原諒，光憑幾句話並不能令我信服。賓利先生祖護他自己朋友的那些話，也許說得很有力；不過，他既然弄不清這件事的某些情節，而且另外一些情節又是聽他朋友自己說的，那麼，我還是不願意改變我原來對他們兩位先生的看法。"

她於是換了一個話題，使她們兩人都能談得更稱心。她們在這方面的意見是完全一致的。伊莉莎白高興地聽着珍妮談起，她在賓利先生身上雖然不敢存奢望，卻寄託着幸福的心願；她於是盡心竭力說了許多話來增加姐姐的信心。不久，賓利先生走到她們這裏來了，伊莉莎白便退到盧卡斯小姐身邊去。盧卡斯小姐問她跟剛才那位舞伴跳得是否愉快，她還沒有來得及回答，只見柯林斯先生走上前來，欣喜欲狂地告訴她們說，他極其幸運地發現了一件至關重要的事。

他說："這真是完全出乎我意料之外，我竟然發現這舞廳裏有一位是我女恩人的至親。我湊巧聽到一位先生跟主人家的那位小姐說，他自己的表妹德·包爾小姐和他的姨母凱瑟琳夫人。這些事真是太巧合了！誰想得到我會在這次的舞會上碰到凱瑟琳·德·包爾夫人的外甥呢！謝天謝地，我這個發現正是時候，還來得及去問候他，我打算現在就去，相信他一定不會怪我沒有早些去問候他吧。

我根本就不知道有這門親戚，因此還有道歉的餘地。"

"你不打算去向達西先生自我介紹嗎？"

"我當然打算去。我一定去求他原諒，請他不要怪我沒有早些問候他。我相信他是凱瑟琳夫人的外甥。我可以告訴他說，上星期我還見到老夫人，她身體着實健康。"

伊莉莎白竭力勸他不要那麼做，她說，他如果不經過別人介紹就去招呼達西先生，達西先生一定會認為他冒昧唐突，而不會認為他是奉承他姨母，又說雙方根本不必打交道，即使要打交道，也應該由地位比較高的達西先生先來結交他。柯林斯先生聽她這麼說，便顯出一副堅決的神氣，表示非照着自己的意思去做不可，等她說完了，他回答道：

"親愛的伊莉莎白小姐，你對於一切問題都有卓越的見解，我非常敬佩，可是請你聽我說一句：世俗人的禮節跟教士們的禮節大不相同。請聽我說，我認為從尊嚴方面看來，一個教士的位置可以比得上一個君侯，只要你能同時保持相當的謙虛。所以，這一次你應該讓我照着我自己良心的吩咐，去做好我認為應當做的事情。請原諒我沒有領受你的指教，要是在任何其他的問題上，我一定把你的指教當作座右銘。不過對於當前這個問題，我覺得，由於我還算讀書明理，平日也曾稍事鑽研，由我自己來決定比由你這樣一位年輕小姐來決定要合適些。"他深深鞠了一躬，便離開了她，去糾纏達西先生了。於是她迫不及待地望着達西先生，看他怎樣對待這種冒失行為，料想達西先生對於這種問候方式一定要大為驚訝。只見她這位表兄先恭恭敬敬地對達西鞠了個躬，然後再開口跟他說話。伊莉莎白雖然一句也沒聽到他說些甚麼，卻又好像聽到了他所有的話，因為從他那蠕動嘴唇的動作看來，他無非口口聲聲盡說些"道歉"、"漢斯福"、"凱瑟琳・德・包爾夫人"之類的話。她看到表兄在這樣的一個人面前出醜，心中好不氣惱。達西先生帶着毫不掩飾的驚奇目光斜睨着他，等到後來柯林斯先生嘮叨夠了，達西才帶着一副敬而遠之的神情，敷衍了他幾句。柯林斯先生卻並不因此而灰心掃興，不再開口。等他第二次開口嘮叨的時候，達西先生的輕蔑的神氣顯得更露骨了。他說完以後，達西先生隨便欠了欠身子就走開了。柯林斯先生這才回到伊莉莎白面前來。

他跟伊莉莎白說："告訴你，他那樣接待我，我實在沒有理由感到不滿意。達西聽到我的殷勤問候，好像十分高興。他禮貌周全地回答了我的話，甚至恭維我說，他非常佩服凱瑟琳夫人的眼力，沒有提拔錯了人。這的確是個聰明的想法。大體上說，我很滿意他。"

伊莉莎白既然對舞會再也沒有甚麼興致，於是幾乎把全部注意力都轉移到她的姐姐和賓利先生身上去了。她把當場的情景都看在眼裏，想像出了許多可喜的事情，幾乎跟珍妮感到同樣的快活。她想像着姐姐做了這莊園的主婦，夫婦之間恩愛彌篤，幸福無比。她覺得如果真有這樣一天，那麼，連賓利的兩個姐妹，她也可以盡量對她們產生好感。她看見她母親很明顯也轉着同樣的念頭，因此決定不要冒險走到母親面前去，免得又要聽她嘮叨個沒完。因此當大家坐下來吃飯的時候，她看到母親的座位跟她隔得那麼近，覺得真是受罪。只見母親老是跟那個人（盧卡斯太太）在信口亂說，毫無忌諱，而且盡談些她怎樣盼望珍妮馬上跟賓利先生結婚之類的話，這讓伊莉莎白更加氣惱。她們對這件事越談越起勁，班奈特太太不停說着這段姻緣有多少多少好處。首先，賓利先生是那麼英俊的一個青年，那麼有錢，住的地方離她們只有三英里路，這些條件令人十分滿意。其次，他的兩個姐妹非常喜歡珍妮，一定也像她一樣地希望能夠結成這頭親事，這一點也很令人快慰。再其次，珍妮的親事既然攀得這麼稱心如意，那麼，幾個小女兒也就有希望碰上別的闊人。最後再說到她那幾個沒有出嫁的女兒，關於她們的終身大事，從此也可以委託給大女兒，不必要她自己再為她們去應酬交際了。於情於理，這都是一件值得高興的事，怎奈班奈特太太生平就不慣於守在家裏。她又預祝盧卡斯太太馬上也會有同樣的幸運，其實她明明是在趾高氣昂地料定她沒有這個福份。

伊莉莎白一心想要挫挫她母親的談鋒，便勸她談起得意的事情來要放輕聲浪，因為達西先生就坐在她們對面，大部份的話都讓他聽到了。可惜事與願違，她的母親只顧罵她廢話，她真是說不出的氣惱。

"我倒請問你，達西先生與我有甚麼關係，我為何要怕他？我沒有理由要在他面前特別講究禮貌，難道他不愛聽的話我就不能說嗎？"

"看老天爺份上，媽媽，小聲點說吧。你得罪了達西先生有甚麼好處？你這樣做，他的朋友也不會看得起你的。"

不過，任憑她怎麼說都不奏效。她的母親偏偏要揚聲發表高見。伊莉莎白又羞又惱，臉色紅了又紅。她禁不住一眼望着達西先生，每望一眼就更加證實了自己的疑慮，因為達西雖然並沒有老是看着她的母親，卻肯定是一直在留心聽她高談闊論。他臉上先是顯出氣憤和厭惡的表情，慢慢地變得冷靜莊重，一本正經。

後來班奈特太太話說完了，盧卡斯太太聽她談得那樣志得意滿，自己又沒有份，早已呵欠連連，現在總算可以來安心享用一點冷肉冷雞了。伊莉莎白現在也算鬆了口氣。可惜她耳朵裏並沒有清靜多久，因為宵夜一吃完，大家就談起要唱唱歌。伊莉莎白眼看着瑪莉經不起別人稍微慫恿一下就答應了大家的請求，覺得很難受。她曾經頻頻向瑪莉打眼色，又再三地默默勸告她，竭力讓她不要這樣討好別人，可惜始終枉費心機。瑪莉絲毫不理會她的用意。這種出風頭的機會她是求之不得的，於是她就開始唱起來了。伊莉莎白極其痛苦地盯着她，帶着焦慮的心情聽她唱了幾節。等到唱完了，她的焦慮絲毫沒有減輕，因為瑪莉一聽到大家對她稱謝，還有人隱約表示要她再賞他們一次臉。於是休息了半分鐘以後，她又唱起了另一支歌。瑪莉本身是不適宜於這種表演的，因為她嗓子細弱，態度又不自然。伊莉莎白真急得要命。她看了看珍妮，看看她是不是受得了，只見珍妮正在安安靜靜地跟賓利先生談天。她又看見賓利先生的兩位姐妹正在彼此擠眉弄眼，一面對着達西做手勢，達西依舊板着面孔。她最後對自己的父親望了一眼，求他來攔阻一下，免得瑪莉整夜唱下去。父親領會了她的意思，他等瑪莉唱完了第二支歌，便大聲說道：

"你已經做得很好了，孩子。你使我們開心得夠久了。留點時間給別的小姐們表演表演吧。"

瑪莉雖然裝做沒聽見，心裏多少有些不自在。伊莉莎白為她感到不好受，也為她爸爸的那番話感到不好受，生怕自己一片苦心完全白費。幸好這時大家請別的人來唱歌了。

柯林斯先生說："假如我僥倖會唱歌，那我一定樂意給大家高歌一曲；我認為音樂是一種高尚的娛樂，和牧師的職業絲毫沒有牴觸。不過我並不是說，我們應該在音樂上花上太多的時間，因為的確還有許多別的事要做。負責一個教區的主管牧師有許多事要做。首先，他得制訂什一稅 [21] 的條例，既要訂得於自己有利，又要不侵犯恩人的利益。他得自己編寫道文，之後剩下的時間就不多了。他還得利用這點時間來安排教區裏的事務，照料和收拾自己的住宅——住宅總少不了要盡量弄得舒舒服服。還有一點我認為也很重要：他對待每一個人都得殷勤和藹，特別是那些提拔他的人。我認為這是他應盡的責任。再說，遇到恩人的家屬親友，凡是在應該表示尊敬的場合下，總得表示尊敬，否則是不像話的。"他說到這裏，向達西先生鞠了一躬，算是結束了他的話。他這一席話說得那麼響亮，半個舞廳裏的人都聽得見。許多人看呆了，許多人笑了，可是沒有一個人像班奈特先生那樣聽得有趣，他的太太卻一本正經地誇獎柯林斯先生的話真說得合情合理，她湊近了盧卡斯太太說，他顯然是個很聰明優秀的青年。

伊莉莎白覺得她家裏人好像是約定今天晚上到這裏來盡量出醜，而且可以說是從來沒有那樣起勁，從來沒有那樣成功。她覺得姐姐和賓利先生真算幸運，有些出醜的場面沒有看到，而幸好賓利先生即使看到了一些可笑的情節，也不會輕易感到難受。不過他的兩個姐妹和達西先生竟抓住這個機會來嘲笑她的親人，這已經是夠難堪的了。至於那位先生無聲的蔑視和兩位小姐無禮的嘲笑，究竟哪一樣更令人難堪，她不能斷定。

晚會的後半段時間也沒有給她帶來甚麼樂趣。柯林斯先生一直不肯離開她身邊，還一直和她打趣。雖然他無法請她再跟他跳一次舞，可是卻弄得她也無法跟別人跳。她要求他跟別人去跳，並且答應給他介紹一位小姐，可是他不肯。他告訴她說，講到跳舞，他完全沒有興趣，他的主要用意就是要小心侍候她，好博得她的歡心，因此他打定主意整個晚上留在她身邊。無論怎樣跟他解釋也沒用。幸好她的朋友盧卡斯小姐常常來到他們身邊，好心好意地和柯林斯先生攀談攀談，她才算覺得解脫一些。

至少達西先生可以不再來惹她生氣了。他雖然常常站得離她很近，邊上也沒有人，卻一直沒有走過來跟她說話。她覺得這可能是因為她提到了韋翰先生的緣故，她因此不禁暗自慶幸。

在全場賓客中，朗伯恩一家人最後走，而且班奈特太太還用了點手腕，藉口等候馬車，一直等到大家走完了，她們一家人還多留了十五分鐘。她們在這一段時間裏看到主人家有些人非常指望她們趕快走。赫斯托太太姐妹兩人除了抱怨簡直不開口說話，顯然是在下逐客令了。班奈特太太一開口想跟她們攀談，就被她們拒絕了，弄得大家都沒精打采。柯林斯先生儘管在發表長篇大論，恭維賓利先生和他的姐妹們，說他們家的宴席多麼精美，他們對待客人多麼殷勤有禮，可是他的話也沒有能給大家增加一些生氣。達西一句話也沒有說。班奈特先生同樣沒作聲，站在那裏袖手旁觀。賓利先生和珍妮站得離大家遠一些，正在親親密密地交談。伊莉莎白像赫斯托太太和賓利小姐一樣，始終不開口。連麗迪亞也覺得太疲乏了，沒有說話，只是偶然叫一聲：「天啊，我多麼疲倦！」接着便大聲打了一個呵欠。

後來她們終於起身告辭了，班奈特太太懇切備至地說，希望在最短期間以內，賓利先生闔府都到朗伯恩去玩，又特別對賓利先生本人說，要是哪天他能上她們家去吃頓便飯，也不要正式下請帖，那她們真是榮幸之至。賓利先生欣喜異常，連忙說，他明天就要動身到倫敦去住一小段時期，等他回來以後，一有機會就去拜訪她。

班奈特太太滿意極了，走出屋來，一路打着如意算盤：不出三四個月時間，她就可以看到自己的女兒在尼德斐莊園找到歸宿了，她少不了要準備一些財產、嫁妝和新的馬車。她同樣相信另一個女兒一定會嫁給柯林斯先生，然而這頭親事雖然沒有大女兒的那頭親事般高興，她可也是相當滿意了。在所有的女兒裏面，她最不喜歡伊莉莎白。儘管姑爺的人品和門第，配她已經綽綽有餘，可是比起賓利先生和尼德斐莊園來，就顯得黯然失色了。

第十九章

第二天，朗伯恩發生了一件新的事情。柯林斯先生正式提出婚約了。他的假期到下星期六就期滿，於是決定不再耽擱時間，況且當時他絲毫也不覺得有甚麼不好意思，便有條不紊地着手進行起來。凡是他認為必不可少的正常步驟，他都照辦了。剛一吃過早飯，看到班奈特太太、伊莉莎白和一個小妹妹在一起，他便對那位做母親的這樣說：

"太太，今天早上我想要請令嬡伊莉莎白賞光，跟我作一次私人談話，你贊成嗎？"

伊莉莎白驚奇得漲紅了臉，還沒來得及有所表示，班奈特太太連忙回答道：

"噢，好極了，當然可以。我相信莉茲也很樂意的，我相信她不會反對。——來，凱蒂；跟我上樓去。"她把針線收拾了一下，便匆匆忙忙走開了，這時伊莉莎白叫起來了：

"親愛的媽媽，別走。我懇求你別走。柯林斯先生一定會原諒我。別人不用聽的話，他也不要跟我說。我也要走了。"

"不，不；你別胡扯，莉茲。我要你留在你原來的地方。"只見伊莉莎白又惱又窘，好像真要逃離的樣子，於是她又說道："我非要你留在這裏聽柯林斯先生說話不可。"

伊莉莎白不便違抗母命。她考慮了一下，覺得能夠趕快悄悄地把事情解決了更為上策，於是她重新坐了下來，時時刻刻當心着，不讓啼笑皆非的心情流露出來。班奈特太太和凱蒂走開了，她們一走，柯林斯先生便開口說話：

"說真的，伊莉莎白小姐，你害羞怕臊，非但對你沒有絲毫損害，而且更增加了你的魅力。要是你不這樣稍稍推諉一下，我反而不會覺得你這麼可愛了。可是請你允許我告訴你一聲，我這次跟你求婚，是獲得了令堂大人的允許的。儘管你天性羞怯，假癡假呆，可是我對你的百般殷勤，已經表現得非常明顯，你一定會明白我說話的用意。我差不多一踏進朗伯恩，就挑中了你做我的終身伴侶。不過關於這個問題，也許最好趁我現在還控制得住我自己情感的時候，先談談我要結婚的理由，更要談一談我來到赫福德郡擇偶的打算，因為我的確是存着那種打算的。"

想到柯林斯這麼一本正經的樣子，居然會控制不住他自己的感情，伊莉莎白不禁覺得非常好笑，因此他雖然說話停了片刻，她可沒有來得及阻止他往下說：

"我之所以要結婚，有這樣幾點理由：第一，我認為凡是像我這樣生活寬裕的牧師，理當給全教區樹立一個婚姻的好榜樣；其次，我深信結婚會大大地促進我的幸福；第三，這一點或許我應該早點提出來，我三生有幸，能夠侍候上這樣高貴的一個女恩人，她特別提議並贊成我結婚。蒙她兩次替我在這件事情上提出了意見（而且並不是我請教她的！）。就在我離開漢斯福的前一個星期六晚上，我們正在玩牌，詹金森太太正在為德·包爾小姐安放腳凳，夫人對我說：'柯林斯先生，你必須結婚。像你這樣的一個牧師，必須結婚。好好去挑選吧，為了我，也為了你自己，挑選一個賢內助；人要活潑生動，要能做事，不求出身高貴，但要會持家，把一筆小小的收入安排得妥妥貼貼。這就是我的意見。趕快找個這樣的女人來吧，把她帶到漢斯福來，我自會照料她的。'好表妹，讓我說給你聽吧：凱瑟琳·德·包爾夫人對我的體貼照顧，也可以算是我一個優越的條件。她的為人我真無法形容，有一天你會體驗得到。我想，你這樣聰明活潑一定會討她喜歡，只要你在她那樣身份高貴的人面前顯得穩重端莊些，她就會特別喜歡你。大體上我要結婚就是為的這些打算；現在還得說一說，我們自己村裏多的是年輕可愛的小姐，我為甚麼看中了朗伯恩，而沒有看中我自己村莊的呢？事情是這樣的：往後令尊過世（但願他長命百歲），得由我繼承財產，因此我打算娶他一個女兒作家室，使得將來這件不愉快的事發生的時候，你們的損失可以盡量減輕一些，否則我實在過意不去。當然，正如我剛才說過的，這事情也許要在許多年以後才會發生。我的動機就是這樣，好表妹，恕我不揣冒昧地說一句，你不至於因此就看不起我吧。現在我的話已經說完，除非是再用最激動的語言把我最熱烈的感情向你傾訴。說到妝奩財產，我完全無所謂，我決不會在這方面向你父親提出甚麼要求。我非常了解，他的能力也辦不到，你名下應得的財產，一共不過是一筆年息四厘的一千鎊存款，還得等你媽媽死後才歸你所得。因此關於那個問題，我也一聲不響，而且請你放心，我們結婚以後，我決不會說一句小氣話。”

現在可是非打斷他的話不可了。

“你太心急了吧，先生，”她叫了起來。“你忘了我根本沒有回答你呢。別再浪費時間，就讓我來回答你吧。謝謝你的誇獎。你的求婚使我感到榮幸，可惜我除了謝絕之外，別無辦法。”

柯林斯先生鄭重其事地揮了揮手回答道：“年輕的小姐們遇到第一次求婚，即使心裏願意答應，口頭上總是拒絕；有時候甚至會拒絕兩次三次。這樣看來，你剛才所說的話決不會讓我灰心，我希望不久就能領你到神的祭壇前去呢 [22]。”

伊莉莎白大聲說道：“不瞞你說，先生，我既然話已經說出了口，你還要存着指望，那真太奇怪了。老實跟你說，如果世上真有那麼膽大的年輕小姐，拿自己的幸福去冒險，要別人提出第二次請求，那我也不是這種人。我的謝絕完全是嚴肅的。你不能使我幸福，而且我相信，我也絕對不能使你幸福。唔，要是你的朋友凱瑟琳夫人認識我的話，我相信她一定會發覺，我無論在哪一方面，都不配做你的太太。”

柯林斯先生嚴肅地說：“就算凱瑟琳夫人會有這樣的想法，我想她也決不會不贊成你。請你放心，我下次有幸見到她的時候，一定要在她面前把你的謙虛、節儉以及其他種種可愛的優點,大大誇獎一番。"

"說實話,柯林斯先生,任你怎麼誇獎我,都是浪費唇舌。我自己的事自己會有主張,只要你相信我所說的話,就是賞我的臉了。我祝你生活幸福富裕。我之所以謝絕你的求婚,也就是為了幫你了卻心願。而你呢,既然向我提出了求婚,那麼,你對於我家裏的事情,也就不必再感到有甚麼不好意思了,將來朗伯恩的莊園一旦輪到你做主人,你就可以取之無愧了。這件事就這樣一言為定吧。"她一面說,一面站起身來,要不是柯林斯先生向她說出下面的話,她早就走出去了。

"要是下趟我有幸再跟你談到這個問題,我希望你能夠給我一個比這次滿意點的答覆。我不怪你這次冷酷無情,因為我知道,你們這些小姐們對於男人第一次的求婚,照例總是拒絕。也許你剛剛所說的一番話,正符合女人微妙的性格,反而足以鼓勵我繼續追求下去。"

伊莉莎白一聽此話,不免有些氣惱,便大聲叫道:"柯林斯先生,你真弄得我太莫名其妙了。我的話已經說到這個地步,要是你還覺得這是鼓勵你的話,那我可不知道該怎麼樣謝絕你,才能使你死心。"

"親愛的表妹,請允許我說句自不量力的話:我相信你拒絕我的求婚,不過是照例說說罷了。我之所以會這樣想,簡單說來,有這樣幾點理由:我覺得我向你求婚,並不見得不值你接受,我的家產你也決不會不放在眼裏。我的社會地位,我同德·包爾府上的關係,以及跟你府上的親戚關係,都是我非常優越的條件。我得提請你考慮一下:儘管你有許多吸引人的地方,不幸你的財產太少,這就把你的可愛、把你許多優越的條件都抵消了,不會有另外一個人再向你求婚了。因此我就不得不認為你這一次並不是真正地拒絕我,而是仿效一般高貴女性的慣例,欲擒故縱,想要更加博得我的喜愛。"

"先生，我向你保證，我決沒有冒充風雅，故意作弄一位有面子的紳士。但願你相信我說的是真話，我就很有面子了。承蒙不棄，向我求婚，我真是感激不盡，但要我接受，是絕對不可能的。我感情上怎麼也辦不到。難道我說得還不夠明白嗎？請你別把我當作一個故作矜持的高貴女子，而要把我看作一個說真心話的平凡人。"

他大為狼狽，又不得不裝出滿臉的殷勤神氣叫道："你始終都那麼可愛！我相信只要令尊令堂做主應承了，你就決不會拒絕。"

他再三要存心自欺欺人，伊莉莎白可懶得再去理他，馬上不聲不響地走開了。她打定了主意：倘若他一定要把她的再三拒絕看作是有意討好他，有意鼓勵他，那麼她就只得去求助於她的父親，讓他斬釘截鐵地回絕他。柯林斯總不見得再把她父親的拒絕，看作一個高貴女性的裝腔作勢和賣弄風情了吧。

第二十章

柯林斯先生獨自一個人默默地幻想着美滿的姻緣，可是並沒有想多久，因為班奈特太太一直留在走廊裏混時間，等着聽他們兩人商談的結果。現在看見伊莉莎白開了門，匆匆忙忙走上樓去，她便馬上走進飯廳，熱烈地祝賀柯林斯先生，祝賀她自己，説是他們今後大有親上加親的希望了。柯林斯先生同樣快樂地接受了她的祝賀，同時又祝賀了她一番，接着就把他跟伊莉莎白剛才的那場談話，一五一十地講了出來，説他有充份的理由相信，談話的結果很令人滿意，因為他的表妹雖然再三拒絕，可是那種拒絕，自然是她那羞怯淑靜和嬌柔細緻的天性的流露。

這一個消息可讓班奈特太太嚇了一跳。當然，要是她的女兒果真是口頭上拒絕他的求婚，骨子裏卻在鼓勵他，那她也會同樣覺得高興的，可是她不敢這麼想，而且不得不照直説了出來。

她説："柯林斯先生，你放心吧，我會讓莉茲懂事一些的。我馬上就要親自跟她談談。她是個固執的傻孩子，不明白好歹；可是我會讓她理解的。"

"對不起，讓我插句嘴，太太，"柯林斯先生叫道；"要是她果真又固執又傻，那我就不知道她是否配做我理想的妻子了，因為像我這樣地位的人，結婚自然是為了要幸福。這麼説，如果她真的拒絕我的求婚，那倒是不要勉強她好，否則，她脾氣方面有了這些缺點，她對於我的幸福決不會有甚麼好處。"

班奈特太太吃驚地説："先生，你完全誤會了我的意思，莉茲不過在這類事情上固執些，可是遇到別的事情，她的性子再好也沒有了。我馬上去找班奈特先生，我們一下子就會把她這個問題談妥的，我有把握。"

她不等他回答，便急忙跑到丈夫那裏去，一走進他的書房就大聲說道：

"噢，我的好老爺，你得馬上出來一下；我們鬧得天翻地覆了呢。你得來勸勸莉茲嫁給柯林斯先生，因為她賭咒發誓不要他；假如你不趕快來打個圓場，他就要改變主意，反過來不要她了。"

班奈特先生見她走進來，便從書本上抬起眼睛，安然自得、漠不關心地望着她的臉。他聽了她的話，完全不動聲色。

她說完以後，他便說道："抱歉，我沒有聽懂你究竟說些甚麼。"

"我說的是柯林斯先生和莉茲的事。莉茲表示不要柯林斯先生，柯林斯先生也開始說他不要莉茲了。"

"這種事我有甚麼辦法？看來是件沒有指望的事。"

"你去同莉茲說說看吧。就跟她說，你非要她嫁給他不可。"

"叫她下來吧。讓我來跟她說。"

班奈特太太拉了下鈴，伊莉莎白小姐給叫到書房裏來了。

爸爸一見她來，便大聲說："上這裏來，孩子，我叫你來談一件要緊的事。我聽說柯林斯先生向你求婚，真有這回事嗎？"伊莉莎白說，真有這回事。"很好。你把這件婚事回絕了嗎？"

"我回絕了，爸爸。"

"很好，我們現在就進入正題。你的媽媽非要你答應不可。我的好太太，不是嗎？"

"是的，否則我再也不要看到她了。"

"擺在你面前的是個很不幸的難題，你得自己去抉擇，伊莉莎白。從今天起，你不和父親成為陌路人，就要和母親成為陌路人。要是你不嫁給柯林斯先生，你的母親就不要再見你，要是你嫁給他，我就不要再見你了。"

伊莉莎白聽到了那樣的開端和這樣的結論，不得不笑了一笑；不過，這可苦了班奈特太太，她本以為丈夫一定會照着她的意思來處理這件事的，哪裏料到反而讓她大失所望。

"你這話是甚麼意思，我的好老爺？你事先不是答應了我，非讓她嫁給他不可嗎？"

"好太太，"丈夫回答道，"我有兩件事要求你幫幫忙。第一，請你允許我自由運用我自己對此事的見解來處理這件事；第二，請你允許我自由使用我自己的書房。我真希望早日在自己書房裏圖個清閒自在。"

班奈特太太雖然碰了一鼻子灰，可是並不心甘情願。她一遍又一遍想說服伊莉莎白，又哄騙，又威脅。她想盡辦法拉着珍妮幫忙，可是珍妮偏不願意多管閒事，極其委婉地謝絕了。伊莉莎白應付得很好，一會情意懇切，一會又是嬉皮笑臉，方式儘管變來換去，決心卻始終如一。

這時，柯林斯先生獨自把剛才的那一幕沉思默想了一番。他太高估自己了，因此弄不明白表妹拒絕他，原因究竟何在。雖說他的自尊心受到了傷害，可是除此之外他絲毫也不覺得難過。他對她的好感完全是憑空想像的，他又以為她的母親一定會責罵她，因此心裏便也不覺得有甚麼難受了，因為她挨她母親的罵是活該，不必為她過意不去。

正當這一家人鬧得亂紛紛的時候，夏綠蒂‧盧卡斯上她們這裏來玩了。麗迪亞在大門口碰到她，立刻奔上前去湊近她說道："你來了我真高興，這裏正鬧得有趣呢！你知道今天上午發生了甚麼事？柯林斯先生向莉茲求婚，莉茲偏偏不肯要他。"

夏綠蒂還沒來得及回答，凱蒂就走到她們面前來了，把同樣的消息報導了一遍。她們走進起坐間，只見班奈特太太正獨自一人在那裏，馬上又和她們談到這話題上來，要求盧卡斯小姐憐恤憐恤她，勸勸她的朋友莉茲順從全家人的意思。"求求你吧，盧卡斯小姐，"她又用痛苦的聲調說道，"誰也不站在我這一邊，大家都故意欺負我，一個個都對我狠心極了，誰也不能體諒我的心情。"

夏綠蒂正要回答，恰巧珍妮和伊莉莎白走進來了，因此沒有開口。

「嘿，她來了，」班奈特太太接下去說。「看她一臉滿不在乎的
神氣，一點不把我們放在心上，好像是冤家對頭，任她自己獨斷獨
行。——莉茲小姐，讓我老實告訴你吧：如果你一碰到求婚，就像
這樣拒絕，那你一生一世都休想找到一個丈夫。等你爸爸去世以後，
還有誰來養你？我是養不活你的，得事先跟你聲明。我從今以後再
也不管你的事了。你知道，剛剛在書房裏，我就跟你說過，我再也不
要跟你說話了，我說得出就做得到。我不願意跟不孝順的女兒說話。
老實說，跟誰說話都不大樂意。像我這樣經歷精神上的折磨的人，
都不會有多大的興致說話。誰也不知道我的苦楚！不過天下事總是
這樣的。你嘴上不訴苦，就沒有人可憐你。」

女兒們一聲不響，只是聽着她發牢騷。她們都明白，要是你想
跟她評評理，安慰安慰她，那就等於火上加油。她嘮嘮叨叨往下說，
女兒們沒有一個來岔斷她的話。最後，柯林斯先生進來了，臉上的
神氣比平常顯得更加莊嚴，她一見到他，便對女兒們這樣說：

「現在我要你們一個個都住嘴，讓柯林斯先生跟我談一會。」

伊莉莎白靜悄悄走出去了，珍妮和凱蒂跟着也走了出去，只有
麗迪亞站在那裏不動，正要聽聽他們談些甚麼。夏綠蒂也沒有走，
先是因為柯林斯先生仔仔細細地問候她和她的家庭，所以不便即走，
隨後又為了滿足她自己的好奇心，便走到窗邊，去偷聽他們談話。
只聽到班奈特太太開始怨聲怨氣地把預先準備好的一番話談出來：
「哦，柯林斯先生。」

「親愛的太太，」柯林斯先生說，「這件事讓我們再也別提了吧。
我決不會怨恨令嬡這種行為。」他說到這裏，聲調中立刻流露出極其
不愉快的意味：「我們大家都得逆來順受，像我這樣年少得志，年紀
輕輕就得到器重，特別應該如此，我相信我一切都聽天由命。即使
蒙我那位美麗的表妹不棄，答應了我的求婚，或許我仍然免不了要
懷疑，是否就此會獲得真正的幸福，因此我一向認為，幸福一經拒

絕，就不值得我們再加重視。遇到這種場合，聽天由命是再好不過的辦法。親愛的太太，我這樣收回了對令嬡的求婚，希望你別以為這是對您和班奈特先生不恭敬的表示，別怪我沒要求你們出面代我調停一下。只不過我並不是遭到您拒絕，而是遭到令嬡拒絕，這一點也許值得遺憾。可是人人都難免有個陰錯陽差的時候。我對於這件事始終是一片好心好意。我的目的就是要找一個可愛的伴侶，並且適當地考慮到府上的利益；假如我的態度方面有甚麼地方應當受到責備的話，就讓我當面道個歉吧。"

第二十一章

關於柯林斯先生求婚問題的討論，差不多就要結束了，現在伊莉莎白只感到一種難免伴隨的不愉快，有時候還要聽她母親埋怨一兩聲。說到那位先生本人，他可並不顯得沮喪，也沒有表現出要迴避她的樣子，只是氣憤地板着臉，默然無聲。他幾乎不跟她説話，他本來的那一股熱情，到下半天都轉移到盧卡斯小姐身上去了。盧小姐蠻有禮貌地聽着他説話，這讓大家都鬆了口氣，特別是她的朋友。

班奈特太太直到第二天還是同樣不高興，身體也沒有復元。柯林斯先生也還是那樣又氣憤又傲慢的樣子。伊莉莎白原以為他這樣一氣，就會早日離開此地，誰知道他決不因此而改變原來的計劃，他説好星期六才走，便決定要留至星期六。

吃過早飯，小姐們上麥里頓去打聽韋翰先生回來了沒有，同時為了他沒有參加尼德斐莊園的舞會而去向他表示惋惜。她們一走到鎮上就遇見了他，於是他陪着小姐們上她們姨媽家裏去，他在那裏把他的歉意，他的煩惱，以及他對於每個人的關注，談了個暢快。不過他卻在伊莉莎白面前自動説明，那次舞會的確是他自己不願意去參加。

他説："當舞會日漸迫近，我心裏想，還是不要碰見達西先生的好；我覺得要同他聚在同一屋簷下的舞會上好幾個小時，那會讓我受不了，而且可能會鬧出些笑話來，弄得彼此都不歡愉。"

她非常讚美他的涵養。當韋翰和另一位軍官跟她們一起回朗伯恩來的時候，一路上他特別照顧她，因此他們有充份的空暇來討論這個問題，而且還客客氣氣地彼此恭維了好一陣子。他之所以要送她們，是為了兩大好處：一來可以讓她高興高興，二來可以利用這個大好機會，去認識她的雙親。

她們剛回到家裏，班奈特小姐就接到一封從尼德斐莊園寄來的信。她把信立刻拆開了，裏面裝着一張小巧、精緻、熨燙得很平滑的信箋，字跡是出自一位小姐娟秀流利的手筆。伊莉莎白看到姐姐讀信時變了臉色，又看到她全神貫注在某幾段上面。頃刻之間，珍妮又鎮靜了下來，把信放在一旁，像平常一樣高高興興地跟大家一起聊天；可是伊莉莎白仍然為這件事焦急，因此對韋翰也分了心。韋翰和他的同伴一走，珍妮便對她使了個眼色，讓她跟她上樓去。一到了她們自己房裏，珍妮就拿出信來，說道：

"這是卡洛琳‧賓利寫來的，信上的話真讓我大吃一驚。她們一家人現在已經離開尼德斐莊園上城裏去了，再也不打算回來了。你看看她怎麼說的吧。"

於是她先把第一句唸出來，那句話就是說，她們已經決定立刻追隨她們的兄弟上城裏去，而且要在當天趕到格魯斯汶納街[23]吃飯，原來赫斯托先生就住在那條街上。接下去是這樣寫的："最親愛的朋友，離開赫福德郡，除了你的友誼以外，我真是毫無留戀。不過，我們希望將來有一天，還是可以像過去那樣愉快地來往，同時也希望能經常通信，無話不談，以抒離別之傷。臨筆不勝企盼。"伊莉莎白對這些浮話奢詞，只是姑妄聽之；雖說她們這一次突然的遷走令她感到驚奇，可是她並不覺得真有甚麼可以惋惜的地方。她們離開了尼德斐莊園，並不等於賓利先生不會再在那裏住下去；至於說到跟她們沒有了來往，她相信珍妮只要跟賓利先生時常見面，也就無所謂了。

停了片刻，伊莉莎白說道："不幸得很，你朋友們臨走以前，你沒有來得及去看她們一次。可是，賓利小姐既然認為將來還有重聚的歡樂，難道我們不能希望這一天比她意料中來得更早一些嗎？將來做了姑嫂，不是比今天做朋友更滿意嗎？賓利先生不會被她們久留在倫敦的。"

"卡洛琳肯定地説，她們一家人，今年冬天誰也不會回到赫福德郡來了。讓我唸給你聽吧：

我哥哥昨天和我們告別的時候，還以為他這次上倫敦去，只要三四天就可以把事情辦好；可是我們認為辦不到，同時我們相信，查理斯一進了城，決不肯馬上就走，因此我們決定追隨前去，免得他冷冷清清住在旅館裏受罪。我很多朋友都上倫敦去過了；親愛的朋友，我本來還希望聽到你進城去的消息，結果不如我所料。我真摯地希望你在赫福德郡照常能夠愉快地度過聖誕節。希望你有很多英俊的男朋友，免得我們一走，你便會因為少了三個朋友而感到難過。"

"這明明是説，"珍妮補充道，"他今年冬天不會回來了。"

"這不過説明賓利小姐不要他回來罷了。"

"你為甚麼這樣想？那一定是他自己的意思。他自己可以做主。可是你還沒有知道全部呢。我一定要把那特別令我傷心的一段讀給你聽。我對你完全不必忌諱。'達西先生急於要去看看他的妹妹；説老實話，我們也差不多同樣熱切地希望和她重逢。我認為喬治安娜·達西無論在容貌方面、舉止方面、才藝方面，的確再也沒有人能夠比得上。路易莎和我都大膽地希望她以後會做我們的嫂嫂，因此我們對她便更加關切了。我不知道以前有沒有跟你提起過我對這件事的感覺，可是當此離開鄉村之際，我不願意不把這些感覺説出來，我相信你不會覺得這是不合情理的吧。我的哥哥已經深深地愛上了她，他現在可以時常去看她，他們自會更加親密起來；雙方的家庭方面都同樣盼望着這頭親事能夠成功。我想，如果我説，查理斯最善於博取任何女人的歡心，這並不是出於做姐妹的偏心，瞎説一陣。既是各方面都贊成這段姻緣，而且事情毫無阻礙，那麼，最親愛的珍妮，我衷心希望這件人人樂見的事能夠實現，總沒錯吧？'你覺得這一句怎麼樣，親愛的莉茲？"珍妮讀完了以後説。"説得還不夠清楚嗎？這不是明明白白地表明她們不希望、也不願我做她們的嫂嫂嗎？不是説明了她完全相信他的哥哥對我無所謂嗎？而且不也是説明了：假如她懷疑到我對他有感情，她就要勸我（多謝她這樣的好心腸！）當心些嗎？這些話還能有別的解釋嗎？"

"當然可以有別的解釋；我的解釋就和你的解釋完全兩樣。你願意聽一聽嗎？"

"非常願意。"

"這只要三言兩語就可以説明白。賓利小姐看出她哥哥愛上了你，可是她卻希望他和達西小姐結婚。她跟着他到城裏去，為的就是要把他絆在那裏，而且竭力想來説服你，讓你相信他對你沒有好感。"

珍妮搖搖頭。

"珍妮，你的確應該相信我。凡是看見過你們兩人在一起的人，都不會懷疑到他的感情。我相信賓利小姐也不會懷疑，她不是那麼一個傻瓜。要是她看到達西先生對她的愛有這樣的一半，她就要辦嫁妝了。可是問題是這樣的：在她們家裏看來，我們還不夠有錢，也不夠有勢，她之所以急於想把達西小姐配給她的哥哥，原來還有一個打算，那就是説，結上了這頭親事以後，再來個親上加親就省事了。這件事當然很費了一些心機，我敢説，要不是德·包爾小姐從中作梗，事情是會成功的。可是，最親愛的珍妮，你千萬不要因為賓利小姐告訴你説，她哥哥已經深深地愛上了達西小姐，你就以為賓利先生自從星期二和你分別以來，對你的傾心有絲毫變卦，也別以為她真有本領使她哥哥不愛你，而去愛上她那位女朋友。"

"假如你我對賓利小姐的看法是一致的，"珍妮回答道，"那麼，你這一切想法也許會大大讓我安心。可是我知道你這種説法很偏心。卡洛琳不會故意欺騙任何人，我對這件事只能存一個希望，那就是説，一定是她自己想錯了。"

"這話説得對。我的想法既然不能安慰你，你自己居然想得出這樣的好念頭來，那是再好也沒有了。 你就相信是她自己想錯了吧。

現在你算是對她盡了禮節，再也用不着煩惱。”

“可是，親愛的妹妹，即使從最好的方面去着想，我答應了這頭親事，而他的姐妹和朋友們都希望他跟別人結婚，這樣我會幸福嗎？”

“那就得看你自己的主張如何，”伊莉莎白説。“如果你考慮成熟以後，認為得罪了他的姐妹們所招來的痛苦，比起做他的太太所得到的幸福來得更多，那麼，我勸你還是拒絕了他算了。”

“你怎麼説得出這種話？”珍妮微微一笑。“你要知道，即使她們的反對使我萬分難受，我還是不會猶豫的。”

“我並沒有説你會猶豫；既然如此，我就可以不必再為你擔心了。”

“倘若他今年冬天不回來，我就用不着左思右想了。六個月裏會有多少變動啊！”

所謂他不會回來，這種想法伊莉莎白大不以為然。她覺得那不過是卡洛琳一廂情願。她認為卡洛琳這種願望，無論是露骨地説出來也罷，委婉地説出來也罷，對於一個完全無求於人的青年來説，決不會產生絲毫影響。

她把自己對這個問題的感想，解釋給她姐姐聽，果然一下子就收到了很好的效果，她覺得非常高興。珍妮這樣的性子，本來不會輕易意志消沉，從此便漸漸產生了希望，認為賓利先生一定會回到尼德斐莊園來，使她稱心如意，儘管有時候她還是懷疑多於希望。

最後姐妹兩人一致主張，這事在班奈特太太面前不宜多説，只要告訴她一聲，這一家人已經離開此地，不必向她説明他走的原因；可是班奈特太太光是聽到這片段的消息，已經大感不安，甚至還哀嘆起來，埋怨自己運氣太壞，兩位小姐剛剛跟她相識相知就走了。不過傷心了一陣以後，她又用這樣的想法來安慰自己：賓利先生不久就會回來，到朗伯恩來吃飯；最後她心安理得地説，儘管只不過邀他來吃便飯，她都一定要費心安排，請他吃兩大道菜。

第二十二章

這一天班奈特全家都被盧卡斯府上請去吃飯，又多蒙盧卡斯小姐一片好意，整日陪着柯林斯先生談話。伊莉莎白利用了一個機會向她道謝。她說："這樣可以令他精神痛快些，我對你真是說不盡的感激。"夏綠蒂說，能夠替朋友效勞，非常樂意，雖然花了一點時間，卻得到了很大的快慰。這真是太好了；可是夏綠蒂的好意，遠非伊莉莎白所能意料：原來夏綠蒂是有意要盡量引柯林斯先生跟她自己談話，免得他再去向伊莉莎白獻殷勤。她這個計謀看來進行得十分順利。晚上大家分手的時候，夏綠蒂幾乎滿有把握地感覺到，要不是柯林斯先生這麼快就要離開赫福德郡，事情一定能夠成功。但是她這樣的想法，未免太不了解他那如火如荼、獨斷獨行的性格。第二天一大早，柯林斯就採用了相當狡猾的辦法，溜出了朗伯恩，趕到盧家莊來向她屈身求愛。他惟恐給表妹們碰到了。他認為，假若讓她們看見他走開，那就必定會讓她們猜中他的打算，而他不等到事情有了成功的把握，決不願意讓人知道。雖說他當場看到夏綠蒂對他頗有情意，因此覺得這事十拿九穩可以成功，可是從星期三那場冒險以來，他不敢太魯莽了。不過這次他倒是受人巴結。盧卡斯小姐從樓上窗戶看見他向她家裏走來，便連忙到那條小道上去接他，又裝出是偶然相逢的樣子。她萬萬想不到，柯林斯這一次竟然給她帶來了說不盡的千情萬愛。

在短短的一段時間裏，柯林斯先生長篇大論了一番，於是兩人之間便一切都講妥了，而且雙方都很滿意。一走進大宅，他就誠懇地要求她擇定吉日，使他成為世界上最幸福的人；雖說這種請求，暫時應該置之不理，可是這位小姐並不想要拿他的幸福當兒戲。他天生一副蠢相，求起愛來總是打動不了女人的心，女人一碰到他求愛,總是請他碰壁。盧卡斯小姐之所以願意答應他,完全是為了財產打算,至於那筆財產何年何月可以拿到手,她倒不在乎。

他們兩人立刻就去請求威廉爵士夫婦加以允許,老夫婦連忙高高興興地答應了。他們本來沒有甚麼嫁妝給女兒,論柯林斯先生目前的境況,真是再適合不過的一個女婿,何況他將來一定會發一筆大財。盧卡斯太太立刻帶着前所未有的興趣,開始盤算着班奈特先生還有多少年可活;威廉爵士一口斷定說,只要柯林斯先生一旦得到了朗伯恩的財產,他夫婦兩人就大有覲見國王的希望了。總而言之,這件大事讓全家人都快活極了。幾位小女兒都滿懷希望,認為可以早一兩年出去交際了,男孩子們再也不擔心夏綠蒂會當老處女了。只有夏綠蒂本人倒相當鎮定。她現在初步已經成功,還有時間去仔細考慮一番。她想了一下,大致滿意。柯林斯先生固然既不通情達理,又不討人喜愛,和他相處實在是件討厭的事,他對她的愛也一定是空中樓閣,不過她還是要他做丈夫。雖然她對於婚姻和夫婦生活,期待都不甚高,可是,結婚到底是她一貫的目標:大凡家境不好而又受過相當教育的青年女子[24],總是把結婚當作僅有的一條體面的退路。儘管結婚並不一定會讓人幸福,但總算給她自己安排了一個最可靠的儲物室,可以讓她日後不致受凍受飢。她現在就獲得了這樣一個儲物室了。她今年二十七歲,人長得又不標緻,能有如此收穫已經使她覺得無比幸運。只有一件事令人不快——那就是說,伊莉莎白·班奈特肯定會對這頭親事感到驚奇,而她又是一向把伊莉莎白的交情看得比任何人的交情都重要。伊莉莎白一定會詫異,說不定還要埋怨她。雖說她一經下定決心便不會動搖,然而別人非難起來一定會使她難受。於是她決定親自把這件事告訴她,囑咐柯林斯先生回到朗伯恩吃飯的時候,不要在班奈特家裏任何人面前透露一點風聲。對方當然惟命是從,答應保守秘密。其實秘密很難保守,因為他出去得太久了,一定會引起大家的好奇心。因此他一回去,大家立刻向他問長問短,他得要有幾分能耐才能夠遮掩過去,加上他又迫切盼望把此番情場得意的喜訊宣揚出去，因此他好不容易才克制住自己。

他明天一大早就要啟程，來不及向大家辭行，所以當夜太太小姐們就寢的時候，大家便相互話別；班奈特太太極其誠懇、極其有禮貌地說，以後他要是有空再來朗伯恩，到她們那裏去探訪探訪，她們都會非常高興和歡迎。

他回答道：＂親愛的太太，承蒙邀約，不勝感激，我也正希望能領受這份盛意；請你放心，我一有空就來看你們。＂

大家都吃了一驚，尤其是班奈特先生，根本不希望他馬上又來，便連忙說道：

＂賢姪，你不怕凱瑟琳夫人不贊成嗎？你最好把親戚關係看得淡一些，免得擔那麼大的風險，得罪了你的女恩人。＂

柯林斯先生回答道：＂堂叔，我非常感激你這樣好心地提醒我，請你放心，這樣重大的事，不得到老夫人的同意，我決不會冒昧從事。＂

＂多加小心百利而無一害。甚麼事都不要緊，可千萬不能讓她不高興。要是你想到我們這裏來，而她卻不高興讓你來（我覺得這是非常可能的），那麼你大可安份留在家裏。你放心，我們決不會因此而見怪的。＂

＂堂叔，請相信我，蒙你這樣好心地關注，真令我感激不盡。你放心好了，你馬上就會收到我一封謝函，感謝你這一點，感謝我在赫福德郡蒙你們對我的種種照拂。至於諸位表妹，雖然我去不了多少日子，且請恕我冒昧，就趁着現在祝她們健康和幸福，伊莉莎白表妹也不例外。＂

太太小姐們便行禮如儀，辭別回房；大家聽說他竟打算很快就回來，都感到驚訝。班奈特太太滿以為他是打算向她的哪一個小女兒求婚，也許能勸動瑪莉去應承他。瑪莉比任何姐妹都看重他的能力。他思想方面的堅定很令她傾心；他雖然比不上她自己那樣聰明，可是只要有一個像她這樣的人作為榜樣，鼓勵他讀書上進，那他一定會成為一個稱心如意的伴侶。只可惜一到第二天早上，這種希望就完全破滅了。盧卡斯小姐剛吃過早飯就來訪，私下跟伊莉莎白把前一天的事說了出來。

早在前一兩天，伊莉莎白就一度想到，柯林斯先生可能一廂情願，自以為愛上了她這位朋友。可是，要說夏綠蒂會慫恿他，那未免太不可能，正如她自己不可能慫恿他一樣。因此她現在聽到這件事，不禁大為驚訝，連禮貌也不顧了，竟大聲叫了起來：

"跟柯林斯先生訂婚！親愛的夏綠蒂，那怎麼行！"

盧卡斯小姐乍聽得這一聲心直口快的責備，鎮靜的臉色不禁變得慌張起來，好在這也在她意料之中，因此她立刻就恢復了常態，從容不迫地說：

"你為甚麼這樣驚奇，親愛的伊麗莎？柯林斯先生不幸沒有得到你的賞識，難道他就不能得到別的女人的賞識嗎？"

伊莉莎白這時候已經鎮定下來，便竭力克制着自己，用相當肯定的語氣預祝他們兩人將來良緣美滿，幸福無疆。

夏綠蒂回答道："我明白你的感受，你一定會感到奇怪，而且是感到非常奇怪，因為在不久以前，柯林斯先生還在想跟你結婚。可是，只要你空下來把這事情細細地想一下，你就會贊成我的做法。你知道我不是個羅曼蒂克的人，我決不是那樣的人。我只希望有一個舒舒服服的家。論柯林斯先生的性格、社會關係和身份地位，我覺得跟他結了婚，也能夠獲得幸福，並不下於一般人結婚時所誇耀的那種幸福。"

伊莉莎白心平氣和地回答道："那倒也是。"她們兩人彆彆扭扭地沉默了一會，便和家人一起坐下。夏綠蒂沒有過多久就走了；伊莉莎白獨自把剛才聽到的那些話仔細想了一下。這樣不合適的一頭親事，真使她難受了好久。說起柯林斯先生在三天之內求了兩次婚，本就夠稀奇了，如今竟會有人答應他，實在是更稀奇。她一向覺得，夏綠蒂關於婚姻問題方面的見解，跟她頗不一致，卻不曾料想到一旦事到臨頭，她竟會完全不顧高尚的情操，來屈就一些世俗的利益。夏綠蒂竟做了柯林斯的妻子，這真是天下最丟人的事！她不僅為這樣一個朋友的自取其辱、自貶身價而感到難過，而且她還十分痛心地斷定，她朋友選的這條路，決不會給她自己帶來多大的幸福。

第二十三章

伊莉莎白正跟母親和姐妹坐在一起，回想剛才所聽到的那件事，決定不了是否可以把它告訴大家。就在這時候，威廉·盧卡斯爵士來了。他是受了女兒的拜託，前來班府上宣佈她訂婚的消息。他一面敍述這件事，一面又大大地恭維了太太小姐們一陣，說是兩家能結上親，他真感到榮幸。班府上的人聽了，不僅感到驚異，而且不相信真有這回事。班奈特太太再也顧不得甚麼禮貌，竟一口咬定他弄錯了。麗迪亞一向是又任性又撒野，不由得叫道：

"天哪！威廉爵士，你怎麼會說出這番話來？你不知道柯林斯先生想要娶莉茲嗎？"

遇到這種情形，只有像朝廷大臣那樣能夠逆來順受的人，才不會生氣。好在威廉爵士頗有素養，竟沒有把它當一回事。雖然他要求她們相信他說的是實話，可是他卻使出了極大的忍耐力，蠻有禮貌地聽着她們無理的談吐。

伊莉莎白覺得自己有責任幫助他來打開這種僵局，於是挺身而出，證明他說的是實話，說是剛剛已經聽到夏綠蒂本人談起過了。為了盡力使母親和妹妹們不再大驚小怪，她便誠懇地向威廉爵士道喜，珍妮馬上也替她幫腔，又用種種話來說明這婚姻是何等幸福，柯林斯先生品格又非常好，漢斯福和倫敦相隔不遠，往返方便。

班奈特太太在威廉爵士面前，實在氣得說不出話；可是他一走，她那一肚子牢騷便馬上發洩出來。第一，她堅決不相信這回事；第二，她斷定柯林斯先生受了騙；第三，她相信這一對夫婦決不會幸福；第四，這頭親事可能會破裂。不過，她卻從整個事件上簡單地得出了兩個結論——一個是：這場鬧劇全都是伊莉莎白一手造成的；另一個是，她自己受盡了大家的欺負虐待；在那一整天裏，她所談的大都是這兩點。無論怎麼也安慰不了她，平不了她的氣。直到晚上，怨憤依然沒有消散。她見到伊莉莎白就罵，一直罵了一個星期之久。她同威廉爵士或盧卡斯太太說起話來，總是粗聲粗氣，一直過了一個月才平和起來；至於對夏綠蒂，她竟過了好幾個月才寬恕了她。

至於班奈特先生，對這件事心情卻完全心平氣和，據他說，這次所經過的一切，真使他精神上舒暢得很。他說，他本以為夏綠蒂・盧卡斯相當懂事，哪知道她簡直跟他太太一樣蠢，比起他的女兒來就更要蠢了，他實在覺得高興！

珍妮也承認這婚姻有些奇怪，可是她嘴上並沒說甚麼，反而誠懇地祝他們兩人幸福。雖然伊莉莎白再三剖白給她聽，她卻始終以為這場婚姻未必一定不會幸福。凱蒂和麗迪亞根本不羨慕盧卡斯小姐，因為柯林斯先生不過是個傳教士而已；這件事根本影響不了她們，除非把它當作一件新聞，帶到麥里頓去傳播一下。

再說到盧卡斯太太，她既然也有一個女兒獲得了美滿的姻緣，自然衷心快慰，因而也不會不想趁此去向班奈特太太反唇相譏一下。於是她拜訪朗伯恩的次數比往常更加頻繁，說是她如今是多麼高興，不過班奈特太太滿臉的酸相，滿口不中聽的話，也足夠令她掃興了。

伊莉莎白和夏綠蒂之間從此竟有了一層隔膜，彼此都不便提到這件事。伊莉莎白斷定她們兩人再也不會像從前那樣推心置腹。夏綠蒂既然令她失望，她便寧願更加熱切地關注自己的姐姐。她深信姐姐為人正直，作風優雅，她這種看法決不會動搖。她關心姐姐的幸福一天比一天來得迫切，因為賓利先生已經走了一個星期，卻沒有聽到一點他要回來的消息。

珍妮很早就給卡洛琳寫了回信，現在正在數着日子，看看還得過多少天才可以再次接到她的信。柯林斯先生事先答應寫來的那封謝函星期二就收到了。信是寫給她們父親的，信上說了許多感激的話，看他那種過甚其辭的語氣，就好像在他們府上叨擾了一年似的。他在這方面表示了歉意以後，便用了歡天喜地的措辭，告訴他們說，他已經有幸獲得他們的芳鄰盧卡斯小姐的歡心了。他接着又說，為了要去看看他的心上人，他可以趁便來看看他們，免得辜負他們善意的期望，希望能在兩個禮拜以後的星期一到達朗伯恩；他又說，凱瑟琳夫人衷心地贊成他趕快結婚，並且希望越早越好，他相信他那位心上人夏綠蒂決不會反對及早定出佳期，使他成為天下最幸福的人。

對班奈特太太來說，柯林斯先生的重返朗伯恩，如今並不是甚麼令人快意的事了。她反而跟她丈夫一樣地大為抱怨。說也奇怪，柯林斯不去盧家莊，卻要來到朗伯恩，這真是既不方便，又太麻煩。她現在正處於健康失調，因此非常討厭客人上門，何況這些癡情種子都是再討厭不過的人。班奈特太太整天嘀咕着這些事，除非想到賓利先生一直不回來而使她感到更大的痛苦時，她才住口。

珍妮跟伊莉莎白都為這個問題大感不安。一天又一天，聽不到一點關於他的消息，麥里頓紛紛傳言，說他今年整個冬天再也不會上尼德斐莊園來了。班奈特太太聽得非常生氣，總是加以駁斥，說那是誣衊性的謠言。

連伊莉莎白也開始恐懼起來了，她並不是怕賓利薄情，而是怕他的姐妹們真的絆住了他。儘管她不願意有這種想法，因為這種想法對於珍妮的幸福既有不利，對於珍妮心上人的忠貞，也未免是一種侮辱，可是她還是往往禁不住要這樣想。他那兩位無情無義的姐妹，和那位足以制服他的朋友同心協力，再加上達西小姐的窈窕嫵媚，以及倫敦的聲色娛樂，縱使他果真對她念念不忘，恐怕也掙脫不了那個圈套。

至於珍妮，她在這種動盪不安的情況下，自然比伊莉莎白更加感到焦慮，可是她總不願意把自己的心事暴露出來，所以她和伊莉莎白一直沒有提到這件事。偏偏她母親不能體貼她的苦衷，過不了一個小時就要提到賓利，說是等待他回來實在等待得心焦了，甚至硬要珍妮承認——要是賓利果真不回來，那她一定會覺得自己受了薄情的虐待。幸虧珍妮臨事從容不迫，柔和鎮定，好容易才忍受了她這些讒言誹語。

柯林斯先生在兩個禮拜以後的星期一準時到達，可是朗伯恩卻不像他初來時那樣熱烈地歡迎他了。他實在高興不過，也用不着別人獻殷勤。這真是主人家走運，幸好他的戀愛成功，這才使別人能夠清閒下來，不必再去跟他周旋。他每天把大部份時間消磨在盧家莊，一直等到盧府上快要睡覺的時候，才回到朗伯恩來，向大家道歉一聲，請大家原諒他終日未歸。

班奈特太太着實可憐。只要一提到那頭親事，她就會不高興，而且隨便她走到哪裏，她總會聽到人們談起這件事。她一看到盧卡斯小姐就覺得討厭。一想到盧卡斯小姐將來有一天會接替她做這幢宅子的主婦，她就更加嫉妒和厭惡。每逢夏綠蒂來看她們，她總以為她是來考察情況，看看還要過多少時候就可以搬進來住；每逢夏綠蒂跟柯林斯先生低聲說話的時候，她就以為他們是在談論朗伯恩的家產，是在計議一旦班奈特先生去世，就要把她和她的幾個女兒攆出去。她把這些苦不堪言的心事都説給她丈夫聽。

她說："我的好老爺，夏綠蒂・盧卡斯遲早要做這宅子的主婦，我卻非得讓她不可，眼睜睜看着她來接替我的位置，這可讓我受不了！"

"我的好太太，別去想這些傷心事吧。我們不妨從好的方面去想。說不定我比你的壽命還要長，我們姑且就這樣來安慰自己吧。"

可是這些話安慰不了班奈特太太，因此她非但沒有回答，反而像剛才一樣地訴苦訴下去。

"我一想到所有的產業都得落到他們手裏，就受不了。要不是為了繼承權的問題，我才不在乎呢。"

"你不在乎甚麼？"

"甚麼我都不在乎。"

"讓我們謝天謝地，你頭腦還沒有不清楚到這種地步。"

"我的好老爺，凡是有關繼承權的事，我決不會謝天謝地的。隨便哪個人，怎麼肯昧着良心，不把財產傳給自己的女兒們？我真弄不懂，何況一切都是為了柯林斯先生的緣故！為甚麼偏偏要他享有這份遺產？"

"我讓你自己去想吧。"班奈特先生説。

第二十四章

賓利小姐的信來了，疑慮消除了。信上第一句話就說，她們決定在倫敦過冬，結尾是替他哥哥道歉，說他在臨走以前，沒有來得及向赫福德郡的朋友們辭行，深感遺憾。

希望破滅了，徹底破滅了。珍妮繼續把信讀下去，只覺得除了寫信人那種裝模作樣的親切之外，就根本找不出可以自我安慰的地方。滿篇都是讚美達西小姐的話，絮絮叨叨地談到她的千嬌百媚。卡洛琳又欣喜地說，她們兩人之間已經一天比一天來得親熱，而且竟大膽地作出預言，說是她上封信裏所提到的那些願望，一定可以實現。她還得意非凡地寫道，她哥哥已經住到達西先生家裏去，又歡天喜地地提到達西先生打算添置新傢具。

珍妮立刻把這些事大都告訴了伊莉莎白，伊莉莎白聽了，怒而不言。她真傷心透了，一方面是關懷自己的姐姐，另一方面是怨恨那幫人。卡洛琳信上說她哥哥鍾情於達西小姐，伊莉莎白無論如何也不相信。她仍舊像以往一樣，相信賓利先生真正喜歡珍妮。伊莉莎白一向很看重他，現在才知道他原來是這樣一個容易輕信而沒有主見的人，以致被他那批詭計多端的朋友們牽制住了，聽憑他們反覆無常地影響他，拿他的幸福做犧牲品——一想到這些，她就不能不氣憤，甚至不免有些看不起他。要是只有他個人的幸福遭受到犧牲，那他愛怎麼胡搞都可以，可是這裏面畢竟還牽涉着她姐姐的幸福，她相信他自己也應該明白。簡單來說，反覆的思索，對於這個問題最終都是沒有辦法。她想不出甚麼別的了。究竟是賓利先生真的變了心呢，還是他的朋友們逼得他無可奈何？他究竟看出了珍妮的一片真心呢，還是根本不知道？雖然對她來說，她應該辨明其中的是非曲直，然後才能斷定他是好是壞，可是對她姐姐來說，反正都是一樣的痛心疾首。

過了一兩天，珍妮才鼓起勇氣，把自己的心事説給伊莉莎白聽。那天班奈特太太像往常一樣説起尼德斐莊園和它的主人，嘮叨了老半天，後來總算走開了，只剩下她們姐妹兩人，珍妮這才禁不住説道：

"噢，但願媽媽多控制她自己一些吧！她不知道她這樣時時刻刻提起他，讓我多麼痛苦。不過我決不怨誰。這局面不會長久的。他馬上就會被我們忘掉，我們還是會一如既往。"

伊莉莎白半信半疑而又極其關切地望着姐姐，一聲不響。

"你不相信我的話嗎？"珍妮微微紅着臉大聲説道。"那你真是毫無理由。他在我的記憶裏可能是個最可愛的朋友，但也不過如此而已。我既沒有甚麼奢望，也沒有甚麼擔心，更沒有甚麼要責備他的地方。多謝上帝，我還沒有那種苦惱。因此，稍微過一些時候，我一定就會慢慢克服過來的。"

她立刻又用更堅強的聲調説道："我立刻就可以安慰自己説：這只怪我自己不該瞎想，好在並沒有損害別人，只損害了我自己。"

伊莉莎白連忙叫起來了："親愛的珍妮，你太善良了。你那樣好心，那樣處處為別人着想，真像天使一般；我不知道應該怎麼跟你説才好。我覺得我從前對你還不夠好，愛你還不夠深。"

珍妮竭力否認這一切言過其實的誇獎，反而用這些讚美的話來讚揚妹妹的熱情。

"別那麼説，"伊莉莎白説，"這樣説是不公平的，你總以為天下都是好人。我只要説了誰一句壞話，你就難受。我要把你看作一個完美無瑕的人，你就來駁斥。請你放心，我決不會説得過份，你有權利對四海之內的人一視同仁，我也不會干涉你。你用不着擔心。至於我，我真正喜歡的人沒有幾個，我心目中的好人就更少了。世事經歷得越多，我就越對世事不滿；我一天比一天相信，人性都是見異思遷，我們不能憑着某人表面上一點點長處或見解，就去相信他。

最近我碰到了兩件事：其中一件我不願意說出來，另一件就是夏綠蒂的婚姻。這簡直是莫名其妙！任你怎樣看，都是莫名其妙！"

"親愛的莉茲，不要這樣胡思亂想吧。那會毀了你的幸福的。你對於各人處境的不同和脾氣的不同，體諒得不夠。你且想一想柯林斯先生的身份地位和夏綠蒂的謹慎穩重吧。你得記住，她也算是一個大家閨秀，說起財產方面，倒是一頭挺適當的親事。你且顧全大家的面子，只當她對我們那位表兄確實有幾分敬愛和器重吧。"

"要是看在你的份上，我幾乎可以隨便對甚麼事都願意信以為真，可是這對於任何人都沒有益處；我現在只覺得夏綠蒂根本不懂得愛情，要是再讓我去相信她是真的愛上了柯林斯，那我又要覺得她簡直毫無見識。親愛的珍妮，柯林斯先生是個自高自大、喜愛炫耀、心胸狹窄的蠢漢，這一點你和我懂得一樣清楚；你也會跟我一樣地感覺到，只有頭腦不健全的女人才肯嫁給他。雖說這個女人就是夏綠蒂·盧卡斯，你也不必為她辯護。你千萬不能為了某一個人而改變原則，破格遷就，也不要千方百計地說服我，或是說服你自己去相信，自私自利就是謹慎，糊塗膽大就等於幸福有了保障。"

"講到這兩個人，我認為你的話說得太過火，"珍妮說。"但願你日後看到他們兩人幸福相處的時候，就會相信我的話。這件事可也談夠了，你且談另外一件吧。你不是舉出了兩件事嗎？我不會誤解你，可是，親愛的莉茲，我求求你千萬不要以為錯是錯在那個人身上，千萬不要說你看不起他，免得我感到痛苦。我們決不能隨隨便便就以為別人在有意傷害我們。我們決不可能指望一個生龍活虎的青年會始終小心周到。我們往往會因為我們自己的虛榮心，而給弄迷了心竅。女人們往往會把愛情這種東西幻想得太不切實際。"

"因此男人們就故意逗她們那麼幻想。"

"如果這件事真的是存心安排好了的，那實在是他們不應該；可是世界上是否真如某些人所想像的那樣，到處都是計謀，我並不知道。"

"我決不是說賓利先生的行為是事先有了計謀的，"伊莉莎白說。"可是，即使沒有存心做壞事，或者說，沒有存心讓別人傷心，事實上仍然會做錯事情，引起不幸的後果。凡是粗心大意、看不出別人的好心好意，而且自己缺乏果斷，都一樣能害人。"

"你看這件事也得歸到這類原因嗎？"

"當然——應該歸於最後一種原因。可是，如果讓我再說下去，說出我對於你所器重的那些人是怎麼看法，那也會讓你不高興的。趁着現在我能夠住嘴的時候，且讓我住嘴吧。"

"那麼說，你斷定是他的姐妹們操縱了他了。"

"是的，而且是跟他那位朋友共同謀劃的。"

"我不相信。她們為甚麼要操縱他？她們只有希望他幸福；要是他果真愛我，別的女人便無從使他幸福。"

"你第一個想法就錯了。她們除了希望他幸福之外，還有許多別的打算：她們會希望他更加有財有勢；她們會希望他跟一個出身高貴、親朋顯赫的闊女人結婚。"

"毫無疑問，她們希望他選中達西小姐，"珍妮說；"不過，說到這一點，她們也許是出於一片好心，並不如你所想像的那麼惡劣。她們認識她比認識我早得多，難怪她們更喜歡她。可是，不管她們自己的願望如何，她們總不至於違背她們兄弟的願望吧。除非有了甚麼太看不順眼的地方，哪個做姐妹的會這樣冒昧？要是她們相信他愛上了我，她們決不會想要拆散我們；要是他果真愛我，她們要拆散也拆散不成。如果你一定要以為他對我真有感情，那麼，她們這樣的做法，便是既不近人情，又荒謬絕倫，我也就更傷心了。不要用這種想法來使我痛苦吧。我決不會因為一念之差而感到羞恥——即使感到羞恥也微乎其微，倒是一想起他或他的姐妹們無情無義，我真不知道要難受多少倍呢。讓我從最好的方面去想吧，從合乎人情事理的方面去想吧。"

伊莉莎白無法反對她這種願望，從此以後，她們就不大提起賓利先生的名字。

班奈特太太見他一去不回，仍然不斷地納悶，不斷地抱怨，儘管伊莉莎白幾乎沒有哪一天不給她解釋個清楚明白，然而始終無法使她減少些煩憂。女兒盡力說服她，盡說一些連她自己也不相信的話給母親聽，說是賓利先生對於珍妮的鍾情，只不過是出於一時高興，根本算不上甚麼，一旦她不在他眼前，也就置之度外了。雖然班奈特太太當時也相信這話不假，可是事後她又每天舊事重提，最後只有想出了一個聊以自慰的辦法，指望賓利先生來年夏天一定會回到這裏來。

班奈特先生對這件事可就抱着兩樣的態度。有一天他對伊莉莎白說："嘿，莉茲，我發覺你的姐姐失戀了。我倒要祝賀她。一個小姐除了結婚以外，總喜歡不時地嘗點失戀的滋味。那可以使她們有點東西去想想，又可以在朋友們面前出點風頭。甚麼時候輪到你呢？你也不大願意讓珍妮趕在前面太久吧。現在你的機會來了。麥里頓的軍官們很多，足夠使這個村莊裏每一個年輕的小姐失意。讓韋翰做你的對象吧。他是個有趣的傢伙，他會用很體面的辦法把你遺棄呢。"

"多謝您，爸爸，差一些的人也能使我滿意了。我們可不能都指望交上珍妮那樣的好運氣。"

"不錯，"班奈特先生說；"不管你交上了哪一種運氣，你那位好心的媽媽反正會盡心竭力來成全的，你只要想到這一點，就會感到安慰了。"

朗伯恩府上因為近來出了幾件不順利的事，好些人都悶悶不樂，幸好有韋翰先生跟他們來往來往，把這陣悶氣消除了不少。她們常常看到他，對他讚不絕口，又說他坦白爽直。伊莉莎白所聽到的那一套話——說甚麼達西先生有多少地方對他不起，他為達西先生吃了多少苦頭——大家都公認了，而且公開加以談論。每個人一想到自己在完全不知道這件事情時，早就十分討厭達西先生，便不禁非常得意。

　　只有班奈特小姐以為這件事裏面一定有些蹊蹺，還不曾為赫福德郡的人們弄清楚。她是個性子柔和、穩重公正的人，總是要求大家多多體察實情，認為事情往往可能給弄錯，可惜別人全把達西先生看作天下再混帳不過的人。

第二十五章

談情說愛，籌劃好事，就這樣度過了一星期，終於到了星期六，柯林斯先生不得不和心愛的夏綠蒂告別。不過，他既已作好接新娘的準備，離別的愁苦也就因此減輕了。他只等下次再來赫福德郡，訂下佳期，使他成為天下最幸福的男子。他像上次一樣隆重其事地告別了朗伯恩的親戚們，祝賀表妹們健康幸福，又答應給她們的父親再來一封謝函。

下星期一，班奈特太太的弟弟和弟婦照例到朗伯恩來過聖誕節，班奈特太太很是欣喜。賈汀納先生是個通情達理、頗有紳士風度的人物，無論在個性方面，以及在所受的教育方面，都遠勝他姐姐。他原是出身商界，見聞不出貨房堆疊之外，竟會這般有教養，這般討人喜愛，要是讓尼德斐莊園的太太小姐們看見了，實在難以相信。賈汀納太太比班奈特太太以及菲力普太太，都要小好幾歲年紀，也是個和藹聰慧、而又很文雅的女人。朗伯恩的外甥女們都很喜歡她，兩個大外甥女跟她特別親切。她們常常進城去在她那裏住一陣子。

賈汀納太太剛到這裏，第一件事就是分發禮物，講述最時新的服裝式樣。做過這件事以後，她便坐在一旁，靜聽班奈特太太跟她說話。班奈特太太有許多牢騷要發，又有許多苦要訴。自從上年她弟婦走了以後，她的家庭受到欺侮。兩個女兒本來快要出嫁了，最終只落得一場空。

"我並不怪珍妮，"她接下去說，"因為珍妮要是能夠嫁給賓利先生，她早就嫁了。可是莉茲——唉，弟婦呀！要不是她自己那麼拗性子，說不定她已做了柯林斯先生的夫人了。他就在這間房子裏向她求婚的，她卻把他拒絕了。結果倒讓盧卡斯太太有個女兒比我的女兒先嫁出去，朗伯恩的財產從此就得讓別人來繼承。的確，盧卡斯一家人手腕才高明呢，弟婦。他們都是為了要撈進這一筆財產。我本來也不忍心這樣來說他們的不是，不過事實的確是如此。我在家裏既然過得這樣不稱心，又偏偏碰到這些只顧自己不顧別人的鄰居，真弄得我精神緊張，人也病了。你可來得正是時候，給了我極大的安慰，我非常喜歡聽你講的那些……長袖子 25 的事情。"

賈汀納太太遠在跟珍妮以及伊莉莎白通信的時候，大體上就已經知道了她們家裏最近發生的這些事情，又為了體貼外甥女們起見，只稍微敷衍了班奈特太太幾句，便把這個話題岔開了。

後來伊莉莎白跟她兩人在一起的時候，又談到了這件事。她說："這倒也許是珍妮的一頭美滿親事，只可惜告吹了。可是這種情形往往難免！像你所說的賓利先生這樣的青年，往往在不到幾個星期的時間裏，就會愛上一位美麗的小姐，等到有一件偶然的事故把他們分開了，他也就很容易把她忘了，這種見異思遷的事情多的是。"

"你這樣的安慰完全是出於一片好心，"伊莉莎白說。"可惜安慰不了我們。我們吃虧並不是偶然的。一個獨立自主的青年，幾天以前剛剛跟一位小姐打得火熱，現在遭到了他自己朋友們的干涉，就把她丟了，這事情倒不多見。"

"不過，所謂'打得火熱'，這種話未免太陳腐，太籠統，太不切合實際，我簡直抓不住一點概念。這種話通常總是用來形容男女一見鍾情的場面，也用來形容一種真正的熱烈感情。請問，賓利先生的愛情火熱到甚麼程度？"

"我從來沒有看見過像他那樣的一往情深：他越來越不去理會別人，把整個的心都放在她身上。他們兩人每見一次面，事情就越顯得明朗，越惹人注目。在他自己所開的一次舞會上，他得罪了兩三位年輕的小姐，沒有邀請她們跳舞；我找他說過兩次話，他也沒有理我。這還不能算是盡心盡意嗎？寧可為了一個人而得罪大家，這難道還不是戀愛場上最可貴的地方？"

"噢，原來如此！這樣看來，他的確對她情深意切。可憐的珍妮！我真替她難受，照她的性子看來，決不會一下子就把這件事情淡忘。莉茲，要是換了你，倒要好些，你自會一笑置之，要不了多少時候就會淡忘。不過，你看我們能不能勸她到我們那裏去小住一陣？換換環境也許會有好處；再說，離開了家，鬆口氣，也許比甚麼都好。"

伊莉莎白非常贊成這個建議，而且相信姐姐也會贊成。

賈汀納太太又說："我希望她不要因為怕見到這位青年小伙子而拿不定主意。我們雖然和賓利先生同住在一個城裏，可是不住在同一個地區，來往的親友也不一樣；而且，你知道得很清楚，我們很少外出。因此，除非他上門來看她，他們兩人就不大可能見到面。"

"那是絕對不可能的，因為他現在被朋友們軟禁着，達西先生也不能容忍他到倫敦這樣的一個地區去看珍妮！親愛的舅母，你怎麼會想到這上面去了？達西先生也許聽到過恩典堂街這樣一個地方，可是，如果他真的到那裏去一次，他會覺得花上一個月的時間也洗不淨他身上所染來的污垢；請你放心好了，他絕不會讓賓利先生單獨行動。"

"那就更好。我希望他們兩人再也不要見面。可是，珍妮不還是在跟他妹妹通信嗎？賓利小姐也許難免要來拜訪呢。"

"她絕不會跟她再來往了。"

伊莉莎白雖然嘴上說得這麼果斷，認為賓利先生一定被他的姐妹朋友挾制住了，不會讓他見到珍妮，這事情實在可笑，可是她心裏想來想去，還是覺得事情未必已經完全絕望。她有時候甚至認為賓利先生非常可能對珍妮舊情重燃，他朋友們的影響也許敵不過珍妮的感情所加在他身上更為自然的影響。

班奈特小姐樂意地接受了舅母的邀請，她心裏並沒有怎麼想到賓利一家人，只希望卡洛琳不和她哥哥同住，那麼她就可以偶爾到卡洛琳那裏去玩上一個上午，而不至於撞見她的哥哥。

賈汀納夫婦在朗伯恩住了一個星期，沒有哪一天不赴宴會，有時候在菲力普府上，有時候在盧卡斯府上，有時候又在軍官們那裏。班奈特太太周到地為她的弟弟和弟婦安排充實的節目，以致他們夫婦不曾在她家裏吃過一頓便飯。家裏有宴會的日子，必定就有幾位軍官到場，每次總是少不了韋翰。在這種場合下，伊莉莎白總是熱烈地讚揚韋翰先生，使得賈汀納太太起了疑心，仔細注意起他們兩人來。從她親眼看到的情形來說，她並不以為他們兩人真正地愛上了，不過相互之間顯然已經產生了好感，這令她很是不安，她決定在離開赫福德郡以前，要把這件事和伊莉莎白談個明白，並且要解釋給她聽，要是這樣的關係發展下去，實在太莽撞。

可是韋翰討好起賈汀納太太來，另有一套辦法，這和他吸引別人的本領完全不同。遠在十多年以前賈汀納太太還沒有結婚的時候，曾在德比郡他所出生的那個地區住過好些時候，因此她跟他有許多共同的朋友。雖說自從五年前達西先生的父親去世以後，韋翰就不多到那地方去，可是他卻能向賈汀納太太報導一些有關她以前的朋友們的消息，比她自己打聽得來的還要新鮮。

賈汀納太太曾經親眼見過龐百利，對於老達西先生也是久聞大名，光是這件事，就是個談不完的話題。她把韋翰先生所詳盡描述的龐百利和她自己記憶中的龐百利比較了一下，又把龐百利已故主人的德行稱讚了一番，談的人和聽的人都各得其樂。她聽到他談起現在這位達西先生對他的虐待，便竭力去回想那位先生小時候的個性如何，是否和現在相符。她終於記起了從前確實聽人說過，費茨威廉・達西先生是個脾氣很壞又很高傲的孩子。

第二十六章

賈汀納太太一碰到有適當的機會和伊莉莎白單獨談話，就善意地對外甥女進行忠告，把心裏的話老老實實講了出來，然後又接下去說：

"你是個非常懂事的孩子，莉茲，你不至於因為別人勸你談戀愛要當心，你就偏偏要談；因此我才敢向你說個明白。說正經話，你千萬要小心。跟這種沒有財產作為基礎的人談戀愛，實在非常莽撞，你千萬別讓自己墜入情網，也不要費盡心機使他墜入情網。我並不是說他的壞話——他倒是個再有趣不過的青年；要是他得到了他應當得到的那份財產，那我就會覺得你這頭親事最好不過。事實既是如此，你大可不必再對他想入非非。你很聰明，我們都希望你不要辜負了自己的聰明。我知道你父親信任你品行好，又果斷，你千萬不可令他失望。"

"親愛的舅母，你真是鄭重其事。"

"是呀，我希望你也能夠鄭重其事。"

"唔，你不用着急。我自己會當心，也會當心韋翰先生。只要我避免得了，我決不會讓他跟我戀愛。"

"伊莉莎白，你這話可就不鄭重其事了。"

"請原諒。讓我重新講一講。目前我可並沒有愛上韋翰先生；我的確沒有。不過在我所看見的人當中，他的確是最可愛的一個，任誰也比不上他；如果他真會愛上我——我相信他還是不要愛上我才好。我看出了這件事很莽撞。噢！那可惡的達西先生！父親這樣器重我，真是我最大的榮幸，我要是辜負了他，一定會覺得遺憾。可是我父親對韋翰也有成見。親愛的舅母，總而言之，我決不願意讓你們任何人為了我而不快活；不過，青年人一旦愛上了甚麼人，決不會因為暫時沒有錢就肯撒手。要是我也被人打動了心，我又怎能免俗？甚至我又怎麼知道拒絕他是不是上策？因此，我只能答應你不倉促行事就是了。我決不會一下子就認為我自己是他最中意的人。我雖然和他來往，可是決不會心存這種幻想。總而言之，我一定盡力而為。"

"假如你不讓他來得這麼勤，也許會好些；至少你不必提醒你母親邀他來。"

伊莉莎白羞怯地笑笑說："就像我那天的做法一樣，的確，最好是不要那樣。可是你也不要以為他是一直來得這麼勤。這個星期倒是為了你才常常請他來的。你知道媽的主意，她總以為她自己的朋友非得經常有人陪着不可。可是請你相信我好了，我總會想出最聰明的辦法去應付的；我希望你總該滿意了吧。"

舅母告訴她說她滿意了；伊莉莎白謝謝她好心的指點，於是二人就分別了——在這種問題上給別人提出意見而沒受抱怨，這次倒可算是一個稀罕的例子。

賈汀納夫婦和珍妮剛剛離開了赫福德郡，柯林斯先生就回到赫福德郡了。他住在盧卡斯府上，因此班奈特太太並沒有多大的不方便。他的婚期已經迫近，因此班奈特太太不但終於死了心，認為這頭親事是免不了的，甚至還三番四次惡意地說："但願他們可能會幸福吧。"星期四就是佳期，盧卡斯小姐星期三到班府上來辭行。當夏綠蒂起身告別的時候，伊莉莎白一方面由於母親那些陰陽怪氣的吉利話，使她聽得不好意思，另一方面自己也委實頗有感觸，便不由得送她走出房門。下樓梯的時候，夏綠蒂說：

"我相信你一定會常常給我寫信的，伊麗莎。"

"這你放心好了。"

"我還要你賞個臉。你願意來看看我嗎？"

"我希望我們能夠常常在赫福德郡見面。"

"我可能暫時不會離開肯特郡[26]。還是答應我上漢斯福來吧。"

伊莉莎白雖然預料到這種拜訪不會有甚麼樂趣，可又沒法推辭。

夏綠蒂又說：「我的父親和瑪麗亞三月裏要到我那裏去，我希望你跟他們一起來。真的，伊麗莎，我一定像歡迎他們一樣歡迎你。」

婚禮完結，新郎新娘從教堂門口直接動身往肯特郡去，大家總是照例你一句我一句的要說上許多話。伊莉莎白不久就收到了她朋友的來信，從此她們兩人的通信便極其正常，極其頻繁！不過，要像從前一樣地暢所欲言，毫無顧忌，那可辦不到了。伊莉莎白每逢寫信給她，都免不了感覺到過去那種推心置腹的快慰已經不復存在；雖說她也下定決心，不要把通信疏懶下來，不過，那與其說是為了目前的友誼，倒不如說是為了過去的交情。她對於夏綠蒂的前幾封信都盼望得很迫切，那完全是出於一種好奇心，想要知道夏綠蒂對於她的新家庭觀感如何，她是不是喜歡凱瑟琳夫人，是不是覺得自己幸福，雖然讀了她那幾封信以後，伊莉莎白就覺得夏綠蒂所說的話，處處都和她自己所預料的完全一樣。她的信寫得充滿了愉快的情調，講到一件事總要讚美一句，好像她真有說不盡的快慰。凡是住宅、傢具、鄰居、道路，樣樣都令她稱心，凱瑟琳夫人待人接物又是那麼友善，那麼親切。她只不過把柯林斯先生所誇耀的漢斯福和洛欣莊園的面貌，稍微說得委婉一些罷了；伊莉莎白覺得，一定要等到親自去那裏拜訪，才能了解原委。

珍妮早已寄了一封短信給伊莉莎白，說她已經平安抵達倫敦；伊莉莎白希望她下次來信能夠講述一些有關賓利家的事。

第二封信真等得她焦急，可是總算沒有白等。信上說，她已經進城一個星期，既沒有看見卡洛琳，也沒有收到卡洛琳的信。她只得認為她上次從朗伯恩寄給卡洛琳的那封信，一定是在路上遺失了。

她接下去寫道：「明天舅母要上那個地區去，我想趁這個機會到格魯斯汶納街去登門拜訪一下。」

珍妮拜訪過賓利小姐並且和她見過面以後，又寫了一封信來。她寫道：「我覺得卡洛琳精神不大好，可是她見到我卻很高興，而且怪我這次到倫敦來為甚麼事先不通知她一下。我果然沒有猜錯,我上次給她的那封信,她真的沒有收到。我當然問起她們的兄弟。據說他近況很好,不過和達西先生過從太密,以致姐妹兄弟很少機會見面。聽說達西小姐要上她們那裏去吃飯,我但願能和她見見面。我這一次拜訪的時間並不太久,因為卡洛琳和赫斯托太太都要出去。也許她們馬上就會上我這裏來看我。"

伊莉莎白讀着這封信,不由得搖頭。她相信,除非有甚麼偶然的機會,賓利先生決不會知道珍妮來到了倫敦。

四個星期過去了,珍妮還沒有見到賓利先生的影子。她竭力寬慰自己說,她並沒有因此而覺得難受;可是賓利小姐的冷淡無情,她到底看明白了。她每天上午都在家裏等賓利小姐,一直白等了兩個星期;每天晚上都替賓利小姐編造一個藉口,最後那位貴客才算上門來了,可是只逗留了片刻便告辭而去,而且她的態度也前後判若兩人,珍妮覺得再不能自己騙自己了。她把這一次的情形寫了封信告訴她妹妹,從這封信裏可以看出她當時的心情:

我最最親愛的莉茲妹妹:現在我不得不承認,賓利小姐對我的關注完全是騙我的。我相信你一定不會因為你的見解比我高明而幸災樂禍。親愛的妹妹,雖然如今事實已經證明你的看法是對的,可是,我如果從她過去的態度來看,我依舊認為,我對她的信任以及你對她的懷疑,同樣都是合情合理的,請你不要以為我固執。我到現在還不明白她從前為甚麼要跟我親近;如果再有同樣的情況發生,我相信我還會受到欺騙。卡洛琳一直到昨天才來看我,她沒來以前不曾給我片紙隻字的訊息,來了之後又顯出十分不樂意的樣子。她只是照例敷衍了我一句,說是沒有早日來看我,很是抱歉,此外根本就沒有提起她想要再見見我的話。她在種種方面都前後判若兩人,因此,當她臨走的時候,我就下定決心和她斷絕來往,雖說我禁不住要怪她,可是我又可憐她。只怪她當初不該對我另眼看待;我可以問心無愧地說，我和她的交情都是由她主動一步一步進展起來的。可是我可憐她，因為她一定會感覺到自己做錯了，我斷定她之所以採取這種態度，完全是由於為她哥哥擔心的緣故。我用不着為自己再解釋下去了。雖然我們知道這種擔心完全不必要，不過，倘若她真的這樣擔心，那就足以說明她為甚麼要這樣對待我了。既然他確實值得他妹妹珍惜，那麼，不管她替他擔的是甚麼憂，那也是合情合理，親切可喜。不過，我簡直不懂她到現在還要有甚麼顧慮，要是他真的有心於我，我們早就會見面了。聽她的口氣，我肯定他是知道我在倫敦的；然而從她談話的態度看來，就好像她確信他是真的傾心於達西小姐似的。這真讓我弄不明白。要是我大膽地下一句刻薄的斷語，我真忍不住要說，其中一定大有蹊蹺。可是我一定會竭力打消一切痛苦的念頭，只去想一些能使我高興的事——比如想想你的親切以及親愛的舅父母對我始終如一的關懷。希望很快就收到你的信。賓利小姐說起他再也不會回到尼德斐莊園來，說他打算放棄那幢房子，可是說得並不怎麼肯定。我們最好不必再提起這件事。你從漢斯福我們那些朋友那裏聽到了許多令人愉快的事，這使我很高興。請你跟威廉爵士和瑪麗亞一起去看看他們吧。我相信你在那裏一定會過得很舒適。

姐字

這封信使伊莉莎白感到有些難過；不過，一想到珍妮從此不會再受到他們的欺蒙，至少不會再受到那個妹妹的欺蒙，她又高興起來了。她現在已經放棄了對那位兄弟的一切期望。她甚至根本不希望他再來重修舊好。她越想越看不起他；她倒真的希望他早日跟達西先生的妹妹結婚，因為照韋翰說來，那位小姐往後一定會令他後悔，後悔當初不該把本來的意中人甩了，這一方面算是給他一種懲罰，另一方面也可能有利於珍妮。

大約就在這時候，賈汀納太太把上次伊莉莎白答應過怎樣對待韋翰的事，又向伊莉莎白提醒了一下，並且問起最近的情況如何；伊莉莎白回信上所說的話，雖然自己頗不滿意，可是舅母聽了卻很滿意。原來他對她的顯著的好感已經消失，他對她的殷勤也已經過去——他愛上別人了。伊莉莎白很留心地看出了這一切，可是她雖然看出了這一切，在信上也寫到這一切，卻並沒有感到甚麼痛苦，她只不過稍微有些感觸。她想，如果她有些財產，早就成為他惟一的意中人了——想到這裏，她的虛榮心也就得到了滿足。拿他現在所傾慕的那位小姐來說，她最顯著的魅力就是使他可以獲得一萬英鎊的意外鉅款；可是伊莉莎白對自己這件事，也許不如上次對夏綠蒂的事那麼看得清楚，因此並沒有因為他追求物質享受而怨怪他。她反而以為這是再自然不過的事；她也想像到他捨棄她一定頗費躊躇，可又覺得這對於雙方都是一種既聰明而又理想的辦法，並且誠心誠意地祝他幸福。

她把這一切都對賈汀納太太說了。敍述了這些事以後，她接下去這樣寫道：“親愛的舅母，我現在深深相信，我根本沒有怎樣愛他，假如我真的有了這種純潔而崇高的感情，那我現在一聽到他的名字都會覺得討厭，而且希望他倒盡了霉。可是我情緒上不僅對他沒有一絲芥蒂，甚至對金小姐也毫無成見。我根本不覺得恨她，並且極其願意把她看作一個很好的小姐。這件事完全算不上戀愛。我的小心提防並不是枉然的；要是我狂戀着他，親友們就一定會把我看作一個更有趣的話柄了，我決不因為別人不十分器重我而感到遺憾。太受人器重有時候需要付出很大的代價。凱蒂和麗迪亞對他的缺點計較得比我厲害。她們在人情世故方面還幼稚得很，還不懂得這樣一個有失體統的信條：美少年和凡夫俗子一樣，也得有飯吃，有衣穿。”

第二十七章

朗伯恩這家人除了這些事以外，再沒有別的大事；除了到麥里頓去散散步以外，再沒有別的消遣。時而雨水泥濘、時而寒風刺骨的正月和二月，就這樣過去了。三月裏伊莉莎白要上漢斯福去。開始她並非打定主意前往；可是她立刻想到夏綠蒂對於原來的約定寄予了很大的期望，於是她也就帶着比較樂意和比較肯定的心情來考慮這個問題了。離別促進了她想和夏綠蒂重逢的願望，也消除了她對柯林斯先生的厭惡。這個計劃多少總有它新奇的地方；再説，家裏有了這樣的母親和這樣幾位不能融洽相處的妹妹，自難完美無缺，換換環境也好。趁着旅行的機會也可以去看看珍妮；總之，時日迫近了，她反而有些等不及了。好在一切都進行得很順利，最後依舊照了夏綠蒂原先的意思，跟威廉爵士和他的第二個女兒一起去做一次客。後來又補充了一下，決定在倫敦住一夜，這個計劃就更加完美了。

只有和父親離別使她感到痛苦，父親一定會記掛她。説起來，他根本就不願意讓她去，既是事情已經決定，只得叫她常常寫信給他，而且幾乎答應親自給她寫回信。

她跟韋翰先生告別時，雙方都十分客氣，韋翰比她還要客氣。他目前雖然在追求別人，卻並沒有因此就忘了伊莉莎白是第一個引起他注目的人，第一個值得他注目的人，第一個聽他傾訴衷情，第一個可憐他，第一個博得了他愛慕的人；他向她告別，祝她萬事如意，又對她説了一遍德·包爾夫人是怎樣的一個人，他相信他們兩人對那位老夫人的評價，對每一個人的評價，一定完全吻合。他説這話的時候，顯得很是熱誠，很是關切，這種盛情一定會使她對他永遠懷着極其深摯的好感。他們分手以後，她更相信不管他結婚也罷，單身也罷，他在她的心目中始終會是一個極其和藹可親而又討人喜歡的人。

第二天和她同路的那些人，也並沒有使韋翰在她心目中相形見絀。威廉爵士簡直說不出一句中聽的話，他那位女兒瑪麗亞雖然脾氣很好，腦子卻像她父親一樣空洞，也說不出一句中聽的話。聽他們父女兩人說話，就好像聽到車輛的轆轆聲一樣無聊。伊莉莎白本來愛聽無稽之談，不過威廉爵士那一套她實在聽得膩了。他談來談去總不外乎覲見國王以及榮膺爵士頭銜之類的奇聞，翻不出甚麼新花樣來；他那一套禮貌舉止，也像他的言談一樣，已經陳腐不堪。

這段旅程不過二十四英里路[27]，他們啟程很早，為的是要在正午趕到恩典堂街。他們走近賈汀納先生的大門時，珍妮正從會客室的窗戶望着他們。他們走進過道時，珍妮正等在那裏迎接他們，伊莉莎白真摯地仔細望了望珍妮的臉，只見那張臉龐還是像往常一樣地健康美麗，她覺得很高興。男男女女的孩子們為了急於要見到表姐，容不下在客廳裏等侯，又因為一年沒見面，不好意思下樓去，便都在樓梯口靜侯。到處是一片歡樂與和善的氣氛。這一天過得極其愉快：上午亂哄哄地忙作一團，又要出去買東西；晚上則到戲院去看戲。

伊莉莎白在舅母身旁坐下來。她們兩人首先就談到她姐姐。她仔細問了許多話，舅母回答她說，珍妮雖然竭力提起精神，還免不了有情緒低落的時候，她聽了並不十分詫異，卻很憂鬱。幸好這種情緒低落的現象不會持續多久。賈汀納太太也跟伊莉莎白談起賓利小姐拜訪恩典堂街的一切情形，又把珍妮跟她好幾次的談話重述了一遍給她聽，這些話足以說明珍妮的確打算再也不和賓利小姐來往了。

賈汀納太太然後又談起韋翰拋棄伊莉莎白的話，把她外甥女笑話了一番，同時又讚美她的忍耐力。

她接着又說：「可是，親愛的伊莉莎白，金小姐是怎麼樣的一個女子？我可不願意把我們的朋友看作一個見錢眼開的人啊。」

「請問你，親愛的舅母，拿婚姻問題來講，見錢眼開與動機正當究竟有甚麼不同？做到甚麼地步為止就算知禮，打哪裏起就要算是貪心？去年聖誕節你還生怕我跟他結婚，怕的是不鄭重其事，而現在呢，他要去跟一個只不過有一萬鎊財產的小姐結婚，你就要說他見錢眼開了。」

「只要你告訴我，金小姐是怎麼樣一個女子，我就知道該怎麼說話了。」

「我相信她是個好女孩。我說不出她有甚麼壞處。」

「可是韋翰本來完全不把她放在眼裏，為甚麼她祖父一去世，她做了這筆家產的主人，他就會看上了她呢？」

「沒有的事，他為甚麼要那樣？要是說，他不願意跟我相愛，就是因為我沒有錢，那麼，他一向不關心的一個小姐，一個同樣窮的小姐，他又有甚麼理由要去跟她談戀愛呢？」

「不過，她家裏一發生這件變故，他就去向她獻殷勤，這未免不像話吧。」

「一個處境困難的人，不會像一般人那樣有閒，去注意這些繁文縟節。只要她不反對，我們為甚麼要反對？」

「她不反對，並不說明他就做得對。那只不過說明了她本身有甚麼缺陷，不是見識方面有缺陷，就是感覺方面有缺陷。」

「哦，」伊莉莎白叫道：「你愛怎麼說就怎麼說吧，說他貪財也好，說她傻也好。」

「不，莉茲，我才不這麼說呢。你知道，在德比郡住了這麼久的一個青年，我是不忍心說他壞話的。」

「噢，要是光光就憑這點理由，我才看不起那些住在德比郡的青年人呢，他們住在赫福德郡的那批知己朋友們，也好不了多少，他們全都讓我討厭。謝謝老天爺！明天我就要到一個地方去，我將要在那裏見到一個一無可取的人，他無論在風度方面，在見解方面，都不見長。話說到尾，只有那些傻瓜值得你去跟他們來往來往。」

"當心些，莉茲；這種話未免說得太消沉了些。"

她們看完了戲，剛要分手的時候，舅父母又邀請她參加他們的夏季旅行，這真是一件意外的樂事。

賈汀納太太說："至於究竟到甚麼地方去，我們還沒有最後決定，也許到湖區 [28] 去。"

對伊莉莎白來說，任何的計劃也不會比這個計劃更合她心意了，她毫不猶豫地接受了這個邀請，而且非常感激。"我的好舅母，親舅母，"她歡天喜地地叫了起來，"多高興，多幸福！你給了我新的生命和活力。我再也不沮喪和憂鬱了。人比起高山大石來，算得了甚麼？我們將要度過一些多麼快樂的時日啊！等到我們回來的時候，一定不會像一般遊人那樣，甚麼都是浮光掠影。我們一定會知道到過甚麼地方——我們看見過的東西一定會牢記。湖泊山川決不會在我們腦子裏亂七八糟地混做一團；我們要談到某一處風景的時候，決不會連位置也弄不明白，彼此爭論不休。但願我們一回來敍述起遊蹤浪跡的時候，不要像一般旅客那樣陳腔濫調，讓人聽不入耳。"

第二十八章

二天旅途上的每一樣事物，伊莉莎白都感到新鮮有趣；她精神很愉快，因為看到姐姐氣色那麼好，可以不用再為她的健康擔心，加上一想到去北方的旅行，她就更加高興。

當他們離開了大路，走上一條通往漢斯福的小徑時，每一隻眼睛都在尋找着那幢牧師住所；每拐一個彎，都以為就要看到那幢房子。他們沿着洛欣莊園的柵欄往前走。伊莉莎白想到外界所傳聞的那家人的種種情形，不禁微笑。

終於看到那幢牧師住所了。大路斜對面的花園、花園裏的房子、綠的柵欄以及桂樹圍籬——每一樣東西好像都在宣佈他們快到了。柯林斯先生和夏綠蒂走到門口來了。在賓主頻頻點頭脈脈微笑中，客人們在一道小門前停下了車，從這裏穿過一條短短的鵝卵石鋪道，便能直達正屋。很快，他們都下了車，賓主相見，無限歡欣。柯林斯太太笑容滿面地歡迎自己的朋友，伊莉莎白受到這麼親切的歡迎，就更加滿意這次的作客了。她立刻看到她表兄並沒有因為結了婚而改變態度，他還是完全和以往一樣地拘泥禮節，在門口耽擱了她好幾分鐘，問候她全家大小的起居安好。聽到她一一回答了之後，他才滿意。於是他就沒有再耽擱他們，只指給他們看看門口是多麼整潔，便把客人們請進了門；等到客人一走進客廳，他又對他們作了第二次的歡迎，極其客氣地說，這次承蒙諸位光臨寒舍，真是不勝榮幸，並且一次又一次把他太太送上來的點心遞給客人。

伊莉莎白早就料到他會那樣得意非凡，因此當他誇耀那牧師住所的優美結構、式樣以及一切陳設的時候，她不禁想到他是特地講給她聽的，好像要令她明白，她當初拒絕了他，是多麼大的一個損失。雖說樣樣東西的確都那麼整潔和舒適，她可千萬不能流露出一點點後悔的痕跡來讓他得意；她甚至帶着詫異的目光看着夏綠蒂，她弄不明白夏綠蒂和這樣的一位伴侶相處，為甚麼還會那麼高興。柯林斯先生有時竟會說些很不得體的話，令他自己的太太聽了也不免難為情，而且這類話又說得並不少。每逢這種場合，伊莉莎白就不由自主地要向夏綠蒂望一眼。有一兩次她看見夏綠蒂微微臉紅了，不過一般總是很聰明地裝作沒有聽見。大家在屋裏坐了好久，欣賞着每一件傢具，從食器櫥一直欣賞到壁爐架，又談了談一路上的情況以及倫敦的一切情形，然後柯林斯先生就請他們到花園裏去散散步。花園很大，佈置得也很好，一切都是由他親手照料的。他最高尚的娛樂就是收拾花園。夏綠蒂說，這種勞作有益於健康，她盡可能鼓勵他這樣做；她講起這件事的時候，非常鎮定自若，真讓伊莉莎白佩服。他領着他們走遍了花園裏的曲徑小道，看遍了每一處景物，每看一處都得瑣瑣碎碎地講一陣，美不美倒完全不在他心上，看的人即使想要迎合他，讚美幾句，也插不上嘴。他數得出每一個方向有多少田園，連最遠的樹叢裏有多少棵樹他也講得出來，可是，不論是他自己花園裏的景物也好，或者是這整個鄉村甚至全國的名勝古蹟也好，都萬萬比不上洛欣莊園的景色。洛欣莊園差不多就在他住宅的正對面，四面是樹，從樹林的空隙處可以望見裏面。那是一幢漂亮的近代建築，聳立在一片高地上。

柯林斯先生本來想把他們從花園裏帶去看看他的兩塊草坪，但是太太小姐們的鞋子抵擋不住那殘餘的白霜，於是全都走回去了，只剩下威廉爵士陪伴着他。夏綠蒂陪着自己的妹妹和朋友參觀住宅，她能夠撇開丈夫的幫忙，有機會讓她自己顯顯身手，真是高興極了。房子很小，但是建築結實，使用也很方便；一切都佈置得很精巧，安排得很協調，伊莉莎白對夏綠蒂誇獎備至。只要不想起柯林斯先生，便真正有了一種非常舒適的氣氛。伊莉莎白看見夏綠蒂那樣得意，便不由得想到她平常一定不把柯林斯先生放在心上。

伊莉莎白已經打聽到凱瑟琳夫人還在鄉下。吃飯的時候又談起了這件事，當時柯林斯先生立即插嘴說：

"正是，伊莉莎白小姐，星期日晚上你就可以榮幸地在教堂裏見到凱瑟琳・德・包爾夫人，你一定會喜歡她的。她為人極其謙和，絲毫沒有架子，我相信那天做完禮拜之後，你就會很榮幸地受到她的注目。我可以毫不猶豫地說，只要你住在這裏，每逢她賞臉請我們做客的時候，總少不了要請你和我的小姨子瑪麗亞。她對待我親愛的夏綠蒂真是好極了。我們每星期去洛欣莊園吃兩次飯，老夫人從來沒有哪一次讓我們步行回家，總是派自己的馬車送我們——我應該說，是派她的某一輛馬車，因為她有好幾輛車子呢。"

夏綠蒂又說："凱瑟琳夫人的確是個可尊敬的、通達情理的女人，而且是位極其殷勤的鄰居。"

"說得很對，親愛的，你真說到我心裏去了。像她這樣一位夫人，你無論對她怎樣尊敬，依舊會感到有些欠缺。"

這一晚主要就談論赫福德郡的新聞，又把以前信上所說的話重新再提一遍。大家散了以後，伊莉莎白孤孤單單地在房間裏，不由得默默想起了夏綠蒂對於現狀究竟滿意到甚麼程度，駕馭丈夫的手腕巧妙到甚麼程度，容忍丈夫的度量又大到甚麼程度。她不由得承認，一切都處理得非常好。她又去想像着這次做客的時間將如何度過，無非是：平淡安靜的日常起居，柯林斯先生那種惹人討厭的插嘴打岔，再加上跟洛欣莊園的酬酢來往等等。她那豐富的想像力馬上解決了整個問題。

大約在第二天晌午的時候，她正在房間裏準備出去散散步，忽然聽到樓下一陣喧嘩，馬上這整個住宅裏的人好像都慌亂了起來；很快，就聽到有人急急忙忙飛奔上樓來，大聲叫她。她開了門，在樓梯口遇見了瑪麗亞，只見她激動得氣都喘不過來，大聲說道：

"噢，親愛的伊麗莎呀，請你趕快到餐廳裏去，那裏有了不起的場面值得看呢！可我不告訴你是怎麼回事。趕快呀，馬上下樓來。"

伊莉莎白一遍遍問，也問不出一個究竟來；瑪麗亞多一句也不肯跟她透露；於是她們兩人便奔進那間面臨着大路的餐廳，去看個究竟。原來來了兩位女客，乘着一輛低低的四輪馬車，停在花園門口。

伊莉莎白連忙大聲説道："就是這麼回事嗎？我還以為是豬闖進了花園呢，原來只不過是凱瑟琳夫人母女兩人。"

瑪麗亞聽她説錯了，不禁大吃一驚："哎，親愛的，那不是凱瑟琳夫人。那位老夫人是詹金森太太，她跟她們住在一起的；另外一位是德·包爾小姐。你看看她那副模樣吧。她真是個非常纖小的人兒。誰會想到她會這麼單薄，這麼小！"

"她真太沒有禮貌，風這樣大，卻讓夏綠蒂站在門外。她為甚麼不進來？"

"噢，夏綠蒂説，她很難得進來。德·包爾小姐要是進來一次，那可真是天大的面子。"

"她那副模樣我喜歡，"伊莉莎白一面説，一面又突然起了別的種種念頭。"她看上去身體不好，脾氣又壞。她配他 [29] 真是再好不過呢。她做他的太太極其相稱。"

柯林斯先生和夏綠蒂都站在門口跟那兩位女客談話。伊莉莎白覺得最好笑的是，威廉爵士正恭恭敬敬地站在門口，誠懇地瞻仰着面前的貴客，每當德·包爾小姐朝着他這邊望的時候，他總是一再鞠躬。

後來他們的話全説完了，兩位女客驅車而去，別人都回到屋裏。柯林斯一看到兩位小姐，就恭賀她們走了鴻運；夏綠蒂把他的意思解釋給她們聽，原來洛欣莊園明天要請他們全體去吃飯了。

第二十九章

洛欣莊園這一次請客,真使得柯林斯先生感到洋洋得意。他本來一心要讓這些好奇的賓客們去瞻仰一下他那女恩人的堂皇氣派,看看老夫人對待他們夫婦兩人多麼禮貌周全。他竟會這麼快就得到了如願以償的機會,這件事足以說明凱瑟琳夫人的禮賢下士,使得他不知如何景仰是好。

"説老實話,"他説,"老夫人邀請我們星期日去吃茶點,在洛欣莊園消磨一個下午,我一點也不覺得意外。她一貫為人和藹,我倒以為她真要這樣招待一番的,可是誰料想得到會像這次這樣情意隆重?誰會想到你們剛剛到這裏,就被請到那邊去吃飯(而且全體都邀請了)?"

威廉爵士説:"剛才的事我倒不怎麼覺得稀奇,大人物的為人處事實在都是如此,像我這樣有身份的人,就見識過很多。在顯宦貴族們當中,這類風雅好客的事不足為奇。"

這一整天和第二天上午,簡直只談到去洛欣莊園的事。柯林斯先生預先仔細地一一告訴他們,到那邊去將要看到些甚麼東西,免得他們看到了那樣宏偉的宅院,那樣眾多的僕從,那樣豐盛的菜餚,會造成臨時慌亂,手足無措。

當小姐們正要各自去打扮的時候,他又對伊莉莎白説:

"不要為衣着擔心,親愛的表妹。凱瑟琳夫人才不會要我們穿得華麗呢,這只有她自己和她的女兒才配。我勸你只要在你自己的衣服裏面,揀一件出色的穿上就行,不必過於講究。凱瑟琳夫人決不會因為你衣着樸素就看不起你。她喜歡各人守着自己的本份,分得出一個高低。"

小姐們整裝的時候,他又到各個人的房門口去了兩三次,勸她們快一點，因為凱瑟琳夫人請人吃飯最討厭客人遲到。瑪麗亞・盧卡斯聽說老夫人的為人處事這樣可怕，不由得嚇了一跳，因為她一向不大會應酬。她一想起要到洛欣莊園去拜訪，就誠惶誠恐，正如她父親當年進宮觀見一樣。

天朗氣清，他們穿過花園，作了一次差不多半英里的愉快的散步。各家的花園都各有美妙，伊莉莎白縱目觀賞，心曠神怡，可是並不如柯林斯先生所預期的那樣，被那眼前的景色陶醉得樂而忘形。儘管他數着屋前一扇扇窗戶說，光是這些玻璃，當初曾一共花了路易斯・德・包爾爵士多大一筆錢，她可並不為這些話動心。

他們踏上台階走進穿堂的時候，瑪麗亞一分鐘比一分鐘來得惶恐，連威廉爵士也不能完全保持鎮定。倒是伊莉莎白毫不畏縮。無論是論才論德，她都沒有聽到凱瑟琳夫人有甚麼了不起的地方足以引起她敬畏，光憑着有錢有勢，還不會令她見到了就膽顫心驚。

進了穿堂，柯林斯先生就帶着一副喜極欲狂的神氣，指出這裏的堂皇富麗，然後由傭人們帶着客人走過前廳，來到凱瑟琳夫人母女和詹金森太太的起坐間。夫人極其謙和地站起身來迎接他們。根據柯林斯太太事先跟她丈夫商量好的辦法，當場由太太出面替賓主介紹，因此介紹得很得體，凡是柯林斯先生認為必不可少的那些道歉和感激的話，都一概免了。

威廉爵士雖說當年也曾進宮觀見過國王，可是看到四周圍這般的富貴氣派，也不禁完全給嚇住了，只得彎腰一躬，一聲不響，坐了下來；再說他的女兒，簡直嚇得失魂落魄一般，坐在椅子邊上，眼睛也不知道往哪裏看才好。伊莉莎白倒是完全安然自若，而且從容不迫地細細看着那三位女主人。凱瑟琳夫人是位高大的婦人，五官清楚，也許年輕時很好看。她的樣子並不十分客氣，接待賓客的態度也不能使賓客忘卻自己身份的低微。她嚇人的地方倒不是默不作聲，而是她出言吐語時聲調總是那麼高高在上，自命不凡，這令伊莉莎白立刻想起了韋翰先生的話。經過了這一整天的察言觀色之後，她覺得凱瑟琳夫人的為人，果然和韋翰所形容的完全一樣。

她仔細打量了她一眼，立刻就發覺她的容貌有些像達西先生，然後她就把目光轉到她的女兒身上。只見她女兒長得那麼單薄，那麼瘦小，這使她幾乎和瑪麗亞一樣感到驚奇。母女二人無論體態面貌，都沒有相似之處。德·包爾小姐臉色蒼白、滿面病容，五官雖然長得不算難看，可是並不起眼；她不大說話，除非是低聲跟詹金森太太嘀咕幾句。詹金森太太的相貌沒有一點突出的地方，她只是全神貫注地聽着小姐說話，並且擋在她面前，不讓別人把她看得太清楚。

坐了幾分鐘以後，客人們都被請到窗邊去欣賞外面的風景。柯林斯先生陪着他們，一處處指給他看，凱瑟琳夫人和善地告訴他們說，到了夏天還要好看。

酒席果然特別體面，侍候的僕從以及盛酒菜的器皿，也跟柯林斯先生所形容過的一模一樣，而且正如他事先所料到的那樣，夫人要他和她對席而坐，看他那副神氣，好像人生沒有比這更得意的事了。他邊切邊吃，又興致淋漓地讚不絕口；每一道菜都由他先來誇獎，然後由威廉爵士加以吹噓，原來威廉爵士現在已經完全消除了驚恐，可以做他女婿的應聲蟲了。伊莉莎白看到那種樣子，不禁擔心凱瑟琳夫人怎麼受得了。可是凱瑟琳夫人對這些過份的讚揚好像倒非常滿意，總是顯露出仁慈的微笑，尤其是端上一道客人們沒見過的菜到桌上來的時候，她便格外得意。賓主們都沒有甚麼可談的，伊莉莎白卻只要別人開個頭，總還有話可說，可惜她坐的地方不對頭，一邊是夏綠蒂，她正在用心聽凱瑟琳夫人談話；另一邊是德·包爾小姐，整個吃飯時間不跟她說一句話。詹金森太太主要在注意德·包爾小姐，她看到小姐東西吃得太少，便逼着她吃了這樣再吃那樣，又怕她不舒服。瑪麗亞根本不想講話，男客們只顧一邊吃一邊讚美。

女客們回到會客室以後，只是聽凱瑟琳夫人談話。夫人滔滔不絕地一直談到咖啡端上來為止。隨便談到哪一件事，她總是那麼斬釘截鐵、不容許別人反對的樣子。她毫不客氣地仔細問着夏綠蒂的家常，又給她提供了一大堆關於管理家務的意見。她告訴夏綠蒂説，像她這樣的一個小家庭，一切事情都應該精密安排，又指教她如何照料母牛和家禽。伊莉莎白發覺這位貴婦人只要有機會支配別人，隨便怎麼小的事情也決不肯輕易放過。夫人跟柯林斯太太談話的時候，也偶爾向瑪麗亞和伊莉莎白問幾句話，特別向伊莉莎白問得多。她不大清楚伊莉莎白和她們是甚麼關係，不過她對柯林斯太太説，她是個很斯文、很標緻的小姐。她好幾次問伊莉莎白有幾個姐妹，她們比她大還是比她小，她們中間有沒有哪一個就要結婚，她們長得好看不好看，在哪裏讀書，她們的父親有甚麼樣的馬車，她母親的娘家姓甚麼。伊莉莎白覺得她這些話問得唐突，不過還是心平氣和地回答了她。於是凱瑟琳夫人説：

“你父親的財產得由柯林斯先生繼承吧，我想？”——説到這裏，她又掉過頭來對夏綠蒂説：“為你着想，我倒覺得高興；否則我實在看不出有甚麼理由不讓自己的女兒們來繼承財產，卻要給別人。路易斯‧德‧包爾家裏就覺得沒有這樣做的必要。——你會彈琴唱歌嗎，班奈特小姐？”

“略知一二。”

“噢，如果有機會的話，我們倒想要聽一聽。我們的琴非常好，説不定比——你哪一天來試一試看吧。你的姐妹們會彈琴唱歌嗎？”

“有一個會。”

“為甚麼不大家都學呢？你們應該個個都學。韋伯家的小姐們就個個都會，她們父親的收入還比不上你們父親呢。你們會畫畫嗎？”

“不，一點也不會。”

“甚麼，一個也不會嗎？”

“沒有一個會。”

“這倒很稀奇。我猜想你們是沒有機會學吧。你們的母親應該每年春天帶你們上城裏來投投名師才對。”

"我媽是不會反對的，可是我父親厭惡倫敦。"

"你們的女家庭教師走了嗎？"

"我們從來就沒有請過女家庭教師。"

"沒有女家庭教師！那怎麼行？家裏教養着五個小姐，卻不請個女家庭教師！我從來沒聽到過這樣的事！你媽簡直是做牛做馬地教育你們了。"

伊莉莎白禁不住笑起來了，一面告訴她說，事實並不是那樣。

"那麼誰教導你們呢？誰服侍你們呢？沒有一個女家庭教師，你們不就是沒人照料了嗎？"

"相比而言，我們家裏對待我們可以算是比較懈怠；可是姐妹們中間，凡是好學的，決不會沒有辦法。家裏經常鼓勵我們好好讀書，必要的教師我們都有。誰要是存心偷懶，當然也可以。"

"那是毫無疑問的；不過，女家庭教師的任務也就是為了防止這種事情；要是我認識你們的母親，我一定要竭力勸她請一位。我總以為缺少了按部就班的指導，教育就不會有任何成績，而按部就班的指導就只有女家庭教師辦得到。說起來也很有意思，許多個家庭都是由我介紹女家庭教師的。我一向喜歡好好安插年輕人。詹金森太太的四個姪女都由我給她們介紹了稱心如意的位置；就在前幾天，我又推薦了一位小姐，她不過是有人偶然在我面前提起的，那家人對她非常滿意。——柯林斯太太，我有沒有告訴過你，麥特卡菲夫人昨天來向我道謝？我覺得蒲白小姐真是件珍寶呢。她跟我說：'凱瑟琳夫人，你給了我一件珍寶。'——你的妹妹們有沒有哪一個已經出來交際了，班奈特小姐？"

"有，太太，全都出來交際了。"

"全都出來交際了！甚麼，五個姐妹同時出來交際？真奇怪！你不過是第二個！姐姐還沒有嫁人，妹妹就出來交際了！你的妹妹們一定還很小吧？"

"是的；最小的一個才十六歲。或許她還太小，不適宜多交朋友。不過，太太，要是因為姐姐無法早嫁，或是不想早嫁，做妹妹的就不能有社交和娛樂，那實在太苦了她們。最小的和最大的同樣有享受青春的權利。怎麼能為了這樣的原由，就讓她們死守在家裏！我以為那樣做就不可能促進姐妹之間的感情，也不可能養成溫柔的性格。"

"真想不到，"夫人說，"你這麼小的一個人，倒這樣有主見。請問你幾歲了？"

"我已經有了三個成年的妹妹，"伊莉莎白笑着說。"您總不會再要我說出年紀來了吧。"

凱瑟琳夫人沒有得到直截了當的回答，顯得很驚奇；伊莉莎白覺得敢於和這種沒有禮貌的富貴太太開玩笑，恐怕要推她自己為第一個人。

"你不會超過二十歲，所以你也不必隱瞞年紀了。"

"我不到二十一歲。"

等到喝過了茶，男客們都到她們這邊來了，便擺起牌桌來。凱瑟琳夫人、威廉爵士和柯林斯夫婦坐下來打"誇錐"牌；德·包爾小姐要玩"卡西諾"[30]，因此兩位小姐就很榮幸地幫着詹金森太太，給她湊足了人數。她們這一桌真是枯燥無味，除了詹金森太太問問德·包爾小姐是否覺得太冷或太熱，是否感到燈光太強或太弱以外，就沒有一句話不是說到打牌方面的。另外一桌可就有聲有色得多了。凱瑟琳夫人差不多一直都在講話，不是指出另外三個人的錯處，就是講些自己的趣聞軼事。她說一句，柯林斯先生就附和一句，他贏一次要謝她一次，如果贏得太多，還得向她道歉。威廉爵士不大說話，只顧着將一件件軼事和一個個高貴的名字裝進腦子裏去。

等到凱瑟琳夫人母女兩人玩得不想再玩的時候，兩桌牌就散場了，派馬車送柯林斯太太回去，柯林斯太太很感激地接受了，於是馬上叫人去套馬。大家又圍着火爐，聽凱瑟琳夫人斷定明天的天氣怎麼樣。等到馬車來了，叫他們上車，他們才停止受教。柯林斯先生說了許多感激的話，威廉爵士鞠躬不止，大家這才告別。馬車一走出門口，柯林斯先生就要求伊莉莎白發表她對於洛欣莊園的感想，她看在夏綠蒂面上，便勉強敷衍了他幾句。她雖然勉為其難地說出了一大篇好話，卻完全不能使柯林斯先生滿意，柯林斯沒有辦法，只得立刻親自開口，把老夫人大大地重新讚揚了一番。

第三十章

威廉爵士在漢斯福只住了一個星期，可是經過了這一次短短的拜訪，他大可以放心了：女兒實在是嫁得極其稱心如意，而且有了這樣不可多得的丈夫和難能可貴的鄰居。威廉爵士在這裏作客的時候，柯林斯先生總是每天上午同他乘着雙輪馬車，帶他到郊野去漫遊；他走了以後，家裏又恢復了日常生活。伊莉莎白真要謝天謝地，因為這一次做客，跟她表兄柯林斯朝夕相見的次數並不多。原來他從吃早飯到吃午飯那一段時間裏，不是在收拾花園，就是在自己那間面臨着大路的書房裏看書寫字，憑窗遠眺，而女客的起坐間又在後面那一間。伊莉莎白剛開始很奇怪：這裏的餐廳比較大，位置光線也比較好，為甚麼夏綠蒂不願意把餐廳兼作起居室？可是她立刻看出了她朋友之所以要這樣做的，的確非常有理由，因為假如女客也在一間同樣舒適的起坐間裏，那麼柯林斯先生留在自己房間裏的時間就要比較少了；她很讚賞夏綠蒂這樣的安排。

她們從會客室裏根本看不見外面大路上的情形，幸虧每逢有甚麼車輛駛過，柯林斯先生總是要告訴她們；特別是德·包爾小姐常常乘着小馬車駛過，差不多天天駛過，他沒有哪一次不告訴她們的。小姐常在牧師住所的門前停下車來，跟夏綠蒂閒談幾分鐘，可是主人從來不請她下車。

柯林斯先生差不多每天要到洛欣莊園去一趟，他的太太也是隔不了幾天就要去一次。伊莉莎白總以為他們還有些別的應得的俸祿要去處理一下，否則她就不懂得為甚麼要犧牲那麼多時間。有時候夫人也光臨他們的住宅，來了以後就把無論甚麼事都看在眼裏。她查問他們的日常生活，察看他們的家務，勸他們換個方式處置；又吹毛求疵地說，他們的傢具擺得不對，或者是他們的傭人在偷懶；要是她肯在這裏吃點東西，那好像只是為了要看看柯林斯太太是否持家節儉，不濫吃濫用。

伊莉莎白立刻就發覺，這位貴婦人雖然沒有擔任郡裏的司法職務，可是事實上她就像是她自己這個教區裏最積極的法官，一點點芝麻綠豆的事都由柯林斯先生報告給她。只要哪一個佃戶在吵架，鬧意見，或是窮得活不下去，她總是親自到村裏去調解處理，鎮壓制服，又罵得他們一個個相安無事，不再叫苦歎窮。

洛欣莊園大約每星期要請她們吃一兩次飯；儘管缺少了威廉爵士，而且只有一桌牌，不過每一次這樣的宴會排場都照舊。他們簡直沒有別的宴會，因為附近一般住戶的那種生活派頭，柯林斯還高攀不上。不過伊莉莎白並不覺得遺憾，因為她在這裏大體上是過得夠舒服的了：經常和夏綠蒂愉快地交談半個小時，加上這個季節裏又天氣晴朗，可以常常到戶外去舒暢一下。別人去拜訪凱瑟琳夫人的時候，她總是愛到花園旁邊那座小林子裏去散散步，那裏有一條很美的綠蔭小徑，她覺得那地方只有她一個人懂得欣賞；而且到了那裏，也就可以避免惹起凱瑟琳夫人的好奇心。

她前兩個星期的作客生涯，就這樣安靜地過去了。復活節快到了，節前一星期，洛欣府上要添一個客人。在這麼一個小圈子裏，這當然是件大事。伊莉莎白一到那裏，便聽說達西先生在最近幾個星期裏就要到來。雖然她覺得在她所認識的人裏面，差不多沒有一個像達西這樣討厭，不過他來了卻能給洛欣莊園的宴會上添一個面貌比較新鮮的人，同時可以從他對他表妹的態度看出賓利小姐在他身上的打算要完全落空，那就更有趣了。凱瑟琳夫人顯然已經把他安排給他的表妹，一談到他要來，就得意非凡，對他讚美備至。可是一聽說盧卡斯小姐和伊莉莎白早就跟他認識，又時常見面，就幾乎好像生起氣來。

不久，柯林斯家裏就知道達西來了；因為牧師先生那天整個上午都在漢斯福路旁的門房附近走動，以便盡早獲得確鑿的消息；等到馬車駛進花園,他就鞠了一個躬,連忙跑進屋去報告這重大的新聞。第二天上午,他趕快到洛欣莊園去拜會。他一共要拜會凱瑟琳夫人的兩位外甥,因為達西先生還帶來了一位費茨威廉上校,是達西的舅父(某某爵士)的小兒子。柯林斯先生回家來的時候,把那兩位貴賓也帶來了,大家很是吃驚。夏綠蒂從她丈夫的房間裏看到他們一行三人從大路那邊走過來,便立刻奔進另外一個房間,告訴小姐們説,她們馬上就會有貴客光臨,接着又説:

"伊麗莎,這次的貴客光臨,我得感謝你呀。否則達西先生才不會一下子就來拜訪我呢。"

伊莉莎白聽到這番恭維話,還沒有來得及申辯,門鈴就響了,宣佈貴賓蒞臨。不久,賓主三人一同走進屋來。帶頭的是費茨威廉上校,大約三十歲左右,人長得不英俊,可是從儀表和談吐看來,倒是個地道的紳士。達西先生完全是當初在赫福德郡的那副老樣子,用他往常一貫的矜持態度,向柯林斯太太問好。儘管他對她的朋友伊莉莎白可能另有一種感情,然而見到她的時候,神色卻極其鎮定。伊莉莎白只對他行了個屈膝禮,一句話也沒説。

費茨威廉上校立刻就跟大家攀談起來,口齒伶俐,像個有教養的人,並且談得頗有風趣;可是他那位表兄,卻只跟柯林斯太太把房子和花園稍稍評賞了幾句,就坐在那裏沒有跟任何人説話。終於,他想到了禮貌問題,便向伊莉莎白問候她和她全家人的安好。伊莉莎白照例敷衍了他幾句;停了片刻,她又説:

"我姐姐最近三個月來一直在城裏。你從來沒有碰到過她嗎?"

其實她明明知道他從來沒有碰到過珍妮,只不過為了想要探探他的口風,看看他是否知道賓利一家人和珍妮之間的關係。他回答説,不幸從來未曾碰到過班奈特小姐。她覺得他回答這話時神色有點慌張,這件事沒有再談下去,兩位貴賓立刻就告辭了。

第三十一章

費茨威廉的風度大受牧師家裏人的稱道，女眷們都覺得他會使洛欣莊園的宴會平添上不少情趣。不過，他們已經有好幾天沒有受到洛欣莊園那邊的邀請，因為主人家有了客人，用不着他們了；一直到復活節那一天，也就是差不多在這兩位貴賓到達一星期以後，他們才蒙受到被邀請的榮幸，那也不過是大家離開教堂時，主人家當面約定他們下午去玩玩而已。上一個星期他們簡直就沒有見到凱瑟琳夫人母女。在這段時間裏，費茨威廉到牧師家來拜訪過好多次，但是達西先生卻沒有來過，他們僅僅在教堂裏才見到他。

他們當然都接受了邀請，準時到達了凱瑟琳夫人的會客室。夫人客客氣氣地接待了他們，不過事實很明顯，他們並不像請不到別的客人時那樣受歡迎；而且夫人的心幾乎都在兩位外甥身上，只顧跟他們說話，特別是跟達西說話比跟房間裏任何人都說得多。

倒是費茨威廉上校見到他們好像很高興，因為洛欣莊園的生活實在單調無味，他很想要有點調劑，而且柯林斯太太的這位漂亮朋友更使他十分喜歡。他就坐到她身邊去，那麼有聲有色地談到肯特郡，談到赫福德郡，談到旅行和家居，談到新書和音樂，簡直談得伊莉莎白感覺到在這個房間裏從來沒有受到過這樣的款待；他們兩人談得那麼興致淋漓，連凱瑟琳夫人和達西先生也注意起來了。達西的一對眼睛立刻好奇地一遍遍在他們兩人身上打轉；過了一會，夫人也有了同感，而且顯得更露骨，她毫不猶豫地叫道：

"你們說的是甚麼啊，費茨威廉？你們在談些甚麼？你跟班奈特小姐在說些甚麼話？說給我聽聽看。"

"我們談談音樂，姑母，"費茨威廉迫不得已地回答了一下。

"談音樂！那麼請你們說得大聲一些吧。我最喜愛音樂。要是你們談音樂，就得有我的份。我想，目前在英國，沒有幾個人能像我一樣真正欣賞音樂，也沒有人比我趣味更高。我要是學了音樂，一定會成為一個名家。安妮要是身體好，也一定會成為一個名家的。我相信她演奏起來，一定動人。喬治安娜現在學得怎麼樣了，達西？"

達西先生極其懇切地把他自己妹妹的成就讚揚了一番。

"聽到她彈得這樣好，我真高興，"凱瑟琳夫人說；"請你替我告訴她，要是她不多多練習，那她也好不到哪裏去。"

"姨母，你放心吧，"達西說，"她用不着你這樣的勸告。她經常在練習。"

"那就更好。練習總不怕太多，我下次有空寫信給她，一定要囑咐她無論如何不得偷懶。我常常告訴年輕的小姐們說，要想在音樂上出人頭地，就非要經常練習不可。我已經告訴過班奈特小姐好幾次，除非她再多練習練習，她永遠不會好到哪裏去；我常常對她說，柯林斯太太那裏雖然沒有琴，我卻很歡迎她每天到洛欣莊園來，在詹金森太太房間裏那座鋼琴上彈奏。你知道，在那間房間裏，她不會妨礙甚麼人的。"

達西先生看到姨母這種無禮的態度，覺得有些丟臉，因此沒有去理她。

喝過了咖啡，費茨威廉上校提醒伊莉莎白說，她剛剛答應過彈琴給他聽，於是她馬上坐到琴邊去。他拖過一把椅子來坐在她身旁。凱瑟琳夫人聽了半首歌，便像剛才那樣又跟這一位外甥談起話來，一直談得這位外甥終於避開了她，從容不迫地走到鋼琴前站住，以便把演奏者的美麗的面貌看個清楚明白。伊莉莎白看出了他的用意，彈到一個段落，便停下來，回過頭來對他俏皮地一笑，說道：

"達西先生，你這樣走過來聽，莫不是想嚇唬我？儘管你妹妹的確演奏得很好，我也不怕。我性子倔強，決不肯讓別人把我嚇倒。別人越是想來嚇倒我，我的膽子就越大。"

達西說："我決不會說你講錯了，因為你不會真以為我存心嚇你；好在我認識你很久了，知道你就喜歡説一些口是心非的話。"

伊莉莎白聽到他這樣形容她，便高興地笑了起來，於是對費茨威廉説道，"你表弟竟在你面前把我説成一個多糟糕的人，教你對我的話一句也不要相信。我真晦氣，我本來想在這裏騙騙人，讓人相信我多少有些長處，偏偏碰上了一個看得穿我真正性格的人。——真的，達西先生，你把我在赫福德郡的一些倒霉事都一股腦了出來，你這是不厚道的——而且，請允許我冒昧説一句，你這也是不聰明的——因為你這樣做，會引起我的報復心，我也會説出一些事來，讓你的親戚們聽了嚇一跳。"

"我才不怕你呢，"他微笑地説。

費茨威廉連忙叫道："我倒要請你説説看，他有甚麼不是。我很想知道他跟陌生人一起的時候，行為怎麼樣。"

"那麼我就講給你聽吧；我先得請你不要覺得不中聽。你得明白，我第一次在赫福德郡看見他，是在一個舞會上；你知道他在這個舞會上做些甚麼？他一共只跳了四次舞！我不願意讓你聽了難受，不過事實確是這樣。雖説男客很少，他卻只跳了四次，而且我知道得很清楚，當時在場的女客中間，沒有舞伴而閒坐在一旁的不止一個人呢——達西先生，你不能否認有這件事啊。"

"説來遺憾，當時舞場上除了我自己人以外，一個女客也不認識。"

"不錯，舞場裏是不能請人介紹女朋友的。——唔，費茨威廉上校，再讓我彈甚麼呢？我的手指在等着你吩咐。"

達西説："也許我當時最好請人介紹一下，可是我又不配去向陌生人自我推薦。"

"我們要不要問問你表弟，這究竟是甚麼緣故？"伊莉莎白仍然對着費茨威廉上校説話。"我們要不要問問他，一個有見識、有閱歷、而又受過教育的人，為甚麼不配把自己介紹給陌生人？"

費茨威廉説："我可以回答你的問題，用不着請教他。那是因為他自己怕麻煩。"

達西說:"我的確不像有些人那樣有本領,遇到向來不認識的人也能任情談笑。我也不會像有些人那樣隨聲附和,假意關切。"

伊莉莎白說:"我彈起鋼琴來,手指不像許多女子技巧那麼熟練,也不像她們那麼有力和靈活,也沒有她們彈得那麼有表情。我一直認為這是我自己的缺點,是我自己不肯用功練習的緣故。可是我不信我的手指不及那些比我彈奏得高明的女人。"

達西笑了笑說:"你說得完全對。你花的時間並不多,可見成效卻要好得多。凡是有福份聽過你演奏的人,都覺得你毫無欠缺的地方。我們兩人都不願意在陌生人面前表演。"

說到這裏,凱瑟琳夫人大聲地問他們談些甚麼,打斷了他們的話。伊莉莎白立刻重新彈起琴來。凱瑟琳夫人走近前來,聽了幾分鐘以後,就對達西說:

"班奈特小姐如果再多加練習,能夠請一位倫敦名師指點指點,彈起來就不會有毛病了。雖說她的趣味比不上安妮,可是她很懂得指法。安妮要是身體好,能夠學習的話,一定會成為一位令人滿意的演奏者。"

伊莉莎白望着達西,要看看他聽了夫人對他表妹的這番誇獎,是不是竭誠表示贊同,可是當場和事後都看不出他對她有一絲一毫愛的跡象;從他對待德·包爾小姐的整個態度看來,她不禁替賓利小姐感到安慰:要是賓利小姐跟達西是親戚的話,達西一定也會跟她結婚。

凱瑟琳夫人繼續對伊莉莎白的演奏發表意見,還給了她許多關於演奏和鑒賞方面的指示。伊莉莎白只得極其克制地虛心領教。她聽從了兩位男客的請求,一直坐在鋼琴旁邊,彈到夫人備好了馬車送他們大家回家。

第三十二章

第二天早晨，柯林斯太太和瑪麗亞到村裏辦事去了，伊莉莎白獨自坐在家裏寫信給珍妮。這時候她突然嚇了一跳，因為門鈴響了起來，肯定是有客人來了。她並沒有聽到馬車聲，心想，可能是凱瑟琳夫人來了，於是她就不安地把那封寫好一半的信放在一旁，免得她問些魯莽的話。就在這時，門開了，她大吃一驚，萬萬想不到走進來的是達西先生，而且只有達西先生一個人。

達西看見她單獨一個人，也顯得很吃驚，連忙道歉說，他原以為太太小姐們全都沒有出去，所以才冒昧闖進來。

他們兩人坐了下來，她向他問了幾句關於洛欣莊園的情形以後，雙方便好像都無話可說，大有陷入僵局的危險。因此，非得想點甚麼說說不可；正在這緊張關頭，她想起了上次在赫福德郡跟他見面的情況，頓時便起了一陣好奇心，想要聽聽他對那次匆匆的離別究竟有些甚麼看法，於是她便說道：

"去年十一月你們離開尼德斐莊園時，是多麼突然呀，達西先生！賓利先生看見你們大家一下子都跟着他走，一定相當驚奇吧；我好像記得他比你們只早走一天。我想，當你離開倫敦的時候，他和他的姐妹們一定身體都很好吧？"

"好極了，謝謝你。"

她發覺對方沒有別的話再回答她了，過了一會便又說道：

"我想，賓利先生大概不打算再回到尼德斐莊園來了吧？"

"我從來沒有聽到他這麼說過；不過，可能他不打算在那裏久住。他有很多朋友，像他這樣年齡的人，交際應酬當然一天比一天多。"

"如果他不打算在尼德斐莊園久住，那麼，為了街坊四鄰着想，他最好乾脆退租，讓我們可以得到一個固定的鄰居。不過賓利先生租那幢房子，說不定只是為了他自己方便，並沒有顧念到鄰舍，我看他那幢房子無論是保留也好，退租也好，他的原則都是一樣。"

達西先生說："我料定他一旦買到了合適的房子，馬上就會退租。"

伊莉莎白沒有回答。她惟恐再談到他那位朋友身上去；既然沒有別的話可說，她便決定讓他動動腦筋，另外找個話題來談。

他領會了她的用意，過了一會便說道："柯林斯先生這所房子倒好像很舒適呢。我相信他初到漢斯福的時候，凱瑟琳夫人一定在這上面費了好大一番心血吧。"

"我也覺得，而且我敢說，她的好心並沒有白費，因為天下再也找不出一個比他更懂得感恩戴德的人了。"

"柯林斯先生娶到了這樣一位太太，真是福氣。"

"是呀，的確是福氣；他的朋友們應當為他高興，難得有這樣一個頭腦清楚的女人肯嫁給他，嫁了他又能使他幸福。我這位女朋友是個絕頂聰明的人，不過她跟柯林斯先生結婚，我可並不認為是上策。她倒好像極其幸福，而且，用普通人的眼光來看，她這婚姻當然攀得很好。"

"她離開娘家和朋友都這麼近，這一定會使她很滿意的。"

"你說很近嗎？快五十英里呢。"

"只要道路方便，五十英里能算遠嗎？只要大半天就到了。我認為很近。"

伊莉莎白大聲說道："我從來沒有認為道路的遠近，也成了這婚姻的有利條件之一，我決不會說柯林斯太太住得離家很近。"

"這說明你自己太留戀赫福德郡。我看你只要走出朗伯恩一步，就會嫌遠。"

他說這話的時候，不禁一笑，伊莉莎白覺得自己領會了他這一笑的深意：他一定以為她想起了珍妮和尼德斐莊園吧，於是她紅了臉回答道：

"我並不是説，女人就不許嫁得離娘家太近。遠近是相對的，還得看各種不同的情況來決定。只要你出得起盤纏，遠一些又何妨。這裏的情形卻不是這樣。柯林斯夫婦雖然收入還好，可也經不起經常旅行；即使把目前的距離縮短到一小半，我相信我的朋友也不會以為離娘家近的。"

達西先生把椅子移近她一些，説道："你可不能有這麼重的鄉土觀念。你總不能一輩子住在朗伯恩呀。"

伊莉莎白神色有些詫異。達西也覺得心情有些兩樣，便把椅子拖後一點，從桌子上拿起一張報紙看了一眼，用一種比較冷靜的聲音説：

"你喜歡肯特郡嗎？"

於是他們兩人把這個村莊短短地談論了幾句，彼此都很冷靜，措辭也頗簡潔。不久，夏綠蒂跟她妹妹散步回來了，談話就此終止。夏綠蒂姐妹兩人看到他們促膝談心，都覺得詫異。達西先生把他剛才誤闖進來遇見班奈特小姐的原委説了一遍，然後稍稍坐了幾分鐘就走了，跟誰也沒有多談。

他走了以後，夏綠蒂便説："這是甚麼意思？親愛的伊麗莎，他一定愛上你了，否則他決不會這樣隨隨便便來看我們的。"

伊莉莎白把他剛才那種對坐無言的情形告訴了她，夏綠蒂便覺得自己縱有這番好意，看上去又不像是這麼事事。她們東猜西揣，結果只有認為他這次是因為閒來無聊，所以才出來探親訪友。這種説法倒還算講得過去，因為到了這個季節，一切野外的活動都停止了，留在家裏雖然可以和凱瑟琳夫人談談，看看書，還可以打台球，可是男人們總不能一直不出房門；既然牧師住所相隔很近，順便散散步到這裏來玩玩，也很愉快，況且那人又很有趣味。於是兩位表兄弟在這段作客時期，差不多每天都禁不住要上這裏來走一趟。他們總是上午來，遲早沒有一定，有時候分頭來，有時候一同來，有時姨母也跟他們一起來。女眷們看得非常明白，費茨威廉來訪，是因為他喜歡跟她們在一起——這當然使大家更加喜歡他。伊莉莎白跟他在一起就覺得很滿意,他顯然也愛慕伊莉莎白,這兩重情況使伊莉莎白想起了她以前的心上人喬治·韋翰;雖說把這兩個人比較起來,她覺得費茨威廉的風度沒有韋翰那麼溫柔迷人,然而她相信他也許知識面更廣。

可是達西先生為甚麼常到牧師家裏來,這仍然讓人不容易明白。他不可能是為了要熱鬧,因為他老是在那裏坐上十分鐘一句話也不說,說起話來也好像是迫不得已的樣子,而不是真有甚麼話要說——好像是在禮貌上委曲求全,而不是出於內心的高興。他很少有真正興高采烈的時候。柯林斯太太簡直弄不懂他。費茨威廉有時候笑他呆頭呆腦,可見他平常並不是這樣,柯林斯太太當然弄不清其中的原委。她但願他這種變化是戀愛所造成的,而且戀愛的對象就是她的朋友伊莉莎白,於是她一本正經地動起腦筋來,要把這件事弄個明白。每當她們去洛欣莊園的時候,或是他來到漢斯福的時候,她總是注意着他,可是毫無效果。他的確常常望着她的朋友,可是他那種目光究竟深意何在,還值得商榷。他望着她,的確很誠懇,可是柯林斯太太還是不敢斷定他的目光裏面究竟含有多少愛慕的情意,而且有時候那種目光簡直是完全心不在焉的樣子。

她曾經有一兩次向伊莉莎白暗示過,說他可能傾心於她,可是伊莉莎白老是一笑置之;柯林斯太太覺得不應該在這個問題上糾纏不休,不要撩撥得伊莉莎白動了心,最後卻只落得一個失望;在她看來,只要伊莉莎白自己覺得已經把他抓在手裏,那麼,毫無疑問,一切厭惡他的情緒自然都會消失的。

她好心好意地處處為伊莉莎白打算,有時候也打算把她嫁給費茨威廉。他真是個最有風趣的人,任何人也比不上他;他當然也愛慕她,他的社會地位又是再適當不過了;不過,達西先生在教會裏有很大的權力,而他那位表親卻根本沒有,相比之下,表親這些優點就無足輕重了。

第三十三章

伊莉莎白在花園裏散步的時候，曾經好多次出乎意料地碰見達西先生。別人不來的地方他偏偏會來，這真是不幸，她覺得好像是命運在故意跟她鬧彆扭。她第一次就對他說，她喜歡獨自一人到這地方來散步，當時的用意就是不讓以後再有同樣的事情發生。如果會有第二次，那才叫怪呢。然而畢竟有了第二次，甚至還有了第三次。看上去他好像是故意跟她過不去，否則就是有心要來賠不是；因為這幾次他既不是跟她敷衍幾句就啞口無言，也不是一下子就走開，而是真的掉過頭來跟她一起走走。他從來不多說話，她也懶得多講，懶得多聽；可是第三次見面，她覺得他問了她幾個稀奇古怪、毫無關連的問題。他問她住在漢斯福快活不快活，問她為甚麼喜歡孤孤單單一個人散步，又問起她是不是覺得柯林斯夫婦很幸福。談起洛欣莊園，她說她對於那家人不大了解，他倒好像希望她以後每逢有機會再到肯特郡來，也會去那裏小住一陣，從他的話裏面聽得出他有這層意思。難道他在替費茨威廉上校着想？她想，如果他的話真有弦外之音，那他一定是暗示那個人對她有些動心。她覺得有些惆悵，幸好已經走到牧師住所對面的圍牆門口，因此又覺得很高興。

有一天，她正在一面散步，一面重新讀着珍妮上一次的來信，把珍妮心灰意冷時所寫的那幾段仔細咀嚼着，這時候又讓人嚇了一跳，可是抬頭一看，只見這次並不是達西，而是費茨威廉上校正迎面走來。她立刻收起了那封信，勉強擠出一副笑臉，說道：

"沒想到你也會到這裏來。"

費茨威廉回答道："我每年都是這樣，臨走以前總得要到花園裏各處去兜一圈，最後上牧師家來拜訪。你還要往前走嗎？"

"不，我馬上就要回去了。"

於是她果真轉過身來，兩人一同朝着牧師住所走去。

"你真的星期六就要離開肯特郡嗎？"她問。

"是的，只要達西不再拖延。不過我得聽他調遣。他辦起事情來只是憑他自己高興。"

"即使不能順着他自己的意思去安排，至少也要順着他自己意思去選擇一下。我從來沒有看見過哪一個人，像達西先生這樣喜歡當權做主，為所欲為。"

"他太任性了，"費茨威廉上校回答道。"可是我們全都如此。只不過他比一般人有條件，可以那麼做，因為他有錢，一般人窮。我說的是真心話。你知道，一個小兒子可就不得不克制自己，依靠別人[31]。"

"在我看來，一個伯爵的小兒子，對這兩件事簡直就一點不懂。再說，我倒要問你一句正經話，你又懂得甚麼叫做克制自己和依靠別人呢？你有沒有哪一次因為沒有錢，而想去的地方去不成，愛買的東西買不了？"

"你問得好，或許我在這方面也是不知艱苦。可是遇到重大問題，我可能就會因為沒有錢而吃苦了。小兒子往往有了意中人而不能結婚。"

"除非是愛上了有錢的女人，我認為這種情形他們倒往往會碰到。"

"我們花錢花慣了，因此不得不依賴別人，像我這樣身份的人，結起婚來能夠不講錢，那可數不出幾個了。"

"這些話都是對我說的嗎？"伊莉莎白想到這裏，不禁臉紅；可是她立刻恢復了常態，用一種很活潑的聲調說道："請問，一位伯爵的小兒子，通常值多少身價？我想，除非哥哥身體太壞，你討起價來總不會超過五萬鎊。"

他也用同樣的口吻回答了她，這事便不再提。可是她又怕這樣沉默下去，他會以為她是聽了剛才那番話心裏難受，因此過了一會，她便説道：

"我想，你表親把你帶來留在他身邊，主要就是為了要有個人聽他擺佈。我不懂他為甚麼還不結婚，結了婚不就是可以有個人一輩子聽他擺佈了嗎？不過，目前他有個妹妹也許就可以了；既然現在由他一個人照料她，那他就可以愛怎麼對待她就怎麼對待她了。"

"不，"費茨威廉上校説，"這份好處還得讓我分享。我也是達西小姐的監護人。"

"你真的是嗎？請問，你這位監護人當得怎麼樣？你們這位小姐相當難侍候吧？像她那樣年紀的小姐，有時候真不大容易對付；假若她的脾氣也和達西一模一樣，她自然也會事事都憑她自己高興。"

她説這話的時候，只見他在情懇意切地望着她。他馬上就問她説，為甚麼她會想到達西小姐可能使他們感到棘手。她看他問這句話的神態，就更加斷定自己果真猜想得很接近事實。她立刻回答道：

"你不必慌張。我從來沒有聽到過她有甚麼缺點；而且我敢説，她是世界上最聽話的一位小姐。我的女朋友們中有幾個人，比如赫斯托太太和賓利小姐，都非常喜歡她。我好像聽你説過，你也認識她們的。"

"我和她們不大熟。她們的兄弟是個富有風趣的紳士派人物，是達西的好朋友。"

"噢，是呀，"伊莉莎白冷冷地説；"達西先生對賓利先生特別好，也照顧得他萬二分周到。"

"照顧他！是的，我的確相信，凡是他想不出辦法的事情，達西先生總是會替他想出辦法。我們到這裏來，路上他告訴了我一些事情，我聽了以後，便相信賓利先生確實應該感激他。可是我得請他原諒，我沒有權利猜想他所説的那個人就是賓利。那完全是瞎猜罷了。"

"你這話是甚麼意思？"

"這件事達西先生當然不願意讓大家知道，免得傳到那位小姐家裏去，惹得她不痛快。”

“你放心好了，我不會説出去的。”

“請你記住，我並沒有足夠的理由猜想他所説的那個人就是賓利。他只不過告訴我，他最近使一位朋友沒有結成一門冒昧的婚姻，免卻了許多麻煩，他覺得這件事值得慶幸，可是他並沒有提到當事人的姓名和其中的細節；我之所以會懷疑到賓利身上，一則因為我相信像他那樣的青年，的確會招來這樣的麻煩，二則因為我知道，他們在一起度過了整整一個夏天。”

“達西先生有沒有説他為了甚麼理由要管別人的閒事？”

“我聽説那位小姐有些條件太不合適。”

“他用甚麼手段把他們兩人拆開的？”

費茨威廉笑了笑説：“他並沒有説明他用的是甚麼手段，他講給我聽的，我剛才全都講給你聽了。”

伊莉莎白沒有回答，繼續往前走，心頭義憤填膺。費茨威廉望了她一下，問她為甚麼這樣思慮重重。

她説：“我在回想你剛才説給我聽的話，我覺得你那位表弟的做法不大好。憑甚麼要他做主？”

“你認為他的干涉完全是多管閒事嗎？”

“我真不懂，達西先生有甚麼權利斷定他朋友的戀愛合適不合適；憑着他一個人的意思，他怎麼就能指揮他的朋友要怎樣去獲得幸福。”她説到這裏，便平了一下氣，然後繼續説下去，“可是，既然我們不明白其中的底細，那麼，我們要指責他，也就難免不公平。也許這一對男女中間根本就沒有甚麼愛情。”

“這種推斷倒不能説不合情理。”費茨威廉説。“只是給你這樣一説，表弟的功勞可要大大地打折扣了。”

他這句話本是説着打趣的，可是她倒覺得，這句話正好是達西先生的一幅逼真的寫照，她因此不便回答，便突然改變了話題，盡談些無關緊要的事，邊談邊走，不知不覺來到了牧師住所的門前。客人一走，她就回到自己房裏閉門獨坐，把剛才聽來的一番話仔細思量。他剛剛所提到的那一對男女，一定跟她有關。世界上決不可能有第二個人會這樣無條件服從達西先生。提到用盡手段拆散賓利先生和珍妮的好事，一定少不了有他的份，她對於這一點從來不曾懷疑過；她一向認為主要是賓利小姐的主意和擺佈。如果達西先生本人並沒有給虛榮心衝昏頭腦，那麼，珍妮目前所受的種種痛苦，以及將來還要受下去的痛苦，都得歸罪於他，歸罪於他的傲慢和任性。世界上一顆最親切、最慷慨的心，就這樣讓他一手把幸福的希望摧毀得一乾二淨；而且誰也不敢說，他造下的這個冤孽何年何月才能了結。

"這位小姐有些條件差太遠了，"這是費茨威廉上校說的；這些差太遠的條件，也許就是指她有個姨丈在鄉下當律師，還有個舅舅在倫敦做生意。她想到這裏，不禁大聲叫了起來："至於珍妮本身，根本就不可能有甚麼缺陷，她真是太可愛太善良了——她見解高明，修養好，風度又動人；我父親也沒有甚麼可指摘的，他雖然有些怪癖，可是他的能力是達西先生所不能藐視的，說到他的品德，達西先生也許永遠趕不上。"當然，當她想到她母親的時候，她的信心不免稍有動搖；可是她不相信那方面的弱點對達西先生會有甚麼大不了的影響。最傷害他自尊心的莫過於讓他的朋友跟門戶低微的人結親，至於跟沒有見識的人結親，他倒不會過份計較。她最後得出一些結論：達西一方面是被這種最惡劣的傲慢心理支配着，另一方面是為了想要把賓利先生配給他自己的妹妹。

她越想越氣，眼淚直流，最後弄得頭痛起來了，晚上痛得更厲害，再加上她不願意看到達西先生，於是決定不陪她的表兄嫂上洛欣莊園去赴茶會。柯林斯太太看她確實有病，也就不便勉強她去，而且盡量不讓丈夫勉強她去；但是柯林斯先生禁不住有些慌張，生怕她不去會惹凱瑟琳夫人生氣。

第三十四章

伊莉莎白等柯林斯夫婦走了以後，便把她到肯特郡以來所收到的珍妮的信，全都拿出來一封封仔細閱讀，好像是為了故意要跟達西做冤家做到底似的。信上並沒有寫甚麼真正埋怨的話，既沒有提起過去的事情，也沒有訴說目前的痛苦。她素性嫻靜，心腸仁愛，因此她的文筆從來不帶一些陰暗的色彩，總是歡欣鼓舞的心情躍然紙上；可是現在，讀遍了她所有的信，甚至讀遍了她每一封信的字裏行間，也找不出這種歡欣的筆調。伊莉莎白只覺得信上每一句話都流露着不安的心情，因為她這一次是用心精讀的，比上一次仔細多了，所以注意到了這種地方。達西先生恬不知恥地誇口說，使人受罪是他的拿手好戲，這使她更加深刻地體會到姐姐的痛苦。幸好達西後天就要離開洛欣莊園，她總算稍覺安慰；而更大的安慰是，不到兩個星期，她又可以和珍妮在一起了，而且可以用盡一切情感的力量，去幫助她重新振作起精神來。

一想起達西就要離開肯特郡，便不免記起了他的表兄也要跟着他一起走；可是費茨威廉已經表明他自己決沒有甚麼意圖，因此，他雖然挺討人喜歡，她卻不至於為了他而不快活。

她正在轉着這種念頭，突然聽到門鈴響，她以為是費茨威廉來了，心頭不由得跳動起來，因為他有一天晚上就是來得很晚的，這回可能是特地來問候她。但是她立刻就知道猜錯了，出乎她的意料，走進屋來的是達西先生，於是她情緒上又是另一種感覺。他立刻匆匆忙忙地問她身體好了沒有，又說他是特地來祝她身體早日康復的。她客客氣氣地敷衍了他一下。他坐了幾分鐘，就站起身來，在房間裏踱來踱去。伊莉莎白心裏很奇怪，可是嘴上一言未發。沉默了幾分鐘以後，他帶着激動的神態走到她面前說："我實在沒有辦法死撐下去了。這怎麼行。我的感情再也壓制不住了。請允許我告訴你，我多麼敬慕你，多麼愛你。"

伊莉莎白真是說不出的驚奇。她瞪着眼，紅着臉，滿腹狐疑，沉默不語。他一看這情形，便認為她是在慫恿他講下去，於是立刻把目前和以往對她的種種好感全都和盤托出。他說得很動聽，除了傾訴愛情以外，又把其他種種的感想也原原本本說出來了。他一方面滔滔不絕地表示深情蜜意，但是另一方面卻又說了許許多多傲慢無禮的話。他覺得她出身低微，覺得自己是遷就她，而且家庭方面的種種障礙，往往會使得他的見解和他的心願不能相容並存——他這樣熱烈地傾訴，雖然顯得他這次舉動的慎重，卻未必能使他的求婚受到歡迎。

儘管她對他的厭惡之心根深蒂固，她終究不能對這樣一個男人的一番盛情，漠然無動於衷；雖說她的意志不曾有過片刻的動搖，可是她剛開始倒也體諒到他將會受到痛苦，因此頗感不安。然而他後來的那些話卻引起了她的怨恨，她那一片憐惜之心便完全化成了憤怒。不過，她還是竭力鎮定下來，以便等他把話說完，耐心地給他一個回答。末了，他跟她說，他對她的愛情是那麼強烈，儘管他一再努力克制，結果還是克服不了，他又向她表明自己的希望，說是希望她肯接受他的求婚。她一下子就看出他說這些話的時候，顯然自認為她毫無疑問會給他滿意的回答。他雖然口裏說他自己又怕又急，可是表情上卻是一副萬無一失的樣子。這只有惹得她更加憤怒；等他講完話以後，她就紅着臉說：

"遇到這一類的事情，通常的方式是這樣的：別人對你一片好心好意，你即使不能給以同樣的方式報答，也得表示一番感激。按照人情事理來說，感激之心是應該有的，要是我果真覺得感激，現在就得向你表示謝意。可惜我沒有這種感覺。我從來不稀罕你的抬舉，何況你抬舉我也是十分勉強。我從來不願意讓任何人感到痛苦，即使惹得別人痛苦，也是根本出於無心，而且我希望很快就會事過境遷。你跟我說，以前你顧慮到種種方面，因此沒有能夠向我表明你對我的好感，那麼，現在經過我這番解釋之後，你一定很容易把這種好感克制下來。"

達西先生本是斜倚在壁爐架上，一雙眼睛盯住了她看，聽到她這番話，好像又是氣憤又是驚奇。他氣得臉色鐵青，從五官的每一個部位都看得出他內心的煩惱。他竭力裝出鎮定的樣子，一直等到自以為已經裝像了，然後才開口說話。這片刻的沉默使伊莉莎白心裏非常害怕。最後達西才勉強沉住了氣說道：

"我很榮幸，竟得到你這樣一個回答！也許我可以請教你一下，為甚麼我竟會遭受到這樣沒有禮貌的拒絕？不過這也無關緊要。"

"我也可以請問一聲，"她回答道，"為甚麼你明明白白存心要觸犯我，侮辱我，嘴上卻偏偏要說甚麼為了喜歡我，竟違背了你自己的意志，違背了你自己的理性，甚至違背了你自己的性格？要是我果真沒有禮貌，那麼，這還不夠作為我沒有禮貌的理由嗎？可是我還有別的氣惱。你也知道我有的。就算我對你沒有反感，就算我對你毫無芥蒂，甚至就算我對你有好感吧，那麼請你想一想，一個毀了我姐姐的幸福的人，怎麼會打動我的心去愛他呢？我最心愛的姐姐的幸福，也許就這麼被永遠地毀了。"

達西先生聽了她這些話，臉色大變；不過這種感情的激動，只持續了一會就過去了，他聽着她繼續說下去，一點不想打岔。

"我有足夠的理由對你懷恨在心。你對待那件事完全無情無義，不論你是出於甚麼動機，都令人無可原諒。說起他們兩人的分離，即使不是你一手造成的，也是你主使的，這你不敢否認，也不能否認。你使得男方被大家指責為朝三暮四，使女方被大家嘲笑為奢望空想，你令他們兩人受盡了痛苦。"

她說到這裏，只見他完全沒有一點悔恨的意思，真使她氣得非同小可。他甚至還假裝出一副不相信的神氣在微笑。

"你能否認你這樣做過嗎？"她又問了一遍。

他故作鎮靜地回答道:"我不想否認。我的確用盡了一切辦法,拆散了我朋友和你姐姐的一段姻緣;我也不否認,我對自己那一次的成績覺得很得意。我對他總算比對我自己多盡了一份力。"

　　伊莉莎白聽了他這篇文雅的辭令,表面上並不願意顯出很注意的樣子。這番話的用意她當然明白,可是再也平息不了她的氣憤。

　　"不過,我還不止在這一件事情上面厭惡你,"她繼續說道,"我很早就厭惡你,對你有了成見。好幾個月以前聽了韋翰先生說的那些話,我就明白了你的品格。這件事你還有甚麼可說的?看你再怎樣來替你自己辯護,把這件事也異想天開地說是為了維護朋友?你又將怎麼樣來顛倒是非,欺世盜名?"

　　達西先生聽到這裏,臉色變得更厲害了,說話的聲音也不像剛才那麼鎮定,他說:"你對於那位先生的事的確十分關心。"

　　"凡是知道他的不幸遭遇的人,誰能不關心他?"

　　"他的不幸遭遇!"達西輕蔑地重複了一遍。"是的,他的確太不幸了。"

　　"這都是你一手造成的,"伊莉莎白激動地叫道。"你害得他這樣窮——當然並不是太窮。凡是指定由他享有的利益,你明明知道,卻不肯給他。他正當年輕力壯,應該獨立自主,你卻剝奪了他這種權利。這些事都是你做的,可是別人一提到他的不幸,你還要鄙視和嘲笑。"

　　"這就是你對我的看法!"達西一面大聲叫道,一面向房間那頭走去。"你原來把我看成這樣的一個人!謝謝你解釋得這樣周到。這樣看來,我真是罪孽深重!不過,"他停下腳步,轉過身來對她說:"只怪我老老實實地把我以前一誤再誤、遲疑不決的原因說了出來,所以傷害了你的自尊心,否則你也許就不會計較我得罪你的這些地方了。要是我要一點手段,把我內心的矛盾掩藏起來,一味恭維你,使你相信我無論在理智方面、思想方面,以及種種方面,都是對你懷着無條件的、純潔的愛,那麼,你也許就不會有這些苛刻的責罵了。可惜無論是甚麼樣的矯飾，我都痛恨。我剛才所說出的這些顧慮，我也並不以為可恥。這些顧慮是自然的，正確的。難道你指望我會為你那些微賤的親戚而歡欣鼓舞嗎？難道你以為，我要是攀上了這麼些社會地位遠不如我的親戚，倒反而會自己慶幸嗎？"

伊莉莎白越來越憤怒，然而她還是盡量平心靜氣地說出了下面這段話：

"達西先生，倘若你有禮貌一些，我拒絕了你以後也許會覺得過意不去；除此以外，倘若你以為這樣向我表白一下，會在我身上起別的作用，那你可想錯了。"

他聽到這番話，吃了一驚，可是沒有說甚麼，於是她又接着說下去：

"你用盡一切辦法，也不能打動我的心，讓我接受你的求婚。"

他又顯出很驚訝的樣子，他帶着痛苦和詫異的神情望着她。她繼續說下去：

"從一開始認識你的時候起，幾乎可以說，從認識你的那一剎那起，你的舉止行為，就使我覺得你非常狂妄自大、自私自利、看不起別人，我對你不滿的原因就在這裏，以後又有了許許多多事情，使我對你深惡痛絕；我還沒有認識你一個月，就覺得像你這樣一個人，在全天下的男人中我最不願意嫁的就是你。"

"你說得夠了，小姐。我完全理解你的心情，現在我只有對我自己那些顧慮感到羞恥。請原諒我耽擱了你這麼多時間，請允許我極其誠懇地祝你健康和幸福。"

他說了這幾句話，便匆匆走出房間。過了一會，伊莉莎白就聽到他打開大門走了。

她心裏紛亂無比。她不知道怎樣撐住自己，她非常軟弱無力，便坐在那裏哭了半個小時。她回想到剛的一幕，越想越覺得奇怪。達西先生竟會向她求婚，他竟會愛上她好幾個月了！不管她有多少缺點，竟會那樣地愛慕她，要和她結婚。何況她自己的姐姐正是由於這些缺點而受到他的阻撓，不能跟他朋友結婚，何況這些缺點對他至少具有同樣的影響——這真是一件不可思議的事！一個人能在不知不覺中博得別人這樣熱烈的愛慕，也足夠自慰了。可是他的傲慢，他那可惡的傲慢，他居然恬不知恥地招認他自己是怎樣破壞了珍妮的好事，他招認的時候雖然並不能自圓其說，可是令人難以原諒的是他那種自以為是的神氣，還有他提到韋翰先生時那種無動於衷的態度，他一點也不打算否認對待韋翰的殘酷——一想到這些事，縱使她一時之間也曾因為體諒到他一番戀情而觸動了憐憫的心腸，這時候連絲毫的憐憫也蕩然無存了。

她這樣迴腸百轉地左思右想，直到後來聽到凱瑟琳夫人的馬車聲，她才感覺到自己這副模樣，不能去見夏綠蒂，便匆匆回到自己房裏去了。

第三十五章

伊莉莎白昨夜一直沉思默想到合上眼睛睡覺為止,今天一大早醒來,心頭又湧起了這些沉思默想。她仍然對那件事感到詫異,無法想到別的事情上去;她根本無心做事,於是決定一吃過早餐就出去好好地透透氣,散散步。她正想往那條心愛的走道上走去,忽然想到達西先生有時候也上那裏來,於是便止了步。她沒有進花園,卻走上那條小路,以便和那條有柵門的大路隔得遠些。她仍舊沿着花園的圍柵走,不久便走過了一道園門。

她沿着這一段小路來回走了兩三趟,禁不住被那清晨的美景吸引得在園門前停住了,朝園裏望望。她到肯特郡五個星期以來,鄉村裏已經有了很大的變化,早春的樹一天比一天綠了。她正要繼續走下去,忽然看到花園旁邊的小林子裏有一個男人正朝這裏走來;她怕是達西先生,便立刻往回走。但是那人已經走得很近,可以看得見她了;只見那人急急忙忙往前跑,一面還叫着她的名字。她本來已經掉過頭來走開,一聽到有人叫她的名字,雖然明知是達西先生,也只得走回到園門邊來。達西這時候也已經來到園門口,拿出一封信遞給她,她不由自主地收下了。他帶着一臉傲慢而從容的神氣說道:"我已經在林子裏踱了一會,希望碰到你。請你賞個臉,看看這封信,好不好?"於是他微微鞠了一躬,重新走進草木叢中,立刻就不見了。

伊莉莎白拆開那封信;這是為了好奇,並不是希望從中獲得甚麼愉悅。使她更驚奇的是,信封裏裝着兩張信紙,以細緻的筆跡寫得密密麻麻。信封上也寫滿了字。她一面沿着小路走,一面開始讀信。信是早上八點鐘在洛欣莊園寫的,內容如下:

小姐：接到這封信時，請你不必害怕。既然昨天晚上向你訴說衷情和求婚，結果只有使你極其厭惡，我自然不會又在這封信裏舊事重提。我曾經衷心地希望我們雙方會幸福，可是我不想在這封信裏再提到這些，免得使你痛苦，使我自己受委屈。我之所以要寫這封信，寫了又要勞煩你去讀，這無非是拗不過自己的性格，否則便可以雙方省事。因此你得原諒我那麼冒昧地擾你清神，我知道你決不會願意勞神的，可是我要求你心平氣和一些。

　　你昨夜曾把兩件性質不同、輕重不等的罪名加在我頭上。你第一件指責我拆散了賓利先生和令姐的好事，完全不顧他們兩人之間如何情深意切，第二件指責我不顧體面，喪盡人道，蔑視別人的權益，毀了韋翰先生那指日可待的富貴，又斷送了他美好的前途。我竟無情無義，拋棄了自己小時候的朋友，一致公認為先父生前的寵兒，一個無依無靠的青年，從小起就指望我們施恩的人——這方面的確是我的一種遺憾；至於那一對青年男女，他們不過只有幾星期的交情，就算我拆散了他們，也不能同這件罪過相提並論。現在請允許我把我自己的行為和動機一一剖白一下，希望你弄明白了其中的原委以後，將來可以不再像昨天晚上那樣對我嚴詞苛責。在解釋這些必要的事情時，如果我迫不得已，要表述我自己的情緒，因而使你情緒不快，我只得向你表示歉意。既是出於迫不得已，那麼，再道歉未免就嫌可笑了。我到赫福德郡不久，就和別人一樣，看出了賓利先生在當地所有的少女中偏偏看中了令姐。但是一直等到在尼德斐莊園開舞會的那個晚上，我才顧慮到他真的對令姐有了愛戀之意。說到他的戀愛方面，我以前也看得很多。在那次舞會上，當我很榮幸地跟你跳舞時，我才聽到威廉·盧卡斯偶然說起賓利先生對令姐的殷勤已經弄得滿城風雨，大家都以為他們就要談到嫁娶問題。聽他說起來，好像婚事已定，只是遲早的問題罷了。從那時起，我就密切注意着我朋友的行為，於是我看出了他對班奈特小姐的鍾情，果然和他往常的戀愛情形大不相同。我也注意着令姐。她的神色和風度依舊像平常那樣落落大方，和藹可親，並沒有鍾情於任何人的跡象。根據我那一個晚上仔細觀察的情形看來，我確實認為她雖然樂意接受他的殷勤，可是她並沒有用深情蜜意來報答他。要是這件事你沒有弄錯，那麼錯處一定在我；你對於令姐既有透徹的了解，那麼當然可能是我錯了。倘若事實果真如此，倘若果真是我弄錯了，以致造成令姐的痛苦，那當然難怪你氣憤。可是我可以毫不猶豫地說，令姐當初的風度極其灑脫，即使觀察力最敏銳的人，也難免以為她儘管性情柔和，可是她的心不容易打動。我當初確實希望她無動於衷，可是我敢說，我雖然主觀上有我的希望，有我的顧慮，可是我的觀察和我的推斷並不會受到主觀情感的影響。我認為，令姐決不會因為我希望她無動於衷，她就真的無動於衷；我的看法大公無私，我的願望也合情合理。我昨天晚上說，遇到這樣不是門當戶對的婚姻，輪到我自己身上的時候，我必須用極大的情感上的力量加以壓制；至於說到他們兩人的婚姻，我之所以要反對，還不光光是為了這些理由，因為關於門戶高低的問題，我朋友並不像我那麼重視。我之所以反對他們的婚姻，還有別的一些令人忌憚的原因——這些原因不但到現在還存在，而且在兩件事裏面同樣存在着，可是我早就盡力把它忘了，因為好在眼不見為淨。這裏必須把這些原因說一說，即使簡單地說一說也好。你母親的娘家親族雖然令人不太滿意，可是比起你們自己家裏人那種完全沒有體統的情形來，便簡直顯得無足輕重。你三個妹妹都是始終一貫地做出許多沒有體統的事情來，有時候甚至連你父親也難免。請原諒我這樣直言不諱，其實得罪了你，也使我自己感到痛苦。你的骨肉至親有了這些缺點，當然會使你感到難受，我這樣一說，當然會令你更不高興。可是你只要想一想，你自己和你姐姐舉止優雅，別人非但沒有責難你們兩人，而且對你們褒獎備至，還賞識你們的見識和個性，這對於你不失為一種安慰吧。我還想跟你說一說：我那天晚上看了那種種情形，不禁更加確定了我對各個人的看法，更加加深了我的偏見，覺得一定要阻止我的朋友，不讓他締結這門最不幸的婚姻。他第二天就離開尼德斐莊園到倫敦去了，我相信你一定記得，他本來打算去一下便立刻回來。我得在這裏把我當初參與這件事的經過說明一下。原來他的姐妹們當時跟我一樣，深為這件事感到不安。我們立刻發覺了彼此有同感，都覺得應該趕快到倫敦去把她們這位兄弟隔離起來，於是決定立刻動身。我們就這樣走了。到了那裏，便由我負責向我朋友指出，他如果攀上了這頭親事，必定有多少多少壞處。我苦口婆心，再三勸說。我這一番規勸雖然動搖了他的心願，使他遲疑不決，可是，我當時要不是那麼十拿九穩地說，你姐姐對他並沒有傾心，那麼這番規勸也許不會產生這樣大的效力，他們的婚姻也許最終也阻擋不住。在我沒有進行這番勸說以前，他總以為令姐即使沒有以同樣的鍾情報答他，至少也是在竭誠期待着他。但是賓利先生天性謙和，遇到任何事情，只要我一出主意，他總是相信我勝過相信他自己。我輕而易舉地說服了他，使他相信這事情是他自己一時糊塗。他既然有了這個信念，我們便進一步說服他不要回到赫福德郡去，這當然不費吹灰之力。我這樣做，自己並沒覺得有甚麼不對。今天回想起來，我覺得只有一件事做得不能讓自己安心，就是令姐來到城裏的時候，我竟不擇手段，把這個消息瞞住了他。這件事不但我知道，賓利小姐也知道，然而她哥哥一直到現在還蒙在鼓裏。要是讓他們兩人見了面，可能也不會有壞的後果，可是我當時認為他並沒有完全死心，見到她未必能免於危險。我這樣隱瞞，這樣欺騙蒙混，也許失掉了我自己的身份。然而事情已經做了，而且完全是出於一片好意。關於這件事，我沒有甚麼可以再說的了，也無需再道歉，如果我傷了令姐的心，也是出於無意；你自然會以為我當初這樣做，理由不夠充足，可是我到現在還沒有覺得有甚麼不對。現在再談另外一件更重的罪名：毀了韋翰先生的前途。關於這件事，我惟一的駁斥辦法，只有把他和我家的關係全部說給你聽，請你評判一下其中的是非曲直。我不知道他特別指責我的是哪一點；但是我要在這裏陳述的事實真相，可以找出不少信譽卓著的人出來做見證。韋翰先生是個值得尊敬的人的兒子。他父親在龐百利管了好幾年產業，極其盡職，這自然使得先父願意幫他的忙；因此先父對他這個教子喬治・韋翰恩寵有加。先父供給他上學，後來還供給他進劍橋大學——這是對他最重要的一項幫助，因為他自己的父親被他母親吃光用窮，無力供給他受高等教育。先父不僅因為這位年輕人風度翩翩而喜歡和他來往，而且非常器重他，希望他從事教會職業，並且一心要替他安插一個位置。至於說到我自己之所以對他印象轉壞，那已經是好多好多年的事了。他為人放蕩不羈，惡習重重，他雖然十分小心地把這些惡習遮掩起來，不讓他最好的朋友察覺，可是逃不過一個和他年齡相仿的青年人的眼睛，他一個不提防就給我看到了漏洞，機會多的是——當然老達西先生決不會有這種機會。這裏我不免又要引起你的痛苦了，痛苦到甚麼地步，只有你自己知道。不論韋翰先生已經引起了你怎樣的感情，我卻要懷疑到這些感情的本質，因而我也就不得不對你說明他真正的品格。這裏面甚至還難免別有用心。德高望重的先父大約去世於五年前；他寵愛韋翰先生始終如一，連遺囑上也特別向我提到他，要我斟酌他的職業情況，極力提拔他，要是他受了聖職 [32]，俸祿優厚的位置一有空缺，就讓他替補上去。另外還給了他一千鎊遺產。他自己的父親不久也去世了。這幾件大事發生以後，不出半年時間，韋翰先生就寫信跟我說，他已最後下定決心，不願意去受聖職；他既然不能獲得那個職位的俸祿，便希望我給他一些直接的經濟利益，要我不要以為他這個要求不合理。他又說，他倒有意學法律，要我明白，要他靠了一千鎊的利息去學法律，當然非常不夠。與其說，我相信他這些話靠得住，不如說，我但願他這些話靠得住。不過，我無論如何還是願意答應他的要求。我知道韋翰先生不適宜當牧師。因此這件事立刻就談妥條件，獲得解決：我拿出三千鎊給他，他不再要求我幫助他獲得聖職，算是自動放棄權利，即使將來他有資格擔任聖職，也不再提出請求。從此我和他之間的一切關係，便好像一刀兩斷。我非常看不起他，不再請他到龐百利來玩，在城裏也不和他來往。我相信他大部份時間都住在城裏，但是他的所謂學法律，只不過是一個藉口罷了；現在他既然擺脫了一切羈絆，便整天過着浪蕩揮霍的生活。我大約連續三年簡直聽不到他的消息，可是後來有個牧師逝世了，這份俸祿本來是可以由他接替的，於是他又寫信給我，要我薦舉他。他說他境遇不能再窘，這一點我當然不難相信。他又說研究法律毫無出息，現在已下定決心當牧師，只要我肯薦舉他去接替這個位置就可以了。他自以為我一定會推薦他，因為他看準我沒有別的人可以補缺，況且我也不能疏忽先父生前應承他的一片好意。我沒有答應他的要求，他再三請求，我依然拒絕，這你總不見得會責備我吧。他的境遇越困苦，怨憤就越深。毫無疑問，他無論在我背後罵我，或是當面罵我，都是一樣狠毒。從這個時期以後，連一點點表面上的交情都完結了。我不知道他是怎樣生活的，可是說來痛心之至，去年夏天他又引起了我的注意。我得在這裏講一件我自己也不願意記起的事。這件事我本來不願意讓任何人知道，可是這一次卻非得一說不可。說到這裏，我相信你一定能保守秘密。我妹妹比我小十多歲，由我母親的內姪費茨威廉上校和我做她的監護人。大約在一年以前，我們把她從學校裏接回來，把她安置在倫敦居住。去年夏天，她跟那位管家楊格太太到蘭斯蓋特鎮[33]去了。韋翰先生跟着也趕到那邊去，顯然是別有用意，因為他和楊格太太早就認識，我們很不幸上了她的當，看錯了人。依靠楊格太太的縱容和附和，他向喬治安求愛。可惜喬治安娜心腸太好，還牢牢記着小時候他對待她的親切，因此竟被他打動了心，自以為愛上了他，答應跟他私奔。她當時才十五歲，我們當然只能原諒她年幼無知。她雖然糊塗膽大，可是總算幸虧她親口把這件事情告訴了我。原來在他們私奔之前，我出乎意料地來到他們那裏；喬治安娜一貫把我這樣一個哥哥當作父親般看待，她不忍心讓我傷心受氣，於是把這件事向我和盤托出。你可以想像得到，我當時做何感想，又採取了怎樣的行動。為了顧全妹妹的名譽和情緒，我沒有把這件事公開揭露出來；可是我寫了封信給韋翰先生，要他立刻離開那個地方，楊格太太當然也被解僱了。毫無疑問，韋翰先生主要是看中了我妹妹的三萬鎊財產，可是我也不禁想到，他也很想借這個機會大大地報復我一下。他差一點就報仇成功了。小姐，我在這裏已經把所有與我們有關的事，都老老實實地談過了；如果你並不完全認為我在撒謊，那麼，我希望從今以後，你再也不要認為我對待韋翰先生殘酷無情。我不知道他是用甚麼樣的謊言，甚麼樣的手段來欺騙你的；不過，你以前對於我們的事情一無所知，那麼，他騙取了你的信任，也不足為奇。你既無從探聽，又不喜歡懷疑。你也許不明白為甚麼我昨天晚上不把這一切當面告訴你。可是當時我自己也不確定，不知道哪些話可以講，哪些話應該講。這封信中所說的一切，是真是假，我可以特別請你問問費茨威廉上校，他是我們的近親，又是我們的至交，而且是先父的遺囑執行人之一，他對於其中的一切詳情自然都十分清楚，他可以來作證明。假如說，你因為厭惡我，竟把我的話看得一文不值，你不妨把你的意見說給我的表弟聽；我之所以要想盡辦法找機會把這封信一大早就交到你手裏，就是為了讓你可以去和他商量一下。我要說的話都說完了，願上帝祝福你。

費茨威廉・達西

第三十六章

當達西先生遞給伊莉莎白那封信的時候，伊莉莎白即使並沒有想到那封信裏是重新提出求婚，她也根本沒想到信裏會寫些甚麼。既然一看見這樣的內容，你可想而知，她當時想要讀完這封信的心情是怎樣迫切，她的情感上又給引起了多大的矛盾。她讀信時的那種心情，簡直無法形容。剛開始讀到他居然還自以為能夠獲得原諒，她就不免吃驚；再讀下去，又覺得他無從辯解，而且處處都流露出一種欲蓋彌彰的羞慚心情。她一讀到他所寫的關於當日發生在尼德斐莊園的那段事情，就對他的一言一語都存着極大的偏見。她迫不及待地讀下去，因此簡直來不及細細咀嚼；她每讀一句就急於要讀下一句，因此往往忽略了眼前一句的意思。他所謂她的姐姐對賓利本來沒有甚麼情意，令她立刻斷定他在撒謊；他說那頭親事確確實實存在着那麼些非常糟糕的缺陷，這使她簡直氣得不想把那封信再讀下去。他對於自己的所作所為，並沒有覺得過意不去，這當然使她無從滿意。他的語氣真是盛氣凌人，絲毫沒有悔悟的意思。

接下去讀到他關於韋翰先生那一段事情的剖白，她才多少比剛才神志清醒一些，其中許多事情和韋翰親口自述的身世十分相同，假如這些都是真話，那就會把她以前對韋翰的好感一筆勾銷，這真是使她更加痛苦，更加心亂。她感到十分驚訝和疑慮，甚至還有幾分恐怖。她恨不得把這件事全都當作他捏造出來的，她一次次說着："一定是他在撒謊！這是不可能的！這是荒謬絕倫的謊話！"——她把全信讀完以後，幾乎連最後的一兩頁也記不起說些甚麼了，連忙把它收拾起來，而且口口聲聲發誓說，決不把它當作一回真事，也決不再去讀那封信。

她就這樣心煩意亂地往前走，真是千頭萬緒，不知從哪裏想起才好。可是不到半分鐘，她又按捺不住，從信封裏抽出信來，聚精會神地忍痛讀着講述韋翰的那幾段，逼着自己去玩味每一句話的意思。其中講到韋翰跟龐百利的關係的那一段，簡直和韋翰自己所說的毫無出入；再說到老達西先生生前對他的好，信上的話也和韋翰自己所說的話完全符合，雖說她並不知道老達西先生究竟對他好到甚麼地步。到這裏為止，雙方所述的情況都可以互相印證，但是當她讀到遺囑問題的時候，兩個人的話就大不相同了。韋翰說到牧師俸祿的那些話，她還記得清清楚楚；她一想起他那些話，就不免感覺到，他們兩個人之間總有一個人說的是假話，於是她一時之間，倒高興起來了，以為自己這種想法不會有錯。接着她又極其仔細地一讀再讀，讀到韋翰藉口放棄牧師俸祿從而獲得了三千鎊一筆款項等等情節的時候，她又不由得猶豫起來。她放下那封信，把每一個情節不偏不倚地推敲了一番，把信中每一句話都仔仔細細考慮了一下，看看是否真有其事，可是這樣做也毫無用處。雙方都是各執一詞。她只得再往下讀。可是越讀越糊塗：她本以為這件事任憑達西先生怎樣花言巧語，顛倒是非，也絲毫不能減輕他自己的卑鄙無恥；哪裏想得到這裏面大有文章可做，只要把事情改變一下說法，達西先生就可以把責任推卸得一乾二淨。

達西竟毫不遲疑地把驕奢淫逸的罪名加在韋翰先生身上，這使她極其驚駭——更何況她又提不出反證，於是就更加驚駭。在韋翰先生參加某某郡的民兵團之前，伊莉莎白根本沒有聽到過他這個人。至於他之所以要參加民兵團，也只是因為偶然在鎮上遇見了以前一個泛泛之交的朋友，勸他加入的。講到他以前的為人處世，除了他自己所說的以外，她完全一無所知。至於他的真正的人品，她即使可以打聽得到，也並沒有想要去追根究底。他的儀態音容，令人一眼看去就覺得他身上具備了一切美德。她竭力要想起一兩件足以說明他品行優良的事實，想起他一些為人誠實仁愛的特性，使達西先生對他的誹謗可以不攻自破，至少也可以使他的優點遮蓋得住他偶然的過失。他所謂的偶然過失，都是因着達西先生所指責的連年來的懶惰和惡習而造成的，可惜她就是想不出他的好處來。她眨下眼睛就可以看到他出現在她面前，風度翩翩，辭令優雅；但是，除了鄰里的讚賞之外，除了他用交際手腕在夥伴之間贏得的敬慕之外，她可想不起他有甚麼更具體的優點。她思考了一段時間以後，又繼續讀信。可是天哪！接下去就讀到他對達西小姐的企圖，這只要想一想昨天上午她跟費茨威廉上校的談話，不就是可以證實了嗎？信上最後要她把每一個細節都問問費茨威廉上校本人，問問他是否真有其事。以前她就曾經聽費茨威廉上校親自說起過，他對他表弟達西的一切事情都極其熟悉，同時她也沒有理由去懷疑費茨威廉的人格。她一度幾乎下定了決心要去問他，但是問起這件事不免又會尷尬，想到這裏，她便把這個主意暫時擱置了下來。後來她又想到，如果達西先生拿不準他表弟的話會和他自己完全一致，那他決不會冒失地提出這樣一個建議，於是她就乾脆打消了這個主意。

那個下午她跟韋翰先生在菲力普先生家裏第一次見面所談的話，現在都能一五一十地記得清清楚楚。他許許多多的話到現在還活靈活現地出現在她的記憶裏。於是她突然想到他跟一個陌生人講這些話是多麼冒昧，她奇怪自己以前為甚麼這樣疏忽。她發覺他那樣自稱自讚，是多麼有失體統，而且他又是多麼言行不一。她記起了他曾經誇口說他自己並不是怕看到達西先生，又說達西先生要走就走，他可決不肯離開此地；然而，下一個星期在尼德斐莊園開的舞會，他卻沒有敢去。她也還記得在尼德斐莊園那家人沒有搬走以前，他從來沒跟另外一個人談起過他自己的身世，可是那家人一搬走以後，這件事就到處議論紛紛了。雖然他曾經向她說過，為了尊重達西先生的先父，他老是不願意揭露那位少爺的過錯，可是他後來還是肆無忌憚，毫不猶疑地在破壞達西先生的名譽。

凡是有關他的事情，怎麼這樣前後懸殊！他向金小姐獻殷勤一事，現在看來，也完全是從金錢着眼，這實在可惡；金小姐的錢並不多，可是這並不能說明他慾望不高，卻只能證實他一見到錢就起貪心。他對待她自己的動機也不見得好：不是他誤會她很有錢，就是為了要博得她的歡心來滿足他自己的虛榮；只怪她不小心，竟讓他看出了她對他有好感。她越想就越覺得他一無可取，她禁不住又想起當初珍妮向賓利先生問起這事時，賓利先生說，達西先生在這件事情上毫無過失，於是她更覺得達西先生有理了。儘管達西的態度傲慢可厭，可是從他們認識以來（特別是最近他們時常見面，她對他的行為作風也更加熟悉），她從來沒有見過他有甚麼品行不端或是蠻不講理的地方，沒有看見過他有任何違反教義或是傷風敗俗的惡習；他的親友們都很尊敬他，器重他，連韋翰也承認他不愧為一個好哥哥，她還常常聽到達西愛撫備至地說起他自己的妹妹，這說明他還是個重情理的人。假如達西的所作所為真的像韋翰說的那樣壞，那麼，他種種胡作非為自然難以掩盡天下人的耳目；一個為非作歹到這樣地步的人，竟會跟賓利先生那樣一個好人交成朋友，真是令人不可思議。

她越想越慚愧得無地自容。不論想到達西也好，想到韋翰也好，她總是覺得自己以往未免太盲目，太偏心，對人存了偏見，而且不近情理。

她不禁大聲叫道：“我做得多麼卑鄙！我一向自負有知人之明！我一向自以為有本領！一向看不起姐姐那種寬大的胸襟！為了滿足我自己的虛榮心，我對人老是不着邊際地猜忌多端，而且還要做得使我自己無懈可擊。這是我多麼可恥的地方！可是，這種恥辱又是多麼活該！即使我真的戀愛了，也不該盲目到這樣該死的地步。然而我的愚蠢，並不是在戀愛方面，而是在虛榮心方面。剛剛認識他們兩位的時候，一個喜歡我，我很高興，一個怠慢我，我就生氣，因此造成了我的偏見和無知，遇到與他們有關的事情，我就不能明辨是非。我到現在才算有了自知之明。”

她從自己身上想到珍妮身上，又從珍妮身上想到賓利身上，她的思想聯成了一條直線，使她立刻想起了達西先生對這件事的解釋非常不夠；於是她又把他的信讀了一遍。第二遍讀起來效果就大不相同了。她既然在一件事情上不得不信任他，在另一件事上又怎能不信任他呢？他說他完全沒想到她姐姐對賓利先生有意思，於是她不禁想起了從前夏綠蒂一貫的看法。她也不能否認他把珍妮形容得很恰當。她覺得珍妮雖然愛心熾烈，可是表面上卻不露痕跡，她平常那種安然自得的神氣，實在讓人看不出她的多愁善感。

當她讀到他提起她家裏人的那一段時，其中措辭固然傷人感情，然而那一番責難卻也入情入理，於是她更加覺得慚愧。那真是一針見血的指責，使她否認不得；他特別指出，尼德斐莊園那次舞會上的種種情形，是第一次造成他反對這婚姻的原因——老實說，那種種情形不僅使他難以忘懷，自己也同樣難以忘懷。至於他對她自己和對她姐姐的恭維，她也不是無動於衷。她聽了很舒服，可是她並沒有因此而感到安慰，因為她家裏人不爭氣，招來他的非議，並不能從恭維中得到補償。她認為珍妮的失望完全是自己的至親骨肉一手造成的，她又想到，她們兩姐妹的優點也一定會因為至親骨肉的行為失禮而受到損害，想到這裏，她感到從來沒有過的沮喪。

她沿着小路走了兩個小時，前前後後地左思右想，又把好多事情重新考慮了一番，判斷一下是否確有其事。這一次突然的變故，實在事關緊要，她得盡量面對事實。她現在覺得疲倦了，又想到出來已久，應該回去了。她希望走進宅院的時候臉色能像平常一樣愉快，又決定把那些心事抑制一下，免得跟人談起話來態度不自然。

一回去，她即被告知在她外出的時候，洛欣莊園的兩位先生都來看過她了。達西先生是來辭行的，只坐了幾分鐘就走了，費茨威廉上校卻跟她們在一起坐了足足一個小時，盼望着她回來，幾乎想要跑出去找到她才肯罷休。伊莉莎白雖然表面上裝出很惋惜的樣子，內心裏卻因為沒有見到這位訪客而感到萬分高興。她心目中再也沒有費茨威廉了，她想到的只有那封信。

第三十七章

那兩位先生第二天早上就離開了洛欣莊園；柯林斯先生在門房附近等着給他們送行，送行以後，他帶了一個好消息回家來，說是這兩位貴客雖然剛剛在洛欣莊園滿懷離愁，身體卻很健康，精神也很飽滿。然後他又趕到洛欣莊園去安慰凱瑟琳夫人母女；回家來的時候，他又得意非凡地把凱瑟琳夫人的口信帶回來——說夫人覺得非常沉悶，極希望他們全家去同她一起吃飯。

伊莉莎白看到凱瑟琳夫人，就不禁想起：要是自己願意，現在已經成了夫人的沒有過門的姪媳婦了；而且她想到夫人那時將會怎樣氣憤，就不禁好笑。她不斷地想出這樣一些話來跟自己打趣："她將會說些甚麼話呢？她將會有些甚麼舉動呢？"

他們一開始就談到洛欣莊園人丁稀疏的問題。凱瑟琳夫人說："告訴你，我真十分難受。我相信，誰也不會像我一樣，為親友的離別而傷心得這麼厲害。我特別喜歡這兩個年輕人，我知道他們也非常喜歡我。他們臨去的時候真捨不得走。他們一向都是那樣。那位可愛的上校到最後才算打起了精神；達西看上去最難過，我看他比去年還要難受，他對洛欣莊園的感情真是一年比一年深。"

說到這裏，柯林斯先生插進了一句恭維話，又舉了個例子，母女兩人聽了，都粲然一笑。

吃過中飯以後，凱瑟琳夫人看到班奈特小姐好像不大高興的樣子；她想，班小姐一定是不願意馬上就回家去，於是說道：

"你要是不願意回去的話，就得寫封信給你媽媽，請求她讓你在這裏多住些時候。我相信柯林斯太太一定非常樂意跟你在一起的。"

伊莉莎白回答道："多謝你好心的挽留，可惜我不能領受盛情。我下星期六一定要進城去。"

"哎，這麼說來，你在這裏只能住六個星期了。我本來指望你住上兩個月的。你沒有來以前，我就這樣跟柯林斯太太説過。你用不着這麼急於要走。班奈特太太一定會讓你再多留兩個星期的。"

"可是我爸爸不會同意的。他上星期就寫信來催我回去。"

"噢，只要媽媽同意，爸爸自然會同意的。做爸爸的決不會像媽媽一樣，把女兒當做寶貝看待。我六月初要去倫敦住一個星期；要是你能再住滿一個月，我就可以把你們兩個人當中順便帶一個去，道森[34] 既不反對駕四輪馬車，那自然可以寬寬敞敞地帶上你們一個；要是天氣涼快，我當然不妨把你們兩個都帶去，幸好你們個子都不大。"

"你真是太好心了，太太；可惜我們要依照原來的計劃行事。"

凱瑟琳夫人不便強留，便説道：

"柯林斯太太，你得派一個傭人送她們。我説話一向心直口快，我不放心讓兩位年輕的小姐趕遠路。這太不像話了，我最看不慣的就是這種事，你千萬得派一個人送送她們。對於年輕的小姐們，我們總得按照她們的身份好好照顧她們，侍候她們。我的外甥女喬治安娜去年夏天上蘭斯蓋特去的時候，我非得要她有兩個男傭人伴送不可。要知道，她身為龐百利的達西先生和安妮夫人的千金小姐，不那樣便難免有失體統。我對於這一類的事特別留意。你得派約翰送送這兩位小姐才好，柯林斯太太。幸虧我發覺了這件事，及時指出，否則讓她們孤零零地自己走，把你的面子也丟光了。"

"我舅舅會派人來接我們的。"

"噢，你的舅舅！他真有男傭人嗎？我聽了很高興，總算有人替你想到這些事。你們打算在哪裏換馬呢？當然是在布羅姆利鎮了。你們只要在貝爾驛站上提一提我的名字，就會有人來招待你們。"

提到她們的旅程，凱瑟琳夫人還有許多話要問，而且她並不完全都是自問自答，因此你必須留心去聽。伊莉莎白倒覺得這是她的運氣，否則，她這麼心事重重，一定會忘了自己的做客身份呢。有心事應該等到單獨一個人的時候再去想。每逢沒有第二個人跟她在一起的時候，她就翻來覆去地想個痛快；她沒有哪一天不獨自散步，一邊走一邊老是回想着那些不愉快的事情。

達西那封信，她簡直快要背得出了。她把每一句話都反覆研究過，她對於這個寫信人的感情也是忽冷忽熱。記起他那種筆調口吻，她到現在還是説不盡的氣憤；可是只要一想到以前怎樣錯怪了他，錯罵了他，她的氣憤便轉到自己身上來了。他那沮喪的情緒反而引起了她的同情。他的愛戀引起了她的感激，他的性格引起了她的尊敬，可是她無法對他產生好感。她拒絕他以後，從來不曾有過片刻的後悔，她根本不想再看到他。她經常為自己以往的行為感到苦惱和悔恨，家庭裏面種種不幸的缺陷更令她苦悶萬分。這些缺陷是無法補救的。她父親對這些缺陷只是一笑置之，懶得去約束他那幾個小女兒的狂妄輕率的作風；至於她母親，她本身既是作風失檢，當然完全不會感覺到這方面的危害。伊莉莎白常常和珍妮同心合力，約束凱瑟琳和麗迪亞的冒失，可是，母親既然那麼縱容她們，她們還會有甚麼長進的機會？凱瑟琳意志薄弱，容易氣惱，她完全聽憑麗迪亞指揮，一聽到珍妮和伊莉莎白的規勸就要生氣；麗迪亞卻固執任性，粗心大意，她根本不聽她們的話。這兩個妹妹既無知，又懶惰，又愛虛榮，只要麥里頓來了一個軍官，她們就去跟他勾搭。麥里頓跟朗伯恩本來相隔不遠，她們一天到晚往那裏跑。

她還有一件大心事，那就是替珍妮擔憂；達西先生的解釋固然使她對賓利先生恢復了以往的好感，同時也就更加感覺到珍妮受到的損失太大。賓利對珍妮一往情深，他的行為不應該受到任何指責，萬一要指責的話，最多也只能怪他過份信任朋友。珍妮有了這樣理想的一個機會，既可以得到種種好處，又可望獲得終身的幸福，只可惜家裏人愚蠢失檢，把這個機會斷送了，令人想起來怎麼不痛心！

每逢回想起這些事情，難免不連帶想到韋翰品格的變質。於是，以她這樣一個向來心情愉快而難得消沉沮喪的人，心裏也受到莫大的刺激，連強顏歡笑也幾乎辦不到了，這是可想而知的。

　　她臨走前的一個星期裏面，洛欣莊園的宴會還是和她們剛來時一樣頻繁。最後一個晚上也是在那裏度過的，老夫人又仔細問起她們旅程的細節，指示她們怎麼樣收拾行李，又再三說到禮服應當怎麼樣安放。瑪麗亞聽了這番話之後，一回去就把早上整理好的箱子完全翻了開來，重新收拾了一遍。

　　她們告別的時候，凱瑟琳夫人紆尊降貴地祝她們一路平安，又邀請她們明年再到漢斯福來。德·包爾小姐甚至還向她們行了個屈膝禮，伸出手來跟她們兩個人一一握別。

第三十八章

星期六吃早飯時，伊莉莎白和柯林斯先生在飯廳裏相遇，原來他們比別人早來了數分鐘。柯林斯先生連忙利用這個機會向她鄭重話別，他認為這是決不可少的禮貌。

他說："伊莉莎白小姐，這次蒙你光臨敝舍，我不知道內人有沒有向你表示感激；不過我相信她不會不向你表示一番謝意就讓你走的。老實告訴你，你這次來，我們非常領情。我們自知舍下簡陋，無人樂意光臨。我們生活清苦，居處侷促，侍僕寥寥無幾，再加上我們見識淺薄，像你這樣一位年輕小姐，一定會覺得漢斯福這地方極其枯燥乏味。不過我們對於你這次賞臉，實在感激萬分，並且竭盡綿薄之力，使你不至於過得興味索然，希望你能見諒。"

伊莉莎白連聲道謝，說是這次作客，非常快活，這六個星期來真是過得高興極了，跟夏綠蒂住在一起真有樂趣，加上主人家對待她又那麼殷勤懇切，實在令她感激萬分。柯林斯先生一聽此話，大為滿意，立刻顯出一副笑容可掬的樣子，鄭重其事地回答道：

"聽到你並沒有過得不稱心，我真滿意到極點。我們總算盡了心意，而且感到最幸運的是，能夠介紹你跟上流人來往。寒舍雖然微不足道，但幸虧高攀了洛欣府上，使你住在我們這種苦地方，還可以經常跟他們來往來往，免得單調，這一點倒使我可以聊以自慰，覺得你這次到漢斯福來不能算完全失望。凱瑟琳夫人府上對我們真是特別優待，特別愛護，這種機會是別人求之不得的。你也可以看出我們是處於怎樣的地位。你看我們簡直無時無刻不在他們那邊作客。老實說，我這所牧師住所雖然異常簡陋，諸多不便。可是，誰要是住到裏邊來，就可以和我們共享洛欣莊園的盛情厚誼，這不能說是沒有福份吧。"

他滿腔的高興實在非言語所能形容；伊莉莎白想出了幾句簡簡單單、真心實意的客氣話來奉承他，他聽了以後，簡直快活得在房間裏打轉。

"親愛的表妹，你完全可以到赫福德郡去給我們傳播傳播好消息。我相信你一定辦得到。凱瑟琳夫人對內人真是殷勤備至，你是每天都親眼看到的。總而言之，我相信你的朋友並沒有看走眼——不過這一點不說也好。請你聽我說，親愛的伊莉莎白小姐，我打從心底裏誠懇地祝你將來的婚姻也能同樣的幸福。我親愛的夏綠蒂和我真是同心合意，無論遇到哪一件事莫不是意氣相投，心心相印。我們這一對夫婦真是天造地設。"

伊莉莎白本來可以放心大膽地說，他們夫婦這樣相處，的確是很大的幸福，而且她還可以用同樣誠懇的語氣接下去說，她完全認為他們家裏過得很舒適，她也沾了一份光。不過話才說到一半，被說到的那位太太走了進來，打斷了她的話。她倒並不覺得遺憾。夏綠蒂好不可憐！要她跟這樣的男人朝夕相處，實在是一種痛苦。可是這畢竟是她自己睜大了眼睛挑選的。她眼看着客人們就要走了，不免覺得難過，可是她好像並不要求別人憐憫。操持家務，飼養家禽，教區裏的形形色色，以及許許多多附帶的事，都還沒有使她感到完全乏味。

馬車終於來了，箱子給繫上車頂，包裹放進車廂，一切都準備好了，只準備出發。大家戀戀不捨地告別以後，便由柯林斯先生送伊莉莎白上車。他們從花園那裏走出去，他一路托她回去代他向她全家請安，而且沒有忘了感謝他去年冬天在朗伯恩受到的款待，還請她代為問候賈汀納夫婦，其實他根本就不認識他們。然後他扶她上車，瑪麗亞跟着走上去，正當車門快要關上的時候，他突然慌慌張張地提醒她們說，她們還忘了給洛欣莊園的太太小姐留言告別呢。

"不過，"他又說，"你們當然想要向她們傳話請安，還要感謝她們這些日子以來的殷勤款待。"

伊莉莎白沒有表示反對，車門這才關上，馬車就開走了。

沉默了幾分鐘以後，瑪麗亞叫道："天啊！我們好像到這裏來才不過一兩天，可是事情倒發生了不少啊！"

她的同伴歎了口氣說："實在不少。"

"我們在洛欣莊園一共吃了九次飯，另外還喝了兩次茶！我回去有多少事要講啊！"

伊莉莎白心裏說："可是我回去有多少事要瞞啊！"

她們一路上沒有說甚麼話，也沒有受甚麼驚，離開漢斯福不到四個小時，就到了賈汀納先生家裏。她們要在那裏耽擱幾天。

伊莉莎白看到珍妮氣色很好，只可惜沒有機會仔細觀察一下她的心情是不是好，因為多蒙她舅母一片好心，早就給她們安排好了各式各樣的節目。幸好珍妮就要跟她一起回去，到了朗伯恩，多的是閒暇的時間，那時候再仔細觀察觀察吧。

不過，她實在等不及到朗伯恩以後再把達西先生求婚的事情告訴珍妮，好容易才算耐住了性子。她知道她自己有本領說得珍妮大驚失色，而且一說以後，還可以大大地滿足她自己那種不能從理智上克服的虛榮心。她真恨不得把它說出來，只是拿不定主意應該怎樣跟珍妮說到適可而止，又怕一談到這個問題，就免不了多多少少要牽扯到賓利身上去，也許會讓她姐姐格外傷心。

第三十九章

五月已經到了第二個星期，三位年輕小姐一起從恩典堂街出發，到赫福德郡的某某鎮去；班奈特先生事先就為她們約定了一家小客棧，派了馬車在那裏接她們。剛一到那裏，她們就看到凱蒂和麗迪亞從樓上的餐廳裏望着她們，這表明車夫已經準時到了。這兩位小姐已經在那裏等了一個多小時，高高興興地光顧過對面的一家帽子店，看了看站崗的哨兵，又調製了一些胡瓜沙拉。

她們歡迎了兩位姐姐之後，便一面得意洋洋地擺出一些菜來（都是小客棧裏常備的一些冷盤），一面大聲説道："這多麼好？你們想也沒想到吧？"

麗迪亞又説："我們存心做東，可是要你們借錢給我們，我們自己的錢都在那邊鋪裏花光了。"説到這裏，她便把買來的那些東西拿給她們看。"看，我買了這頂帽子。我並不覺得太漂亮；可是我想，買一頂也好。一到家我就要把它拆開來重新做過，你們看我會不會把它收拾得好一些。"

姐姐們都説她這頂帽子很難看，她卻毫不在乎地説："噢，那家鋪裏還有兩三頂，比這一頂還要難看得多。讓我去買點顏色漂亮的緞子來，把它重新裝飾一下，那就過得去了。再説，某某郡的民兵團，兩星期之內就要開走了，他們一離開麥里頓之後，夏季隨便你穿戴些甚麼都無所謂。"

"他們就要開走了，真的嗎？"伊莉莎白極其滿意地説道。

"他們就要駐紮到布萊頓[35]去；我真希望爸爸帶我們大家到那裏去消暑！這真是個妙極的打算，或許還用不着花錢。媽媽也一定非要去不可！你想，否則我們這一個夏天多苦悶呀！"

"話説得是，"伊莉莎白想道；"這真是個好打算，馬上就會讓我們忙死了。老天爺啊！光是麥里頓一個可憐的民兵團和每個月開幾次舞會，就弄得我們神魂顛倒了，怎麼當得起布萊頓和那整營整營的官兵！"

大家坐定以後，麗迪亞說："現在我有點消息要告訴你們，你們猜猜看是甚麼消息？這是個絕妙的消息，頭等重要的消息，說的是關於我們大家都喜歡的某一個人。"

珍妮和伊莉莎白面面相覷，便讓那個堂倌走開。於是麗迪亞笑笑說："你們真是小心謹慎，謹守規矩，怕給侍應聽到，好像他存心要聽似的！我相信他平常聽到的許多話，比我要說的這番話更是不堪入耳。不過他是個醜八怪！他走開了，我倒也高興。我生平沒有見到過他那樣長的下巴。唔，現在我來講新聞了——這是關於可愛的韋翰的新聞；侍應不配聽，是不是？韋翰再不會有跟瑪麗·金結婚的危險了——真是個了不起的消息呀！那位小姐上利物浦[36]她叔叔那裏去了——一去不回來了。韋翰安全了。"

"應該說瑪麗·金安全了！"伊莉莎白接着說，"她總算逃過了一段冒失的姻緣。"

"要是她喜歡他而又走開，那真是個大傻瓜呢。"

"我但願他們雙方的感情都不十分深，"珍妮說。

"我相信他這方面的感情是不會深的。""我可以擔保，他根本就沒有把她放在心上。誰看得上這麼一個滿臉雀斑的討厭的小東西？"

伊莉莎白心想，她自己固然決不會有這樣粗魯的談吐，可是這種粗魯的見解，正和她以前執迷不悟的那種成見無異，她想到這裏，很是驚愕。

吃過了飯，姐姐們結了賬，便吩咐着手準備馬車；經過了好一番安排，幾位小姐，連帶自己的箱子、針線袋、包裹以及凱蒂和麗迪亞所買的那些不受歡迎的東西，總算都放上了馬車。

"我們這樣擠在一起，多有趣！"麗迪亞叫道。"我買了頂帽子，真是高興，就算特地添置了一隻帽盒，也很有趣！好吧，讓我們再假緊來舒服舒服，有說有笑地回到家裏去。首先，請你們講一講，你們離家以後遇到了些甚麼事情。你們見到過一些中意的男人嗎？有沒有跟他們調情？我真希望你們哪一位帶了個丈夫回來呢。我說，珍妮馬上就要變成一個老處女了。她快二十三歲了！天哪！我要是不能在二十三歲以前結婚，那多麼丟臉啊！菲力普姨媽要你們趕快找丈夫，你們可沒有想到吧。她說，莉茲要是嫁給柯林斯先生就好了，我倒不覺得那會有多大的趣味。天哪！我真希望比你們哪一個都先結婚！我就可以領着你們上各種舞會去。我的老天爺！那天在弗斯托上校家裏，我們那個玩笑開得真大啊！凱蒂和我那天都準備在那裏玩上一整天，弗斯托太太答應晚上開個小型的舞會（說起來，弗斯托太太跟我是多麼好的朋友！）；她於是請哈林頓家的兩位都來參加。可是海麗病了，因此潘不得不獨自來啦；然後，你們猜我們怎麼辦？我們把錢柏倫穿上了女人衣服，讓別人當他是個女人。你們想想看，多有趣啊！除了上校、弗斯托太太、凱蒂和我以及姨媽等人以外，誰也不知道；說到姨媽，那是因為我們向她借禮服，她才知道的。你們想像不到他扮得多麼像啊！丹尼、韋翰、普拉特和另外兩三個人走進來的時候，他們根本認不出是他。天哪！我笑得好厲害，弗斯托太太也笑得好厲害。我簡直要笑死了。這才讓那些男人們起了疑心，他們不久就識穿了。"

麗迪亞就這樣說說舞會上的故事，講講笑話，另外還有凱蒂從旁給她添油加醋，使得大家一路上很開心。伊莉莎白盡量不去聽，但是總免不了聽到一聲聲提起韋翰的名字。

家裏人極其親切地接待她們。班奈特太太看到珍妮姿色未減，十分快活；吃飯的時候，班奈特先生不由自主地一次又一次跟伊莉莎白說：

"你回來了，我真高興，莉茲。"

他們飯廳裏人很多，盧卡斯府上差不多全家人都來接瑪麗亞，順便聽聽新聞，還問到各種問題。盧卡斯太太隔着桌子向瑪麗亞問起她大女兒日子過得好不好，雞鴨養得多不多；班奈特太太格外忙，因為珍妮正坐在她下首，她便不斷向她打聽一些時尚，然後再去傳給盧卡斯家幾位年輕小姐去聽；麗迪亞的嗓子比誰都高，她正在把當天早上的趣事逐一說給愛聽的人聽。

"噢，瑪莉，"她說，"你要是跟我們一起去了多有趣！我們一路去的時候，凱蒂和我放下了車簾，看上去好像是空車，要是凱蒂沒有暈車，就會這樣一直到達目的地。我們在喬治客棧實在做得夠漂亮，我們用世界上最美的冷盤款待她們三位；假如你也去了，我們也會款待你的。我們臨走的時候，又是那麼有趣！我以為這樣一輛車無論如何也裝不下我們。我真要笑死了。回家的路上又是全程開心作樂！我們有說有笑，聲音大得十英里路以外都能聽見！"

瑪莉聽到這些話，便一本正經地回答道："我的好妹妹，並不是我故意要煞你們的風景，老實說，你們這些樂趣當然會迎合一般女子的愛好，可動不了我的心，我覺得讀書要有趣得多。"

可是她這番話麗迪亞一個字也沒有聽進去。別人說話她很少聽滿半分鐘，對於瑪莉，她就從來沒有認真聽過。

到了下午，麗迪亞硬要姐姐們陪她上麥里頓去，看看那邊的朋友們近況如何，可是伊莉莎白堅決反對，為的是不讓別人說閒話，說班奈特家的幾位小姐在家裏坐不上半天，就要去追逐軍官們。她之所以反對，還有一個理由。她怕再看到韋翰。她已經下定決心，能夠和他避而不見就盡量避而不見。那個民兵團馬上就要調走了，她真是感覺到說不出的快慰。不出四個星期，他們就要走了，她希望他們一走以後，從此平安無事，使她不會再為韋翰受到折磨。

她到家沒有幾個小時，就發覺父母在反覆討論上布萊頓去玩的計劃，也就是麗迪亞在客棧裏給她們提到過的那個計劃。伊莉莎白看出她父親絲毫沒有讓步的意思，不過他的回答卻是模棱兩可，因此她母親雖然慣常碰釘子，可是這一次卻並沒有死心，還希望最後能如她的願。

第四十章

伊莉莎白非把那件事告訴珍妮不可了，再也忍耐不住了，於是她決定把牽涉到姐姐的地方，都一概不提。第二天上午就把達西先生跟她求婚的那一幕，選主要情節說了出來。她料定珍妮聽了以後，一定會感到詫異。

班奈特小姐對伊莉莎白手足情深，覺得她妹妹被任何人愛上了都是理所當然的事情，因此開始雖然吃驚，過後便覺得不足為奇了。她替達西先生惋惜，覺得他不應該用那種很不得體的方式來傾訴衷情；但她更難過的是，她妹妹的拒絕會給他造成怎樣的難堪。

她說："他那種十拿九穩會成功的態度實在不應該，他至少不能讓你看出這種態度，可是你倒想一想，你的拒絕會使他失望到甚麼地步啊。"

伊莉莎白回答道："我的確萬分替他難過；可是，他既然還有那麼些顧慮，他對我的好感可能不久就會完全消失。你總不會怪我拒絕了他吧？"

"怪你！噢，不會的。"

"可是我幫韋翰說話幫得那麼厲害，你會怪我嗎？"

"不怪你；我看不出你那樣說有甚麼錯。"

"等我把第二天的事告訴了你，你就一定看得出有錯了。"

於是她就說起那封信，把有關喬治·韋翰的部份，都一點一滴講了出來。可憐的珍妮聽得多麼驚奇！她即使走遍天下，也不會相信人間竟會有這許多罪惡，而現在這許多罪惡竟集中在這樣一個人身上。雖說達西的剖白使她感到滿意，可是既然發現了其中有這樣一個隱情，她也就不覺得安慰了。她誠心誠意地想說明這件事可能與事實有出入，竭力想去洗清這一個的冤屈，又不願讓另一個受到委屈。

伊莉莎白說：「這怎麼行，你絕對沒有辦法兩全其美。兩個裏面你只能選一個。他們兩個人一共只有那麼多優點，勉強才夠得上一個好人的標準，近來這些優點又在兩個人之間移來動去，轉變得非常厲害。對我來講，我比較偏向於達西先生，覺得這些優點都是他的，你可以隨你自己的意思。」

過了一會，珍妮臉上才勉強露出笑容。

她說：「我生平最吃驚的事莫過於此，韋翰原來這麼壞！這幾乎令人不能相信。達西先生真可憐！親愛的莉茲，你想，他會多麼痛苦。他遭受到這樣的一次失望！而且他又知道了你看不起他！還不得不把他自己妹妹的這種私事都講出來！這的確令他太痛苦了，我想你也會有同感吧。」

「沒有的事；看到你對他這樣惋惜和同情，我反而心安理得了。我知道你會竭力幫他講話，因此我反而越來越不把它當一回事。你的寬宏大量造成了我的感情吝嗇；要是你再為他歎息，我就會輕鬆愉快得要飛起來了。」

「可憐的韋翰！他的樣貌那麼善良，他的風度那麼文雅。」

「那兩位年輕人在教養方面，一定都有非常欠缺的地方。一個擁有全部的好處卻藏得隱密，一個則只是表面上看似滿是優點。」

「你以為達西先生儀表方面有所欠缺，但我從來不這麼想。」

「不過，我是想賣弄下聰明才智才這樣的無緣無故地厭惡他，這樣做足以激勵人的天才，啟發人的智慧。例如，你不斷地罵人，當然說不出一句好話；你要是常常取笑人，倒很可能偶然想到一句妙語。」

「莉茲，你第一次讀那封信的時候，我相信你對待這件事的看法一定和現在不同。」

「當然不同，我當時十分難受。我非常難受——可以說是很不快活。我心裏有許多感觸，可是找不到一個人可以傾訴，也沒有個珍妮來安慰安慰我，説我並不像我自己所想像的那樣懦弱，虛榮和荒誕！噢，我真少不了你啊！"

"你在達西先生面前説到韋翰的時候，語氣那麼強硬，這真是多麼不幸啊！現在看起來，那些話實在顯得不怎麼得體。"

"的確如此。我確實不應該説得那麼刻毒，可是我既然事先存了偏見，自然難免如此。有件事我要請教你。你説我應不應該把韋翰的品格公諸於親朋戚友們？"

班奈特小姐想了一會才説道："當然用不着令他太難堪。你的意見如何？"

"我也覺得不必如此。達西先生並沒有允許我把他所説的話公開向外界聲張。他反而吩咐我説，凡是牽涉到他妹妹的事，都要盡量保守秘密；説到韋翰其他方面的品行，我即使盡量對別人説老實話，又有誰會相信？一般人對達西先生都存着那麼深的成見，你要讓別人對他有好感，麥里頓有一半人死也不願意。我真沒有辦法。好在韋翰馬上就要走了，他的真面目究竟怎樣，與任何人都無關。總會有一天真相大白，那時候我們就可以譏笑人們為甚麼那麼蠢，沒有早些知道。目前我可絕口不提。"

"你的話對極了。要揭露他的錯誤，可能就會斷送了他的一生。也許他現在已經後悔，痛下決心，重新做人。我們千萬不要弄得他走投無路。"

這番談話以後，伊莉莎白煩亂的心境平靜了下來。兩星期以來，這兩件秘密一直壓在她的心頭，如今總算放下了一塊大石頭。她相信以後要是再談起這兩件事來，不論其中哪一件，珍妮都會願意聽。可是這裏面還有些蹊蹺，為了謹慎起見，她不敢説出來。她不敢談到達西先生那封信的另外一半，也不敢向姐姐説明他那位朋友對姐姐是多麼真心實意。這件事是不能讓任何人知道的，她覺得除非把各方面的情況裏裏外外都弄明白了，這最後的一點秘密才可以揭露出來。她想："這樣看來，如果那件不大可能的事一旦居然成了事實，我便可以把這件秘密說出來，不過到那時候，賓利先生自己也許會說得更動聽。要說起這番隱情，不等到事過境遷，才輪不到我呢！"

現在既然到了家，她就有閒暇的時間來觀察姐姐的真正心情。珍妮心裏並不快活。她對賓利仍然未能忘情。她先前甚至從未想到自己會對他鍾情，因此她的柔情蜜意竟像初戀那樣熱烈，而且由於她的年齡和品性的關係，她比初戀的人們還要來得堅貞不移。她癡情地盼望着他能記住她，她把他看得比天下任何男人都高出一等。幸虧她很識大體，看出了她朋友們的關切之情，這才沒有多愁多恨，否則一定會毀了她的健康，也擾亂她們的安寧。

有一天，班奈特太太這麼說："喂，莉茲，你對於珍妮這件傷心事怎麼看呢？我可已經下定決心，再也不在任何人面前提起。我那天就跟我妹妹說過，我知道珍妮在倫敦連他的影子也沒有見到，唔，他是個不值得鍾情的青年，我看她這一輩子休想嫁給他了。也沒有聽人談起他夏天會回到尼德斐莊園來，凡是可能知道些消息的人，我都一一問過了。"

"我看他無論如何不會再住到尼德斐莊園來。"

"哎，隨他的便吧。誰也沒有要他來，我只是覺得他太對不起我的女兒。要是我是珍妮，我才嚥不下這口氣。好吧，我也總算有個安慰：我相信珍妮一定會傷心得把命也送掉，到那時候，他就會後悔當初不該那麼狠心了。"

伊莉莎白沒有回答，因為這種想入非非的指望，並不能使她得到安慰。

沒過多久，她母親又接下去說："這麼說來，莉茲，柯林斯夫婦日子過得很舒服啊，不是嗎？唔，那麼就，但願他們天長地久。他們每天的飯菜怎麼樣？夏綠蒂一定是個了不起的管家婆。她只要有她媽媽一半那麼精明，就夠省儉的了。他們的日常生活決不會有甚麼浪費。"

"當然，絲毫也不浪費。"

"他們一定是管家管得好極了。不錯，不錯。他們會小心謹慎，不讓他們的支出超過收入，他們是永遠不愁沒有錢的，希望對他們有幫助吧！據我猜想，他們一定會常常談到你父親去世以後，來接收朗伯恩。要是這一天到了，我看他們真會把它看作他們自己的財產呢。"

"這件事，他們當然不便當着我的面提。"

"當然不便，要是提了，那才叫怪呢。可是我相信，他們自己一定會常常談到的。唔，要是他們拿了這筆非法的財產能夠心安理得，那是再好也沒有了。倘若要我來接受這筆法庭硬派來的財產，我才會害羞呢。"

第四十一章

她們回家後一下子就過了一個星期，現在已經開始過第二個星期了。過了這個星期，駐紮在麥里頓的那個民兵團就要開拔了，附近的年輕小姐們立刻一個個垂頭喪氣起來。幾乎處處都是心灰意冷的氣象。只有班奈特家的兩位大小姐照常飲食起居，照常各幹各的事。可是凱蒂和麗迪亞已經傷心到極點，便不由得常常責備兩位姐姐冷淡無情。她們真不明白，家裏怎麼竟會有這樣鐵石心腸的人！

她們老是無限悲痛地大聲說道："老天爺呀！我們這下還成個甚麼樣子呢？我們該怎麼辦呢？你還好意思笑得出來，莉茲？"她們那位慈祥的母親也跟了她們一起傷心；她記起二十五年以前，自己也是為了差不多同樣的事情，忍受了多少痛苦。

她說："我一點沒記錯，當初米勒上校那一團人調走的時候，我整整哭了兩天。我簡直心碎了。"

"我相信我的心是一定要碎的，"麗迪亞說。

"要是我們能上布萊頓去，那多麼好！"班奈特太太說。

"對啊——如果能上布萊頓去多麼好！可是爸爸偏偏要作對。"

"洗一洗海水浴就會使我一輩子身體健康。"

"菲力普姨母也說，海水浴一定會對我的身體大有好處。"凱蒂接着說。

朗伯恩的這兩位小姐，就是這樣沒完沒了地長嗟短歎。伊莉莎白想把她們笑話一番，可是羞恥心打消了她一切的情趣。她重新又想到達西先生的確沒有冤枉她們，他指出她們的那些缺陷的確是事實，她深深感覺到，實在難怪他要干涉他朋友和珍妮的好事。

但是麗迪亞的憂鬱不多久就煙消雲散了，因為弗斯托團長的太太請她陪她一起到布萊頓去。這位貴友是位很年輕的夫人，新近才結婚的。她跟麗迪亞都是好興致，好精神，因此意氣相投；雖然才只有三個月的友誼，卻已經做了兩個月的知己。

麗迪亞這時候是怎樣歡天喜地，她對於弗斯托太太是怎樣敬慕，班奈特太太又是怎樣高興，凱蒂又是怎樣難受，這些自然都不在話下。麗迪亞根本沒有注意到姐姐的心情，只顧自己手舞足蹈。在房間裏跳來蹦去，要大家都來祝賀她，大笑大叫，比往常鬧得更加厲害；不走運的凱蒂卻只能繼續在小客廳裏怨天尤人，說話蠻不講理，發着小脾氣。

“我不明白弗斯托太太為甚麼不讓我和麗迪亞一同去，”她說，“即使我不是她特別要好的朋友，又何妨也邀我一同去？照理說我比她大兩歲，面子也得大些呢。”

伊莉莎白把道理講給她聽，珍妮也勸她不必生氣，她都不理睬。再說伊莉莎白，她對於這次邀請，完全不像她母親和麗迪亞那樣興高采烈，她只覺得麗迪亞縱然還沒有糊塗到那種地步，這一去可算完全給毀了。於是她只得暗地裏讓她父親不許麗迪亞去，也顧不得事後要是讓麗迪亞知道了，會把她恨到甚麼地步。她把麗迪亞日常行為舉止失檢的地方都告訴了父親，說明和弗斯托太太這樣一個女人做朋友毫無益處，跟這樣的一個朋友到布萊頓去，也許會變得更荒唐，因為那邊的誘惑力一定比這裏大。父親用心聽她把話講完，然後說道：

“麗迪亞非到公共場所之類的地方去出一出醜，是決不肯罷休的。她這次要去出醜，既不必花家裏的錢，又用不着家裏麻煩，真難得有這樣的機會呢。”

伊莉莎白說：“麗迪亞那樣輕浮冒失，一定會引起外人注目，會使我們姐妹吃她的大虧——事實上已經吃了很大的虧——你要是想到了這一點，那你對這件事的看法就會截然不同了。”

“已經使你們吃了大虧！”班奈特先生重複了一遍。“這話怎麼說：她把你們的情人嚇跑了不成？可憐的小莉茲呀，不用擔心。那些經不起一點小風浪的挑三揀四的小伙子，不值得你去惋惜。我倒要問問你：究竟有過多少傻小子，因為看見了麗迪亞的放蕩行為，而不敢向你們問津？」

「你完全弄錯了我的意思。我並不是因為吃了虧才來埋怨。我也說不出我究竟是在埋怨哪一種害處，只覺得害處很多。麗迪亞這種放蕩不羈、毫不自制的性格，確實對我們的體面有損，一定會影響到我們的社會地位。我說話爽直，請你千萬要原諒。好爸爸，你得想辦法管教管教她這種撒野的脾氣，使她明白，不能夠一輩子都這樣到處追逐，否則她馬上就要無可救藥了。一旦她的性格定型以後，就很難改過來。她才不過十六歲，就成了一個十足的浪蕩女子，弄得她自己和家庭都惹人笑話，而且她還輕佻浪蕩到極端下賤無恥的地步。她只不過年紀還輕，略有幾分姿色，此外就一無可取。她愚昧無知，頭腦糊塗，只知道博得別人愛慕，結果到處令人看不起。凱蒂也有這種危險。麗迪亞要她東就東，西就西。她既無知，又愛虛榮，生性又懶惰，完全是沒有一點家教的樣子！哎，我的好爸爸呀，她們隨便走到甚麼地方，只要有人認識她們，她們就會受人指責，受人輕視，還時常連累到她們的姐姐們也丟臉，難道你還以為不會這樣嗎？」

班奈特先生看到她鑽進了牛角尖，便慈祥地握住她的手說：

「好孩子，放心好了。你和珍妮兩個人，隨便走到甚麼有熟人的地方，大家都會尊敬你們，器重你們；你們決不會因為有了兩個──甚至三個傻妹妹，就失掉了體面。這次要是不讓麗迪亞到布萊頓去，我們在朗伯恩就不得安寧。還是讓她去吧。弗斯托上校是個有見識的人，不會讓她闖出甚麼禍事來的；幸虧她又太窮，誰也不會看中她。布萊頓跟這裏的情形兩樣，她即使去做一個普通的浪蕩女子，也不夠資格。軍官們會找到更中意的對象。因此，我們但願她到了那裏以後，可以得到些教訓，知道她自己沒有甚麼了不起。無論如何，她再壞也壞不到哪裏去，我們總不能把她一輩子關在家裏。」

伊莉莎白聽到父親這樣回答，雖然並沒有因此改變主張，卻也只得表示滿意，悶悶不樂地走開了。以她那樣性格的人，也不會盡想着這些事自尋煩惱。她相信她已經盡了自己的責任，至於要她為那些無法避免的害處去鬱悶，或者是過份焦慮，那她可辦不到。

　　倘若麗迪亞和她母親知道她這次跟父親談話的內容，她們一定要氣得跳腳，即使她們兩張利嘴同時夾攻，滔滔不絕地大罵一陣，也還消不了她們的氣。在麗迪亞的想像中，只要到布萊頓去一次，人間天上的幸福都會獲得。她幻想着在那華麗的浴場附近，一條條街道上都擠滿了軍官。她幻想着幾十個甚至幾百個素昧生平的軍官都對她獻殷勤。她幻想着堂皇富麗的營帳，帳幕整潔美觀，裏面擠滿了血氣方剛的青年小伙子，都穿着燦爛奪目的大紅軍服。她還幻想到一幅最美滿的情景，幻想到自己坐在一個帳篷裏面，同時跟好多個軍官在柔情蜜意地賣弄風情。

　　倘若她知道了她姐姐竟要想妨害她，不讓她去享受到這些美妙的遠景和美妙的現實，那要她怎麼受得了？只有她母親才能體諒她這種心境，而且幾乎和她有同感。她相信丈夫決不打算到布萊頓去，她感到很痛苦，因此，麗迪亞能夠去一次，對她這種痛苦實在是莫大的安慰。

　　可是她們母女兩人完全不知道這回事，因此，到麗迪亞離家的那一天為止，她們一直都是歡天喜地，沒有受到半點打岔。

　　現在輪到伊莉莎白和韋翰先生最後一次會面了。她自從回家以後，已經見過他不少次，因此不安的情緒早就消失了；她曾經為了從前對他有過情意而感到不安，這種情緒現在更是消失得無影無蹤。他以往曾以風度文雅而博得過她的歡心，現在她看出了這裏面的虛偽做作，陳腔濫調，覺得十分厭惡。他目前對待她的態度，又造成了她不愉快的一個新的根源；他不久就流露出要跟她重溫舊好的意思，殊不知經過了那一番冷暖之後，卻只會使她生氣。她發覺要跟她談情說愛的這個人，竟是一個遊手好閒的輕薄公子，因此就不免對他心灰意冷；而他居然還自以為只要能夠重溫舊好，便終究能夠滿足她的虛榮，獲得她的歡心，不管他已經有多久沒有向她獻過殷勤，其中又是為了甚麼原因，都不會對事情本身產生任何影響。她看到他那種神氣，雖然表面上忍住了氣不作聲，可是心裏卻正在對他罵不絕口。

民兵團離開麥里頓的前一天，他跟別的一些軍官們都到朗伯恩來吃飯；他問起伊莉莎白在漢斯福那一段日子是怎麼度過的。伊莉莎白為了不願意和他好聲好氣地分手，便趁機提起費茨威廉上校和達西先生都在洛欣莊園消磨了三個星期，而且還問他認識不認識費茨威廉。

他頓時氣急敗壞，大驚失色，可是稍稍鎮定了一下以後，他便笑嘻嘻地回答她説，以前常常見到他的。他説費茨威廉是個很有紳士風度的人，又問她喜歡不喜歡他。她熱情地回答他説，很喜歡他。他立刻又帶着一副滿不在乎的神氣説道：“你剛剛説他在洛欣莊園住了多久？”

“差不多有三個星期。”

“你常常和他見面嗎？”

“常常見面，差不多每天見面。”

“他的風度和他表弟大不相同。”

“的確大不相同；可是我想，達西先生跟人熟悉了也就好了。”

只見韋翰頓時顯出吃驚的神氣，大聲説道：“那可怪了，對不起，我是否可以請問你一下——”説到這裏，他又控制住了自己，把説話的聲調變得愉快些，然後接下去説：“他跟人説話時，語氣是否好了些？他待人接物是否比以前有禮貌些？因為我實在不敢指望他——”他的聲調低下去了，變得更嚴肅了，“指望他從本質上變好過來。”

“沒那回事！”伊莉莎白説。“我相信他的本質還是和過去一樣。”

韋翰聽到她這一番話，不知道應該表示高興，還是應該表示不相信。韋翰見她説話時臉上有種形容不出的表情，心中不免有些害怕和焦急。她又接下去説：

"我所謂達西先生跟人熟悉了也就好了，並不是説他的思想和態度會變好，而是説，你跟他相處得越熟，你就越了解他的個性。"

韋翰一聽此話，不禁心慌起來，頓時便紅了臉，神情也十分不安。他沉默了好幾分鐘以後，才收斂住了那副窘相，轉過身來對着她，用極其溫和的聲調説：

"你很了解我心裏對達西先生是怎樣一種感覺，因此你也很容易明白：我聽到他居然也懂得在表面上裝得像個樣子了，這讓我多麼高興。那種驕傲即使對他自己沒有甚麼益處，對別人也許倒有好處，因為他既然有這種驕傲，就不會有那種惡劣行為，讓別人吃盡我當年的苦頭了。我只怕他雖然收斂了一些(你大概就是説他比較收斂了一些吧)，事實上只不過為了要在他姨母面前做做樣子，讓他姨母看得起他，説他的好話。我很明白，每逢他和他姨母在一起的時候，他就免不了戰戰兢兢，這多半是為了想和德·包爾小姐結婚，我敢説，這是他念念不忘的一件大事。"

伊莉莎白聽到這些話，不由得微微一笑，她只稍微點了一下頭，並沒有作聲。她看出他又想在她面前把那個老問題拿出來發一通牢騷，她可沒有興致去慫恿他。這個晚上就這樣過去了，他表面上還是裝得像平常一樣高興，可沒有打算要逢迎伊莉莎白；最後他們兩人客客氣氣地分了手，也許雙方都希望永遠不再見面了。

他們分手以後，麗迪亞便跟弗斯托太太回到麥里頓去。他們打算明天一早從那裏動身。麗迪亞和家裏分別的時候，與其説是有甚麼離愁別恨，還不如説是熱鬧了一場。只有凱蒂流了眼淚，可是她這一場哭泣卻是為了煩惱和嫉妒。班奈特太太口口聲聲祝她女兒幸福，又千叮萬囑地要她不要錯過了及時行樂的機會——這種囑咐，女兒當然會去遵命照辦；她得意非凡地對家裏人高聲辭別，於是姐妹們低聲細氣地祝她一路平安的話，她聽也沒有聽見。

第四十二章

倘若要伊莉莎白根據她自己家庭的情形，來說一說甚麼叫做婚姻的幸福，甚麼叫做家庭的樂趣，那她一定說不出好話來。她父親當年就因為貪戀青春美貌，而往往青春美貌會給人帶來很大的情趣，因此娶了這樣一個智力貧乏而又小心眼的女人，以致結婚不久，他對太太的深摯的情意便完結了。夫婦之間的互敬互愛和推心置腹，都永遠消失得無影無蹤；他對於家庭幸福的理想也完全給推翻了。換作別的人，凡是因為自己的冒失而招來了不幸，往往會以荒唐或是不正當的逸樂來安慰自己，可是班奈特先生卻不喜歡這一套。他喜愛鄉村景色，喜愛讀書自娛，這就是他最大的樂趣。說到他的太太，除了她的無知和愚蠢可以供他開心作樂之外，他對她就再沒有別的恩情了。一般男人是不會希望在妻子身上去找這一種樂趣的，可是大智大慧的人既然沒有辦法去找別的樂趣，那也只好將就現成的了。

不過，伊莉莎白並不是看不出父親這方面的缺德。她看到這情況，老是覺得痛苦；可是她尊重他的才能，又感謝他對自己的寵愛，因此，本來不能無視的地方，她也想忘掉作罷。而且，縱使父親不該讓孩子們看不起媽媽，以致使他們老夫婦一天比一天不能夠互敬互愛地相處，她也盡量不去想它。但是，說到不美滿的婚姻給兒女們帶來的不利，她從前決沒有像現在體驗得這樣深刻；再說，父親的才能使用不得當因而造成種種害處，這一點她也從來沒有像現在這樣看得透徹。要是父親的才能運用得當，即使不能夠擴展母親的見識，至少也可以保存女兒們的體面。

韋翰走了固然使伊莉莎白感到快慰，然而，這個民兵團開拔以後，並沒有甚麼別的地方令她滿意。外面的宴會不像以前那麼多那麼有趣了，在家裏又是成天只聽到母親和妹妹口口聲聲埋怨生活沉悶，使家裏籠罩了一層陰影；至於凱蒂，雖說那些鬧得她心猿意馬的人已經走了，她不久就會恢復常態；可是還有那另外一個妹妹，秉性本就不好，加上現在又身處在那兵營和浴場的雙重危險的環境裏，自然會更加大膽放蕩，闖出更大的禍事來。因此從大體上來說，她發覺到（其實以前有一度她早就發覺到）她眼巴巴盼望着到來的一件事，等到真正到來了，總不像她預期的那麼滿意。因此她不得不把真正幸福的開端寄託於未來，找些別的東西來寄託她的希望和心願，在期待的心情中自我陶醉一番，暫時安慰自己一下，準備着再次遭受到失望。她現在心裏最得意的一件事便是不久就可以到湖區去旅行，因為既然母親和凱蒂心裏不快活，吵得家裏雞犬不寧，當然一想起出門便使她獲得了最大的安慰；如果珍妮也能參加這次旅行，那就十全十美了。

她心裏想："總還算幸運，我還可以存些指望。假如處處都安排得很完美，我反而要感到失望了。姐姐不能夠一同去，我自然會時時刻刻都感到遺憾，不過也反而可以使我存着一分希望，因此我所期待的愉快也可能會實現。十全十美的計劃總不會成功；只有稍微帶着幾分苦惱，才可以大體上防止了失望。"

麗迪亞臨走的時候，答應常常給母親和凱蒂寫信來，詳詳細細地告訴她們一路上的情形。可是她走了以後，家裏老是等了好久才接到她一封信，而每封信又往往只是寥寥數行。她給她母親寫的那些信，無非說說她們剛剛從圖書館回來，有許多軍官們陪着她們一起去，她們在那裏看到許多漂亮的裝飾品，使她眼紅極了，或者說是她買了一件新的禮服，一把陽傘，她本來可以把這些東西詳詳細細地描寫一番，可是弗斯托太太在叫她了，她們馬上就要到兵營裏去，等等。至於她寫給凱蒂的信，雖然要長得多，可是也很空洞，因為有許多重要的話不便於寫出來。

她走了兩三個星期以後，朗伯恩又重新恢復了愉快歡樂的氣象。一切都欣欣向榮。上城裏過冬的那些人都搬回來了，人們都穿起了夏天的新裝，到處是夏天的約會。班奈特太太又像往常一樣動不動就發牢騷。到了六月中旬，凱蒂完全恢復了常態，到麥里頓去完全可以不掉眼淚了，伊莉莎白看到真高興，她希望到了聖誕節，凱蒂會變得相當有理智，不至於每天三番五次地提到軍官們，除非作戰部不管人們死活，又來一次惡作劇，重新調一團人駐紮到麥里頓來。

他們北上旅行的日期已經迫近，只剩下兩個星期了，不料這時候賈汀納太太卻寄來了一封信，使行期耽擱了下來，旅行範圍也得縮小。信上說，因為賈汀納先生有事，行期必須延遲兩個星期，到七月裏才能動身，又因為他只能外出旅行一個月便得回到倫敦，日期很短促，不能照原來的計劃作長途旅行，飽餐山川景色，至少不能照原來所安排的那樣悠閒自在地去遊覽；湖區必須放棄，旅程必須縮短，只能到德比郡為止。其實德比郡也就足夠供他們遊覽，足夠他們消磨短短三星期的旅行日程，而且賈汀納太太非常嚮往那個地方。她以前曾在那裏住過幾年，現在能夠舊地重遊，盤桓數日，便不禁對於馬特洛克 37、恰滋華斯 38、鴿谷 39、秀卓 40 的風景名勝，心醉神往。

這封信使伊莉莎白非常失望。她本來一心想去觀賞湖區風光，到現在還覺得時間很充裕。不過，她既沒有權利可以反對，她的心境又很瀟脫，不多一會，便又接受起來了。

一提到德比郡，就免不了勾起許多聯想。她看到這個地名，就不禁想到龐百利和龐百利的主人。她說："我一定可以大搖大擺地走進他的故鄉，趁他不知不覺的時候，攫取幾塊透明的晶石 41。"

行期一延再延。舅父母還得過四個星期才能來。可是四個星期畢竟過去了，賈汀納夫婦終於帶着他們的四個孩子來到朗伯恩。四個孩子中間有兩個女孩子，一個六歲，一個八歲，另外兩個男孩子年紀還小。孩子們都將留在這裏，由他們的表姐珍妮照顧，因為他們都喜歡珍妮，加上珍妮舉止穩重，性情柔和，無論是教孩子們讀書，跟他們遊戲，以及照顧他們，都非常適合。

賈汀納夫婦只在朗伯恩住了一夜，第二天一大早就帶着伊莉莎白去探新獵異，尋歡作樂。這幾個旅伴確實非常適合，所謂適合，就是說大家身體健壯，性子隨和，路上遇到不方便的地方可以忍受得了，這實在令人稱心如意。他們一個個都生氣勃勃，這自然可以促進愉快，而且他們感情豐富，人又聰明，萬一在外地碰到了甚麼掃興的事情，互相之間仍然可以過得很快活。

本書不打算詳細描寫德比郡的風光，至於他們的旅程所必須經過的一些名勝地區，例如牛津、布榜恩 [42]、瓦立克 [43]、凱尼爾沃思 [44]、伯明罕 [45] 等，大家都知道得夠多了，也不打算寫。現在只講一講德比郡的一小部份。有個小鎮名叫蘭姆頓，賈汀納太太從前曾在那裏住過，她最近聽說還有些友人依舊住在那邊，於是看完了鄉間的一切名勝古蹟之後，便繞道到那裏去看看。伊莉莎白聽見舅母說，離開蘭姆頓不到五英里路就是龐百利，雖然不是路過必經之處，可是也不過彎了一兩英里路。前一個晚上討論旅程的時候，賈汀納太太說是想到那邊再去看看。賈汀納先生表示願意，於是他們便來徵求伊莉莎白同意。

舅母對她說："親愛的，那個地方你是久聞大名的，願意去看看嗎？你的許多朋友都跟那地方有關係。韋翰的整個少年時代都是在那裏度過的，你知道。"

伊莉莎白給説得窘極了。她覺得不必到龐百利去，便只得說不想去。她說大宅雄偉建築、錦氈繡幃，已經見識得夠多了，實在無意再去瀏覽。

賈汀納太太笑她蠢，她說："要是光光只有一幢富麗堂皇的房子，我也不會把它放在心上；可是那裏的庭園景色實在可愛，那裏的樹林是全國最美麗的樹林。"

伊莉莎白不作聲了，可是她心裏仍舊不敢贊同。她立刻想到，如果到那裏去欣賞風景，很可能碰到達西先生，那多糟糕！她想到這裏就羞紅了臉，自以為還不如把事情跟舅母開誠佈公地說個明白，免得要擔這麼大的風險。可是這也不妥當；她最後決定先暗地裏打聽一下達西先生家裏有沒有人，如果有人，那麼，她再來用這最後一招也不遲。

晚上臨睡的時候，她便向侍女打聽龐百利地方好不好，主人姓甚名誰，又心驚膽顫地問起主人家是否要回來消暑。她這最後一問，竟得到了她所求之不得的回答：他們不回來。她現在用不到再怕甚麼了，又逐漸產生了極大的好奇心，想親眼去看看那幢房子；第二天早上舊話重提，舅母又來徵求她的意見，她便帶着一副毫不在乎的神氣馬上回答說，她對於這個計劃沒有甚麼不贊成，於是他們就決定上龐百利去了。

第四十三章

他們坐着車子一直向前去。龐百利的樹林一出現在眼前，伊莉莎白就有些心慌；等到走進了莊園，她更加心神不定。

花園很大，只見裏邊高卓低窪，氣象萬千。他們揀一個最低的地方走進了園，在一座深邃遼闊的美麗的樹林裏坐着車子走了好久。

伊莉莎白滿懷感觸，無心説話，可是看到了每一處、每一角的美景，她都讚賞不止。他們沿着上坡路慢慢走了半英里左右，最後來到了一個相當高的山坡上，這也就是樹林子盡頭的地方，龐百利大宅馬上映入眼簾。房子在山谷那邊，有一條相當陡斜的路曲曲折折地通到谷中。這是一幢很大很漂亮的石頭建築物，屹立在高壟上，後面枕着一連片樹林茂密的高高的小山崗；屋前一泓頗有天然情趣的溪流正在漲潮，沒有一絲一毫人工的痕跡。兩岸的點綴既不呆板，也不做作。伊莉莎白高興極了。她從來不曾看到過一個地方比這裏更能體現大自然的鬼斧神工，也沒有見過任何地方的自然之美能像這裏一樣的不落俗套。大家都熱烈地讚賞不已，伊莉莎白頓時不禁覺得：在龐百利當個主婦也還不錯吧。

他們下了山坡，過了橋，一直駛到大宅門前，欣賞那附近一帶的景物，伊莉莎白這時候不免又起了一陣疑懼，生怕闖見主人。她擔心旅館裏的侍女弄錯了。他們請求進去參觀，立刻便被請進客廳；大家都在等着管家，這時候伊莉莎白才想起身在何處。

管家來了，是一個態度端莊的老婦人，遠不如她想像中那麼有風姿，可是禮貌的周到倒出乎她的想像。他們跟着她走進了餐廳。那是一間寬敞舒適的大房間，佈置得很精緻。伊莉莎白稍稍看了一下，便走到窗口欣賞風景。他們望着剛才下來的那座小山，只見叢林密佈，從遠處望去更加顯得陡峭，真是個美麗的地方。處處都配搭得很美觀。她縱目四望，只見一彎河道，林木夾岸，山谷蜿蜒曲折，真看得她心曠神怡。他們再走到別的房間裏去看，每換一個房間，景致總會兩樣，可是不管她走到哪扇窗戶，都自有秀色可餐。一個個房間都高大美觀，傢具陳設也和主人的身價頗為相稱，既不俗氣，又不過份奢華，比起洛欣莊園來，可以說是豪華不足，風雅有餘，伊莉莎白看了，很佩服主人的情趣。

她心裏想：“我差一點就做了這裏的主婦呢！這些房間也許早就讓我走熟了！我非但不必以一個陌生的身份來參觀，而且還是擁有這一切的女主人，把舅父母當做貴客歡迎。可是不行，”她忽然想了起來，“這是萬萬辦不到的事：那時候我就見不到舅父母了，他決不會允許我邀他們來。”

她幸虧想起了這一點，才沒有後悔當初的事。

她真想問問這位女管家，主人是否真不在家，可是她沒有勇氣，只得作罷。不過她舅父終於代她問出了這一句話，使她大為慌張，連忙轉過頭去，只聽見雷諾太太回答道，他的確不在家。接着又說：“可是他明天會回家，還要帶來許多朋友。”伊莉莎白聽了真高興，幸虧他們沒有遲一天到這裏來。

她的舅母叫她去看一張畫像。她走近前去，看見那是韋翰的肖像，和另外幾張小型畫像夾在一起，掛在壁爐架的上方。舅母笑嘻嘻地問她覺得好不好。管家太太走過來說，畫像上這位年輕人是老主人的賬房的兒子，由老主人一手把他栽培起來的。她又說道：“他現在到軍隊裏去了，我怕他已經變得很浪蕩了。”

賈汀納太太笑吟吟地對她外甥女望了一眼，可是伊莉莎白實在笑不出來。

雷諾太太指着另一張畫像說：“這就是我的小主人，畫得像極了。跟那一張是同時畫的，大約有八年了。”

賈汀納太太望着那張畫像說：“我常常聽人說，你的主人堂堂一表人才，他這張臉龐的確英俊。——可是，莉茲，你倒說說看，畫得像不像。"

雷諾太太聽到伊莉莎白跟她主人相熟，便好像更加敬重她。

"這位小姐原來跟達西先生相熟？"

伊莉莎白臉紅了，只得説："不太熟。"

"你覺得他是位很英俊的少爺嗎，小姐？"

"是的，很英俊。"

"我敢説，我沒見過這樣英俊的人；樓上畫室裏還有一張他的畫像，比這張大，畫得也比這張好。老主人生前最喜愛這個房間，這些畫像的擺法，也還是照從前的老樣子。他很喜歡這些小型畫像。"

伊莉莎白這才明白為甚麼韋翰先生的像也放在一起。

雷諾太太接着又指給他們看達西小姐的一張畫像，那還是她八歲的時候畫的。

"達西小姐也跟她哥哥一樣好看嗎？"賈汀納先生問道。

"噢，那還用説——從來沒見過這樣漂亮的小姐，又那麼多才多藝！她成天彈琴唱歌。隔壁房間裏就是剛剛替她買來的一座新鋼琴，那是我主人給她的禮物，她明天會跟他一起回來。"

那位女管家看見賈汀納先生為人那麼隨和，便跟他有問有答。雷諾太太非常樂意談到她主人兄妹兩人，這或者是由於為他們感到驕傲，或者是由於和他們感情深厚。

"你主人每年留在龐百利的日子多嗎？"

"並沒有我所盼望的那麼多，先生，他每年大概可以在這裏住上半年；達西小姐總是在這裏消夏。"

伊莉莎白心想："除非到蘭斯蓋特去就不來了。"

"要是你主人結了婚，你見到他的時候就會多些。"

"是的，先生；不過我不知道這件事幾時才能如願。我也不知道哪家小姐配得上他。"

賈汀納夫婦都笑了。伊莉莎白不由得説，"你會這樣想，真使他太有面子了。"

女管家説："我説的全是真話，認識他的人都是這樣説，"伊莉莎白覺得這話實在講得有些過份。那女管家又説道："我一輩子沒聽過他説一句重話，從他四歲起，我就跟他在一起了。"伊莉莎白聽得更是驚奇。

這句褒獎的話説得最出人意料，也令她最難想像。她早就斷定達西是個脾氣不好的人，今日乍聽此話，不禁引起了她深切的注意。她很想再多聽一些。幸喜她舅舅又開口説道：

"當得起這樣恭維的人，實在沒有幾個。你真是運氣好，碰上了這樣一個好主人。"

"你説得是，先生，我自己也知道運氣好。我就是走遍天下，再也不會碰到一個更好的主人。我常説，小時候脾氣好，長大了脾氣也會好；他從小就是個脾氣最好、修養氣度最大的孩子。"

伊莉莎白禁不住瞪起眼來看她。她心裏想："達西先生真的是這樣一個人嗎？"

"他父親是個了不起的人，"賈汀納太太説。

"太太，你説得是，他的確是個了不起的人；他兒子完全像他一樣——也像他那樣體貼窮苦人。"

伊莉莎白一直聽下去，先是奇怪，繼而懷疑，最後又很想再多聽一些，可是雷諾太太再也想不出別的話來引起她的興趣。她談到畫像，談到房間的大小，談到傢具的價格，可是她都不愛聽。賈汀納先生覺得，這個女管家之所以要過甚其辭地誇獎她自己的主人，無非是出於家人的偏愛，這倒也使他聽得很有趣，於是馬上又談到這個話題上來了。她一面起勁地談到他的許多優點，一面領着他們走上大樓梯。

"他是個開明的莊主，又是個最好的主人；"她説，"他不像現在一般撒野的青年，一心只為自己打算。沒有一個佃戶或傭人不稱讚他。有些人説他傲慢；可是我從來沒看到過他有哪一點傲慢的地方。據我猜想，他只是不像一般青年人那樣愛説話罷了。"

"他被你説得多麼可愛！"伊莉莎白想道。

她舅母一邊走，一邊輕輕地説："只聽到説他的好話，可是他對待我們那位可憐的朋友卻是那種樣子，好像與事實不大符合。"

"我們可能是受到蒙蔽了。"

"這不大可能；我們的根據太可靠了。"

他們走到樓上那個寬敞的穿堂，就給領進一間漂亮的起坐間，這起坐間新近才佈置起來，比樓下的許多房間還要精緻和清新，據説那是剛剛收拾起來專供達西小姐享用的，因為去年她在龐百利看中了這個房間。

"他確實是一個好哥哥，"伊莉莎白一面説，一面走到一個窗戶前面。

雷諾太太估計達西小姐一走進這個房間，將會怎樣高興。她説："他一向就是這樣，凡是能使他妹妹高興的事情，他馬上就辦到。他從來沒有一件事不依她。"

剩下來只有畫室和兩三間主要的寢室要指給他們看了。畫室裏陳列着許多優美的油畫，可惜伊莉莎白對藝術方面完全是外行，覺得這些畫好像在樓下都已經看到過，於是她寧可掉過頭去看看達西小姐所畫的幾張粉筆畫，因為這些畫的題材一般都比較耐人尋味，而且比較容易看得懂。

畫室裏都是家族的畫像，陌生人看了不會感到興趣。伊莉莎白走來走去，專門去找那個面熟的人的畫像；她終於看到了有張畫像非常像達西先生，只見他臉上的笑容正像他從前看起她來的時候那種笑容。她在這幅畫像前站了幾分鐘，欣賞得出了神，臨出畫室之前，又走回去看了一下。雷諾太太告訴他們説，這張畫像還是他父親在世的時候畫的。

伊莉莎白不禁對畫裏那個人立刻起了一陣親切之感，即使從前她跟他見面最多的時候，她對他也從來沒有過這種感覺。我們不應當小看了雷諾太太對她主人的這種稱讚。甚麼樣的稱讚會比一個聰明的下人的稱讚更來得寶貴呢？她認為他無論是作為一個兄長，一個莊主，還是一家之主，都一手操縱着多少人的幸福；他能夠帶給人多少快樂，又能夠帶給人多少痛苦；他可以行多少善，又可以做多少惡。那個女管家所提出的每一件事情，都足以説明他品格的優良。她站在他的畫像面前，只覺得他一雙眼睛在盯着她看，她不由得想起了他對她的鍾情，於是一陣從來沒有過的感激之情油然而生，她一記起他鍾情的殷切，便不再去計較他求愛的唐突了。

凡是可以公開參觀的地方，他們都走遍了，然後走下樓來，告別了女管家，女管家便吩咐一個園丁在大廳門口送他們。

他們穿過草地，走向河邊，伊莉莎白這時候又掉過頭來看了一下，舅父母也都停住了腳步，哪知道她舅舅正想估量一下這房子的建築年代，忽然看到屋主人從一條通往馬廄的大路上走了過來。

他們只相隔二十碼路左右，他這樣突然出現，讓人簡直來不及躲避。頃刻之間，四隻眼睛碰在一起，兩個人臉上都漲得血紅。只見主人吃驚非凡，竟愣住在那裏一動不動，但是他立刻定了一定心，走到他們面前來，跟伊莉莎白説話，語氣之間即使不能算是十分鎮靜，至少十分有禮貌。

伊莉莎白早就不由自主地走開了，可是見他既然已經走上前來，她便不得不停住腳步，又窘又羞地接受他的問候。再説舅父母，他們即使一見了他還認不出是他，或是明明看出他和剛才那幅畫像有相似的地方，卻還看不出他就是達西先生，只要看看那個園丁眼見主人歸來而驚奇萬狀的神氣，也應該立刻明白了。舅父母看到他在跟他們的外甥女談話，便稍稍站得遠一點。他客客氣氣地問候她家裏人的平安，她卻詫異慌張得不敢抬起眼睛來朝他臉上看一眼，簡直不知道自己回答了他幾句甚麼話。他的態度跟他們兩人上一次分手的時候完全兩樣，這使她感到驚奇，因此他每説一句話都使她更加覺得窘；她腦子裏左思右想，覺得闖到這裏來被人發現，真是有失體統，這短短的幾分鐘竟成了她生平最難熬的一段光陰。他也不見得比她從容，説話的聲調也不像往常那麼鎮定。他問她是幾時從朗伯恩出發，在德比郡停留了多久，諸如此類的話問了又問，而且問得很是慌張，這足以説明他是怎樣的心神錯亂。

最後他好像已經無話可説，默默無言地站了幾分鐘，突然又定了一下心，告辭而去。

舅父母這才走到她面前，説他的儀表令他們很是仰慕，伊莉莎白滿懷心事，一個字也沒聽進去，只是默默無言地跟着他們走。她真是説不出的羞愧和懊惱。她這次上這裏來，真是天下最不幸、最不明智的事。他會覺得多麼奇怪！以他這樣傲慢的一個人，又會怎樣看不起這件事！她這次好像是重新自己送上門來。天哪，她為甚麼要來？或者説，他怎麼偏偏就出人意料地早一天趕回家來？他們只要早走十分鐘，就會走得遠遠的，他就看不見了；他顯然是剛巧來到，剛巧跳下馬背或是走出馬車。想起了剛才見面時那種彆扭的情形，她臉上不禁紅了又紅。他的態度完全和從前兩樣了——這是怎麼回事呢？他居然還會走上前來跟她説話，光是這一點，就令人夠驚奇的了；何況他出言吐語，以及問候她家裏人的平安，又是那麼彬彬有禮！這次邂逅，他的態度竟這般謙恭，談吐竟這般柔和，她真是從來也沒有見過。上次他在洛欣莊園裏交給她那封信的時候，他那種措詞跟今天成了怎樣的對比！她不知道如何去想才好，也不知道怎樣去解釋這種情景。

他們現在已經走到河邊一條美麗的小徑上，地面逐漸低下去，眼前的風光便更加顯得壯麗，樹林的景色也更加顯得幽雅，他們慢慢地向前走，舅父母沿途一再招呼伊莉莎白欣賞如此這般的景色，伊莉莎白雖然也隨口答應，把眼睛朝着他們指定的方向張望一下，可是她好久都辨別不出一景一物，簡直無心去看。她一心只想着龐百利大宅的一個角落裏，不管是哪一個角落，只要是達西先生現在所處的地方。她真想知道他這時候在想些甚麼，他心目中怎樣看待她，儘管發生了那麼一連串事情，他是否依舊對她有好感。他也許只是自以為心頭一無牽掛，所以對她特別客氣，可是聽他說話的聲調，自有一種說不出的意味，又不像是一無牽掛的樣子。她不知道他見了她是痛苦多於快樂，還是快樂多於痛苦，可是看他那副樣子，決不像是心神鎮定。

後來舅父母怪她怎麼心不在焉，這才提醒了她，覺得應該裝得像樣一點。

他們走進樹林，踏上山坡，跟這彎溪流暫時告別。從樹林的空隙間望出去，可以看到山谷中各處的景色。對面一座座的小山，有些小山上都長滿了整片的樹林，蜿蜒曲折的溪流又不時映入眼簾。賈汀納先生想在整個園林裏兜個圈子，可是又怕走不動。園丁帶着得意的笑容告訴他們說，兜一圈有十英里路呢。這事情只得作罷，他們便沿着平常的途徑東兜西轉，過了一段時間，才在懸崖上的小林子裏下了坡，又來到河邊，這是河道最狹窄的一部份。他們從一座簡陋的小橋上過了河，只見這座小橋和周圍的景色很是和諧。這地方比他們所到過的地方要樸素些，山谷到了這裏也變成了一條小夾道，只能容納這彎溪流和一條小徑，小徑上灌木夾道，參差不齊。伊莉莎白很想循着曲徑去探幽尋勝；可是一過了橋，眼見離開住宅已經那麼遠，不擅長走路的賈汀納太太已經走不動了，一心只想快一些上馬車。外甥女只得依從她，大家便在河對岸抄着近路向住宅那邊走。他們走得很慢，因為賈汀納先生很喜歡釣魚，平常卻很少能夠過癮，這時看見河面上常常有鱒魚出現，便又跟園丁談魚談得很投契，因此時常站着不動。他們就這樣慢慢溜達，不料又吃了一驚，尤其是伊莉莎白，她幾乎詫異得跟剛才完全沒有兩樣。原來他們又看見達西先生向他們這邊走來，而且快要來到面前了。這一帶的小路不像對岸那樣隱蔽，因此他們隔得很遠便可以看見他。不過伊莉莎白不管怎麼詫異，至少比剛剛那次見面有準備得多，因此她便下定決心：如果他真的要來跟他們碰頭，她便索性放得鎮定些，跟他攀談一番。她剛開始倒以為他也許會轉到別的一條小道上去。她之所以會有這種想法，只因為道路拐彎的時候，他的身影被遮住了，他們看不見他。可是剛一拐彎，他馬上便出現在他們面前。她偷偷一看，只見他正像剛才一樣，沒有一點失禮的地方，於是她也仿效着他那彬彬有禮的樣子，開始讚賞這地方的美麗風光，可是她剛剛開口說了幾聲"動人"、"嫵媚"，心裏又起了一個不愉快的念頭。她想，她這樣讚美麗百利，不是會讓人曲解嗎？想到這裏，她不禁又紅了臉，一聲不響。

賈汀納太太站在稍微後面一點；正當伊莉莎白默不作聲的時候，達西卻要求她賞個臉，把她這兩位親友給他介紹一下。他這樣的禮貌周到，真是完全出乎她的意料；想當初他向她求婚的時候，他竟那樣傲慢，看不起她的某些親友，而他現在所要求介紹的卻正是這些親友，相形之下，她簡直忍不住要笑出來。她想："要是他知道了這兩位是甚麼樣的人，他不知會怎樣吃驚呢！他現在大概把他們錯看作上流人了。"

不過她還是立刻替他介紹了；她一面跟他說明這兩位是她的至親，一面偷偷地瞟了他一眼，看他是不是受得了。她想他也許會撒腿就跑，避開這些丟臉的朋友。他弄明白了他們的親戚關係以後，顯然很吃驚。不過他總算沒給嚇壞，非但不走開，反而陪了他們一起走回去，又跟賈汀納先生攀談起來。伊莉莎白自然又是高興，又是得意。她可以讓他知道，她也有幾個不丟臉的親戚，這真令她快慰。她十分留心地聽着他跟賈汀納先生談話，幸喜他舅父的舉止談吐，處處都足以令人看出他頗有見識，趣味高尚，風度優雅。

他們不久就談到釣魚，她聽見達西先生非常客氣地跟他說，他既然住在鄰近，只要不走，隨時都可以來釣魚，同時又答應借釣具給他，又指給他看，這條河裏通常哪些地方魚最多。賈汀納太太跟伊莉莎白挽着手走，對她做了個眼色，表示十分驚奇。伊莉莎白沒有說甚麼，可是心裏卻得意極了，因為這番殷勤當然都是為了討好她一個人。不過她還是極端詫異；她一遍遍地問自己："他的為人怎麼變得這麼快？這是由於甚麼原因？他不見得是為了我，看在我的面上，態度才會這樣溫和吧？不見得因為我在漢斯福罵了他一頓，就會使他這樣面目一新吧？我看他不見得還會愛我。"

他們就這樣兩位太太小姐在前，兩位先生在後，走了一會。後來為了要仔細欣賞一些稀奇的水草，便分頭走到河邊，等到恢復原來位置的時候，前後次序就改變了。原來賈汀納太太因為一上午走累了，覺得伊莉莎白的臂膀支持不住她的重量，還是挽着自己丈夫走舒服些。於是達西先生便代替了她的位置，和她外甥女並排走。兩人先是沉默了一陣，後來還是小姐先開口說話。她想跟他說明一下，這一次他們是事先打聽他不在家然後再到這裏來遊覽的，因此她第一句話就談起他這次回來非常出人意料。她接下去說："因為你的女管家告訴我們，你一定要到明天才會回來；我們離開巴克威爾以前，就打聽到你不會一下子回到鄉下來。"他承認這一切都是事實，又說，因為要找賬房有事，所以比那批同來的人早來了幾個小時。他接着又說："他們明天一大早就會和我見面，他們中間也有你認識的人，賓利先生和他的姐妹們都來了。"

伊莉莎白只稍微點了一下頭。她立刻回想到他們兩人上一次提到賓利時的情形；從他的臉色看來，他心裏這時候也在想着上一回的情形。

停了片刻，他又接下去說："這些人裏面，有個人特別想要認識你，那就是舍妹。我想趁你在蘭姆頓的時候，介紹她跟你認識認識，不知道你是否肯賞臉，是否認為我太冒昧？"

這個要求真使她受寵若驚；她不知道應該怎樣答應才好。她立刻感覺到，達西小姐之所以要認識她，無非是出於她哥哥的慫恿；只要想到這一點，就足夠令她滿意了。她看到他雖然對她不滿，可是並沒有因此就真的對她懷着厭惡感，心裏覺得很快慰。

他們兩人默不作聲地往前走，各人在想各人的心事。伊莉莎白感到不安；這一切好像不大可能；可是她覺得又得意，又高興。他想要介紹妹妹給她認識，這真是給足她面子。他們立刻就走到賈汀納夫婦前面去了；當他們快走到馬車那裏的時候，賈汀納夫婦還距離他們好一段路呢。

他請她到大宅裏去坐坐，她說並不累，兩個人便一起站在草地上。在這種時候，雙方應當有多少話可以談，不作聲可真不像樣。她想要說話，可是甚麼話都想不起來。最後她想起了自己正在旅行，兩個人便大談起馬特洛克和鴿谷的景物。然而時間過得真慢，她舅母也走得真慢，這場知心的密談還沒結束，她卻早已心也慌了，話也完了。賈汀納夫婦趕上來的時候，達西先生再三請大家一起進大宅裏去休息一下，可是客人們謝絕了，大家極有禮貌地告辭分手。達西先生扶着兩位女客上了車。直到馬車開駛，伊莉莎白還目送他慢慢走進屋去。

舅父母現在開始評長論短了；夫婦兩人都說他的人品比他們所料想的不知要好多少。舅父說："他的舉止十分優雅，禮貌也極其周到，而且絲毫不擺架子。"

舅母說："他的確有點高高在上的樣子，不過只是風度上稍微有這麼一點罷了，並不令人討厭。現在我真覺得那位女管家的話說得一點不錯：雖然有些人說他傲慢，我可完全看不出來。"

"他竟那樣款待我們，真是萬萬料想不到。這不僅是客氣，而是真正的殷勤；其實他用不到這樣殷勤，他跟伊莉莎白不過是泛泛之交。"

舅母說："莉茲，他當然比不上韋翰那麼好看，或者可以說，他不像韋翰那樣談笑風生，因為他的容貌十分端莊。可是你怎麼會跟我們說他十分討厭呢？"

伊莉莎白竭力為自己辯解，她說她那次在肯特郡遇見他時，就比以前對他有好感，又說，她從來沒有看見過他像今天上午那麼和藹可親。

舅父說："不過，他那麼殷勤客氣，也許靠不大住，這些貴人大都如此；他請我常常去釣魚，我也不能信他的話，也許有一天他會變了主意，不許我進他的莊園。"

伊莉莎白覺得他們完全誤解了他的性格，可是並沒說出口來。

賈汀納太太接着說："從我們看到他的一些情形來說，我真想像不出，他竟會那樣狠心地對待可憐的韋翰。這人看上去心地不壞。他說起話來，嘴上的表情倒很討人喜歡。至於他臉上的表情，的確有些尊嚴，不過人們也不會因此就說他心腸不好。只有帶我們去參觀的那個女管家，倒真把他的性格說得天花亂墜。有幾次我幾乎忍不住要笑出聲來。不過，我看他一定是位很慷慨的主人；在一個傭人的眼睛裏看來，一切的德性就在於這一點上面。"

伊莉莎白聽到這裏，覺得應該替達西說幾句公道話，辯明他並沒有虐待韋翰；她便小心翼翼地把事情的原委說給舅父母聽。她說，達西在肯特郡的有些親友曾告訴她，他的行為和別人所傳說的情形大有出入；他的為人決不像赫福德郡的人們所想像的那麼荒謬，韋翰的為人也決不像赫福德郡的人們所想像的那麼厚道。為了證實這一點，她又把他們兩人之間金錢往來上的事情，一五一十地講了出來，雖然沒有指明這話是誰講出來的，可是她斷定這些話很可靠。

這番話使賈汀納太太聽得既感驚奇，又極擔心，只是大家現在已經走到從前她喜愛的那個地方，於是她一切的心事都煙消雲散，完全沉醉在甜蜜的回憶裏面。她把這周圍一切有趣的處所一一指給她丈夫看，根本無心想到別的事上面去。雖然一上午的步行已經使她感到疲倦，可是一吃過飯，她又動身去探訪故友舊交。這一晚過得真有意思，正所謂：連年怨闊別，一朝喜重逢。

至於伊莉莎白，白天裏所發生的種種事情對她來說實在太有趣了，她實在沒有心情去結交任何新朋友；她只是一心一意地在想，達西先生今天為甚麼那樣禮貌周全，尤其使她詫異的是，他為甚麼要把他妹妹介紹給她。

第四十四章

伊莉莎白料定達西先生的妹妹一到龐百利，達西先生隔天就會帶着她來拜訪她，因此決定那天整個上午都不離開旅館，至多在附近走走。可是她完全猜錯了，原來她跟舅父母到達蘭姆頓的當天上午，那批客人就到了龐百利。他們到了蘭姆頓，便跟着幾個新朋友到各處去逛了一轉，剛剛回到旅館去換衣服，以便到一家朋友那裏去吃飯，忽然聽到一陣馬車聲，他們便走到窗前，只見一男一女，坐着一輛雙輪馬車，從大街上往這邊來。伊莉莎白立刻就認出了馬車夫的號衣，心裏有數，於是告訴舅父母說，她就要有貴客光臨。舅父母聽了都非常驚訝。他們看見她說起話來那麼窘迫，再把眼前的事實和昨天種種情景前前後後想一想，便對這件事有了一種新的看法。他們以前雖然完全蒙在鼓裏，沒有看出達西先生愛上了他們的外甥女，可是他們現在覺得一定是這麼回事，否則他這百般的殷勤就無法解釋了。他們腦子裏不斷地轉着這些新的念頭，伊莉莎白本人也不禁越來越心慌意亂。她奇怪自己怎麼會這樣坐立不安。她前思後想，很是焦急，怕的是達西先生為了愛她的緣故，會在他妹妹面前把她捧得太高；她越是想要討人喜歡，便越是懷疑自己沒有討人喜歡的本領。

她為了怕讓舅父母看見，便從窗前退縮回來，在房間裏踱來踱去，竭力裝出心神鎮定的樣子，但見舅父母神色詫異，這下可更糟了。

達西兄妹終於走進了旅館，大家鄭重其事地介紹了一番。伊莉莎白看到達西小姐也和自己同樣顯得不好意思，不禁頗感驚奇。自從她來到蘭姆頓以來，總是聽說達西小姐為人非常傲慢，可是這時她只觀察了她幾分鐘，就斷定她不過是過份羞怯畏縮。達西小姐除了簡單地回答一兩個字外，此外你休想再逼得出她一字一句來。

達西小姐個子很高，身材比伊莉莎白大一號，她雖然才十六歲，可是已經發育完全，一舉一動都像個大人，端莊大方。她比不上她哥哥好看，可是她的臉龐長得聰明有趣，儀表又謙和文雅。伊莉莎白本以為她看起人來也像達西一樣尖酸刻薄，不留情面，現在見她並不如此，倒放下了心。

　　他們見面不久，達西先生就告訴伊莉莎白說，賓利也要來拜候她；她正要說一聲不勝榮幸，可是話未出口，就聽見賓利先生上樓梯的急促的腳步聲，轉眼間，他就進來了。伊莉莎白本來已經對他心平氣和，縱使餘怒未消，只要看他這次來訪，情懇意切，對重逢表示喜悅，即使有氣也煙消雲散了。他親切地問候她全家安好，雖然只說了幾句很平常的話，可是他的容貌談吐，卻完全和從前一樣安詳愉快。

　　賈汀納夫婦也和她有同感，認為他是個耐人尋味的人物。他們早就想見見他。眼前這些人確實引起了他們極大的興趣。他們因為懷疑達西先生跟他們外甥女的關係，便禁不住偷偷地仔細觀察雙方的情形，觀察的結果，他們立刻確定兩個人中間至少有一個已經嚐到了戀愛的滋味。小姐的情意一時還不能斷定，可是先生方面顯然是情意綿綿。

　　伊莉莎白自有事情忙於應付。她既想弄清在場賓客中每個人對她觀感如何，又要確定她自己對他們的觀感如何，還要博得大家的好感。她最怕不能博得大家的好感，可是效果偏偏非常好，因為她要討好的那些人，沒來之前都已對她懷着好感。賓利存心要和她交好，喬治安娜極想和她親近，達西非要討好她不可。

　　看到了賓利，她一切的念頭自然都轉到自己姐姐身上去了，她多麼想要知道他是不是也同她一樣，會想到她姐姐！她有時候覺得他比從前說話說得少了，不過一兩次，當他看着她的時候，她又覺得他竭力想在她身上看出一點和她姐姐相似的地方。這也許是她自己的憑空假想，不過有一件事她可看得很真切：大家都說達西小姐是珍妮的情敵，其實賓利先生對達西小姐並沒有甚麼情意。他們兩人之間看不出有甚麼特別鍾情的地方。無論甚麼地方，都不能證明賓利小姐的願望一定會實現。伊莉莎白立刻就覺得自己這種想法頗近情理。賓客們臨走以前，又發生了兩三件小事，伊莉莎白因為愛姐心切，便認為這兩三件小事足以說明賓利先生對珍妮依然舊情難忘，而且他還想多攀談一會，以便談到珍妮身上去，只可惜他膽量甚小，未敢如此。他只有趁着別人在一起談話時，才用一種萬分遺憾的語氣跟她說：“我和她好久不曾相見，真是福薄緣淺。”她還沒有來得及回他的話，他又說道：“有八個多月沒見面了。我們是十一月二十六日分別的，那一次我們大家都在尼德斐莊園跳舞。”

伊莉莎白見他對往事記得這麼清楚，很是高興；後來他又趁着別人不在意的時候，向她問起她的姐妹們現在是不是全在朗伯恩。這前前後後的一些話，本身並沒有甚麼深意，可是說話人的神情態度，卻大可玩味。

她雖然不能常常向達西先生顧盼，可是她只要隨時看他一眼，就看見他臉上總是那麼親切，她聽他談吐之間既沒有絲毫的高傲習氣，也沒有半點蔑視她親戚的意味，於是她心裏不由得想道：昨天親眼看到他作風大有改進，那即使是一時的改變，至少也保持到了今天。幾個月以前他認為和這些人打交道有失身份，如今他卻這樣樂於結交他們，而且要博得他們的好感；她看到他不僅對她自己禮貌周全，甚至對那些他曾經聲言看不入眼的親戚們，禮貌也頗周全。上次他在漢斯福牧師家裏向她求婚的那一幕，還歷歷在目，如今對比起來，真是前後判若兩人。這種種情形，實在使她極度激動，使她幾乎禁不住把心裏的驚奇流露到臉上來。她從來沒見過他這樣一心要討好別人，無論是在尼德斐莊園和他那些好朋友們在一起的時候，或是在洛欣莊園跟他那些高貴的親戚在一起的時候，也不曾像現在這樣虛懷若谷，有說有笑，何況他這樣的熱情並不能增進他自己的體面，何況他現在殷勤招待的這些人，即使攀上了交情，也只會落得尼德斐莊園和洛欣莊園的太太小姐們嘲笑指摘。

這些客人在他們這裏逗留了半個多小時，臨走的時候，達西先生讓他妹妹跟他一起向賈汀納夫婦和班奈特小姐表示，希望他們在離開這裏以前，上龐百利去吃頓便飯。達西小姐雖然對於邀請客人還不大習慣，顯得有些畏縮不前，可是她卻立刻照做了。於是賈汀納太太望着外甥女，看她是不是願意去，因為這次請客主要是為了她，不料伊莉莎白轉過頭去不響。賈汀納太太認為這樣故意迴避是一時的羞怯，而不是不喜歡這次邀請；她又看看自己的丈夫，他本來就是個愛交際的人，這時更顯得完全願意去的樣子，於是她就大膽答應了，日期定在後天。

賓利表示十分高興，因為他又可以多一次看到伊莉莎白的機會，他還有許多話要和她談，還要向她打聽赫福德郡某些朋友的情況。伊莉莎白認為這一切都只是因為，他想從她嘴裏探聽她姐姐的消息，因此心裏很快活。凡此種種，雖然她當時倒並不怎麼特別歡欣，可是客人們走了以後，她一想起剛才那半個小時的情景，就不禁得意非凡。她怕舅父母再三追問，很想迴避，所以她一聽完他們把賓利讚揚了一通以後，便趕快去換衣服。

可是她沒有理由害怕賈汀納夫婦的好奇心，因為他們並不想強迫她講出心裏的話。她跟達西先生的交情，顯然不是他們以前所猜想的那種泛泛之交，他顯然愛上了她，舅父母發現了許多蛛絲馬跡，可又實在不便過問。

他們現在一心只想到達西先生的好處。他們和他認識到現在為止，從他身上找不出半點錯處。他那樣的客氣，使他們不得不感動。要是他們光憑着自己的感想和那個女管家的報導來稱道他的為人，而不參考其他人的意見，那麼，赫福德郡那些認識他的人，簡直辨別不出這是講的達西先生。大家現在都願意去相信那個女管家的話，因為她在主人四歲的那年就來到他家，當然深知主人的為人，加上她本身的舉止也令人起敬，那就決不應該貿貿然把她的話置若罔聞，何況根據蘭姆頓的朋友們跟他們講的情形來看，也覺得這位女管家的話沒有甚麼不可靠的地方。達西除了傲慢之外，別人指摘不出他有任何錯處。說到傲慢，他也許果真有些傲慢，縱使他並不傲慢，那麼，那個小鎮上的居民們見他全家終年足跡不至，自然也要說他傲慢。不過大家都公認他是個很大方的人，濟苦救貧，慷慨解囊。

再說到韋翰，他們立刻就發覺他在這個地方並不十分受人器重；雖然大家不大明瞭他和他恩人的兒子之間的主要關係，可是大家都知道他離開德比郡時曾經欠下了許多債務，後來都是由達西先生替他償還的。

伊莉莎白這個晚上一心一意只想到龐百利，比昨天晚上還要想得厲害。這雖然是一個漫漫的長夜，可是她還是覺得不夠長，因為龐百利大宅裏那個人弄得她心裏千頭萬緒，她在牀上整整躺了兩個小時睡不着覺，左思右想，還弄不明白對他究竟是愛是憎。她當然不會恨他。決不會的；恨早就消了。如果說她真的一度討厭過他，她也早就為當初這種心情感到慚愧。她既然認為他具有許多高尚的品質，自然就尊敬起他來，儘管她剛開始還不大願意承認，事實上早就因為尊敬他而不覺得他有絲毫討厭的地方了。她現在又聽到大家都說他的好話，昨天她又親眼看到了種種情形，看出他原來是個性格很柔順的人，於是尊敬之外又添上了幾分親切。但是問題的關鍵還不在於她對他尊敬和器重，而在於她還存着一片好心好意，這一點不能忽略。她對他頗有幾分感激之心。她之所以感激他，不僅因為他曾經愛過她，而且因為當初她雖然那麼意氣用事，斬釘截鐵地拒絕過他，錯怪過他。如今他卻決不計較，反而依舊愛她。她本以為他會恨她入骨，決不會再理睬她，可是這一次邂逅，他卻好像急不待緩地要跟她重修舊好。提到他們兩人本身方面的事情，他雖然舊情難忘，可是語氣神態之間，卻沒有粗鄙怪癖的表現，只是竭力想要獲得她親友們的好感，而且真心誠意地要介紹她和他的妹妹認識。這麼傲慢的一個男人，會一下子變得這樣謙虛，這不僅令人驚奇，也讓人感激，這不能不歸根於愛情，濃烈的愛情。她雖然不能千真萬確地把這種愛情説出一個所以然來，可是她決不覺得討厭，而且還被深深的打動，覺得應該讓這種愛情滋長下去。她既然尊敬他，器重他，感激他，便免不了極其關心到他的幸福。她問她自己究竟是否願意放心大膽地來掌握他給予的幸福；她相信自己依舊有本領讓他再來求婚，問題只在於她是否應該放心大膽地施展出這副本領，以便達到雙方的幸福。

晚上她和舅母商談，覺得達西小姐那麼客氣，回到龐百利已經是吃早飯的時候，卻還當天就趕來看她們，她們即使不能像她那樣禮貌周全，至少也應該稍有禮貌，去回訪她一次。最後她們認為，最好是明天一大早就上龐百利去拜候她。她們決定就這麼辦。伊莉莎白很是高興，不過她要是問問自己為甚麼這樣高興，卻又答不上來了。

吃過早飯以後，賈汀納先生馬上就出去了，因為上一天他又重新談到了釣魚的事，約定今天中午到龐百利去和幾位紳士碰頭。

第四十五章

伊莉莎白現在認為，賓利小姐之所以一向厭惡她，原因不外乎和她吃醋。她既然有了這種想法，便不禁覺得這次到龐百利去，賓利小姐一定不會歡迎她；儘管如此，她倒想看看這一次舊雨重逢，那位小姐是否會多少顧全一些大體。

到了龐百利大宅，家人們就帶着她們走過穿堂，進入客廳，只見客廳北面景色非常動人，窗戶外邊是一片空地，屋後樹林茂密，崗巒聳疊，草地上種滿了美麗的橡樹和西班牙栗樹，真是賞心悅目的夏日風光。

達西小姐在這間客廳裏接待她們，跟她一同來接她們的還有赫斯托太太、賓利小姐，以及那位在倫敦跟達西小姐住在一起的太太。喬治安娜對她們禮貌非常周全，只是態度頗不自然，這固然是因為她有幾分羞怯，生怕有失禮的地方，可是在那些自以為身份比她低的人看來，便容易誤會她為人傲慢矜持，幸虧賈汀納太太和她外甥女決不會錯怪她，反而還同情她。

赫斯托太太和賓利小姐只對她們行了個屈膝禮。她們坐定以後，賓主之間許久不曾交談，實在彆扭。後來還是安涅斯雷太太第一個開口說話。這位太太是個和藹可親的大家閨秀，你只要看她竭力想出話來攀談，便可以知道她確實比另外兩位有教養得多。全靠她同賈汀納太太先攀談起來，再加上伊莉莎白不時地插幾句嘴助興，談話才算沒有冷場。達西小姐好像想說話而又缺乏勇氣，只是趁着別人聽不見的時候支吾一兩聲，也總算難得。

伊莉莎白立刻發覺賓利小姐在仔細地看着她，注意她的一言一行，特別注意她跟達西小姐攀談。如果伊莉莎白跟達西小姐的座位隔得很近，攀談起來很方便，她決不會因為畏忌賓利小姐而就不和達西小姐攀談，可是既然毋須多談，再加她自己也正心事重重，所以也並不覺得遺憾。她時時刻刻都盼望着會有幾位男客走進來，而且盼望這一家的主人也會跟着男客們一同進來。可是她雖然盼望，卻又害怕，她究竟是盼望得迫切，還是害怕得厲害，她自己也幾乎説不上來。伊莉莎白就這樣坐了十五分鐘之久，沒有聽到賓利小姐發表一言半語，後來忽然之間嚇了一跳，原來是賓利小姐冷冰冰地問候她家裏的人安好。她也同樣冷冷淡淡簡簡單單地敷衍了她幾句，對方便也就不再開口。

她們來了不久，傭人們便送來了冷切肉、點心以及各種應時鮮果。本來達西小姐一直忘了叫人端來，幸虧安涅斯雷太太頻頻向她使着眼色，裝着微笑，才提醒了她做主人的責任。這下大家都有事情可做了。雖然不是每個人都健談，可是每個人都會吃；大家一看見那大堆大堆美麗的葡萄、油桃和桃子，一下子就聚攏來圍着桌子坐下。

吃東西的時候，達西先生走了進來，伊莉莎白便趁此辨別一下自己的心情，究竟是希望他在場，還是害怕他在場。辨別的結果，雖然自以為盼望的心情多於害怕的心情，可是他進來了不到一分鐘，她卻又認為他還是不進來比較好。

達西原先跟自己家裏兩三個人陪着賈汀納先生在河邊釣魚，後來一聽到賈汀納太太和她外甥女當天上午就要來拜訪喬治安娜，便立刻離開了他們，回到家裏來。伊莉莎白見他走進來，便隨機應變，下定決心，促使自己千萬要表現得從容不迫，落落大方。她下定這個決心，確實很必要，只可惜事實上不大容易做到，因為她看到全場人都在懷疑他們兩人；達西一走進來，幾乎沒有一隻眼睛不在注意着他的舉止。雖然人人都有好奇心，可是誰也不像賓利小姐那麼露骨，好在她對他們兩人中間隨便哪一個談起話來，還是滿面笑容，這是因為她還沒有嫉妒到不顧一切的地步，也沒有對達西先生完全死心。達西小姐看見哥哥來了，便盡量多説話；伊莉莎白看出達西極其盼望她跟他妹妹相熟起來，他還盡量促進她們雙方多多攀談。賓利小姐把這些情形看在眼裏，很是氣憤，也就顧不得唐突，顧不得禮貌，一有機會便冷言冷語地說：

"請問你，伊莉莎白小姐，麥里頓的民兵團是否離去了嗎？府上一定覺得這是一個很大的損失吧。"

她只是不敢當着達西的面明目張膽地提起韋翰的名字，可是伊莉莎白立刻懂得她指的就是那個人，因此不禁想起過去跟他的一些來往，一時感到很難過。這是一種惡意的攻擊，伊莉莎白非要狠狠地還擊她一下不可，於是她立刻用一種滿不在乎的聲調回答了她那句話。她一面説，一面不由自主地對達西望了一眼，只見達西漲紅了臉，懇切地望着她，達西的妹妹更是萬分慌張，低頭無語。賓利小姐如果早知道這種不三不四的話會使得她自己的意中人這樣痛苦，她自然就決不會説出口了。她只是存心要讓伊莉莎白煩惱，她以為伊莉莎白過去曾傾心於那個男人，便故意説了出來，使她獻醜，讓達西看不起她，甚至還可以讓達西想起她幾個妹妹曾經為了那個民兵團鬧出多少荒唐的笑話。至於達西小姐想要私奔的事情，她一點也不知情，因為達西先生對這件事一向盡量保守秘密，除了伊莉莎白小姐以外，沒有向任何人透露過。他對賓利的親友們隱瞞得特別小心，因為他認為以後要和他們攀親，這也是伊莉莎白意料中的事。他的確早就有了這個打算；也許就是為了這個原因，便對賓利先生的幸福更加關心，可並不是因此而千方百計地去拆散賓利先生和班奈特小姐的好事。

達西看到伊莉莎白不動聲色，這才安下心來。賓利小姐苦惱失望之餘，不敢再提到韋翰，於是喬治安娜也很快恢復了正常的神態，只不過一時之間還不好意思開口説話。她害怕看到她哥哥的眼睛，她哥哥倒沒有留意她也牽涉在這件事情裏面。賓利小姐這次本來已經安排好神機妙算，要使得達西回心轉意，不再眷念伊莉莎白，結果反而使他對伊莉莎白更加念念不忘，更加有情意。

這一問一答以後，客人們沒有隔多久就告辭了。當達西先生送她們上馬車的時候，賓利小姐便趁機在他妹妹面前大發牢騷，把伊莉莎白的人品、舉止和服裝都一一批評。喬治安娜可並沒有接嘴，因為她哥哥既然那麼推崇伊莉莎白，她當然便也對她有了好感。哥哥的看法決不會錯；他把伊莉莎白捧得令喬治安娜只覺得她又親切又可愛。達西回到客廳裏來的時候，賓利小姐又把剛才跟他妹妹說的話，重新說了一遍給他聽。

她大聲說道：「達西先生，今天上午伊麗莎·班奈特小姐的臉色多難看！從去年冬天以來，她真變得太厲害了，我一輩子也沒看見過哪個人像她這樣。她的皮膚變得又黑又粗糙，路易莎和我簡直不認識她了。」

這種話儘管不合達西的心意，他卻還是冷冷地敷衍了她一下，說是他看不出她有甚麼變化，只不過皮膚黑了一點，這是夏天旅行的結果，不足為奇。

賓利小姐回答道：「老實說，我覺得根本看不出她有甚麼美。她的臉太瘦，皮膚沒有光澤，眉目也不清秀。她的鼻子也很平常，線條一點不突出。她一口牙齒勉強還過得去，可是也不過普普通通；講到她的眼睛，人們有時候都把它說得有多麼美，我可看不出有甚麼大不了。她那雙眼睛有些尖刻相，又有些惡毒相，我才不喜歡呢；而且拿她的整個風度來說，完全是自命不凡，其實卻不登大雅之堂，真令人受不了。」

賓利小姐既然早已斷定達西愛上了伊莉莎白，又要用這種辦法來博得他的喜歡，實在不太高明；不過人們在一時氣憤之下，往往難免有不明智的時候。她看到達西終於被弄得多少有些神色煩惱，便自以為打響了如意算盤。達西卻咬緊牙關，一聲不響，她為了非要他說幾句話不可，便又往下說：

「我還記得我們第一次在赫福德郡認識她的時候，聽說她是個有名的美人，我們都覺得十分奇怪；我特別記得有一個晚上，她們在尼德斐莊園吃過晚飯以後，你說：'她也算得上一個美人！那麼她媽媽也算得上一個天才了！'可是你以後就對她印象好起來了，你也有一個時期覺得她很好看。"

達西真是忍無可忍了，只得回答道："話是說得不錯，可是，那是我剛認識她時候的事情；最近好幾個月以來，我已經把她看做我認識的女人當中最漂亮的一個。"

他這樣說過以後，便走開了，只剩下賓利小姐一個人。她逼迫他說出了這幾句話，本以為可以借此得意一番，結果只是自討沒趣。

賈汀納太太和伊莉莎白回到寓所以後，便把這次作客所遇到的種種事情詳細談論了一番，只可惜大家都感興趣的那件事卻偏偏沒有談到；凡是她們所看到的人，她們都拿來一個個評頭論足，又一一談到各人的神情舉止，只可惜她們特別留意的那個人卻沒有談到。她們談到了他的妹妹、他的朋友、他的住宅、他請客人們吃的水果——樣樣都談到了，只是沒有談到他本人，其實外甥女真希望舅母大人談談對那個人印象如何，舅母大人也極其希望外甥女先扯到這個話題上來。

第四十六章

伊莉莎白到蘭姆頓的時候，因為沒有立即接到珍妮的來信，感到非常失望；第二天早上又感到同樣的失望。可是到了第三天，她就再也不用焦慮了，再也不埋怨她的姐姐了，因為她這一天收到了姐姐兩封信，其中一封註明曾經送錯了地方。伊莉莎白並不覺得詫異，因為珍妮確實把位址寫得很潦草。

那兩封信送來的時候，他們剛剛要出去溜達；舅父母自己走了，讓她一個人去靜靜地讀信。誤投過的那封信當然要先讀，那還是五天前寫的。信上先講了一些小規模的宴會和約會之類的事，又報導了一些鄉下的新聞；後一半卻報導了重要消息，而且註明是下一天寫的，顯而易見寫信人提筆時心緒很亂。後半封內容如下：

親愛的莉茲，寫了上半封信之後，發生了一件極其出人意料、極其嚴重的事；可是我又怕嚇壞了你。請放心吧，家人都安好，我這裏要說的是關於可憐的麗迪亞的事。昨天晚上十二點鐘，我們正要睡覺的時候，突然接到弗斯托上校一封快信，告訴我們說，麗迪亞跟他部下的一個軍官跑到蘇格蘭去了；說實在，就是跟韋翰私奔了！你試想像我們當時多麼驚惶。不過凱蒂卻認為這件事並非完全出人意料。我真難受。這兩個男女就這樣冒冒失失地配成了一對！可是我還是願意從最好的方面去着想，希望別人都是誤解了他的人品。我固然認為他為人輕率冒昧，不過他這次的舉動未必就是存心不良（讓我們但願如此吧）。至少他這麼做不是為了有利可圖，因為他一定知道父親沒有一分錢給她。可憐的母親傷心得要命。父親總算還支持得住。謝天謝地，好在我們從來沒有讓兩位老人知道外界對他的議論，我們自己也不必把它放在心上。據大家猜想，他們大概是星期六晚上十二點鐘走的，但是一直到昨天早上八點鐘，才發現這兩個人失蹤了。於是弗斯托上校連忙寫信告訴我們。親愛的莉茲，他們所經過的地方離開我們一定不滿十英里。弗斯托上校說，他一定立刻就到我們這裏來。麗迪亞留了一封短信給弗斯托太太，把他們兩人的意圖告訴了她。我不得不停筆了，因為我不能離開母親太久。我怕你一定會覺得莫名其妙吧，我自己也簡直不知道在寫些甚麼。

伊莉莎白讀完了這封信以後，幾乎說不出自己是怎樣的感覺，想也沒有想一下，便連忙抓起另外一封信，迫不及待地拆開就看。這封信比第一封信遲寫一天。

親愛的妹妹，你現在大概收到了我那封倉促寫成的信了吧。我希望這封信會把問題說得明白些；不過，時間雖然並不急促，我的頭腦卻糊裹糊塗，因此並不能擔保這封信一定會寫得有條有理。我親愛的莉茲，我簡直不知道該寫些甚麼，但是我總得把壞消息告訴你，而且事不宜遲。儘管韋翰先生和我們可憐的麗迪亞的婚姻是多麼荒唐，可是我們卻盼望着聽到他們已經結婚的消息，因為我們非常擔心他們並沒有到蘇格蘭去。弗斯托上校前天寄出那封快信以後，稍隔數小時即由布萊頓出發到我們這裏來，已於昨日抵達。雖然麗迪亞給弗太太的那封短信裏說，他們兩人要到格利那草場[46]去，可是根據丹尼透露出來的口風，他相信韋翰決不打算到那裏去，也根本不打算跟麗迪亞結婚。弗上校一聽此話，大為駭異，便連忙從布萊頓出發，希望能追到他們。他一路追蹤覓跡，追到克拉普汗，這倒還不費甚麼事，可是再往前追便不容易，因為他們兩人到達此地後，便把從艾普桑[47]僱來的馬車退了，重新僱了出租馬車。以後的行蹤便頗難打聽，只聽見有人說，看見他們繼續往倫敦那方向去。我不知道應該怎樣想。弗上校在倫敦竭力仔細打聽了一番以後，便來到赫德福郡，在沿路的關卡上以及巴納特和海菲德兩地所有的旅館裏，通通探尋了一遍，可是不得要領而返。大家都説沒有看見這樣的人走過。他無限關切地來到了朗伯恩，把他的種種疑慮全都誠心誠意地告訴了我們。我實在替他和弗太太難過；誰也不能怪他們夫婦兩人。親愛的莉茲，我們真是痛苦到極點。父親和母親都以為，這事情的下場勢必糟透極了，可是我卻不忍心把他看作那麼壞。也許為了種種緣故，他們覺得在城裏私下結婚，比較合適，故未按照原來計劃進行；縱使他欺侮麗迪亞年幼無知，沒有顯親貴戚，因而對她存心不良，難道麗迪亞自己也會不顧一切嗎？這件事絕對不可能！不過，聽到弗上校不大相信他們兩人會結婚，我又不免傷心。我把我的心願説給他聽，他只是頻頻搖頭，又説韋翰恐怕是個靠不住的人。可憐的媽真要病倒了，整天不出房門。要是她能勉強克制一下，事情也許要好些，可惜她無法辦到。説到父親，我一輩子也沒見過他這樣難受。可憐的凱蒂也很氣憤，她怪她自己沒有把他們兩人的親密關係預先告訴家裏人；但是他們既然信任她能夠保守秘密，我也不便怪她沒有早講。最親愛的莉茲，我真替你高興，這些痛苦的場面對你來説，真是眼不見為淨。不過，最開始的一場驚險既已過去，我很希望你回來，你不會覺得我這是不合情理吧？如果你不方便，自然我也不會太自私，非要逼你回來不可。再見吧！剛剛才告訴過你，我不願意逼你回來，現在我又要拿起筆來逼你了，因為照目前情況看來，我不得不誠懇地請求你們盡可能快些回來。舅父母和我相知頗深，決不會見怪，我因此才大膽提出要求，而且我還有別的事要求舅父幫忙。父親馬上就要跟弗斯托上校到倫敦去想辦法找她。他的具體打算我無從知道，可是看他那麼痛苦萬狀，就知道他辦起事來決不會十分穩妥，而弗斯托上校明天晚上就得回布萊頓。情況如此緊急，萬萬非請舅父前來協助指示不可。我相信他一定會體諒我此刻的心情，我相信他一定肯來幫忙。

伊莉莎白讀完信以後，不禁失聲叫道："舅父到哪裏去了？"她連忙從椅子上跳起來，急急去找尋舅父。時間太寶貴，一分鐘也不能錯過。她剛走到門口，恰逢傭人把門打開，達西先生走了進來。他看見她臉色蒼白，神情倉皇，不由得吃了一驚。他還沒有定下心來說一句話，她卻因為一心只想到麗迪亞的處境，連忙叫起來了：「對不起，不能奉陪。我有要緊的事要去找賈汀納先生，一分鐘也不能耽擱。」

他抑制不住一時的感情衝動，便也顧不得禮貌，大聲說道：「老天爺啊，這究竟是怎麼回事？」他讓自己定了一下心，然後接下去說：「我不願意耽擱你一分鐘；不過還是讓我去替你找賈汀納先生夫婦吧，或是讓傭人去也好。你身體不好；你不能去。」

伊莉莎白猶豫不定，但是她已經雙膝發抖，也覺得自己沒有辦法去找他們。她只得叫傭人來，派他去把主人和太太立刻找回來。她說話的時候上氣不接下氣，幾乎讓人聽不清楚。

傭人走出去以後，她便坐下來，達西見她身體已經支持不住，臉色非常難看，簡直不放心離開她，便用了一種溫柔體貼的聲調跟她說：「讓我把你的女傭人叫來吧。你能不能吃點東西，使你自己好過一些？要我給你弄一杯酒嗎？你好像生病了呢。」

她竭力保持鎮靜，回答他道：「不用，謝謝你。我沒有甚麼。我很好；只是剛剛從朗伯恩傳來了一個不幸的消息，使我很難受。」

她說到這裏，不禁哭了起來，半天說不出一句話。達西一時摸不着頭腦，只得含含糊糊說了些慰問的話，默默無言地望着她，心裏很是同情。後來她便向他吐露實情：「我剛剛收到珍妮一封信，告訴了我一個非常不幸的消息，反正這也瞞不住任何人。告訴你，我那最小的妹妹離棄了她所有的親友——私奔了——落入了韋翰先生的圈套。他們兩人是從布萊頓逃走的。你深知他的為人，下文也就不必提了。她沒錢沒勢，沒有任何地方足以滿足他——麗迪亞一生完了。」

達西給嚇呆了。伊莉莎白又用一種更激動的聲調接下去說：「我本來是可以阻止這一件事的！我知道他的真面目！我只要把那件事的一部份——我所聽到的一部份，早說給家裏人聽就好了，要是大家都知道了他的品格，就不會弄得一團糟了，但現在事已太遲。"

達西叫道："我真痛心，又痛心又驚嚇。但是這消息靠得住嗎，完全靠得住嗎？"

"當然靠得住！他們是星期日晚上從布萊頓出走的，追他們一直追到倫敦，可是無法再追下去。他們一定沒有去蘇格蘭。"

"那麼，有沒有想甚麼辦法去找她呢？"

"我父親到倫敦去了，珍妮寫信來，要舅父立刻回去幫忙，我希望我們在半個小時之內就能動身。可是事情毫無辦法，我認為一定毫無辦法。這樣的一個人，有甚麼辦法對付得了？又想得出甚麼辦法去找他們？我實在不敢存一線的希望。想來想去真可怕。"

達西搖搖頭，表示默認。

"我當初本已看穿了他的人品，只怪我一時缺乏果斷，沒有大膽去辦事。我只怕做得太過火，這真是千不該萬不該！"

達西沒有回答。他好像完全沒有聽到她的話，只是在房間裏踱來踱去，煞費苦心地在沉思默想。他雙眉緊蹙，滿臉憂愁。伊莉莎白立刻看到了他這副面容，隨即明白了他的想法。她對他的魅力一步步在消退了；家庭這樣不爭氣，招來了這樣的奇恥大辱，自然處處都被人一天比一天看不起。她絲毫不覺得詫異，也不怪別人。她即使姑且認為他願意委曲求全，也未必就會感到安慰，未必就會減輕痛苦。這反而足以使她懂得了自己的心事。現在千恩萬愛都已落空，她倒第一次感覺到真心真意地愛他。

她雖然難免想到自己，卻並不是完全只想到自己。只要一想到麗迪亞給大家帶來的恥辱和痛苦，她立刻就打消了一切的個人顧慮。她用一條手絹掩住了臉，便一切都不聞不問了。過了一會，她聽到她朋友的聲音，這才神志清醒過來。只聽到達西說話的聲調裏滿含着同情，也帶着一些拘束："我恐怕你早就希望我走開了吧，我實在沒有理由留在這裏，不過我無限地同情你，雖然這種同情無濟於事。天哪，我但願能夠說幾句甚麼話，或是盡我一份力量，來安慰安慰你這樣深切的痛苦！可是我不願意說些空洞的漂亮話，讓你受罪，這樣做倒好像是我故意要討好你。我恐怕這件不幸的事，會使得你們今天不能到龐百利去看我妹妹了。」

「哦！是呀，請你替我們向達西小姐道個歉吧。就說我們有緊要的事，非立刻回家不可。請你把這一件不幸的事盡可能多隱瞞一些時候，儘管我也知道隱瞞不了多久。」

他立刻答應替她保守秘密，又重新說他非常同情她的痛苦，希望這一件事會得到比較圓滿的結局，不至於像現在所想像的這樣糟糕，又請她代為問候她家裏人，然後鄭重地望了她一眼，便告辭了。

他一走出房門，伊莉莎白就不禁想到：這一次居然能和他在德比郡見面，而且好幾次見面都蒙他竭誠相待，這簡直是出人意料。她又回想了一下他們整個一段交情，真是矛盾百出，千變萬化；她以前曾經迫切地想要斷絕這一段交情，如今卻又希望能繼續下去，想到這種顛三倒四的地方，不由得歎了口氣。

如果說，大凡一個人愛上一個人，都是因為先有了感激之心，器重之意，那麼，伊莉莎白這次感情的變化當然既合情理，又使人無可非議。反而言之，世人有所謂一見傾心的場面，也有雙方未曾交談三言兩語就相互傾心的場面；如果說，由感激和器重而產生的愛情，比起一見傾心的愛情來，顯得不近人情事理，那我們當然就不能夠再袒護伊莉莎白，不過還有一點可以替她交代清楚一下：當初韋翰使她動心的時候，她也許多少就採用了一些一見傾心的辦法，結果事情不妙，她只得退而求其次，採用了另一種比較乏味的戀愛方式。這且不提，卻說她看見達西走了，真是十分惆悵；麗迪亞這次的醜行，一開始就造成了這樣嚴重的惡果，再想起這件糟糕的事，她心裏更加痛苦。自從她讀了珍妮的第二封信以後，她再也不指望韋翰會存心和麗迪亞結婚了。她想，只有珍妮會存這種希望，此外誰都不會。關於這件事的發展趨勢，她絲毫不覺得奇怪。當她讀到第一封信的時候，她的確覺得太奇怪，太驚訝——韋翰怎麼會跟這樣一個無利可圖的女子結婚？麗迪亞又怎麼會愛上他？實在令人不可理解。可是現在看來，真是再自然也沒有了。像這一類的苟合，麗迪亞的風流嫵媚可能也就足夠了。她雖然並不以為麗迪亞會存心私奔而不打算結婚，可是麗迪亞無論在品德方面或見識方面，的確都很欠缺，當然經不起別人勾引，這也是她意料中事。

民兵團駐紮在赫福德郡的時候，她完全沒有看出麗迪亞對韋翰有甚麼傾心的地方，可是她深深認識到麗迪亞只要隨便哪個人勾引一下，就會上鈎。她今天喜歡這個軍官，明天又喜歡那個軍官，只要你對她獻殷勤，她就看得中你。她平常的情感極不專一，可是從來沒有缺少過談情說愛的對象。這只怪一向沒有家教，對她任意縱容，結果使這樣的一個小姐落得這般下場。天哪！她現在實在體會太深了！

她非回家不可了——要親自去聽聽清楚，看看明白，要趕快去給珍妮分擔一份憂勞。家裏給弄得那麼糟，父親不在家，母親撐不起身，又隨時要人侍候，千斤重擔都壓在珍妮一個人身上。關於麗迪亞的事，她雖然認為已經無計可施，可是她又認為舅父的幫助是極其重要的，她等他回來可謂萬分焦急。賈汀納夫婦聽了僕人的話，還以為是外甥女得了急病，便連忙慌慌張張趕回來。伊莉莎白見到他們，馬上說明並非得了急病，他們這才放心。她又連忙講清楚找他們回來的原因，把那兩封信讀出來，又氣急敗壞地唸着第二封信後面補寫的那一段話。雖然舅父母平常並不喜愛麗迪亞，可是他們卻不得不感到深切的憂慮，因為這件事不單是牽涉到麗迪亞，而是與大家都息息相關。賈汀納先生剛開始大為駭異，感慨不已，然後便一口答應竭盡一切力量幫忙到底。伊莉莎白雖然料到舅父必定不會推辭，可還是感激萬分。於是三個人協力同心，一會就把行裝收拾妥當，只等上路。他們要走得越快越好。"可是怎樣向麗百利交代呢？"賈汀納太太大聲地說："約翰[48] 跟我們說，當你在找我們的時候，達西先生正在這裏。這是真的嗎？"

"是真的；我已經告訴過他，我們不能赴約了。這件事算是交代清楚了。"

"這件事算是交代清楚了，"舅母一面重複了一遍，一面跑回房間去準備。"難道他們兩人的交情已經好到這步田地，她可以把事實真相都説給他聽了嗎？哎唷，我真想弄明白這究竟是怎麼回事！"

可惜她這個願望落空了，最多不過在這匆匆忙忙、慌慌亂亂的一個小時裏面，寬慰了一下她自己的心。縱使伊莉莎白能夠偷閒跟她談談，在這種狼狽不堪的情況下，哪裏還會有閒情逸致來談這種事，何況她也和她舅母一樣，有許多事情要處理：別的且不説，蘭姆頓所有的朋友們就得由她寫信去通知，捏造一些藉口，説明他們為甚麼要突然離去。好在一小時以後，樣樣事情都已經安排妥當，賈汀納先生也和旅館裏算清了賬，只等動身。伊莉莎白苦悶了整整一個上午，想不到在極短的時間裏，就能坐上馬車，向朗伯恩出發了。

第四十七章

他們離開那個城鎮的時候，舅父跟伊莉莎白說："我又把這件事想了一遍，認真地考慮了一番，更加認同你姐姐的看法。我認為無論是哪個青年，決不會對這樣一位小姐存着這樣的壞心眼，她又不是無依無靠，何況她就住在上校家裏，因此我要從最好的方面去着想。難道他以為她的親友們不會挺身而出嗎？難道他還以為這一次冒犯弗斯托上校以後，還好意思回到民兵團裏去嗎？我看他不見得會癡情到冒險的地步。"

伊莉莎白的臉色立刻顯得高興起來，連忙說道："你果真這樣想嗎？"

賈汀納太太接嘴說："你相信我好了，我也開始贊成你舅舅的看法了。這件事太不知羞恥，太不顧名譽和利害關係了，他不會這樣膽大妄為。我覺得韋翰未必會這樣壞。莉茲，你能夠完全把他看透，相信他會做出這種事嗎？"

"他也許不會不顧全自己的利害關係。除此以外，我相信他全不在乎。但願他能有所顧忌。可是我不敢存這個奢望。要是真像你所想的那樣，那他們為甚麼不到蘇格蘭去呢？"

賈汀納先生回答道："第一，現在並不能完全證明他們沒有到蘇格蘭去。"

"哎！可是他們把原來的馬車退了，換上了出租的馬車，光是憑這一點就可想而知！此外，到巴納特去的路上，也找不到他們的蹤跡。"

"那麼就假定他們在倫敦吧。他們到那裏去也許是為了暫時躲避一下，不會別有用心。他們兩個人都沒有多少錢；也許他們都會想到，在倫敦結婚雖然比不上在蘇格蘭結婚來得方便，可是要省儉些。"

"可是為甚麼要這樣秘密？為甚麼怕給人發覺？為甚麼結婚要偷偷摸摸？哦，不，不，你這種想法不切合實際。你不是看到珍妮信裏說嗎——連他自己最好的朋友也相信他不會跟她結婚。韋翰絕不會跟一個沒有錢的女人結婚的。他根本辦不到。麗迪亞除了年輕、健康、愛開玩笑之外，有甚麼辦法、有甚麼吸引力，可以令他為了她而放棄掉結婚致富的機會？至於他會不會怕這次羞恥的私奔使他自己在部隊裏丟面子，便把行為檢點一下，那我就無法判斷了，因為我無從知道他這一次的行為究竟會產生甚麼樣的後果。但是你說的另外一點恐怕站不住腳。麗迪亞的確沒有個親兄弟為她出頭，他又看到我父親平日為人懶散，不管家事，便以為他遇到這類事情，也會跟別人的父親的一樣，不肯多管，也不肯多想。"

"可是你認為麗迪亞為了愛他，竟會不顧一切，可以不跟他結婚而跟他同居嗎？"

伊莉莎白眼睛裏湧起了眼淚說道："說起來真是駭人聽聞，一個人居然懷疑到自己親妹妹會不顧體面，不顧貞操！可是我的確不知道該怎麼說才好。也許是我冤枉了她。她很年輕，又從來沒有人教她應該怎樣去考慮這些重大的問題；半年以來——不，整整一年以來——她只知道開心作樂，愛好虛榮。家裏縱容她，讓她盡過些輕浮浪蕩的日子，讓她隨便遇到甚麼事情都是輕信盲從。自從民兵團駐紮到麥里頓以後，她滿腦子只想到談情說愛，賣弄風情，勾搭軍官。她先天就已經夠多情了，再加上老是想這件事，談這件事，想盡辦法使自己的感情更加——我應該說更加怎麼呢？——更加容易被人誘惑。我們都知道韋翰無論在儀表方面，辭令方面，都有足夠的魅力可以迷住一個女人。"

"可是你得明白，"她的舅母說，"珍妮就不把韋翰看得那麼壞，她認為他不會存這種心腸。"

"珍妮何時把任何人看作壞人？不管是甚麼樣的人，無論他過去的行為怎樣，除非等到事實證明了那個人確實是壞，她怎麼會相信別人會存這種心腸？可是説到韋翰的底細，珍妮卻和我一樣清楚。我們兩人都知道他是個不折不扣的淫棍，他既沒有人格，又不顧體面，一味虛情假意，柔聲媚氣。”

這番話使賈汀納太太起了極大的好奇心，想要弄明白外甥女怎麼知道這些事情的，便大聲問道：“這些情形你真的都了解嗎？”

伊莉莎白紅着臉回答道：“我當然了解，那一天我已經把他對待達西先生的無恥行為説給你聽過。達西先生對他那麼寬宏大量，可是你上次在朗伯恩的時候，曾經親耳聽到過他是以怎樣的態度談到達西的。還有許多事情我不便於説，也不值得説，可是他對於龐百利府上造謠中傷的事實，真是數説不盡。他把達西小姐説成那樣一個人，使得我原先完全把她當做一位驕傲冷酷、惹人討厭的小姐。然而他自己也知道事實完全相反。他心裏一定明白，達西小姐正像我們所看到的那樣和藹可親，一些也不裝腔作勢。”

“難道麗迪亞完全不知道這些事嗎？既然你和珍妮都了解得那麼透徹，她自己怎麼會完全不知道？”

“糟就糟在這裏。我自己也是到了肯特郡以後，常常跟達西先生和他的親戚費茨威廉上校在一起，才知道真相。等我回到家來，某某郡的民兵團已經準備在一兩個星期以內就要離開麥里頓了。當時我就把這情形在珍妮面前全盤托出，珍妮和我都覺得不必對外聲張，因為街坊四鄰既然都對韋翰有好感，如果讓大家對他印象轉壞，這會對誰有好處？甚至於到決定讓麗迪亞跟弗斯托太太一起走的時候，我還不想讓麗迪亞了解他的人品。我從來沒想到她竟會被他欺騙。你可以相信，我萬萬想不到會造成這樣的後果。”

“那麼説，他們開拔到布萊頓去的時候，你還是毫不在意，沒想到他們兩人已經愛上了吧？”

“根本沒有想到。我記得他們誰都沒有流露出相愛的意思，要知道，當初只要看出了一點形跡，在我們那樣的一個家庭裏是不會不談論的。他剛到部隊裏來的時候，她就對他十分愛慕，當時我們大家都是那樣。在前一兩個月裏面，麥里頓一帶的小姐們沒有哪一個不為他神魂顛倒；可是他對她卻不曾另眼相看。後來那一陣濫愛狂戀的風氣過去了，她對他的幻想也就消失了，因為民兵團裏其他的軍官們更加看重她，於是她的心又轉到他們身上去了。」

＊

他們一路上把這個有趣的話題翻來覆去地談論，談到哪些地方值得顧慮，哪些地方還可以寄予希望；揣想起來又是如何如何；實在再也談不出甚麼新花樣來了，只得暫時住口。可是過了不久，又談到這件事上面來了；這是可想而知的。伊莉莎白的腦子裏總是擺脫不開這件事。她為這件事自怨自艾，沒有一刻能夠安心，也沒有一刻能夠忘懷。

他們匆匆忙忙趕着路，在中途住宿了一夜，第二天吃中飯的時候就到了朗伯恩。伊莉莎白感到快慰的是，總算沒有讓珍妮等得心焦。

他們進了圍場，買汀納舅舅的孩子們一看見一輛馬車，便趕到台階上站着；等到馬車趕到門口的時候，孩子們一個個驚喜交集，滿面笑容，跳來蹦去，這是大人們回來時第一次受到的愉快熱誠的歡迎。

伊莉莎白跳下馬車，匆匆忙忙把每個孩子親吻了一下，便趕快向門口奔去，珍妮這時候正從母親房間裏跑下樓來，在那裏迎接她。

伊莉莎白熱情地擁抱着她，姐妹兩人都熱淚滾滾。伊莉莎白一面又迫不及待地問她是否聽到那一對私奔的男女的下落。

「還沒有打聽到下落，」珍妮回答道。「幸好親愛的舅舅回來了，我希望從此以後一切都會順利。」

「爸爸進城去了嗎？」

「進城去了，他是星期二走的，我信上告訴過你了。」

「常常收到他的信嗎？」

"只收到他一封信。是星期三寄來的，信上三言兩語，只說他已經平安抵達，又把他的詳細地址告訴了我，這還是他臨走時我特別要求他寫的。另外他只說，等到有了重要消息，再寫信來。"

"媽好嗎？家裏人都好嗎？"

"我覺得媽還算好，只不過精神上受了很大的挫折。她在樓上；她看到你們回來，一定非常快活。她還在她自己的化粧室裏呢。謝天謝地，瑪莉和凱蒂都非常好。"

"可是你好嗎？"伊莉莎白又大聲問道。"你臉色蒼白。一定吃了不少苦！"

姐姐告訴她安然無恙。姐妹兩人趁着賈汀納夫婦忙於應付孩子們的時候，剛剛談了這幾句話，只見他們一大羣男女老幼都走過來了，於是談話只得終止。珍妮走到舅父母面前去表示歡迎和感謝，笑一陣又哭一陣。

大家都走進會客室以後，舅父母又把伊莉莎白剛才問過的那些話重新問了一遍，立刻就發覺珍妮沒有甚麼消息可以奉告。珍妮因為內心善良，總是從樂觀的方面去着想，即使事到如今，她還沒有心灰意冷，她還在指望着一切都會有圓滿的結局：總有哪一天早上她會收到一封信，或者是父親寫來的，或者是麗迪亞寫來的，信上會把事情進行的經過詳細報告一番，或許還會宣佈那一對男女的結婚消息。

大家談了一會以後，都到班奈特太太房裏去了。果然不出所料，班奈特太太見到他們便熱淚盈眶，長嗟短歎。她先把韋翰的卑劣行為痛罵了一頓，又為自己的病痛和委屈抱怨了一番，她幾乎把每個人都罵到了，只有一個人沒罵到，而那個人卻正是盲目溺愛女兒，使女兒鑄成大錯的主要原因。

她說："要是當初能夠依了我的打算，讓全家人都跟着到布萊頓去，那就不會發生這種事了。麗迪亞真是又可憐又可愛。問題就出在沒有人照應。弗斯托夫婦怎麼竟放心讓她離開他們眼前呢？我看，一定是他們太怠慢了她。像她那樣一個小姐，要是有人好好地照料她，她是決不會做出那種事來的。我一直覺得他們不配照顧她；可是我一直要受人擺佈。可憐的好孩子呀！班奈特先生已經走了，他一碰到韋翰，一定會跟他拼個死活，他一定會給韋翰活活打死，那讓我們大家可怎麼辦？他屍骨未寒，柯林斯一家人就要把我們攆出去；兄弟呀，要是你不幫幫我們的忙，我就真不知道怎麼是好了。"

大家聽到她這些可怕的話，都失聲大叫；賈汀納先生先告訴她說，無論對她本人，對她家裏人，他都會盡心照顧，然後又告訴她說，他明天就要到倫敦去，盡力幫助班奈特先生去找麗迪亞。

他又說："不要過份焦急，雖說也應該從最壞的方面去想，可也不一定會落得最壞的下場。他們離開布萊頓還不到一個星期。再過幾天，我們可能會打聽到一些有關他們的消息。等我們把事情弄明白了，要是他們真的沒有結婚，而且不打算結婚，那時候才談得上失望。我一進城就會到姐夫那裏去，請他到恩典堂街我們家裏去住，那時候我們就可以一起商量出一個辦法來。"

班奈特太太回答道："噢，好兄弟，這話正說到我心裏。你一到城裏，千萬要把他們找到，不管他們在哪裏也好；要是他們還沒有結婚，一定讓他們結婚。講到結婚的禮服，讓他們用不着等了，只告訴麗迪亞說，等他們結婚以後，她要多少錢做衣服我就給她多少錢。至關重要的是，別讓班奈特先生跟他打架。還請你告訴他，我真是在活受罪，簡直給嚇得神經錯亂了，渾身發抖，東倒西歪，腰部抽搐，頭痛心跳，從白天到夜裏，沒有一刻能夠安心。請你跟我的麗迪亞寶貝說，讓她不要自作主張做衣服，等到和我見了面再說，因為她不知道哪一家衣料店最好。噢，兄弟，你真是一片好心！我知道你會想出辦法來把每樣事情都辦好。"

賈汀納先生雖然又重新寬慰了她一下，說他一定會認真盡力地去效勞，可是又讓她不要過份樂觀，也不要過份憂慮。大家跟她一直談到吃中飯才走開，反正女兒們不在她面前的時候，有女管家侍候她，她還可以去向女管家發牢騷。

雖然她弟弟和弟婦都以為她大可不必和家裏人分開吃飯，可是他們並不打算反對她這樣做，因為他們考慮到她說話不謹慎，如果吃起飯來讓好幾個傭人一起來侍候，那麼她在傭人們面前把心裏的話全說了出來，未免不大好，因此最好還是只讓一個傭人——一個最靠得住的傭人侍候她，聽她去敍述她對這件事是多麼擔心，多麼牽掛。

他們走進飯廳不久，瑪莉和凱蒂也來了，原來這兩姐妹都在自己房間裏忙着各人自己的事，一個在讀書，一個在化妝，因此沒有早一些出來。兩人的臉色都相當平靜，看不出有甚麼變化，只是凱蒂講話的聲調比平常顯得暴躁一些，這或者是因為她丟了一個心愛的妹妹而感到傷心，或者是因為這件事也使她覺得氣憤。至於瑪莉，她卻自有主張，等大家坐定以後，她便擺出一副嚴肅的面孔，跟伊莉莎白低聲說道：

"家門不幸，遭此慘禍，很可能會引起外界議論紛紛。人心惡毒，我們一定要及時防範，免得一發不可收拾。我們要用姐妹之情來安慰彼此創傷的心靈。"

她看到伊莉莎白不想回答，便又接下去說："此事對於麗迪亞雖屬不幸，但亦可以作為我們的前車之鑒。大凡女人一經失去貞操，便無可挽救，這真是一失足成千古恨。美貌固然難於永葆，名譽亦何嘗容易保全。世間多的是輕薄男子，豈可不寸步留神？" [49]

伊莉莎白抬起眼睛來，神情很是詫異；她心裏實在太鬱悶，所以一句話也答不上來。可是瑪莉還在往下說，她要從這件不幸的事例中闡明道德的精義，以便聊以自慰。

到了下午，兩位年紀最大的小姐有了半個小時的時間可以在一起談談心。伊莉莎白不肯錯過機會，連忙向珍妮問東問西，珍妮也連忙一一回答，好讓妹妹放心。兩姐妹先把這件事的不幸的後果共同歎息了一番。伊莉莎白認為一定會產生不幸的後果，珍妮也認為難免。於是伊莉莎白繼續說道：「凡是我不知道的情節，請你全部說給我聽。請你談得再詳細一些。弗斯托上校怎麼說的？他們兩人私奔之前，難道看不出一點形跡可疑的地方嗎？應該經常可以看到他們兩人在一起呀。」

「弗斯托上校說，他也曾懷疑過他們兩人有感情，特別是懷疑麗迪亞，可是他並沒有看出有甚麼形跡可疑，因此沒有及時留意。我真為他難受。他為人極其殷勤善良。遠在他想到他們兩人並沒有到蘇格蘭去的時候，他就打算上我們這裏來慰問我們。等到人心惶惶的時候，他連忙便趕來了。」

「丹尼認為韋翰不會跟她結婚嗎？他是否知道他們存心私奔？弗斯托上校有沒有見到丹尼本人？」

「見到的；不過他問到丹尼的時候，丹尼絕口否認，說是根本不知道他們私奔的打算，也不肯說出他自己對這件事究竟怎樣看法。丹尼以後便沒有再提起他們兩人不會結婚之類的話，照這樣看來，但願上一次是我聽錯了他的話。」

「我想，弗斯托上校沒有到這裏以前，你們誰都沒有懷疑到他們不會正式結婚吧？」

「我們的腦袋裏怎麼會有這種念頭呢！我只是覺得有些不安心，有些顧慮，怕妹妹跟他結婚不會幸福，因為我早就知道他的品行不太端正。父親和母親完全不知道這種情形，他們只覺得這頭親事非常冒昧。凱蒂當時十分好勝地說，她比我們大家都熟悉內幕情形，麗迪亞給她的最後一封信上就已經隱隱約約透露出了一些口風，準備來這一招。看凱蒂那副神氣，她好像遠在好幾個星期以前，就知道他們相愛了。」

「總不見得在他們去到布萊頓以前就看出了吧？」

「不見得，我相信不見得。」

「弗斯托上校是不是顯出看不起韋翰的樣子？他了解韋翰的真面目嗎？」

"這我得承認，他不像從前那樣器重他了。他認為他行事荒唐，又愛奢華，這件傷心的事發生以後，人們都傳說他離開麥里頓的時候，還欠下了好多債，我但願這是謠言。"

"哎，珍妮，要是我們當初少替他保守一點秘密，把他的事情照直說出來，那也許就不會發生這件事了！"

珍妮說："說不定會好些，不過，光是揭露別人過去的錯誤，而不尊重別人目前的為人，未免有些說不過去。我們待人接物，應該完全好心好意。"

"弗斯托上校能不能把麗迪亞留給他太太的那封短信逐字逐句背出來？"

"那封信他是隨身帶來給我們看的。"

於是珍妮從口袋裏掏出那封信，遞給伊莉莎白。全文如下：

親愛的海麗[50]：

明天一大早你發現我失蹤了，一定會大為驚奇；等你弄明白了我上甚麼地方去，你一定又會發笑。我想到這裏，自己也禁不住笑出來了。我要到格利那草場去。如果你猜不着我是跟誰一起去，那我真要把你看成一個大傻瓜，因為這世界上只有一個男人是我心愛的，他真是一個天使。沒有了他，我決不會幸福，因此，你別以為我這次去會惹出甚麼禍來。如果你不願意把我出走的消息告訴朗伯恩我家裏人，那你不告訴也罷。我要使他們接到我信的時候，看到我的簽名是"麗迪亞・韋翰"，讓他們更覺得事出意外。這個玩笑真開得太有意思！我幾乎笑得無法寫下去了！請你替我向普拉特道個歉，我今天晚上不能赴約，不能和他跳舞了。我希望他知道了這一切情形以後，能夠原諒我；請你告訴他，下次在舞會上相見的時候，我一定樂意和他跳舞。我到了朗伯恩就派人來取衣服，請你告訴莎蕾一聲，我那件細洋紗的禮服裂了一條大縫，讓她替我收拾行李的時候把它補一補。再見。請代問候弗斯托上校。願你為我們的一路順風而乾杯。

你的好朋友

麗迪亞‧班奈特

伊莉莎白讀完了信以後叫道:"好一個沒腦的麗迪亞!遇到這樣重大的事,竟會寫出這樣一封信來!但是至少可以説明,她倒是把這一次旅行看成一件正經事。不管他以後會誘惑她走到哪一步,她可沒有存心要做出甚麼丟臉的事來。可憐的爸爸!他對這件事會有多少感觸啊!"

"他當時驚駭得那種樣子,我真是一輩子也沒見過。他整整十分鐘説不出一句話來。媽一下子就病倒了,全家都給弄得心神不寧!"

"噢,珍妮,"伊莉莎白叫道。"豈不是所有的傭人當天都知道了這件事的底細嗎?"

"我不清楚,但願他們並非全部都知道。不過在這種時候,即使你當心,也很難辦到。媽那種歇斯底里的毛病又發作了,我雖然盡了我的力量去勸慰她,恐怕還是有不夠周到的地方。我只怕會出甚麼意外,因此嚇得不知如何是好。"

"你這樣侍候她,真夠你累的。我看你臉色不怎麼好。樣樣事都由你一個人操心煩神,要是我跟你在一起就好了!"

"瑪莉和凱蒂都非常好心,願意替我分擔,可是我不好意思讓她們受累,因為凱蒂很纖弱,瑪莉又太用功,不應該再去打擾她們休息的時間。幸好星期二那天,父親一走,菲力普姨媽就到朗伯恩來了,蒙她那麼好心,一直陪我到星期四才走。她幫了我們不少的忙,還安慰了我們。盧卡斯太太對我們也好,她星期三早上來慰問過我們,她説,如果我們需要她們幫忙,她和她女兒們都樂意效勞。"

伊莉莎白大聲説道:"她留在自己家裏更合適吧,她也許真是出於一片好意,但是遇到了這樣一件不幸的事,誰還樂意見到自己的鄰居?他們幫我們忙幫不成功,慰問我們反而會使我們難受。讓她們在我們背後去高興得意吧。"

然後她又問起父親這次到城裏去，打算採用甚麼方法去找到麗迪亞。

珍妮説："我看他打算到艾普桑去，因為他們兩人是在那裏換馬車的，他要上那裏去找找那些馬車夫，看看能不能從他們嘴裏探聽出一點消息。他的主要目的就是要去查出他們在克拉普汗所搭乘的那輛出租馬車的號碼。那輛馬車本來是從倫敦載了客人來的；據他的想法，一男一女從一輛馬車換上另一輛馬車，一定會引人注目，因此他準備到克拉普汗去查問。他只要查出那個馬車夫在哪家門口卸下先前那位客人，他便決定上那裏去查問一下，也許能夠查問得出那輛馬車的號碼和停車的地方。至於他有甚麼別的打算，我就不知道了。他急急忙忙要走，心緒非常紊亂，我能夠從他嘴裏問出這麼些話來，已經算是不容易了。"

第四十八章

第二天早上，大家都指望班奈特先生會寄信來，可是等到郵差來了，卻沒有帶來他的片紙隻字。家裏人本來知道他一向懶於寫信，能夠拖延總是拖延；但是在這樣的時候，她們都希望他能夠勉為其難一些。既是沒有信來，她們只得認為他沒有甚麼愉快的消息可以告知，但即使如此，她們也希望把事情弄個清楚明白。賈汀納先生也希望在動身以前能夠看到幾封信。

賈汀納先生去了以後，大家都認為，今後至少可以經常聽到一些事情進行的經過情形。他臨走的時候，答應一定去勸告班奈特先生盡可能馬上回來。她們的母親聽了這話，很是安慰，她認為只有這樣，才能保證她丈夫不會在決鬥中被人打死。

賈汀納太太和她的孩子們還要在赫福德郡多住幾天，因為她覺得，留在這裏可以讓外甥女們多一個幫手。她可以幫着她們侍候班奈特太太，等她們空下來的時候，又可以安慰安慰她們。姨媽也常常來看她們，而且據她自己說，她來的目的是為了讓她們高興高興，好振作起來，不過，她沒有哪一次來不談到韋翰的奢侈淫逸，每次都可以舉出新的事例。她每次走了以後，總是令她們比她沒有來以前更加意志消沉。

三個月以前，差不多整個麥里頓的人們都把這個男人捧到天上；三個月以後，整個麥里頓的人都說他的壞話。他們說，他在當地每一個商人那裏都欠下了一筆債；又給他加上了誘騙婦女的惡名，又說每個商人家裏都受到過他的糟蹋。每個人都說他是天下最壞的青年；每個人都開始發覺自己一向就不信任他那偽善的面貌。伊莉莎白雖然對這些話只是半信半疑，不過她早就認為妹妹會毀在他手裏，現在當然更是深信無疑。珍妮本來連半信半疑也談不上，現在也幾乎感到失望——因為時間已經過了這麼久，如果他們兩人真到蘇格蘭去了，現在也應該有消息了，這樣一想，縱使她從來沒有覺得完全失望，現在當然也難免要感到失望。

賈汀納先生是星期日離開朗伯恩的。星期二他太太接到他一封信。信上說，他一到那裏就找到了姐夫，把他勸到恩典堂街去。又說，他沒有到達倫敦以前，班奈特先生曾到艾普桑和克拉普汗去過，可惜沒有打聽到一點滿意的消息；又說他決定到城裏各大旅館去打聽一下，因為班奈特先生認為，韋翰和麗迪亞一到倫敦，可能先住旅館，然後再慢慢尋找房子。賈汀納先生本人並沒有指望這種辦法會獲得甚麼成績；既是姐夫非要那樣做不可，也只有幫助他着手進行。信上還說，班奈特先生暫時根本不想離開倫敦，他答應不久就會再寫一封信來。這封信上還有這樣的一段附言：

我已經寫信給弗斯托上校，請他盡可能在民兵團裏把那個年輕小伙子的好朋友找幾個來打聽一下，韋翰有沒有甚麼親友知道他躲藏在這個城裏的哪一個區域。要是我們有這樣的人可以請教，得到一些線索，那是大有用處的。目前我們還是無從捉摸。也許弗斯托上校會盡他所能為我們尋找線索。但是，我又想了一下，覺得莉茲也許比任何人都了解情況，會知道他現在還有些甚麼親戚。

伊莉莎白究竟為甚麼會受到這樣的抬舉，她自己完全知道，只可惜她不能提供甚麼令人滿意的信息，所以也就受不起這樣的恭維。

她除了聽到韋翰談起過他自己的父母以外，從來不曾聽到他有甚麼親友，況且他父母也都已去世多年。他在某某郡民兵團裏的一些朋友，或許能提供一些資料，她雖說並不能對此存着過份的奢望，但不妨試一試。

朗伯恩一家人每天都過得非常心焦，最焦急的時間莫過於等待郵差的那一段時間。大家每天早上所急的第一件大事，就是等着郵差送信來。不管信上報導的是好消息還是壞消息，總是要通傳給大家，而且大家都盼望着第二天會有重要的消息傳來。

賈汀納先生雖然還沒有給她們寄來第二封信，可是她們卻收到了別的地方寄來的一封信，原來是柯林斯先生寄來了一封信給她們的父親。珍妮事前曾受到父親的囑託，代他拆閱一切信件，於是她便來拜讀這一封信。伊莉莎白也知道柯林斯先生的信總是寫得奇奇怪怪，便也湊在珍妮身旁一同拜讀。信是這樣寫的：

親愛的堂叔：

昨接赫福德郡來信，借悉先生目前正值心煩意亂，不勝苦悲。小姪夫婦聞之，無論對先生個人或尊府老幼，均深表同情。以小姪之名份職位而言，自當聊申悼惜之意，何況與尊府忝為葭莩，益覺責無旁貸。此次不幸事件自難免令人痛心疾首，蓋家聲一經敗壞，便永無清洗之日，傷天下父母之心，孰有甚於此者？早知如此，但冀其早日夭亡為幸耳。小姪惟有曲盡言辭，備加慰問，聊寬尊懷。據內人夏綠蒂言，令嬡此次淫奔，實為由於平日過份溺愛所致，此尤其可悲者也。惟小姪以為令嬡年紀尚幼，竟而鑄成大錯，亦足見其本身天性之惡劣，先生固不必過於引咎自責。日前遇凱瑟琳夫人及其千金小姐，曾以此事奉告，夫人等亦與小姪夫婦有所同感。多蒙夫人與愚見不謀而合，認為令嬡此次失足，辱沒家聲，遂使後之攀親者望而卻步，殃及其姐終生幸福，堪慮堪慮。念言及此，禁憶及去年十一月間一事，則又深為慶幸，否則木已成舟，勢必自取其辱，受累不淺。敬祈先生善自寬慰，任其妄自菲薄，自食其果，不足憐惜也。

　　　　　　　　　　　　　　　姪　威廉・柯林斯拜上

賈汀納先生一直等到接到弗斯托上校的回信以後，才寫第二封信到朗伯恩來。信上並沒有一點喜訊。大家都不知道韋翰是否還有甚麼親戚跟他來往，不過倒知道他確確實實已經沒有一個至親在世。

他以前交遊頗廣，只是自從進了民兵團以後，看來跟他們都已疏遠，因此找不出一個人來可以打聽一些有關他的消息。他這次之所以要保守秘密，據說是因為他臨走時拖欠了一大筆賭債，而他目前手頭又非常拮据，無法償還，再則是因為怕讓麗迪亞的親友發覺。弗斯托上校認為，要清償他在布萊頓的債務，需要有一千多英鎊才夠。他在本鎮固然欠債很多，但賭債則更可觀。賈汀納先生並不打算把這些事情瞞住朗伯恩這家人。珍妮聽得心驚膽跳，不禁叫道："好一個賭棍！這真是完全出人意料；我想也不曾想到。"

賈汀納先生的信上又說，她們的父親明天（星期六）就可以回家來了。原來他們兩人再三努力，毫無成績，情緒十分低落，因此班奈特先生答應了他大伯的要求，立刻回家，一切事情都留給賈汀納相機而行。女兒們本以為母親既是那樣擔心父親會被人打死，聽到這個消息，一定會非常滿意，誰知並不盡然。

班奈特太太大聲說道："甚麼！他沒有找到可憐的麗迪亞，就這樣一個人回來嗎？他既然沒有找到他們，當然不應該離開倫敦。他一走，還有誰去跟韋翰決鬥，逼他跟麗迪亞結婚？"

賈汀納太太也開始想要回家了，決定在班奈特先生動身回朗伯恩的那一天，她就帶着孩子們回倫敦去。動身的那天可以由這裏派一部馬車把她送到第一站，然後趁便接主人回來。

賈汀納太太走了以後，對伊莉莎白和德比郡她那位朋友的事，還是糊裏糊塗，從當初在德比郡的時候起，就一直弄不明白。外甥女從來沒有主動在舅父母面前提起過他的名字。她本以為回來以後，那位先生就會有信來，可是結果並沒有。伊莉莎白一直沒有收過從龐百利寄來的信。

她看到外甥女情緒消沉；可是，家裏既然出了這種不幸的事情，自然難免如此，不必把這種現象牽扯到別的原因上面去。因此她還是摸不着一點邊際。只有伊莉莎白自己明白自己的感受，她想，要是不認識達西，那麼麗迪亞這件丟臉的事也許會讓她多少好受些，也許可以使她減少幾個失眠之夜。

班奈特先生回到家裏，仍然是那一副樂天安命的樣子。他還是像平常一樣不多說話，完全不提起他這次外出是為了甚麼事情，女兒們也過了好久才敢提起。

一直到下午，他跟她們一起喝茶的時候，伊莉莎白才大膽地談到這件事。她先簡單地說到他這次一定吃了不少的苦，這使她很難過，他卻回答道："別說這種話吧。除了我自己之外，還有誰該受罪呢？我自己做的事應該自己承擔。"

伊莉莎白勸慰他說："你千萬不要過份埋怨自己。"

"你勸我也是白勸。人的本性就是會自怨自艾！不，莉茲，我一輩子也不曾自怨自艾過，這次也讓我嘗嘗這種滋味吧。我不怕憂鬱成病。這種事一下子就會過去的。"

"你以為他們會在倫敦嗎？"

"是的，還有甚麼別的地方能讓他們藏得這樣好呢？"

凱蒂又在一旁補充了一句："而且麗迪亞老是想要到倫敦去。"

父親冷冷地說："那麼，她可得意了，她也許要在那裏住一陣子呢。"

沉默了片刻以後，他又接下去說："莉茲，五月間你勸我的那些話的確沒有勸錯，我決不怪你，從目前這件事看來，你的確有見識。"

班奈特小姐進來打斷了他們的談話，她要端茶上去給她母親。

班奈特先生大聲叫道："這真所謂享福，舒服極了；居然倒霉也不忘風雅！哪一天我也要有樣學樣，坐在書房裏，頭戴睡帽，身穿寢衣，盡量找人麻煩；要不就等到凱蒂私奔了以後再說。"

凱蒂氣惱地說："我不會私奔的，爸爸，要是我上布萊頓去，我一定比麗迪亞規矩。"

"你上布萊頓去！你即使要到東伯恩那麼近的地方去，要我跟人打五十鎊的賭，我也不敢！不，凱蒂，我至少已經學會了小心，我一定要讓你看看我的厲害。今後哪個軍官都不許進我家門，甚至不許從我們村裏經過。絕對不許你們去參加舞會，除非你們姐妹們之間自己跳跳；也不許你走出家門一步，除非你在家裏每天至少有十分鐘規規矩矩，像個人樣。"

凱蒂把這些威嚇的話信以為真，不由得哭了起來。

班奈特先生連忙説道："行了，行了，別傷心吧。假如你從今天起，能做上十年好孩子，那麼，等到十年期滿的時候，我一定帶你去看閲兵典禮。"

第四十九章

班奈特先生回來兩天了。那天珍妮和伊莉莎白正在屋後的矮樹林裏散步，只見管家太太朝她們兩人走來，以為是母親派她來叫她們回去的，於是迎面走上前去。到了那個管家太太面前，才發覺事出意外，原來她並不是來召喚她們的。她對珍妮説："小姐，請原諒我打斷了你們的談話，不過，我料想你們一定獲得了從城裏來的好消息，所以我來大膽地問一問。"

"你這話怎麼講，希爾？我們沒有聽到一點城裏來的消息。"

希爾太太驚奇地説道："親愛的小姐，賈汀納先生派了一個專差給主人送來一封信，難道你們不知道嗎？他已經來了半個小時了。"

兩位小姐拔腳就跑，急急忙忙跑回家去，話也來不及説了。她們兩人跑進大門口，來到起坐間，再從起坐間來到書房，兩處地方都沒有見到父親，正要上樓到母親那裏去找他，又碰到了男管家，他説：

"小姐，你們是在找主人吧，他正往小樹林裏去散步呢。"

她們聽到這話，又走過穿堂，跑過一片草地，去找父親，只見父親正在從容不迫地向圍場旁邊的一座小樹林走去。

珍妮沒有伊莉莎白那麼玲瓏，也沒有她那麼會跑，因此一下子就落後了，只見妹妹已經上氣不接下氣地跑到了父親面前，迫不及待地叫道：

"爸爸，有了甚麼消息？甚麼消息？你接到舅父的信了嗎？"

"是的，他派專人送了封信來。"

"唔，信裏説些甚麼消息呢——好消息還是壞消息？"

"哪來好消息？"他一面説，一面從口袋裏掏出信來。"也許你倒願意看一看。"

伊莉莎白性急地從他手裏接過信來。珍妮也趕上來了。

"唸出來吧，"父親説，"我也不知道信上講些甚麼。"

親愛的姐夫：

　　我終於能夠告訴你一些有關外甥女的消息了，希望這個消息大體上能讓你滿意。總算僥倖，你星期六走了以後，我立刻打聽出他們兩人在倫敦的住址。詳細情況等到見面時再告訴你。你只要知道我已經找到了他們就夠了。我已經看到了他們——

　　珍妮聽到這裏，不禁叫了起來："那麼這次我可盼望到了！他們結婚了吧！"

　　伊莉莎白接着讀下去：

　　我已經看到了他們兩人。他們並沒有結婚，我也看不出他們有甚麼結婚的打算；可是我大膽地向你提出條件來，要是你願意照辦的話，他們不久就可以結婚了。我要求你的只有一點。你本來已經為你女兒們安排好五千鎊遺產，準備在你和姐姐歸天以後給她們，那麼請你立刻就把這位外甥女應得的一份給她吧。你還得和她訂定一個契約，在你生前每年再津貼她一百鎊。這些條件我已經再三考慮，自以為有權力可以代你做主，因此便毫不遲疑地答應了。我特派專人前來送給你這封信，以便可以馬上得到你的回音。你了解了這些詳情以後，就會明白韋翰先生並不如一般人所料想的那麼生計維艱，一籌莫展。一般人都把這件事弄錯了。外甥女除了自己名下的錢以外，等韋翰把債務償清以後，還可得到些剩餘的錢，這使我很高興。你如果願意根據我所説的情況，讓我全權代表你處理這件事，那麼，我立刻就吩咐哈格斯東去辦理財產過戶的手續。你不必再進城，大可以安心地留在朗伯恩。請你放心，我辦起事來既勤快又小心。請趕快給我回信，還要你費神，寫得清楚些。我們以為最好就讓外甥女從寒舍出嫁，想你也會同意。她今天要上我們這裏來。倘若有其他情況，當隨時奉告。

愛德華・賈汀納

八月二日，星期一，寫於恩典堂街

伊莉莎白讀完了信問道："這事情可能嗎？他竟會和她結婚？"

她姐姐說："那麼，韋翰倒並不像我們所想像的那樣不成器。親愛的爸爸，恭喜你。"

"你寫了回信沒有？"伊莉莎白問。

"沒有寫回信，可是立刻就會寫。"

於是她極其誠懇地請求他馬上就回家去寫，不要耽擱。

她大聲說道："親愛的爸爸，馬上就回去寫吧。你要知道，這種事情是一分鐘一秒鐘也不能耽擱的。"

珍妮說："要是你怕麻煩，讓我代你寫好了。"

父親回答道："我的確不大願意寫，可是不寫又不行。"

他一邊說，一邊轉過身來跟她們一同回到屋裏。

伊莉莎白說："我可以問你一句話嗎？我想，他提出的條件你一定都肯答應吧？"

"一口答應！他要得這麼少，我倒覺得不好意思呢。"

"他們兩人非結婚不可了！然而他卻是那樣的一個人。"

"是啊！怎麼不是，他們非結婚不可。沒有別的辦法。可是有兩件事我很想弄個明白——第一件，你舅舅究竟拿出了多少錢，才促成了這件事；第二件，我以後有甚麼辦法還他這筆錢？"

珍妮叫道："錢！舅舅！你這是甚麼意思，爸爸？"

"我的意思是說，一個頭腦清楚的人是不會跟麗迪亞結婚的，因為她沒有哪一點地方可以讓人看中。我生前每年給她一百鎊，死後只有五十鎊。"

伊莉莎白說："那倒是實話，不過我以前卻從來沒有想到過。他的債務償清了以後，還會多下錢來！噢，那一定是舅舅幫他處理好的！好一個慷慨善良的人！我就怕苦了他自己。這樣一來，他得花費不少錢呢。”

父親說：“是啊，韋翰要是拿不到一萬鎊就答應娶麗迪亞，那他才是個大傻瓜呢。我與他剛剛攀上親戚關係，照理本不應該多說他的壞話。”

“一萬鎊！天理不容！即使半數，又怎麼還得起？”

班奈特先生沒有回答。大家都轉着念頭，默不作聲。回到家裏，父親到書房裏去寫信，女兒們都走進飯廳裏去。

姐妹兩人一離開父親，妹妹便大聲說道：“他們真要結婚了！這真稀奇！不過我們也大可以謝天謝地。他們究竟結婚了。雖然他們不一定會過得怎麼幸福，他的品格又那麼壞，然而我們畢竟不得不高興。哦，麗迪亞！”

珍妮說：“我想了一下，也覺得安慰，要不是他真正愛麗迪亞，他是決不肯跟她結婚的。好心的舅舅即使替他清償了一些債務，我可不相信會墊付了一萬鎊那麼大的數目。舅舅有那麼多孩子，也許以後還要生養兒女。就是要他拿出五千鎊，他又怎麼能夠拿出來？”

“我們只要知道韋翰究竟欠下了多少債務，”伊莉莎白說，“用他的名義給我們妹妹的錢有多少，那我們就會知道賈汀納先生幫了他們多大的忙，因為韋翰自己一點錢也沒有。舅舅和舅母的恩典今生今世也報不了。他們把麗迪亞接回家去，親自保護她，給她爭面子，這犧牲了他們自己多少利益，真是一輩子也感恩不盡。麗迪亞現在一定到了他們那裏了！要是這樣一片好心還不能使她覺得慚愧，那她可真不配享受幸福。她一見到舅母，該多麼難為情啊！”

珍妮說：“我們應該把他們兩人過去的事盡力忘掉，我希望他們還是會幸福，也相信會這樣。他既然答應跟她結婚，這就可以證明他已經往正路上去想。他們能夠互敬互愛，自然也都會穩重起來。我相信他們兩人從此會安安穩穩、規規矩矩地過日子，到時候人們也就會把他們過去的荒唐行為忘了。”

"他們既然已經有過荒唐行為，"伊莉莎白回答道，"那麼無論你我，無論任何人，都忘不了。也不必去談這種事。"

兩姐妹想到她們的母親也許到現在還完全不知道這回事，於是便到書房裏去，問父親願意不願意讓母親知道。父親正在寫信，頭也沒抬起來，只是冷冷地對她們說：

"隨你們的便吧。"

"我們可以把舅舅的信拿去讀給她聽嗎？"

"你們愛拿甚麼去就拿甚麼，快走開。"

伊莉莎白從他的書桌上拿起那封信，姐妹兩人一起上了樓。瑪莉和凱蒂兩人都在班奈特太太那裏，因此只要傳達一次，大家就都知道了。她們稍微透露出了一點好消息，便把那封信唸出來。班奈特太太簡直喜不自禁。珍妮一讀完麗迪亞可能就在最近就要結婚的那一段話，她就高興得要命，越往下讀她越高興。她現在真是無限歡喜，極度興奮，正如前些時候是那樣無限煩惱，坐立不安。只要聽到女兒快要結婚，她就心滿意足。她並沒有因為顧慮到女兒得不到幸福而心神不安，也並沒有因為想起了她的不當行為而覺得丟臉。

"我的麗迪亞寶貝呀！"她叫了起來："這太令人高興了！她就要結婚了！我又可以和她見面了！她十六歲就結婚！感謝我那好心好意的弟弟！我早就知道事情不會弄糟——我早就知道他有辦法把每件事情都辦好。我多麼想要看到她，看到親愛的韋翰！可是衣服，嫁妝！我要立刻寫信跟弟婦談談。莉茲，乖寶貝，快下樓去，問問你爸爸願意給她多少陪嫁。等一下，等一下；還是我自己去吧。凱蒂，去拉鈴叫希爾來。我馬上就會穿好衣服。麗迪亞我的寶貝呀！等我們見面的時候，會有多麼高興啊！"

大女兒見她這樣得意忘形，便談起她們全家應該怎樣感激賈汀納先生，以便讓她分分心，讓她精神上輕鬆一下。

珍妮又接下去說："全靠他一片好心，才會有這樣圓滿的結局。我們都認為是他答應拿出錢來幫韋翰先生的忙。"

"哎，"母親叫道，"這真是好極了。要不是親舅父，誰肯幫這種忙？你要知道，他要不是有了自己的家庭，他所有的錢都是我和我的孩子們的了；他以前只送些禮物給我們，這一次我們才算真正得到他的好處。哎！我太高興啦。過不了多久，我就有一個女兒出嫁了。她就要當上韋翰太太了！這個稱呼多麼動聽！她到六月裏才滿十六歲。我的珍妮寶貝，我太激動了，一定寫不出信！還是我來講，你替我寫吧。關於錢的問題，我們以後再跟你爸爸商量，可是一切東西應該馬上就去預訂好。"

於是她就一五一十地報出一大篇布的名目：細洋紗、印花布、蔴紗，恨不得一下子就把所有貨色都購置齊全。珍妮好不容易才勸住了她，要她等到父親有空的時候再商量，又説，遲一天完全無關緊要。母親因為一時太高興了，所以也不像平常那麼固執。她又想起了一些別的花樣。

"我一穿好衣服，就要到麥里頓去一次，"她説，"把這個好消息説給我妹妹菲力普太太聽。我回來的時候，還可以順路去看看盧卡斯太太和郎格太太。凱蒂，快下樓去，吩咐他們給我備好馬車。外出透透氣，一定會使我精神爽快得多。孩子們，有甚麼事要我替你們在麥里頓辦嗎？噢！希爾來了。我的好希爾，你聽到好消息沒有？麗迪亞小姐快要結婚了。她結婚的那天，我們大家都可以喝一碗'潘趣酒[51]'歡喜歡喜。"

希爾太太立即表示非常高興。她向伊莉莎白等一一道賀。後來伊莉莎白對這個蠢局實在看得討厭透了，便躲到自己房間裏去自由自在地思量一番。

可憐的麗迪亞，她的處境再好也好不到哪裏去，可是總算沒有糟到不可收拾的地步，因此她還得謝天謝地。她確實要謝天謝地；雖説一想到今後的情形，就覺得妹妹既難得到應有的幸福，又難享受到世俗的富貴榮華，不過，只要回想一下，兩個小時以前還是那麼憂慮重重，她就覺得目前的情形真要算是萬幸了。

第五十章

班奈特先生在很久以前，就希望每年的進款不要全部花光，能夠積蓄一部份，讓女兒們往後不至於衣食匱乏，如果太太比他長命，也能衣食無憂。拿目前來說，他這個希望比以往來得更迫切。要是他在這方面早就安排好了，那麼這次麗迪亞挽回面子名譽的事，自然就不必要她舅舅為她花錢；也不必讓她舅舅去說服全英國最差勁的一個青年和她確定夫婦的名份。

這事情對任何人都沒有好處，如今卻得由他大伯獨自拿出錢來成其好事，這實在令他太過意不去；他決定要竭力打聽出舅爺究竟幫了多大的忙，以便儘快報答這筆人情。

班奈特先生剛結婚的時候，完全不必省吃儉用，因為他們夫婦自然會生兒子，等到兒子成了年，外人繼承產權的這件事就可以取消，寡婦孤女也就衣食無慮了。可是五個女兒接連出世，兒子還不知道在哪裏；麗迪亞出世許多年以後，班奈特太太還一直以為會生兒子。這個指望終於落了空，如今省吃儉用已經太遲了。班奈特太太不慣於節省，幸好丈夫自有主張，才算沒有入不敷支。

當年老夫婦的婚約上規定了班奈特太太和子女們一共應享有五千鎊遺產。至於子女們究竟怎樣分，得由父母在遺囑上規定。關於這個問題，至少麗迪亞應享有的部份必須立刻解決，班奈特先生毫不猶豫地同意了擺在他面前的那個建議。他回信給他大伯，多謝他一片好心。他的措辭極其簡潔，只說他對一切既成事實都表示贊同，而且舅舅所提出的各項條件，他都願意照辦。原來這次說服韋翰跟他女兒結婚一事，竟安排得這樣好，簡直沒有帶給他甚麼麻煩，這實在是他始料不及的。雖說他每年要付給他們兩人一百鎊，可是事實上他每年還損失不了十鎊，因為麗迪亞在家裏也要吃用開銷，外加她母親還要貼錢給她花,計算起來每年幾乎也不下於一百鎊。婚約上所載事項大都是關於財產方面的,由結婚當事人於結婚前妥為簽署,以便作為結婚時授予妻子財產之根據。

還有一個驚喜,那就是辦起這件事來,他自己簡直可以不費甚麼力氣,他目前最希望麻煩越少越好。他開始也曾因為一時衝動,親自去找女兒,如今他已經氣平怒消,自然又變得像往常一樣懶散。他把那封回信立刻寄出去;他雖然做事喜歡拖延,可是只要他肯動手,倒也完成得很快。他在信上請他大伯把一切代勞之處詳詳細細告訴他,可是說起麗迪亞,實在使他太氣惱,因此連問候也沒有問候她一聲。

好消息立刻在全家傳開了,而且很快便傳到鄰居們耳朵裏去。四鄰八舍對這件事都抱着相當超然的態度。當然,如果麗迪亞·班奈特小姐親自上這裏來了,或者說,如果她恰恰相反,遠離塵囂,住到一個偏僻的農村裏去,那就可以給人們增加許多話題。不過她的出嫁問題畢竟還是使人議論紛紛。麥里頓那些惡毒的老太婆,原先總是一番好心腸,祝她嫁個如意郎君,如今雖然眼看着情境變了,也還是在起勁地談個不休,因為大家看到她嫁了這麼一個丈夫,都認為必定會有悲慘的下場。

班奈特太太已經有兩個星期沒有下樓,遇到今天這麼快樂的日子,她歡欣若狂,又坐上了首席。她並沒有覺得羞恥,自然也不會掃興。遠從珍妮十六歲那年起,她的第一個心願就是嫁女兒,現在她快要如願以償了。她的思想言論都完全離不了婚嫁的漂亮排場:上好的細洋紗,新的馬車,以及男女傭僕之類的事情。她還在附近一帶到處奔波,要給女兒找一所適當的住宅;她根本不知道他們有多少收入,也從來沒有考慮到這一點。她看了多少處房子都看不中,不是因為空間太小,就是嫌不夠氣派。

她說:"要是戈丁家能遷走,海夜花園倒還合適;斯托克那幢大房子,要是會客室大一些,也還可以,可是阿西渥斯離這裏太遠!我不忍心讓她同我隔開十英里路；講到柏衛苑，那閣樓實在太糟了。"

　　每當有傭人在的時候，她丈夫總是讓她講下去，不去岔斷她的話。可是傭人一出去，但他老實不客氣地跟她說了："我的好太太，你要為你的女兒和女婿租房子，不管你要租一幢也好，或是把所有的房子都租下來也好，都得讓我們事先談清楚問題。鄰近的房子，一幢也不許他們來住。他們不要妄想我會在朗伯恩招待他們！"

　　這話一說出口，兩人便爭吵不休；可是班奈特先生說一不二，於是又吵了起來；後來班奈特太太又發覺丈夫不肯拿出一分錢來給女兒添置一些衣服，不禁大為驚駭。班奈特先生堅決聲明，麗迪亞這一次休想得到他半點疼愛，這實在讓他太太弄不懂。他竟會氣憤到這樣深惡痛絕的地步，連女兒出嫁都不肯優待她一番，簡直要把婚禮弄得不成體統，這確實太出乎她的意料。她只知道女兒出嫁而沒有嫁妝是件丟臉的事情，至於她的私奔，她沒有結婚以前就跟韋翰同居了兩個星期，她倒絲毫不放在心上。

　　伊莉莎白目前非常後悔：當初實在不應該因為一時痛苦，竟讓達西先生知道了她自己家裏為她妹妹擔憂的經過，因為妹妹既然馬上就可以名正言順地結婚，了卻那一段私奔的風流孽債，那麼，開始那一段不體面的事情，她們當然希望最好不要讓局外人知道。

　　她並不是擔心達西會把這事情向外界傳開。講到保守秘密，簡直就沒有第二個人比他更能使她信任；不過，這一次如果是別的人知道了她妹妹的醜行，她決不會像現在這樣難受。這倒不是生怕對她本身有任何不利，因為她和達西之間反正隔着一條跨不過的鴻溝。即使麗迪亞能夠體體面面地結婚，達西先生也決不會跟這樣的門戶攀親，因為這家人本來已經缺陷夠多，如今又添上了一個一向為他所不齒的人做他的至親，那當然一切都不必談了。

　　她當然不怪他對這頭親事望而卻步。她在德比郡的時候就看出他想要博得她的歡心，可是他遭受了這一次打擊以後，當然不會不改變初衷。她覺得丟臉，她覺得傷心；她後悔了，可是她又幾乎不知道在後悔些甚麼。如今她已經不能再想攀附他的身份地位,卻又忌恨他的身份地位;如今她已經沒有機會再聽到他的消息,她可又偏偏希望能夠聽到他的消息;如今他們兩人已經再也不可能見面,可她又認為,如果他們能夠朝夕聚首,那會多麼幸福。

她常常想:才不過四個月以前,她那麼高傲地拒絕了他的求婚,可如今又心悅誠服地盼望他再來求婚,這要是讓他知道了,他會感到怎樣的得意!她完全相信他是個極其寬宏大量的男人。不過,他既然是人,當然免不了要得意。

她開始理解到,他無論在個性方面和才能方面,都百份之百是一個最適合她的男人。縱使他的見解、他的脾氣,和她自己不是一模一樣,可是一定能夠令她稱心如意。這個結合對雙方都有好處:女方從容活潑,可以把男方陶冶得心境柔和,作風優雅;男方精明通達,閱歷頗深,也一定會使女方得到莫大的裨益。

可惜這件幸福的婚姻已經不可能實現,天下千千萬萬想要締結真正幸福婚姻的有情人,從此也錯過了一個借鑒的榜樣。她家裏立刻就要締結一門另一種意味的親事,也就是那頭親事破壞了這頭親事。

她無從想像韋翰和麗迪亞究竟怎麼樣獨立維持生活。可是她倒很容易想像到另一方面:這種只顧情欲不顧道德的結合,實在很難得到久遠的幸福。

*

賈汀納先生馬上又寫了封信給他姐夫。他先對班奈特先生信上那些感激的話簡潔地應酬了幾句,再說到他極其盼望班奈特府上的男女老幼都能過得舒舒服服,末了還要求班奈特先生再也不要提起這件事。他寫這封信的主要目的是,要把韋翰先生已經決定脫離民兵團的消息告訴他們。

他這封信接下去是這樣寫的:

我非常希望他婚事一定奪之後就這樣辦。我認為無論為他自己着想，為外甥女着想，離開民兵團的確是一個非常高明的選擇，我想你一定會同意我的看法。韋翰先生想參加正規軍，他從前的幾個朋友都願意協助他，也能夠協助他。駐紮在北方的某將軍麾下的一個團，已經答應讓他當旗手。他離開這一帶遠些，只會有利於他自己。他前途頗有希望，但願他們到了人地生疏的地方能夠爭點面子，行為稍加檢點一些。我已經寫了信給弗斯托上校，把我們目前的安排告訴了他，又請他在布萊頓一帶通知一下韋翰先生所有的債主，就說我一定信守諾言，馬上就償還他們的債務。是否也可以麻煩你就近向麥里頓的債主們通知一聲？隨信附上債主名單一份，這都是他自己說出來的。他把全部債務都講了出來，我希望他至少沒有欺騙我們。我們已經委託哈格斯東在一星期以內將所有的事統統辦好。那時候你如果不願意請他們上朗伯恩來，他們就可以直接到軍隊裏去。聽見內人說，外甥女很希望在離開南方之前跟你們見見面。她近況很好，還請我代她向你和她母親請安。

　　　　　　　　　　　　　　　　　　　　愛·賈汀納

　　班奈特先生和他的女兒們都和賈汀納先生同樣地看得明明白白，認為韋翰離開某某郡有許多好處。只有班奈特太太不甚樂意。她正在盼望着要跟麗迪亞痛痛快快、得意非凡地過一段時間，不料她卻要住到北方去，這真讓她太失望。到現在為止，她還是決定要讓女兒和女婿住到赫福德郡來。再說，麗迪亞剛剛在這個民兵團裏和大家相熟了，又有那麼多人喜歡她，如今遠去他方，未免太可惜。

　　她說："她那麼喜歡弗斯托太太，把她送走可太糟了！而且還有好幾個年輕小伙子，她也很喜歡。某某將軍那個團裏的軍官們未必能夠這樣討她喜歡。"

　　她女兒要求在去北方之前，再回家來看一次，這其實應算作她自己的要求，不料一開始就遭到她父親的斷然拒絕。幸虧珍妮和伊莉莎白顧全到妹妹的心情和身份，一致希望她的婚姻會受到父母的重視，再三要求父親，讓妹妹和妹婿一結婚之後，就到朗伯恩來。她們要求得那麼懇切，那麼合理，又那麼婉轉，終於把父親說動了心，同意了她們的想法，願意照着她們的意思去辦。母親這下可真得意：她可以趁着這個嫁出去的女兒沒有充軍到北方去之前，把她當作寶貝似的炫耀給街坊四鄰看看。於是班奈特先生寫回信給他大伯的時候，便提到讓他們兩人回來一次，講定讓他們行過婚禮就立刻到朗伯恩來。不過伊莉莎白倒是驚訝於韋翰會同意這樣的做法；如果單是為她自己着想，那麼，跟韋翰見面實在是萬不得已的事。

第五十一章

妹妹的婚期到了，珍妮和伊莉莎白都為她擔心，恐怕自己比妹妹擔心得還要厲害。家裏派了一部馬車到某某地方去接新婚夫婦，吃中飯時他們就可以來到。兩位姐姐都怕他們來，尤其是珍妮怕得厲害。她設身處地地想：要是麗迪亞這次的醜行發生在她自己身上，她一定會感觸萬千，再想到妹妹心裏的難受，便更加覺得不好過。

新夫婦來了。全家都集合在起居室裏迎接他們。當馬車停在門前的時候，班奈特太太滿面堆着笑容，她丈夫卻板着臉。女兒們又是驚奇又是焦急，而且十分不安。

只聽到門口已經有了麗迪亞說話的聲音，一會，門給打開了，麗迪亞跑進屋來。母親高興得要命，連忙走上前來歡迎她，擁抱她，一面又帶着親切的笑容把手伸給韋翰（他走在新婦後面），祝他們夫婦兩人快活。班太太的話講得那麼響亮，說明她相信他們兩人一定會幸福。

然後新夫婦轉身走到班奈特先生面前，他對他們可沒有他太太那麼熱誠。只見他的臉色顯得份外嚴峻，連嘴也不張一下。這一對年輕夫婦那種安然自得的樣子，實在令他生氣。伊莉莎白覺得厭惡，連珍妮也禁不住感到驚駭。麗迪亞還是麗迪亞——不安份，不害羞，撒野吵鬧，天不怕地不怕的。她從這個姐姐面前走到那個姐姐面前，要她們一個個恭喜她。最後大家都坐下來了，她連忙掃視了一下這間房間，看到裏面稍稍有些改變，便笑着說，好久不曾到這裏來了。

韋翰更沒有一點難受的樣子。他的儀表一向親切動人，要是他為人正派一些，娶親合乎規矩一些，那麼，這次來拜見岳父母的家，他那笑容可掬、談吐安詳的樣子，自然會討大家歡喜。伊莉莎白從來不相信他竟會這樣厚顏無恥，她坐下來思忖道：一個人不要起臉來可真是漫無止境。她不禁紅了臉，珍妮也紅了臉；可是那兩位當事人，別人都為他們難為情，他們自己卻面不改色。

這個場合確實是不愁沒有話談。新娘和她母親只覺得有話來不及說；韋翰湊巧坐在伊莉莎白身旁，便向她問起附近一帶的熟人近況如何，問得極其和顏悅色從容淡定，弄得她反而不能對答如流。這一對夫婦儼然心安理得，毫無羞恥之心。他們想起過去的事，心裏絲毫不覺得難受；麗迪亞又不由自主地談到了許多事情——要是換了她姐姐們，這種事情是無論如何也說不出口的。

只聽見麗迪亞大聲說道："想想看，我已經走了三個月了！好像還只有兩個星期呢；可是時間雖短，卻發生了許多事情。天啊！我走的時候，的確想也沒想到這次要結了婚再回來，不過我也想到：如果真就這樣結了婚，倒也挺有趣的。"

父親瞪着眼睛。珍妮很難受，伊莉莎白啼笑皆非地望着麗迪亞；可是麗迪亞，凡是她不願意知道的事，她一概不聞不問，她仍然得意洋洋地說下去："噢，媽媽，附近的人們都知道我今天結婚了嗎？我怕他們還不見得都知道；我們一路來的時候，追上了威廉·戈丁的雙輪馬車，我為了要讓他知道我結婚了，便把我自己車子上的一扇玻璃窗放了下來，又脫下手套，把手放在窗戶上，好讓他看見我手上的戒指，然後我又對他點點頭，笑得甚麼似的。"

伊莉莎白實在忍無可忍了，只得站起身來跑到屋外去，一直聽到她們走過穿堂，進入飯廳，她才回來。來到她們這裏，又見麗迪亞匆匆忙忙大搖大擺地走到母親右邊，一面對她的大姐姐說："喂，珍妮，這次我要坐你的位子了，你得坐到下首去，因為我已經出嫁了。"

麗迪亞既然從一開始就完全不覺得難為情，這時候當然更是若無其事。她反而越來越不在乎，興致越來越高。她很想去看看菲力普太太，看看盧卡斯全家人，還要把所有的鄰居都統統拜訪一遍，讓大家都叫她韋翰太太。吃過午飯，她立刻把結婚戒指給希爾太太和其他兩個女傭人看，誇耀她自己已經結了婚。

　　大家都回到起居室以後，她又說道："媽媽，你覺得我丈夫怎麼樣？他不是挺可愛嗎？姐姐們一定都要羨慕我。但願她們有我一半運氣就好了。誰讓她們不到布萊頓去。那裏才是個找丈夫的地方。真可惜，媽媽，我們沒有大家一起去！"

　　"你講得真對；要是按照我的意見，我們早就應該一起都去。可是，麗迪亞寶貝，我不願意你到那麼遠的地方去。你難道非去不可嗎？"

　　"天啊！當然非去不可，那有甚麼關係。我真高興極了。你和爸爸，還有姐姐們，一定要來看我們呀。我們整個冬天都住在紐卡斯爾 [52]，那裏一定會有很多舞會，而且我一定負責給姐姐們找到很好的舞伴。"

　　"那我真是再喜歡也沒有了！"母親說。

　　"等你動身回家的時候，你可以讓一兩個姐姐留在那裏；我擔保在今年冬天以內就會替她們找到丈夫。"

　　伊莉莎白連忙說："謝謝你的關懷，可惜你這種找丈夫的方式，我不太欣賞。"

　　新夫婦只能和家裏人相聚十天。韋翰先生在沒有離開倫敦之前就已經受到了委任，必須在兩星期以內就到團部裏去報到。

　　只有班奈特太太一個人惋惜他們的行期太倉促，因此她盡量抓緊時間，陪着女兒到處走訪親友，又常常在家裏宴客。這些宴會大家都歡迎：沒有心事的人固然願意赴宴，有心事的人更願意借這個機會出去解解悶。

　　果然不出伊莉莎白所料，韋翰對麗迪亞的恩愛比不上麗迪亞對韋翰的那樣深厚。從一切事實上都可以看出來，他們的私奔多半是因為麗迪亞熱戀韋翰，而不是因為韋翰熱戀麗迪亞，這在伊莉莎白看來，真是一件顯而易見的事。至於說，他既然並不十分愛她，為甚麼還要跟她私奔，伊莉莎白一點也不覺得奇怪，因為她斷定韋翰這次為債務所逼，本來非逃跑不可；那麼，像他這樣一個青年，路上有一個女伴陪他，他當然不肯錯過機會。

麗迪亞太喜歡他了，她每說一句話就要叫一聲親愛的韋翰。誰也比不上他。他無論做甚麼事都是天下第一。她相信到了九月一日那一天，他射到的鳥一定比全國任何人都要多。

他們來到這裏不久，有一天早晨，麗迪亞跟兩位姐姐坐在一起，對伊莉莎白說：

"莉茲，我還沒有跟你說起過我結婚的情形呢。我跟媽媽和別的姐姐們說的時候，你都不在場。你難道不想要聽聽這場喜事是怎麼辦的嗎？"

"不想聽，真不想聽，"伊莉莎白回答道；"我認為這件事談得不算少了。"

"哎呀！你這個人太奇怪！我一定要把經過情形告訴你。你知道，我們是在聖克利門教堂結婚的，因為韋翰住在那個教區裏面。大家約定十一點鐘到那裏。舅父母跟我一起去的，別的人都約定在教堂裏碰頭。唔，到了星期一早上，我真是慌張得要命。你知道，我真怕會發生甚麼意外，把婚期耽擱了，那我可真要發狂了。我在打扮，舅母一直不住嘴地講呀，說呀，好像是在傳道似的。她十句話我最多聽進一句，你可以想像得到，我那時一心在惦記着我親愛的韋翰。我一心想要知道，他是不是穿着他那件藍色的禮服去結婚。

"唔，像平常一樣，我們那天是十點鐘吃早飯的。我只覺得一頓飯老是吃不完，說到這裏，我得順便告訴你，我住在舅父母那裏的一段時期，他們一直很不高興。說來你也許不信，我雖在那裏住了兩個星期，卻沒有出過家門一步。沒有參加過一次宴會，沒有一點消遣，真過得無聊極了。老實說，倫敦雖然並不太熱鬧，不過至少那個小戲院 53 還是開着。言歸正傳，那天馬車來了，舅父卻讓那個名叫斯東先生的討厭傢伙叫去辦事。你知道，他們兩人一碰頭，就不想分手。我真給嚇壞了，不知道如何是好，因我需要舅父主婚；要是我們誤了時間，那天就結不成婚。幸虧他不到十分鐘就回來了，於是我們一起動身。不過我後來又想起來了，要是他真被纏住了不能分身，婚期也不會延遲，因為還有達西先生可以代勞。”

伊莉莎白大驚失色，又把這話重複了一遍：“達西先生！”

“噢，是呀！他也要陪着韋翰上教堂去呢。天哪，我怎麼完全給弄糊塗了！這件事我應該隻字不提才對。我早已在他們面前保證不說的！不知道韋翰會怎樣怪我呢？這本來應該嚴格保守秘密的呀！”

“如果是秘密，”珍妮説，“那麼，就請你再也不要説下去了。你放心，我決不會再追問你。”

“噢，一定不追問你，”伊莉莎白嘴上雖是這樣説，心裏卻非常好奇。“我們決不會盤問你。”

“謝謝你們，”麗迪亞説；“要是你們問下去，我當然會把底細全都告訴你們，那韋翰就要生氣了。”

她這話明明是慫恿伊莉莎白問下去，伊莉莎白便只得跑開，讓自己要問也無從問起。

但是，這件事是不可能不聞不問的，至少也得去打聽一下。達西先生竟會參加了她妹妹的婚禮！那樣一個場面，那樣兩個當事人，他當然萬萬不願意參與，也絕對沒有理由去參與。她想來想去，把各種各樣古怪的念頭都想到了，可還是想不出一個所以然來。她當然願意從最好的方面去想，認為他這次是胸襟寬大，有心表示好意，可是她這種想法又未免太不切合實際。她無論如何也摸不着頭腦，實在難受，於是連忙拿起一張紙，寫了封短短的信給舅母，請求她把麗迪亞剛才無意中洩露出來的那句話解釋一下，只要與原來保守秘密的計劃能夠並行不悖就是了。

她在信上寫道：“你當然很容易了解到，他跟我們非親非故，而且跟我們家裏相當陌生，竟會跟你們一同參加這次婚禮，這讓我怎麼能夠不想打聽一下底細呢？請你立刻回信，讓我把事情弄明白。如果確實如麗迪亞所説，此事非保守秘密不可，那我也只得不聞不問了。"

　　寫完了信以後，她又自言自語地説："親愛的舅母，如果你不老老實實告訴我，我迫不得已，便只有千方百計地去打聽了。"

　　珍妮是個十二萬分講究信用的人，她無論如何也不肯把麗迪亞嘴裏漏出來的話暗地裏去説給伊莉莎白聽。伊莉莎白很滿意她這種作風。她既然已經寫信去問舅母，不管回信能不能使她滿意，至少在沒有接到回信以前，最好不要向任何人透露心事。

第五十二章

伊莉莎白果然如願以償，很快就接到了回信。她一接到信，就跑到那清靜的小樹林裏去，在一張長凳上坐下來，準備讀個痛快，因為她看到信寫得那麼長，便斷定舅母沒有拒絕她的要求。

親愛的甥女：

剛剛接到你的來信，我便決定以整個上午的時間來給你寫回信，因為我估計三言兩語不能夠把我要跟你講的話講個明白。我得承認，你所提出的要求很使我詫異，我沒有料到提出這個要求的竟會是你，請你不要以為我這是生氣的話，我不過是説，我實在想像不到你居然還要來問。如果你一定裝作聽不懂我的話，那只有請你原諒我失禮了。你舅父也跟我同樣地詫異，我們都認為，達西之所以要那樣做，完全是為了你的緣故。如果你真的一點也不知道，那也只好讓我來跟你説個明白了。就在我從朗伯恩回家的那一天，有一個意想不到的客人來看你舅父。那人原來就是達西先生，他跟你舅父關起門來，密談了好幾個小時。等我到家的時候，事情已經過去了，我當時倒並沒有像你現在這樣好奇。他是因為發覺了你妹妹和韋翰的下落，特地趕來告訴賈汀納先生一聲。他説，他已經看到過他們，而且跟他們談過話——跟韋翰談過好多次，跟麗迪亞談過一次。據我看，我們離開德比郡的第二天，達西就動身趕到城裏來找他們了。他説，事情弄到如此地步，都怪他不好，沒有及早揭露韋翰的下流品格，否則就不會有哪一位正派小姐會把他當作知己，會愛上他了。他慨然引咎自責，認為這次的事情都得怪他當初太傲慢，因為他以前認為韋翰的品格自然而然會讓別人看穿，不必把他的私人行為都一一揭露出來，免得使他自己有失體統。他認為這都是他自己一手造成的罪惡，因此他這次出面調停，設法補救，實在是義不容辭。他自己承認他要干預這件事的動機就是如此。如果他真的別有用心，也不會使他丟臉。他在城裏逗留了好幾天才找到他們；可是他有線索可找，我們可沒有。他也是因為自信有這點把握，才下定決心緊跟着我們而來。好像有一位楊格太太，她早先做過達西小姐的家庭教師，後來犯了甚麼過錯（他沒有講明），被解僱了，便在愛德華街弄了一幢大房子，分租過活。達西知道這位楊格太太跟韋翰極其相熟，於是他一到城裏，便上她那裏去打聽他的消息。他花了兩三天時間，才從她那裏把事情探聽明白。我想，楊格太太早就知道韋翰的下落，可是不給她賄賂她決不肯講出來。他們兩人確實是一到倫敦便到她那裏去，要是她能夠留他們住，他們早就住在她那裏了。我們這位好心的朋友終於探聽出了他們在某某街的住址，於是他先去看韋翰，然後他又非要看到麗迪亞不可。據他說，他第一件事就是勸麗迪亞改邪歸正，一等到和家裏人說通了，就趕快回去，還答應替她幫忙到底。可是他發覺麗迪亞決意要堅持下去，家裏人一個都不在她心上。她不要他幫助，她無論如何也不肯丟掉韋翰。她斷定他們兩人遲早總要結婚，早一天遲一天毫無關係。於是他想，他第一次跟韋翰談話的時候，明明發覺對方毫無結婚的打算，如今既是麗迪亞存着這樣的念頭，當然只有趕快促成他們結婚。韋翰曾經親口承認，他當初之所以要從民兵團裏逃出來，完全是由於為賭債所逼，至於麗迪亞這次私奔所引起的不良後果，他竟毫不猶豫地把它完全歸罪於她自己的愚蠢。他說他馬上就要辭職。講到事業前途，他簡直不堪設想。他應該到一個甚麼地方去找份差事，可是又不知道究竟去哪裏，他知道他快要沒有錢生活下去了。達西先生問他為甚麼沒有立刻跟你妹妹結婚，雖然班奈特先生算不上甚麼大闊人，可是也能夠幫他一些忙，他結婚以後，境況一定會有利一些。但是他發覺韋翰回答這話的時候，仍然指望到別的地方去另外攀門親，以便扎扎實實地賺進一筆錢。

不過，他目前的情況既是如此，如果有救急的辦法，他也未必不會
心動。他們見了好幾次面，因為有好多地方都得當面商討。韋翰
當然漫天討價，結果總算減少到一個合理的數目。他們之間一切都
商談好了，達西先生的下一個步驟就是把這件事告訴你舅父，於是
他就在我回家的前一天晚上，到恩典堂街來進行第一次訪問。當時
賈汀納先生不在家；達西先生打聽到你父親那天還住在這裏，不
過第二天早晨就要走。他認為你父親不是像你舅父那樣一個好商
量的人，因此，決定等到你父親走了以後，再來看你舅父。他當時
沒有留下姓名，直到第二天，我們還只知道有位某某先生到這裏來
過，找他有事。星期六他又來了。那天你父親已經走了，你舅父在
家，正如我剛才說過的，他們兩人便在一起談了許久。他們星期天
又見了面，當時我也看見他的。事情一直到星期一才完全談妥。一
談妥之後，就派專人送信到朗伯恩來。但是我們這位貴客實在太
固執了。莉茲，我以為說到他的性格，惟一的缺點畢竟還是固執。
人們都紛紛指責他的錯處，今天說他有這個錯處，明天又說他有那
個錯處，可是這一個才是他真正的錯處。每件事情都非得由他親
自來辦不可；其實你舅父非常願意全盤包辦（我這樣說並不是為了
討好你，所以請你不要跟別人提起）。他們為這件事爭執了好久，
其實對當事人來說，無論是男方女方，都不配享受這樣的對待。可
是你舅父最後還是不得不依從他，以致非但不能替自己的外甥女稍
微盡點力，而且還要無勞居功，這完全和他的心願相違；我相信你
今天早上的來信一定會使他非常高興，因為這件掠人之美的事，從
此可以說個清楚明白，使那應該受到讚美的人受到讚美。不過，莉
茲，這件事只能讓你知道，最多只能說給珍妮聽。我想你一定會深
刻了解到，他對那一對青年男女盡了多大的力。我相信他替他償還
的債務一定遠在一千鎊以上，而且除了她自己名下的錢以外，另外
又給她一千鎊，還給他買了個官職。至於這些錢為甚麼得由他一個
人付，我已經在上面說明理由。他說這都怪他自己不好，怪他當初

考慮欠妥，矜持過份，以致讓別人不明了韋翰的人品，結果使人上了當，把他當做好人。這番話或許真有幾分道理；不過我卻覺得，這種事既不應當怪他矜持過份，實在是也不應當怪任何人矜持過份。親愛的莉茲，你應當明白，他的話雖然說得這樣動聽，我們要不是鑒於他別有苦心，你舅父決不肯依從他。一切事情都決定了以後，他便回到龐百利去應酬他那些朋友，大家同時說定，等到舉行婚禮的那天，他還得再到倫敦來，辦理一切有關金錢方面的最後手續。現在我把所有的事情都講給你聽了。這就是你所謂會使你大吃一驚的一番敍述；我希望至少不會讓你聽了不痛快。麗迪亞上我們這裏來住過，韋翰也經常來。他完全還是上次我在赫福德郡見到他時的那副老樣子。麗迪亞住在我們這裏時，她的種種行為舉止，的確令我很不滿。我本來不打算告訴你，不過星期三接到珍妮的來信，我才知道她回家依然故態復萌，那麼，告訴了你也不會使你有甚麼新的難過。我多次一本正經地跟她說，她這件事做得大錯特錯，害得一家人都痛苦悲傷。哪裏知道，我的話她聽也不要聽。有幾次我非常生氣，但是一記起了親愛的伊莉莎白和珍妮，看在她們份上，我還是容忍着她。達西先生準時來到，正如麗迪亞所告訴你的，他參加了婚禮。他第二天跟我們在一起吃飯，星期三或星期四又要進城去。親愛的莉茲，要是我利用這個機會說，我多麼喜歡他（我以前一直沒有敢這樣說），你會生我的氣嗎？他對待我們的態度，從任何方面來說，都跟我們在德比郡的時候同樣討人喜愛。他的見識，他的言論，我都很喜歡。他沒有任何缺點，只不過稍欠活潑；關於這一點，只要他娶妻得當，他也許會讓她給教好的。我認為他嘴緊得很，因為他幾乎沒有提起過你的名字。但是嘴緊倒好像成了時下的一種風氣。如果我說得太放肆了，還得請你原諒，至少不要處罰得我太厲害，將來連龐百利也不許我去啊。我要把那個花園逛遍了，才會心滿意足。我只要弄一輛矮矮的雙輪小馬車，駕上一對漂亮的小馬就可以了。我無法再寫下去，孩子們已經喊着要我要了半個小時。

舅母手書

九月六日寫於恩典堂街

　　伊莉莎白讀了這封信，真是百感交集。她這種心情，讓人弄不明白她究竟是高興多於痛苦，還是痛苦多於高興。她本來也曾隱隱約約、疑疑惑惑地想到達西先生可能會成全她妹妹的好事，可是又不敢往這方面多想，怕他不可能好心到這個地步；另一方面她又顧慮到，如果他真的這樣做了，那又未免情意太重，報答不了他，因此她又感到痛苦。如今這些揣測卻成了千真萬確的事實！想不到他那天竟會跟隨着她和舅父母趕到城裏去。他不惜承擔起一切的麻煩和艱苦，來打探這件事。他不得不向一個他所深惡痛絕、極其鄙視的女人去求情。他不得不委曲求全，與一個他極力要加以迴避、而且連名字也不願意提起的人去見面，並且是常常見面，跟他說理規勸他，最後還不得不賄賂他。他這般仁至義盡，只不過是為了一個他既無好感又不器重的女子。她心裏輕輕地說，他這樣做，都是為了她。但是，再想到一些別的方面，她立刻就不敢再存這個希望。她馬上感覺到，她本可以從虛榮心出發，認為他確實愛她，可是她哪能存着那麼大的虛榮心，指望他會愛上一個已經拒絕過他的女人！他不願意跟韋翰做親戚，這種情緒本來也極其自然，又哪能指望他去遷就！何況是跟韋翰做連襟！凡是稍有自尊心的人，都容忍不了這種親戚關係。毫無疑問，他為這件事付出了很多。她簡直不好意思去想像他究竟付出了多少。他之所以要過問這件事，理由已經由他自己加以說明，你不必多費思索就可以深信無疑。他怪他自己當初做事欠妥，這自然講得通；他很慷慨，而且有資格可以慷慨；雖然她不願意認為他這次主要就是為了她，可是她也許可以相信，他對她依舊未能忘情，因此遇到這樣一件與她的心境息息相關的事情，他還是願意盡心竭力。一想起這樣一個人對她們深情重義，而她們卻無法報答他，這真是痛苦，說不盡的痛苦。麗迪亞能夠回來，能夠保全了人格，這一切都得歸功於他。她一想起自己以前竟會那樣厭惡他，竟會對他那樣出言唐突，真是萬分傷心！她不勝自愧，同時又為他感到驕傲。驕傲的是，他竟會存着同情之心，重情重義，委曲求全。於是她把舅母信上恭維他的那段話讀了又讀，還嫌說得不夠，可是也足以讓她十分高興。她發覺舅父母都斷定她跟達西先生情深意切，推心置腹。她雖然不免因此而感到幾分懊惱，卻也頗為得意。

這時已經有人走近前來，打斷了她的沉思，使她從座位上站起來；她剛要從另一條小徑走過去，卻見韋翰趕了上來。

他走到她身邊說道："我怕我打擾了你清靜的散步吧，親愛的姐姐。"

她笑着回答道："的確是這樣，不過，打擾未必就不受歡迎。"

"要是這樣，我真過意不去。我們一向是好朋友，現在更加親近了。"

"對。他們都出來了嗎？"

"不知道。媽媽和麗迪亞乘着馬車到麥里頓去了。親愛的姐姐，聽舅父母說起，你真的到龐百利去玩過了。"

她說，真的去過了。

"你這份眼福幾乎令我嫉妒，可惜我又消受不了，否則，我到紐卡斯爾去的時候，也可以順道一訪。我想，你看到了那位年老的管家太太吧？可憐的雷諾太太！她從前老是那麼喜歡我。不過，她當然不會在你面前提起我的名字。"

"她倒提到了。"

"她怎麼說的？"

"她說你進了軍隊，就怕——就怕你情形不大好。路隔得那麼遠，傳來的話十分靠不住。"

"當然。"他咬着嘴唇說。伊莉莎白滿以為這下可以令他住嘴了；

但是過不了一會，他又說道：

"上個月真出乎意料，在城裏碰到了達西。我們見了好幾次面。我不知道他到城裏有甚麼事。"

"或許是準備跟德・包爾小姐結婚吧，"伊莉莎白說。"他在這樣的季節到城裏去，一定是為了甚麼特別緊要的事。"

"毫無疑問。你在蘭姆頓見到過他嗎？聽賈汀納夫婦說，你見過他的。"

"見過，他還把我們介紹給他的妹妹。"

"你喜歡她嗎？"

"非常喜歡。"

"真的，我聽說她這一兩年來有了很大的長進。以前看到她的時候，我真覺得她沒有甚麼出息。你喜歡她，我很高興。但願她能夠改好，像個人樣。"

"她一定會那樣；她那最容易惹禍的年齡已經過去了。"

"你們經過金普頓嗎？"

"我記不得是否到過那個地方。"

"我之所以要提到那個地方，就因為我當初應該得到的一份牧師俸祿就在那裏。那是個非常好玩的地方！那所牧師住所也好極了！各方面都適合我。"

"你竟喜歡講道嗎？"

"喜歡極了。我本當把它看作我自己本份的職務，即使開始要費點力氣，過不了多久也就無所謂了。一個人不應該後悔；可是，這的確是我的一份好差事！這樣安閒清靜的生活，完全合乎我幸福的理想！只可惜已經事過境遷。你在肯特郡的時候，有沒有聽到達西談起過這件事？"

"聽到過的，而且我認為他的話很靠得住，聽說那個位置給你是有條件的，而且目前這位恩主 [54] 可以自由處理。"

"你聽到過！不錯，這話也有些道理；我一開始就告訴過你，你可能還記得。”

“我還聽説，你過去有一個時期，並不像現在這樣喜歡講道，你曾經鄭重其事地宣佈過，決定不要當牧師，於是這件事就此解決了。”

“你真聽説過！這話倒不是完全沒有根據。你也許還記得，我們第一次談起這件事的時候，我也提起過的。”

他們兩人現在快要走到家門口了，因為她有意走得很快，想要擺脱他；不過看在妹妹份上，她又不願意使他生氣，因此她只是和顏悦色地笑了笑，回答道：

“算了吧，韋翰先生；你要知道，我們現在已是兄弟姐妹。不要再為了過去的事爭論吧。但願將來一直不會有甚麼衝突。”

她伸出手來，他親切而殷勤地吻了一下，雖然這時候他的表情十分尷尬。他們就這樣走進了大宅。

第五十三章

韋翰先生對於這場談話感到完全滿意，從此他便不再提起這件事，免得自尋苦惱，也免得惹他親愛的大姨子伊莉莎白生氣；伊莉莎白見他居然給說得不再開口，也覺得很高興。

轉眼之間，他和麗迪亞的行期來到了，班奈特太太不得不和他們分離，而且至少要分別一年，因為班奈特先生堅決不贊同她的計劃，不肯讓全家都搬到紐卡斯爾去。

她哭了："哦，我的麗迪亞寶貝，我們到哪一天才能見面呢？"

"天哪！我也不知道。也可能兩三年不能見面。"

"常常寫信給我吧，好孩子。"

"我盡可能常寫信來。可是你知道，結了婚的女人是沒有甚麼時間來寫信的。姐妹們倒可以常常寫信給我，反正她們無事可做。"

韋翰先生一聲聲的道別比他太太叫得親切得多。他笑容滿面，儀態萬方，又說了許多漂亮話。

他們一走出門，班奈特先生就說："他是我生平所看到的最好看的一個人。他既會假笑，又會癡笑，又會跟大家調笑。我真為他感到莫大的驕傲。我敢說，連盧卡斯爵士也未必拿得出一個更寶貝的女婿。"

女兒走了以後，班奈特太太鬱悶了好幾天。

她說："我常常想，跟自己的親人離別，真是再難受不過的事；他們走了，我好像失去了歸宿。"

伊莉莎白說："媽媽，你要明白，這就是嫁女兒的下場，幸好你另外四個女兒還沒有人要，一定會讓你好受些。"

"完全不是那麼回事。麗迪亞並不是因為結了婚而要離開我，而是因為她丈夫的部隊湊巧駐紮得那麼遠。要是近一點，她就用不着走得這樣快了。”

這事雖然使班奈特太太精神頹喪，不過沒有過多久也就好了，因為這時候外界正流傳着一件新聞，使她的精神又振作了起來。原來風聞尼德斐莊園的主人一兩天內就要回到鄉下來，打幾個星期的獵，他的管家太太 [55] 正在奉命收拾一切。班奈特太太聽到這消息，簡直坐立不安。她一會望望珍妮，一會笑笑，一會又搖搖頭。

“好極了，賓利先生居然要來了，妹妹，”（因為第一個告訴她這消息的正是菲力普太太。）“好極了，實在太好了。不過我倒並不在乎。你知道，我們一點也不把他放在心上，我的確再也不想見到他了。不過，他既然願意回到尼德斐莊園來，我們自然還是歡迎他。誰知道會怎麼樣呢？反正與我們無關。你知道，我們早就協議，再也不提這件事。還有的是，他真的會來嗎？”

她的妹妹説：“你放心好了，尼可爾斯太太昨天晚上去過麥里頓。我親眼看見她走過，便特地跑出去向她打聽，是不是真有這回事；她告訴我説，的確真有這回事。他最晚星期四就會來，很可能星期三就來。她又説，她正要到肉店去訂點肉，準備星期三做菜，她還有六隻鴨子，已經可以宰來吃。”

班奈特小姐聽到他要來，不禁變了臉色。她已經有好幾個月沒有在伊莉莎白面前提起過他的名字；可是這一次，一等到只有她們姐妹兩人在一起的時候，她就説道：

“莉茲，今天姨母告訴我這消息的時候，我看到你直望着我，我知道我當時神色很難看；可是你千萬別以為是為了這一類的傻事，只不過當時我覺得大家都在盯着我看，所以一時之間有些心亂。老實告訴你，這個消息既不使我感到愉快，也不使我感到痛苦。只有一點使我感到高興——這次他是一個人來的，因此我們看到他的機會就會比較少。我本身並沒有甚麼顧慮，而是怕別人閒言閒語。”

伊莉莎白對這件事不知道怎麼想才好。如果她上次沒有在德比郡見到他，她也許會以為他此來並非別有用心。可是她依舊認為他對珍妮未能忘情。這次他究竟是得到了他朋友的允許才來的呢，還是他自己大膽跑來的？這實在讓她無從斷定。

她有時候不由得這麼想："這可憐的人，回到自己租定的房子裏來，卻引起別人這樣紛紛猜測，想起來着實令人難受。我也別去管他吧。"

不管她姐姐嘴上怎麼説，心裏怎麼想，是否盼望他來，伊莉莎白卻很容易看出了她姐姐心情上受到了影響，比往常更加心魂不定，神色不安。

大約在一年以前，父母曾經熱烈地爭論過這個問題，如今又要舊事重提了。

班奈特太太又對她丈夫説："我的好老爺，賓利先生一來，你一定要去拜訪他呀。"

"不去，不去，去年你硬逼着我去看他，説甚麼只要我去看了他，他就會挑中我們的某一個女兒做太太，可是結果只落得一場空，我再也不幹這種傻事了。"

他太太又説，那位貴人一回到尼德斐莊園，鄰居們都少不了要去拜候他。

他説："我恨透了這一類的禮節，要是他想跟我們來往，讓他自己找上門來好了。他又不是不知道我們的住址。鄰居們每次來來去去，都得要我來迎送，我可沒有時間。"

"唔，你不去拜訪他，那就是太不知禮。不過，我還是可以請他到這裏來吃飯，我已經決定要請他來。我們本當早些請郎格太太和戈丁一家人來，加上我們自己家裏的人，一共是十三個，所以正好留個位子給他。"

她決定了這麼做，心裏就覺得快慰了些，因此丈夫的無理也就讓她好受了些；然而，這樣一來，結果就會使鄰居們比他們先看到賓利先生。他來的日子迫近了。

珍妮對她妹妹説："我現在反而覺得他還是不要來的好。其實別無他的，我見到他也可以裝得若無其事，只是聽到別人老是談起這件事，我實在有些受不了。媽媽是一片好心，可是她不知道（誰也不知道）她那些話使我多麼難受。但願他不要在尼德斐莊園再住下去，我就滿意了！」

伊莉莎白說：「我真想說幾句話安慰安慰你，可惜一句也說不出。你一定明白我的意思。我不願意像一般人那樣，看到別人難受，偏偏勸他要有耐性一些，因為你一向就有極大的耐性。」

賓利先生終於來了。班奈特太太由於有傭人們加以協助，最早獲得消息，因此煩神也煩得最久。既然及早去拜訪他的計劃已告失望，她便屈指計算着日子，看看還得再隔多少天才能送請帖。但他來到赫福德郡的第三天，班奈特太太便從化粧室的窗戶看見他騎着馬走進圍場，朝她家裏走來。

她喜出望外，急急忙忙喚女兒們來分享她這種快樂。珍妮毅然坐在桌邊不動。伊莉莎白為了讓她母親滿意，便走到窗前望了一望，只見達西先生也跟他一同來了，於是她便走回去坐在姐姐身旁。

凱蒂說：「媽媽，另外還有位先生跟他一起來了呢，那是誰呀？」

「我想，不外乎是他朋友甚麼的，寶貝，我的確不知道。」

「看！」凱蒂又說。「活像以前跟他在一起的那個人。記不起他的名字了，就是那個非常傲慢的高個子呀。」

「天哪，原來是達西先生！肯定是的。老實說，只要是賓利先生的朋友，這裏總是歡迎的；要不然，我一見到這個人就討厭。」

珍妮極其驚奇、極其關心地望着伊莉莎白。她完全不知道妹妹在德比郡跟達西會面的事，因此覺得妹妹自從收到他那封解釋的信以後，這回第一次跟他見面，一定會覺得很窘迫。姐妹兩人都不十分好受。她們彼此體貼，各有隱衷。母親依舊在嘮叨不休，說她頗不喜歡達西先生，只因為看他究竟還是賓利先生的朋友，所以才客客氣氣地接待他一番。這些話姐妹兩人都沒有聽見。其實伊莉莎白心神不安，的確還另有原因，這是珍妮所不知道的。伊莉莎白始終沒有勇氣把賈汀納太太那封信拿給珍妮看，也沒有勇氣向珍妮敍述她對他感情變化的經過。珍妮只知道他向她求婚，被她拒絕過，她還低估過他的長處，殊不知伊莉莎白的隱衷絕不僅如此而已，她認為他對她們全家都有莫大的恩典，因此對他另眼看待。她對他的情意即使還抵不上珍妮對賓利那樣深切，至少也像珍妮對待賓利一樣地合情合理，恰到好處。達西這次回到尼德斐莊園，並且自動到朗伯恩來重新找她，確實使她感到驚奇，幾乎像她上次在德比郡看見他作風大變時一樣地感到驚奇。

時間已經過了這麼久，而他的情意，他的心願，竟始終不渝；一想到這裏，她那蒼白的臉便重新恢復了血色，而且顯得更加鮮豔，她不禁喜歡得笑逐顏開，容光煥發。可是她畢竟還是放心不下。

她想：「讓我先看看他的舉止行動如何，然後再存指望還不遲。」

她坐在那裏專心做針線，竭力裝得鎮靜，連眼睛也不抬起來一下，等到傭人走近房門，她才性急起來，抬起頭來望望姐姐的臉色，只見珍妮比平常稍微蒼白了一些，可是她的端莊持重，頗出乎伊莉莎白的意料。兩位貴客到來的時候，她的臉漲紅了；不過她還是從容不迫、落落大方地接待他們，既沒有顯露半點怨恨，也並不做得過份殷勤。

伊莉莎白沒有跟他們兩人攀談甚麼，只不過為了顧全禮貌，照例敷衍了幾句，便重新坐下來做針線，而且做得特別起勁。她只是大膽地瞟了達西一眼，只見他的神色像往常一樣嚴肅，不像在龐百利時的那副神情，而是像他在赫福德郡時的那副神氣。這也許是因為他在她母親面前，不能像在她舅父母面前那樣不拘禮節。她這種揣測固然是煞費苦心，但也未必不近情理。

她也望了賓利一眼，立即就看出他又是高興，又是侷促不安。班奈特太太對他那樣禮貌周到，而對他那位朋友，卻是勉強敷衍，十分冷淡，相形之下，使她兩個女兒覺得很是過意不去。

其實她母親對待這兩位貴客完全是輕重倒置，因為她心愛的一個女兒幸虧得到了達西先生的搭救，才能免於身敗名裂，伊莉莎白對這事的經過知道得極其詳細，所以特別覺得難受。

達西向伊莉莎白問起賈汀納夫婦，伊莉莎白回答起來不免有些慌張。以後達西便沒有再說甚麼。他之所以沉默寡言，也許是因為他沒有坐在她身邊的緣故，不過上次在德比郡，他卻不是這樣。記得上次他每逢不便跟她自己說話的時候，就跟她舅父母說話，可是這一次，卻接連好幾分鐘沒聽見他開口。她再也抑制不住好奇心了，便抬起頭來望望他的臉，只見他不時地看着珍妮和她自己，大部份時間又總是對着地面發呆。可見這一次比起他們兩人上次見面的時候，他更加心事重重，卻不像上次那樣急於博得別人的好感。她感到失望，同時又怪自己不應該失望。

她想："怎麼料到他竟是這樣？那他何必要來？"

除了他以外，她沒有興致跟別人談話，可是她又沒有勇氣向他開口。

她向他問候他的妹妹，問過以後，又是無話可說。

只聽到班奈特太太說："賓利先生，你走了好久了。"

賓利先生連忙說，的確好久了。

"我原先還擔心你一去不回。人們都說，你打算一到米迦勒節，就把房子退租，我但願不會如此。自從你走了以後，這一帶發生了好多事情。盧卡斯小姐結婚了，有了歸宿了，我自己一個女兒也出了嫁。我想你已經聽到過這件事，你一定在報紙上看到了吧。我知道《泰晤士報》和《快報》上都有消息，不過寫得不成體統。那上面只說：'喬治‧韋翰先生將於最近與班奈特小姐結婚，'關於她的父親，她住的地方，以及諸如此類的事，一個字也沒有提到。這是我弟弟賈汀納擬的稿，我不懂他怎麼會做得這樣糟糕。你看到了嗎？"

賓利說他看到了，又向她道賀。伊莉莎白連眼睛也不敢抬起來，因此也不知道達西先生此刻表情如何。

班奈特太太接下去說："的確，順利地嫁出了一個女兒，真是件開心的事，可是，賓利先生，她離開了我身邊，我又覺得難受。他們到紐卡斯爾去了，在很遠的北方，他們去了以後也不知道多久才能回來。他的部隊在那裏。他已經脫離了某某民兵團，加入了正規軍，你大概也知道吧。謝天謝地！他總算也有幾個朋友，不過憑他的品德，他還可以多幾個朋友呢。"

伊莉莎白知道她這話是有意說給達西先生聽的，真是難為情得要命，幾乎坐也坐不住了。不過這番話倒是比甚麼都有效用，使她能夠勉為其難地跟客人攀談起來。她開始問賓利是否打算暫時在鄉下小住，他說，要住幾個星期。

她母親說："賓利先生，等你打完你自己莊園裏的雀鳥以後，請到班奈特先生的莊園裏來，你愛打多少就打多少。我相信他一定非常樂意讓你來，而且會把最好的鷓鴣都留給你。"

伊莉莎白聽她母親這樣廢話連篇，討好賣乖，更加覺得難受。想起了一年以前，她們曾經滿懷希望，沾沾自喜，如今雖然眼見得又是好事在即，然而只要一轉眼的時間，便會萬事落空，徒感懊喪。她只覺得無論是珍妮也好，她自己也好，即使今後能夠終身幸福，也補償不了這幾分鐘的痛苦難堪。

她心裏想："我只希望今後永遠不要跟他們兩人來往。跟他們做朋友雖然愉快，可是實在抵償不了這種難堪的局面。但願再也不要見到他們！"

不過話說回來，雖然終身的幸福也抵償不了眼前的痛苦，可是不到幾分鐘，她看到姐姐的美貌又打動了她先前那位情人的心，於是她的痛苦便大大減輕了。賓利剛進來的時候，簡直不大跟珍妮說話，可是不久便越來越殷勤。他發覺珍妮還是像去年一樣漂亮，性格溫順，態度自然，只是不像去年那麼愛說話。珍妮一心只希望別人看不出她跟從前有甚麼兩樣，她自以為她依舊像從前一樣健談。其實她是心事太重，因此有時候沉默起來，連她自己也沒有覺察到。

班奈特太太早就打算向貴客稍獻殷勤，當他們告辭的時候，她記起了這件事，便立即邀請他們過幾天到朗伯恩來吃飯。

於是她便說道："賓利先生，你還欠我一次回訪呢，你去年冬天上城裏去的時候，答應一回來就上我們這裏來吃頓便飯。你要知道，我一直把這事放在心上，你卻一直沒有回來赴約，真使我大失所望。"

提起這件事來，賓利不禁呆了起來，後來才說，因為有事情耽擱了，極為抱歉。然後兩人便告辭而去。

班奈特太太本來一心一意打算當天就請他們吃飯，然而她又想到，家裏平常的飯菜雖然也很不錯，可是對方一個是她極想攀親的人，一個每年的收入達一萬鎊之多，那麼，不添兩道佳餚，怎麼好意思呢？

第五十四章

他們一走，伊莉莎白便到屋外去溜達溜達，好讓自己精神舒暢一下，換句話說，也就是不停地去想那些足以使她精神更加沉悶的念頭。達西先生的行為讓她驚奇，也使她煩惱。

她想："要是他這次來是為了要沉默寡言，莊嚴冷淡，那他又何必來？"

她想來想去，總是不愉快。

"他在城裏的時候，對我的舅父母依舊很和氣，很討人喜歡，怎麼反而對我兩樣？如果他見我就怕，他又何必要來？如果他已經無心於我，又何必有話不說？好一個作弄人的男子！今後我再也不去想念他了。"

姐姐走近前來，使她不得不把這個念頭暫時擱在一旁。她一見姐姐神色欣然，便知道這兩位貴客雖使她自己失意，卻使她姐姐較為得意。

姐姐說："第一次見面總算過去了，我倒覺得非常自在。這次我既然能夠應付，等他下次再來，我便不會發窘。他星期二能到這裏來吃飯，我倒很高興，因為到那時候，大家都會看出，我和他不過是無所謂的普通朋友。"

伊莉莎白笑着說："好一個無所謂的朋友！珍妮，還是當心點好！"

"親愛的莉茲，你可別以為我那麼軟弱，到現在還會招來甚麼危險。"

"我看你有極大的危險，會讓他如醉如癡地愛着你。"

*

直到星期二，她們才又見到那兩位貴客。班奈特太太因為上次看到賓利先生在那短短的半小時拜訪過程中，竟然興致極高，禮貌又好，因此這幾天來便一直在打着如意算盤。

那天朗伯恩來了許多客人；主人家最盼望的兩位嘉賓都準時而到，作為狩獵者，他們果真做到了信守時刻。兩人一走進飯廳，伊莉莎白連忙注意賓利先生，看他是不是在珍妮身旁坐下，因為從前每逢有宴會，他都是坐在那個位子上。她那精明的母親也有同感，因此並沒有請他坐到她自己身邊去。他剛走進飯廳的時候，好像頗有些猶豫，幸虧珍妮湊巧回過頭來，湊巧在微笑，他這才拿定主意，在她身邊坐下。

伊莉莎白看得很是得意，不由得朝他那位朋友望了一眼，只見達西落落大方，若無其事。她要不是恰巧看見賓利先生又驚又喜地也對達西先生望了一眼，她還以為他這次之所以能夠稱心如意，是事先得到達西先生恩准的呢。

吃飯的時候，賓利先生果然對她姐姐流露出了愛慕之意。雖然這種愛慕表現得沒有從前那樣露骨，可是伊莉莎白卻覺得，只要能夠完全讓他自己做主，珍妮的幸福和他自己的幸福一定馬上就可以十拿九穩。雖然她不敢心存奢望，可是看到他那樣的態度，實在讓她高興。她當時心情雖然並不十分愉快，這個場景卻使她精神上得到了極大的鼓舞。達西先生的座位和她隔得那麼遠，他和她母親坐在一起。她覺得這無論是對於達西，對於她母親，都是興味索然，兩不方便。座位隔得遠了，她自然聽不清達西跟她母親講些甚麼，可是她看得出他們兩人很少談話，談起來又非常拘泥，非常冷淡。看看母親對他那樣敷衍應酬，再想想他對她們家裏情深義重，她當然份外難受。有幾次她真恨不得能夠告訴他說，她家裏並不是沒有人知道他的好處，並不是全家都對他忘恩負義。

她但願這個晚上彼此能夠親近一些，多談些話，不要辜負了他這一場拜訪，不要讓他只是在進門時聽到她循例地招呼一聲，便一無所獲。她感到萬分焦急不安，因此在兩位貴客沒有走進會客室之前，她幾乎厭倦沉悶得快要發脾氣了。她一心盼望他們進來，因為整個晚上的興致完全在此一舉。

她想：＂假如那時候他依舊不到我面前來，我只好永遠把他放棄。＂

兩位貴賓進來了；看他那副神情，她倒覺得他不會辜負她一片心意。可是天哪！班奈特小姐在桌子上斟茶，伊莉莎白在倒咖啡，女客們卻把這張桌子團團圍住，大家擠在一起，擺一張椅子的空地方也沒有。他們進來以後，有一個小姐又向伊莉莎白身邊更靠近一些，跟她低聲說道：

＂我決不讓這般男人來把我們分開，不管哪個男人，我們都不讓他來，好不好？＂

達西只得走開。伊莉莎白的眼睛盯着他看，隨便看到甚麼人跟他說話，她都覺得嫉妒。她幾乎沒辦法耐着性子給客人們倒咖啡了。過了一會，她又埋怨自己不該這樣癡心。

＂他是一個被我拒絕過的男人！我怎麼蠢到這般地步，竟會指望他重新愛上我？哪一個男人會這樣沒有骨氣，向一個女人求第二次婚？他們決不屑做這種丟面的事！＂

這時只見他親自把咖啡杯送回來，因此她總算稍微高興了一些，立即抓住這個機會跟他說話：

＂你妹妹還在龐百利嗎？＂

＂還在，她一直要在那裏住到聖誕節。＂

＂只有她一個人嗎？她的朋友都走了沒有？＂

＂安涅斯雷太太跟她在一起。別的人都在三個星期以前上斯卡巴[56]去了。＂

她想不出別的話可說了，不過，只要他願意跟她談話，他自有辦法。可是，他默默無言地在她身旁站了幾分鐘，後來那位年輕的小姐又跟伊莉莎白咬起耳朵來，他又只得走開。

等到茶具撤走、牌桌全擺好以後，女客們都站起身來，這時伊莉莎白更希望他立刻就到自己身邊來，但見她母親在四處硬拉人打"惠斯特"，他也情面難卻，頃刻之間就和眾賓客一同坐上牌桌，於是她一切的希望都落了空。她滿懷的興致都變成了泡影。今晚她已毫無指望。兩個人只得各自坐在一張牌桌上，達西的眼睛頻頻向她這邊看，結果兩個人都打輸了牌。

班奈特太太本來打算留尼德斐莊園的這兩位貴客吃宵夜，不幸的是，他們吩咐傭人備車比誰都要快，因此她沒有機會留他們。

客人們一走，班奈特太太便說："孩子們，今天過得快活嗎？告訴你們，我覺得一切都非常順利。飯菜烹調得從來沒有那麼好過。鹿肉燒得恰到好處，大家都說，從來沒見過這麼肥的腰肉。說到湯，比起我們上星期在盧卡斯家裏吃的，那可不知要好多少。連達西先生也承認鷓鴣燒得美極了，我看他自己至少用了三個法國廚子呢。再說，親愛的珍妮，我從來沒有看見你比今天更美。郎格太太也這麼說，因為我在她面前問過你美不美。你猜她還說了些甚麼？她說：'呃！班奈特太太，她一定會嫁到尼德斐莊園去的。'她真是這麼說的。我覺得郎格太太這個人真是太好了；她的姪女兒們都是些規規矩矩的好女孩，只可惜長得一點也不好看。我真喜歡她們。"

總而言之，班奈特太太今天的確高興極了。她把賓利對珍妮的一舉一動全看在眼裏，因此相信珍妮一定會把他弄到手。她一時高興，便不禁想入非非，一心只指望這頭親事會給她家裏帶來多少多少好處，等到第二天不見他來求婚，她又大失所望。

班奈特小姐對伊莉莎白說："今天一天過得真有意思，來吃飯的客人都挑選得那麼好，大家都很投機。我希望今後我們能夠常常聚會。"

伊莉莎白笑了笑。

"莉茲，請你千萬不要笑，千萬不要疑心我。這會使我難受。告訴你吧，我只不過很欣賞這樣一位聰明和藹的年輕人的談吐，並沒有存別的非份之想。他的整個舉止作風中間，有一點我完全感到滿意，那就是他絕對沒有想要博得我的歡心。只不過他的談吐實在比別人美妙，而且他也比別人隨和。"

妹妹說："你真狠心，你不讓我笑，又偏偏要時時刻刻引我發笑。"

"有些事是多麼不容易令人相信！"

"又有些事簡直不可能令人相信！"

"可是，你為甚麼偏要逼我，認為我沒有把真心話全說出來呢？"

"這話可令我無從回答了。我們都喜歡替別人出主意，可是出了主意，別人又不領情。算我對不起你。如果你再三要說你對他沒有甚麼意思，可休想讓我相信。"

第五十五章

這次拜訪以後，沒有過幾天，賓利先生又來了，而且只有他一個人來。他的朋友已經在當天早上動身上倫敦去，不過十天以內就要回來。他在班府上坐了一個多小時，顯然非常高興。班奈特太太留他吃飯，他一再道歉，說是別處已經有約在先。

班奈特太太只得說："希望你下次來的時候，能夠賞賞我們的臉。"

他說他隨時都樂意來，只要她不嫌麻煩，他一有機會就來看她們。

"明天能來嗎？"

可以，由於他明天沒有約會，於是他爽爽快快地接受了她的邀請。

第二天他果然來了，來得非常早，太太小姐們都還沒有打扮好。班奈特太太身穿晨衣，頭髮才梳好一半，連忙跑進女兒房間裏去大聲叫道：

"親愛的珍妮，快些下樓去。他來了。賓利先生來了。他真來了。趕快，趕快。我說，莎蕾，趕快上大小姐這裏來，幫她穿衣服。你別去管莉茲小姐的頭髮了。"

珍妮說："我們馬上就下去，也許凱蒂比我們兩個都快，因為她上樓有半個小時了。"

"哦，別去管凱蒂吧！關她甚麼事？快些，快些！好孩子，你的腰帶在哪裏？"

母親走了以後，珍妮再三要一個妹妹陪着她下樓去。

到了晚上，顯而易見班奈特太太又一心要成全他們兩人在一起。喝過了茶，班奈特先生照着他平常的習慣，到書房裏去了，瑪莉上樓彈琴去了。班太太看見五個障礙除了兩個，便立即對伊莉莎白和凱瑟琳擠眉弄眼，可惜她們半天都沒領會她的用意，伊莉莎白看也不看她一眼，凱蒂終於很天真地說："怎麼了，媽媽？你為甚麼老是對我眨眼？你要我做甚麼呀？"

"沒甚麼，孩子，沒甚麼。我沒有對你眨眼。"於是她又多坐了五分鐘，實在不願意再錯過這大好的機會，她便突然站起來，對凱蒂說：

"來，寶貝，我跟你說句話，"說過這話，她便把凱蒂拉了出去。珍妮立刻對伊莉莎白望了一眼，意思說，她受不住這樣的擺佈，請求伊莉莎白不要也這樣做。轉眼間，只見班奈特太太打開了半邊門，喊道：

"莉茲，親愛的，我要跟你說句話。"

伊莉莎白只得走出去。

一走進穿堂，她母親就對她說："我們最好不要去打擾他們，凱蒂和我都上樓到我化粧室裏去了。"

伊莉莎白沒有跟她爭辯，靜靜地留在穿堂裏，等母親和凱蒂走得看不見了，才又回到會客室來。

班奈特太太這一天的打算沒有如願。賓利樣樣都討人喜愛，只可惜沒有公然以她女兒的情人自居。他安然自若，神情愉快，在她們晚間的家庭聚會上，人人都喜歡他。雖然班奈特太太不知分寸，多管閒事，他卻竭力忍受；儘管她講出多少蠢話，他也一點不動聲色，很有耐性地聽着，這特別讓那女兒滿意。

他幾乎用不到主人家邀請，便自己留下來宵夜；他還沒有告辭，便又順應着班奈特太太的意思，將計就計，約定明天來跟她丈夫打鳥。

自從這一天以後，珍妮再也不說對他無所謂了。姐妹兩人事後一句也沒有談起賓利，可是伊莉莎白上牀的時候，心裏很是快活，覺得只要達西先生不準時趕回來，這件事很快便會有眉目。不過她又認為事到如今，達西先生一定早已表示同意。

　　第二天，賓利準時赴約，依照事先約定，跟班奈特先生在一起消磨了整個上午。班奈特先生和藹可親，實在遠遠出乎賓利先生的意料。這是因為，賓利沒有甚麼傲慢或愚蠢的地方惹他嘲笑，或是令他討厭得不肯理睬他。比起賓利上次跟他見面的情形來，他這次更加健談，也不像以前那樣古怪。不用說，賓利跟他一同回來吃了晚飯，晚上班奈特太太又設法把別人都遣開，讓他跟她女兒在一起。伊莉莎白今晚有一封信要寫，吃過茶以後便到起坐間去寫信，因為她看到別人都坐下來打牌，不便再和她母親作對。

　　等她寫好了信回到客廳裏來的時候，一看那種情景，不由得大吃一驚，認為母親果然比她聰明得多。她一走進門，只見姐姐和賓利一起站在壁爐前，看來正談話談得起勁，如果這情形還沒有甚麼可疑，那麼，只要看看他們兩人那般的臉色，那般慌慌張張轉過身去，立即分開，你心裏便有數了。他們窘態畢露，可是她自己卻更窘。他們坐了下來，一言不發；伊莉莎白正想走開，只見賓利突然站起身來，跟她姐姐悄悄地說了幾句話，便跑出去了。

　　珍妮心裏有了快活的事情，向來不瞞伊莉莎白，於是她馬上抱住妹妹，極其熱情地承認她自己是天下最幸福的人。

　　她又說：「太幸福了！實在太幸福了。我不配。哎，為甚麼不能人人都像我這樣幸福呢？」

　　伊莉莎白連忙向她道喜，真誠熱烈，歡欣異常，實在非筆墨所能形容。她每說一句親切的話，就增加珍妮一分幸福的感覺。可是珍妮不能跟妹妹多糾纏了，她要說的話還沒有說到一半，可是不能再說下去了。

　　「莉茲，親愛的，我要跟你說句話。」珍妮說：「我得馬上到媽媽那裏去，我千萬不能辜負她一片好心好意，我要親自去把這件事說給她聽，不要別人轉告。他已經去告訴爸爸了。噢，莉茲，你知道，家裏人聽到我這件事，一個個會覺得多麼高興啊！我怎麼受得了這樣的幸福！"

於是她就連忙到母親那裏去，只見母親已經特地散了牌場，跟凱蒂坐在椅子上。

伊莉莎白一個人留在那裏，心想：家裏人為了這件事，幾個月來一直在煩神擔心，如今卻一下子便得到了解決，她想到這裏，不禁一笑。

她說："這就是他那位朋友處心積慮的結局！是他自己的姐妹自欺欺人的下場！這個結果真是太幸福、太圓滿、太有意思了！"

沒過幾分鐘，賓利就到她這裏來了，因為他跟她父親談得很簡潔扼要。

他一打開門，便連忙問道："你姐姐在哪裏？"

"在樓上我媽那裏，馬上就會下來。"

他於是關上了門，走到她面前，接受她的道喜。伊莉莎白真心誠意地說，她為他們兩人未來的美滿姻緣感到欣喜。兩人親切地握了握手。她只聽到他講他自己的幸福，講珍妮的十全十美，一直講到珍妮下樓為止。雖然這些話是出於一個情人之口，可是她深信他那幸福的願望一定可以實現，因為珍妮絕頂聰明，脾氣更是好得不能再好，這便是幸福的基礎，而且他們彼此的性格和趣味也十分相近。

這一晚大家都非常高興，班奈特小姐因為心裏得意，臉上也顯得鮮豔嬌美，容光煥發，比平常更加漂亮。凱蒂笑一笑，忍一忍；忍一忍，笑一笑，一心只希望這樣的幸運趕快輪到自己頭上。班奈特太太和賓利足足談了半個小時之久，她滿口嘉許，極力讚美，可總覺得不能夠把滿腔的熱情充份表達出來；班奈特先生跟大家一起吃宵夜的時候，但看他的談吐舉止，便可以看出他也快活到了極點。

不過他當時對這件事卻隻字不提，等到貴客一走，他又連忙轉過身來對大女兒說：

"珍妮，我恭喜你。你可成了一個無比幸福的女子了。"

珍妮立刻走上前去吻他，多謝他的好意。

他説："你是個好孩子；想到你這樣幸福地解決了終身大事，我真高興。我相信你們一定能夠和睦相處。你們的性格很相近。你們遇事都肯遷就，結果會弄得樣樣事都拿不定主張；你們那麼好説話，結果會弄得每個傭人都欺負你們；你們都那麼慷慨，一定會入不敷支。"

"但願不會如此。我要是在銀錢問題上粗心大意，那是不可原諒的。"

他的太太叫道："入不敷支！我的好老爺，你這是甚麼話？他每年有四五千鎊收入，可能還不止呢。"她又對大女兒説："我的好珍妮，親愛的珍妮，我太高興了！我今天晚上休想睡得着覺。我早就知道會這樣，我平常老是説，總有這一天的到來。我一向認為你決不會白白地生得這樣好看。他去年初到赫福德郡的時候，我一看到他，就覺得你們兩個一定會成雙配對。天哪！我一輩子也沒見過像他這樣英俊的男人！"

她早把韋翰和麗迪亞忘了。珍妮本來就是她最寵愛的女兒，現在更是誰也不在她心上了。妹妹們馬上都簇擁着珍妮，要她答應將來給她們多少好處。

瑪莉請求使用尼德斐莊園的藏書室，凱蒂硬要她每年冬天在那裏開幾次舞會。

從此以後，賓利自然就成了朗伯恩家每天必來的客人。他總是早飯也沒吃就趕來，一直要留到吃過宵夜才走——除非有哪一家不識大體、不怕人討厭的鄰居，再三請他吃飯，他才不得不去應酬一下。

伊莉莎白簡直沒有機會跟她姐姐談話，因為只要賓利一來，珍妮的心就想不到別人身上去。不過他們兩人總還是有時候不得不分開一下。珍妮不在的時候，賓利老愛跟伊莉莎白談話；賓利回家去了，珍妮也總是找她一起來消遣，因此她對於他們兩人還是大有用處。

有一個晚上，珍妮對她説："他説今年春天完全不知道我也在城裏，這話讓我聽了真高興。我以前的確不相信會有這種事。"

伊莉莎白答道："我以前也疑心到這一點，他有沒有說明是甚麼緣故？"

"那一定是他的姐妹們佈置好了的，她們當然不贊成他和我好，我也不奇怪，因為他大可以選中一個樣樣都比我強的人。可是，我相信她們總有一天會明白，她們的兄弟跟我在一起是多麼幸福，那時候她們一定又會慢慢地回心轉意，跟我恢復原來的交情，不過決不可能像從前那樣知心了。"

"我生平只聽到你講了這樣一句氣量小的話。你真是個好心的女子！老實說，要是又看到你去受那假仁假義的賓利小姐的騙，那可真要氣死我了！"

"莉茲，我希望你相信，他去年十一月裏到城裏去的時候，的確很愛我，他要不是信了別人的話，以為我真的不愛他，那他無論如何早就回來了！"

"他實在也有些不是，不過那都是因為他太謙虛。"

珍妮聽了這話，自然又讚美起他的虛心來，讚美他雖然具有許多優秀的品德，可並不自以為了不起。

伊莉莎白高興的是，賓利並沒有把他朋友阻擋這件事的經過洩露出來，因為珍妮雖然寬宏大量，不記仇隙，可是這件事如果讓她知道了，她一定會對達西有成見。

珍妮又大聲說道："我確實是古往今來最幸福的一個人！哦，莉茲，家裏這麼多人，怎麼偏偏是我最幸福？但願你也會同樣地幸福！但願你也能找到這樣一個人！"

"你即使給我幾十個這樣的人，我也決不會像你這樣幸福。除非我脾氣也像你這樣好，人也像你這樣好，我是無論如何也不會像你這樣幸福的。不會，決不會，還是讓我來自求多福吧，如果我運氣好，到時候我也許又會碰到另外一個柯林斯。"

朗伯恩這家人的事瞞人也瞞不了多久。先是班奈特太太得到了特許，偷偷地講給了菲力普太太聽，菲力普太太沒有得到任何人的許可，就大膽地把它傳遍了麥里頓的街坊四鄰。

　　記得就在幾星期以前，麗迪亞剛剛私奔，那時大家都認為班奈特府上倒盡了霉，如今這樣一來，班奈特家竟在頃刻之間成了天下最有福氣的一家人了。

第五十六章

有一天上午，大約是賓利和珍妮訂婚之後的一個星期，賓利正和女眷們坐在飯廳裏，忽然聽到一陣馬車聲，大家都走到窗口去看，只見一輛四馬大轎車駛進園裏來。這麼一大早，理當不會有客人來，再看看那輛馬車的配備，便知道這位訪客決不是他們的街坊四鄰。馬是驛站上的馬，至於馬車本身，車前侍從所穿的制服，他們也不熟悉。賓利既然斷定有人來訪，便馬上勸班奈特小姐跟他避開，免得被這不速之客纏住，於是珍妮跟他走到矮樹林裏去了。他們兩人走了以後，另外三個人依舊在那裏猜測，可惜猜不出這位來客是誰。最後門開了，客人走進屋來，原來是凱瑟琳・德・包爾夫人。

大家當然都十分詫異，萬萬想不到會有這樣出奇的事。班奈特太太和凱蒂跟她素昧生平，可是反而比伊莉莎白更感到受寵若驚。

客人走進屋來的那副神氣非常沒有禮貌。伊莉莎白招呼她，她只稍微側了一下頭，便一屁股坐下來，一句話也不說。她走進來的時候，雖然沒有要求介紹，伊莉莎白還是把她的名字告訴了她母親。

班奈特太太大為驚異，不過，這樣一位了不起的貴客前來登門拜訪，可又使她得意非凡，因此她便極其有禮貌地加以招待。凱瑟琳夫人不聲不響地坐了一會，便冷冰冰地對伊莉莎白說：

"我想，你一定過得很好吧，班奈特小姐。那位太太大概就是你母親？"

伊莉莎白簡簡單單地回答了一聲正是。

"那一位大概就是你妹妹吧？"

班奈特太太連忙應聲回答："正是，夫人，"她能夠跟這樣一位貴夫人攀談，真是得意。"這是我第四個女兒。我最小的一個女兒最近出嫁了，大女兒正和她的好朋友在附近散步，那個小伙子不久也要變成我們自己人了。"

凱瑟琳夫人沒有理睬她，過了片刻才說："你們這裏還有個很小花園呢。"

"哪能比得上洛欣莊園，夫人，可是我敢說，比威廉·盧卡斯爵士的花園卻要大得多。"

"到了夏天，這間房間夜裏做起居室一定很不適宜，窗子都朝西。"

班奈特太太告訴她說，她們每天吃過晚飯以後，從來不坐在那裏，接着又說：

"我是否可以冒昧請問您夫人一聲，柯林斯夫婦都好嗎？"

"他們都很好。前天晚上我還看見他們的。"

這時伊莉莎白滿以為她會拿出一封夏綠蒂的信來；她認為凱瑟琳夫人這次到這裏來，決不可能為了別的原因。可是並不見夫人拿信出來，這真令她完全不明白是怎麼回事了。

班奈特太太恭恭敬敬地請貴夫人隨意用些點心，可是凱瑟琳夫人甚麼也不肯吃，謝絕得非常堅決，非常沒有禮貌，接着又站起來跟伊莉莎白說：

"班奈特小姐，你們這塊草地的那一頭，好像頗有幾分荒野的景色，倒很好看。我很想到那裏去逛逛，可否請你陪我走一走？"

她母親連忙大聲對她說："你去吧，乖孩子，陪着夫人到各條小徑上去逛逛。我想，她一定會喜歡我們這個幽靜的小地方。"

伊莉莎白聽從了母親的話，先到自己房間裏去拿了一把陽傘，然後下樓來侍候這位貴客。兩人走過穿堂，凱瑟琳夫人打開了那扇通到飯廳和客廳的門，稍稍打量了一下，說是這些房間還算過得去，然後繼續向前走。

她的馬車停在門口，伊莉莎白看見車子裏面坐着她的侍女。兩人默默無聲地沿着一條通到小樹林的鵝卵石鋪道往前走。伊莉莎白只覺得這個老婦人比往常更加傲慢，更加令人討厭，因此拿定主意，決不先開口跟她說話。

她仔細看了一下這老婦人的臉，不禁想道："她哪一點地方像她外甥？"

一走進小樹林，凱瑟琳夫人便用這樣的方式跟她談話：

"班奈特小姐，我這次上這裏來，你一定知道我是為了甚麼原因。你心裏一定有數，你的良心一定會告訴你，我這次為甚麼要來。"

伊莉莎白大為驚訝。

"夫人，你實在想錯了，我完全不明白你這次怎麼這樣看得起我們，會到這種地方來。"

夫人一聽此話，很是生氣："班奈特小姐，你要知道，我是決不肯讓別人來跟我開玩笑的。不管你怎樣不老實，我可不是那樣。我這個人向來心直口快，何況遇到現在這件事，我當然更無需拐彎抹角。兩天以前，我聽到一個極其驚人的消息。我聽說不光是你姐姐將要攀上一頭高親，連你，伊莉莎白‧班奈特小姐，也快要攀上我的外甥，我的親外甥達西先生。雖然我明知這是無稽的流言，雖然我不會那樣看不起他，相信他真會有這種事情，我還是當機立斷，決定上這裏來一次，把我的意思說給你聽。"

伊莉莎白又是詫異，又是厭惡，滿臉漲得通紅。"我真覺稀奇，您既然認為不會有這種事情，何必還要勞煩您親自跑到這麼遠的地方來？請問您究竟有何見教？"

"我一定要你立刻向大家去闢謠。"

伊莉莎白冷冷地說："要是外界真有這種傳言，那麼您趕到朗伯恩來看我和我家裏人，反而會弄假成真。"

"要是真有這種傳言！你難道存心要假癡假呆不成？這不全是你自己拼命傳出去的嗎？難道你不知道這個消息已經鬧得滿城風雨了嗎？"

"我從來沒有聽見過。"

“你能不能説一聲這是毫無根據？”

“我並不冒充我也像您一樣坦白。您儘管問好了，可是我不想回答。”

“豈有此理！班奈特小姐，我非要你説個明白不可。我外甥向你求過婚沒有？”

“您自己剛剛還説過，決不會有這種事情。”

“不應該有這種事情；只要他還有頭腦，那就一定不會有這種事情。可是你千方百計地誘惑他，他也許會一時癡迷，忘了他應該對得起自己，對得起家裏人。你可能已經把他迷住了。”

“即使我真的把他迷住了，我也決不會説給你聽。”

“班奈特小姐，你知道我是誰嗎？你這種話真講得不成體統。我差不多是他最親近的長輩，我有權利過問他一切的切身大事。”

“您可沒有權利過問我的事，而且你這種態度也休想把我逼供出來。”

“好好聽我把話説明白。你好大膽子，妄想攀這門親，那是絕對不會成功——一輩子也不會成功的。達西先生早跟我的女兒訂過婚了。好吧，你還有甚麼話要説？”

“只有一句話要説——如果他當真如此，那你就沒有理由認為他會向我求婚。”

凱瑟琳夫人遲疑了一會，然後回答道：

“他們的訂婚，跟一般情形兩樣。他們從小就配好了對，雙方的母親兩廂情願。他們在搖籃裏的時候，我們就打算把他們配成一對；眼見他們兩人就要結婚，老姐妹兩人的願望就要達到，卻忽然來了個出身卑賤、門戶低微的女人從中作梗，何況這女人跟他家裏非親非眷！難道你絲毫也不顧全他親人的願望？絲毫也不顧全他跟德·包爾小姐默認的婚姻？難道你一點沒有分寸，一點也不知廉恥嗎？難道你沒有聽見我説過，他一生下來，就註定了要跟他表妹成親的嗎？”

"我以前確實聽到過。可是這跟我有甚麼關係？如果你沒有別的理由反對我跟你外甥結婚，那麼，我雖然明知他母親和姨媽要他跟德·包爾小姐結婚，我也決不會因此卻步。你們姐妹兩人費盡了心機籌劃這段婚姻，成功不成功可要看別人。如果達西先生既沒有責任跟他表妹結婚，也不願意跟她結婚，那他為甚麼不能另外挑一個？要是他挑中了我，我又為甚麼不能答應他？"

"無論從面子上講，從禮節規矩上講——不，從利害關係來講，都不允許這麼做。不錯，班奈特小姐，的確是為了你的利害關係着想。要是你有意跟大家都過不去，你就休想他家裏人或是他的親友們看得起你。凡是和他有關的人，都會斥責你、輕視你、厭惡你。你們的結合是一種恥辱；甚至我們連你的名字都不肯提起。"

"這倒真是大大的不幸，"伊莉莎白說。"可是做了達西先生的太太，必然會享受到莫大的幸福，因此，歸根結底，完全用不到懊惱。"

"好一個不識好歹的女孩！我都為你害臊！今年春天我待你不薄，你就這樣報答我嗎？難道你沒有一點感恩之心？

讓我們坐下來詳談。你應該明白，班奈特小姐，我既然上這裏來了，就非達到目的不可；誰也攔不住我。任何人玩甚麼花樣，我都不會屈服。我從來不肯讓我自己失望。"

"那只有使你自己更加難堪，可是對我毫無影響。"

"我說話不許別人插嘴！好好聽我說。我的女兒和我的外甥是天造地設的一對。他們的母系都是高貴的出身，父系雖然沒有爵位，可也都是極有地位的名門世家。兩家都是富豪。兩家親戚都一致認為，他們兩人是前生註定的姻緣；有誰能把他們拆散？你這樣一個女人，無論家世、親戚、財產，都談不上，難道光憑着你的癡心妄想，就可以把他們拆散嗎？是可忍，孰不可忍！假如你腦子明白點，為你自己的利益想一想，你就不會忘了自己的出身了。"

"我決不會為了要跟你外甥結婚，就忘了我自己的出身。你外甥是個紳士，我是紳士的女兒，我們正是旗鼓相當。"

"真說得對。你的確是個紳士的女兒。可是你媽是個甚麼樣的人？你的姨父母和舅父母又是甚麼樣的人？別以為我不知道他們的底細。"

"不管我親戚是怎麼樣的人，"伊莉莎白說。"只要你外甥不計較，便與你毫不相干。"

"爽爽快快告訴我，你究竟跟他訂婚了沒有？"

伊莉莎白本來不打算給凱瑟琳夫人留情面，來回答這個問題，可是仔細考慮了一會以後，她不得不說了一聲：

"沒有。"

凱瑟琳夫人顯得很高興。

"你願意答應我，永遠不跟他訂婚嗎？"

"我不能答應這種事。"

"班奈特小姐，我真是又驚駭又詫異。我沒有料到你是這樣一個不講理的女人。可是你千萬要把頭腦放清楚一些，別以為我會讓步。非等到你答應了我的要求，我就不走。"

"我當然決不會答應你的。這種荒唐到極點的事，你休想嚇得我答應。你只是一心想要達西先生跟你女兒結婚；可是，就算我如了你的意，答應了你，你以為他們兩人的婚姻就靠得住了嗎？要是他看中了我，就算我拒絕他，難道他因此就會去向你表妹求婚嗎？說句你別見怪的話，凱瑟琳夫人，你這種異想天開的要求真是不近情理，你說的許多話又是淺薄無聊。要是你以為你這些話能夠說得我屈服，那你未免太看錯人了。你外甥會讓你把他的事干涉到甚麼地步，我不知道，可是你無論如何沒有權利干涉我的事。因此我請求你不要再為這件事來勉強我了。"

"請你不必這樣性急。我的話根本沒有講完。除了我已經說過的你那許多缺陷以外，我還要加上一件。別以為我不知道你那個小妹妹不要臉私奔的事。我完全知道。那個年輕小伙子跟她結婚，完全是你爸爸和舅舅花了錢買來的。這樣一個女人，也配做我外甥的小姨子嗎？她丈夫是他父親生前的賬房的兒子，也配和他做連襟嗎？上有天下有地！你究竟是打的甚麼主意？龐百利的門第能夠這樣給人糟蹋嗎？」

伊莉莎白恨恨地回答道：「現在你該說完了，你也把我侮辱得夠了。我可要回家去了。」

她一面說，一面便站起身來。凱瑟琳夫人也站了起來，兩人一同往回走去。老夫人真給氣壞了。

「那麼，你完全不顧全我外甥的身份和面子了！好一個沒良心、自私自利的女人！你難道不知道，他跟你結了婚，大家都要看不起他嗎？」

「凱瑟琳夫人，我不想再講了。你已經明白了我的意思。」

「那麼，你非要把他弄到手不可嗎？」

「我並沒有說這種話。我自有主張，怎麼樣做會幸福，我就決定怎麼樣做，你管不了，任何像你這樣的局外人也都管不了。」

「好啊。你堅決不肯依我。你完全喪盡天良，不知廉恥，忘恩負義。你決心要令他的朋友們看不起他，讓天下人都恥笑他。」

伊莉莎白說：「目前這件事情談不上甚麼天良、廉恥、恩義。我跟達西先生結婚，並不觸犯這些原則。要是他跟我結了婚，他家裏人就厭惡他，那我毫不在乎；至於說天下人都會生他的氣，我認為世界上多的是知義明理的人，不見得個個都會恥笑他。」

「這就是你的真心話！這就是你堅定不移的主張！好啊。現在我可知道該怎麼做了。班奈特小姐，別以為你的癡心妄想會達到目的。我不過是來試探試探你，沒想到你竟不可理喻。等着吧，我說得到一定做得到。」

凱瑟琳夫人就這樣一直講下去，走到馬車前，她又急急忙忙掉過頭來說道：

「我不向你告辭，班奈特小姐。我也不問候你的母親。你們都不識抬舉。我真是十二萬分不高興。"

伊莉莎白不去理她，也沒有請她回到宅子裏去坐坐，自己不聲不響地往屋裏走。她上樓的時候，聽到馬車駛走的聲音。她母親在化粧室門口等她等得心急了，這時一見到她，便連忙問她，為何凱瑟琳夫人不回來休息一會再走。

女兒說："她不願意進來，她要走。"

"她是個多麼好看的女人啊！她真太客氣，竟會到我們這種地方來！我想，她這次來，不過是為了要告訴我們一聲，柯林斯夫婦過得很好。她或許是到別的甚麼地方去，路過麥里頓，順便進來看看你。我想，她沒有特別跟你說甚麼話吧？"

伊莉莎白不得不撒了個小謊，因為她實在沒有辦法把這場談話的內容說出來。

第五十七章

這不速之客去了以後，伊莉莎白很是心神不安，而且很不容易恢復平靜。她接連好幾個小時不斷地思索着這件事。凱瑟琳夫人這次居然不怕麻煩，從洛欣莊園這麼遠趕來，原來是她自己異想天開，認為伊莉莎白和達西先生已經訂了婚，所以特地趕來要把他們拆散。這個辦法倒的確很好；可是，關於他們訂婚的謠傳，究竟有甚麼根據呢？這真令伊莉莎白無從想像，後來她才想起了達西是賓利的好朋友，她自己是珍妮的妹妹，而目前大家往往會因為一重婚姻而連帶想到另一重婚姻，那麼，人們自然要生出這種念頭來了。她自己也早就想到，姐姐結婚以後，她和達西先生見面的機會也就更多了。因此盧家莊的鄰居們（她認為只有他們和柯林斯夫婦通信的時候會說起這件事，因此才會傳到凱瑟琳夫人那裏去）竟然把這件事看成十拿九穩，而且好事就在眼前，可是她自己只不過覺得這件事將來有幾分希望而已。

不過，一想起了凱瑟琳夫人那一番話，她就禁不住有些感到不安：如果她硬要干涉，誰也不肯定會造成怎樣的後果。她說她堅決要阻擋這一頭親事，從這些話看來，伊莉莎白就想到夫人一定會去找她的外甥；至於達西是不是也同樣認為跟她結婚有那麼多壞處，那她就不敢說了。她不知道他跟他姨母之間感情如何，也不知道他是否完全聽他姨母的主張，可是按情理來說，他一定會比伊莉莎白看得起那位老夫人。只要他姨媽在他面前說明他們兩家門第不相當，跟這樣出身的女人結婚有多少壞處，那就會擊中他的弱點。凱瑟琳夫人說了那麼一大堆理由，伊莉莎白當然覺得荒唐可笑，不值一駁，可是她那樣看重門第身份，在他看來，也許會覺得見解高明，理由充足。

如果他本來就心裏動搖不定（他好像時常如此），那麼，只要這位至親去規勸他一下，央求他一下，他自會立刻打消猶豫，下定決心，再不要為了追求幸福而貶低自己的身份。如果真是這樣，那他一定再也不會回來。凱瑟琳夫人路過城裏，也許會去找他，他雖然和賓利先生有約在先，答應立即回到尼德斐莊園來，恐怕只能作罷了。

她心裏又想："要是賓利先生這幾天裏就接到他的信，託辭不能赴約，我便一切都明白了，不必再對他存甚麼指望，不必希望他始終如一。當我現在快要愛上他、答應他求婚的時候，如果他並不真心愛我，而只是惋惜我一下，那麼，我便馬上連惋惜他的心腸也不會有。"

＊

她家裏人聽到這位貴客是誰，都驚奇不已；可是她們也同樣用班奈特太太那樣的假想，滿足了自己的好奇心，因此伊莉莎白才沒有被她們問長問短。

第二天早上，她下樓的時候，遇見父親正從書房裏走出來，手裏拿着一封信。

父親連忙叫她："莉茲，我正要找你；你馬上到我房間裏來一下。"

她跟着他去了，可是不明白父親究竟要跟她說些甚麼。她想，父親之所以要找她談話，多少和他手上那封信有關，因此她更加覺得好奇。她突然想到，那封信可能是凱瑟琳夫人寫來的，免不了又要向父親解釋一番，說來真是煩悶。

她跟她父親走到壁爐邊，兩個人一同坐下。父親說：

"今天早上我收到一封信，使我大吃一驚。這封信上講的都是你的事，因此你應該知道這裏面寫些甚麼。我一直不知道我同時有兩個女兒都有結婚的希望。讓我恭喜你情場得意。"

伊莉莎白立刻斷定這封信是那個外甥寫來的，而不是姨媽寫來的，於是漲紅了臉。她不知道應該為了他寫信來解釋而感到高興呢，還是應該怪他沒有直接把信寫給她而生氣，這時她父親接下去說：

"你好像已經心裏有數似的。年輕的小姐們對這些事情總是非常精明；可是即使以你這樣機靈，我看你還是猜不出你那位情人姓甚名誰。告訴你，這封信是柯林斯先生寄來的。"

"柯林斯先生寄來的！他有甚麼話可說？"

"當然說得很徹底。他一開始先恭喜我的大女兒快要出嫁，這消息大概是那愛管閒事的好心的盧家說給他聽的。這件事我姑且不唸出來，免得你不耐煩。與你有關的部份是這樣寫的：——'愚夫婦既為尊府此次喜事竭誠道賀以後，容再就另一事略申數言。此事消息來源同上。據聞尊府一旦大小姐出閣以後，二小姐伊莉莎白也即將出閣。且聞二小姐此次所選如意郎君，確為天下大富大貴之人。'"

"莉茲，你猜得出這位貴人是誰嗎？——'貴人年輕福宏，舉凡人間最珍貴之事物，莫不件件俱有。非但家勢雄厚，門第高貴，抑且佈施提拔，權力無邊。惟彼雖屬條件優越，處處足以打動人心，然則彼若向尊府求婚，切不可遽而應承，否則難免輕率從事，後患無窮，此小姪不得不先以奉勸先生與表妹伊莉莎白者也。'"

"莉茲，你想得到這位貴人是誰嗎？下面就要提到了。"

"'小姪之所以不揣冒昧，戇直陳詞，實因慮及貴人之姨母凱瑟琳·德·包爾夫人對此次聯姻之事，萬難贊同故耳。'"

"你明白了吧，這個人就是達西先生！喂，莉茲，我已經讓你感到詫異了吧。無論是柯林斯也好，是盧卡斯一家人也好，他們偏偏在我們的熟人當中挑出這麼一個人來撒謊，這不是太容易給人揭穿了嗎？達西先生見到女人就覺得晦氣，也許他看都沒有看過你一眼呢！我真佩服他們！"

伊莉莎白盡量迎合着父親打趣，可是她的笑容顯得極其勉強。父親的俏皮幽默，從來沒有像今天這樣不討她喜歡。

"你不覺得滑稽嗎？"

"啊，當然。請你再讀下去。"

"'昨夜小姪曾與夫人提及此次聯姻可能成為事實,深蒙夫人本其平日推愛之忱,以其隱衷見告。彼謂此事千萬不能贊同,蓋以令嬡門戶低微,缺陷太多,若竟而與之聯姻,實在有失體統。故小姪自覺責無旁貸,應將此事及早奉告表妹,冀表妹及其所愛慕之貴人皆能深明大體,以免肆無忌憚,私訂終身!'——柯林斯先生還說:'麗迪亞表妹之不貞事件得以圓滿解決,殊為欣慰。惟小姪每念及其婚前即與人同居,穢聞遠揚,仍不免有所痛心。小姪尤不能已於言者,厥為彼等一經確定夫婦名分,先生即迎之入尊府,誠令人不勝駭異,蓋先生此舉實為助長傷風敗俗之惡習耳。設以小姪為朗伯恩牧師,必然堅決反對。先生身為基督教徒,固當寬恕為懷,然則以先生之本份而言,惟有拒見其人,拒聞其名耳。'——這就是他所謂的基督徒寬恕精神!下面寫的都是關於他親愛的夏綠蒂的一些情形,他們快要生小孩了。怎麼,莉茲,你好像不樂意聽似的。我想,你不見得也有那種小姐腔,假裝正經,聽到這種廢話就要生氣吧。人生在世,要是不讓別人開開玩笑,回頭來又取笑取笑別人,那還有甚麼意思?"

伊莉莎白大聲叫道:"噢,我覺得非常有趣。不過這事情實在古怪!"

"的確古怪——有趣的也正是這一點。如果他們講的是另外一個人,那倒還說得過去。最可笑的是,那位貴人完全沒有把你放在眼裏,你對他又是非常厭惡!我平常雖然最討厭寫信,可是我無論如何也不願和柯林斯斷絕書信往來。唔,我每次讀到他的信,總覺得他比韋翰還要討我喜歡。我那位女婿雖然又冒失又虛偽,還是及不上他。請問你,莉茲,凱瑟琳夫人對這事是怎麼說的?她是不是特地趕來表示反對?"

女兒聽到父親問這句話,只是笑了一笑。其實父親這一問完全沒有一點猜疑的意思,因此他問了又問,也沒有使她感覺到痛苦。伊莉莎白從來沒有像今天這樣為難:心裏想的是一套,表面上卻要裝出另一套。她真想哭，可是又不得不強顏歡笑。父親說達西先生沒有把她放在眼裏，這句話未免太使她傷心。她只有怪她父親為甚麼這樣糊塗，或者說，她現在心裏又添了一重顧慮：這件事也許不能怪父親看見得太少，而應該怪她自己幻想得太多呢。

第五十八章

賓利先生非但沒有如伊莉莎白所料，接到他朋友不能履約的道歉信，而且在凱瑟琳夫人來過以後沒有幾天，就帶着達西一同來到朗伯恩。兩位貴客來得很早。莉茲坐在那裏時時刻刻都擔心，惟恐母親把達西的姨母來訪的消息當面告訴達西，幸好班奈特太太還沒有來得及說這件事，賓利就提議出去散步，因為他要和珍妮單獨在一起。大家都同意。班奈特太太沒有散步的習慣，瑪莉又從來不肯浪費時間，於是一同出去的只有五個人。賓利和珍妮馬上就讓別人走在前頭，自己在後邊走，讓伊莉莎白、凱蒂和達西三個人去相互應酬。三個人都不大說話：凱蒂很怕達西，因此不敢說話；伊莉莎白正在暗地裏下最大的決心；達西或許也是一樣。

他們向盧卡斯家裏走去，因為凱蒂想要去看看瑪麗亞；伊莉莎白覺得用不着大家都去，於是等凱蒂離開了他們以後，她就大着膽子跟他繼續往前走。現在是她拿出決心來的時候了；她便立刻鼓起勇氣跟他說：

"達西先生，我是個自私自利的人，我只想讓自己心裏痛快，也不管是否會傷害你的情感。你對我那位可憐的妹妹情義太重，我再也不能不感激你了。我自從知道了這件事情以後，一心就想對你表示謝意；要是我家裏人全都知道了，那麼，就不止我一個人要感激你了。"

"我很抱歉，我真抱歉，"達西的聲調又是驚奇又是激動，"這件事要是以錯誤的眼光去看，也許會使你覺得不好受，可是想不到竟會讓你知道。我沒有料到買汀納太太這樣不可靠。"

"你不應該怪我舅母。只因為麗迪亞自己不留神，先露出了口風，我才知道你牽涉在這件事情裏面；那麼我不打聽清楚明白，當然不肯罷休。讓我代表我全家人謝謝你，多謝你本着一片同情心，不怕麻煩，受盡委屈，去找他們。”

達西說：“如果你真的要謝我，你只需表明你自己的謝意。不可否認，我之所以做得那麼起勁，除了別的原因以外，也為了想要使你高興。你家裏人不用感謝我。我雖然尊敬他們，可是我當時心裏只想到你一個人。”

伊莉莎白窘得一句話也說不出來。過了片刻，她的朋友又說：“你是個爽快人，決不會開我的玩笑。請你老實告訴我，你的心情是否還是和四月裏一樣。我的心願和情感依然如舊，只要你說一句話，我便再也不提起這件事。”

伊莉莎白聽他這樣表明心跡，更加為他感到不安和焦急，便不得不開口說話。她立刻吞吞吐吐地告訴他說，自從他剛剛提起的那個時期到現在，她的心情已經起了很大的變化，現在她願意以愉快和感激的心情來接受他這一番盛情美意。這個回答簡直使他感到前所未有的快樂，他正如一個熱戀中的人一樣，立刻抓住這個機會，無限乖巧熱烈地向她傾訴衷曲。要是伊莉莎白能夠抬起頭來看看他那雙眼睛，她就可以看出，他那滿臉喜氣洋洋的神氣，使他變得多麼英俊；她雖然不敢看他的臉色，卻敢聽他的聲音；他把千絲萬縷的感情都告訴了她，說她在他心目中是多麼重要，使她越聽越覺得他情感的寶貴。

他們只顧往前走，連方向也不屑去辨別。他們有多少事要想，多少情感要去體會，多少話要談，實在無心去注意別的事情。她馬上就意識識到，這次雙方之所以會取得這樣的諒解，還得歸功於他姨母的一番力量。原來他姨母回去的時候，路過倫敦，果真去找過他一次，把她自己到朗伯恩來的經過、動機，以及和伊莉莎白談話的內容，都一一告訴了他，特別把伊莉莎白的一言一語談得十分詳細，凡是她認為囂張乖僻、厚顏無恥的地方，都重點地說了又說，認為這樣一來，縱使伊莉莎白不肯答應打消這頭親事，她外甥一定會親口承諾。不過，也是老夫人倒霉，效果恰恰相反。

他說："以前我幾乎不敢奢望，這一次倒覺得事情有了希望。我完全了解你的脾氣，我想，假若你真的恨我入骨，再也沒有挽回的餘地，那你一定會在凱瑟琳夫人面前照直招認出來。"

伊莉莎白漲紅了臉，一面笑，一面說："這話不假，你知道我為人直爽，因此才相信我會做到那種地步。我既然能夠當着你自己的面，深惡痛絕地罵你，自然也會在你任何親戚面前罵你。"

"你罵我的話，哪一句不是活該？雖然你的指責都沒有根據，都是聽到別人以訛傳訛，可是我那次對你的態度，實在應該受到最嚴厲的責備。那是不可原諒的。我想起這件事來，就免不了痛恨自己。"

伊莉莎白說："那天下午的事，究竟應該由誰多負責任，我們也用不着爭論了，嚴格說來，雙方的態度都不好，不過自從那次以後，我覺得我們雙方都變得有禮貌些了。"

"我心裏實在過意不去。幾個月以來，一想起我當時說的那些話，表現出的那種行為，那種態度，那種表情，我就覺得說不出的難過。你罵我的話，確實罵得好，讓我一輩子也忘不了。你說：'假如你表現得有禮貌一些就好了。'你不知道你這句話使我多麼痛苦，你簡直無從想像；不過，說實話，我也還是過了好久才明白過來，承認你那句話罵得對。"

"我萬萬想不到那句話對你有那樣大的影響。我完全沒有料到那句話竟會令你難受。"

"你這話我倒很容易相信。你當時認為我沒有一絲一毫真正的感情，我相信你當時一定是那種想法。我永遠也忘不了：當時你竟翻臉，你說，不管我怎樣向你求婚，都不能打動你的心，讓你答應我。"

"哎，我那些話你也不必再提，提起來未免太不像話。告訴你，我自己也早已為那件事覺得難為情。"

達西又提起那封信。他說："那封信——你接到我那封信以後，是否立刻對我有好感一些？信上所説的那些事，你相信不相信？"

她説，那封信對她影響很大，從此以後，她對他的偏見都慢慢地消除了。

他説："我當時就想到，你看了那封信，一定非常難受，可是我實在萬不得已。但願你早把那封信毀了。其中有些話，特別是剛開始那些話，我實在不願意你再去看它。我記得有些話一定會使你恨透了我。"

"如果你認為一定要燒掉那封信，才能保持我的愛情，那我當然一定把它燒掉；不過話説回來，即使我怎樣容易變心，也不會看了那封信就和你翻臉。"

達西説："當初寫那封信的時候，我自以為完全心平氣和，頭腦冷靜；可是事後我才明白，當時確確實實是出於一股怨氣。"

"那封信最開始幾句也許有幾分怨氣，結尾卻並不是這樣。結尾那句話完全是一片大慈大悲 [57]。還是不要再去想那封信吧。無論是寫信的人也好，看信的人也罷，心情都已和當初大不相同，因此，一切不愉快的事，都應該把它忘掉。你得學學我的人生觀。你要回憶過去，也只應當去回憶那些使你愉快的事情。"

"我並不認為你有這種人生觀。對你來説，過去的事情，沒有哪一件應該受到指責，因此你回憶起過去的事情來，便覺得件件滿意，這與其説，是因為你人生觀的關係，倒不如説，是因為你天真無邪。可是我的情形卻不同。我腦子裏總免不了想起一些痛苦的事情，實在不能不想，也不應該不想。我雖然並不主張自私，可是事實上卻自私了一輩子。從小時候起，大人就教我，為人處世應該如此這般，卻不教我要把脾氣改好。他們教我要學這個規矩那個規矩，又讓我學會了他們的傲慢自大。不幸我是一個獨生子（有好幾年，家裏只有我一個孩子），從小給父母親寵壞了。雖然父母本身都是善良人（特別是父親，完全是一片慈善心腸，和藹可親），卻縱容我自私自利，傲慢自大，甚至還鼓勵我如此，教我如此。他們教我，除了自己家裏人以外，不要把任何人放在眼裏，教我看不起天下人，至少希望我去鄙薄別人的見識，鄙薄別人的長處，把天下人都看得不如我。從八歲到二十八歲，我都是受的這種教養。可愛的伊莉莎白，親愛的伊莉莎白，要不是因為你，我可能到現在還是如此！我怎能不感激你呢！你給了我一頓教訓，起初我當然接受不了，可是我實在得益匪淺。你羞辱得我好有道理。當初我向你求婚，以為你一定會答應。幸虧你使我明白過來，我既然認定一位小姐值得我去博得她的歡心，卻又一味對她自命不凡，那是萬萬辦不到的。"

"當時你真以為會博得我的歡心嗎？"

"我的確是那樣想的。你一定會笑我太自負吧？我當時還以為你在指望着我、等待着我來求婚呢。"

"那一定是因為我態度不好，可是我告訴你，我並不是故意要那樣。我決不是有意欺騙你，可是我往往憑着一時的興致，以致鑄成大錯，從那天下午起，你一定是非常恨我！"

"恨你！剛開始我也許很生你的氣，可是過了不久，我便知道究竟應該氣誰了。"

"我簡直不敢問你，那次我們在龐百利見面，你對我怎麼個看法。你怪我不該來嗎？"

"不，哪裏的話；我只是覺得驚奇。"

"你固然驚奇，可是我蒙你那樣抬舉，恐怕比你還要驚奇。我的良心告訴我說，我不配受到你的殷勤款待，老實說，我當時的確沒有料到會受到格外的禮遇。"

達西說："我當時的用意，是要盡量做到禮貌周全，讓你看出我氣量頗大，不計舊怨，希望你知道我已經重視了你對我的責備，誠心改過，能夠原諒我，沖淡你對我的惡感。至於我從甚麼時候又起了別的念頭，實在很難說，大概是在看到你以後的半個小時之內。"

然後他又說，那次喬治安娜非常樂意跟她做朋友，不料交情突然中斷，使她十分掃興；接着自然又談到交情中斷的原因，伊莉莎白這才明白，當初他還沒有離開那家旅館以前，就已下定決心，要跟着她從德比郡出發，去找她的妹妹，至於他當時之所以沉悶憂鬱，並不是為了別的事操心，而是為了這件事在轉念頭。

她又感謝了他一次，但是提起這件事，雙方非常痛苦，所以沒有再談下去。

他們這樣悠閒自在地走了好幾英里路，只顧忙着交談，想不到已走了這麼遠，最後看看錶，才發覺應該回家了。

"賓利和珍妮上哪裏去了？"他們兩人從這句話又談到那另外一對的事情上去。達西早已知道他朋友已經和珍妮訂婚，覺得很高興。

伊莉莎白說："我得問問你，你是否覺得事出意外？"

"完全不覺得意外。我臨走的時候，便覺得事情馬上會成功。"

"那麼說，你早就允許了他了。真讓我猜着了。"雖然他竭力聲辯，說她這種說法不對，她卻認為事實確實如此。

他說："我到倫敦去的前一個晚上，便把這事情向他坦白了，其實早就應該坦白的。我把過去的事都對他說了，使他明白我當初阻擋他那件事，真是又荒謬又冒失。他大吃一驚。他從來沒有想到過會有這種事。我還告訴他說，我從前以為你姐姐對他平平淡淡，現在才明白是我自己想錯了；我立刻看出他對珍妮依舊一往情深，因此我十分相信他們兩人的結合一定會幸福。"

伊莉莎白聽到他能夠這樣輕而易舉地指揮他的朋友，不禁一笑。

她問道："你跟他說，我姐姐愛他，你是你自己看出來的呢，還是春天裏聽我說的？"

"是我自己看出來的。最近我到你家裏去過兩次，仔細觀察了她一下，便看出她對他感情很深切。"

"我想，一經你說明，他也立即明白了吧。"

"的確如此。賓利為人極其誠懇謙虛。他因為膽怯，所以遇到這種迫切問題，自己便拿不定主張，總是相信我的話，因此這次一切都做得很順利。我不得不向他招認了一件事，我估計他在短時間裏當然難免要為這件事生氣。我老實對他説，去年冬天你姐姐進城去住了三個月，當時我知道這件事，卻故意瞞住了他。他果然很生氣。可是我相信，他只要明白了你姐姐對他有感情，他的氣憤自然會消除。他現在已經真心誠意地寬恕了我。"

伊莉莎白覺得，賓利這樣容易聽信別人的話，真是難得；她禁不住要説，賓利真是個太可愛的人，可是她畢竟沒有把這句話説出口。她想起了目前還不便跟達西開玩笑，現在就開他的玩笑未免太早。他繼續跟她談下去，預言着賓利的幸福——這種幸福當然抵不上他自己的幸福。兩人一直談到走進家門，步入穿堂，這才分開。

第五十九章

伊莉莎白一走進家門，珍妮便問她："親愛的莉茲，你們到甚麼地方去了？"等到他們兩人坐下來的時候，家裏所有的人都這樣問她。她只得說，他們兩人隨便逛逛，後來她自己也不知道走到甚麼地方去了。她說話時漲紅了臉，可是不管她神色如何，都沒有引起大家懷疑到那件事上面去。

那個下午平平靜靜地過去了，並沒有甚麼特別的事情。公開了的那一對情人有說有笑；沒有公開的那一對不聲不響。達西生性沉靜，喜怒不形於色；伊莉莎白心慌意亂，只知道自己很幸福，卻沒有確切體味到究竟如何幸福，因為除了眼前這一陣彆扭以外，還有種種麻煩等在前面。她預料事情公開以後，家裏人會有何種感覺。她知道除了珍妮以外，家裏沒有一個人喜歡他，她甚至顧慮到家裏人都會討厭他，哪怕憑他的財產地位，也是無法挽救。

晚上，她把真心話說給珍妮聽。雖說珍妮一向並不多疑，可是對這件事卻簡直不肯相信。

"你在開玩笑！莉茲。不會有這種事！跟達西先生訂婚！不行，不行，你不要騙我；我知道這件事不可能。"

"一開始就這樣糟糕，可真要命！我惟一的希望全寄託在你身上，要是你不相信我，就沒有人會相信我了。我決不是跟你胡說。我說的都是真話。他仍然愛我，我們已經講定了。"

珍妮半信半疑地看着她。"噢，莉茲，不會有這種事的。我知道你非常厭惡他。"

"你一點也不明白這裏面的曲折，這種話不必再提。也許我一向並不像現在這樣愛他。可是這一類的事，總不應該把宿怨記得太牢。我從今以後也一定要把它忘記得乾乾淨淨。"

班奈特小姐仍然顯出非常詫異的樣子。於是伊莉莎白更加一本正經地重新跟她說，這是事實。

珍妮不禁大聲叫道：「老天爺呀！真有這件事嗎？這次我可應該相信你了，我可愛的莉茲，親愛的莉茲，我要恭喜你，我一定得恭喜你；可是，對不起，讓我問你一聲：你能不能斷定——能不能百份之百地斷定，嫁了他是否會幸福？」

「這當然毫無疑問。我們兩人都認為我們是世界上最幸福的一對。可是你高興嗎，珍妮？你願意要這樣一位妹夫嗎？」

「非常非常願意。賓利和我真是再高興也沒有了。這件事我們也考慮過、談論過，都認為不可能。你真的非常愛他嗎？噢，莉茲，甚麼事都可以隨便，沒有愛情可千萬不能結婚。你確實感覺到你應該這樣做嗎？」

「的確如此！等我把詳情細節都告訴了你，你只會覺得我還做得不夠呢。」

「你這話是甚麼意思？」

「唉，我得承認，我愛他要比愛賓利深切。我怕你要生氣吧。」

「好妹妹，請你嚴肅一些。我要聽你嚴肅地談一談。凡是可以對我說的話，趕快對我說個明白，你是否願意告訴我：你愛他有多久了？」

「這是慢慢發展起來的，我也說不出從甚麼時候開始，不過我覺得，應該從我看到龐百利莊園那美麗的園林算起。」

姐姐又叫她嚴肅些，這一次總算產生了效果；她立刻依了珍妮的意見，鄭重其事地把自己愛他的經過講給珍妮聽。班奈特小姐弄明白了這一點以後，便萬事放心了。

她說：「我現在真是太幸福了，因為你也會同我一樣幸福。我一向很器重他。不說別的，光是為了他愛你，我也就要永遠敬重他了；他既是賓利的朋友，現在又要做你的丈夫，那麼，除了賓利和你以外，我最喜歡的當然就是他了。可是莉茲，你太狡猾了，平常連一點口風也不向我吐露。龐百利的事和蘭姆頓的事從來沒有説給我聽過！我所知道的一些情形，都是別人説給我聽的，不是你自己説的。"

伊莉莎白只得把保守秘密的原因告訴了她。原來她以前不願意提起賓利，加上她又心緒不寧，所以也不講起達西，可是現在，她大可不必再把達西為麗迪亞的婚姻奔忙的那段情節，瞞住珍妮了。她把一切的事都和盤托出，姐妹兩人一直談到半夜。

＊

第二天早上，班奈特太太站在窗前叫道："天哪！那位討厭的達西先生又跟着我們的賓利一起上這裏來了！他為甚麼那樣不知趣，老是要上這裏來？我但願他去打鳥，或者隨便去幹點甚麼，可別來吵我們。讓我們拿他怎麼辦？莉兹，你又得同他出去散散步才好，不要讓他在這裏麻煩賓利。"

母親想出個辦法來，正是伊莉莎白求之不得的，她禁不住要笑出來，可是聽到母親老是説他討厭，她亦不免有些氣惱。

兩位貴客一走進門，賓利便意味深長地望着她，熱烈地跟她握手，她一看見這情形，便斷定他準是消息十分靈通；過了一會，他果然大聲説道："班奈特太太，這一帶還有甚麼別的曲徑小道，可以讓莉兹今天再去迷路嗎？"

班奈特太太説："我要勸達西先生、莉兹和凱蒂，今天上午都上奧克漢山去。這一段長路走起來挺有意思，達西先生還沒有見過那裏的風景呢。"

賓利先生説："對他們兩人當然再好也沒有了，我看凱蒂一定吃不消。是不是，凱蒂？"

凱蒂説她寧可留在家裏。達西表示非常想到那座山上去看看四面的風景。伊莉莎白默默表示同意，正要上樓去準備，班奈特太太在她後面説：

"莉兹，我很對不起你，逼你去跟那個討厭的人在一起，你可不要計較。你要知道，這都是為了珍妮；你只要隨便敷衍敷衍他，不必太費心了。」

　　散步的時候，兩人決定當天下午就去請求班奈特先生的允許；母親那裏由伊莉莎白自己去說。她不知道母親是否會贊成。母親實在太厭惡他了，因此伊莉莎白有時候竟會認為，即使以他的財產地位，也挽回不了母親的心。可是，母親對這婚姻無論是堅決反對也好，欣喜若狂也好，她的出言吐語反正都是不得體，讓人覺得她毫無見識。她對達西先生不是欣喜欲狂地表示贊成，便是義憤填膺地表示反對，伊莉莎白想到這裏，心裏實在受不了。

*

　　當天下午，只見班奈特先生剛一走進書房，達西先生便立刻站起身來跟着他走，伊莉莎白看到這情形，心裏焦急到了極點。她並不是怕父親反對，而是怕父親會被弄得不愉快。她想，她是父親最寵愛的女兒，如果她選擇了這個對象，竟會使父親感到痛苦，使父親為她的終身大事憂慮惋惜，未免太不像話。她擔心地坐在那裏，直到達西先生回到她身邊，面帶笑意，她這才鬆了口氣。過了一會，達西走到她跟凱蒂一起坐着的那張桌子前面來，裝作欣賞她手裏的針線，輕聲地跟她說：「快到你爸爸那裏去，他在書房裏等着你。」她於是馬上就去了。

　　她父親正在房間裏踱來踱去，看他那種神氣，既是嚴肅，又是焦急。他說：「莉茲，你在鬧些甚麼？你瘋了嗎，你怎麼會接受這個人？你不是一向都恨他嗎？」

　　她這時候真是焦急非凡。假如她從前不是那樣見解過火，出言不遜，那就好了，那現在就用不到那麼尷尷尬尬地去解釋和剖白了。可是事到如今，既是免不了要費些唇舌，她只得心慌意亂地跟父親說，她愛上了達西先生。

　　「換句話說，你已經打定主意，非嫁他不可了。他當然有的是錢，可以使你比珍妮衣服穿得更高貴，車輛乘得更華麗。難道這就會使你幸福嗎？」

伊莉莎白説：「你認為我對他並沒有感情，除此以外，你還有別的反對意見嗎？」

「一點沒有。我們都知道他是個傲慢而不易親近的人；不過，只要你真正喜歡他，這也無關緊要。」

女兒含淚回答道：「我實在喜歡他，我愛他。他並不是傲慢得沒有道理。他可愛極了。你不了解他真正的為人，因此，我求你不要這樣説他的不是，免得我痛苦。」

父親説：「莉茲，我已經允許他了。像他那樣的人，只要蒙他不棄，有所請求，我當然只有答應。如果你現在已經決定了要嫁他，我當然允許你。不過我勸你還是再仔細想想：我了解你的個性，莉茲。我知道，你除非能真正敬重你的丈夫，認為他高你一等，你便不會覺得幸福，也不會覺得得意。以你這樣了不起的才能，要是婚姻攀得不相稱，那是極其危險的，那你就很難逃得了丟臉和悲慘的下場。好孩子，別讓我以後看到你看不起你的終身伴侶，為你傷心。你得明白，這不是鬧着玩的。」

伊莉莎白更加感動，便非常認真、非常嚴肅地回答他的話；後來她又再三保證，達西先生確實是她選中的對象，説她對他的敬愛已經一步步提高，説她相信他的感情決不是一朝一夕建立起來的，而是經歷了好幾個月才考驗出來的；她又竭力讚揚他種種優秀的品德，這才打消了父親的猶疑，完全贊成了他們的婚姻。

她講完了，他便説道：「好孩子，這麼説，我沒有別的意見了。當真這樣，他的確配得上你。莉茲，我可不願意讓你嫁給一個達不到這種標準的人。」

為了要使得父親對達西先生更有好感，她又把他自告奮勇搭救麗迪亞的事告訴了父親。父親聽了，大為驚奇。

「今天真是無奇不有了！原來一切全靠達西的大力幫忙，他一手撮合他們的婚姻，為他們賠錢，替那個傢伙還債，給他找差事！這好極了。省了我多少麻煩，省了我多少錢。假如這事是你舅舅做的，我就非還他不可，而且可能已經還了他；可是這些熱戀中的年輕人，甚麼事都喜歡自作主張。明天我就提出還他的錢，他一定會大吹大擂，說他怎麼樣愛你疼你，那麼事情就這樣完了。"

於是他記起了前幾天給伊莉莎白讀柯林斯先生那封信的時候，她是多麼侷促不安；他又取笑了她一陣，最後才讓她走了；她正要走出房門，他又說："如果還有甚麼年輕人來向瑪莉和凱蒂求婚，帶他們進來好了，我正閒着呢。"

伊莉莎白心裏那塊大石頭這才算放了下來，在自己房間裏坐了半個小時定了定心以後，便神色鎮定地去和大家聚在一起了。所有歡樂愉快的事情都來得太突然，這個下午就這樣心曠神怡地消磨過去了；現在再也沒有甚麼重大的事情需要擔憂了，反而覺得心安理得，親切愉快。

晚上母親進化粧室去的時候，伊莉莎白也跟着母親一起去，把這個重要的消息告訴她。班奈特太太的反應極好。她初聽到這消息，只是靜靜地坐着，一句話也説不出，過了好久，她才聽懂了女兒的話，才隱隱約約地明白了又有一個女兒要出嫁了，這對於家裏有多少好處。到最後她才完全弄明了是怎麼回事，於是在椅子上坐立不安，站起來又坐下去，既感到詫異，又為自己祝福。

"謝謝老天爺！謝天謝地！且想想看吧！天啊！達西先生！誰想得到啊！真有這回事嗎？莉茲，我的寶貝，你馬上就要大富大貴了！你將要有多少針線錢[58]，有多少珠寶，多少馬車啊！珍妮比起來就差得太遠了——簡直是天上地下。我真高興——真快樂。這樣可愛的丈夫！那麼英俊，那麼魁偉！噢，我的好莉茲！我以前那麼討厭他，請你代我去向他求饒吧！我希望他不會計較。莉茲，我的寶貝。他在城裏有所大住宅！漂亮的東西一應俱全！三個女兒出嫁了！每年有一萬鎊的收入！噢，天啊！我真樂不可支了！我要發狂了！"

這番話足以證明她完全贊成他們的婚姻；伊莉莎白心喜的是，

幸虧母親這些得意忘形的話只有她一個人聽見。不久她便走出房來。可是她走到自己房間裏還沒有三分鐘，母親又趕來了。

母親大聲叫道："我的寶貝，我腦子裏再也想不到別的東西了！一年有一萬鎊的收入，可能還要多！簡直闊綽得像個皇親國戚！而且還有特許結婚證[59]——你當然要用特許結婚證結婚的。可是，我的寶貝，告訴我，達西先生愛吃甚麼菜，讓我明天準備起來。"

這句話不是個好兆頭，看來她母親明天又要在那位先生面前出醜。伊莉莎白心想，現在雖然已經十拿九穩地獲得了他的熱愛，而且也得到了家裏人的同意，恐怕還是難免節外生枝。幸好出人意料之外，第二天的情形非常好，這完全是由於班奈特太太對她這位未來的女婿極其敬畏，簡直不敢跟他說話，只是盡量向他獻些殷勤，或者是恭維一下他的高談闊論。

伊莉莎白看到父親也盡心竭力地跟他親近，覺得很滿意；班奈特先生不久又對她說，他越來越器重達西了。

他說："三個女婿都使我非常得意，或許韋翰是我最寵愛的一個；可是我想，你的丈夫也會像珍妮的丈夫一樣討我喜歡。"

第六十章

伊莉莎白馬上又高興得頑皮起來了，她要達西先生講述愛上她的經過。她問：“你是怎樣走出第一步的？我知道你只要走出了第一步，就會一路順風往前去。可是，你最初究竟怎麼會有這個念頭的？”

“我也不肯定究竟是在甚麼時間，甚麼地點，看見了你甚麼樣的風姿，聽到了你甚麼樣的談吐，而使我開始愛上了你。那是非常久遠的事。等我發覺我自己開始愛上你的時候，我已經走了一半路了。”

“我的美貌並沒有打動你的心，至於我的態度方面，我對你至少不是怎麼有禮貌，我沒有哪一次和你說話不是想要讓你難過一下。請你老老實實說一聲，你是不是愛我的唐突無禮？”

“我愛你的腦子靈活。”

“你還不如說是唐突，十足的唐突。事實上是因為，你對於殷勤多禮的客套，已經感到膩煩。天下有種女人，她們無論是說話、思想、表情，都只是為了博得你稱讚一聲，你對這種女人已經覺得討厭。我之所以會引起你的注目，打動了你的心，就因為我不像她們。如果你不是一個真正可愛的人，你一定會恨我這種性格。可是，儘管你想盡辦法來掩飾你自己，你的情感畢竟是高貴的、正直的，你心目中根本看不起那些拼命向你獻媚的人。我這樣一說，你就可以不必費神去解釋了；我通盤考慮了一下，覺得你的愛完全合情合理。老實說，你完全沒有想到我有甚麼實在的長處；不過，隨便甚麼人，在戀愛的時候，也都不會想到這種事情。”

“當初珍妮在尼德斐莊園病了，你對她那樣溫柔體貼，不正是你的長處嗎？”

“珍妮真是太好了！誰能不好好地對待她？你姑且就把這件事當

作我的德性吧。我一切優秀的品德都全靠你誇獎，你愛怎麼説就怎麼説吧；我可只知道找機會來嘲笑你，跟你爭論；我馬上就開始這樣做，聽我問你：你為甚麼總是不願意直接爽快地談到正題？你第一次上這裏來拜訪，第二次在這裏吃飯，為甚麼見到我就害羞？尤其是你來拜訪的那一次，你為甚麼顯出那副神氣，好像完全不把我放在心上似的？”

“因為你那樣板起了臉，一言不發，使得我不敢和你攀談。”

“可是我覺得難為情呀。”

“我也一樣。”

“那麼，你來吃飯的那一次，也可以跟我多談談了。”

“要是愛你愛得少些，話就可以説得多些了。”

“真不湊巧，你的回答總是這樣有道理，我又偏偏這樣懂道理，會承認你這個回答！我想，要是我不來理你，你不知要拖到甚麼時候；要是我不問你一聲，不知你甚麼時候才肯説出來。這都是因為我拿定了主意，要感謝你對麗迪亞的幫助，這才促成了這件事。我怕促成得太厲害了。如果説，我們是因為打破了當初的諾言⁶⁰，才獲得了目前的快慰，那在道義上怎麼説得過去？我實在不應該提起那件事的。實在是大錯特錯。”

“你不用難過。道義上完全講得過去。凱瑟琳夫人蠻不講理，想要拆散我們，這反而使我消除了種種疑慮。我並不以為目前的幸福，都是出於你對我的一片感恩圖報之心。我本來就不打算等你先開口。我一聽到我姨母的話，便產生了希望，於是決定要立刻把事情弄個清楚明白。”

“凱瑟琳夫人倒幫了極大的忙，她自己也應該高興，因為她喜歡幫別人的忙。可是請你告訴我，你這次上尼德斐莊園來是幹甚麼的？難道就是為了騎着馬到朗伯恩來難為情一番嗎？你有沒有預備要做出些正經大事來呢？”

“我上這裏來的真正目的，就是為了看看你。如果可能的話，我還要想辦法研究研究，是否有希望使你愛上我。至於在別人面前，在我自己心裏，我總是說，是為了看看你姐姐對賓利是否依然有情，如果依然有情，我就決定把這事的原委向他說明。"

"你有沒有勇氣把凱瑟琳夫人的自討沒趣，向她自己宣佈一次？"

"我並不是沒有勇氣，而是沒有時間，伊莉莎白。可是這件事是應該要做的；如果你給我一張信紙，我馬上就來做。"

"要不是我自己有封信要寫，我一定會像另外一位年輕的小姐一樣[61]，坐在你身旁，欣賞你那工整的書法。可惜我也有一位舅母，不能再耽誤回信給她了。"

早前，舅母過高地估計了伊莉莎白和達西先生的交情，伊莉莎白又不願意把事情向舅母說明白，因此賈汀納太太寫來的那封長信一直還沒有回覆，現在有了這個可喜的消息告訴她，她一定會滿心歡喜。可是伊莉莎白倒覺得，讓舅父母遲了三天才知道這個消息，真有些不好意思。她馬上寫道：

親愛的舅母，蒙你寫給我那封親切而令人滿意的長信，告訴了我種種詳情細節，本當早日回信道謝，無奈我當時實在情緒不佳，因而不願意動筆。你當時所想像的情況，實在有些過甚其辭。可是現在，你大可愛怎麼想就怎麼想了。關於這件事，你可以放縱你的幻想，想到哪裏就是哪裏，只要你不以為我已經結了婚，你總不會猜想得太過份。你得馬上再寫封信來把他讚美一番，而且要讚美得大大超過你上一封信。我要多謝你沒有帶我到湖區去旅行。我真傻，為甚麼想到湖區去呢？你說要弄幾匹小馬去遊園，這個打算可真有意思。今後我們便可以每天在那個園裏兜圈子了。我現在成了天下最幸福的人。也許別人以前也說過這句話，可是誰也不能像我這樣名副其實。我甚至比珍妮還要幸福：她只是莞爾微笑，我卻要縱聲大笑。達西先生分一部份愛我之心問候你。歡迎你們到龐百利來過聖誕節。

你的甥女

達西先生寫給凱瑟琳夫人的信，格調和這封信頗不一樣，而班奈特先生寫給柯林斯先生的回信，和這兩封信又是全不相同。

賢姪先生：

　　我得麻煩你再恭賀我一次。伊莉莎白馬上就要做達西夫人了。請多多勸慰凱瑟琳夫人。要是我處在你的位置，我一定要站在外甥一邊，因為他可以給人更大的利益。

愚某手上

　　賓利小姐祝賀哥哥快要結婚的那封信，寫得無限親切，只可惜缺乏誠意。她甚至還寫信給珍妮道賀，又把從前那一套假仁假義的話重提了一遍。珍妮雖然再也不受她蒙蔽，可仍然為她感動；雖說對她不再信任，可還是回了她一封信，措辭極其親切，實在使她受之有愧。

　　達西小姐來信上說，她接到喜訊時，正和她哥哥發出喜訊時一樣歡欣。那封信寫了四張信紙，還不足以表達她內心的喜悅，不足以表明她是怎樣懇切地盼望着嫂嫂會疼愛她。

　　柯林斯先生的回信還沒有來，伊莉莎白也還沒有獲得柯林斯太太的祝賀，這時候朗伯恩全家卻聽說他們夫婦兩人馬上要到盧家莊來。他們突然動身前來的原因，是很容易明白的。原來凱瑟琳夫人接到她外甥那封信，大發雷霆，而夏綠蒂對這門婚事偏偏非常欣喜，因此不得不火速避開一下，等到這場暴風雨過去了以後再說。對伊莉莎白來說，在這樣的佳期，自己的好朋友來了，真是一件無上愉快的事，只可惜等到見了面，看到柯林斯先生對達西先生那種極盡巴結阿諛的樣子，便不免認為這種愉快有些得不償失。不過達西卻非常鎮定地容忍着。還有威廉・盧卡斯爵士，他恭維達西獲得了當地最寶貴的明珠，而且還恭而敬之地說，希望今後能常在宮中見面。達西先生甚至連這些話也聽得進去，直到威廉爵士走開以後，他才聳了聳肩。

　　還有菲力普太太，她為人很粗俗，也許會令達西更加受不了。菲力普太太正像她姐姐一樣，見到賓利先生那麼和顏悅色，於是攀談起來很是隨便，而對達西則敬畏備至，不敢隨便，可是她的言語總還是免不了粗俗。雖說她因為尊敬達西而很少跟達西說話，可是她並不因此而顯得舉止文雅一些。伊莉莎白為了不讓達西受到這些人的糾纏，便竭力使他跟她自己談話，跟她家裏那些不會使他受罪的人談話。雖然這一番應酬大大減少了戀愛的樂趣，可是卻促進了她對未來生活的期望，她一心盼望着趕快離開這些討厭的人物，到龐百利去，和他的家人在一起，舒舒服服地過一輩子風雅有趣的生活。

第六十一章

班奈特太太兩個最值得疼愛的女兒出嫁的那一天，正是她做母親的生平最高興的一天。她以後去拜訪賓利太太，在她面前談起達西太太，是多麼得意，多麼驕傲，這是可想而知的。看在她家庭的份上，我想在這裏作一個說明：她所有的女兒後來都得到了歸宿，她生平最殷切的願望終於如願以償；說來可喜，她後半輩子竟因此變成了一個頭腦清楚、和藹可親、頗有見識的女人；不過她有時候還是神經衰弱，經常都是大驚小怪，這也許倒是她丈夫的幸運，否則他就無從享受這種稀奇古怪的家庭幸福了。

班奈特先生非常捨不得第二個女兒；他因為疼愛她，便常常去看她，他生平從來不肯這樣經常外出作客。他喜歡到龐百利去，而且大都是在別人完全意料不到的時候。

賓利先生和珍妮在尼德斐莊園只住了一年。雖說他的脾氣非常隨和，她的性情亦極其溫柔，可是夫婦兩人都不大願意和她母親以及麥里頓的親友們住得太近。後來他在德比郡鄰近的一個郡裏買了一幢房子，於是他姐妹們的衷心願望總算如願以償；而珍妮和伊莉莎白兩人在萬重幸福之上又添了一重幸福，那就是說，姐妹兩人從此不過相隔三十英里了。

凱蒂受惠最多，大部份時間都消磨在兩位姐姐那裏。從此她所交往的人物都比往常高尚，她本身當然也就大有長進。她本來不像麗迪亞那樣放縱，現在既沒有麗迪亞來影響她，又有人對她加以妥善的注意和照料，她便不像以前那樣輕狂無知和麻木不仁了。當然家裏少不了要小心地管教她，不讓她和麗迪亞來往，免得再受到她的壞影響；韋翰太太常常要接她去住，說是有多少舞會，有多少美少年，她父親總是不讓她去。

後來只剩下瑪莉還沒有出嫁；班奈特太太因為不甘寂寞，自然弄得她這個女兒無從探求學問。瑪莉不得不多多和外界應酬，可是她仍然能夠用道德的眼光去看待每一次的外出作客。她現在再也不用為了和姐妹們爭妍比美而操心了，因此她父親不禁懷疑到，她這種改變是否心甘情願。

說到韋翰和麗迪亞，他們兩人的性格並沒有因為她兩位姐姐的結婚而有所變化。韋翰想起自己對達西種種的忘恩負義、虛偽欺詐的事情，伊莉莎白雖然從前不知道，現在可完全明白了，不過他依舊處之泰然，他多少還指望達西給他一些錢。伊莉莎白結婚的時候，接到麗迪亞一封祝賀信。她看得很明白，即使韋翰本人沒有存那種指望，至少他太太也有那種意思。那封信是這樣寫的：

親愛的莉茲：

祝你愉快。要是你愛達西先生抵得上我愛韋翰的一半，那你一定會非常幸福了。你能這樣富有，真讓人十分快慰；當你閒來無事的時候，希望你會想到我們。我相信韋翰極其希望在宮廷裏找份差事做做。要是再沒有別人幫幫忙，我們便很難維持生計了。隨便甚麼差事都行，只要每年有三四百鎊的收入。不過，要是你不願意跟達西講，那就不必提起。

妹字

伊莉莎白果然不願意講，因此在回信中盡力打消她這種希望，斷了她這一類的念頭。不過伊莉莎白還是盡量把自己平日的用途節省一些，積下錢來去接濟妹妹。她一向都明白，他們的收入那麼少，兩人又揮霍無度，只顧眼前，不顧今後，這當然不夠維持生活；每逢他們搬家，伊莉莎白或是珍妮總是接到他們的信，要求接濟他們一些錢去償付賬款。即使天下太平了，他們退伍回家，他們的生活終究難以安定。他們老是東遷西徙，尋找便宜房子住，結果總是多花了不少錢。韋翰對麗迪亞不久便情淡愛弛，麗迪亞對他比較持久一些，儘管她年輕荒唐，還是顧全了婚後應有的名譽。

雖然達西再三不肯讓韋翰到龐百利來，但是看在伊莉莎白的面上，他依舊幫助他謀了一官半職。麗迪亞每當丈夫到倫敦去或是到巴思[62]去尋歡作樂的時候，也不時到他們那裏去做客；至於賓利家裏，他們夫婦兩人老是一住下來就不想走，弄得連賓利那樣性格溫和的人，也覺得不高興，甚至説，要暗示他們走。

達西結婚時，賓利小姐萬分傷心，可是她又要在龐百利保持作客的權利，因此便把多少怨氣都打消了；她比從前更喜愛喬治安娜，對達西也依舊殷勤，又把以前對伊莉莎白失禮的地方加以彌補。

喬治安娜現在長住在龐百利了；姑嫂之間正如達西先生所料到的那麼情投意合，互尊互愛，甚至融洽得完全合於她們自己的理想。喬治安娜非常推崇伊莉莎白，不過，剛開始看到嫂嫂跟哥哥談起話來，那麼活潑調皮，她不禁大為驚異，幾乎有些擔心，因為她一向尊敬哥哥，幾乎尊敬得超過了手足的情份，想不到現在他竟成為公開打趣的對象。她以前無論如何也弄不懂的事，現在才恍然大悟了。經過伊莉莎白的陶冶，她開始懂得：妻子可以對丈夫放縱，做哥哥的卻不能允許一個比自己小十歲的妹妹調皮。

凱瑟琳夫人對她外甥的婚姻極其氣憤。外甥寫信給她報喜，她竟毫不留情，直言無諱，寫了封回信把他大罵一頓，對伊莉莎白尤其罵得厲害，於是雙方曾有一個短時期斷絕往來。後來伊莉莎白説服了達西，達西才不再計較這次無禮的事，上門去求和；姨母稍稍拒絕了一下便不計舊怨了，這可能是因為她疼愛外甥，也可能是因為她有好奇心，要看看外甥媳婦怎樣做人。儘管龐百利因為添了這樣一位主婦，而且主婦在城裏的那兩位舅父母都到這裏來過，因此使門戶受到了玷污，但她還是屈尊到龐百利來拜訪。

新夫婦跟賈汀納夫婦一直保持着極其深厚的交情。達西和伊莉莎白都衷心喜愛他們，又一直感激他們，感激他們把伊莉莎白帶到德比郡來，才成全了新夫婦這一段姻緣。

完

註解

1 米迦勒節為 9 月 29 日，是英國四結賬日之一，僱用傭人多在此日，租約亦多於此日履行。

2 是伊莉莎白的愛稱。

3 英國內陸之一郡，以玫瑰花圃著稱。該郡的聖阿爾班及白納特曾先後於 1455 年、1461 年及 1471 年為有名的"玫瑰戰爭"的戰場。英國名人如培根、蘭姆、李敦等均出生於此郡。

4 即凱蒂，後者為愛稱。

5 指班奈特家的大小姐，即珍妮，本書中除特別指出者以外，均同此。

6 即盧卡斯小姐。

7 一種法國牌戲。下注後每人發牌三張，其中一張可以根據各個玩牌者之需要在牌堆中調換，直等到有人換妥贏牌為止，通常三張相同者為最大，同花順子次之。

8 指英國軍人。

9 倫敦街名，自聖保羅教堂向東延展，以珠寶商及綢緞商著稱。1666 年大火以前，該處是一露天廣場，為中世紀市集匯聚之地。

10 賓利先生的名字。

11 位於英格蘭北中部。該郡在英國諸郡中人口佔第 19 位，面積佔第 20 位。其北面之高地名秀阜，以風景秀麗著稱。此郡多古代寺院教堂之遺跡，金屬礦藏亦甚豐富，故採礦業頗為發達。關於該郡風景名勝，可參閱第 42 章有關注解。

12 "詩是愛情的食糧"一句，請參閱莎士比亞《第十二夜》開場第一句："如果音樂是愛情的食糧，奏下去吧。"這裏應是套用。

13 法國的一種賭錢的牌戲，每人發牌三至五張。如發五張，則以梅花 J 為最大；如發三張，其大小同"惠斯特"。兩個人玩的一種牌戲，自六以下的牌一般皆除去。

14 意謂求和修好，因橄欖枝是和平的象徵。典出《聖經·創世記》第 8 章第 11 節："到了晚上，鴿子回到他那裏，嘴裏銜着一個新擰下來的橄欖葉子，挪亞就知道地上的水退了。"

15 四個人玩的一種牌戲，風行於 18 世紀初葉。

16 這裏應該指出，英國小說之所以盛行於 18 世紀，是和英國 17 世紀的資產階級革命分不開的。在資產階級革命以前的封建社會裏，英國流行着一種傳奇文學（romance），這是一種非現實的、封建意識形態的文學，它在政治上的作用就是利用一個"理想的"世界來粉飾現實，以鞏固封建統治階級的統治。而 18 世紀一切現實主義的小說都是隨着封建主義的解體而來的，所以都是"反傳奇的"（anti-romance），因此在 18 世紀初，封建貴族都不願意讀小說。柯林斯之所以不讀小說，也正是這種封建意識形態的流露，試比較本書第 8 章達西講到一個多才多藝的女子應具備的條件時，便說："……還應該多讀書，長見識，有點真才實學。"這裏所謂多讀書，是指多讀小說，這也正是當時新興的商業資產階級意識形態的反映。

17 指詹姆斯・弗迪斯，是蘇格蘭的一個牧師，著有《對青年婦女的講道集》，出版於 1765 年，主要內容是向青年婦女灌輸封建道德。奧斯汀在這裏以詼諧諷刺的筆墨對當時的舊道德作了無情的抨擊。

18 一種用骰子比賽的遊戲。

19 指牛津大學或劍橋大學。

20 一種四人玩的牌戲，與橋牌大同小異。

21 指向教會繳納的農作物、牲畜等稅，其稅率約為年產額的十份之一，故名什一。

22 指到教堂裏去結婚。

23 倫敦一條街名，近海德公園，有各式各樣的建築物，是一個有名的住宅區。

24 作者奧斯汀在這裏揭露了當時婦女的悲慘命運，她們沒有獨立自由，惟一的出路只有結婚，做母親的也都逼着她們結婚。奧斯汀的前輩作家哥爾斯密（1728—1774）的《威克斐牧師傳》中所描寫的白琳羅太太便是這種母親的典型。

25 班奈特太太最後想要說句話敷衍敷衍她弟婦，可是一時氣急敗壞，說了上半句又接不上下半句，便順口說出了"你講的那些……長袖子"，是指她弟婦所說關於時裝樣式的事。

26 英格蘭東南部海濱之一郡，富有歷史意義。坎特伯雷大教堂及路徹斯特大教堂均在此郡。瑪麗女王及伊莉莎白女王均出生於此郡，愛德華六世及拿破崙三世死於此郡。彼得大帝曾在此郡學習造船業。此郡又為大文豪狄更斯之故鄉。

27 在奧斯汀時代，英國交通雖比 18 世紀初較為便利，但仍道路崎嶇，旅程艱苦。

28 英國北部的名湖區，風景優美，19 世紀的湖上詩人華茲華斯、騷塞、柯勒律治即居住此地。華茲華斯所著《湖上行》一書，對該處風景名勝有極其詳盡優美的描寫。

29 指達西。

30 一種牌戲，類似 21 點。

31 在封建社會中，財產都由長子繼承，其他的小兒子既無職業，又無生活資源，只得依靠兄長或朋友資助。

32 受聖職是一種儀式，誓願終生為上帝服務。

33 英格蘭肯特郡一港口。

34 是凱瑟琳夫人的侍僕。

35 在英格蘭海濱，是一個幽美的遊憩療養之地。

36 在奧斯汀那個時代，利物浦雖然居民尚不足 10 萬人，卻已成為英格蘭一個極大的港口。

37 德比郡一教區，多溫泉及鐘乳石洞穴。

38 德比郡一名勝地區，以圖書館、美術及雕刻聞名。此間花園亦極其美麗，僅次於凡爾賽。

39 在恰滋華斯附近，是一個美麗無比的小山谷，佈滿着精巧綺麗的岩石和綠葉成蔭的樹木。

40 德比郡西北部的丘陵地帶，鴿谷之水流經此處。面積約為 30 英尺乘 22 英尺。此處有秀阜洞，縱深約達 750 碼。

41 一名"德比郡瑩石"，是德比郡的一種著名礦產。

42 原是德國巴伐利亞州一村莊。1704 年，因西班牙王位繼承問題所引起之戰爭，進展至此地，8 月 3 日，英國馬包羅公爵擊敗法國人與巴伐利亞人於此，安妮女王為紀念此次勝利，遂以 50 萬鎊之鉅資在牛津郡建立馬包羅城堡，中有 130 英尺高之圓柱一根，其上塑馬包羅像，極其宏偉。

43 英格蘭中部一郡名，其森林地帶風景之美麗居於全英國之首，並有瓦立克男爵之城堡，頗為宏偉。

44 瓦立克郡一市鎮，以凱尼爾沃思城堡著稱。1563 年，伊莉莎白女王將此城堡賜予其情人勒西斯特伯爵，伯爵於 1575 年 6 月在此城堡中款待女王 18 日，詳見司各特所着《墜樓記》。

45 瓦立克郡一城市，以鋼鐵及五金業著稱。

46 格利那草場在蘇格蘭鄧弗裏斯郡。自 1754 年以後，秘密結婚者多逃往該地，每年多達 200 起，因為當時適用於英格蘭之婚姻法不適用於蘇格蘭。自 1756 年以後，凡男女結婚，必須在該地居住 3 星期以上始得舉行婚禮。

47 倫敦附近一小鎮，18世紀時是一個遊覽休憩的名勝地方，現在以跑馬場著稱。

48 指男傭人。

49 瑪莉頗有女學究氣，她說的這兩段話在原文中用字造句都十分矯揉造作，故譯文亦盡力保持原來的風格。

50 海麗是弗斯托太太的名字。

51 用檸檬汁、糖和葡萄酒混合而成的一種飲料。

52 英格蘭一港口，英國所產的煤大都由此處運往世界各國。

53 小戲院可能是指朱瑞巷戲院。該戲院舊址原是鬥雞場，至詹姆斯一世時改為戲院，於1663年開幕，1672年被焚，1674年重新開設，由德萊頓致開幕詞。1809年又被焚，1812年重新開幕，由拜倫朗誦揭幕詩。在該院演出之名演員有波士、加里克等人，肯波曾於1782年9月3日在該院初次登台演出《哈姆雷特》。該院於1908年3月25日三度被焚。又海馬克劇院亦稱小戲院。

54 指達西。

55 尼可爾斯太太是賓利家裏的女管家，應是本書第11章所提男管家尼可爾斯之妻子。

56 英格蘭北部一個有名的消暑地區。1620年該地發現溫泉後，更加有名。又因該處環境極為優美，故有"英國溫泉之後"的稱呼。

57 指第35章達西致伊莉莎白那封信的結尾一句："我要說的話都說完了，願上帝祝福你。"達西當初這句話實在含有幾分怨氣，伊莉莎白在這裏是嘲弄他。

58 英國自14世紀剛剛發明針時，極其寶貴，售針僅限於1月1日及1月2日兩天。用針者僅限於富人。故通常結婚時，夫家均給予妻子一筆款項作為購針之用，謂之針線錢。"針線錢"這一名詞今日在英國仍甚普遍，多指貴夫人用以購買奢侈品之錢，或丈夫給予妻女的零用錢。

59 按英國從前的法律，結婚多用結婚通告，由牧師在禮拜天做早禱時，讀完了第二遍《聖經》經文以後，便當眾宣佈，連續宣佈三個禮拜。如男女一方有未成年的，家長或監護人出來反對，結婚通告就不生效。如需提早結婚，則不用通告，而用特許結婚證，特許結婚證只有大主教或主教始有權頒發。凡請求頒給特許結婚證者，男女雙方必須有一方在所在地教區居住十五日以上，並得發誓。

60 這一句極其俏皮，可參閱第34章。

61 伊莉莎白又在這裏說俏皮話了，她指的是從前賓利小姐看達西寫信的事，請參閱第 10 章。

62 英國一個有名的溫泉所在地。